A YEAR IN THE THEATRE

Greater Manchester 2004-05

1 September 2004 – 31 August 2005

FOREWORD BY ROBERT ROBSON
Artistic Director of The Lowry

Compiled by Giles Haworth

Additional Journal Contributions by Alan Kelsey and Bren Francis

Broadfield Publishing

Also Available

A YEAR IN THE THEATRE:- Greater Manchester 2003-2004

The ultimate annual compendium of theatre events in Greater Manchester. Nothing is missed, no detail omitted; the premier theatrical reference book: **Bolton Evening News**

An exhaustive tome of what's been happening on the stages of Greater Manchester; **Bury Times**

A truly amazing record. Another classic edition of this phenomenal book. It gives a comprehensive journey into all dramatic activity: Greater Manchester's theatre world is very much alive and kicking: **NODA Northwest News**

In his Foreword to the 12th edition if Giles Haworth's estimable tome, **Contact** Artistic Director **John McGrath** talks of Manchester's newfound confidence as a city capable of supporting new talent and emerging artists. This sense of possibility has seen the emergence of leftfield, experimental artists like **Ben Faulks** and **Juliet Ellis**, new initiatives like the **RX's Blue Season** and challenging companies like **Richard Gregory's Quarantine.** Best of all, with rise of **Studio Salford** and the **24:7 Festival**, Manchester now has a fringe scene to be proud of. **24:7** gets plenty of detailed coverage in Haworth's book, as does pretty much every other show staged in Manchester last year. The fact the author sees so many productions is amazing; the fact he writes about them in such perceptive detail is nothing short of miraculous: **City Life** **ISNB 0 9543450 1 0 £9.95**

GILES HAWORTH T/A

BROADFIELD PUBLISHING

71 Broadfield Road
Moss Side
MANCHESTER
M14 4WE

0161-227 9265

A YEAR IN THE THEATRE

Many Thanks for buying this book.

If you like it, please invite your friends to buy their **own** copies.

Otherwise, they will sit around reading yours all the time

Best Wishes

Giles Haworth

Giles Haworth

VAT Registration Number: GB 603 5773 46

Also Available

A YEAR IN THE THEATRE:- Greater Manchester 2002-2003

A remarkable compilation: takes in the the big professional blockbusters, the Little Theatre movement, local halls, school productions, you name it. Boundless enthusiasm and a daunting devotion to details: **John Slim in NODA National News, Spring 2004**

Packs in so much information about professional and amateur productions. Bolton gets a good showing and there's particular praise for Marco Players: **Dorothy Crowther in Bolton Evening News, 2 December 2003**

A must for everyone interested in the Theatre. A stirring Foreword by Wyllie Longmore emphasis the continuing importance of live Theatre: **Area News Today, 14 November 2003**

Another fantastic read! You can't get a better record than this: **NODA NorthWest News, January 2004**

Features world famous productions, such as Sunset Boulevard and Beauty And The Beast as well as local offerings at the Bury Met and Bolton Octagon: **Bury Times, 20 December 2003**

Many societies and groups feature in the latest edition of this valuable and interesting publication: **CUES Newsletter of Greater Manchester Drama Federation**

ISBN 0 9543459 0 2 **£9.95**

HOLLAND ENTERPRISE TROPHY

ALL-ENGLAND THEATRE FESTIVAL 1998

On 26 June 1998, A YEAR IN THE THEATRE received the HOLLAND ENTERPRISE TROPHY from the West-Pennine Region of the ALL-ENGLAND THEATRE FESTIVAL, for its recording of Theatre activity in Greater Manchester.

Broadfield Publishing
71 Broadfield Road
Moss Side
MANCHESTER
M14 4WE

0161-227 9265

First Published: October 2005

ISBN 0 9543450 2 9

ISSN 1357 – 6003

Previous Volumes A YEAR IN THE THEATRE: Greater Manchester 1993
ISBN 09521502 04
A YEAR IN THE CITY OF DRAMA: Greater Manchester 1994; ISBN 09521502 1 2
A YEAR IN THE THEATRE: Greater Manchester 1994-95
ISBN 09521502 2 0
A YEAR IN THE THEATRE: Greater Manchester 1995-96
ISBN 09521502 3 9
A YEAR IN THE THEATRE: Greater Manchester 1996-97
ISBN 09521502 4 7
A YEAR IN THE THEATRE: Greater Manchester 1997-98
ISBN 09521502 5 5
A YEAR IN THE THEATRE: Greater Manchester 1998-99
ISBN 09521502 6 3
A YEAR IN THE THEATRE: Greater Manchester 1999-2000
ISBN 09521502 7 5
A YEAR IN THE THEATRE: Greater Manchester 2000-01
ISBN 09521502 8 X
A YEAR IN THE THEATRE: Greater Manchester 2001-02
ISBN 09521502 9 8
A YEAR IN THE THEATRE: Greater Manchester 2002-03
ISBN 09543450 0 2
A YEAR IN THE THEATRE: Greater Manchester 2003-04
ISBN 09543450 1 0
Forthcoming A YEAR IN THE THEATRE: Greater Manchester 2005-06
ISBN 09521502

Typeset by the Compiler in Times New Roman with Word Through Windows

Printed and Bound by Antony Rowe Ltd, Bumpers Farm, Chippenham SN14 6LH

Cover Film Separations: Engraving Services, 21 Radnor Street, Moss Side M15 5RD

CONTENTS

ILLUSTRATIONS

Front Cover: VINCENT IN BRIXTON (1); the opening production in an outstanding year, in which the **Library**, one of the oldest civic theatres in the country, has presented splendid productions, almost all of new work; in the foreground, Sam (**Christopher Pizzey**) and Eugenie (**Hannah Watkins**) rejoice at the new perspectives which Art can bring into their lives, whilst the young Vincent Van Gogh (**Gus Gallagher**) has yet to realise his abilities in the field; Photo: **Gerald Murray**

Spine and Back Cover show some of the latest flood of new talent, which constantly emerges from Manchester's noted Drama Schools and University Theatre Departments: on the rigging – **Lowri Shimmin** as Diana, the constant companion of Gower in this imaginative production of **Pericles (183)** by the **Arden School of Theatre;** Photo: **Ian Tilton**

A. Arden also produced a rare but timely performance of **The Witches of Lancashire (182)** by **Richard Brome** and **Thomas Heywood;** seen here, left to right) are **Tom Harvey** (Seely), **Richard Lee Kirkbride** (Gregory Seely), **Sarah Jones (**Joan Seely) and **Amy Hiscocks (**Winny Seely); Photo: **Ian Tilton**

B. The **University of Manchester's Department of Music and Theatre** has not primarily focussed on performance, although many players of national repute have emerged from it over the years. Several of their most talented recent graduates have formed themselves into **Envision Theatre,** who this year have been invited to be the **Department**'s company in residence; seen here, **Helen Spencer**, as Bet in **April in Paris (344);** Photo: **David Oakes – www.oakesphotograpy.co.uk**

Contents **Page**

C. Ross Grant as Charlie in **Marvin's Room (284)** at the **Manchester Metropolitan University School of Theatre;** Photo: **Baird Media**

D. Richard Sails and **Neville Millar**, as Rumsey and Bates, in the **Arden** production of **Silence (48);** Photo: **Ian Tilton**

E. Lowri Shimmin (Augustinas) and **Vicki Scowcroft** (Bernada) in **The Household of Bernada Alba (184)** at **Arden;** Photo: **Ian Tilton**

Contents Page

Contents **Page**

Contents **Page**

Contents **Page**

Contents | Page

Contents **Page**

Contents	Page

Contents **Page**

Contents **Page**

Contents **Page**

Contents **Page**

ADVERTISERS

HOW THE SYSTEM WORKS

The Most Important Principle: INDEXING IS BY THE Production Numbers given in SECTION 1

Section 1gives the **Page** in **Section 3** upon which **Full Programme Details** can be found.

Section 3 is organised

A by **Boroughs and Cities,** in ALPHABETICAL ORDER (**Bolton, Bury, Manchester, Oldham …**)

B with **Theatres and Venues** in ALPHABETICAL ORDER within **A: (Abbey Hey, Alma, Abraham Moss, Arden …)**

and **C Programme Details** in CALENDAR ORDER of First Nights at each Venue.

Section 3 gives **Theatre Details** for each Venue: **Address, Box Office Telephone Numbers, AZ Map Reference and Access Facilities.** Where a single company regularly uses a public hall, the **telephone number** given will often be that, not of the hall, but of the company's Booking Secretary.

IF YOU WANT TO KNOW ANY OF THESE DETAILS OR ABOUT A PARTICULAR PLAY AT A KNOWN VENUE:

THE EASY WAY: I) Open the book somewhere near the middle II) Work your way forward or back, following the principles **A, B and C** above

Section 3 Programme Details end with

Giving a DATE if a production is described in the **Journal** in **Section 2**, where the entries are given in CALENDAR ORDER

Abbreviations for **Access Facilities** at the various venues are given at the start of **Section 3**

IF YOU WANT TO KNOW THE FULL YEAR'S WORK OF A PARTICULAR THEATRE ARTIST:

a) Sorry; you may not be able to; not all plays have been indexed in **Section 4.**

(There are provisional plans for a comprehensive cumulative Artists Index, covering all the volumes of this record up to the point this made, but that will not be available for at least a couple of years).

b) For as much information as is available in this volume:

i) Look up the name in **Section 4,** the Alphabetical **Artists Index**

ii) This will give you the **Production Numbers** of the Plays in which the Artist was involved; these numbers in **Section 1** will give you the **Pages** upon which further details can be found.

IF Section 1 GIVES SEVERAL PAGES FOR A SINGLE PRODUCTION: Full Programme Details only appear on the Page given in **Bold** Print; the other pages show other places at which the production has appeared.

IF YOU KNOW A PLAY TITLE BUT NOT WHERE IT WAS PERFORMED: Section 5 will give you the **Production Numbers**, from **Section 1**, where you can then learn the **Pages** giving further information.

IF YOU WANT TO KNOW ABOUT THE WORK OF A PARTICULAR COMPANY: Its **Address** and **Telephone Number**, where available, are given in **Section 6**, together with the **Production Numbers** of all plays it has presented in Greater Manchester. From these you can learn the **pages** for further information, through **Section 1.**

IF YOU WANT TO KNOW ABOUT AWARDS WON THIS YEAR: See **Section 7.**

THE RANGE OF CHOICE IS QUITE OUTSTANDING ...

ROBERT ROBSON, Artistic Director of THE LOWRY, outlines its diverse contributions to the dynamic theatrical scene in Greater Manchester.

1.SINGING NUNS

In **The Lowry**'s relatively short life we have already done many things of a high profile and highly artistic nature but we also have a strongly populist streak..........

Just over eighteen months ago, for instance, we presented the only performances south of the border of **Scottish Opera**'s outstanding **Ring Cycle** more or less direct from its success at the Edinburgh Festival and recently we had been considering hosting the **Kirov Opera**'s production of the same epic cycle. For a variety of reasons, this is unfortunately not going to happen but I did travel to Moscow to attend performances of the production at the **Bolshoi Theatre**.

Early one Friday evening, shortly after my return, I was involved in a rather lengthy and involved telephone conversation exploring the complexities of this possible presentation, looking out of my office window at **The Lowry** over the adjacent quayside as I spoke. As the conversation wound on about this highest of pieces of high art, I have to confess that my attention was

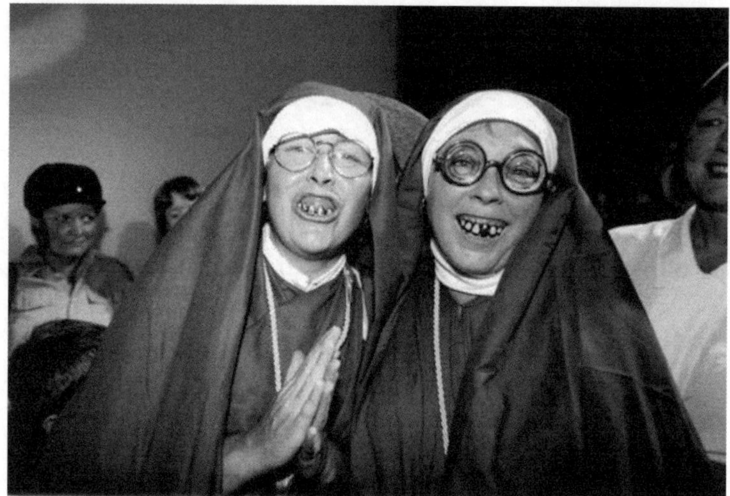

NUN BUT THE BRAVE ...

increasingly taken up by the sight of not only audiences fetching up to the first performance of this year's run by **The Ladyboys of Bangkok** in a tent on a nearby pier but also by hordes of nuns (for the evening) flocking up to attend a performance of **Singalonga Sound of Music** inside our building. It all seemed rather incongruous and to undermine the telephone conversation.

Can we be serious?

2.A SHORT LIFE

In just over five years, **The Lowry** has brought you (and with comparatively modest levels of subsidy) the **Paris Opera** and **Kirov Ballet** companies, a **Ring Cycle**, the truly epic **Tantalus, Kabuki, Dance Theatre of Harlem, Nederlands Dans Theater, Love on the Dole**

... DESERVE THE FAIR (KIROV SWAN LAKE); ROBERT ROBSON writes of how Salford enterprise has made THE LOWRY a premier provider of both Art and Entertainment

as a community play, the hit musical **Taboo, Mark Morris Dance Group**, the **Maly Drama Theatre, Laurie Anderson**, partner companies such as **Birmingham Royal Ballet, Opera North** and **Rambert, Matthew Bourne**'s work, the **Donmar**, the **Young Vic,** the **RSC** and the **National, Northern Broadsides, Peter Brook, Shared Experience**.......... increasing dance attendances in the Greater Manchester area two-and-a-half times along the way ....as well as a host of popular entertainment................not to mention our work in the visual arts and in the community and education field................**LS Lowry**............and over 800,000 visitors a year!

And there's more to come................**Alvin Ailey.................Robert Lepage...........**

3.A DAY IN THE LIFE

……………… of a member of the theatres programming team at **The Lowry.**

You come in most mornings to a list of calls to make, deals to be struck, contracts to be issued, shows to be checked out, meetings to have. These can range from the **Kirov Ballet** to comedy and music agents to choreographers to be in residence (in the new **Studio** spaces we have added to our **Lyric** and **Quays Theatres**) to a local Salford school. And that's exactly as it should be………………………

4.FROM GRANITEVILLE TO LOWRYLAND

After a spell as Festival Director of **Mayfest** (Glasgow's one time international festival), I worked for a number of years at **His Majesty's Theatre** in Aberdeen (the Granite City) before moving to **The Lowry** nearly seven years ago now in 1998 in the period before it opened. In 1994, when **The Lowry** was still probably just a gleam in somebody's eye, I hatched a plan to seek lottery funds to extend the **His Majesty**'s building to add badly needed front of house and rehearsal facilities. That proposed extension is only now nearing completion and, in the intervening period, the funding for **The Lowry** has been found, the construction completed and the building opened and its programme up and running for over five years. This is the best indicator I know for the dynamism of **The Lowry**'s organisation and all those people associated with it.

5.LOOKING AHEAD

The Lowry is of course still to a degree something of the new kid on the block in terms of the theatre scene in Greater Manchester and, as this publication illustrates so well, what a healthy, active, busy and dynamic scene that is! The range of choice for the theatregoer across Manchester and Salford and out to Bolton and Oldham, and elsewhere in the surrounding area, is quite outstanding and I am absolutely convinced that if the work on offer is generally good enough, then there is certainly enough audience to go round. And we can also look forward to the new **Manchester Festival** in 2007 and **Liverpool's City of Culture** year in 2008.

Above all, **The Lowry**'s greatest strength has been the overwhelming public support we have experienced and I am equally convinced that the potential for developing the programme at **The Lowry** and the audience for it is conceivably boundless and only restricted by the financial resources we are currently able to command.

ROBERT ROBSON

29 July 2005

BAKER'S DOZEN

This seems to be it.

I am very unlikely to be able to produce a volume of this book over the coming year.

Being a merry wanderer of the night no longer seems to be consistent with staying awake during the reasonable hours of work required by those who pay my wages. The running costs of producing the book are not vast but they are now beyond what those wages can keep up with.

I had hoped to keep going for at least another year, so that, when retired, I would then have the time to give the book the attention to marketing which it requires to make it viable.

If no one else has taken the book in hand by then, I shall survey my resources at that point and see if they enable me to revive the title. For the coming year, however, I think that producing it is beyond me.

I have been fairly clear in my mind for several months that this must be. During the last few weeks, as I have devoted myself exclusively to the task of putting the present volume together, I have, once again, been impressed by the bountiful quality of Theatre in Greater Manchester, - so much diverse excellent work, created by so many people who deserve to have their achievements recorded and whose stature, in some respects, can only be realised by seeing it gathered together *en masse.*

I am most loath to see even a gap, let alone a cessation, in creating this record. While the vision of how much it needs to be done sways me against the decision that I can no longer do it, I am also aware of factors which may have swayed me towards it. There is another piece of writing which I very much wish to undertake, which I hope, if achieved, would be of some interest to many readers of this volume. Eager as I am to do this, however, I could realistically wait to begin it until the amounts of time brought by my retirement next year become available. So I do not think I would exchange that task for this and this book would properly, in any year, take priority.

This book, however, does not need to be mine. It has been a personal pleasure to compile but I think that, over the past twelve years, it has shown itself to have a value independent of what I, personally, have been able to bring to it. The work could readily be undertaken by other hands.

It does not need to be a one-man-band. That is a possibility but probably not the best one. A group of independent enthusiasts could undertake it, an established local publisher could find it a prestigious and modestly profitable addition to their portfolio, an educational institution could find it a project which enabled students to develop skills in IT inputting and design, journalism, marketing and advertising sales, - let alone understanding of the Performing Arts. Several establishments in Greater Manchester offer this range of disciplines and to take up the title could provide them with a focus both for enthusiasm, experience and wider prestige.

I have only had time for production, which any small business adviser will know it fatal. This book has never made a profit but this does not mean it never could. It has gained quite a deal of recognition and regard. This could be converted, without an impossible degree of effort, into increased sales. The scale of this increase, given the evidence of multiple readership per copy, does not need to be vast for its pages to become a very well focussed advertising medium. The rates could be moderate and still make the book at least modestly profitable.

Once this edition is out, I shall see what can be done to form an editorial board, representing the various interests associated with professional and amateur theatre, training and publishing, who could apply for the resources to establish the book under new management, until it can pay its way. If any readers wish to save me the trouble, by being inspired to put themselves forward to take on the work, and to see that it continues without interruption, I would be more than happy to hear from them. [This is not an impossibly tight timetable. In several years, not a word of the new book has been typed until January but it has still managed to cover the previous four months and to go to press the following September].

Meanwhile, whatever may be the future, I do know what a splendid twelve months the past year has been and I hope that the book does something to reflect this and to enable readers to share the joy. It has been a constant pleasure to see such a variety of excellent work, brought from the furthest corners of the earth and created by a host of local people – **The Lowry**, whose Artistic Director **Robert Robson** has generously donated such a vivid Foreword, is just one local institution which creates both these achievements within its walls.

My thanks to him and to all others who have done so much both to provide such Theatre and to assist me in recording it. I am confident that they will continue to create more excellent work, drawing on the Theatres oldest traditions and constantly amazing us with innovation. I hope their work will continue to be recorded. It deserves to be.

As usual, my especial thanks to **Sheila Waddington** for finding time among her numerous commitments once more to design the cover and to **Geoffrey Clifton** for reducing significantly the number of typing errors in the Journal. My efforts in this have been helpfully added to by **Bren Francis** and **Alan Kelsey**. [Future publishers can know that several have recently expressed their willingness to contribute to this dimension of the work].

This may be Farewell. It should be but it has been a privilege to carry out this work while I could. I still expect to see a lot of Theatre. I hope that someone will be around to record it. **Giles Haworth** **17 September 2005**

Section 1

PRODUCTION

NUMBERS

1. PRODUCTION NUMBERS

No	Play	Venue	Page	Journal
1	VINCENT IN BRIXTON	Library	327	04/10/04
2.	CHAPTER TWO	Curtain	431	04/10/04
3	SPARK	**M6**	**439**	04/10/04
	Cardinal Langley High		430	
	Swinton High	Grange	497	413
	Marple High	Kingsway	504	504
	Prestwich Hi	St Peter's	278	552
	Buile Hill	Balderstone	453	429
	St Joseph's	St Monica's	444	280
4	A CONVERSATION	Royal Ex	372	04/10/04
5	BEYOND BELIEF	Library	328	04/10/04
6.	MERLIN AND THE CAVE OF DREAMS	Library	328	04/10/04
7.	LONDON ASSURANCE	Royal Ex	366	04/10/04
8.	MAYHEM	Royal Ex	373	04/10/04
9.	OFFLINE	Contact	303	13/10/04
10	MOVE OVER MORIATY	**Zion**	**394**	13/10/04
		Library	332	
11	CRAZY LADY	Contact	307	13/10/04
12	MOVING PICTURES	**King's Arms**	**456**	13/10/04
		Midland Hotel	341	
13.	THREE GOBBY COWS	**Contact**	**307**	13/10/04
		Taurus	388	
14	DANNY, KING OF THE BASEMENT	**M6**	**439**	13/10/04
	Falinge Park	St Monica's	434	280
	Oulder Hill	Hayward	434	254
	Marland Hill	Balderstone	441	429
	Bolton Uni	Darnhill	244	432
	Matthew Moss		441	

No	Play	Venue	Page	Journal
15	ANTIGONE	Adelphi	450	18/01/05
16.	ELECTRA	Robert Powell	494	18/01/05
17	STUFF HAPPENS	Adelphi	450	18/01/05
18.	WHEN MEDEA MET ELVIS	Adelphi	450	18/01/05
19.	HOUSE OF ILLUSIONS	Robert Powell	494	18/01/05
20.	POSSIBLY PORN	Totties	542	18/01/05
21	GRAZED KNEES	Solomon Gru	387	18/01/05
22	TWISTED TRAILS or	**Attic**	**286**	18/01/05
	MOULDILOCKS AND THE THREE BIRDS	Bedlam	281	
23	CABBAGES	Attic	285	18/01/05
24	ONE BIRD, TWO STONES	**Jabez Clegg**	**322**	18/01/05
		Bedlam	287	
25	CHAMELEON	Jabez Clegg	322	18/01/05
26	MARBLES	Barca	285	18/01/05
.27.	CHICKEN TIKKA MASALA	Barca	285	18/01/05
.28.	FROM YARD 2 ABROAD	A Fe We	284	18/01/05
29.	UGLY SISTER	Taurus	388	18/01/05
30.	FARNWORTH POND-LIFE	Taurus	388	18/01/05
31	FURTHER THAN THE FURTHEST THING	Capitol	293	18/01/05
32.	THE TRESTLE AT POPE LICK CREEK	Royal Ex	374	18/01/05
33.	PHAEDRA	John Thaw	324	18/01/05
34.	INTERVALS	Coliseum	408	16/03/05
35	THE WORDS LEAVE US	Contact	310	07/03/05
36.	FACE	Contact	310	07/03/05

No	Play	Venue	Page	Journal
37.	10%	Contact	310	07/03/05
38.	RHINOCEROS	Contact	310	
39	HOTEL BABELE	Contact	310	07/03/05
40.	HOMESICK	Contact	311	07/03/05
41	NUNCA NADA DE NINGUEM	Contact	311	07/03/05
42.	A CRIME AGAINST THE LAMBS	Contact	311	07/03/05
43.	SPRING AWAKENING	Contact	311	
44.	EVERYWHERE	John Thaw	324	
45.	DISEMBODIED	Contact	311	07/03/05
46.	A DIFFERENT LANGUAGE	Royal Ex	374	07/03/05
47	THE PILLOWMAN	Lowry	480	07/03/05
48	3 PINTER SHORTS	City Campus	298	07/03/05
49.	THE LIFE OF MOLIERE	Octagon	265	16/02/05
50.	THE FIREWORK MAKER'S DAUGHTER	Lowry	479	16/02/05
51.	OUT OF THE BLUE	Met	277	16/02/05
52.	THE GOSPEL OF MATTHEW	Met	277	16/02/05
53.	RESISTANCE	Contact	312	16/02/05
54.	A RAISIN IN THE SUN	Lowry	482	16/02/05
55.	A TASTE OF HONEY	RNCM	380	16/02/05
56.	BELLS	**Contact**	**312**	16/02/05
		Coliseum	408	
57.	CHAOS	**Contact**	**312**	16/02/05
		Coliseum	408	
58.	IN GOD WE TRUST	**Octagon**	**265**	**16/02/05**
	Coliseum	Contact	403	313
59.	ON THE SHORE OF THE WIDE WORLD	Royal Ex	369	16/02/05

No	Play	Venue	Page	Journal
60.	ELECTRA	Royal Ex	375	18/01/05
61.	POEMS OF ANTIGONE	Capitol	294	18/01/05
62.	LEGEND OF THE WHITE SNAKE	Lowry	469	18/01/05
.63.	FOREST OF THE WILD BOARS	Lowry	469	
.64.	AT THE CROSSROADS	Lowry	470	
.65.	SUICIDE WITH A GOLDEN BRICK	Lowry	470	
.66.	PAPERWORLD	Lowry	468	25/04/05
67.	THE SAFARI PARTY	Library	333	25/04/05
68.	SMILIN' THROUGH	Contact	313	25/04/05
69.	THOROUGHLY MODERN MILLIE	Palace	359	25/04/05
70.	SALAD DAYS	Palace	361	25/04/05
71.	LOOT	Robert Powell	494	25/04/05
.72	WAKE UP LITTLE SUZIE	Coliseum	402	
73.	STRICTLY DANDIA	Lowry	478	
74.	THE REAL THING	Library	330	
75.	ONE TOUCH OF VENUS	Lowry	465	
76.	TURN OF THE SCREW	Coliseum	403	
77.	ARSENIC AND OLD LACE	Lowry	464	
78	WHEN HARRY MET SALLY	Lowry	468	
79.	HELLO, DOLLY	Albert Halls	244	
80.	HOME AND BEAUTY	Bolton Little	245	
.81.	FISH OUT OF WATER	Theatre Chur	276	
82.	CAUGHT IN THE NET	URC	271	
83	OKLAHOMA	Albert Halls	244	
84.	THE LOVE MATCH	St Vincent's	269	

No	Play	Venue	Page Journal
85.	HOT MIKADO	Walmsley	272
.86.	THE GHOST TRAIN	Bolton Little	246
.87.	BEDROOM FARCE	Halliwell	254
88.	JESUS CHRIST SUPERSTAR	Theatre Chur	270
.89.	ALICE IN WONDERLAND	Bolton Lit	249
.90.	DICK WHITTINGTON	Trinity	270
.91.	ALLADIN	Theatre Chur	270
92.	SKYLIGHT	Bolton Little	247
.93.	SEE HOW THEY RUB	Chorley Old R	250
.94.	SOUTH PACIFIC	Theatre Chur	270
95.	DICK BARTON – SPECIAL AGENT	Bolton Little	247
.96.	THE PAJAMA GAME	St Phillip's	268
97.	QUARTET	Halliwell	254
.98.	EDUCATING RITA	URC	271
99.	KISMET	Walmsley	272
100.	KES	Bolton Little	248
101.	ARMED MAN	Albert Halls	244
102.	WEST SIDE STORY	Theatre Chur	270
103.	BRASSED OFF	Bolton Little	248
104.	AN INSPECTOR CALLS	URC	271
105.	LOVE ME SLENDER	St Vincent's	269
106.	ONE O'CLOCK FROM THE HOUSE	Farnworth	252
107.	SUMMER VARIETY SHOW	Bolton Little	249
108,	DIAL M FOR MURDER	Farnworth	251
109.	THE IMPORTANCE OF BEING EARNEST	Farnworth	251
110,	HANS, THE WITCH AND THE GOBBIN	Farnworth	251

No	Play	Venue	Page	Journal
111.	RUMOURS	Farnworth	252	
112.	SHADOWLANDS	Farnworth	251	
113.	GIZMO	**Farnworth**	**251**	
		Club	536	
114..	FLATMATES	**Farnworth**	**251**	
		Club	536	
115.	SAY SOMETHING HAPPENED	Farnworth	251	
116.	TOO LONG AN AUTUMN	Farnworth	252	
117.	ALBERT	Farnworth	252	
118.	GOSFORTH'S FETE	Farnworth	252	
119.	LAST TANGO IN LITTLE GRIMLEY	**Farnworth**	**252**	
		Club	535	
120.	SOAP IN MY EYE	Farnworth	252	
121.	THE LOVER	Farnworth	252	
122.	HOT MIKADO	Theatre Chur	244	
123.	WITH MY LITTLE EYE	Farnworth	252	
124.	OUR BLITZ	Farnworth	252	
125.	LITTLE BROTHER, LITTLE SISTER	Farnworth	252	
126.	SCHOOL JOURNEY TO THE CENTRE OF THE EARTH	Farnworth	252	
127.	GOODBYE IPHIGENIA	Farnworth	252	
128.	RAINDROP FAIRIES	**Farnworth**	**252**	
		Club	535	
129.	WHO CARES	**Farnworth**	**252**	
		Club	535	
130.	CAGE BIRDS	**Farnworth**	**252**	
		Club	536	

No	Play	Venue	Page	Journal
131.	ELEGY FOR A LADY	Farnworth	252	
132.	OH WHAT A LOVELY WAR	Chorley Old	250	
133.	COMMUNICATING DOORS	Chorley Old	250	
134.	VERY LITTLE WOMEN	Octagon	255	
135.	TWELFTH NIGHT	Octagon	256	
136.	DROWNING ON DRY LAND	Octagon	256	
137.	FRANKIE & JOHNNY IN THE CLAIR DE LUNE	Octagon	257	
138.	GEORGE'S MARVELLOUS MEDICINE	Octagon	257	
139..	THE BEAUTY QUEEN OF LEENANE	Octagon	258	
140.	GOING DUTCH	**Octagon**	**260**	
		Lowry	488	
141.	BEAUTIFUL THING	Octagon	260	
142.	SATIN 'N' STEEL	Octagon	261	
143.	TWO	Octagon	261	
144.	EIGHT MILES HIGH	Octagon	263	
145..	RE: GENERATION OF ROAD	Octagon	262	
146.	GARDEN OF THE HEART	**RNCM**	**379**	
	Bill Naughton	PCM	263	505
147.	MEGALOMANIAC	**Bill Naughton**	**263**	
	Green Room	Grange	318	413
148.	ROUGH CUTS	Bill Naughton	264	
149.	MACBETH	**Union Mill**	**271**	
		Vulcan Works	389	

No	Play	Venue	Page	Journal
150.	THE MAGIC SANDALS	Bill Naughton	263	
151.	THE GOLDEN CROWN	Bill Naughton	263	
152.	THE FOOL OF THE WORLD	Bill Naughton	263	
153.	SONYA'S GARDEN	**Bill Naughton**	**264**	
	St Peters	Blue Box	445	288
	Hilltop	Queensway	437	443
	Trinity	St Mary's Ch	448	445
	Holy Family	Chapelfield	437	431
	St Mary's Sch	Rydings	448	443
154.	SISTERS, SUCH DEVOTED SISTERS	**Bill Naughton**	**265**	
		Library	344	
155.	THE UGLY EAGLE	**Octagon**	**155**	
		Waterside	543	
156.	THE OWL AND THE PUSSYCAT	**Bill Naughton**	**265**	
		Waterside	543	
157.	DUDE! WHERE'S MY TEDDY BEAR?	Bill Naughton	265	
158.	RED RIDING HOOD AND THE WOLVES	Bill Naughton	265	
159.	THE IGNATIUS TRAIL	**Bill Naughton**	**266**	
		Royal Ex	375	
160.	CARTWRIGHT CABARET	Bill Naughton	266	
161.	THE BOOTLEGGER'S DAUGHTER	Bill Naughton	266	
162.	THE BUDDING	Bill Naughton	266	
163.	SYD AND FANNY'S CHRISTMAS TURKEY	Bill Naughton	264	
164.	TOP BANANA	Bury Met	276	

No	Play		Venue	Page	Journal
188-200: THE CHORLTON FESTIVAL					
188.	THE CONSTANT WIFE		Chorlton Meth	338	
189.	PLAYBACK THEATRE		St Clement's	383	
190.	FANTASTIC FABLES		Blue Box	287	
191.	COACH G		**Royal Oak**	**459**	
			King's Arms	381	
192.	ADOPTED		St Clements	383	
193.	LAST TURN OF THE NIGHT		**Royal Oak**	**381**	25/05/05
			Late Room	326	
194.	WITHERING LOOKS		Blue Box	288	
195.	COMIC POTENTIAL		St Werburgh's	386	
196.	THE GARDEN IN WINTER		**Blue Box**	**289**	
		Burnley Brow	Byron Street	397	397
		Coppice	Greenhill	409	413
	1	Broadfield	Shawclough	397	446
		Chapelfield	Octagon	431	264
197.	THE NET		Blue Box	287	
198.	THE GREAT BIG JOURNEY		Blue Box	288	
199.	OUR STREET		Blue Box	288	
200.	CHANGE		Blue Box	287	
201-208: IN-FRINGE DRAMA FESTIVAL					
201.	THE INSTALLATION		Council Cham	316	
202.	PUSH UP		Burlington	290	
203.	THE GOAT, OR WHO IS SYLVIA?		Cellar	295	
204.	MIME PIECE		Burlington	290	
205.	GAGARIN WAY		Cellar	295	
206.	EQUUS		Council Cham	316	
207.	A DAY IN THE DEATH OF JOE EGG		Cellar	295	

No	Play	Venue	Page	Journal
208.	THE SWEETEST SWING IN BASEBALL	Burlington	290	
209	YOU DON'T HAVE TO BE JEWISH!	Bury Hebrew	274	
210.	THE ROSES OF EYAM	Blue Box	287	
211.	LIFESPAN	St Clement's	383	
212.	ABU BEN/ADAM	Coliseum	409	25/05/05
213.	EMERGE	Taurus	388	25/05/05
214-217 WRITE 2 FESTIVAL				
214.	PICKERS	Royal Ex	377	25/05/05
215.	LOCUST BEAN GUM	Royal Ex	377	25/05/05
216.	PICTURES OF CLAY	Royal Ex	376	25/05/05
217.	PEACEFULLY, AT HOME	Royal Ex	377	25/05/05
218.	SLAVE TO LOVE	**Royal Ex**	**378**	25/05/05
		Bill Naughton	266	
219.	CATCHING LIGHNING IN A BOTTLE	**Royal Ex**	**378**	25/05/05
		Bill Naughton	266	
220	MUCH ADO ABOUT NOTHING	Wyth Park	390	25/05/05
221.	HAMLET	**Wyth Park**	**390**	25/05/05
		Fletcher Moss	318	
222.	0161 – THE MUSICAL	Contact	314	25/05/05
223.	CHILDREN OF THE MOORS	Coliseum	409	25/05/05
224.	THIS IS HOW IT GOES	Lowry	409	25/05/05
225.	HOOK, LINE AND SINKER	Green Room	320	25/05/05
226.	THE BABY & FLY PIE	Royal Ex	378	25/05/05
227-243 24:7 FESTIVAL, the festival also included productions 12, 22, 24 and 193				
227.	DRINKS WITH NATALIE	Midland Hotel	342	25/05/05

No	Play	Venue	Page	Journal
228.	MILK	Late Room	326	25/05/05
229.	THE FIRST RULE OF COMEDY	Bedlam	286	25/05/05
230.	LAZY DAYS	Life Café	336	25/05/05
231.	THE FALLING	**Midland Hotel**	**342**	25/05/05
		Zion	394	
232.	BOTTLE	Life Café	336	25/05/05
233	THE FRENCH LECTURES	Late Room	326	25/05/05
234.	VODKA KNICKERS	Midland Hotel	326	25/05/05
235.	I'M FRANK MORGAN	Midland Hotel	340	25/05/05
236.	CABBAGES	Midland Hotel	340	25/05/05
237.	SALAD OLVAY	Midland Hotel	343	25/05/05
238.	NOW BREATHE OUT	Midland Hotel	343	25/05/05
239.	HERE IN THE NIGHT	Midland Hotel	341	25/05/05
240.	WHITE WEDDING	Midland Hotel	341	25/05/05
241.	LOVESICK	Midland Hotel	341	25/05/05
242.	THE HANGED MAN	Bedlam	286	25/05/05
243.	NOWHERE MAN	Midland Hotel	343	25/05/05
244.	THE GHOSTS OF CRIME LAKE	Coliseum	407	25/05/05
245.	THE ROOT OF IT	Contact	314	25/05/05
246-255	**BLUE 3 FESTIVAL**			
246.	360 FALLING	Royal Ex	378	25/05/05
247.	VENT	Royal Ex	379	25/05/05
248.	HALF HEAVEN, HALF HEARTACHE	Royal Ex	379	25/05/05
249.	JOURNEY TO THE CENTRE OF YOUR MIND	Royal Ex	379	25/05/05
250.	PEPPERED MOTH	Royal Ex	379	25/05/05
251.	NIGHT PIECE	Royal Ex	379	25/05/05

No	Play		Venue	Page	Journal
252.	THE POETRY OF MATTY P		Royal Ex	379	25/05/05
253.	THE THREE LITTLE ..PIGS		Royal Ex	379	25/05/05
254.	HARRIOT AND I		Royal Ex	379	25/05/05
255.	A WAR IN THE MORNING		Royal Ex	379	25/05/05
256.	IRON		Contact	314	25/05/05
257.	CURRY TALES		**Coliseum**	**406**	25/05/05
		Library	Waterside	327	543
258.	LE STATE		Zion	394	25/05/05
259.	DRACULA – THE BLOOD COUNT		Heaton Park	321	07/08/05
260..	THE IMPORTANCE OF BEING EARNEST		Wyth Park	391	07/07/05
261.	TRANSFORMATIONS		Contact	315	25/05/05
262.	A REVENGE TRAGEDY		Cellar	295	
263.	LOVE AND LULLABIES		**Counthill**	**410**	
		Royton High	Grange	420	415
		Blue Coats	Saddleworth H	396	421
		Radclyffe	Hathershaw	419	413
		Grange High	St Augustines	413	421
		Kaskenmoor	Breeze Hill	415	397
		Crompton Hs	Failsworth	410	412
		South Chad	City Learning	424	398
264.	HIGHS AND LOWS		**Kaskenmoor**	**415**	
			Pakistani Cen	416	
265.	ACTING YOUR AGE		**St Augustine**	**422**	
		Alder High	R'dale Tn Hall	512	447
		Mossley Hollins	Met	521	277
		Breezehill	Saxon Hall	397	
			Royal Ex	375	

No	Play		Venue	Page	
266.	A LIKELY STORY		**All Souls**	**451**	
		Langworthy	Hodge Clough	460	414
		Alexandra Pk	Stansfield Road	396	
		St Hilda's	Freehold	422	412
		Friezeland	Mayfield	412	
		Corpus Christi	St Joseph's	410	423
			St Hugh's	423	
267.	SMASHED		**Two Trees**	**528**	
		Broad Oak	Hyde High	274	522
		St Gabriel's	Hartshead	280	521
		Phoenix	Bolton	267	
		Copley High	West Hill	513	529
		St Damian's	Egerton Park	524	515
		Longdendale	Fairfield	523	515
		Radclyffe	Mossley Hollins	280	521
268.	MACBETH		**Hyde Tech**	**522**	
		Kaskenmoor	Littlemoss	415	522
		Siddal Moor	St James	446	507
		Kingsdown	Stamford High	550	525
		Bolton Boys	Bury CofE High	249	274
		Fred Longworth	G Tomlinson	549	254
		Rivington	Wentworth	267	497
		St Cuthbert's	Wardle	443	448
		Queen Elizabeth	Buile Hill	442	453
		Egerton Park	Thomas Holford	515	534
		Woodhey	Sharples	281	269
		Abraham Guest	St Patrick's	548	496
		Hartshead	Mount St J	521	255
		Stretford Grammar			542
269.	PINOCCHIO		**Our Lady**	**550**	
		Norden	Belfield	442	429
		Benchill	St Joseph's	287	383

No	Play		Venue	Page	
		St Mary's	Dukesgate	384	454
		Romiley	Bp Bilsborrow	507	287
		Castle Hill	St Willibrords	249	387
		St Anthony's	St Thomas	382	
		Sacred Heart	Manley Park	382	338
		Great Moor	All Souls	502	
		Mount Carmel	Forest Park	343	537
		St Cuthbert's	Webster	551	389
		St Alphonsus	Park Road	540	539
270.	FIREBIRD		**Beaver Road**	**286**	
		Butterstile	St Mary's	275	
		Blackshaw	Branwood	396	
		St John Fisher	Seedley		497
		Abram	Bowker Vale	548	289
		St Richard's	Victoria Park	552	542
		Oldham Parish	St James	417	
		Chantlers	St Mary	275	423
		Canon J	Banks Lane	512	500
		The Oaks	Bp Bilsborrow	255	
271.	ROMEO AND JULIET		**Rose Bridge**	**551**	
		Hathershaw	Hulme Girls	413	415
		Offerton	Hulme Boys	504	414
		Fred Longw	Flixton	549	537
		St John Fisher	St John Rigby	551	552
		Broadoak	Bolton Boys	274	241
		Failsworth	Queen Elizabeth	412	442
			City Campus	298	
272.	FAMILY HOLD BACK		Green Room		319
273.	SMOKING GUN		Green Room		319
274.	CUL-DE-SAC		Green Room		319
275.	UNDO		Contact		314
276.	THE LARAMIE PROJECT		Studio Salford		459

No	Play	Venue	Page
680.	CAN I 'AVE A BUDGIE	Hippodrome	526
681.	ANNIE	Hippodrome	527
682.	THE CALCULATING MR ONE	Hippodrome	527
683.	LAUGHIN' ALL OVER THE WORLD	Hippodrome	527
684.	HALFWAY TO PARADISE	Hippodrome	527
685.	THE PIRATES OF THE RIVER ROTHER	Hippodrome	528
686.	A SMALL FAMILY BUSINESS	Alt Garrick	532
687.	KAFKA'S DICK	Alt Garrick	532
688.	MAME	Alt Garrick	532
689.	PERFECT DAYS	Alt Garrick	532
690.	DAD'S ARMY	Alt Garrick	533
691.	BABES IN THE WOOD	Alt Garrick	533
692.	MURDER ON THE NILE	Alt Garrick	533
693.	THE PRICE	Alt Garrick	533
694.	BRASSED OFF	Alt Garrick	533
695.	LES LIASONS DANGEREUSES	Alt Garrick	533
696.	ABIGAIL'S PARTY	Alt Garrick	534
697.	THE WIND IN THE WILLOWS	Alt Garrick	534
698.	MY FAIR LADY	Alt Garrick	534
699.	OLIVER	Alt Garrick	533
700.	FIDDLER ON THE ROOF	Alt Garrick	533
701.	THE IMPORTANCE OF BEING EARNEST	Club	534
702.	THE SNOW QUEEN	Club	534
703.	DEATHTRAP	Club	534
704.	NATURAL CAUSES	Club	534
705.	OLIVER TWIST	Club	535
706.	HARVEY	Club	535
707 – 716 + 113-14, 119, 128-30: HALE ONE-ACT PLAY FESTIVAL			
707.	THE WIZARD OF OZ	Club	535

Section 2

JOURNAL

JOURNAL

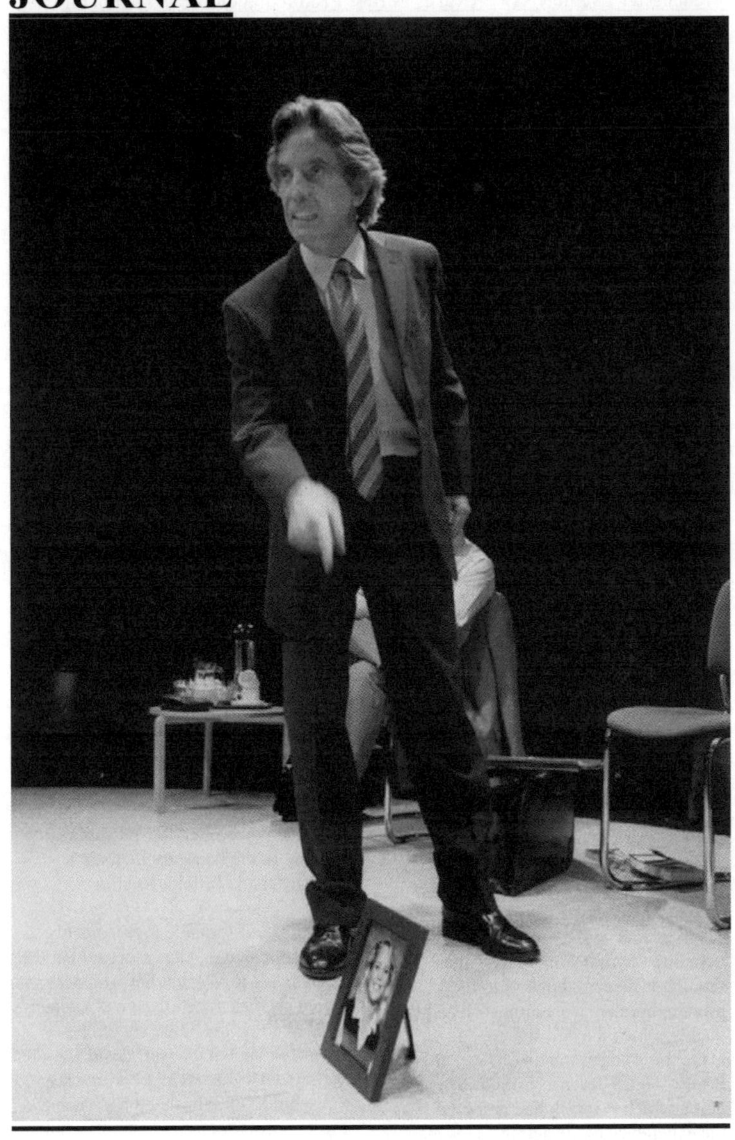

A CONERSATION (4, previous page), within weeks being recognised in the Manchester Evening News Awards as Best Production our of all seen in Greater Manchester in the previous twelve months; here MARTIN TURNER portrays Derek Milsom as blaming everyone in sight for the vicious killing of his daughter.

2004

4 OCTOBER. **VINCENT IN BRIXTON (1);** Library. *6 OCTOBER.* **CHAPTER TWO (2);** Curtain. *7 OCTOBER.* **SPARK (3);** M6. *9 OCTOBER.* **A CONVERSATION (4);** Royal Exchange. *4 NOVEMBER.* **BEYOND BELIEF (5);** Library. *27 NOVEMBER.* **MAYHEM (8);** Royal Exchange. **2005** *7 JANUARY.* **MERLIN AND THE CAVE OF DREAMS (6);** Library. *8 JANUARY.* **LONDON ASSURANCE (7);** Royal Exchange.

The first four of these productions were not quite the first which I saw after sending last year's book of to the printers but they were almost so and the quality which they all shared, and which made them so stimulating to see, after the prolonged absence from theatre-going which that task had enforced, was the excellence of the acting. This may not be true to quite the same degree of all the other productions considered here but it is of most of them and is the primary factor which ties them all together.

This emphasis on performance is not to be divorced from the very significant content of most of the plays. **Vincent In Brixton** was a fascinating exploration of an emerging artistic sensibility, set in a very significant period, and also had much to express about the romantic experience of an older woman. It tells of the young Vincent Van Gogh (**Gus Gallagher)** in London 1873-74. He is not then an artist, although much interested in the field as a junior employee in the London offices of a Dutch firm of art dealers. At the start of the play, he has just become attracted to the house in which he is seeking lodgings by observing a much more adept though still developing artist Sam Plowman, **Christopher Pizzey**) sketching outside and being visited at his task by the attractive young daughter of the house (Eugenie Loyer, **Hannah Watkins**). The action begins when he is being shown around the available lodging in the house by Eugenie's mother Ursula (**Sheila Ruskin**).

That actress' surname is presumably pure coincidence but is most apt, as she emphasises to Vincent how important it is that she has a well-designed kitchen table and that the house should be beautiful, showing a wall-design painted by Sam. This is not a 'working class' household, - her husband had been a professor of languages -, but it is not an affluent one. Now widowed, her modest income comes from running a Dame School on the premises and taking in lodgers. Hearing that Vincent has spotted her house on his way home from church, she stresses she is not religious. When she becomes aware that Vincent has previously made the acquaintance of her daughter, she at first feels it would be inappropriate for him to be a lodger but the closeness of Eugenie's relationship with Sam causes her no concern. She is ready to lend her daughter her wedding-ring in order to make it possible for her and Sam to spend a weekend at a seaside boarding-house as if man and wife. Vincent is able to talk her into allowing a brief trial period of his residence but by the beginning of the second scene this has been well exceeded and what she is amazed to find is that by then Vincent has developed a passion for her. "Have you any idea how old I am?" (56) she exclaims but Vincent bulldozes through, partly inspired by his current enthusiasm for the writings of **Jules Michelet**: "Il n'y a pas de vielle femme!"

We see here the English side of the company remaking its social understanding as the principles of **Ruskin** and **William Morris** supersede those of traditional Christianity. Vincent does not entirely fit into this bracket, - the terms in which he praises what he finds beautiful in Ursula's aging body are not the aesthetics of a Pre-Raphaelite and take her more than somewhat aback but it is the excitement of a time of changing and generally inspirational outlooks which enables a dialogue to evolve between the very distinctive Vincent and the other characters. He had originally got at fierce cross purposes with Sam, who is a craftsman in the building trades, by criticising the perspective in the sketches in his portfolio but the argument not only draws Vincent into trying his own hand at the sketch pad but brings the two of them closer through argument, Vincent coming to be the strongest supporter of Sam's attempt to gain a scholarship which would enable him to take up a place to train at the **Royal Academy**.

At the end of the First Act, therefore, everyone is caught up in exciting and positive developments: Vincent and Ursula's love for each other has grown into an absorbing passion, that of Sam and Eugenie is buoyed up not only by the prospect of his scholarship but his belief that Art can create a more equitable society, reflecting a solid foundation in skilled artisans rather than the images of the idle but fabulously wealthy disporting themselves in elegant ball gowns, which are the most popular works of which Vincent's employers can sell reproductions by the hundred, as working households like to hang them on their walls. **Nicholas Wright**, the author, has slightly adjusted the timing of events, - as suggested by the dates on the extracts from Vincent's letters to his brother which are included in the programme -, so that he can name his scenes after the four seasons. After the prospects and flourishing of Spring and Summer in the First Act, we now get the storms and chill of Autumn and Winter.

At the end of the First Act, Vincent has been insisting on his plan to install his sister Anna into the Loyers' household, preparatory to her finding domestic service in England, after he has brought her over from Holland. He has represented this as a bounty for Ursula, portraying Anna as an unstoppable domestic dynamo who will take over cooking and cleaning for the whole household, - already extremely well handled by Ursula. At the beginning of Act Two we find Anna (**Olivia Darnley**) equipped with bucket and mop and precisely so engaged. She is tackling this so comprehensively that one might imagine her to be already well established. In fact, she is only just off the boat. Unfortunately, it is not only material dirt through which she powers her way. She has soon got to the bottom of the relationship between Vincent and Ursula and her reaction drives Vincent out of the house, uncertain as to whether he will ever return. Months later it is clear that he did not. The emotional turmoil has brought the once highly resilient Ursula to a state of near total collapse. She is unable to keep up her school or the care of her house. Sam and Eugenie, now married and living elsewhere, do what they can to support her but she is so listless that this or that repair really does little to keep the house viable. Their condition too is less hopeful than it had seemed when we last saw them. As Eugenie had become pregnant, Sam has had to turn down his scholarship and to continue working at his old trade in order to provide sufficient income for them to marry and start a household.

In these circumstances, the re-appearance of a dishevelled Vincent is not an especially welcome sight but he is admitted, soaked to the skin as, although once a trim figure well equipped with umbrellas, he now has nothing to protect him from the rain. He has nothing very coherent to say to Ursula about why he left her so abruptly. Words of scripture are more prominent among his utterances but his response to the news from Sam is that concern for a wife and child should not have come between an artist and his calling. He is now living in Paris, has lost his art dealer's job but is taking seriously to painting himself. In an ending somewhat reminiscent, - in re-creating one of the artist's most famous images -, of the one-act play **Tony Benge** wrote for the **Lowry** centenary, when the **Library** still staged lunch-time theatre, he becomes aware of the potential as a still-life of the sopping wet pair of shoes which have been removed from him and placed on a newspaper. He becomes absorbed in trying to sketch them, oblivious of all else in the once familiar kitchen.

Raising the question of whether growing artistic vision could in anyway be linked to a decline in 'ordinary' mental faculties was only one fascinating issue explored by the play. The whole context of a section of the English population discovering if it can live by new principles but finding that fundamental decencies still have to be observed through old conventions and the power to disrupt of even older emotions, makes fascinating material, vividly realised. Certainly the staging helps: the well-equipped kitchen for instance, in which the entire action takes place, enable Ursula to go through all the procedures for preparing a comprehensive family Sunday lunch throughout the first scene with Vincent. Nevertheless, it was the detail and vividness of the acting which was the key ingredient in bringing every aspect of the play to life and making it a fascinating experience to see.

Sheila Ruskin shows Ursula to be thoroughly in command of both her household duties and ideas, utterly confident in both, clear how she should respond to the needs of Sam and Eugenie, at first amazed at Vincent's declaration of love but then tremendously buoyed up by it, at first none too appreciative of the intrusions of Anna but convinced she can survive their inconveniences, totally devastated when she destroys her new-found love but able to fabricate some elements of a response when, unapologetically, he once more re-appears in her life.

Gus Gallagher makes Vincent a distinctive character from the first: still somewhat unfamiliar with the customs of a new country but probably not one who ever fitted very exactly into any social ambience, while still having the confidence, even audacity, to achieve his way of doing things from the first. He is assimilating new ideas throughout the play but always primarily reliant on his own instincts in how things should be done. While in the first scenes he initially seems to be accumulating opportunities for a fuller life, by the end he has lost even the ability to wash or dress himself but perhaps as the cost of attaining an artistic vision on a larger scale than he ever had before.

Eugenie and, especially, Sam had had an artistic vision from the first and one which encompassed the whole ordering of society but, whereas Vincent has abandoned the practical, they have been prepared to forsake their vision for the sake of more mundane practicalities. **Hannah Watkins** showed Eugenie as able to respond to Vincent's initial attraction to her with an amused smile, without for a moment wavering in her commitment to Sam, and when her eventual marriage to him is sooner than they would have wished and burdened from the first not merely with a helpless baby but an unexpectedly helpless mother, she accepts this with a positive resilience also. **Christopher Pizzey** can show real anger as the bumbling Vincent crosses both his artistic and his social vision but also the friendship which grows out of realising that Vincent is someone it is worth talking to about art. Although seeing what is unjust and callous about much of the world in which he lives, he can be affectionate to him as well as towards his future wife and mother-in-law.

The one performance at which I found some disquiet was that of **Olivia Darnley** as Anna but I do not know if that was any fault of the actress. Given that Anna is the agent of the play's massive disruption, it is perhaps natural that one's response to her should include more than an element of unease. Perhaps I sensed artifice from the way she instantly appeared banging about with her mop and bucket. Were we seeing a cartoon of how Vincent had described her just before the interval, rather than a fuller character which she might have been in herself? However, we soon saw that there was far more to her than an automaton broom-wielder. Although at first getting the wrong end of the stick in how the love-lines lay in the household, she batters through to the true situation and has clear moral ideas about how she should respond to them. In having her distinctive ideas and her insistence on following them she was in many ways her brother's true sister. Bringing in a character of completely different pace and style can be perfectly good drama. I am not quite sure why I felt that there was something about this piece of the jigsaw which did not really fit but a sense of the agley was what I did experience.

Whether this was some detail of writing or performance, I am not quite sure but even though this was the key element which completely changed the course of events in the second half, some uneasiness in how this was done did not prevent this being a most absorbing production, dealing with matters of the greatest interest.

Content was a far lesser matter in the **Neil Simon** comedy **Chapter Two.** It did deal with matters of some genuine human concern, - how much a man can fully give himself to a second marriage when his mind is always filled with memories of a blissfully happy first, -which ended tragically, suddenly and early -, and how much a writer, who must not only write but sell his work to Hollywood, can combine this with domestic affection. These are much the issues addressed in **Jake's Women (99:106).** I felt the treatment worked better here, perhaps because it made no bones about being primarily a very funny comedy, whereas I found in **Jake** what seemed somewhat special pleading for the male representing itself as a considered *Apologia Pro Vita Sua.* There the male side had to predominate, as the second wife deliberately took herself out of the story, to see if he could sort himself out in her absence, whereas here Jenny Malone (**Jo Weetman**) is involved throughout. She may primarily be left to be sweetly understanding and tolerant, if often hurt by the touchy behaviour of George Schneider (**John Weetman**), but she has been able to establish herself before they meet as a cheerily resilient person and also one does not feel a sense of imbalance because **Jo Weetman** does such a splendid job of making her an attractive on-stage character, in a way seeming like the clearly "something different" Connie Dayton, nine years on, whom she portrayed so successfully in **Come Blow Your Horn (96:2)** in 1995. **Colin Smith** and **Rachel Mellor** were also strikingly effective in the smaller parts of brother and best friend, whose *amours* are not troubled with the demands of deep commitment and emotion which possess the principals. The play is replete with witty lines and splendidly structured scenes, including the farcical, but for these to be effective one needed the splendid involving acting which we got on all hands and which made the evening such a delight.

These are very experienced actors but all amateurs. On the other side of Rochdale the next night, one could see actors almost half their age but fully professional giving as involving a performance at the **M6 Theatre**. Whereas the four actors at the **Curtain Theatre** each had but as single role, the four in **Mary Cooper**'s **Spark** not only portrayed the four young people who were their primary characters but the parents with whom they came to be on such difficult terms and various other people whom they encountered. It was important that all these characters should be well represented as it was of the essence of the play to understand the position of all parties and for the primarily young audiences for whom the play is intended not only to be able to identify with those of their own age but to see understandable and sympathetic reasons for the behaviour of those senior to them with which they had such difficulty.

Whereas **Chapter Two** had had a comparatively realistic set, showing the two flats where the action took place side by side, (although in reality they were in different districts), with a full range of furnishing and hand props, **Spark** just had the play's title sprayed up on a back screen by a local graffiti artist (**Liam**), the ramp from a skateboard park and four large cardboard boxes, on the otherwise bare forestage, representing the bedrooms of the four main characters. These could be characterised in different ways, for instance by the manner in which they shook when characters shut themselves in on their several returns from school, Sakina's (**Shahena Choudhury**) bouncing all over the place as she danced to *bhangra,* Rachel's (**Sarah Han**) shaking to the unvarying thump of Heavy Metal.

The core difficulties arose because the two boys (**Marlon Lloyd Allen** and

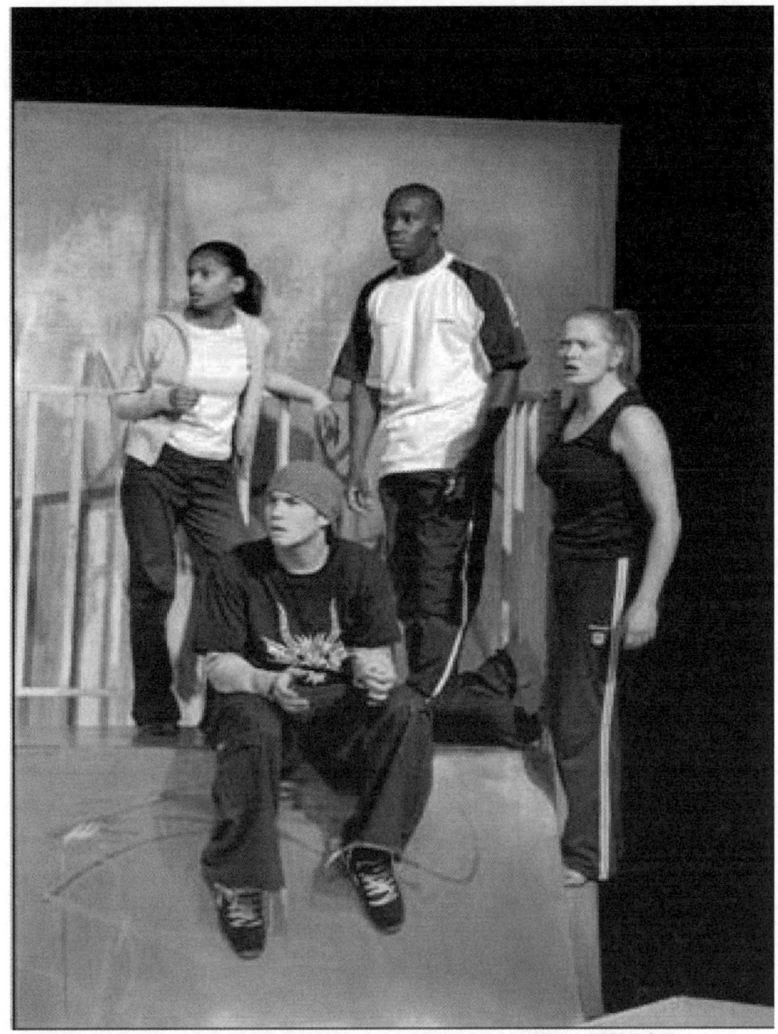

SPARK (3); left to right: SHAHENA CHOUDHURY, JAMES A WILSON, MARLON LLOYD ALLEN, SARAH HAN

Jamie A Wilson) found a satchel containing several hundred pounds on the school bus. There were different ideas over what they should do about it but a couple of ineffective attempts were made to hand it in, frustrated by closed counters and offices. Then, learning that the roughest thugs in the school are aware of their find, they decide that the safest thing to do is to spend the money quick, which leads to all sorts of parental suspicions about how clothing items have been obtained or why they no longer need to shop for the new trainers they have been pleading for. Concerned that this apparent wealth has been obtained by dangerous means, the parents become far more intrusive than the teenagers find tolerable. Some get at such cross-purposes that they try to leave home. Searching for their children brings the parents into closer contact than before and more aware of what different standards of behaviour are allowed in the different houses their children visit. The intertwining of these stories builds up into a very involving experience, the primary means through which this becomes effective being the highly skilful acting, switching briskly from character to character and conveying circumstances through movement as well as more realistic action.

The theme of how massive disagreements can evolve from minor untruths, told with the best of intentions, was the most central to **Mayhem.** Although the setting was far more recent, August 2000 in Los Angeles, the prime impetus, a Liberal's voluble but often ludicrous determination to involve herself in a worthy cause, is one which several American writers would seem to have addressed over at least the previous thirty years. Claire (**Rebecca Egan**), at the beginning of the play is desperate to show solidarity with the women of Afghanistan, oppressed by the Taliban, by constraining her more biddable friend Susan (**Penny Layden**) to attend a meeting. She steam-rollers over Susan's reluctance to leave her husband David (**Sean Gallagher**) at such short notice with responsibility for their baby, claiming that David's touchiness about this is mere male domination, unworthy of respect. Her despite for men would seem not to be very deep as it is apparent enough that her own wish to attend the meeting is greatly stimulated by the fact that it is to be addressed by a Gonzo Journalist (Wesley, **Sean Campion**) with whom she would dearly love to be on intimate terms. Such a liaison could be achieved at after-meeting drinks, the prospect of which is even more undesirable to David, a reformed alcoholic, than the initial chore of being left with the baby. Susan assures him that there will be no going to bars but is constrained to accompany Claire in her attempts to allure Wesley, with a visit to a Chinese restaurant. Her endeavours to hide this from David and then the repercussions of Wesley finding her far more interesting than Claire set in motion the spiral of lies.

It was a rather diffuse play, combining both the satirical, the highly emotional and some concern with genuinely serious issues. It was well acted, making it a reasonably interesting evening's theatre but in terms of being gripping was as nothing in comparison with the previous in-house production in the **Royal Exchange Studio, A Conversation.** This reproduced the circumstances of the Australian practice of community conferencing, which is designed to bring the victims of crime face to face with the offenders in controlled circumstances, so that the latter may fully understand the implications of what they have done and the former may feel that they have had a full chance to express what the events have meant for them.

The meeting we see does not conform entirely to this pattern. There is absolutely no question of the perpetrator of this particular crime, - a brutal murder -, being let out of his cell for such a meeting. He can only submit a tape recording, giving his account of what happened. The meeting has been sought by his mother, who wants the opportunity to express directly to the victim's family their regrets for what has happened. The victim's father (Derek Milsom, **Martin Turner**) is outraged at this temerity, only agreeing to the meeting so that he can leave none of the perpetrator's family in any doubt as to the nature of the crime which was committed and blame everyone in sight, most especially the psychiatrist (Lorin Zemak, **Cate Hamer**) who had recommended that the killer, after previous offences, was safe to be allowed back into the community.

Although he says very little, the meeting's moderator (Jack Manning, **Stuart Goodwin**) is successful in engendering a dialogue between the two families, so that even a few friendly remarks could be exchanged as they left. On reflection afterwards one could be aware of an almost **Inspector Calls**-like schematism in the way absolutely everyone involved, even Derek Milsom, came to admit some degree of responsibility for what had happened. This is not to belittle **Priestley**'s splendid play, only to suggest that **David Williamson**'s affected to evoke a far messier reality, and in performance successfully did so. Performance was of the essence. Although there was great skill in the way the conversation made its way through all the difficulties and tensions, never resorting to obvious artifice in order to move on from an *impasse,* never making anyone inappropriately articulate but always managing to sustain a clear thread of involvement, nevertheless, what was needed to carry this off was high quality acting on all sides, the distinct characters seeming to emerge entirely naturally, the drama evolving and involving without histrionics. Although Jack Manning, in laying down the ground rules at the outset, said "You can get up and move around if you want to," everybody just sat in their distinctive ways, silent or expressing themselves. It was perfect material for a Studio theatre (although the **Royal Exchange** main house could have been just as apt), with the audience sitting on either side, right up to the actors, so one was conscious of being inside a confined room and events developing in a natural environment.

Whilst highly realistic, **A Conversation**, was an entirely facsimilated piece, a fictional drama. **Beyond Belief** drew all its material from the actual records of the Shipman Inquiry, which was conducted just a couple of hundred yards away from the theatre, in Manchester Town Hall. The **Library Theatre** has played host to such re-stagings in the past, for instance **Tricycle Theatre**'s **The Colour of Justice (00.32),** on matters relating to the killing of **Stephen Lawrence**. Being so local, the Shipman Inquiry was a very natural subject for the **Library Theatre** to choose in creating its own drama of this nature and a proper extension of the work sought by those relatives of victims who pushed for the inquiry to be public, so that the details of what happened might be clearly known by all. It was, however, far more difficult material to submit to such treatment. The **Lawrence** inquiry related to one killing, in clearly known circumstances, and had a specific focus on why police investigations had failed to lead to any successful prosecutions. It had taken sixty-nine days. Compressing that into two and a half hours might seem a challenge but the enquiry led by **Dame Janet Smith (Romy Baskerville** in this staging) lasted over two years and had far more foxes to hunt.

Harold Shipman had been formally convicted of killing fifteen of his patients. The enquiry had to try and determine the total extent of his crimes, finding that he killed at least 215 people. It had to examine why, when this long sequence of deaths did eventually raise suspicions which were referred to the police, the action taken was ineffectual, several more killings taking place before his crimes were uncovered. In so far as each success by **Shipman** had depended upon his obtaining death certificates endorsed by other members of the medical profession and large supplies of lethal drugs whose issue is meant to be controlled, the enquiry had to determine what had actually happened in all these particular cases and what better procedures might be more effective in future. As **Shipman** had been publicly convicted earlier in his career of the misuse of drugs, the question had to be examined as to whether the **General Medical Council** had been negligent in allowing him to continue to practice and whether it was an appropriately constituted body to have such authority.

A net cast so wide raised problems of dramatic focus. Whereas **The Colour of Justice** had managed to give the impression of a continuously evolving narrative, **Beyond Belief** was from the first clearly a matter of edited highlights. As this is what it was, it is no slur that it did not make undue pretence to be otherwise. It is just to remark that it had one less card in the dramatic pack. A dramatic card available to **The Colour of Justice** was that it featured grandstanding QCs, such as **Michael Mansfield** (who partly sponsored the production) and **Stephen Kamlish**, who missed no opportunity to pour open scorn on the police officers who appeared before the inquiry and whose incompetence they held responsible for the failed prosecution. This awakened some considerable concern in me, that a police force so treated might be unlikely to receive sympathetically advice from such a source as to how it might conduct its affairs better in future, but, again, this was a dramatic tool which was not available to this production, the lawyers on this occasion usually confining themselves far more circumspectly to eliciting information, even when confronting police officers whose performance may have been as fatally inadequate as that of those brought before the **Stephen Lawrence** inquiry. When Andrew Spink QC (**C P Hallam**) continued to try to establish at considerable length, when Mrs Shipman (**Joan Kempson**) appeared, that, as she still believed in her husband's innocence and intended to take legal action to try to establish this, many might doubt if she would be fully forthcoming when questioned, Dame Janet Smith called him to order, saying that no further questioning along these lines would be appropriate: it ought to be apparent that a woman under considerable stress was doing her best to be helpful.

It was in the human detail of the presentation of the evidence that I found the true strength of the production to lie. I did not take more particular interest in the **Shipman** events than in any other ongoing subject of news but I did not find that on major matters of information or interpretation there was much of which I had been previously unaware. What did make it a very rewarding evening's theatre was to see the skill with which

BEYOND BELIEF (5); ROMY BASKERVILLE as Dame Janet Smith presides over the Shipman Enquiry

each character appearing at the tribunal was presented. From this point of view, the fact that single actors had to take two or even three roles was a positive advantage because one could delight in their ability to take on totally different persona.

As the audience entered, **Simon Molloy** was strolling across the stage, brief under his arm as one of the lawyers, Philip Gaisford, and he then sat chatting with Caroline Swift QC (**Cate Hamer**) who appeared to be the leading counsel to the inquiry (a very fine performance; **Cate Hamer** has had several notable roles recently as professional women, such as Tessa in **Across Oca (04:3)** and Lorin Zemanek in **A Converation** this year; in both of these she had to show her character brought low by accumulated stresses, so it was nice to see her remaining on top of her brief, with only a momentary embarrassment on finding that she has not been exact enough in stating how an inquiry witness was related to one of the victims)

As Philip Gaisford, **Simon Molloy** had only a minor contribution to make to the inquiry but he also portrayed two major witnesses: Chief Superintendent David Sykes, in overall charge of the investigation which was made when suspicions were first raised with the police, and Robert Gray, the final witness we saw, representing the **General Medical Council.** These were both very distinctive performances. It would have been possible for an audience member whose attentions were focussed on other matters not to have realised that they were both being given by the same actor but for those who did there was the additional pleasure of seeing enormous professional skill being deployed in realising the human character of two very different people responding to close criticism of themselves and of their organisations. Ram-rod straight but genially inclined, Chief Superintendent Sykes asserted that he was a police officer of very considerable experience but conceded from the first that this had never involved major matters of detection. He had considered it sufficient to ask the most senior of his few available detectives, (the Detective Chief Superintendent being on leave) to take an informal 'look-see,' when questions about the behaviour of a well respected doctor were raised, receiving general verbal feed back from him a few times a week on how things were going but never thinking this a matter that required formal record to be kept of steps taken and their results. He would be among those of whom the inquiry and the audience saw many which reminded them of others they knew well in various spheres: entirely able and well-meaning, who would have been as likely as many others to have responded inadequately to the possibility of events which were characterised by **Shipman**'s trial judge as "beyond belief."

The penultimate witness we saw, Alison Massey (**KateLayden**), the relative of a victim, described as coherently as she could that one of the ways in which her experiences had left her totally shattered was the feeling that she could never have any confidence again in being well served by any profession, whether medicine or the police –she forbore to mention the law but the lawyers present, led by Dame Janet, quietly indicated very generously that they would have quite understood if she had included them in her feelings that they would always look after their own, rather than allow any objection to be sustained that they had not acted in the best interests of ordinary members of the public.

When **Simon Molloy**'s Robert Gray was asked if he recognised such a viewpoint, he barked emphatically "I do not!" Leaning fully back in his chair, wearing bulky tweeds whose style would have changed less over the past century than the clothes of anyone else appearing at the inquiry and seeing it less than any as a full dress occasion, he represented himself as having a far deeper professional insight into the issues raised than anyone else present had or could have. Addressing the question of whether the general public could have full confidence in doctors being regulated by a body consisting only of doctors, he justified his position by harking back to the establishment of the **General Medical Council** in the mid-Nineteenth Century, when there had been dozens of allegedly professional organisations, representing all sorts of specialisations and training or the lack of it and the public could not have known whether membership of any of them represented anything worthwhile or mere quackery.

Aside from the issue of whether such worthy origins could still act as a sovereign guarantee that the public could have every confidence in doctors being regulated by doctors, - which **Dame Janet**'s Fifth Report, published just after this production, decided it could not (: a doctors' body must always find the interests of its own profession the first call on its loyalties) –the specific question Robert Gray had to answer was why the **GMC** had allowed **Shipman** to continue to practice after his early conviction for misuse of drugs, in that case for his own consumption. Shaw represented this as the reasonable reaction to 'the mistakes of a young man, whose senior colleagues had imposed upon him the chore of having charge of the medical cabinet,' there being every sign that he had been fully re-habilitated and as he had made no endeavour to hide his lapse from future colleagues, who had indeed had the greater confidence in him because of his openness.

The reasonableness of this reply might have stood up better if we had had more chance to hear it in the context of the ramifications of the blunt assertion to the inquiry on this issue of Detective Inspector David Smith (**David Crellin**): "It's a fact. Doctors do steal drugs. I've arrested them for it." I have heard it suggested, before and independent of the **Shipman** case, that, just as many doctors apparently still ease the strains of their profession with greater use of alcohol and cigarettes than they would recommend to their patients, so a resort to the drugs cabinet, especially during the pressures of the early years of the profession, is not that uncommon. In other words, if everyone caught out in this was to be permanently debarred a significant number of fully-trained people would cease to available for work which there is never enough people to do. A professional body which decided that, in many cases, means could be found to benefit from their abilities would have a case for saying that it was acting in the public interest. It could claim that it was acting with more insight than the "Off With His Head!" which might come more naturally to laymen. **Harold Shipman** was so exceptional that his case should not seriously call into question such a general procedure.

If the extracts we saw of the testimony of Robert Shaw did not allow him to make such a claim in full, certainly the vigorous self-confidence and assertive tone with which **Simon Molloy** presented him made a strong dramatic impact and did enable the audience to judge the nature of the case which needs to be addressed.

Whilst it was tremendously impressive to see a single actor discharging three roles to such good effect, this should not detract from the power of such as **Romy Baskerville, Cate Hamer** and **David Crellin**, who each had only a single part. As Chair and Leading Counsel, the first two of these were on stage throughout, **David Crellin** only appeared as a single witness out of many. He was helped to make the impact he did by being the first whose testimony we saw at some considerable length and thus less at hazard from the hydra-headed nature of the subject matter, which I have suggested was something of a problem in helping the audience to find an exact focus. He also triumphed by realising the drama of his position by very vivid characterisation. Many would have seen him as very much a villain of the piece, having been condemned in a preceding Police inquiry into the investigation in which he came up with nothing particular against **Shipman**, after suspicions had first been raised. He had his avenues of research narrowed because of the strong plea from **Dr Reynolds**, who had finally felt that **Dr Shipman**'s frequent requests for countersigned Death Certificates raised questions which must be looked into, that this must be done without making **Shipman** aware that he was being investigated, as she was deeply embarrassed by finding she had to report suspicions about the conduct of a fellow professional. Smith had decided that the best means of search within this constriction would be to look at the coroner's reports on deaths among **Shipman**'s patients. He found that he could not just roll up and look through the files and had to ask the coroner's office themselves to look through a selection of cases which he gave them.

Understandably, this did not prove to be an especially enlightening exercise. However, despite some embarrassment in conceding this, Smith in the testimony we saw held to the view that he might have turned to more revealing procedures if he had been given time to take the case further. He had not used the rigorous procedures of a full enquiry because this had not been asked of him. We got a picture of someone used enough to dealing with the grubby side of human behaviour, conscious that his conduct on this case had been called in question in very serious circumstances but in general confident that he knew more about what his work entailed on a day to day basis than outsiders who questioned him.

Confidence in what her profession entailed was also a primary characteristic of such a witness a Dr Susan Booth, played by **Eileen O'Brien**, in contrast to her other, totally dissimilar role as Carol Chapman, **Shipman's** now shattered surgery clerk, whose mother and grandmother were both killed by him but who never associated him with the cause of their deaths, even just after seeing her mother walk down the corridor well enough into his consulting room, both because such an idea was beyond belief and because the only thought she was capable of, when called to the treatment room was "Me mum's dead." Even a trained surgery nurse (**Alison Burrows**) would not register at the time, when called to help with resuscitation, that **Dr Shipman** was not really instructing the use of the best resources they had for such a purpose. **Beyond Belief** was an apt title to choose.

This was the most unique production of a most distinctive and interesting season which the **Library Theatre** is offering this year and which I hope to see in full. Top-level acting was the core ingredient in realising the virtues of the first two productions. This was not really true of the Christmas production, **Merlin and The Cave of Dreams**, a simpler sketching-in of characters being found more appropriate for a predominantly young audience, but the key resource in realising its distinctive world was to have the title role taken by **Wyllie Longmore**, pronouncing powerfully the lines adapted from a 13th Century Welsh poem "I am Merlin. I dream perfect dreams" and evoking a time in which the forests stretched as far as the sea.

Charles Way has become a most prolific writer of plays for young people and has for some years dominated the **Library**'s Christmas offerings. I find his rather insistent emphasis on adapting ancient myths works better for me on some occasions than others. Last year, I found that the simple folktale structure of **A Spell of Cold Weather (04:246)** at the **Royal Exchange** succeeded more for me than the updating of **The Ghosts of Scrooge (04:364)** at the **Library. Merlin** did not seem to me to have a very effective structure. After Merlin's prologue, we meet the fourteen-year-old Arthur (**Alexander Campbell**) and his brother Cei (**Patrick Connolly)** trying to find their way through the forest, as if it were important to find a particular place. However, it seems later that their mission was a first attempt to hunt for a useful contribution for their parents' pot, for which arriving at a specific glade would not obviously be of great importance. All they in fact achieve is a dream inspired in Arthur by Merlin, both giving him the vision of his drawing the sword from the stone, a legend whose significance this Arthur already knows, and revealing to him the news that King Uther Pendragon is dead

It seems later that Merlin intended Arthur to pass on this news to his apparent parents, Sir Ector (**Duncan Henderson**) and Gwyneth (**Rebecca Steele**) and that they would by now have told him that he was not their natural son. When he comes after the boys' return he has to break both pieces of news himself. Arthur is absolutely shattered by this, rejecting all three members of those he had though of as his family. He rushes out distractedly, unable to attend to Merlin's principal demand that as he is the true son of Uther Pendragon, he must come quickly to draw the sword from the stone, to establish that he is the true king before rival claimants start a vicious civil war, which will spread throughout the land, even to the very door of Sir Ector and Gwynneth, who, in particular, feels that Arthur is far too young for such a calling and that they should have been allowed to keep him until he was old enough to assume responsibilities and for them to explain all these things to him.

Merlin finds him five days later, collapsed in the forest with exhaustion, in particular after spurning Cei's attempts to find him and bring him home, a place that Arthur no longer feels he has. Merlin revives him and urges him that they have only two days left in which to reach the stone and prevent the civil war. Arthur says that he cannot take the decision about becoming king until he has spoken to his real parents, now both dead but which Merlin is able to help him achieve by showing him how to travel to the other world.

Discovery of birth parents and feelings about meeting them have become a major theme since 1986,when the **Children's Act** completely changed policy, which had been that these were people of whose very existence the adopted should know nothing, to enabling them to be kept informed from their earliest years and those adopted earlier to be entitled to know everything about their origins and helped to meet their birth parents if they wish. Plays have been written for all age groups about this but although **Charles Way** shows Arthur greatly distraught by these discoveries he does not seem to explore the issue in any way, least of all one which might be especially helpful for a young audience.

Arthur does meet his mother Igraine (**Helen Kirkpatrich**), who is full of loving encouragement for him to be king, saying it is what she had always dreamed of for her son, but Arthur says he needs to speak to his father also. Igraine warns him that in the other world people appear in their true character, so that, in finding Uther (**Christian Bradley**), he will encounter a fearsome dragon. To protect himself, and stressing it is only for this purpose, she gives him the sword Excalibur. Sons killing fathers is something which has been more openly discussed over the past century than any other, thanks to the influence of **Sigmund Freud.** Whether anything useful could be made of this in a play for children, I rather doubt. The possibility in this context also raised memories of **Martin Beard**'s skit **Romeo and Juliet Deceased (00:467)**, without doing any more to address the question of what could possibly be entailed in re-killing beyond the grave.

Although at first rather enthused by the gift of the sword and excited by his attempts to learn how to use it, when indeed challenged by Uther, - donning a dragon's head and most of the rest of the cast forming itself into his extensive, armour-grey, scaled body, (Movement Direction by **Niamh Dowling**) -, Arthur, after battling for a while, is ultimately unsuccessful. Whether this was because he had not yet mastered how to use a weapon almost as big as he was or because he lacked the killer instinct, was not entirely apparent. As he lay prostrate, about to be devoured, a white knight entered and dispatched the dragon. Removing his helmet, he proved to be his 'brother' Cei. How he came to be in the other world was not explained. Nor did the question apply only to him. As Arthur was about to sink back into the world from which he had come, Cei was joined by the two other characters he had met in the other world, the Washer At The Ford and Rhitta of the Beards, revealing themselves to be Gwyneth and Sir Ector.

Reconciling himself to his debt to his adoptive parents, as a necessary precursor to his kingship, might have been a sensible lesson to draw from the tale but there seemed nothing particular to stress it. The sole episode remaining was to see him draw the sword from the stone and raise it aloft, as Merlin proclaimed that he was to establish a kingdom of order and justice whose principles would endure for hundreds of years. A binding thread to the various events we had seen could have been that his various experiences in the Cave of Dreams had laid the foundations for this, just as the spirit with which the young girl who comes to stay on the farm in **A Spell of Cold Weather** tackles the three daily tasks of milking the cow, collecting the eggs and feeding the donkey, helps the two old people, - whose labours have so drained out of them the abilities to enjoy their lives that they had not even celebrated Christmas -, to welcome the New Year before she leaves with a party featuring the three-fold amusements of song, dance and playing games. I found no such pattern, or other helpful interpretation, in the experiences of Arthur in the Cave. The Washer ,whom he meets on arrival, requests a kiss as a reward for helping him to cross to the island of Avalon, where he can meet Igraine. Despite her wart-covered lips (- the production benefited from very well-made masks for her and Rhitta, although their maker was not credited specifically in the programme-), Arthur steels himself to pay this debt, with no particularly manifest results.

She was not transformed into a beautiful woman, which tales tell as being the experience of some of his knights, and nothing openly underlined the importance of a King being unfailing in keeping his word, even to the meanest of his subjects. Rhitta does remark that it is a good quality to trust, when Arthur, seeking Uther, agrees to lie down by his fire, even after being told that the beards which adorn his costume have been cut from other travellers as they slept, a few of whom this giant has also eaten. Being able to trust subordinates and to take timely rest are indeed valuable qualities for good leadership but some discretion about when to exercise them is also necessary and some of the most famous stories of the royal Arthur show him betrayed by those in whom he placed the greatest trust. Sound principles about when to exercise the force of arms are very proper for a King but I did not see anything very clear emerge in this regard from the fight with Uther.

If the issue was not the making of a king but the responsibilities of a wizard, more hares were started here than were caught. Having proclaimed from the first his ability to dream perfect dreams, Merlin did have to confess that things had not turned out as he foresaw or intended. This is in response to Gwyneth's accusation that Arthur is too young for kingship or to be taken from her, Merlin admitting that he had not foreseen how soon King Uther's death would come. Towards the end, he reveals that the reason he has such a strong emotional commitment to Arthur taking the role he has chosen for him is that, in between his taking him at birth from the dying Igraine, with the promise that he would find the child suitable parents, and his bringing him to Gwynneth and Sir Ector for this purpose, there were two years in which he was responsible alone for Arthur's upbringing. There would be things to say and which it might even be possible to find suitable ways to express to a young audience about the aspirations of a parent for a child but I did not in fact notice anything being made of this.

The play, therefore, broached several emotional hot potatoes without, it seemed to me, making very much of them. It may be thought right to expose the young to tales which have deep implications without wading in detail through their interpretation. It might equally be thought dubious to raise such issues without having determined on a suitable way in which to help shape response to them. I certainly felt unhappy with a play which began by intimating through the use of ancient poetry that it was dealing with mighty issues, and repeating this in refrain

The Sword Is Drawn from The Stone; MERLIN AND THE CAVE OF DREAMS (6) tells the story of what led Arthur (ALEXANDER CAMPBELL) to kingship.

throughout, but following with a ragbag of incident and discussion, - made striking by impressive masks, allusive sound and lighting and a vigorous final battle, and alluring with the emotional pull of family relationships -, which did not seem to me to have the coherence one would expect from a 'proper play,' as distinct from the miscellany of mere amusements available to the same audience in a seasonal panto.

Certainly, the exceptionally bright seven-year-old sitting next to me seemed engaged throughout, crying out "It's his brother!", when the helmeted white knight entered to rescue Arthur and finding much to discuss, or rather outlay her extensive views about, to her adult companion afterwards but I rather gathered she was one able to do that in any circumstances. Some of the 'young' in the audience were considerably older, - mid-teens -, than one might have expected to come to a play which seemed likely to be a relatively juvenile treatment of knights and wizards and they seemed absorbed enough; the emotional issues of the play being quite appropriate for them and not needing any steer on how they should be interpreted. This also would be true for the more adult who found it an absorbing piece and certainly there was much good stage-craft, if one or two oddities (- why an 8mm projector on a tripod on the stage at the outset, for Merlin to handle as he spoke of light breaking through the forest but for him then to remove and it never to be seen again? The use of film later, to suggest his spiritual presence with Arthur in the other world required nothing else by way of paraphernalia and nothing more was included in the production to suggest any connection with our time rather than his).

One might not have thought **London Assurance**, the most obvious play to which to take a seven-year-old but the young boy next to me in the front row on that occasion was absorbed throughout and was rewarded by **Gerald Harper** addressing the last two words of the play directly to him. Having just had Richard Dazzle (**Andrew Langtree**) exemplify the play's title, - which might otherwise be translated as 'bumptious self-confidence' -, through defending his right to be called a gentleman by much the same criteria as might Algernon Montcrieff, - such as the length of his unpaid tailor's bills -, Sir Harcourt Courtley, no neglecter of tailors himself, steps forward to utter the play's most seriously delivered lines, in terms which would have been recognisable to **Thomas Hughes'** Squire Brown: "No. A Gentleman is

GERALD HARPER as Sir Harcourt Courtley in LONDON ASSURANCE

the one title that is not in the gift of kings but is within the reach of every beggar. ... It is bred in the heart of every brave, young Englishman."

This elegant but apt improvisation was a fitting consummation to a performance which depended above all else on fine acting, much of it highly stylised and exactly timed. not least from Sir Harcourt, but always lively and able to adapt to occasion, whether an audience laugh or a rare mishap, such as an expansive gesture from **Jonathan Keeble**, as the appropriately named lawyer, Mark Meddle, sweeping a table ornament into the lap of an audience member, seated immediately behind him in the front row. He had most of the few planned acknowledgements of the presence of the audience, whether indirectly, lacking witnesses to enable an action for slander, by the tone and look with which he exclaimed, "What a pity there's nobody here!", or more directly in using them for cover in his attempts to overhear information which might enable him to bring a profitable court case. The clear visual humour with which he presented his backside in the hope of bringing a charge of assault or the loud whoops with which Charles Courtly (**Charles Aitken**) and Richard Dazzle made their drunken first entry, clanging their collection of pilfered door bells, or Mrs Gay Spanker **(Race Davies**) demonstrated her enthusiasm for the chase might have helped retain the attention of a young audience member, as might the brilliant costumes, designed by **Louise Ann Wilson** and executed with the now long established expertise of the **Royal Exchange** costume department but this is not to suggest that the production was in any way burdened with over obvious effect. A young audience member might have been as much carried along as his elders by the ever constant sense of apt style.

Often from our recent opportunities to see their previous work we can know this aptness of acting to be the result of highly accomplished skills, not reliance on a narrow range of appropriate expressions. At this time last year we saw **Rae Hendrie** as the confused and simple young farmer's wife in **Knives In Hens (04:473)**. Here she is the highly alert Grace Harkaway, at first dismissing the horror of her maid Pert (**Linda Lewis**) at the prospect of her marrying a man almost four times her age, on the grounds that "marriage is conducted nowadays in a most mercantile manner," so the actual character of her husband can be treated as irrelevant, whilst she interests herself in other ways, then smitten for the first time with the pangs of love on meeting the young man she does not at first know to be her intended suitor's son, but, although negotiating in this an entirely new and powerful range of experience, determined not to be taken for granted, if sometimes alarmed that her attempts to distance herself may have been over successful. The almost 'traffic-directing' nature of her hand signallings in her early scenes, marking her points and indicating when others may speak, were a useful way of indicating how very much she intended to keep control of the parts of her life which mattered to her, even if such matters as her marriage must be determined by other forces. That this did not inhibit her from unbridled affection was shown in the unrestrained way in which she rushed to throw her arms about the neck of her loving father (**Jon Cartwright**) on his return from London. The two impulses then had to be mixed afresh in her exposure to love and courtship.

In these variations one can see that although **Dion Boucicault**, the author, might at first seem to be using characters as standardised as the familiar figures in *Commedia del arte,* he is not leaving them to the expression of single Humours. Richard Dazzle may vary little from the single character of a fun-loving young man moving in the best society but **Andrew Langtree** is not only able to point every jape, stratagem or set-back with appropriate expression but to show that as an actor he is capable of a completely different performance from the one which he gave as the sullen young, barely educated, contemporary Australian whom he portrayed in **A Conversation. Race Davies** we also saw last in a contemporary role, the child-seeking Mancunian in **Perfect Days (02:333)** at the **Library Theatre.** Here her initial cavortings, displaying her enthusiasms as a horse-woman, could easily seem over the top but she carries them through with unhesitating vigour and then has time for the variations, if still often at full throttle, of humouring the infatuation of Sir Harcourt which makes him endeavour to elope with her and then facing the possibilities that this may have lost her not only the loyalty of her husband (**Peter Lindford**) but his very life, all this to be followed by heart-felt reconciliations.

The comparison made earlier between Richard Dazzle's expatiations and those of Algernon Montcrieff was specific as it is fascinating how exactly **London Assurance** stands as a midway point between **She Stoops To Conquer** and **The Importance of Being Earnest**, a single continuum in the works of ambitious Irishmen, determined to make their marks in the English Theatre, although **Boucicault** had his great triumph when less than half the age of either **Wilde** or **Goldsmith. London Assurance** is as filled with apophthegms as **Earnest** satirising the assumptions of British society but the scarcely stooping Grace Harkaway is a character several strides nearer to reality than the dedicated romanticism of Cecily Cardew, if rejecting equally impostures in wooing. **London Assurance** represents considerable more than The Mistakes of A Night but if in all three plays, if one's primary awareness is of fun, fun, fun, like almost all the works considered here, their prime requirement in realising their various virtues is acting of the highest order, and that is no trivial matter.

13 OCTOBER. **OFFLINE (9);** Contact. *3 NOVEMBER.* **MOVE OVER MORIATY (10);** Zion. *19 NOVEMBER.* **CRAZY LADY (11);** Contact. *25 NOVEMBER.* **MOVING PICTURES (12);** Studio Salford. **2005** *20 JANUARY.* **THREE GOBBY COWS (13);** Contact. *25 JANUARY.* **DANNY, KING OF THE BASEMENT (14);** M6.

It was interesting to see **Crazy Lady** and **Moving Pictures** within a few days of each other: two completely different works, although sharing so many characteristics – new writing by female authors, about two female characters in comparatively early middle age, notably well acted, performed in studio settings, dealing with matters of great emotional depth but both veined with deep strands of humour.

Although it opens with one of the prolonged bursts of cackling which are a trade mark of Anne (**Denice Hope**), humour is a less frequent feature of **Moving Pictures.** It is, however, most intensely germane to the story as one of the key elements of the drama is the opportunity it gives to the audience to realise how many aspects Anne has inherited of the character of the father whom she has never seen, a sense of humour being one of them. That such matters are not spelt out is an indication of the subtlety of the writing.

If this being inexplicit is one strength, so is the directness with which the key relationship is brought out. The scene we join at the opening is of Anne being

MOVING PICTURES (12): Tina (SUE JAYNES) confronts Anne (DENICE HOPE).

shown around the flat of Tina (**Sue Jaynes**), the half-packed-up state of which showing that she is about to move, Anne representing herself as a prospective new tenant. Her repeated delays in taking her leave suggest to us that she has some other interest but no undue time is wasted building up what this is. Tina reaches the conclusion without waiting for an extensive array of evidence: "You're my sister, aren't you?"

No meal is made of how Anne had managed to track her down. The play just gets on with detailing the experience of the two meeting. Anne had been the first child, put up for adoption as her father had been in the midst of qualifying for the priesthood and he and his wife had felt that then was the time to take on the responsibilities of parenthood. Tina had only found out about her existence by finding a photograph during her childhood which she had managed to get her aunt to explain. She had never had any particular inspiration to track her down but the reason that she felt particularly unwilling to meet Anne now was not only out of a sense of being ambushed but because of her major state of upheaval: both her parents had recently died; this had made her withdrawn, making her partner look for companionship elsewhere and eventually to move out; the reason she is moving too is not only that he works in the same office but her hope that if she takes up a new job and moves to Leeds she will be able to make a new start in life.

Without knowing any of this in advance, Anne had apparently been particularly inspired to seek her out "because I felt worried about you," although she is also interested to pick up further information about her parentage. She had known they were clergy and so had taken an early chance to ask Tina if she was religious. Apart from any doubts she might have had about the value of religious inspiration from the value her birth parents had put upon her, she had been most definitely put off when she had found that it might help her own child to get into a better secondary school if she adopted church membership. She and her nine-year-old son had gone and sat at the back of a service at which the priest was trying to 'involve the children' by getting them to shout out answers to the question "How much to you think you are worth?" and then seeking to endorse the answer "Well, this is what Jesus thinks you are worth!" by getting his Cubs and Brownies to lift up a massive crucifix he had left lying behind the altar, which was surmounted by an exceptionally gory crucified Christ. Anne and her son had looked at each other in repugnance and left.

Unfortunately, the question of how they should pursue his schooling had not had to be answered because he had died abruptly, for no very obvious reason. Although greatly upset, she had been able to adapt to bereavement far more successfully than had yet been possible for her sister: still living with her partner and making a passable living as a portrait painter. Her talent in this line is revealed when Tina shows her a painting made by their father of his church and the technical insight of her comments shows her to be far more highly educated than her 'common' manners had previously led Tina to expect.

This was one of the points at which the relationship between them significantly changes and throughout the movement from unease to acceptance to fury to reconciliation to distancing is most skilfully modulated, creating a highly involving drama, never subverted by obvious artifice. The essential naturalness was most skilfully captured by the direction of **James Foster. Studio Salford** has few technical resources. Its space was comparatively recently residential accommodation, of a primitive nature, so when Tina is showing Anne around her flat, she can walk off through a real door and down a short flight of steps, continuing their dialogue in real other rooms we can half see, and Anne can make her various exits through another real door.

The setting for **Crazy Lady** is far more unusual but the substance of the drama is not without its parallels: we and the characters spend a good deal of our time discovering the background to events and if the depression of Tina following the death of her parents in **Moving Pictures** may have approached the medical, both characters in **Crazy Lady** have had to have some degree of professional support. A painting is also significant in both settings. Whilst that of the church, which proves to be by the father of Anne and Tina, is not especially prominent in the various still unpacked furnishings of Tina's flat, it catches the eye from the first because it has been used on the publicity flyer and this is entirely appropriate as it is a key element in the action through which the drama is finally wound to its conclusion.

The painting which forms the principal item of the setting for **Crazy Lady** is far more prominent, hanging the entire height of **Space Two** at **Contact**, the area between the audience seating on either side otherwise being entirely bare, apart from a few scattered upright chairs, a small bar-room table and a cello by one of the chairs at the far end from the painting. The cellist (**Nikki-Kate Heyes**) is the first figure to enter, in a basic black performance costume, making some acknowledgement of the presence of the audience as she makes a slow circuit towards her chair but otherwise not doing anything particular until the action begins some while later and her presence almost never acknowledged by the other actors. The painting is a large 'primitive' portrait of a woman, presumably giving the name of **Crazy Lady** to the open but apparently totally deserted night club in which the action takes place.

The first impression of both the characters who later enter, separately, is that it looks absolutely ghastly. The first to do so is Claudia (**Heather Peace**}, who is unsurprised as she is coming at the invitation of Jaz (**Shobna Gulati**) who, great as their friendship has once been, she has always recognised as capable of making the most terrible choices, not least in boy friends, not least in the one she eventually decided to marry. We come to learn that they have not met since the wedding, a decade earlier, which Claudia had disrupted with a drunken scene. She had been given to understand by Jaz's husband, who had knocked her up the next morning at the hotel room to which she had gone to collapse and sleep it off, that Jaz never wanted to see her again. Most of this we only learn later as they piece together their experiences. Claudia has led a pretty chaotic life since then, experiencing a variety of doses of counselling to try and sort herself out. This has helped her to realise that she is gay. It has led her into various forms of active Women's Liberation but it takes the naïve perceptions of Jaz, when they now meet again, to make clear that the doctrines through which she and others were urged to free themselves from guilt by abandoning false, male-imposed, preconceptions were still presumptions of female inferiority, in portraying them as especially subject to such delusions. She comes to realise that she was not merely gay but specifically enamoured of Jaz, perceiving by the end, when she might well wish that circumstances had not made her aspirations finally come true, that what she had really been dreaming of, throughout the years of their youthful friendship, was a time when just they two could be together and she would be the one to whom Jaz would always turn for support.

It eventually emerges that the circumstances in which Jaz has at long last sought to renew contact is that she has finally killed her husband and needs someone "to help me with my body." It has been a pretty unhappy marriage, him accusing her of being a witch and she passing in and out of hospital to receive medication, which she continues to have to take. She first of all comes dashing in when Claudia has gone off in search of a drink and groans in horror at the sight of the painting, "Oh No! She'll think it's terrible!" She has never been there before either, had just spotted it from the bus after her killing and thought of it as a possible meeting place as she has been ringing Claudia's mother to try to find out how to get in touch, Claudia not having been home for ages but her sister knowing her number.

Jaz tries to put herself into a condition to meet Claudia by taking some of her medication and **Shobna Gulati** performs a wonderful extended mime of her endeavours to swallow her tablets without any water being available to ease them down. A great strength of the production was **Gulati'**s splendid performance. This was a double tonic to me as it was not only fine in itself but, whilst many praised her in the full production of **Dancing Within Walls (04:16)** last year, on the night I went it did not work for me, in no way matching either her earlier workshop performance in the play **(01:55)** or the dozen or so other performances I had seen her in over the previous fifteen or more years. I had wondered if having to dash round to the theatre after her duties on **Coronation Street** was a viable way in which to create work of the standard we had previously seen.

I may just have been wrong about last year. Certainly there was no shortfall on this occasion. It was a different type of stage part than I had seen from her before, - perhaps closer to her **Coronation Street** character, which I have not seen: an indubitably local and adult character. It also drew upon her notable dance skills as she portrayed for Claudia the various meanings which could be put upon her husband calling her a witch. The readiness to move into this mode, combined with the presence of the cellist, showed how the production was unlike the unfaltering realism of **Moving Pictures.** Perhaps no night club sets out to look entirely everyday and its amenities may seem especially unusual on a deserted afternoon. As both Claudia and Jaz wander off independently through its subterranean recesses, as they search for a drink while waiting for the other to arrive, they find **Alice In Wonderland**-like notices on the bars, and later in the lavatories, over **Warhol**-style multiple reproductions of portraits of bar-maids, reading not "Drink Me" but "Go Ahead. You Deserve It."

Light Ensemble are also able to incorporate a sense of the strange into what could be every day. Their first piece had been as much choreography as anything else and had included the poetry of **Domsta Monsta**, who has now re-emerged as **Dominic Berry**, and thus supplied himself with the facility to take two roles, as Dom and Nick, - it being part of the style of the company that their plays' characters should have the same names as the actors portraying them.

It was not the aspiration of this piece to eschew realism completely or to portray its concerns as unrealistic. After the first forty-five minutes of action in **Space Two**, the characters withdrew to drown their sorrows in the bar, where we were invited to follow them and to endeavour to engage them in conversation. I did have some words with Mel **(Melanie Hughes**) in her secluded corner, where she successfully maintained herself in role, as doubtless did the other characters with whom some managed to speak but so far as I know they never re-coalesced into a company giving more universally apparent fulfilment to the intention which I later saw on a flyer, that the play would 'have a different ending every night.'

I felt this rather an anti-climax but this did not totally cancel out the excellent quality of what we had seen before. Much of this lay in the writing. Most of the characters were highly self-absorbed, so even when meant to be interacting with others it was natural material for each to have written their own parts: Nick is more morbid and monosyllabic than Eeyore, so whatever bubblingly bright remarks Carly (**Carly Henderson**), the Temp who is meant to be shadowing him to gain experience, comes up with are unlikely to be greatly modified by what he has to say and when she takes over the presentation which was meant to have been made by Mel to the distinguished potential clients for their agency's new advertising campaign, her cascade of crudely trivial slogans is meant to be unstoppable and is. Mel's most extensive speeches, highly amusing and characterful, are direct narration to the audience, and so naturally self-penned, but her second concern at the opening, in addition to preparing her presentation, is whether she should take up a blind-date from a lonely hearts column, something to which she goes with more or less nil expectations. The way she and Dom interact to show a most natural conversation being sparked up and the grounds being established for a relationship which she would very much have liked to continue was a very impressive and engaging joint performance.

The lonely hearts column is a burgeoning section of almost all newspapers and magazines and so doubtless is a sufficiently widespread feature of our society to be worthy of dramatic treatment, **Mr Wonderful (01:84)**, for instance having become a highly popular element in our local repertoires (eg **03:479, 574, 618; 04: 646, 692**). The possibility of video dating is now making an entry upon our stages, being the subject of the third contribution to**Three Gobby Cows** and an extended element of **Chameleon (25** described under 18/1/05).

Gobby Cows was all self-penned monologues by the performers, the first two of whom included this title as a self-description by the characters, in apology to us for chattering on so long.

The first was a rewritten version of **Women's Little Christmas (03:14)**, by **Louise Twomey.** It has lost the main dimension which made the original a very effective small drama, as there is now no contrast between the social expectations which the character finds when she comes to England and those she had known in her native Cork. Now the whole narrative takes place there, leaving an engaging set of anecdotes, interspersed with a couple of songs, which is enjoyable but more inconsequential.

This tale, however, was very effectively used as the setting for the whole performance, most ably directed by **Chris Sudworth.** The company's publicity must have been excellent as al the Regne of Manchester Femenye had turned out in force, so far as I know for all four nights of the run, with the result that, although there were about four men present, the general impression was of the all-female social gather which takes place in Cork on 6 January. The space had been crowded with bar-room tables around which the audience sat and the various performers popped up on various points of the periphery to tell their stories. There was a large screen, which was most germane to the third narrative, on which as we entered film could be seen of a bedraggled **Kate Henry** walking on her misfortune-dogged way to work, about which she told us in the second episode, but a large screen is a feature of many bar-rooms now, so it did not look out of place. Her tale, too, was essentially a collection of anecdotes, enjoyably told and holding the interest but not really amounting to much more.

Deborah Brian's essay on video dating did have more dramatic point. Our presence was not so directly acknowledged as in the other two pieces, although it was as much a narrative about why she was attempting to make the video as examples of her direct-to-camera endeavours. The basic situation was that she was desperate to be married and would like to have children. The dramatic nub was that in order to achieve this she was willing entirely to negate herself. "I can be anything you like, really," is said specifically in regard to hair colour but in fact applies to the whole range of the lengths to which she is prepared to go in order to secure a male companion. She is ready to wave the formality of marriage, if this discourages him, settling for "long-term," and will not push the issue of children.

There was the material here for a strong drama but I did not feel that the piece really managed to build up into this, remaining a well-presented collection of gaffes and reflections, many of which were cast in very familiar patterns. There is a drama to be made about a character being imprisoned in a set of conventional views but there is a problem in how to realise this: to show the situation which lies under such views being rehearsed.

If one wanted to see the full effect to which **Deborah Brian**'s very real talents as a performer can be put, it was possible to do so almost immediately, as she was just about to open in **Danny, King of The Basement** with **M6.** The emotional lives of neither of the mothers she portrayed was no more satisfactory but she had a far fuller and more distinctive character in the mother of Danny himself (**Harley Bartles**), besides rushing on from time to time as one of the numerous taxi-drivers, as which almost all the cast took their turn.

The play begins with her being about to flee from yet another unsatisfactory relationship, this time a dangerously violent one. The ten-year-old Danny is quite used to this and does not really mind, partly because he is so adept at living in his fantasy world as a secret agent, which he can take with him and use to gain friends anywhere, and also because, as frequently disrupted schooling has left him badly behind on basic skills, changing schools yet again can put off the day when anyone might notice this. And on some skills he is far superior to his mum. He has to keep the purse if she is to have any idea of how much money they have left and avoid frittering it away on inessentials. She has, however, the resilience to hunt out a job, so that they can have some income and to keep it when difficulties arise. She also does have to assert over the ever-confident Danny that there are some issues on which an adult must decide. This builds up into into a far wider range of character and dramatic issues and **Deborah Brian** succeeds in making sure that they all have full weight. **Paul Mallon** and **Jo Pridding** effectively portray the two very different children who are Danny's neighbours in his new home, whom he first of all succeeds in bringing together into a happy relationship through friendship with him and who finally combine to make Danny realise that he must find the strength to face up to the challenges of staying in one place long enough to undertake some serious schooling.

Theatre-in-Education companies nowadays seem to be constrained to tackle clear "Issues" relevant to personal and social education, whereas I am inclined to think that there is a lot of good education in just bringing high class performance up to the very toenails of the young in their school hall but this play certainly fulfils that objective and is highly amusing, whilst proving plenty of occasion for 'discussion', either spontaneously in the playground after seeing it or more formally in the classroom.

The *doyennes* of self-penned pieces by women for their own performance are **Maggie Fox** and **Sue Ryding** as **Lip Service.** I have missed seeing their three latest pieces, either because of an impossible clash between their local performance dates and when this book has to go to press or, last year, through sheer incompetence on my part in reading the calendar. I am not quite sure how we got a one-night revival of **Move Over, Moriaty** last November (I thought maybe because they like to accompany their latest work in Edinburgh with a golden oldie and decided we might as well have the chance to benefit but I have now seen details of a Spring Tour coming back to the **Library Theatre**). Certainly, I was delighted to get the chance to see it. It was far better than I remember it first time around. The chief delight is in their constantly witty detail in the performance but this is given every chance to shine through the elaborately ludicrous satire on the chosen *genre* and

MOVE OVER MORIARTY (10); MAGGIE FOX and SUE RYDING

the regular feature of a set which may look simple, even rudimentary, at first sight but proves to have the most amazing flexibility in ever refolding itself into new dimensions. Their work may essay none of the serious dimensions to be found in the work of many of the female writers and performers described here but, excellent though most of this was in its various ways, none excel this talented and prolific pair in sheer skill and amusement.

2005

18 JANUARY. **ANTIGONE (15);** Adelphi. *19 JANUARY.* **ELECTRA (16);** Robert Powell Theatre. *26 JANUARY.* **STUFF HAPPENS (17);** *28 JANUARY.* **WHEN MEDEA MET ELVIS (18);** Adelphi. *29 JANUARY.* **HOUSE OF ILLUSIONS (19);** Robert Powell Theatre. *30 JANUARY.* **POSSIBLY PORN (20);** Totties. *31 JANUARY.*

GRAZED KNEES (21); Solomon Grundy's. *1 FEBRUARY.* **TWISTED TALES (22); CABBAGES (23);** Attic. *2 FEBRUARY.* **ONE BIRD, TWO STONES (24); CHAMELEON (25);** Jabez Clegg. *3 FEBRUARY.* **MARBLES (26); CHICKEN TIKKA MASALA (27);** Barca. *4 FEBRUARY.* **FURTHER THAN THE FURTHEST THING (31);** Capitol. *5 FEBRUARY.* **FROM YARD 2 ABROAD (28);** A Fe We. **UGLY SISTER (29); FARNWORTH POND-LIFE (30);** Taurus. *9 FEBRUARY.* **THE TRESTLE AT POPE LICK CREEK (32);** Royal Exchange. *11 FEBRUARY.* **PHAEDRA (33);** John Thaw Theatre. *28 MARCH.* **ELECTRA (60).** Royal Exchange. *11 MAY.* **POEMS OF ANTIGONE (61);** Capitol. *12 MAY.* **THE LEGEND OF THE WHITE SNAKE (62);** Lowry.

After a week of seeing the self-devised pieces by graduating students from the **Arden School of Theatre**, despite some of them being remarkably fine, one was struck, on visiting their opposite numbers at the **Capitol** by being reminded, through seeing their production of **Zinnie Harris' Further Than The Furthest Thing**, what an extra dimension there is to seeing a fully formed play, beyond the episode of a essentially devised piece. There had been reminders within the **Arden** miscellany of the variety of forms which the Theatre can effectively take, from the opening collection of Thoughts on Masturbation in **Possibly Porn**, through the single real-time episode of **Grazed Knees**, which nevertheless ranged back through reminiscences for much of its length and, while incorporating significant events, was essentially a mood piece, as, in its very different way was **Twisted Trails**, guying every 'Fairy Tale' tradition, with the extra discipline of lively doggerel verse, to be followed by **Cabbages**, a thoroughly-plotted and **Kafka**-like tale of abductions, in which mood was certainly important but an endeavour was also made to link the proceedings to the philosophy of **Kant.**

By the end of the week, we were back to masturbation but whereas **Possibly Porn** had focussed on those who make quite a meal of it, through all sorts of mental and physical elaborations, for

TRESTLE AT POPE LICK CREEK (32); Pace (HANNAH STOREY) tries to lure Dalton (STEPHEN WRIGHT) into trying to outrun the train

those experiencing the forms of **Farnworth Pond-Life** evoked by **Victoria Brown** it is just matter-of-factly included, as a judicious preliminary to certain episodes of courtship. One could say that the student-created contributions focussed on the groin, whereas the more fully evolved plays considered here dealt with passion of the heart but that is not the real dividing line. The division may be between the older and newer works. **The Trestle At Pope Lick Creek** ends with an act of male masturbation (all the **Arden** treatments concentrating on the female) and it is also a key element of **Lee Hall**'s **Cooking With Elvis**, one of the main ingredients of **Salford Performing Arts'** creation **When Medea Met Elvis.** The settings of **Chicken Tikka Masala** and **Jean Genet**'s **The Balcony** are broadly comparable, - brothels where the main perspective on them of the proprietors is as a money-making business. That in **Chikken Tikka** is a pokey little two-hand operation off Oldham Road, with the emphasis on quick turn-around, - prices for twenty or thirty minutes being the main detail quoted to telephone enquirers -, although allowing that some clients do require an indirect route to stimulation, - at least the pretence that the girl selected is under fourteen or the exercise of the urino-genital organs for their non-specifically-sexual purposes -, whereas **The Balcony** is an elaborately equipped **House of Illusions.**

The translations and productions of the classical Greek plays produced by **Salford** can emphasise the carnal, -"I don't see any virgins here" – is the sort of line given to her chorus in **Liz Lochhead**'s translation/adaptation of **Medea** used in their conflation, (whereas "We're all friends here" is the kind of term used in other translations in which they express their mutual understanding of Medea's plight) and the idea of making the Chorus in **Antigone** cleaning ladies allows them to use their dusting rods as phalli when portraying Man's Folly as a specifically male delinquency. This is not necessarily out of place, as the Greeks had great fun with phalli in their comedies and **Antigone** is one of the tragedies in which comedy can fairly be found to counterpoint the grim but it does say something about the style of the productions. The primary passion found in the **Antigone**, however was a moral/political one, as in its way was the **Electra**, and one of the great interests in seeing the **Phaedra** shortly after **The Trestle At Pope Lick Creek** was to see how well the former did manage to combine the passionate with the political, which **Trestle** did not seem to me to succeed in doing.

It is set during the American Depression, specifically in 1936. The trestle in this remote rural settlement, - albeit containing a few small factories -, is that over which the goods trains regularly rumble at some speed. A programme essay draws our attention to the fact that about a third of the hundreds of thousands of unemployed who jumped aboard such trains at points where they slowed down, in the hope of being carried to where they might find at least temporary work, were teenagers. This is the age of the two leading characters in the play, - Dalton (**Stephen Wight**) and Pace (**Hannah Storey**) -, but this is not how they seek to use the trains. She is a great enthusiast for the power of steam, not only having read about engines in great detail in the school library and made a model as a project but her obsession is to try and race ahead of them over the trestle, on which there is no side room to escape if she is overtaken. She is determined to essay this again, despite the boy she originally ran with being killed. She now tries to persuade Dalton to accompany her on a second attempt.

We know from almost the outset that she was unsuccessful as we begin with Dalton in the county jail, accused of, and indeed admitting, to killing her. This gives an awful sense of inevitability, which overwhelmed most of my other feelings throughout the First Act. The predominant element of the play is the distinctive young love affair between Dalton and Pace. This is built up in a insightful way and despite the final act of masturbation is dealt with at a more imaginative level. She gets him to stimulate her without his touching her and he, while having physical aspirations, is held by a more general growing fascination.

This is a persuasive portrait but the play did not fully work for me. The other main element is the picture built up, mainly through the scenes between Dalton's parents (**DeNica Fairman** and **Julian Prothero**), of the effect of the Depression, he now a recluse who cannot bear to go out of the house after being depersonalised by losing the job in the factory he had worked in all his life, she at first hanging onto hers but the employers using the desperate situation as grounds to require dangerous working practices and she then joining a group who decide that the only way to keep work going is to occupy and run themselves a glass factory which has closed down, (the identity of industry and harsh management proving a very natural and imaginative link with the splendid revival of **Githa Sowerby's Rutherford and Son** being performed in parallel in the **Royal Exchange** main house).

There is a connection between this wider situation and the relationship of Dalton and Pace. One of their first exchanges is him saying "Teacher says I'm smart enough to go to college" and her replying "If your mother can't buy you new shoes, you're not going to college." Young people who see no future for themselves are the more likely to take part in dangerous sports. However, I did not find that the two themes were enabled to grow together in a way which strengthened them both. The final act of masturbation did not really seem to me the natural climax of the play. There was important material in the scene but where it got to seemed more to be winding up a plot point resulting from the tale being told non-chronologically than giving full impact to the tragic fate of individuals in a tragic age. That is what the substance of the play seemed to me to be about but for me the full potential of a combined dramatic focus was not achieved.

In **Phaedra**, it was. This was an incredibly detailed production, not elaborate but with appropriate steps being taken to emphasise every detail. The translation by **Julie Rose** was very informal, not even, I think, in verse. Thus it was very different from the exact metre of **Racine**'s original but still robust enough for us always to be conscious that we were behind the scenes at a royal palace and the acting on all hands constantly gave full force to both the personal passions and the political intrigues, whether these were voiced openly or, more frequently, had to be suppressed. Phaedra (**Susanna Fiore**), the wife of Theseus, is sick with passion for Hippolytus (**David Oakes**), her husband's son by his previous wife, the Amazon Hippolita. In dedication to her, he has chosen a life of celibacy but now finds himself passionately in love with Aricia (**Charlotte Gascoyne**), a state prisoner, held in the palace of the subsidiary kingdom of Troezen, where the royal family is staying. The principal political manipulator is the palace official Oenone (**Helen Spencer**), who, when Phaedra has desperately declared her passion to Hippolytus and been rejected,turns her lust to hate by persuading her that his Amazon origins make him inevitably antipathetic to women and she should denounce him to Theseus as having tried to assail her, a message that she is ready to communicate to the king herself.

The political is also seen in Hippolytus himself, however, as, when Theseus is earlier presumed dead, he is elected by the citizens as king of Troezen but not of Athens, whose electors instead choose the infant son of Phaedra, making it seem for a while as though she will hold the senior monarchy. While he does think himself king, Hippolytus acts in what he takes to be common justice, freeing Aricia from an unjust imprisonment, though uncertain if he can distinguish this act from his personal passion for her, which he in fact blurts out when bringing her word of his release. Declaring this love to the returned Theseus as evidence that the charges of his attempting to rape Phaedra must be false cuts initially no ice, as Theseus would regard this love for his enemy as equally criminal if he believed it. It does show Oenone, however, that the grounds on which she misjudged Hippolytus must be false and she retracts her story about the attack on Phaedra. Theseus does try to withdraw his death sentence on Hippolytus but in vain.

It was very interesting to see this **Phaedra** so soon after the **Euripedes Hippolytus (04:92)**, brought by **Actors**

PHAEDRA (33); SUSANNA FIORE

of Dionysus last year. As with all dramatic retellings of the Greek myths, the interpretation was significantly different. Both productions had some problems with being in modern dress. Here the overall look very effectively achieves with limited resources a suitably stylish setting. The difficulty can often be overcome of weaponry from one period being referred to in the text and something more modern being on view but here the 'sword' Phaedra takes from Hippolytus is his pen-knife, in order to extract which from his pocket she has to come initimately close, without resistance, which makes it harder for the audience to understand how she can see herself as so heartlessly spurned. She has several useful changes of attire and Oenone is given the opportunity to make herself look more formal in preparation for the expected entrance of Theseus, so one would have thought that Hippolytus, who takes so actively to the kingship of Troezen for the brief while that he assumes he has it, might have re-enforced this by sprucing himself up at least slightly to present himself to the electorate.

Mention of these oversights, as I would take them to be, however, should not be taken to obscure one of the supreme virtues of the production, directed by **Susannah Tresilian**: the close attention to visual and aural detail throughout in giving a controlled sense of emphasis in every development of the text, from the introductory tableaux to the variations within each utterance. **Envision Theatre**, all of whose core members are recent graduates of **Manchester University** and currently the company in residence in the Drama Department there, are developing a very distinctive style. One feature of this is a notably evolved incorporation of music, in this case making use of a full score, composed and probably mostly played by **Vincent Migliorisi.** I am not competent to comment on the virtues of this in detail. There seemed to me a rather abrupt change of style from that which accompanied the opening tableaux to that which introduced the first action and one or two passages which effected changes of scene in Act Two, as the drama heightened, did seem to me to be slightly reminiscent of traditional 'chase' music but even this seemed to make a valid contribution to the overall role of a stylish heightening of dramatic emphasis.

If the schemer in the **Euripedes** version was the goddess Aphrodite, here the intervention which led to so many human passions having their worst effect was through the political instincts of Oenone. The political was especially to the fore in the **Antigone**, among the Greek plays undertaken by the **Salford** students, but the most political of their presentations which I saw was the scoop of having so early a production of **David Hare**'s **Stuff Happens**, his very recent history play on events leading to the 2003 invasion of Iraq. In many ways this was a very bold production as it took licence from **Hare**'s assertion that, while "Nothing in the narrative is knowingly untrue", ""this is surely a play, not a documentary," to essay the production with a cast ten out of whose eleven members were female. The characters kept their historical male names but were presented as women. There was no insuperable difficulty in this as there was no political role portrayed which has not already had a woman occupant or could not now be seen as having one. The more distracting consideration in our current theatre was to see two cracking parts for Black actors, - **Colin Powell** and **Condoleeza Rice** – undertaken by members of an all-white cast. This was not because **Salford** totally lacks Black actors who could have undertaken the roles, as **Simone Randall** and **Charles Denton** showed in their accomplished portrayals of Medea and Jason a couple of nights later, but simply that they were not available on this occasion.

If one allows the principle of "non-traditional casting" to cut both ways and to excuse the decision to present the play with these resources, one significant difficulty was not to my mind overcome: there was no single portrayal which I would class in itself as inadequate and many had very real strengths; nevertheless, the effect of this was largely lost to my mind because the range of voices was too narrow to represent the variety of character needed for effective drama. Many of the characters are in extreme disagreement with each other. The sense of conflict was lost in all speaking in very similar tones or approximations to an American accent. Even when one gets voices from outside the American Administration, such as Tony Blair (**T Henderson**) or De Villepin (**Laura Croft**), they do not sound different enough for the contrast to come out. Whether, if more consideration had been given to this in production, this cast could have managed it, I do not know. In the event, they didn't.

This should not disguise the fact that within the far too even tone and tempo, good acting was going on: **T Henderson**'s Tony Blair having to try to explain to George Bush (**Gabby Sanderson**) that one reason he had limited political capital to expend on pushing through an unpopular policy was because of difficulties over fox-hunting; the President maintaining a constant air of confident authority and being able to give effect to a line by the speed with which she confirmed "We Are Not!", in response to Wolfowitz (**Crecy Yorke**) commenting "but, of course, we're not the Clinton Administration."

She wore cowboy clothing throughout, though only the hat when this was appropriate on his Crawford Ranch and when she marched on for the curtain call, contributing to an occasional sense that we were seeing a cartoon version, which, although **Hare** does include the laughably ridiculous, I do not think was intended. So far as one could judge the play on this performance, it does seem fairly conventionally 'anti-Bush/Blair,' but I do not think it was meant to be so on too callow grounds. His Note stresses "events have been authenticated from multiple sources, both public and private." As such, I thought that I would learn rather more than I did, as one who has followed the news with reasonable diligence and interest but not taken exceptional steps to study the matter. In a radio review I heard of the original London production, it was said Tony Blair came across as an implausibly feeble character. In **T Henderson**'s portrayal, I got far more of a sense of someone conscious of being a junior partner but being as effective as possible in that position in trying to have an influence. Where (s)he did seem somewhat overweening in early encounters was portraying himself as the more experienced partner: "Of course, I've been in office some time. I know all these people …" (Heads of other major countries); "You know, it sometime happens in politics, - it probably hasn't happened to you yet -, but …" **Gabby Sanderson**'s Bush took this with a plausibly gracious tolerance.

The suggestion which was new to me was that the French said privately in pre-invasion discussions with Powell (**Mackayla Cuthbert**) and Negroponte (**Aaisha Moffatt**) that if America just went ahead and attacked without seeking a second resolution in the United Nations, giving specific authorisation, France would not make too much of a stink about it. What she could not do was give such a resolution her open support. Blair was in the opposite position. He desperately needed such formal authorisation to give the invasion any hope of popular support in Britain. Because of his loyalty on other matters, Bush authorised the lengthy and eventually unsuccessful pursuit of a second resolution.

Only two Middle Eastern voices were heard in the play, either side of the Second Act. The first was probably in the original script: a Palestinian woman (**Aaisha Moffatt**) saying how her people looked on every international initiative with suspicion. The second had only been on the radio that day, an Iraqi woman (**Mackayla Cuthbert**) on the prospect of the elections due the next week-end. So the cast were involved enough to set the play in the context of on-going events. I could not really be sure how good a play it is. It is probably rather better than it seemed in this performance but this is not to deny that, character for character, there was some very creditable acting going on. I just felt that, cumulatively, the play proved to be beyond their range. No disgrace for their enterprise in giving it a good try, however.

Contemporary political relevance was openly sought for in the production of **Antigone.** "Somewhere in the world every day, on a larger or smaller stage, the real life drama of **Antigone** is being enacted" was the slogan on the publicity and **Bush, Blair, Ken Bigley,** Tsunami were said in the programme all to have come up spontaneously in discussions in the referral room. The production was not linked to any specific circumstances, indeed it was generalised by all characters having facial paintings, most of them small and black on the major characters but nearer to grotesque clowns in the case of the Chorus and the main soldier (**Pip Harvey).** She went full out for the humour in the guard who scarcely dares to tell Creon (**Natalie O'Brien**) that, against her orders, a grave has been dug for Polynices, and later making sure she gets all the credit for capturing the person who has done it (Antigone, **Jude Williams**), pushing aside the other guard (**Michael H Corbett**), so he will get no acknowledgement.

He is so constantly left standing aside that one might have thought that the actor had got a pretty thankless part but, of course, it is the Messengers in **Sophocles** who get the really plum dramatic speeches, telling how the major characters have died off stage, **Michael H Corbett** here most effectively doing the honours for Antigone, Haemon (**Daniel Boarer**) and Eurydice. He had chance of having this speech stolen from him by **Pip Harvey**, as she also played Eurydice, in complete contrast to her former role: the one character to appear without exaggerated make-up, quiet and shattered by the other deaths. **Don Taylor**'s consciously contemporary translation here had one of its effectively colloquial moments, the guard saying after her exit, "She'll be alright," before later deciding "I'll take a look," to find that she is no such thing.

The decision to present the Chorus (**Donna Basnett, Sam Crump, Rosie Greenhalgh** and **Beth Spano**) as cleaning ladies posed one major question which I thought had been brilliantly resolved by Creon on her entry addressing all of us in the audience as "Senators," a title to which the cleaning ladies did not seem obviously entitled. This had the valuable effect that we were directly challenged as to what we would make of Creon's pronouncements. For some reason this was not maintained throughout, as once or twice later on the Chorus were so addressed. This did not significantly reduce the impact of the piece, several un-dry eyes being perceivable in the surrounding audience. This was despite the chief beneficiary of these, Antigone, seeming to me as if she might have had her part some what trimmed, as I only really registered her opening dialogue with Ismene (**Emma McCullagh**) and one scene after her capture.

Certainly the play was not significantly shortened. It was performed in two acts and there was more than enough material before and after the interval to justify this division. All parts were performed strongly: **Natalie O'Brien** being a good tough female Creon, giving a constant impression through sinister re-entries of keeping a very close watch over the state she now leads, **Daniel Boarer** making an effective transition from the apparently submissive "Of course I respect you, Mother .." with which Haemon first appears to the direct challenge to which he comes, **Sue Hodgkinson** being an imposing Teiresias, **Emma McCullagh** re-appearing unrecognisably as the strange, agile, crawling 'boy' who acts as her guide.

If the **Antigone** company had gone to some trouble to create a surreal modern look, **Electra** was played in robes quite compatible with the original Greece. Jason and Medea also wore clothes which were consistent with that period but their Chorus (**Nancy Bray, Louise Tarver, Naringer Chohan** and **Felicity Caddick**), in keeping with the whole mixing / re-editing character of **When Medea Met Elvis**, were in elegant, black, sharp-cut suits, with dark hats tilted over their eyes. They were given dramatic movement and dance steps with which to emphasise their views but the production which really went to town on this was the **Electra**, with a Chorus of nine, making up three-fifths of the cast. They had extensively choreographed pieces, in Greek style. It does not seem to have been thought appropriate to include their final hymn to "Freedom restored," (**Bush** still getting no votes in Salford),which meant that the performance seemed to me rather to peter out. The splendid **Compass Theatre** production of this **Sophocles** version **(99.11)**, which we saw in 1999, had not used this final chorus either but had left Orestes looking so shattered and horrified after killing Aegisthus that we could see the full weight of the Euripedean **Oresteia** about to fall on his head. Here he shows up, does the killing, end of story. There is lots of splendidly dramatic stuff along the way, for instance, in addition to the constantly impressive work of the Chorus, **Nic James** as Pylades, despite looking rather younger than the Orestes (**Johnny Beck**) whom he is meant to have raised from infancy, giving a vivid account of his supposed death. **Beck** having a light Irish accent was eminently suitable for a character brought up away from his native land. **Jo Higson** as Electra is greatly distraught when she supposes him to be dead and then overwhelmed when she realises that she is speaking to him face to face. **Rachel Forrest** was a fearsomely evil Clytemnestra.

If Irish was an effective trace element in the **Aspects Electra**, it was absolutely all pervasive in the complete re-writing by **Jo Combes** which she directed at the **Royal Exchange**, totally re-set on the West Coast of Ireland of the 1950's. It is a close parallel to the **Sophocles**' version but it is an understatement to call it 'adapted.' It is a very effective new play, as bold in its retelling of the legend as any classical Greek writer would have been expected to be.

It too dispenses with any final sense of "Freedom restored" but uses at least two adaptations to intensify the final feeling of guilt about the actions of Restes (**William Ash**) and Electra (**Penny Layden**). The Chorus is replaced by the single role of Bridgid (**Maggie Shevlin**), a former servant of this farming family who left and became a nun when Aengus (**Drew Carter-Main**) insinuated himself into the household and property as the partner of Nestra (**Stella McCusker**) during her husband's absence, fighting in the British Army during the Second World War, slaying him on his return and having the wherewithal to prevent the local representatives of Church and State looking into the matter too closely. Bridgid has a deep affection for all the children and visits Electra and Chrissy (**Amy Huberman**) covertly whenever she is back in the village from her convent. Restes had been helped to escaped by Electra and she is delighted to see him too when he reveals himself on his secret return but then horrified at the determination of him and Electra to be revenged on Aengus and Nestra by slaying them.

We, therefore, have her repugnance at the killing constantly before us as Restes and Electra constantly re-affirm to each other the rightness of their plans.

Bridgid has tried to tell Electra "Your father wasn't all good," of which anyone with a passing knowledge of the Agamemnon of tradition would be well aware, so in a way it does not add much to our knowledge when Nestra in her final words to Electra stresses this point by revealing to her that when she had picked up her father's mass book, after his return, what had fallen from it had been the letters from the woman with whom he had been consistently unfaithful to her during his absence in the army. However, this is not only something that would have been less obvious to the young Electra than Agamemnon marching in with Cassandra on his arm, it is an element in **Stella McCusker**'s very strong performance which she can use to present Nestra as a woman sinned against as well as sinning, who has struggled to reconstitute a household for herself. Obviously Electra's ceaseless opposition to her life with Aengus has been a strain for both of them. Indeed, the reason Aengus " has blessed Limerick with his presence this day" is that he has gone to make arrangements for her to be taken into a Home for Distressed Women if she will not agree to more restrained behaviour.

If all this and many other changes involved considerable re-writing, nevertheless the intention and effect was for the most part to create a very close parallel to the work by **Sophocles**, for instance, using religious practices associated with the Catholic church to provide corresponding observances at the graveside and to invoking the gods. For their joint **MA Course** production, the **Manchester Metropolitan University School of Theatre** and **Teatr Piesn Kozla**, from Wroclaw in Poland, used only **Socrates**' words, often in the original Greek and, like the **Aspects Electra**, used costumes and, very extensively, dance styles reminiscent of Ancient Greece. Their very powerful **Poems of Antigone**, however, only sought to be a work "inspired by" **Sophocles**' play, rather than a direct presentation of it. The dominance of dance and music did not mean that these skills displaced others. As each of the four episodes was inspired by particular words, their effect would have been greatly reduced if the performers, whether Polish or British, had not had the skills to make these heard distinctly amid the music and general chanting.

The first poem, entitled 'Dawn' was built on Antigone's words in the four lines at the opening of the play: "Dear Sister. Dear Ismene / How many griefs our father Oedipus handed down! / Do you know one, I ask you, one grief / That Zeus did not perfect for the two of us."

The stage was dark at the first (lighting by **Arkadiussz Chrusciel**). It was also completely bare, with a plain, dark back wall, the only furnishing being a small tiered rostrum and three stout stools, which, if not laid aside, could be used singly or built up on top of each other, at this point forming a mound, stage right. The first thing we could see was a figure seated at its foot playing a cello, then that there was also a figure at the top, of whom we could then see no detail. The words were not coming from them. We could hear them being sung chorically and repetitively from off-stage left, from which, down stage, ten of the rest of the cast then danced on sideways, linked, cross-handed, in a single line.

It was still very dark, so one could not distinguish details for some time. It then did emerge that they were classically dressed but not masked. Half were male, in dark red, the women in pale blue. They formed a single line but all the men first, then the women. The general effect was already sorrowful but after some time the words came to be accompanied by increasingly loud wails which could soon be seen, as the lights rose on her, to be coming from the female figure in agony on top of the mound.

If this was, for the moment, specifically Antigone, it was not the manner of the performance to identify any particular actor with an individual character for long. The opening words were identifiably those of Antigone but had been represented by the whole cast.

The next development seemed to me rather odd. The **Aspects Antigone** had shown that there are comic and light-hearted strands in the original play which it can be effective to acknowledge. However I could not see how this production at this stage was doing anything other than build up a terrible situation. Nevertheless, the chorus, still singing the same words, suddenly quickened the tempo of its singing and footwork, making it sound rather jolly. In the fourth 'Poem' there was a very effective episode of delivering the words in a contrary spirit to their apparent sense but I could not apprehend what the intended effect was meant to be here. The next episode continued the appropriate emphasis on the grim. The Chorus withdrew to the side, leaving one solitary female figure crouching in the shadows, up stage left. The figure on top of the mound, now descended and crossed over to her, as if she might have been Antigone going to speak to Ismene. Although the words used were those of Creon in the original play, pronouncing his judgement, they were entirely suitable for the news Antigone brings: "As for his blood brother. Polynices / - A proclamation has forbidden the city / To dignify him with burial, mourn him at all. / No, he must be left unburied, his corpse / Carrion for birds and dogs to tear." The way, however, in which the actresses shared and repeated the words between them did not allow one to identify one of them alone as Antigone.

This had established the opening situation of the play with great power. As a more severe male figure took centre stage, one assumed at first that we were now seeing a representation of Creon. There was a direct continuation in subject matter, as he was talking about the disfigured body of Polynices but we soon realised that what we were hearing did not fit with an early Creon view of the matter: "I escorted your lord, I guided him / To the edge of the plain where the body lay, / Polynices, torn by the dogs and still unmourned. / And saying a prayer to Hecate of the Crossroads, / Pluto too, to hold their anger and be kind, / We washed the dead in a bath of holy water / And plucking some fresh branches, gathering / What was left of him, we burned them all together / And raised a high mound of native earth." Were we getting Antigone's account of her early actions in a male voice? Some details did not fit that. As the speech continued we realised that we had jumped almost to the end of the play and were hearing the Messenger's account of how Creon himself buried Polynices, then went to rescue Antigone, found her already dead and witnessed the ensuing end of his own son Haemon.

This was the main point in the performance at which we got an extensive speech from the original, used to something like its initial purpose. Music, chanting and movement from the chorus reinforced the effect but the basic power was in the continuously delivered speech.

It now seemed as if we had the beginning and end of the story and presumed the remaining two Poems were to fill in the middle. Doubtless, in some sense they did, but for long enough in the next episode I did not have much idea of how they were doing it. This was because, for a long way in, the words used were in the original Greek, possibly also partly in Polish, - two languages whose general sound I thought I would be able to distinguish but on this occasion I could not. The sound and movement continued to be as adept as ever but everywhere else in the production these were fortified by a clear indication from the words of what they were meant to express. At this stage this was not provided in a form which was accessible to me.

Movement by a few characters was accompanied by two male figures seated on two stools, as if discussing and the rest seated in rows chanting on the steps of the rostrum. The main thing which struck me about their disposition was that women were making up one of the rows alongside the men. Up to this point it had rather seemed to me as if a distinction was being made between the behaviour of men and the behaviour of women. Certainly, these two sections of the company had up to then seemed to be grouped separately and the next bit of the text we got in English appeared still to be on this theme. A Creon figure shouted "I'm not the man, not now: she is the man / If this victory goes to her and she goes free." In the full play he has plenty to say in this vein, for instance to Haemon: "Never let some woman triumph over us/ … never be rated / Inferior to a woman, never," and one could reasonably take this line in this production as representing all the rest.

Quite in what context here the issue is raised, because of the language was not entirely apparent to me. The action had come to include an actor taking a handful of strips of cloth, most of which he used to lay across the shoulders of those sitting on the rostrum., as though they were wearing a sash, but one he used to blindfold one of the men sitting on the stools. At first I took this to be a reference back to the griefs of our father Oedipus. On reflection, I suppose it was as likely to be an indication of Tiresias. Because of the language and the lack of any other clues I could decipher, I have not really got a clue.

The final Poem was far clearer as to its contents, somewhat strange in its presentation but undoubtedly powerful in its impact. Its central feature was a dialogue between two female figures, one of whom spoke lines derived from Creon in the original play and in a manner which seemed quite contrary to their content. She was kneeling on the floor, speaking them most solicitously to a figure who had Antigone's lines, whose head she cradled on her knees and who breathed her lines quietly, as if at her last extremity, in acceptance of her end and in a reasonable degree of sympathy with her interlocutor. The main lines were:

CREON: Tell me briefly, no long speeches - / Were you aware a decree had forbidden this?

ANTIGONE: Well aware. How could I avoid it? It was public.

CREON: And still you had the gall to break this law?

ANTIGONE: Of course I did. It wasn't Zeus, not in the least /Who made this proclamation – not to me. / Nor did Justice, dwelling with the gods / Beneath the earth, ordain such laws for men. / Nor did I think your edict had such force / That you, a mere mortal, could override the gods, the great unwritten, unshakable traditions. / They are alive, not just today or yesterday: / They live forever, from the first of time, / And no one knows when they first saw the light.

CREON: The mind convicts itself

ANTIGONE: Creon, what more do you want / Than my arrest and execution?

CREON: Nothing. Then I have it all.

ANTIGONE: Then why delay? Your moralising repels me, / Every word you say – pray god it always will.

I do not think that any reasonable grounds could be found for speaking these lines in this manner, even with the excision from them of the much more vicious lines supplied for Creon in the full text, which include the "I am not the man … if she goes free" shouted so angrily in this production earlier. No harm in a de-constructed production showing how the same lines can be taken different ways but that is not what is being done here. 'Reasonable' or not, it is undeniably effective. The quiet speaking of the lines enables one to concentrate on their meaning, even if the tone is quite against their sense. Maybe this contrast even, in some strange way, helped to bring it out. It makes a very powerful end to a potent production. The elements filleted from the **Sophocles** text provided a very robust backbone but, as was entirely appropriate as a Masterpiece for performers, the whole effect was created through the unwavering excellence in the way it was done. At every moment, the movement, music, word and imagery were perfectly co-ordinated so as to create unceasing and cumulative impact. Most of the resources were in essence fairly simple but nothing was lacking from the overall effect.

The resources of the **National Beijing Opera Company** are infinitely grander, dazzling costumes being available in glittering number and several of the painted backdrops being detailed work in classical style. Nevertheless, the bedrock skill was highly evolved and disciplined physical performance, also closely integrated with music and song, if not to the same degree as in **Poems of Antigone.** Its folk legend source is not so evolved as in the major writers of Greek tragedy. What struck me, however, as the most vivid link was the appeal to unwritten laws by the heroine Bai (**Li Shengsu).** The holy man Fa Hai (**Yang Yanyi**) repeatedly tries to persuade her husband Xu (**Zhang Wei**), who reveres him, that, as she is a Snake Goddess in disguise, she is only waiting for the time when she can swallow him whole. Outraged at his repeated attempts to use his religious authority to separate them, she declares that, however holy a man he may be, his nostrums cannot rightly override the absolutely fundamental principles of enduring love and the duty of constant support between a man and his wife, -

and her husband should have been able to perceive this in any circumstances.

Although not only the stories but many of the techniques of **Beijing Opera** doubtless go back more than a millennium, it seems to have evolved very rapidly into its present form over the past century, which may mean that, together with always having been a popular art, its accessibility to a Western audience is greater than that of a more refined art form. Any audience anywhere would be dazzled by the athleticism of the great battle at the end of Act I, after Bai and her sister Qing (**Huang Hua**) go to try and rescue Xu from the monastery in which Fa Hai has imprisoned him. When Fa Hai calls down the Army of The Gods to support him, Bai and Qing turn themselves back into snakes, flood the temple and bring in an army of fishes. Some of the earlier sword fighting had been fairly stylised twirling and missing but, apart from the dazzling back-somersaults with which many champions in the Army of The Gods whizz across the stage, **Huang Hua** gives a dazzling display of taking them all on single-handed, leaping to kick back twirling spears, thrown at her simultaneously from all directions.

However, they are also able to make the original courtship of Xu highly amusing and the prolonged argument at the start of Act Two, - in which the two sisters accuse Xu of disloyalty and he pleads how he was misled by Fa Hai and how strong his prison was inside the monastery, so that he could not escape unaided -, came across for me as significantly moving, even though I would not really undertand the music and certainly not the language. (There were surtitles, somewhat erratically projected, which did seem to me to convey usefully not only general sense but often poetic imagery, although I passed two Chinese at the interval, who seemed to be native speakers of English, who were laughing to each other that the inaccuracy of the translations was "the funniest thing.")

The opening scenes I found very funny. The two sisters enter, singing of how they have come down from the mountain to walk beside the lake, nothing at this stage apparently being said about this having been their abode as Snake Goddesses, although those with trained eyes, as well as prior knowledge of the legend, might perhaps have picked up clues from their costumes. They are clearly there to "eye up the talent" or, as they explain themselves more discretely towards the end of the play, "drawn by human longing." There is nothing raucous about this, as there are several mentions throughout the play of the importance of refinement, but several of the eye-movements, emphasised by their white face make-up, would be directly recognisable in certain sorts of Lancashire Lassies. They talk of how they have definitely come to the right place as everybody is walking about in couples, presumably encouraging an atmosphere of togetherness. They then spot a handsome man, Xu, on his own and wonder how they can attract his attention. Providentially it begins to rain, so they are able to make him realise that it would be a courteous act to share his umbrella, He goes further and commissions a boat to drop them off at their gate of the city before taking him on to his. Though they are crushed up close in the boat, he observes propriety by keeping his back to them, although Qing does catch him in the act of stealing a glance at Bai. He lets himself be persuaded to call at their house another day to reclaim his umbrella.

LEGEND OF THE WHITE SNAKE (62) Bai (LI SHENGSU) battles to save her husband

The comedy in this scene is gentle, the place leisurely. Much of the fun in the next scene is in the speed of development. When he calls he is met by Qing, representing herself as Bai's maid, who immediately says that her mistress wants to know if he is married. He says he is just a poor apothecary's apprentice and cannot think of marriage yet. Qing says that Bai's father has left her very well provided for, so that is not a problem. She is learned in medicinal arts, so it would be a very compatible arrangement and she would very much like to marry him. Xu says he has not even the money for an engagement gift but Qing says he has already given her his umbrella, which is very suitable. He asks her family name and is then amazed that Qing already knows his, until Qing points out that he had painted it in very large characters on his umbrella. He says he should talk to his elder sisters about the possibility of engagement but Qing says why not get engaged first and tell them later. Bai enters in robes ready for an engagement ceremony and Xu is led off as rapidly and as bemused as Sebastian being dragged to her chapel by Olivia.

Apparently the Woman Warrior is a familiar figure in Chinese folk lore and performance. The forward female wooer is known in some more Western tales but not often from such an independent skills base. By the next scene, Bai is well established as a doctor, noted for her skill and dedication in treatment of the poor but also apparently treating enough with ability to pay to provide an adequate business for Xu in dispensing the medicines she prescribes. He is by no means her match as a warrior. Although Bai and Qing upbraid him for not having supported them in their battle against Fa Hai, it is unlikely that he could have contributed significantly. When he is present and Fa Hai makes his final assault to capture Bai, she sees that the most valuable act he can undertake is to escape with their new-born child, so as to bring him up in safety. In fairness, knowing the power of the Golden Alms Bowl with which Fa Hai finally overcomes her, she urges Qing, - of whose prowess as a warrior there is no doubt -, to flee also, which does enable her to return many years later, at the play's conclusion, with sufficient forces to overturn the pagoda under which Fa Hai had imprisoned Bai.

If some of the central episodes of the story, - threat, struggle, freedom, recapture, escape, recapture, final freedom -, would seem similar to a pretty roughly constructed Western melodrama and some elements of the acting are as obvious, - Xu when he is afraid stretches out very visibly trembling hands -, overall the level of appeal is far more elevated. Fa Hai is not a mostacio-twirling, black-caped, cackling villain. The nature-imagery in songs, evoking virtues or describing scenery, may possibly be conventional but seemed to me to be more sustained and several notches above what most melodrama writers in our land would occasionally have thrown into the pot, even in the country songs they would sometimes have included. If both the Ancient Greeks and Chinese used divine legends as the initial basis for many of their dramas, both developed them in distinctive if sometimes analogous ways. One might find several parallels between the use of music and dance in Greek comedies and Beijing Opera and if both developed very exact conventions both have shown themselves to have created works capable of sustaining very considerable development in performance.

If the **Aspects Electra** was a Greek tragedy in traditional style which did what it says on the tin, and none the worse for that, it was amazing how the cut-and-mix style of **When Medea Met Elvis** allowed the original strengths of the constituent plays to show through, rather than to totally disappear and to re-emerge, for better or worse, as something completely different. To have had the courage to expose a play of the stature of **Euripedes' Medea** to such a hazard was a bold move but an entirely successful one. I am not quite sure what happened to the elements supposedly derived from **Caryl Churchill**'s **Lives of The Great Poisoners**, as I do not know the play and did not spot a fourth major constituent on the scale of those from **Medea, Cooking With Elvis** and **Neil LaBute**'s **Bash**. I had known nothing previously of the latter play either but we seemed to get a pretty complete narrative. **Lee Hall**'s **Cooking ...** I had seen **(04:199)** and thought that in this edited-down version it emerged as a stronger play. The main strength of the original I had felt was in its very real portrayal of the emotions involved in a woman no longer having an effective husband but still needing male companionship and the revulsion against this of her young teenage daughter. The full play, however, had seemed to me to package this amidst a disproportionate amount of smut. There is still plenty of this in the condensed version seen here but not at the expense of getting on with a powerful narrative. The power in the narrative of **Medea** is well known and, in the distinctive contemporary voice of **Liz Lochhead**, it lost none of this by having to share stage space and running time with the other plays.

Betrayed love was the linking theme which the company found in all the plays it merged. I could not, after one viewing, summarise the full effectiveness of each point where one narrative passes into another but certainly it seemed entirely appropriate as one went along. The Chorus from **Medea** was always downstage right and the kitchen from **Elvis** downstage left. Dad (**Liam Greenfield**) was usually perched in his wheelchair at the top of a ramp behind them but came down centre stage for his performances as Elvis, where the same actor sometimes transformed directly into being Kreon, the one direct linking of the performance of the various narratives. This was the spot for his encounters with Medea and of hers with the Chorus and with Jason but the wall behind them could become transparent, to reveal him offstage, alone or with Glauke (**Jennifer Cooper**). Debbie (**Jennifer Sharrocks**) ,the only on-stage character and narrator of **Bash**, came to tell us the end of her tale sitting centre-stage, having told most of it to camera from a third level stage-left, above the usual position of Dad. We saw her there, sitting in profile, her full-face image being shown on a large screen at the same height, centre stage. In the final episodes, it was Glauke sitting in this position, as if on a throne, and being filmed, as she received the fatal presents from children.

The grieved women triumphing through ruthless acts was the linking pattern in all the stories, although Horace the Tortoise was the only outright fatality in the **Elvis**, Jill (**Maria Blackburn**) more succeeding in achieving the expulsion of Stuart (**Chris Bowler**) by inducing him to give to her what he has been recruited to supply to her mother (**Abby Simmons**), **Maria Blackburn** maintaining a wonderfully unchanged mask of boredom whilst she continues to eat chocolate cake at Stuart's point of delivery.

Bash is apparently consciously shaped by **Medea**, Debbie wreaking her revenge on the man who betrayed her (- her school teacher, a circumstance which seems to be appearing in an increasing number of our plays, for instance also featuring in **Kate Henry**'s contribution to **Three Gobby Cows (13)** and being the fate of the Debbie in **Tom Stoppard**'s **The Real Thing**). **Labute**'s Debbie slays the child for whom she has developed such an affection, after ensuring that her betrayer came to love him too. The linking passion is the suppression of passion, - mustering the strength to kill her child. In **Bash**, this is very much the act of a free citizen, taking justice into her own hands. In **Medea**, the context is doubly political, Medea living in a polity where a woman needs a male protector and her being abandoned by Jason is primarily an affair of state.

In **House of Illusions (The Balcony)** the clients may have a passion to gain their sexual excitements in a particular way. For the staff, as in **Chicken Tikka Masala,** it is just a routine day's work, of no especial interest. In **Chicken Tikka** the whores may not be especially free citizens but they are outside the workings of the state, unable to call on its resources, even when subject to criminal attack. I suspect that its main aspiration was to be documentary, in a passably entertaining way. It may be that many houses of resort are currently run on such a basis and have clients of the general type shown. Straight reality would probably be more unpleasant as well as more tedious but to try and make it lighter also makes it less authentic. Reflections that their trade does no harm and may be more honest than marriages continued for services rendered but where feelings are predominantly bitter may be common in the business but, by the same token, do not spring off the stage with the freshness of being new-minted. **Laura Bestley** and **Emanuel Greco** as the workers and **Christian Knott** as their various clients created a reasonable drama which kept moving and included some characterful interactions.

The Balcony is a far more major drama but began with improvised material which provided a background for the main clients which was not geographically very far from the activities in **Chicken Tikka Masala.** These were quite good in themselves but did not mesh very well with the unadapted parts of the play, which clearly still took place in a city with a palace and a monarch in residence. I do not know if the whole play could have been reset in Manchester. We have had some high profile Chief Constables, though it would certainly be taking them some way from their public image to suggest that their deepest desire was to find themselves among the public authority figures whom clients at the brothel aspired to impersonate in lewd scenarios. Also we do not have anywhere in this country a Catholic Bishop so closely identified with the establishment that his impersonation could be a natural inspiration for turning the tide of a revolution. It had to be Catholic as the attraction for the brothel client in taking on his persona was the opportunity to hear alluring confessions and prescribe penances. In this production he considered it rank prejudice that he had been barred from obtaining such opportunities by joining the priesthood, - on the grounds that he was a Protestant. The suggestion that he could have overcome this by conversion he found scandalous.

This possibility was put to him by the Madam who welcomed us all and bid us be at our ease, as it was the lot of everyone to have secrets about which, in a less sympathetic environment, we might be embarrassed. The production did not run to having a printed programme, so I cannot record any of the actors. This was a very well characterised performance, although if the number of knowing looks had been cut by about half it might have vastly increased the sense of allure. There was much that was lively and well done about the production, although I did come to feel that it could usefully have been trimmed a little in length.

The honour for which the police chief would have been willing to settle, if no brothel client had wished to impersonate him, would have been a vast public statue in the shape of a phallus. Despite this being the sort of area in which the interests of most of the characters essential lay, - even the female client who had to be equipped with a massive dildo to fulfil her fantasies as a Captain of Horse -, the considerations of the play ranged far more widely. Female fantasies as an adjunct to masturbation did play their part in **Possibly Porn**, although **Francesca Larkin** and **Lowri Shimmin** often focussed more specifically upon the deed itself. As, however, there are apparently boyfriends, who consider it a reasonable expectation to be allowed to watch them doing it, and are more enticed by what they imagine this to involve than actual practice, the boundaries of the 'real' and the fantasised become blurred. A more involving portrait came in the final episode in which **Francesca Shimmin** represented a character so addicted to the sexual act that she brushed aside any attempt by males to show any individual interest in or tenderness towards her, just urging them to get on with it, afterwards feeling so revolted with herself that she determines never to seek such a liaison again but immediately after that beginning to plan how she can do so. This was so isolated an element, however, that it did not have the scope to develop its full dramatic potential. The bulk of the piece concentrated on what a woman can do for herself.

It is not that obvious to me that this is a subject on which there is all that much of interest to be said, - even the acclaimed **Vagina Monologues (02: 516, 03:497, 526** etc) seem to me not really able to sustain their running time -, but as it is indulged in by the articulate as much as by any others, from time to time people will essay comment or explication on an involving occupation. That said, the creators of **Possibly Porn** did show themselves to be able performers, both in their balletic and movement skills, in stage confidence and in being able to change mood swiftly, - for instance, from the involved to the dismissive.

Variation of stage mood was of the essence of **Grazed Knees.** The title and the poster suggest that the original focus was on memories of childhood but in fact the eventual focus proved to be on the context in the present. The basement at **Solomon Grundys** seems to have been trimmed up quite a bit since I last saw a play there, when it was pretty dingy, but **Sarah Jones** and **Rebecca Blackshaw** had still taken trouble to furnish it appropriately to become a well-kept if rudimentary flat, including having a calendar showing the appropriate date on the back wall, even if this was not prominent enough to be that noticeable to the audience.

We began with a courageously long frozen image of **Rebecca Blackshaw**, seated motionless at her kitchen table, grasping her cleaning equipment. We do not know until the end why she should be so paralysed in thought or why, once she returns to motion, she should spring to it with such reckless energy or spray her anti-bacterial surface cleaner so thoughtlessly near the teacups laid out on the side-table beside her cooker. It is while she is scouring away at this, with a vigour which might well have shaken the cups to the floor, that a much more trimly-dressed **Sarah Jones** enters behind her, with a suitcase, and tiptoes forward to surprise her. **Rebecca Blackburn** squeals with delight as they embrace, but it is the visiting **Sarah** who seems the more conscious that there is a baby in the bedroom who must not be disturbed. She would like to stay over the Christmas holiday but is concerned that **Rebecca**'s partner would object. **Rebecca** assures her that he will be alright with her if she is alright with him and urges **Sarah** that she wants her to stay. She does not make a very good job of brewing them tea and also adamantly refuses when **Sarah** says that she wants her and her baby to go with her to their parents on Christmas Day itself: she knows this will just provoke their father into going on about her living with a “bloody Paki.”

This leads to a resentful silence between them but they agree to make up as **Rebecca** sets the tea on the table. **Sarah** has brought her a very generous cheque as a Christmas present. **Rebecca** is disconcerted that she has got nothing for **Sarah** but then has the happy inspiration to dash out and bring in a boxful of their childhood playthings and photographs, over which they merrily reminisce. **Rebecca** now says that her partner is away, so she has little food in the house, but they agree that she should telephone for the delivery of a take-away meal while **Sarah** nips up to the bathroom. **Rebecca** does not phone. She reverts to something near the lethargy in which we first found her. She does manage eventually to lift the teacups off the table but becomes anchored again in much the position she was when **Sarah** first entered. **Sarah** enters again but this time in silent horror. When **Rebecca** turns round she rushes at her, shaking her and beating her about the head and shouting out "What have you done?" She had taken the opportunity to go in and look at the baby and had found it dead, - obviously killed. The context, which tearfully emerges in fragments, is that **Rebecca**'s partner is not merely away: he has left her. It would seem that the killing was not a Medea-like act of revenge but a desperate, meaningless, emotional reaction. The play ends with the sisters realising that they have a shared and overwhelming problem.

As far as it took things, this was very well done. It held one absorbed throughout and managed all of its changes of mood. It was not developed enough to become a full drama, on the scale of the issues involved but it was fully successful in setting out its stall and could, for instance, effectively be used as it stands in certain sorts of educational work.

Twisted Trails had no aspiration to be a 'full drama' but made equally full use of highly-evolved dramatic skills. It might have been subtitled "**Stephen Sondheim**, Eat Your Heart Out!" for its rapid concatenation of umpteen 'Fairy' Tales. Brief extracts of adapted songs from Musicals were among the ingredients but essentially the material was guyed in every way possible. Our friend the phallus occasionally made his appearance but the fun was not primarily in the lewd references, of which there several, but the speed and skill with which they were incorporated: low-slung forearms in the appropriate position or a raised crooked little finger aptly suggesting the designated organ in an instant, before the performance dashed on to other matters. A non-traditional intimation of an interest in carnal knowledge or other bodily functions was just one of the caricatures. At least as frequent was "This is ridiculous," "I know this is ridiculous," "You know this is ridiculous" and "This looks even more ridiculous if you put it in the context of this completely different story." The main verbal element was doggerel verse, with glaring, but often very witty, puns, wilful anachronisms and sometimes yer actual lewd reference. Song origins came not only from musicals but other mangled traditions, such as Teddy Bears Picnic.

It was all done in basic black performance costumes on a bare stage but with effective use of a limited range of carefully made or selected props or costume adjuncts: a 'tree' which could also serve as a cottage door, after passing through or behind which an actor could emerge as a different character, or faces or other elements could protrude, to enable four actors to suggest the presence of a full complement of Seven Dwarves. A two-sided mask could allow the simultaneous presentation of both a wolf and a piglet. Somewhat more realistically, a peaked hat could enable

TWISTED TRAILS (22); Who's Afraid?

the suitably tall **Amy Hiscocks** to convey instantly that she had become Prince Charming, a cloak helped **Richard Sails** to become the Wicked Witch. It all rattled through in about thirty minutes. I am not sure that it would not have been even better at twenty-five, as I think by then most of the changes had been very effectively rung. All the effect was in the doing of it but this was so skilful that the net impact was not just that it was hilariously funny throughout but highly impressive.

The guyed 'Fairy' Tale was also the substance of the one play of this **Arden** season not to be composed by its performer, **Ugly Sister** by **Joanne Harris. Catia Soteiro** had heard this performed as a wireless play and had found that it was a monologue/short story in the author's book **Jigs and Reels.** The **Arden External Projects** regulations currently allow any work not previously seen on a stage, so **Catia Soteiro** had set to to adapt it for live performance. It was set in the dressing room of a theatre in which the Ugly Sister still gets seasonal work portraying the version of herself known through pantomime. She protests that this is a traduction of her historical reality but does it for the money. Being constantly booed at every appearance is wearing on the spirit so, when a grey, stooped gentleman indicates from the front row that she should meet him outside the Stage Door, she rushes to throw herself into his arms, notices what big teeth he has, as he consolingly says, "Call me Wolfie." It was a jolly little piece, perfectly well carried off.

It was staged with some elaboration, entering in grotesque Ugly Sister costume and make-up, which she gradually removed as she told her tale. **Victoria Brown** followed with complete informality. Instead of making an entrance, as **Catia Soteiro** had done, she just casually began to address us whilst the audience was settling down, as if she too had been passing the performance area to find a seat or stepped on to it to adjust the setting, which was just the remnants of the previous performance. She was entirely successful in gaining and holding our attention on her chosen subject of **Farnworth Pondlife,** although some of the effect of this being told in doggerel rhyme was lost to me, I think not through my accumulated ear wax but by some of it being taken at such a speed that I missed some of the verbal detail.

The primary subject was the depraved mores of her home town, very recognisable as that of **Jim Cartwright**'s **Road**, although full of fresh and lively detail. All age groups were portrayed as most active in injestion and its consequent expulsions, alcohol and the products of the chippy being universal, sexual fluids being absorbed as regularly by the younger. That taken through the neck emerged in comparable bulk as often through the same orifice as it did lower down, in either case, whether on or within the doorstep, it being that task of others to clean up. Home is no single location as parents are unlikely to stay together. Whether they get hospitalised by getting beaten up or byfalling down stairs depends on who is telling the story.

That the sordid can clearly retain this character whilst being so laughable doubtless owes much to the character of the narrator but may well be helped by now seeing it from outside. In Manchester, she finds that recognisable **Pondlife** characteristics still exist but she also has a new range of friends.

This was the note on which **Destiny Thomas** ended her more clearly autobiographical narrative **From Yard 2 Abroad**, beginning with her childhood in Jamaica up to her present life in Manchester. She now has a clear direction, after gaining education and Drama training, first at **Abraham Moss** and now **Arden**, but even more important in her finally summary is the friends she still has, who helped her through after finding she was pregnant shortly after she had arrived alone in England and after a later marriage had proved to be extremely short-lived. She attracted a good community audience at **A Fe We**, as glad to recognise and to show to their locally-born children her Jamaica experiences of mischief-making, schooling, passing in and out of church and first meeting boys as her tale of her life in this country. It was a good straight-forward piece, vividly performed.

In a completely different style from the content of **Victoria Brown**'s performance had been the quotation from **Aristotle** in her programme, "The soul is characterised by these capacities: self-nutrition, sensation, thinking and movement," the point probably being that such a dimension as the soul, such activities as thinking, let alone such vocabulary as "capacities," are scarcely discernible in the **Pondlife** which she describes. The programme for **Cabbages** was largely taken up with an extensive document on The Unity of Substance and The Natural Order, which I take to be summarising the thinking of **Immanuel Kant**, even though the thinker being discussed is only referred to in the text as "???." I make this attribution, not because I can instantly recognise the work of this philosopher but because he seems the logical person to quote after seeing the last scene of the play. In this the joint authors, **Mark Winstanley** and **Lawrence Ghorra,**, are the two orderlies sitting around while whatever fearsome scientific process The Institute concerns itself with is presumably turning Godfrey (**Alan Dickie**) into a mental cabbage:

"Wot you reading?"

"Kant." (titter from elements of the audience who may not have heard too exactly, or may have seen the legitimate joke.)

"Wot's it abaht?"

"Philosophy."

"I read some philosophy once."

"?"

""Man Is Born Free But Everywhere He Is In Chains.""

"Where you read that?"

"Found it in a fortune cookie. Dunno what it means."

"It's abaht Free Will, innit?"

"?" …prompting the orderly played by **Lawrence Ghorra** to go off into a long exposition, which is even more impenetrable than the text in the programme and on which he is still engaged when the play ends.

This, which followed on in a double-bill from the high jinks of **Twisted Trails**, was the first play of the Arden season which had the feel of a conventionally structured drama, with a sequence of scenes and narrative development. Even within this form, however, it had three very distinct styles. It began almost as a cartoon, with two bespectacled library assistants sitting on a park bench, cooing at each other "I love you, Audrey," … "I love you too, Godfrey." They exchanged sweet nothings about how she (**Trees Maessen**) admired his cataloguing skills and how grateful he was for her using her more senior position to allow him to extend his loan on the books he wanted to borrow.

The scene then abruptly ended in a blackout, with Godfrey reappearing in more or less the same position but now flanked by two highly sinister policemen (**Steve Bezzina** and **Lawrence Ghorra**), questioning him about the disappearance of Audrey, about which he professes to know nothing. After learning nothing useful, the Police decide that, although their psychologist has pronounced him sane, they intend to send him to The Institute for observation. There he meets various strange patients, one of whom (Eric, **Lawrence Ghorra**) claims to have been there long enough to have found where the library is but the book he has borrowed proves to have pages which are completely blank. At one stage Godfrey believes that he sees Audrey, apparently engaged at her old profession, but entirely mute, not recognising him and tending shelves on which the books have pages as blank as in the one clasped by Eric. Godfrey comes to recall that the bench on which he had last spoken to Audrey had been on a hill near The Institute and that the last he had seen of her had been when a strange light had seemed to come out of the building.

Godfrey's questioning on these matters is resented by the medical staff (Nurse Hart,**[Trees Maessen]** and Dr Spinoza **[Steve Bezzina]**), who have always behaved in a most sinister way, and the

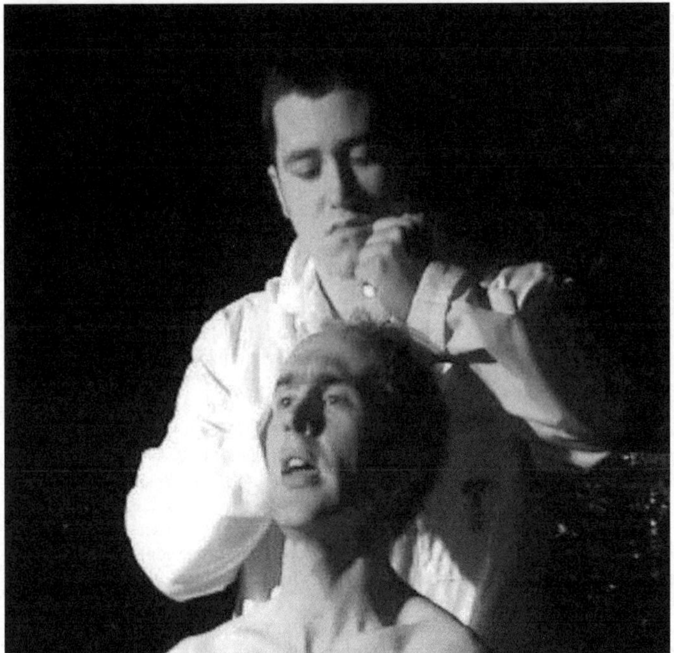

CABBAGES (23); Godrey (ALAN DICKIE) gets the treatment from Dr Spinoza (STEVE BEZZINA)

doctor declares that he is going to send him for treatment. When Godfrey protests that he is there for observation, not treatment, the doctor says that things have moved on and, anyway, they have the power to do whatever they like. One infers that the real work of The Institute is some form of experimentation which leaves those subjected to it as mindless as the briefly rediscovered Audrey.

All this central part of the play had been highly sinister, in a manner reminiscent of **Kafka.** We now jumped to the scene with the two orderlies discussing Philosophy while Godfrey apparently takes longer than most to be processed in 'the tank.' I am not sure that the piece was quite tight enough to be fully dramatically effective. More writers and actors seem to think scenes of the mentally destabilised are good theatrical material than they often seem to me to be and the **Kafta / Pinter** style of 'threat.' can by now seem a little familiar. Nevertheless, it was an interesting endeavour and I believe that the authors have been inspired by their opportunity to attempt further works in future, for which I think it will be worth keeping on the watch.

The somewhat surreal effect of their deliberate mixture of styles made me forget the initial impression I had had of at last seeing a 'proper play,' so that the feeling of freshness in 'at last seeing' a conventionally structured piece was able to exert itself again on seeing **One Bird, Two Stones.** In truth, it did not have that much more plot than **Grazed Knees** and varied its style by having at least the first character we met, Gus (**Neville Millar**), address us directly as well as having the characters talk to each other. Also the conclusion cannot exactly be called naturalistic, which overall the bulk of the play was, nor can it be said that it brought the piece to a very specific conclusion, which, after their fashions, **Grazed Knees** and **Cabbages** both more or less had. Nevertheless, the piece showed that some traditional script-writing is still a valuable resource upon which to be able to draw.

Instead of making use of the large upper room at **Jabez Clegg**, which performers in the past have often found a useful space to which to gain access, this company used a secondary bar-room downstairs, for the excellent reason that the bulk of the play was set on just such premises. Gus entered from the Ladies lavatories, explaining to us that he has just been cleaning them out at the start of a new day, he and his not-yet-wife Bernie (**Victoria Scowcroft**) living on the premises. She is not assisting him on this merry morn as it is her day off, on which she is entitled to lie in and have him prepare her breakfast. With nattering to us and pursuing his other duties he does not make great progress with this. He has made her coffee but by the time she shows herself it has got cold as he has been distracted from taking it up to her by the early arrival of Mr T (**Darren Langford**), more of a friend than a customer, indeed not thinking of paying for the drink he requests, early in the day though it is.

He is especially amiable to Bernie, whom he may have known longer, and hopes she will play a game of three-dimensional noughts-and-crosses with him, the kit for which is in a bar table, as if for the recreation of customers. They do not make much progress with that as Bernie is ribbing Gus about her lack of breakfast and about the female underwear sticking out of his back-pocket, which had been the subject of his first disquisition to us, on the things he finds when cleaning up. He relays to Bernie his suspicions of which loose-living customer may have left them. When she teases him by asking how he knows they are not hers, he not only replies, "You're not like that," but "You've put all that behind you." There are various suggestions about Bernie having had some form of difficult past from which Gus takes some credit for having helped her escape.

An item of clothing he does recognise is to be hers is her future wedding dress and they talk on how much she is to spend on this. The cost is formidable but Gus only lightly questions it before conceding. [It seemed at this stage as though they were still thinking of Dublin as using Pounds, although in later conversation the Euro was recognised. This may recognise a continuing duality in daily conversation or have been a slip by a not especially Irish group of writers]. Gus takes the attitude that "It's your big day," and seems ready to concede almost any expense to his beloved. She sets forth for her day of alleged retail therapy but we next meet her in a state of undress, admiring her own charms in the mirror in the rooms of a single gentleman (James, also **Darren Langford**, who is able to distinguish himself clearly from Mr T not only by adept difference of facial expression and hairstyle but because the latter has a well represented paralysed arm and neck, resulting from some incident in the past, which may have had something to do with Bernie's unhappy years). James emerges from the bathroom, brushing his teeth, and is keen to engage her in "shenanigans," which, while accepting intimate embraces, she wishes to postpone in all its fullness, as she apparently still does have some retail therapy in mind. Jamie pursues his quest with expressions of devotion, which extend to a proposal of marriage. This, after very little sparring, she appears to accept with sincerity.

Where this leaves her in relation to the devoted Gus, does not become explicit. He is not oblivious to the possibility of a rival but more seems to see this in the presence of Mr T. Back in the bar, his conversation with him is becoming less amiable, telling him that he should not presume on his relationship with Bernie in the past: it is he, Gus, who got her out of her difficulties then; it is he who is going to marry her. He tells Mr T that he is to cease his visits to the bar and that his current one should end there and then. Mr T withdraws without much expostulation. Bernie returns, laden with her shopping. There is no suggestion of any disruption to their wedding plans but as they discuss these, James enters, presumably representationally, and she stands framed between them as the play ends.

How their lives might have continued is not suggested. I rather suspect the ending of being a 'got-to-end-it-somehow' artifice, rather than one felt to sum everything up. Nevertheless, the piece otherwise did make an effective drama. This is primarily a tribute to the acting. There is good deal of light-hearted banter, which it is amusing to hear, and there is much that is intriguing about what the relationships really are and about what has happened and may happen but as the play in its present form cannot take these considerations very far they cannot develop into a matter of lasting interest. As not all that much in plot terms actually happens it is a tribute to the performers that our interests are sustained as well as they are. It need not have been all that interesting for us in the audience to observe the exchanges of people we did not know all that much about but the creators of the piece succeeded in making it so and it was well worth seeing..

I am not sure I can say as much for the second half of the double-bill, **Chameleon**, but a great many in the audience audibly got a lot of pleasure out of it, so it was obviously fine for them.

The main live-action elements were two police interviews following a killing in a southern state of the USA, the plays two creators, **Steve Blower** and **Richard Kirkbride**, alternating the roles of suspect and detective. In the first half, the suspect is English (Krakak Anderson, **Blower**), as is the victim, the incriminating circumstance being that he had got to know her through an unsuccessful approach via the Last Chance Video Dating Agency. The main fun of this half was to see his bumbling attempts to make his video and was indeed reasonably amusing. His explanation for why he had pursued the woman who rejected him to America was that he had indeed subsequently found love and his new partner had suggested they come out and say there was no ill-feeling. It emerged that his first love had managed to find employment in a small-scale recording studio and when **Steve Blower** took his turn to play a detective, his suspect (Bengle Bo Thomas, **Richard Kirkbride**) was a singer who had applied for an audition at the studio and been rejected. This was where most of the audience got a lot of fun but I did not. The amusement to be got out of people singing badly seems to me to be limited but we got a double helping: the tape of Bengle's disastrous audition and then a live action performance to round the piece off. There was wit here and there but not, it seemed to me, all that much. The detectives were deliberately exaggerated caricatures of southern Americans, with what seemed to me a disproportionately small amount of material to extend over the amount of time they had to threaten their suspects with shouts of "Boy!" It seemed to me rather small beer and not really worthy of the steel of graduating students from such a college but a lot of people did get fun out of it.

The audience were far more deeply moved by a play of even simpler repeating structure, also created by its two performers: **Marbles.** Although glass spheres are being played with by one of the children in the first scene, the primary reference of the title is to something which we lose. In that scene the children are visiting their grandmothers in a retirement home, well evinced by rough-edged life-sized sculptures made from newspaper, sitting in arm chairs. The children's attention is divided between some attempts at interaction with their relatives and their games. They are frank about their perception of their grandmothers' condition and as interested in whether they can share their sweets or food.

Half a lifetime passes between each scene. For the middle episode, the performers (**Kate Hazlewood** and **Kathryn Haycock**) transform themselves into adult family women, now visiting their own mothers in the same day room, unable to respond to their wish to be taken home or even to communicate very clearly with their rambling minds. Thirty years further on it is they who are now the residents, equally uncertain about what day or time it is, able to draw on their life-long friendship to have some jolly chat and to confide about their bodily functions and the attractions of the male nurses but also very lost about what is going on. The performers very ably represented themselves as being of the three different ages shown and created a most telling fusion of showing what could be amusing in the ramblings of the very old without reducing the overall feeling of sadness which left many eyes undry.

If this was so successful, why did I open this account by commenting on the "extra dimension" of a "fully formed" play? Partly because **Marbles** was only twenty minutes out of a full week of short pieces, partly because I saw them in this single week, so even though there were several pieces of near comparable quality and a great deal of variety, to return to the enjoyment of a full-length play was a pleasure which was increased by being different in so many ways from the other work experienced in the week in which I saw it. The difference is not to denigrate the quality of either body of work but just to say that the contrast quickened one's appreciation.

Further Than The Furthest Thing did not use its additional length to investigate character in greater detail than had been possible in the shorter works, nor did it have a significantly more complex plot, nor, with a cast of five, was it on a very different scale in that regard either. It did have the resources of a purpose-built theatre and benefited from a highly atmospheric set, although the only furnishing, - a small table and a couple of chairs -,was on much the same level as most of the small scale works. These had had only limited control of their atmosphere, setting themselves up in what corner they might of licences premises, where sounds of other activities could not be fully excluded and nor could occasional incursions by bar-staff or other patrons, lighting control only being a limited resource. Apparently there was trouble with the lighting at the **Capitol** also on the night I went: we were kept waiting considerably while they tried to sort it out and then we were told this had not been resolved, with the hope that this would not spoil our enjoyment. What we missed, I do not know but that the atmosphere was darker than in some of the production photographs on view in the foyer seemed to me entirely in keeping with the mood of the piece, let alone the atmosphere of an island covered in volcanic dust in the central episode of the play and the resources certainly remained to enhance this with an appropriate red glow, repeated in the boiler-room of the factory in which many of the islanders gain employment after being evacuated to 'Hingland.' **Victoria Brown** and **Richard Kirkbride** had had the skills to enhance their pieces through their talents as actor-musicians but, - aside from **Kirkbride**'s contributions being deliberately bad -, they had not had the resources to make this as major a contribution to atmosphere as **Iain Jackson**'s extensive score, composed specifically for **Further Than the Furthest Thing.**

The atmosphere of this play was so distinctive and so strange that I was surprised to see in the programme that it was set specifically on Tristan da Cunha and was directly representing the events of 1961, rather than just being inspired generally by them. It seemed more as if another world had been created by artistry, rather than by a remoteness of History and Geography. Ultimately, of course, as it reached us in the audience, this was an artistic creation but real History also seems to have been nearer than I would have thought.

The real can seem an artifice. The language of the islanders does much to create the atmosphere of strangeness but **Hywel Evans**, the director, assures us in the programme note that this is not a construct but the authentic dialect of people on a very remote and originally uninhabited island in the South Atlantic, whose population has been made up over recent centuries by seafarers from all quarters of the globe. Apart from unfamiliar structures, the most noticeable feature is the intrusive aspirate. In the opening scene, Mill (**Claire Jones**) is welcoming back one of the few islanders (her son Francis, **Gareth Bayliss**) who has ever boarded a ship to leave the island. The main delicacy which she has to offer him is "Heggs," gathered from wild birds. Given the extreme hunger which we learn that the islanders have been experiencing, after exceptionally bad weather had prevented the supply ship on which they depended arriving the previous year, that two of these 'heggs' get broken might have been made to seem an even more tragic event but, despite Mill's desperation to make Francis stay on the island, now he has returned, her extreme hospitality in fact leads her to serve the one remaining hegg to the guest (Mr Hanson, **Graeme Brookes**) whom Francis has brought back with him. It proves not to be exactly to his taste and he does not complete eating it but never the less he and Mill do strike up an amiable rapport, partly aided by his skill as a conjurer in most skilfully making the hegg appear and disappear in a variety of traditional ways.

This, however, is only a minor, personal, sideline to his real interests as an all-purpose capitalist. He has come because Francis, after meeting him in South Africa, had persuaded him that the islanders would be willing to let him establish a factory there. After learning that they will not, he promptly takes his leave and would have passed out of the story had it not been his ship which was passing the island at the time the volcano was erupting. He rescues them, despite the conflict between his perception that they need to leave immediately and their communal solidarity meaning that Mill gives priority to the decent burial of the still-born child of Rebecca (**Ruth E Cockburn**). The higher hope she had had of this baby had been to induce Rebecca to name Francis as the father, in the hope that this would prevent him leaving the island again.

These extremes of solidarity in the islanders' culture, however, were not ones which excluded ruthlessness when necessary to preserve the community. We learn that the first response to the lack of a supply ship had been an absolutely equal division of the resources which remained between all the islanders. When it was calculated, however, that the portions thus arrived at could not possibly be sufficient to allow any individual to survive, in order that some might live, about half the population, selected by lot, had been taken round to the barren far side of the island by boat and left there, their share of the supplies being redistributed to the remainder.

In Hingland, Mr Hanson provides them with housing and work in his factory. Neither, particularly the housing, is particularly attractive but he does undertake to obtain government grants to provide far more suitable accommodation and to keep the rent for this within what they can afford from their wages. He still accepts Mill as his friend, which means that she can act as spokeswoman for the community, particularly about their concern to return to their island. He tells them that this has been completely destroyed but when the workers build up a fund from their wages to pay a few representatives to return to witness the disappearance of their lost home, he has to confess that he lied, - that the island is in not much worse condition than when they left it.

Whether he deceived them to try to obtain a source of cheap labour or whether he could not conceive that it was in the best interests of anybody to live on such a barren rock, we do not really know. It was not the nature of the play to fill in such detail, giving us more an impressive series of portraits of what the characters did and said to each other. Found out, he is deeply apologetic and undertakes that never during his life will a supply ship ever fail to arrive to sustain those who choose to return. This all except Francis elect to do. Not all are able to do this, as his factory has not been a very safe working environment for them and Bill (**Scott Bradley**) has not been able to maintain the right pressure in the boiler room.

He had been recognised by the islanders as their chaplain and had also had the burden of transporting those who drew the unfavourable lots in the winter of starving. **Scott Bradley** and **Graeme**

Brookes were very successful in portraying characters considerably older than they are naturally, as they were, as William and Crampton, in the splendid production of **You Never Can Tell.** **Claire Jones** had been entirely successful there as Mrs Clandon but as Mill it would probably have helped if she could have seemed older, very effective though the performance was in other ways.

I would tend to think of actors and script as the prime ingredients for good theatre. Some of the best we see in Manchester often being workshop versions of new work in which almost no other resource is brought into play. We saw some very good work in the minimally resourced **Arden** projects but certainly the **Salford** and, still more, the **Capitol** work did show, by contrast, what a useful contribution controlled lighting, sound, costume and staging can make. **Further Than The Furthest Thing** is a highly allusive piece and would not easily have had the same impact if, in addition to a strong cast, it had not had the assistance of light and sound in creating atmosphere. **The Trestle At Pope Lick Creek** at the **Royal Exchange** had, of course, had all these resources in abundance but if it seemed to me to have less overall success than the **Phaedra**, this is probably because the latter is a better structured play. The contribution of the Greeks had here been taken some distance from its source as, even more so, had **When Medea Met Elvis** but these seasons of work combined to show not only how valuable it is that we have the classics of two-and-a-half-thousand years ago alongside the new but how able a set of fresh interpreters we have emerging from our drama schools.

16 FEBRUARY. **THE LIFE OF MOLIERE (49);** Bill Naughton. *5 MARCH.* **THE FIREWORK-MAKER'S DAUGHTER (50);** Lowry. **OUT OF THE BLUE (51);** *16 MARCH.* **THE GOSPEL OF MATTHEW (52);** Bury Met. *5 APRIL.* **CHAOS (57);** *7 APRIL.* **RESISTANCE (53);** *8 APRIL.* **BELLS (56);** Contact. *9 APRIL.* **A RAISIN IN THE SUN (54);** Lowry. **A TASTE OF HONEY (55);** RNCM. *13 APRIL.* **IN GOD WE TRUST (58);** Bill Naughton. *19 APRIL.* **ON THE SHORE OF THE WIDE WORLD (59);** Royal Exchange.

It was sheer theatrical delight to see both **The Firework-Maker's Daughter** and **Out of The Blue** on the same day. There was not much connection in the subject matter or in the level at which their concerns were addressed but the uniting factor was that the greater part of their effect was the skill and co-operation of the actors.

It was not that the productions lacked any other resources but that their utilisation to produce impact depended entirely on the performers. When Hamlet, the white elephant (**Malcolm Ridley**), enters in **The Firework-Maker's Daughter**, the way in which the great bulk of his body is represented is the instant re-configuration of the umbrellas of the wind-swept visitors to the market, from beneath which elephants droppings then began to land, to the geat delight of the youngest members of the audience. The stage for **Out of The Blue** is littered with all sorts of predominantly-metal objects, such as a mangle and the base of a treadle-operated sewing machine, which do give a late-1930's period feel in their own right but the way they are used to convey the impression not only of a submerged submarine but of various settings on the surface and on land is mainly the work of the actors.

From the moment the trap-door in front of the curtain bangs open at the beginning to reveal the tousled head of the ever-active **Ayesha Antoine, The Firework-Maker's Daughter** sweeps one along with its invention and vigour. Like **Sue Devaney**, another actress who is more than common small, no matter how far up-stage or outside the main focus of the action she may be, **Antoine** is always vigorously in action. In the final grand firework contest, on her winning which the life of her father (**Johannes Flaschberger)** depends, while Dr Puffenflasch (**Gregory Gudgeon**) and Colonel Harry Sparkington (**Jason Webb**) are unleashing all their expertise centre-stage, **Antoine**, as Lila, can be glimpsed to one-side, giving properly sporting applause as due recognition of prowess, whilst manifestly wishing that that the opposition she was up against was nowhere near so keen.

The vivid word-descriptions in the book are a triumph of creating vivid images in the mind's eye of the displays created by the different competitors. There Lila and her father triumph by creating a far subtler display than the whizzes and bangs of their German and American (and there also Italian) competitors. That the contest should be decided by the volume of applause is a natural theatrical opportunity but the way this was ensured in the play was not to downplay the other competitors, whose acting out of their displays was much enjoyed by the audience, but because this method, - which was used from the play's opening when **Amanda Lawrence,** as Fuse, rushed on with red-tinsel-draped finger-nails to portray the effect of Lila lighting her first device-, was finally abandoned and the whole stage erupted in fountain-like cascades of real fireworks.

Such effects and the gaily coloured costumes gave no impression of the production being under-resourced but in truth most of the effects were gained with basic skill rather than hi-tec: the bespectacled **Malcolm Ridley** curling his lip contemptuously at each display of ignorance by mere mortals or Lila's great friend Chulak (Manchester-trained **Mo Zainal**, cf **02: 21, 25, 207, 212)209**) not only able to give a constant sense of his dogged pursuit of her interests but able to interpolate into his interrogation by the dreaded monarch (**Joanne Howarth**) that he could answer his enquiries into his making away with Hamlet much more ably if the King's Special and Particular Bodyguard (**Amanda Lawrence**) removed his foot from his neck. **Lucian Msamati** led a motley crew who constantly re-appear in different guises as, "Like a Flash!", he has yet another idea of how they can make their fortunes: too incompetent and soft-

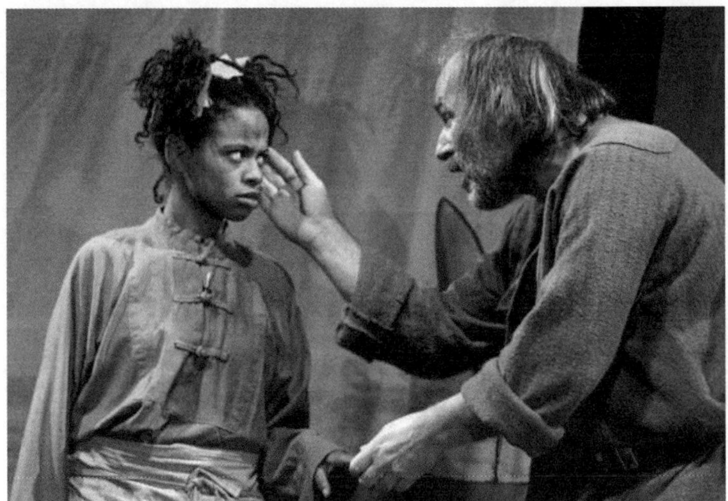

THE FIREWORK MAKER'S DAUGHTER (50, AYESHA ANTOINE) is most reluctant to hear any suggestion that she is not able to become as skilled in the profession as her father (JOHANNES FLASCHBERGER).

hearted to be pirates, not finding an adequate customer base for setting up Rambashi's Jungle Grill and dubiously equipped to become festive singers.

The voyage in **Out of The Blue** was a much more serious matter than that of the supposed river taxi aboard which the aspirant pirates endeavoured to ply their trade and which Lila had far more idea of how to steer clear of predatory crocodiles and to defend from tigers. It was the ill-fated maiden voyage of the submarine **HMS Thetis**, which not only carried the souls of men into the other world beneath the sea, as doubtless those who named her hoped, but most of them to their graves. The moment at which she became water-logged was vividly evoked by a silk parachute seeming to spring from the mangle as Lieutenant Woods (**Ben O'Sullivan**) opened the final torpedo tube to discover why the craft was not submerging as readily as intended. We had seen him assess the safety of opening the tube by the same procedure as that adopted for all the rest, by first opening a test cock. The reason why this had seemed as negative as all the rest, we saw later being discovered, was that it had been blocked by a spot of enamel paint, explaining why a grainy newsreel shot of paint being applied at the same time as drilling into metal had repeatedly appeared on the screen early in the performance. (The first version of this performance was originally called **Achilles Heel**, an apt reference to the small omission through which Thetis failed to protect the life of her son in the manner which she had hoped).

The story was not told chronologically, so we knew from early on that the voyage had been a disaster. Act I ended with the triumph of the sailors on-board fabricating means to pump out the excess water, so that the craft could rise from the sea bed to the surface. We saw newsreel footage of the stern sticking out of the water but the escape hatches remained submerged, so only a few of the crew were able to make their way out before she once again sank, the rescue craft which eventually arrived on the scene being unable to support her. There was vivid material here of lack of communication between the coast guard and the navy and the considerable difficulty of locating the vessel, even though it had sailed such a little distance. Nevertheless, I did wonder at half-time what more could be made from the story of heroic tragedy than had been done competently half a century ago by such as **John Mills** in **Morning Departure.**

The answer was, a great deal. The British films of that era focussed mainly on the officer class. Here the social spectrum is far wider, the view of society is far bleaker. A Welfare Fund for the families of the dead, predominantly the low-waged on Merseyside, immediately begins to be gathered in the local pub and doubtless from more affluent contributors also. Access to its resources, however, is scarcely made easy for those from such a background, having to apply through a highly formal legal tribunal. The son of a dead sailor has been offered an apprenticeship, through which he could come to support himself and then the rest of his family. To take this up, however, he needs to be able to equip himself with tools. The court is ready to consider this as an appropriate use of funds but cannot release them for six months, by which time the place will no longer be available. The wife of one of the dead men (**Fionnuala Dorrity**) is so aggrieved by the harsh way in which the local Catholic priest (**Tim Hibberd**) tries to claim monopoly of ministering to her grief that she withdraws her daughter Kathleen (**Julie Walker**) from the Catholic school. The alternative requires the purchase of a new uniform, well beyond her means but rejected as a valid claim by the judge (**Ben O'Sullivan**).

We have seen a good deal of Kathleen, playing in the street with her hoop and always glad to see the return home of her father (**Sean Kearney**), to teach her new tricks to play with it. Aged 9, however, his death traumatises her less outwardly than her mother. Kathleen is still able to play the game of submission to the priest, urging her mother "You only have to say Yes," when he has demanded her resumed attendance at Mass and she has only been able to sit in shaken silence until finally provoked into ordering him to leave her house. Once possessed of her new uniform, through the personal generosity of one of her teachers (**Fionnuala Dorrity**), however, Kathleen is able to defy the nuns (**Nicholas Collett, Sean Kearney**) who challenge her when they find her teaching herself to whistle in the street. Overall, a very detailed picture is built up of what parts of society pulled together and what did not.

The entire strength in the way this powerful story had its effect was in the quality of the acting, through which the various little shards of the event were made to shine and welded together into a striking picture. That **The Gospel of Matthew** is seen as a work of enormous significance is the reason that it has remained widely available and read for almost two thousand years but among the various motivations which led **George Dillon** to present it as a performance was his realisation of its dramatic potential. This had had its spark when he was reading of the Gospel whilst waiting at Euston Station in 1985, (presumably on his way up to Manchester where he had continued to act, most notably in **Berkoff**'s **Decadence** and **Greek**, since his graduation from the University Drama Department in 1983). He had been interrupted by a loud dramatic cry from a drunk, "Eeeyah! It's Saint Bob!", pointing out the rapid transit of the concourse by **Bob Geldof** as he tried to get to his train. This reminded him of the equally blunt terms in which **Geldof** had appealed for support for Ethiopia whilst organising **Live Aid** and although the example of righteous anger which he was reading at the time was Jesus' cleansing of the temple the connection which the drunk's outcry made in his mind was "the astonishment of those fishermen when they were interrupted in their work by **Jesus** two thousand years ago."

This may explain why the description "He called them," as he sees his first disciples by the sea of Galilee, is illustrated here with a loud cry of "Oy!" This does not mean, however, that we predominantly get a shouting Jesus, rather the reverse. From the moment he squats down, cross-legged like the Buddha, on the mountainside to teach shortly afterwards, the principal tone is to present what he had to say as quiet common sense. Up to that point, he had certainly held the attention, with a variety of emphases on a strong text but I had not really been able to perceive any overall direction.

It is not a full-text presentation: he had found that took him about three hours and he gets through in ninety minutes. He begins, however, with the complete seventeen verses of genealogy, which might be many people's first cut. This seems to be to set it firmly in an

historical context, both to link it to our war-torn age and to emphasise what he takes to be the 'original' character of the Gospel, a teaching of a purified Judaism, in which not one dot or comma of The Law would pass away. **George Dillon** has always emphasised features of his performances with well-planned lighting but the overall impression has simple been of an actor alone on a bare stage, without scenery. Here, very considerable use is made of large projections on the rear wall, behind the still bare performance area. A chronology is used during his declamation of the genealogy: "2010 BC: Abraham; 1010BC: David; 5BC: Birth of Jesus; 30AD: Crucifixion; 70AD: Destruction of Jerusalem; 100AD: Gospel of Matthew." This sets the book not only in the context of specifically Jewish history but of wars and rumours of wars, which are the subject of the only use of newsreel film among the various projections, a montage linking the Nuremburg rally to

American fighter-bombers streaking over Asian locales in the wake of the burning of the World Trade Centre. This, **Dillon** says, "was the final trigger for my long-planned production of **The Gospel of Matthew.**"

Nevertheless, this does not mean a performance primarily characterised by "righteous anger." It seems more inspired by the spirit of his performance of **Dostoevsky**'s **Dream of A Ridiculous Man (03:154)**, 'a commitment to spreading a message of hope.' This does not mean he avoids hard sayings, least of all in giving emphasis to what he takes to be the original character of the gospel. His prelude to sending out The Twelve to the lost sheep of the house of Israel is "Don't go to the Gentiles, - or the Samaritans. Don't bother with them." He sees the final emphasis on a "gospel for all nations" as the results of an incomplete re-editing, attempting to turn the work into one of "blatant Pauline propaganda" but gives both due emphasis in his performance, oddly enough, on this occasion at any rate, (I wondered if it was a slip), in answering the question "Who is the greatest in the Kingdom of Heaven?", he has Jesus set before them not a child but a Gentile.

Dillon has prepared his own text for his performance, working directly from the original Greek as well as consulting established English translations. It sounded to me as though he had mainly used the **New Revised Standard Version** but made adjustments, as he says, towards "simple, everyday English I was comfortable with speaking." This does not exclude blunt effect, however. Approached by those on his left in the Parable of The Sheep and The Goats, the first detail from "And he will answer them …" is a loud raspberry.

Here, too, the projection screen is used to great effect. During the first accounts of the hungry and unwelcomed stranger there has been a photograph which one might think had been selected almost at random from an agency, showing one of our contemporary roadside beggars. During the second recitation, however, the camera moves into close-up, so we can see, while he says "Just as you did not do it to one of the least of these, you did not do it to me," that the unshaved face of the beggar in fact bears remarkably Christ-like features.

In this performance, I did not gain very much from his treatment of the Lord's Prayer. Perhaps to show that this should be a private activity he went fully upstage left, turned his back on us and addressed himself to the heavens somewhere above the wings. I did not notice anything particular about the form of words used, which seemed familiar enough, but apparently it did strike several of those who wrote reviews and in his programme notes **Dillon** says that one of his discoveries, working with the original Greek, was that "Forgive us our wrongs as we forgive others" means not "in the same way as" but "at the same time as." I failed to notice how he brought this out (or the meaning he says he found in the prayer for Daily Bread) but doubtless he found a comparable sense in the "Just as ..." of the sheep and goats.

A major use of the screen was to project in burning letters, - first Hebrew, then in Greek, then in English -, the text of Old Testament prophecies which **Matthew** cites as being fulfilled in **Jesus.** These did not seem to be shown in exact synchronicity with the gospel episodes in which he includes them. Fire was a recurrent image in the film, not only appearing in the texts and in the wars footage but in a shimmering graphic of a flaming circle in the heavens, which was used both at the time of **Jesus**' baptism and at that of his Resurrection.

It is a most impressive performance but very likely still evolving. (**Dillon** plans to keep it in his repertoire for at least ten years). I was not convinced that absolutely every verbal emphasis was striking an indubitably apt target but certainly a great many were. For the central character one would have to see the performance on further occasions to assess the interpretation. Where I was definitely unsure that the right method had been found was in the full supporting cast. The disciples seemed to be consistently represented as thickos, - "Urr. … 'ow often should I forgive my bruvver?" - , and the Lawyers and Bishops (as the 'Scribes and Pharisees' are denominated) as devious scumbags. This is nearer a traditional interpretation but an attempt to look at matters afresh might have found less obvious Aunt Sallies and characters it might be more of a challenge today to ask to reconsider their ways. Any establishment faced with a wild young man, liable to bring a shouting mob into the temple and turn it over, even if only the outer courtyard, would feel that this was something to which it had to put a stop. 'Seeking to trap him in his words' would be a fairly civilised way to try and deflate his reputation. If that was ineffective, the fact that slapping an Anti-Social Behaviour Order on him in those days meant crucifixion does not mean that the basic approach was very different from what many would recommend today. Whether any of them would recognise themselves in the contorted bodies and speech with which **Dillon** endows them, I rather doubt. Making them such obvious baddies might be the view of the original text but I do not think it is dictated by the words. More subtle characters would be better drama and a more significant challenge to people today.

What those despised by the establishment had to undergo and the effect this had upon them is revealed in two brilliant plays of the late 1950's: **A Raisin In The Sun** and **A Taste of Honey.** Both are set in single, vermin-infested rooms, having to accommodate a whole household, - a mother and her daughter, or whoever her companion may be, in Salford, three generations in South Side Chicago. There ,the determining factor in keeping them there and in poverty is being Black, a depth to which Helen in **A Taste of Honey** cannot think of herself descending, the realisation that this is to be the colour of her grandchild being the factor which finally, it seems, drives her out of her daughter Jo's life.

Analysis of their situation is not the strong suit of the Salford household. "I blame the parents," is the formula to which Jo is most likely to revert, even when it is increasingly imminent that she is about to become one herself. "We're Communists!" she and her firm friend Geoffrey chorus at one point but this more out of defiance of Helen, even if based on a certain sense of communal sharing between them. **Lorraine Hansberry**, the author of **A Raisin In The Sun**, was indeed a Communist, with as well-informed a grasp of her reasons for being so as the most zealous Marxist theoretician could desire and at the heart of her play is a series of arguments, as her full range of characters set out their positions.

It could even be considered a structural fault that half-a dozen times a key figure says "Now listen …!" and then holds forth at length, in virtual monologue, on his or her perception of their situation. That this fails to appear as artifice or to lose dramatic impetus is primarily due to the emotional vigour with which each contrasting viewpoint is put forwards but also because **Lorraine Hansberry** is as skilled in using dialogue for small detail as for great expositions, for instance Mama (**Novella Nelson**) inquiring of her exhausted daughter-in-law Ruth **Noma Dumezweni**) what she has given her son Travis (**Matthew Hodge**) for breakfast. The views do not have to be consistent to have power: Walter Lee Travis (**Lennie James**) can rage that what holds back the Black Man is the lack of ambition in the Black Woman but later wonders why his sister Beneatha (**Nicola Charles**) should set her heart on being a surgeon rather than accept the role of being a nurse, in which many Black Women have established themselves, if she wants to look after people.

People also consciously change their views, but not by way of discovering a great Truth which the author wishes to propagate. Beneatha not only aspires to be a surgeon but despises as Assimilationist anyone who adopts the White-dominated mores of North America when they have the Great Heritage of Africa to which they could turn. After being shattered by seeing her brother completely lose without any benefit whatsoever to a corrupt colleague the thousands of dollars for which he has ceaselessly begged Mama when she has received her husband's life insurance, Beneatha completely loses her faith that things can ever improve, now accusing her great inspiration, the African student Joe Asagai (**Javone Prince**), of pursuing a worthless dream in seeking Independence for his country: it will only result in his people being exploited by from their own leaders, rather than by colonialists. J His name carefully pronounced "A-Saa-Gee" in this production, to make him more plausibly the Yoruba he professes to be, {whereas, after seeing the magnificent production of **Les Blanks (01:53)** at the **Royal Excahnge,** I had come to assume the various details about him to be another of **Hansberry**'s deliberate Pan-African constructs), Joe dismisses this: ending colonialism is the demand of today; the character of future rulers is the problem to be faced tomorrow. He accuses Benaetha's "Nothing Ever Changes" despair of being the pessimist's circular view of History: the optimist sees a line vanishing into the distance, - new problems indeed to be discovered as we advance along it but always in the confidence that they can be overcome (neatly reversing conventional generalisation about which cultures have cyclical and which linear views of Time).

This re-inspires Beneatha to renew her aspiration to become a surgeon but to take these skills as Joe's bride to Africa. Mama briskly dismisses this as "You're too young to marry anyone," but it means that Beneatha is now back in the positive mood to join in the great act of family collective defiance in determining to move to the house in the 'White' area on which Mama had spent a third of the insurance money before entrusting the rest to Walter Lee and from which their future neighbours had tried to buy them out. **Lorraine Hansberry** knew from personal experience what violent opposition the family was likely to face once it arrived but the ending, as they audaciously clear the room of every item and march out to the waiting truck, is one of great triumph.

RAISIN IN HE SUN (53); NOMA DUMEZWENI and LENNIE JAMES as Ruth and Walter Lee Younger

A core reason for this is that they are now doing this as a family. What had determined Mama first of all to buy the house and then to entrust Walter Lee was the sight of the family "falling apart": the exhausted Ruth willing to kill her unborn child, which she cannot believe she can provide for and finding no way in which she can talk to her husband Walter Lee about this or any other issue; he so disheartened at the loss of his dreams for opening a liquor store that he does not have the sense of raising a family to discourage the abortion; Beneatha neither able to accept her mother's religion nor her brother's view of women and Black destiny.

There is a very comparable sense of family relationships withering in **On The Shore of The Wide World, Simon Stephen**'s latest play at the **Royal Exchange.** Whereas in **Port (03:29)** he had focussed on the generation growing into adulthood, but without any real experience of family life along the way, here three generations receive almost equal attention and they do have some sense of family connection to lose. Charlie Holmes (**David Hargreaves**) is conscious that he may not have been too good a dad to Peter (**Nicholas Gleaves**) but he believes Peter has been a much better dad to Alex (**Thomas Morrison**) and Chris (**Steven Webb**), whose company he enjoys, and believes that Alex will be a yet better dad in his turn. Chris is not included in this reckoning because by Part Two (of the four play sections) he is dead. We are left ignorant of this for two scenes, as the house-owner, Susan Reynolds (**Susannah Harker**), who employs Peter to restore her timbers is also unaware for some time of why it has been Charlie showing up on so many occasions to do the work.

Chris has died in a road accident for which no-one can really be held to blame but for which Peter does blame himself as even before the Saturday bicycle ride on which Chris was killed he had been conscious that he ought to be spending more time with him but had always found work weariness and television had superseded. Chris had specifically invited him to join him on the ride to Manchester Airport, to watch the aeroplanes, but he had turned down the opportunity, despite being free to take it up.

CARLA HENRY as Sarah and THOMAS MORRISON as Alex

The invitation shows that he had been a perfectly approachable father to his son and this was true for both of them. Chris (15) had been able to confide in him about feeling overwhelmingly in love with his brother's girlfriend Sarah (**Carla Henry**) and Alex (18)had felt able to ask his parents to let her stay overnight at the family home with him. They had not raised any of the traditional objections, Alice (**Siobhan Finneran**) mainly being discomposed to find how old it makes her feel but finding Sarah likeable and being ready to have a word with Peter, to reinforce her confidence that "They'll be careful."

The death of Chris is obviously a major strain but not the only one we hear of. We first meet Charlie Holmes and his wife Ellen (**Eileen O'Brien**) just after the death of his old friend. This only partially increases his lethargy, which primarily results from drinking disproportionately, which had led to his passing over his business to Peter several years before. Ellen, however, comes to feel that she wants to get out more and on one occasion when he is not in the mood for this he tries to force the car keys from her at the moment that Chris walks in. This shatters the pedestal of affection upon which Chris and Alex have always held them and, after the death of Chris, with whom Alex had a very close bond, contributes to making him feel he must get away to London with Sarah. Also shattered by the death of Chris, his parents feel that this is the last moment at which they want to lose him too but, seeing he cannot be dissuaded, do their best to give them God Speed.

Despite this endeavour to preserve a decent friendly relationship, the sense of the family being torn apart is already at an intense pitch at this point, the interval. Traditional strains now assert themselves. Susan becomes very attracted by the well-built Peter working on her roof-beams, wearing only his singlet above the waist, and finds herself saying so. Alice has been approached by the driver of the car (**Roger Morlidge**) which killed Chris, wishing to express his apologies and becoming very drawn to her. Neither yields unduly but Peter certainly becomes suspicious of whom she may be seeing. Chris, troubled by his own feeling for his brother's girl-friend had had the nerve to ask if he had ever been unfaithful to their mother and Peter finds himself asking the same question of Charlie, when the latter is in hospital with suspected cancer. Neither of them it seems ever had, beyond a single kiss to a works secretary, to whom, out of deference to Ellen, Charlie had never spoken another word, while confessing that he has always longed for her ever since.

It may be that this frankness between generations, which would not have been thinkable in recent times, contributed to the play being able to end on a more optimistic note. Alex and Sarah have also had their rows in London, the strain being made yet keener for him as the good friend (**Matt Smith**)who had allowed them to sleep on his floor, being well into the London drug scene, had endeavoured to burn the house down and was now facing charges of arson. Sarah at first feels very aggrieved and Alex ineffectively apologetic to her but the suggestion of a properly cooked Sunday lunch at the home of Peter and Alice, - take-aways having been the staple of all three generations -, does seem to be successful in bringing everyone together. Chairs which would fit the dining room table which is now put on Stage have been around the performance area throughout, characters sitting on them when not directly involved in scenes. They are not brought forward before the end of the final scene, in what could have been a concluding image of reconstitution, but Charlie being asked by Peter to lay the cutlery in the way he would have remembered from his youth does suggest the possibility that it is as likely that things will get better as that the stresses will become intolerable. As in **A Raisin In The Sun**, the family together does not mean a future without problems but it does mean that they might be overcome.

When Walter Lee finds it in himself to tell Karl Lindler (**Jim Dunk**), the representative of their new neighbours, who has tried to persuade them that they "would be happier somewhere else," he does so on the basis of being a member of a family which has been in North America for six generations, not spelling out that someone with a name like Lindler has probably been there significantly less, but drawing on the emphasis in the title of the book then just published on the History of The Black Man in America by **Lerone Bennett Jr, Before The Mayflower**, that they have an ancestry going back before that claimed by the White 'Founding Fathers.' They have the pride, therefore, which can make them confident good neighbours, which they will try to be. The Communist **Lorraine Hansberry** would recognise the significance of economic power but she portrays the Ten Thousand Dollars which the Younger family gained and lost as a weaker reed than the family solidarity which made them determined to improve their lot, come what may.

Jo in **A Taste of Honey** has never known much in the way of family solidarity and by the end, left alone, would seem to have none whatsoever. I would not previously have thought of this play as remotely comparable in stature with the highly wrought achievement of **A Raisin In The Sun** but after seeing the production by **NorthFace Theatre Company** I would be more ready to consider the plays as being in the same league, if perhaps at different ends of it. This is principally on the basis of the performances of **Amanda Crossley** and **Sarah**

McDonald Hughes as Helen and Jo. This is not to belittle the contributions of **David Judge**, as a suitably young Jimmie, for a lad still doing his National Service, **Martin Gibbons** as a thoroughly callow Peter, - again being plausibly young, as he need be no more than thirty, and **Alan Neal** as a very dedicated Geof.

I was interested to read in the programme note by the director, **Jason Hudson,** that **Shelagh Delaney** originally wrote the piece as a two-hander for Helen and Jo, all the other parts being created under the influence of **Theatre Workshop.** If the original still exists, it would be very interesting to see how it plays, as certainly this production shows these two characters to be the heart of the work. The two-hander would presumably not be entirely direct conversation between them as a great deal of the effectiveness of these performances is the natural way in which both actresses address so many lines directly to us in the audience, "What does she think …?" being a typical way in which each lets us know how hopeless they think the other is.

Several current writers, such as **Catherine Kay** (eg **04:45**) and **Christine Marshall (02:140)**, have been keen to portray both the grim poverty and the humour of life in Salford but **A Taste of Honey** shows **Shelagh Delaney** to have been there well before them, **Sarah McDonald Hughes** not only being an entirely plausible school girl but naturally capturing the 'Not bothered' idiom which is still very recognisable today. In **A Raisin In The Sun**, the grindingly poor Ruth Younger can scarcely comprehend that if the seriously rich George Murchison (**Mark Theodore**) is interested in Beneatha , she should concern herself with any of his other qualities. Likewise, however much Helen in **A Taste of Honey**, may value a male companion, the size of Peter's wallet is definitely the deciding factor in her going off with him. She is a character of many dimensions. Whether having a cold or having a daughter is of more concern to her varies but **Amanda Crossley** by addressing so many of her concerns directly to us gives us a vivid sense of the resilience and also the humour with which she makes what she can of a difficult life. "Getting out" is the sovereign aspiration both of the Younger family and of generations of characters created by Salford writers, from **Harold Brighouse** to **Catherine Kay**. Jo is the one ready to forego making her move geographical. Whereas even Helen thinks "You can't 'ave a baby in 'ere," Jo is ready to believe that her tidying up with Geof can convert the decayed room into a 'Manchester maisonette.' However dirty Pippin Hill, a Pretty Miss can be found there. Her desperate belief in this seems hardly likely to convince the audience.

If being Black is a major factor in keeping the Youngers and Jo's child in straightened circumstances, this is not the problem which being Brown presents for the main families seen in **Bells** and **Chaos**, both of whom have done comparatively well for themselves in Britain. It does have a significant influence on their lives and both these plays and **In God We Trust** begin with the performance of the Muslim Daily Prayers. Especially following the violence generated in the Sikh community following the staging of **Behtzi**, (from which there is a veteran in the cast of **Chaos**), it was refreshing to see the young Muslims who wrote all these plays, being able to be critical of their own communities, to show disputes within Islam and to be watched appreciatively by audiences containing Muslims of several generations and varieties of social standing. In fairness to the Sikhs who revolted against **Behtzi**, their public spokespersons claimed that they would have been happy to see a play raising all these difficulties in relation to their own faith. The one thing they could not tolerate was to see disgraceful acts taking place in a Gurdwara, the central function of which is the housing of the Guru Granth Sahib in conditions of the utmost reverence. They professed that they would be entirely happy for the play to be staged in some other setting. Speaking also from a position of faith, its author, **Gurpreet Kaur Bhatti**, felt that "the setting was crucial and valid for the story."

Alarming though the outcome was of this conflict of principle, it was confined to a circumscribed issue and need not of itself lead to a restriction which many feared of what is permissible in the theatre. That is, of course, a concern for every reader of this book but is a narrower issue than the readiness to use violence which is very much a current feature of our society, on any issue or none. Some Christians are using it to oppose television drama they dislike but the restrictions this could lead to would be as nothing compared to the edict of Liverpool City Council that theatres they licence must not portray people smoking, on the grounds that they must avoid 'negative role models.' That principle, universally applied, would wipe out virtually all established Theatre. The Puritan Commonwealth tried that, on the highest authority, and other regimes in recent centuries have sought to be as restrictive. However concerned we may be about unleashed depravities, a great many of us prefer not to live in such a state, not least those who have experienced them. Aside from those who actually enjoy depravities, there are those of us who insist that we can learn from unfettered expression, needing to know what people will say if they can.

Whatever some may fear of imams or ayatollahs, these plays show young Muslim writers well able to present publicly debate within their own communities as well as their difficulties with the wider societies in which they live. "Difficulties" is, of course, an understatement for the circumstances faced by the two British characters we see in **In God We Trust**, who have been detained in Guantanamo Bay, but most of what we hear them talking about is their understanding as Muslims of their position. It is very possible that neither of them had anything to do with armed conflict. Babar Rizvi (**Marc Elliott**) in **Chaos** is indeed inspired by his faith in the post-"9:11" circumstances to feel that he must take up arms to defend fellow believers subject to American attack and he sees the willingness of the Labour Party to allow his father to stand as their candidate in the Wembley Local Council elections as entirely false: "Does he really think anyone wants him because of his policies? Do you think that the people voting bother to find out what they are? He's a brown face – that's all that matters to them – and his 'supporters' know it. He's as gullible as a baby. I don't like seeing my father being taken for a fool."

This is not a full picture of his father, Jameel Rizvi,'s character. One of the most skilful achievements of the author, **Azma Dar**, in her first full-length play, is showing his very real abilities as a politician, most ably represented by

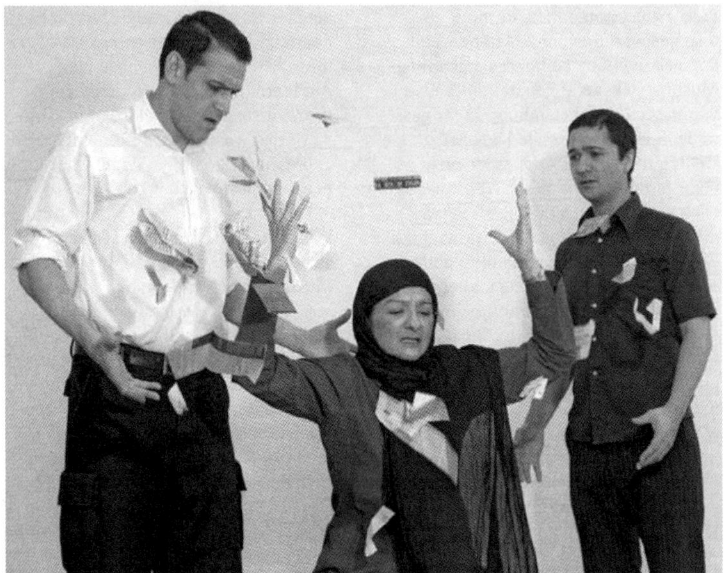

CHAOS (5); Mr Rizvi (NICHOLAS KHAN, left) and his son Salim (DAMIAN ASHER) are able to find diplomatic answers to many challenges but not when the many frustrations of Mrs Rizvi (SHELLEY KING) burst into incontrollable frenzy.

Nicholas Khan, in being able to find an instant courteous response in apparent agreement with any view with which anyone may challenge him. He is not able to head off Babar from flying out to Afghanistan and the potential political difficulties of his outwardly more loyal son Salim (**Damian Asher**) having a child by a white non-Muslim whom he has not yet married is something which has already happened, - although he only now discovers it -, but he does succeed in keeping it secret for the duration of the election campaign.

It being discovered would have been a problem in the first instance with his own community but losing standing with them would have lost his status with his sponsors in the Labour Party. A challenge from within his own community is by far the greatest concern to Ashraf in **Bells** (a splendidly contrasted performance by **Nicholas Khan** from the smooth Jameel Rizvi in **Chaos**). The Mujra he is running is essentially a brothel, which might seem very reasonable grounds for the mosque to object. One of the things which sickened the author, **Yasmin Whittaker Khan** (who is working on a play for our local **M6 Theatre Company**), as she came to find out the reality behind the glamorized Murjas she had seen in the dancing films she had watched throughout her youth, was how "even religious men visit Murja clubs – condemning these vulnerable women in public whilst pursuing them in private." Nevertheless, what makes them especially vulnerable in this country is not only the ruthless steps which have been taken to disgrace the girls in their own eyes and those of their families, to whom they feel, often validly, that they can, therefore, no longer return, but the British visa system, which means that if they escape from this "employment" in this country they will face deportation to one in which they will at best be outcasts and, at worst, subject to fatal attack. This is ruthlessly pointed out by Madam (**Sharona Sassoon**) to Charles (**Damian Asher**) the thoroughly anglicised and affluent young accountant of Hindu origins who becomes besotted with the most attractive young dancer Aiesha (**Shivan Ghai**) and first of all innocently asks Ashraf and Madam for her hand in marriage, then seeking to drag her away when he discovers her real status.

He is eventually successful in doing so because Madam, - who despite her ruthless commercial interest in Aiesha also has motherly feelings for her -, fights off the muscular Ashraf with a whip (which it seems no well-appointed brothel should be without), when he seeks to prevent Charles by force. She is mother to no child of her own because, although she married Ashraf willingly out of love and retains a reasonable business partnership with him, she discovered that his sexual interests were entirely with men. These are currently directed towards the transvestite dancer Pepsi (**Marc Elliott**) He, in his male attire of jeans and tee-shirt, is the one character in the household, seen at the play's opening, who is not making the dawn daily prayers, listening instead to pop music on his headset. This, however, is not because Islam is the religion he has rejected. His origins are Sikh but his mother's despair at his constantly wearing her saris is a nightmare of repudiation which recurs to him throughout the play. Muslim observance is an ingrained part of the life of Ashraf and Madam. Despite their ruthlessness as procurers, Madam believes "We have much better family values" and, although Ashraf perceives "The English are very civilised in their own way," he certainly does not see himself as ethically behind them.

Those found praying at the start of **In God We Trust** and **Chaos** (Hamza, **Gary Stoner**, and Mrs Rizvi [Safia], **Shelley King**) do so from a much less compromised position, although Mrs Rizvi's faith comes to seem as though it may be verging on dementia. She is convinced that her husband's constant socialising, in furtherance of his political objectives, is cover for frequent adultery. She does indeed discover a notebook full of exotic descriptions of female bodies, although it may be that these are an imaginative relief from his no longer finding himself able to get much tender loving from her, not delineations of actual paramours. She has already been confining herself to the home, not by external constraint but through her understanding of what a respectable woman should do. Her isolated view of the world is then further battered by her discovery of Salim's child, Barbar's departure and then his apparent death in an air-raid. If Madam can restrain Ashraf with a whip, she can finally go for Mr Rizvi with a kitchen knife and endeavour to constrain Salim and their close friend Aunty Moonah (**Jamila Massey**) to stone him to death for adultery, with gravel she has collected from his prized new drive. The news that Babar may still be alive deflates her outrage and it may be that Mr Rizvi has the skills to restore their relationship at least to what it was before. He has represented this as something of a penance, "married to the high priestess. Forever being subjected to her fatal fatwas. You'll roast on God's barbecue if you eat a bacon crisp."

His summary has been "Safia's never understood that true faith comes from the heart," and his response to Babar's determination to fly to Afghanistan is "I know how you feel son, believe me. But jihad doesn't have to be with the sword – any struggle in the way of God is jihad." This is probably genuinely held and informed belief, although not as theologically rigorous as that of Hamza in **In God We Trust**, who would seem to have a very clear understanding of the primacy of the Jihad of The Heart and to have made very fair progress in waging it. He complies without comment to the procedural demands of his captors and makes no complaint against their deliberately spilling most of his daily water ration on the floor, in reaction to his clearly unbroken spirit. He tries to establish decently amiable relationships both with an unseen prisoner, Tariq (**Roikhsaneh Ghawam Shahidi**), and with Sarfraz (**Asif Khan**). The latter, a Blackburn Asian, initially rejects all overtures, both being racially disgusted at being placed in the next cell to a Black and determined to establish his innocence with the guards through constant deferential petitions that they should ring his college lecturer and keeping his cell spick and span. Hamza both asks him "Why bother?" on the former but offers him his toothpaste, pointing out that it is a very good substitute for polish if he is determined to bring up a shine on his iron bedstead. Sarfraz rejects this but then decides to experiment with the contents of his own tube. He never has the chance to see the effect of this as the guards (**Stoner** and **Shahidi**) decide this is an opportune moment to beat him to pulp.

The motivation for this was not too clear to me. It looked like just the sort of beating up which those with the power to carry one out often inflict in almost any circumstances. The accompanying dialogue seemed to suggest that he was being required to confess to terrorist activities, being told "We already know what you've done." There was no sign of there being any provision to record anything he might have said, so maybe this was just idle dressing on a brutal cake.

In this scene, Safraz still protests, while he can speak at all, that he is just a well-meaning innocent who has done nothing. Once he has regained the power to speak and move, however, he not only begins to observe the daily prayers and to read the Koran, matters with which Hamza has been the only one previously to concern himself, but to engage with Hamza's sympathetic attentions. He does this by characterising their captors as evil unbelievers who must be violently opposed. Hamza will not concur with this. Aside from regarding the perpetration of 9:11 as so complete a distortion of true religion as to be almost beyond belief, he neither rejects the non-Muslim world in its totality, - devoting much of his time for reflection to wondering how **Manchester City** may be faring in the League -, nor sees the Jihad of the Sword as the primary or most appropriate way in which to oppose what must be opposed. At one stage he does seem to get into a bout of Scriptural Snap, swapping Qur'anic texts with Sarfraz in a manner almost comparable with the much less scholarly Rizvis, when Jameel tries to head off Babar from flying to

IN GOD WE TRUST (58); Hamza (GARY STONER) and Sarfraz (ASIF KHAN) imprisoned in Guantanamo Bay.

Afghanistan: "God says that killing one man is like killing the whole of humanity …" "God also says protect yourselves from those who attack you and your homes…"

Avaes Mohammad, the author of **In God We Trust**, confesses to anger at "how the very same sources, Qur'an and Hadith, that have been used by the Sufis and other Muslims to teach love and peace could also be used to teach hate and bloodshed." **Navid Kermani**, in his fascinating article in **The Times Literary Supplement** of 1 October 2004 points out that "Classical Muslim interpreters agree that no verse of the Qur'an can be reduced to one single, absolute meaning." This follows from its highly poetic nature, which from the first was taken as evidence of its divine authorship, as no mortal could have written in comparable style. **Kermani** says that although at first it is highly impressive to hear **Osama bin Laden**, with his exquisite grasp of Classical Arabic, quoting the Qur'an without the poetic lilting of the traditional scholar, what sounds initially as persuasively fresh and direct comes to appear as "the assertion of a single, eternally valid, literal interpretation." This would, theoretically, avoid the practice which distresses of **Avaes Mohammad** of the same texts being used to support contrary practices and any possibility of Scriptural Snap. The 'single, eternally valid, literal interpretations' perceived by **bin Laden** would not always square, however, with **Avaes**' realisation of 'the beautifully simple importance of good conduct."

Despite his cumulative bout of text swapping with Sarfraz, Hamza has always insisted on the meaning behind the tradition and the importance of the poetic. He recites **Bulleh Shah** in his cell, which the almost juvenile Tariq, - who remains amazingly happy-go-lucky despite their circumstances -, says "doesn't rhyme" but still finds interesting, while remaining pretty carefree about their religion. To Hamza it is of supreme importance but for what it signifies, not its formularies. A more characteristic challenge to Sarfraz, when he rejects the common aim within all communities, is to ask him why he rolls up the bottoms of his trousers when he resumes making the daily prayers. Sarfraz says because the Prophet wore his trousers above the ankle. Hamza persists in asking why he should role up his trousers. Sarfraz insists he does know the reason and eventually expresses this in a formulaic statement about 'because this was the practice of the Prophet and I will not allow my standards to fall below his standards.' Hamza insists that this is meaningless without the knowledge that the practice of important people in the days of the Prophet was to wear long flowing robes and that the only way these could be kept out of the dirt was by having little Black slaves from Africa running along behind, holding them up. The Prophet, therefore, was making a Fashion Statement against such subjection. To continue the practice without this knowledge is utterly meaningless..

Although the prolonged and heated bout of text-swapping with Sarfraz which follows is uncharacteristic of Hamza's methods, it does in time have its effect. Sarfraz brakes off highly disgruntled and he takes to his bed in some rage. However, he rises the next morning repentant. His saying "Sorry" to Hamza is accepted. They are united in outrage to the guard that Tariq should have been made away with overnight without explanation and the play ends with them combining for the first time in making the dawn prayers together.

The focus of **In God We Trust** has been on "Honesty and self-critique," **Avaes Mohammad** believing that this could 'help the Muslim and the world's cause," whereas "a play purely about American injustice would not." Nevertheless, this is very much the play's context. The American government would doubtless resist any comparison between Camp X-Ray and a Stalinist Gulag or the Lubianka but parallel columns of their features might show as many similarities as distinctions. **Talia Theatre**;s **The Life of Moliere** is very much set in that context as it is inspired by the novel by **Mikhail Bulgakov**, in which the picture he drew of the tight control by **Louise XVI** of allowable artistic expression was seen as unduly critical of the similar control exercised by **Joseph Stalin. Stalin** in fact stopped short of the actual arrest or execution of **Bulgakov** but placed him in official positions in which his work could be closely monitored and frequently suppressed. The play is set within the framework of two plain clothes policemen (**Julia Rounthwaite** and **Carys Williams**) arriving at the house of Bulgakov after he has written to Stalin, requesting permission to leave the country and he is now in trepidation that this will be deemed treasonable. Interspersed are scenes in which we first see the fascination of the young Moliere (**Benedict Power**) with the touring theatres and his disastrous attempts to establish himself as a tragedian and then his later work as a comic satirist, in which he has clearly found his *metier* but is also potentially dangerous enough to attract constant monitoring.

Talia describe their production as "exquisite physical performances and a story that will keep you riveted." In the performance I saw, which was the first ever of a newly constructed work, the story element did not seem to have developed to the point at which it could make its contribution to this. The Moliere elements did not seem to contribute to holding us but riveted we certainly were by the excellence of the physical performances. **Talia** are great devotees of the principles of Biomechanics, evolved a century ago by the Russian director **Vsevolod Meyerhold**, who ran into comparable difficulties to those of **Bulgakov** during the 1930's, and they are regularly directed themselves, as in this production, by **Gennadi Bogdanov**, who was himself taught by **Meyerhold**'s student **Nikolai Kustov.** In the pure form of this theory, the actors should be as totally controlled and constrained in their movements as if they were puppets (presumably marionettes) operated by the director. In this production some characters, notably the policemen, are masked but otherwise the actors, notably **Terence Mann** as Bulgakov and the old Moliere, are allowed a wider range of facial expression than such a theory would suggest, from the self-loving reverie in which we first find him to the desperation as to what fatal message the telephone may bring, before and after the arrival of the police. This only complements the effect of the highly expressive and stylised movement, whether he is huddled in his chair or taking exaggeratedly giant steps to hurl himself in slow motion towards the telephone or to be spread-eagled by his guards.

All this could have been most effective means for conveying the perilous times in which both of the main protagonists lived and the humour with which they chose to confront them. I did not find that the extracts from the life of Moliere were very effective in pointing the significance which it seemed intended to place upon them. Maybe this has been worked up since, as the theory of contrasting the two lives seemed full of dramatic potential. Nevertheless, although I did not feel that this total effect was realised, the performance remained spell-binding in the dexterity of its style alone.

Style can sometimes be found where one might least expect it. In the same theatre eight years ago, when the **Octagon** had a **Deaf Youth Theatre**, their production **Hand To Mouth (97:52)** was preceded by a most impressive and distinctive percussive musical overture. Comparably, I would not have expected that the great binding strength, giving full impact to **Maria Oshodi**'s play **Resistance,** would have been its powerful visual style, as **Extant**, the company she has set up, is for blind and partially sighted actors. The great creed of the play's hero, **Jacques Lusseyran**, is that blindness is not an infirmity which entails privation nor a deficiency which needs to be compensated for but simply a different state of perception. The regime under which he lived throughout the main events of this play, that of Nazi Germany, was one notoriously intolerant of human differences but despite all the efforts he made to take a major part in its overthrow, what he found was "undoubtedly the hardest battle of my life" was the seventeen succeeding years during which he struggled (successfully) to overcome the surviving laws of the Vichy regime which barred him from the teaching profession.

What we see in the play is the seventeen previous years, particularly from 1940-43, during which he was still at school, making every effort to gain the highest possible marks in his examinations but simultaneously setting up an underground network to distributed Free French newspapers, initially duplicated, eventually printed on proper presses, producing over half a million copies. The danger of this work was the more apparent to me as I saw the play at the same time as I was reading the chapters in **Interesting Times** in which **Eric Hobsbawm** tells of the very real dangers for him and his school fellows in Berlin as they dedicated themselves to distributing Communist Party literature in the elections of 1932, during which the results would have been fatal if they had encountered Nazi Party members on the stairways of blocks of flats where they made a point of pushing them through every letterbox. The great triumph for **Lusseyan** was having his team distribute so many copies in broad daylight among such crowds as those emerging from the metro, under the very eyes of Nazi soldiers. This might have given him especial pleasure in contemplating the limitations of those having the sight of the eyes, although he does not explicitly make the connection in the play.

The one thing which might have made a stronger impact in the play, for those of us having the sight of the eyes, might have been if the actor playing the younger Lusseyan in the play had been clearly a teenager, so that we could have been mindful of at what a young age he had made these great achievements. Nevertheless, **Mark Scales**, who is centre stage throughout most of the performance, gives the part and the narrative tremendous power. The action is framed by extracts from his interrogation by the Gestapo in 1943, in which he felt able to tell some of his tale but not what they really wanted to know, so he was sent off to a concentration camp where it was expected that deprivation would make him more forthcoming. It did not but fortunately Allied troops arrived before he and his fellows had quite expired, Viewpoints from later in his life were interposed from time to time by his much elder self (**John Wilson Goddard**) but the story up to 1943 was told piecemeal, between elements of the interrogation. **Maria Oshodi** feels that this "reflects the fractured way that blind people gather fragments about the visual environment, often piecing these together backward to add up to a sense of the whole" and it certainly made an effective dramatic method.

Strong though the story was, for the sighted a decisive impact was the visual style. There were two tall metal towers, which could be climbed and had platforms. Towards the end they were reconfigured, to reflect the compartments in which Lusseyan hid or was transported or the camp in which so many were confined. The main variations in visual effect, however, were through lighting. The basic resource was simple but a decisive factor in giving the story the power it deserved. This was not the total theatre of **The Firework Maker's Daughter** or **Out of The Blue**, not the way in which every detail of the **Young Vic**'s production of **A Raisin In The Sun** had been thought out and achieved to bring out the effect of a most detailed play, - every support from sound and items of clothing, every detail of characterisation, whether line by line or what was done between lines. Nevertheless, like all the plays considered here it was using the full range of dramatic resources to bring effective life to plays, most of them new, dealing dramatically with matters of the widest significance.

7 MARCH. **WORDS LEAVE US (35); FACE** (36); *8 MARCH.* **10%** (37); *10 MARCH.* **HOTEL BABELE (39);** Contact. *11 MARCH.* **A DIFFERENT LANGUAGE (46);** Royal Exchange. *12 MARCH.* **THE PILLOWMAN (47);** Lowry. **MOUNTAIN LANGUAGE; SILENCE; PARTY TIME (48);** City Campus. *14 MARCH.* **HOMESICK (40);** *15 MARCH.* **A CRIME AGAINST THE LAMBS (42);** *18 MARCH.* **DISEMBODIED (45);** Contact,

The majority of these productions formed part of the **Palaver Festival of Language and Performance**, jointly organised by **Contact, Envision Theatre**, - currently in residence at the **University of Manchester**'s **Department of Music and Drama** -, and by the newly enlarged and restructured University's Schools of **Arts Histories** and of **Languages, Literatures and Cultures**. The other plays considered here are included either because they were similar in nature to the works seen in the Festival, because they were linked by theme to some of the works presented or because they are linked to the links in a similar way.

In addition to the plays discussed here, the Festival also included the productions presented annually by the University's French, German and Portuguese Departments (**38, 41, 43**), a production devised by **Quarantine Theatre** with the University's Drama students (**44**) and mid-day seminars led by such noted practitioners as **David Glass** and **Jatinder Verma**, on the Language of Theatre and on multi-language performance, and on the use of Theatre in Literacy Teaching, both in Brazil and in Manchester. The latter item was to have been linked to a performance, **Manchester Babel**, celebrating the more than twenty languages in use in the homes of the students at the nearby **Manchester Academy**, but, for whatever reason, this contribution unfortunately had to be cancelled.

What exactly the overall linking factor was amongst all this material did not reveal itself to me too precisely. Clearly the great majority of works presented had their origins in speakers of other tongues and some were presented in them, but not always in those languages. That some were presented by people of mixed inheritance and some by casts involving persons normally resident in different countries may have been saying that, contrary to the great principle of several notable groups who tried to establish themselves as nations during the Twentieth Century, - No People Can Be A Nation Without Their Own Language -, many people and organisations now naturally co-operate across natural boundaries and within those boundaries many languages flourish. Some of the blurbs refer to the Language of Theatre as though this were a single entity and one which can be thought of as taking its place along side those defined by linguistics and verbal structures. Certainly the Festival contained several productions which made no use of spoken language whatsoever and the majority particularly emphasised physical expression. It was not, however, a festival celebrating Language Without Language. Apart from the well-known texts by **Ionesco** and **Wedekind**, the outstanding contribution to the Festival was the script-in-hand World Premier performance by **Envision Theatre** of **A Crime Against The Lambs**, by the Mexican playwright **Carlos Prieto.**

In the opening work, by the French **Cadmium Compagnie, Words Leave Us,** the words had totally left. Apart from the accompanying music, it was entirely silent, essentially a balletic piece. Two young female dancers stood at opposite corners of a bare rectangular performance area, one facing out, one down the margin. They slowly began to move independently around the border, completing many laps and without any recognition of each other. As they proceeded at different speeds, they did eventually come alongside and one overtook, still without any apparent acknowledgement. This seemed to me to become the dramatic focus: - whether they would establish any relationship. Some brief signs of potential co-operation did eventually emerge, - so we were not just observing the erratic movement of electrons around a nucleus -, but these did not evolve into any closer relationship. The two figures parted and proceeded as independently as before.

One could just have accepted this as a pleasant piece of abstract dance, lasting about twenty minutes, but apparently "using as a point of departure the atmosphere of **Becket**'s famous play **Happy Days**" it sought "to experiment, through movement, the immobility and poetic universality of the central character Winnie." I do not have any great insight into the interpretations of this work but I found it hard to make any connections. I would not know if **Les Mots Nous Lachent**, the French title of this piece, is the original of Winnie's asseveration in the English version "Words fail."

The sketch on the programme cover shows the two figures on the hands of a clock but, although Winnie's existence is obviously cyclical and has a great deal to do with the passing of time, this image was not very apparent to me in performance: one was more aware of it taking place in a square than a circle and the movement was counter-clockwise. Although Winnie seems by and large to be acceptant of her solitary existence, any sign of attention from Willie seems to be what can make a really Happy Day, 'just to feel he is there within earshot' is important, so she is "not to be just babbling away on trust as it were." Any signs of his interest seem to be greeted with an effusiveness I did not detect in the brief moments of encounter in **Words Leave Us** (where both figures were probably meant to be aspects of Winnie, rather than he and she).

Elements of **Happy Days** and a **Becket** manner seemed far more closely related to other productions which we saw during the week. **David Glass**, in his **Disembodied**, has a very Clov-like aspect as he makes his way, bent-kneed in pyjamas and stark make-up, down the steps of the auditorium, searching for seat Number 11. This proves to be in the middle of the stage but when, - despite advising the (invisible) neighbours he has climbed over to reach it that the play they can then try to watch is "Very Good," – he falls asleep, he descends onto a very **Becket**-like rubbish tip. Like Winnie he is awoken by a bell and endeavours to essay his toilet but in an infinitely less refined way. The toothbrush and paste he excavates from the tip are not too dissimilar to hers but he then deploys them as if electric-powered. The hair brush he is then content to use is the abandoned attachment from a vacuum cleaner.

Even more directly reminiscent of **Happy Days**, is the central trait of the principal character, Beni (**Alessandro Mauro**), in **Ted Moore**'s **10%**, which replaced **Words Leave Us** in **Contact**'s compact **Space 2**, the next day. The inspiring proposition apparently was that "approximately 10% of all communication is verbal and nearly 90% non-verbal." Beni, arriving in this country from some unspecified point of origin, seems determined to get his full ten percent as he spells out what is written on every poster or notice he passes, in a manner reminiscent of Winnie squinting without her glasses at her toothbrush, determined to decipher "fully guaranteed … genuine … pure … hog's setae" or Willie regularly reading out the classified Jobs announcements in **Reynold's News:** "Opening for Smart Youth," "Wanted bright boy."

Quite where he is from is a little hard to determine, as he is obviously not entirely unfamiliar with the workings of a society such as ours but does find making his way around a matter of some difficulty. He is surprised that he has to pay, - let alone so much -, for a

ALESSANDRO MAURO

bottle of water he picks up off a kiosk in the arrivals hall but knows how to identify and use a rubbish bin and a water closet. When spelling his way through the items on offer at a take-away food outlet, he can correctly pronounce Hawaiian but is uncertain either how to say "Burger," or what he will get if he orders what one had thought had become the world's most universally available, and so designated, food stuff. Although socially very compliant, he is not so naïve as to accept every notice he encounters as an order. Spelling out "Insert Coins Here" on the nearby pin-ball machine as he waits for his burger, he deliberates and then decides "I don't think I will."

Brushing such considerations aside, however, this was an enjoyably performed odyssey, as Beni wandered through a strange city in our strange land. One of **Contact**'s young volunteers told me after that she could just see all the various people and places he encountered and indeed these were vividly realised but through the revealing lens of bringing out all the ludicrous details of our slogan-strewn environment. Having proceeded through this in a manner behind which we could see the realism, however, the play finally drifted away in a surreal cloud. Having pursued as well as he could the address he thought he had of his friend Petra, Beni finally found himself passing through a minor urban park. Seeing a small shelter he responded by finding a way to climb up onto the roof and sat there contemplating the mysterious city, happy just to envisage the possibility of endless new discoveries, such practical matters as how to find his friend and making his money last having floated to a more distant corner of his mind. It was a very engaging performance by **Alessando Mauro**, carried out in a bare space, with the occasional use of a couple of plain chairs.

This was an exploration of the use of English by one supposedly not very familiar with its workings and thereby being revelatory to those who thought themselves more acquainted with the tongue. The challenge was the other way round in **Face,** the more extensive performance on the first night, following **Words Leave Us.** A detail which was not widely announced in advance was that its was more than eighty percent in Cantonese. Luckily a good number of native speakers of this language had heard of this and had a very jolly time. The rest of us could see a lively performance going on but, as it was predominantly a verbal narrative, missed a lot.

The play was primarily the personal life story of its author and performer, **Victoria Needa**, up to the point at which she won a scholarship to leave her native Hong Kong, to come and train at the **Bristol Old Vic Drama School.** She had a largely bare performance area but behind a small Chinese arch was a large projection screen on which in the early stages there appeared photographs of some of her nineteenth-century and early twentieth-century commercial ancestors, British and Chinese, and of herself in infancy but no attempt was made to use this to portray a wide picture of life in Hong Kong at the period. That was entirely done in the narrative, so far as I could judge from the brief episodes in English. These primarily came at the point at which she went to a suitable academy for young ladies, the drive to school being evoked by her taking a model VolksWagen and running it over the sides and top of the arch whilst naming the unsurfaced and pot-holed streets on her daily route. Of what happened in school I do not think that we heard very much but she seems to have got home by walking to her mother's flower shop, where she represented the telephone being answered either in English or Cantonese, according to the Language of the customer. She then climbed the stairs to her father's club, where, on a not always perfectly observed vow of absolute silence, she was occasionally admitted to watch some of the games in the strictly men-only pool room.

After that the narrative reverted entirely to Cantonese, so I missed most of the detail, not even assimilating how she came to be interested in theatre before we saw her scholarship audition. It was so verbal a piece that I did look up from time to time to see if there were projected sur-titles, but there were none. The play had originally been written in English and then translated into Cantonese for performance in Hong Kong and elsewhere in the Far East, both languages being equally those of the author. The style was predominantly one of informal conversation with the audience, not the elaborately physical performance of much in the festival. Obviously many theatrical performances can be effective regardless of the language being spoken but others cannot. An other-language performance of **Shakespeare** has never worked for me, where the text has kept its appropriate prominence. Here one could see that there was a lively performance going on but without a knowledge of Cantonese I was excluded from most of its impact.

The Italian company **Petit Soleil**, presenting **Hotel Babele** at first gave the impression that they would be avoiding such exclusion by forgoing speech altogether. Three couples appeared in masks reminiscent of **Commedia del Arte** but with no such jolliness in their appearance, as their distorted clothing was entirely tatty and grey. After miming their connubial slumbers they were aroused for their daily duties and some limited use began to be made of speech, which was in English. We learned that they were the staff of a hotel, expecting guests, for whom they must prepare. After they departed to commence this, the guests began to appear, in far more normal and brighter clothing and without masks, though often with exaggerated make-up. They were played by the same actors as those we had already seen, which meant that after the staff had re-assembled and sat hopelessly waiting for the guests, one of them had to advise her colleagues, in a manner like Hugo reading from Frederick's letter in **Ring Around The Moon** "for reasons which will by now be apparent, I cannot at this moment appear before you", "The guests cannot arrive unless we leave."

This part was taken by **Sussanah Tresilian**, the Artistic Director of **Envision Theatre**, who seem to have been the primary instigators of the Festival and to have used their personal connections from performing abroad to have invited the companies who came from overseas for the festival, to present work on which they had previously collaborated. She also presented the first of the guests to appear, an American communications consultant and veteran of five marriages. Whilst her initial impression was an extremely vivid physical characterisation, it did strikc mc that it was not a persona with scope for enough elaboration to retain comparable interest in her ensuing scenes. This may have been of necessity, as it emerged that the nature of the 'Hotel' was, as summarised in the blurb, "where recently-dead citizens of the world are received in order to come to terms with the fact that they have died, before they move on." Except in this particular regard therefore, it may be that it would be inappropriate for the character to have scope to develop and also, despite her high status job, her arrival was occasioned by a life of sufficient emptiness to be ended by a lonely, hotel-room surfeit of bourbon and barbiturates. We got to know this as when they were finally sat down to supper they eventually disappeared beneath the table, their bare feet reappearing above it with mortuary tags on their big toes and their voices uttering their cause of death, presumably their moment of "coming to terms."

In a way, therefore, with the grotesque make-up and exaggerated action, the effect was somewhat like a **Huis Clos** on acid. The next to enter was a tall man in evening dress (**Andrea Neami**), to whom the American tried to make herself attractive, as she did also to the next male to appear (**Sergio Pancaldi**) and probably would have done to any other.. The other women were a far more diffident female (**Silvia Melotti**) and one who stalked on in khaki (**Lucia Gadolini**), smoking a cigar, which appeared as a Latin American image to me but was apparently a European Big Game Hunter on another continent, who announced her cause of death in the mortuary scene as "a lion, - a very fierce lion."

This was an interesting development of the **Commedia / Buffo** traditions, not, I thought, rising to the heights of engaging activity which these can but certainly showing that they are alive and well and leading to innovative work.

The next night, at the **Royal Exchange**, it was not only the title of the piece, **A Different Language**, which made one feel that one was still at the Festival. It was a joint work created by the Glasgow-based **Suspect Culture** and **il Rossetti** from Venice, performed by one actor from each company, using both languages. The theme was of introductions effected through a dating agency, beginning with each insecure applicant completing a detailed personal profile, and them alternating in role between remaining that applicant and being their assured interviewer from The Agency. It was nicely ambiguous whether this venerated institution was just a front, to enable each applicant to make their own contacts, perhaps enabled by this status to achieve the confidence which otherwise they lacked. This was not an especially coherent way in which to understand the material but the piece was not a naturalistic one, being effective both through the vivid

A DIFFERENT LANGUAGE (46); SERGIO ROMANO and SELINA BOYACK

exchanges in the script, for instance bringing out the ludicrous in the opening questionnaire, and through the characterful performance of the actors, showing the discrepancy between their words and their feelings and moving nimbly between their two main persona. It was clever rather than deep but with the proliferation of dating agencies observable in every advertising medium it was satirising a world in which there is obviously a lot currently going on.

Meanwhile, back at the Festival, we were still in Italy, with **Homesick**, a three-part presentation by **Progretto 47** and **ServidiScena.**

There was nothing especially Italian about the first episode that we saw, **Waiting**, which was set in a basic hotel bedroom of the type which can now doubtless be found anywhere in the world and it was an English newspaper and book which were available to the room's occupant, **Jacopo Lanteri**, who also created the piece. This was described as **azione performative teatrale**, so one was not looking for the most convincing Method Acting of a man trying to get to sleep, and the four neat rectangles cut out of the first pages of the newspaper he tried to read showed some element of the surreal in the generally naturalistic setting. This meant that a photographer visibly circling the action to record it was not out of place.

Often with performance art one only realises its significance later, so when, after about ten minutes the actor finally drew himself under the coverlet and looked as if he had finally got to sleep, there was quite a bit of joking as we were led out of one door and waited to be re-admitted through another: "Boy, that was a real cliff-hanger!", "I can't wait to see the next episode!" What we saw on re-entering was a cleaner **(Davide Passera)** standing by the bed with a mop and bucket, a supply of waste bags and other equipment. This did for me have the instant impact of stressing "Someone's got to clean up," as the room occupant had indeed been most profligate in casting onto the floor first the scattered pages of his newspaper and later the scrumpled pages he had torn from his book, in lieu of reading it, and then rolled into balls to try his hand, most inexpertly, at throwing them into the inverted shade he had detached from the bedside light and also left lying on the floor. The cleaner first of all took himself to tidying up in a moderately business-like way but then allowed himself at a much more leisurely pace than I should imagine would be allowed to most low-paid contract cleaners to become diverted by the newspaper, which, after scanning he reconstituted and folded upon the bed-side table. He became far more interested in the torn pages of the book, which he smoothed out and read, kneeling reverentially at the bed side. Finally resuming his duties, he discovered the four rectangles cut from the newspaper pages under one of the pillows and placed them back with the folded paper.

This episode, **Sunday Morning**, was in fact labelled Number Three. Whether its opening would have had the same impact if seen after by far the longest episode (some forty minutes), Number Two, **Supper At Eight**, set elsewhere, I cannot tell. This, performed down in the bar, included the most significant acting. A long dining table had been set out with two elegantly dressed but utterly woebegone ladies (**Lucia Gadolini** and **Susannah Tresilian**) at either end. Despite the refinement of the setting it seemed that the only sustenance being offered to the former character by the waiter (**Jacopo Lanteri**) was baby food, to be eaten from a plastic bowl with plastic cutlery. He seemed to offer a far more varied range of dishes to the second diner but without raising in her any real interest, surveying each dish as it was offered and nodding her unenthusiastic assent, with a wonderfully sustained sense of *Bon Soir, Tristesse.* It appeared that it was even her Birthday, as he brought her a card, sang to her silently and invited her to dance. None of this for a second relieved her melancholy. On only two occasions did she take any initiative. After being brought a cigarette, she first of all tried to light it on the one surreal item which had been added to the setting: an electric iron sitting near her on the table cloth. This proving ineffective, she spoke the one word of audible dialogue in the whole evening, asking the waiter, in Italian, for a light.

This was graciously supplied. What was received with outrage was the point at which she finally declined to accept a further dish of food placed before her. The waiter had throughout insisted that both diners continue eating, that plates and glasses remained full. When the first diner had thrown all her plastic cutlery into her bowl of Allenbury's, he had wiped clean all but her spoon with his napkin and replaced them on the tablecloth, using the spoon to scrape around the bowl and to feed her as if she was still a baby in a high chair. When **Susannah Tresilian**'s character felt she could eat no more, however, he seized back from her all tokens of esteem, - the birthday card and cake, the cigarette supply -, and transferred them to the other diner, leaving her with only a plastic spoon and the bowl of slop.

Both the Italian productions in the festival appeared to be set in some sort of limbo beyond the grave, more temporary than the absolute hell of **Huis Clos** in **Hotel Babele** but condemnation to an eternity of ingestion seeming to be the setting of **Supper At Eight.** In both the sufferers seemed to have condemned themselves by being blinded to life's true possibilities by excess of wealth. This did not seem to be the problem for the protagonists in **Disembodied** by the acclaimed mime-artists **David Glass**, which the **ServidiScena** company turned out in force to see from the audience. Here both **Glass**' own character, already described, and his fellow performer **Jonathan Cooper** appeared to be citizens of comparatively humble means in a world whose spacial geography is simply not what most of us are used to. After **Glass**' descent to his rubbish tip, **Cooper**, of somewhat **Harry Langdon**-like aspect, descended stairs on the opposite side of the stage, for the humble purpose, it proved, of making use of a not very well appointed public lavatory. It lacked washing facilities, so when he realised this after meeting his primary need, he gained a good deal of laughter by endeavouring to dry his hands on his trousers. The premises did, however, have a mirror, made up of several small rectangular segments. After pausing to straighten his hat in this and apparently preparing to leave, he returned his attention to the mirror and pulled out first one segment and then another. In the dark on the opposite side of the stage, it could be seen that matching rectangles were disappearing from the wall above the sleeping **Glass. Cooper** them removed one of the tiles below the mirror and stretched through the resulting aperture while, simultaneously, a hand appeared through a comparable hole above the rubbish tip and reached over the prostrate body to retrieve an oboe from the debris. **Cooper** then retracted, his hand, now also holding an oboe, and thence forward his contributions were mainly musical, accompanying **Glass**' actions, first on the oboe and then, after demolishing more of his wall, but without comparable effect on the far side of the stage, revealed the greater part of a piano, thenceforward making this his instrument.

This combined music and mime (**Supper At Eight** had been accompanied by Italian Grand Opera) certainly held the attention and was often clever, - for instance, **Glass** cradling his right shin in his arms as if he was nursing a baby -, but did not really seem to me create an overall vision in which I could espy great significance or to match the tremendous acclaim which his visits have attracted in recent years, **Unheimlich Spine**

(02.229) being nominated for a **Manchester Evening News Award.** I had not seen any since **Red Thread (00.348)** five years ago, his ghostly and menacing development of the Hansel and Gretel theme, as part of his Lost Child sequence. There was a ghostly element in this production also, in the shadowy and distorted agonised faces which occasionally appeared on the folds of the curtains on either side of **David Glass** whenever he managed to make his way back to the chair on which he had sat at the beginning of the performance.

Despite the title, **Disembodied**, I doubt if these were meant to signify that we were once again seeing matters beyond the grave. The outstanding production of the festival, however, **A Crime Against The Lambs**, while truly concerned with much more present-life realities, at one point nicely tricked us into thinking matters were continuing in such a realm. "How would you like it if your daughter killed you?" we saw the leading capitalist Berneto asking his psychiatrist at the beginning of Act Three, just after we had seen him and many of the other most interesting characters die in a hail of bullets at the end of Act Two, just before the interval. Life beyond the grave is a perfectly mainstream tradition in Mexican art, as those who saw the return of **Horse and Bamboo**'s **A Strange And Unexpected Event (.., plus 94:278)** will have been reminded but this is not the resource upon which this most talented playwright, **Carlos Prieto**, was drawing here.

This was his last play out of a fair-sized canon so it is not surprising that it is a work of considerable skill but that he should use this particular style in the circumstances of its inspiration is evidence of notable mental resilience and imaginative stature. He began to write after being shattered by the death of his youngest daughter at the age of nineteen, after a very short career in the armed revolutionary group, the **Frente de Liberacion Nacional**, he had done much to inspire, who have since evolved into the **Zapatistas**. As evidenced in the quotation above, much of the play is very funny. Its title points to a harsh doctrine, the advice of **Georges Clemenceau** to **Benito Juarez**, after he had liberated Mexico from the rule of **Maximilian Hapsburg:** "To Spare the Wolf Is A Crime Against The Lambs." Nevertheless, although this is the conviction which leads to its final act, it does not, like **Ariel Dorfman**, in another insider's response to a regime of rapine and torture in Latin America, **Death And The Maiden,** foreground the wish for a violent reaction and make this its primary dramatic activity. He is like **Bernard Shaw**, not only in his humour but in his setting and his characterisation. However, much the concern may be for the peasants and workers, the action is primarily in an upper middle class household and its ruthless capitalists are as socially perceptive and as blunt and jovial in their arguments as Andrew Undershaft.

There are no great Shavian perorations, as exchanges are generally much more terse but these bring out distinctions within capitalism in a way that writer would have recognised. The businessman Berneto is aware, like Undershaft, that his commercial control makes him a true ruler of the country, beside which that of the Minister of Labour is of total insignificance. He does recognise, however, a higher power in the overwhelming financial might of the USA, although one of the few things which can make him lose his cool is the arrogance of the 'gringo'

CIA operative, Parker. The Minister is sublimely unaware of his inferiority. When Parker upbraids him for making the place unsafe to do business by 'the way you people are screwing your peasants,' he waffles about the 'very real reforms' his government is, gradually, making. When both he and Parker are kidnapped by a revolutionary group, the one concession he refuses to make is to be ransomed for a lesser sum than the American.

Courteously though both he and Parker are treated by their captors, a full staging of the play would probably have necessitated having a fair amount of ordnance about the stage during the Second Act. I suspect that it was a positive strength of the simplified, script-in-hand presentation, that this could be omitted. The second main artistic tradition upon which the play drew was the Classical Greek awareness that the really nasty is the more terrible for being kept off stage. In **Envision Theatre**'s celebration of new European work last year (**04: 358-360**), **Susannah Tresilian** had been noticeably successful in directing a script-in-hand performance of **Caresses** by **Sergi Belbel**, because in avoiding the sight of the seamier side of life being exposed in its fullest detail, she could allow concentration on what the nature of that seaminess actually is. Here, the playwright's daughter, **Ayari Prieto**, in a most helpful introduction to the play, stressed that one of the reasons why it was still most important to be seen was the resurgence of torture as an admitted practice in states which until recently would have been among the first to condemn it and to treat it as a procedure which should have disappeared from the planet. That it is a known practice of the government they oppose is a constant awareness of the revolutionaries throughout the play and that it is finally inflicted upon the one least likely to be able to sustain it, the young student Dario, is an important element of the play's conclusion. We hear the methods likely to be used and their effect intimated, we see him fearing it as the prospect becomes immediate and we learn the results but the actual deeds are kept off-stage. So is most of the gunfire at the ends of Acts Two and Three. That on stage is confined to two shots and the gun which is produced to fire them is one of the very few hand props deployed.

The style is one of the utmost simplicity. A couple of chairs and a table are all the furnishing. The ten characters can be portrayed in any combination by a cast of six through having them all in basic black performance costume and taking a single supplementary item of clothing, associated with each character from a rack. Every actor plays every role. The great strength of the performance is the excellence with which this is done but the method also enables the audience to concentrate upon the essence of the piece. This is most definitely not because the characters are the simplified figures of Agitprop: - The Wicked Capitalist, The Brave Revolutionary … . This is not the play for the deepest plumbing of the depths of the human soul but that most of its varied characters are conceived in considerable detail and interact with some complexity is what makes the drama itself one of considerable force.

We might assume that we are going to see on-stage violence in **The Pillowman**, not only because that is not unusual in a **Martin McDonagh** play but because, in the second of the two almost identical, stark, threatening police interrogation cells in which it

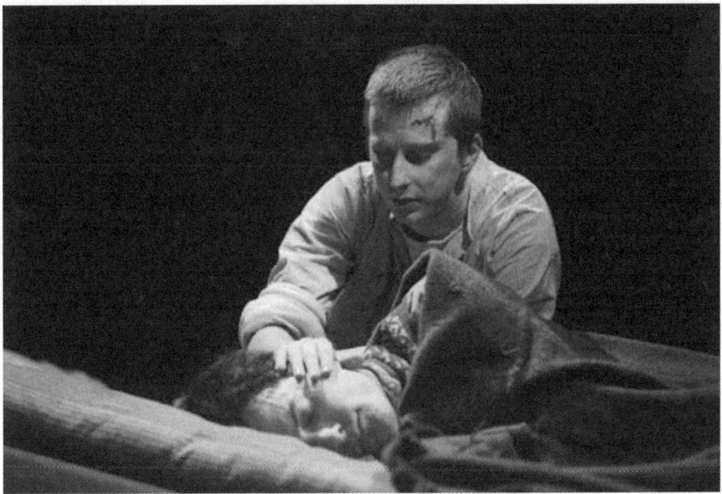

THE PILLOWMAN (47); Karturian (LEE INGLEBY) cares for his brother Michal (EDWARD HOGG)

takes place, there is a palliasse stained with blood which one might presume to be left over from a previous performance. Certainly there have been screams and groans from the neighbouring cell, which have led us to believe that torture has been taking place and the second policeman, (Ariel, **Ewan Stewart**) has made his first contribution to the enquiry the announcement that the only real question is "How long will it be before we start beating you up?" He has a broad Irish accent but that is the only link with the setting of all **McDonagh**'s previous work. The location here is deliberately more generalised but probably meant to suggest somewhere nearer to where names such as Tupolski and Katurian are rather more common, without limiting what it shows to that particular region. "What do you expect? You're living in a f***ing Police Dictatorship," the principal interrogator (Tupolswki, **Jim Norton**) pronounces, presuming upon an internationally recognisable set of principles. "By the way, I'm the Good Cop. He's the Bad Cop, in case you hadn't realised," he throws in for good measure.

Dispensing with these preliminaries, on the grounds that we know it all already, in fact leaves **McDonagh** free to raise issues of substance, despite the cartoon elements of his style. The biggest fish he has to fry is the Responsibility of The Artist, being ruthless on the argument against this having anything to do with social outcomes and strong on the primacy of this being exclusively to create and preserve his work. The social outcomes from the work of the writer Karturian (**Lee Ingleby**) have been the most dire imaginable. The police in any state would be expected to pursue them and many of the most vocal in this country would advocate investigation as ruthless and punishment as summary as that seen here. There have been a series of brutal child murders and these seem to be deliberate imitations of the violent deaths in the writings of Karturian. As only one of his short stories has ever been published, the enquiry very naturally starts with him and his retarded brother Michal (**Edward Hogg**) with whom he lives.

As there is an interweaving of stories and stage narrative and as neither investigators nor the investigated see it initially in their interest to be entirely frank, I thought at first that there was to be more play with the uncertainty of truth and fiction but there did not seem to be any eventual ambiguity as to What Actually Happened. Karturian had been entirely unaware for his first fifteen or so years that he had a younger brother. He had been indulged and encouraged by apparently devoted parents. When his abilities turned to writing, he first of all wrote naturally happy stories but then the house became permeated with loud screams and groans, which turned his imagination in more sinister directions. We saw the briefest of flashes of what was actually happening in the next-door bedroom but when Karturian himself eventually investigated, he found his happy, smiling parents sitting there, displaying the electric drill and other noisy instruments with which they convinced him that they had made the sinister sounds, in order to inspire him towards the writing of more horrific stories, with which indeed he did win an award in a prestigious competition for child writers. It was only later that Karturian found this to be a partial truth, by discovering the corpse-like body of the tortured Michal under the bedding in the neighbouring room. He had reacted by suffocating his parents in their sleep, throwing their bodies down the well and devoting his life to trying to restore affection to that of Michal and to arranging for him to get some belated schooling. Unfortunately, Michal had become so inspired by the stories Karturian read to him that he had successfully tried to re-enact several of them.

One he had not got round to carrying out himself was that of The Pillowman of the title. This creature, constructed entirely from several pillows, had made it his vocation to visit children destined to lead unhappy lives, reveal to them the horrors which lay ahead and lovingly get their agreement to his suggestion that it would be better if he smothered them on the spot. In the last seconds before he is executed for his involvement, Karturian tells us, (**McDonagh** showing he is not ready to leave after-death experiences to the Italians), that he was formulating a tale in which such an offer had been made to Michal but it had been refused, Michal saying he knew the torture of his infancy was going to be terrible and that going on to get his brother into trouble for his later killings was very bad but as he was so much going to enjoy listening to the stories which Karturian told him, he wanted to be allowed to live.

The shown brutality of a Police Dictatorship is thus only the context for a wider theme in **The Pillowman,** if an extremely apposite one. **A Crime Against The Lambs** shows that those who have direct experience of such a polity are quite well able to use humour in portraying its nature, so the persistent comedy running through **McDonagh**'s dark portrait does nothing to invalidate it. Failing to take such bold steps may be why I felt **Harold Pinter** in **Mountain People** and **Party Time** did not make a useful contribution in trying to portray such circumstances. The latter has an extremely apt and clever title, as the rich of a country such as Mexico meet socially and discuss the luxuries available through joining the club. The occasional sound of gunfire from the streets shows that an unhappier world exists immediately outside their enclave but any brief notice taken of it is set aside with the assurance that control is being restored. It is far more disruptive that one of the wives present (**Nicola Hayes**) should continually intrude into the conversation with the demand to know the whereabouts of one of their relatives, who has become one of the disappeared. The main action to shut her up is the demand that her husband (**Geoff Morton**) should take appropriate action to discipline her once they get home. For the wider maintenance of social order, a final sustained lifting of every right arm in salute demonstrates that the entire company looks to The Party.

Luis Bunuel, in works with such titles as The Discrete Charm of The Avenging Angel, long ago created distinct and far more persuasive portrayals of such circumstances and **Carlos Prieto** can paint a vivid picture of their nature from the inside. That new residencies in our cities are fortified with increasingly Medieval battlements, that "Safe Strolling Areas" are promised around them (acknowledging that everyone else will have to put up with being pretty unsafe) by councillors for whom the Institutionalised Revolutionary Party might seem to many not an unsuitable name and that their national counterparts are willing to countenance any restriction in the name of Security might seem to make this an apt topic. Once again I have failed to see that Our Greatest Living Playwright has made an effective play. The accompanying play, **Silence,** some sort of poetic evocation of the relationship of two very different men (**Richard Sails** and **Neville Millar**) with a young woman (**Rebecca Blackshaw**), may possible have had rather more to it but whatever it was did not come across to me. In this play particularly, there were some nice performances from the **Arden** students, so I do not think that the author could claim to have been ill served. I would be surprised if, given a morning to improvise, the actors could not have come up with a piece as telling as **Mountain Language** from scratch, on the theme of man's inhumanity, in the setting of a military road block and holding centre.

The inclusion of the word 'Language' in the title related to a form of 'ethnic cleansing' in attempts to suppress a local tongue. As a writer, **Pinter** doubtless cares deeply about this, as well as the other human issues addressed, but, although raising it might have been sufficient to make his play eligible for inclusion in the **Palaver Festival**, it did not seem to me to make very much of it, Karurian , once aware that he himself is to be destroyed, devotes all his efforts to endeavouring to ensure that at least his written works will be preserved in the Police archives. As, in retelling some of his stories, he had seemed willing to paraphrase and to speak loosely, also, on one occasion, to indicate that he realised that in "unpaintoverable" he might not have found the *mot juste*, it was not entirely clear in what he saw he saw his literary heritage to lie, as he seemed to accept, - while he stood by his artistic inspiration -, that his choice of subject matter might not have been entirely fortunate.

Carlos Prieto was bi-lingual and prepared his own English Language version of **A Crime Against The Lambs**, after originally writing it in

Spanish. The role of those two tongues is the only language issue to receive some direct attention in the play but, as one concerned about the fate of local communities, amongst whom the **Zapatistas** have since had their main successes, he probably had his views on the importance of minority languages

He knew intimately about the issues of class oppression, about which, by comparison, **Pinter**, merely seems to be trying his hand. **Prieto** undoubtedly had the ability to turn his concerns into a finely wrought drama. If it may have been hard to see the exact theoretical defining principle of the **Palaver Festival ,** there can be no doubt that presenting his work so well was sufficient in itself to make it a very notable occasion. Much else was of interest. This was outstanding.

16 MARCH.
INTERVALS (34);
Coliseum Studio

This was a really enjoyable evening's Theatre and of an impressively high standard.

Several of our local professional theatres now have their Outreach Programmes, providing to all sections of their communities the same access to their professional skills which for a rather longer period of time most of them have made available through their Youth Theatres. **Activ8** at the **Octagon** have produced some impressive performances from their older age groups (eg **02: 33, 34** and **03: 150**) but, although participants had a considerable input into the contents of the scripts, their final form was usually created by such established professional writers as **Neil Duffield** and **Mandy Precious**. In **My Place (04:139), Jennifer Farmer** was only credited as "Associate Writer" but this was such a collective work by the company that individual writing skills were a little hard to descry. No harm in that, since there are many ways to make a play, but, as much Theatre shows, individual authorship is a valuable strength and it was good to see it developed to such an impressive degree in the current programme at the **Coliseum.**

Oldham Wakes Week (03:457) a couple of years ago had been a jolly evening but had had to be made up to a full programme with a variety of popular songs and recitations. I did not manage to see the same group's **Counterproductive (04:536)** last year, so I cannot tell if the notable advances in stagecraft since two years ago, from several of the same writers and performers, has been part of a steady progression or a consolidation of gains already made some while back. Certainly, however, impressive levels have now been reached.

The unifying theme of the evening's work proved to be a particularly fertile one: - the **Coliseum** itself. This had plenty of links to the most popular subject material of these local writers, the heritage of their own community, but also scope to escape from one of their most frequent traps, - letting the subject matter take over, so that the actors can be left with little to do but sit and reminisce, often in monologue, the attractions of memory lane and distinctive local turns of phrase being left to bear the whole dramatic weight, which they have frequently done to pleasant effect but still leaving some sense of a restricted use of the theatrical pallet. It may be that **Neil Duffield**, as the Writing Tutor who assisted the authors in the development of their pieces, had helped guide them towards a wider use of stage action and also away from the characters emphasised by the title of the theatre history compiled by the **Coliseum**'s recent Marketing Director, **Mark Llewellin, They Started Here**, (which many found a useful starting point), concentrating instead on those off-stage, - the theatrical landlady, wardrobe mistress, parents of child performers, the **Chronicle** theatre correspondent, theatre cleaners and audience members -, territory which several of the writers found most congenial.

The evening was also assisted notably towards achieving its full dramatic potential by the **Coliseum** making it a major project for its Trainees, so that, for instance, instead of the rather makeshift provision for **Oldham Wakes Week,** there was appropriate costuming for a wide range of characters, gathered and adapted by **Kat Meredith**, and a very serviceable basic set, providing useful different levels and a central frame of plain electric light-bulbs, which could be switched on at appropriate moments to suggest either a dressing-room mirror or the stage for a variety show, designed by **Caroline Smith**, who also contributed appropriate sound effects when required, amidst her general operation of the Lighting and Sound during the performance.. These provisions were not especially elaborate but they had sufficient style and practical value to make a real contribution. The acting was not only undertaken by **Full Circle** members but BTEC and HND Performing Arts students at **Oldham College,** so the full range of performers for characters of various ages was available and some very able individual and collective work was achieved.

The various items were not presented in Historical order but still knit together very effectively to present a tapestry of the **Coliseum**'s one-hundred-and-twenty years. Not having read the programme in advance, - as I prefer to see plays ignorantly and let them make their own impression -, I was not aware of the theme until some way into the performance. Seeing the opening hilarious image of a character in a large ruff (**Antony Clowes**) sitting at a computer keyboard, I at first assumed that we were going to get **William Shakespeare**'s version of **The Crafty Art of Playmaking.** In fact, the character proved to be **Harold Norman**, the theatre's Ghost since his unfortunate demise as a result of an accident during a 1947 production of The Scottish Play. He was communicating by e-mail with his opposite number at the **Bradford Alhambra (Kevin Lennox)** about the possibility of holding their annual congress at that establishment. Amidst his struggle with appropriate Inboxes and Send keys he communicated that they had been hoping to foregather at the **Tameside Hippodrome** but it had seemed sensible to postpone this because of **Metrolink**'s failure to complete the expected loop. He also complained about current lack of recognition: when he had entered the theatre's Annual General Meeting, through the wall, the only response to the noticed chill had been a request to close the window. This was one of several brief pieces contributed by **Pam Maddock** and it got the evening off to a pleasantly droll start.

The author of the second piece, **Peter Connolly**, had unfortunately reached the end of his allotted span before his play, **Don't They Know There's A War On**, could be performed, so the evening was dedicated to his memory,

DON'T THEY KNOW THERE'S A WAR ON; MICHAEL SEAN O'DONNELL (left) has to get off to perform but MARK STEPHEN GALVIN (centre) now rarely has such grounds for leaving the lodgings; the Landlady, JEAN ETCHELLS, however, is only to happy to have him about the house.

he having been an active member of **Full Circle** since it began. One feature of the evening was the notably smooth transition between the various episodes, partly by keeping furnishings to a minimum. All the adjustment which was needed to the set was for the actors to remove the computer keyboards and for others to bring on a couple of sofa cushions but a small bridging scene had been created to tell us where we were and **Jane Cawdon** entered as a theatre cleaner, telling us that the outbreak of war probably would not affect her job, as people would still be wanting to come to the theatre, although there might be less sweet-papers and cigarette ends, because of rationing. Her rambling remarks introduced us to the likes of Stella, a boarding-house landlady, taking in all sorts of theatrical people, whether variety artists or actors.

The scene now established itself in her sitting-room, with two performers wedged onto her sofa. A third, **Osman Tosum**, entered from his bedroom, saying he would be back in late, as he had some business after the performance. This was generally understood to be black-market dealing but he assured Stella (**Jean Etchells**) that he was not subverting the war effort as the parachute silk he was selling, whilst still very acceptable as ladies' underwear, was torn and so no longer suitable for its original purpose.

The second performer (**Michael Sean O'Donnell**) was clasping his ventriloquist's dummy, which **Caroline**

Smith may well have co-opted from the recently concluded **Wake Up Little Suzie** in the main house. He withdrew to attempt some repairs to its jaw before his evening performance, for which he later left, leaving **Mark Stephen Galvin**, the one actor actually associated with the **Coliseum**, - Oldham having several theatres in those days -, but only rather tenuously so, as he has not been cast in the current production or the next one and has not had a substantial part for some time. He reacts with the typical horror of the dedicated actor at Stella's suggestion that he should realistically be thinking of some other activity. She has a personal interest, as she becomes increasingly open in saying that she would much prefer his presence in the house to become based on a far closer domestic relationship. She suggests that he could still do work related to the theatre if he took up a post with a theatrical agent of her acquaintance, which would also provide good opportunities for making contact with suitable future boarders. **Mark Steven Galvin** presents a very good image of a dreamy, impractical man, who finally assimilates that she is making an offer of marriage. He goes off into an extended ramble about maybe needing to face up to reality and consider new possibilities. I would have thought that Stella's prompt response, when his words eventually peter out, "Shall I take that as a Yes, then?", was a phrase that had become current in rather more recent decades than the 1940's but **Peter Connolly** will have had a fuller recollection of those times than I and **Jean Etchells**' timing certainly makes it a very funny line.

The main piece to focus on the historical contributions of a famous performer was **Jean Alexander**, another piece out of five composed by **Pam Maddock.** Essentially a monologue, it was made more fully dramatic by the title character (**Joyce Blake**) being made up, somewhat rapidly but with the tempo kept professionally calm, by her dresser (**Alex Brady**) The reason for the speed is that having been invited back in the 1960's for one of the **Coliseum**'s many re-launches, to perform in **Arsenic And Old Lace**, she and several of her fellow performers in **Coronation Street**, had managed to get a week off filming for the actual run, - still in the days on weekly rep -, but the production having been so successful that the run had been extended, meaning she had to rush up from **Granada** daily, particularly as she was first on, once having only fourteen minutes to complete preparations which to do properly she would normally reckon to take twice as long.

Alex Brady had very much the subsidiary role in this but was the main performance in another **Pam Maddock** piece seen later, **Parent In The Bar**, also in a rush as the more unsung hero, the mother of a child performer whom she must be available to take home as soon as the curtain comes down. The bar tender is brisk to supply her with a cup of coffee, without being asked, to help her settle, whilst she talks about the problems of taking home such a mucky child, - as they are meant to have been down the coal mine, - "Thank goodness the Costume people take care of the clothes!"-, but obviously all concerned having enjoyed the experience.

This was the piece I had most trouble dating: I would have thought it pretty contemporary and the bag in which the mother brought her child's going-home clothes seemed of very recent design, - **Kat Meredith** and **Caroline Smith** seeming to be pretty careful in this

THE AUDITION; Douglas Emery (MARK STEVEN GALVIN, right) wants to celebrate the end of the War by firing a young lady (SARAH CROMWELL, left) from a cannon; at twelve shillings a time, her mother (SARAH WHITMORE) is more than willing.

regard to give us a valid feel for the various periods shown -, but I did not recognise the play poster and title which was displayed as being in the recent repertory. We knew exactly when we were for the other piece with a mother whose daughter had the chance of an appearance: immediately post-War in **The Audition** by **Ken Williams.** Whereas the involvement in **Parent In The Bar** was a known social opportunity, for **The Audition** it was to enter a very unfamiliar world. What Douglas Emery (**Mark Stephen Galvin**) required was a girl ready to be fired from a cannon in a post-Victory celebration. As all his engineers were also working at AVRO, he could guarantee the reliability of the equipment and he would make sure the mesh in the safety net was not too wide for her to fall through. The mother (**Sarah Whitmore**) was initially willing enough, then reluctant to the point of being ready to withdraw as she became unconvinced of the safety and then, when Douglas Emery mentioned the fee was twelve shillings a performance, able instantly to calculate what this would mean for sixteen performances over two weeks and would clearly have been ready to allow anything short of having her daughter boiled in oil for such munificent sums.

This was all discussed over the head of the daughter herself (**Sarah Cromwell**) magnificently sullen and gawky in hand-me-down clothes, never uttering a word, completely different in effect from when she re-appeared a couple of the plays later in a rich crimson dress, as the keeper of the eponymous **Baldwin Monkey.** This was one of the variety acts to appear at the late-Victorian "Colosseum," a picture of which parachuting, from a poster, was the inspiration for the author, **Frank Gibbons.** The play was the least naturalistic of the productions, almost everyone involved in any of the plays, plus a few more, swirling on, as if disporting themselves in Alexandra Park. If they had done this in their stage costumes it would doubtless have been a more obviously promotional activity and, although the Fairy Godmother was ready enough to sweep forward to urge us to respond to "Oh No It Isn't!" they mainly seemed to be there to refresh themselves.

The main incident was that the adored pussy cat of the wife of the proprietor of the **Oldham Chronicle** escaped from her loving arms and ran up a tree. A couple of acrobats from the company (**Chris Hayhurst** and **Norman Nevitt**) volunteered to climb up in its pursuit but, after many contortions, failed. The monkey's keeper then volunteered that he should undertake the task. After he was produced, invisibly, from his cage, his ascent was avidly watched. Having captured the cat, it was feared that he had opened the parachute too late, but he landed safely, albeit with a well-timed thump, and the happiness of all was restored.

Obviously the main entertainment here was in the action, belying the instincts of many beginner playwrights (-although **Frank Gibbons** by now has written several such sketches -) that their job is to provide a constant stream of lines to speak. Effective though it may be to reduce the amount of dialogue that actors have to get through, one of the best contributions to this programme was **Intermission** by **Jean Etchells**, in which everyone was brimming over with things they wanted to say, with the result that they were all prevented from saying them. It is set in the bar during the interval of **Babes In The Wood**, the **Coliseum**,s most recent panto. The grandmother (**Jean Backhouse**) has been coming for more than sixty years and recognises everyone, pointing our "her, who used to be in **Coronation Street** but is now in **Emmerdale**" and "Kevin; he's the director. He's in charge here now: very young but ever so good," the laughs being all the louder because most people knew that **Kevin Shaw** was in the audience that night. She absolutely dominates the conversation. Her daughter, **Jane Cawdron**, is next most successful in saying something of how important she thinks it is that, now her son is out of the house, she has got herself a full-time job which she thinks accords with her abilities and which she is starting on Monday morning. This registers so little with her mother that she swims straight on into presuming her daughter will be taking her to the hairdressers next Wednesday.

For the first time in a generation her son-in-law is not part of the party to see the panto, having given up his ticket so that his son (**Daniel Couller**) can bring his girlfriend (**Mary Grainger**). She is very eager that he tells their news to his mum and gran but he bottles out of it, the couple of times in which there is a half-second in which he might have been able to intervene. To keep all the overlapping conversations and non-sequiturs flowing at high speed throughout, with all the looks between those who cannot get a word in, was very talented acting, four distinct characters being established and a replete script justifying its every word.

MEMOIRS OF A WARDROBE MISTRESS; MARIE HANSON

The two further **Pam Maddock** monologues, which ended each half of the performance, were completely different from each other in tone. In **Memoirs of A Wardrobe Mistress, Marie Hanson** just sat quietly stitching away at the eiderdown she had intended to give her daughter for her wedding but might just about now have ready for her grand-daughter's. In Wardrobe at the **Coliseum** they had to work to less flexible timetables and repeatedly so but the two great rewards were the constant teamwork among those whom she had joined shortly after leaving school, with the principal skill of good plain stitching, and the regular success, which this co-operation enabled them to achieve, of the costumes looking as good on the last night of a run as they did on the first.

The concluding piece, **By A Local Newspaper Reporter**, went back to the earliest days of the "Colosseum," after its opening in 1885. Equestrian events in its wooded amphitheatre were the first staple and before **Buffalo Bill Cody** brought his own Wild West Show ten years later, a local man from Greenfield thought he could give as good a representation of "Indian Attacks" and "Feats of Shooting" with local talent. This final piece consisted essentially of the **Chronicle**'s report but was far from a static reading of the text. As he ripped his copy from the upright typewriter at the play's opening, the journalist (**Chris Hayhurst**) began to clatter around the set, leaping and whooping, as he re-enacted the events his report described. He paused briefly as this ended, once more to address his typewriter and to hammer out an extremely brief letter of resignation, on the grounds that he had been invited to join the show, seizing a cowboy hat from the stand and vaulting into the wings with a loud "Yee-Ha!"

25 APRIL. **THOROUGHLY MODERN MILLIE (69);** Palace. *28 APRIL.* **PAPERWORLD (66);** Lowry. *29 APRIL.* **THE SAFARI PARTY (67);** Library. *3 MAY.* **SALAD DAYS (71);** Palace. *6 MAY.* **SMILIN' THROUGH (68);** Contact. *14 MAY.* **LOOT (71);** Robert Powell.

All these productions were enormously entertaining, some of them with no aspiration to be anything else, some of them with a darker world deliberately in the background or very prominently in the foreground.

Loot originally was pushing boundaries in putting the unpleasant on the stage but is now thoroughly mainstream and enjoyed as such by comfortable audiences. The two great strengths of this self produced performance by final-year **Salford University Performing Arts** students were admirable pace and absolute clarity in constantly bringing out the humour in the very witty lines in appropriate context. They had trimmed the play slightly, so as to be able to present it in one act, - a very tricky operation to carry out effectively on an intricately constructed farce -, and managed this most successfully. While achieving these key aspects of their performances very effectively, not all the acting was sophisticated in every respect but all made a good contribution to bringing things off. **Sarah Burke** was notably strong in giving amusing and distinctive character to every line and action by Fay. Having **Luisa Omeilan** play Truscott raised the interesting question of what would have been the effect of playing the character as a woman, which she didn't. I have seen some pretty steely policewomen and it might work very well.

Revealing how great a number of well-turned lines there are in **Loot**, as against the general humour of the situation, was paralleled for me in discovering how many laugh-out-loud lines there are in **Salad Days**. I had only seen this previously in what I think was probably a pretty run-down version of the original production, when it eventually reached **The Rex** in Wilmslow after its five-and-a-half years in London and its extensive ensuing tour. Despite whatever shortcomings there may have been in that performance, I have remembered the basis of a good many of the songs over the years and several lines. The basic plot does not take much remembering and I thought that this Fiftieth Anniversary revival would be a mildly pleasant evening's entertainment, which it was. A lot of it was very well done. I am not sure that every aspect of the production was well advised but the great bonus was how funny many of the lines were. Some were well within the tone I remembered: - Electron (**Kate Buxton**) explaining that she cannot steer the Flying Saucer on her own "because she's only a Saucerer's Apprentice." Others were much sharper. When Jane and Timothy come down from university they don't have any particular idea of what they are to do but the general expectation is that she will get married and he will get a respectable career through family connections. When asked what he would like this to be, he replies, "I don't know: something exciting, challenging, - and NOT permanent" (he can't bear the idea of going out of the house to the same job every day for the rest of his life}. Jane responds, "Yes. I feel the same about marriage."

The innocence with which this is said is of the essence of the piece and for the most part the production plays to this very effectively. Occasionally, however, it loses its touch, sometimes just resulting in a wobble, sometimes to more sustained ill-effect. The most obvious example of the latter is in the deliberate changes to the opening: This is justified in the programme as "Fifty years on, the prim language and behaviour might seem a little odd to younger members of the audience. The **MTP** production has the two leads open the show as very 21st –century youngsters who find themselves drawn into **Slade** and **Reynolds**' weird world." What this meant in practice was a slow start, of a large packing-case being seen very partially illuminated through a gauze, the light fading-out again and the case then re-appearing flanked by two motionless capped and overalled removal men, this fading out yet again, the next re-appearance showing the case partially opened to reveal what we later come to recognise as Minnie, the Magic Piano, - rather an enclosed existence for one once so dedicated to an outgoing, active life on the road. At this point the "very twenty-first-century youngsters (**Helen Power** and **Jamie Read**)" make their appearance, which just means that they have loose black tee-shirts and slacks, - clothing that does not place them very exactly in recent chronology - , and quietly playing **Slade** overture music on trumpets. Other characters wander on in academic gowns and playing other wind instruments. They place a mortar-board on the head of each of the trumpeters, who react with mild surprise, whilst continuing to play. There is then another blackout, while the removal men shift the packing case, to enable the rest of the cast to eventually get into the lively opening chorus of The Things That Are Done By A Don, with which they could normally have got the show off with a bang from curtain up.

As I now have a bit more idea of what a Don is than when I first saw the play, I was hoping to pick up a bit more wit but unfortunately not all of this was sung for perfect clarity. The cast were OK on diction in later songs, so it may just have been a wobbly first night. There were one or two occasions where there seemed to be fluffed lighting cues on scene-changes, so perhaps what appeared as the unproductive sequence of fades up and down were just something which had not been smoothed out in time, but the whole sequence seemed to me to contribute nothing. It had not provided any clear twenty-first century hook for anybody who might have needed one and when **Power** and **Read** ran on after the opening song, now suitably girt in college scarves and sweaters to be Jane and Timothy, they gave no hint of any more recent existence and indeed gave very well characterised and lively 1950's performances for the rest of the show.

Marriage as the necessary destiny for the young woman was also the prevailing social assumption of the American 1920's as represented in **Thoroughly Modern Millie**, although, unlike **Salad Days**, this is not an inside job from its own era but as it was represented in a 1960's film. This is not to the exclusion of employment which is, rather, represented as the route to marriage for the enterprising young woman making her way in life. The "Modern" of the title relates to the perception that reaching this goal has nothing to do with love. The gentler world of **Salad Days** also notes this separation but in a different way. In order to avoid the tedium of being introduced to an infinite range of rich young men whom her family think suitable for her, Jane decides it would be better to nip off to a registry office with someone she gets on with , - Timothy -, and see if they fall in love later. "Actually that then happened quite quickly," they concede subsequently. Wedding a rich man is the primary objective for the Modern in **Millie** but the route to this for those outside the affluent circle is to gain employment where one can marry the boss.

The glitter of the city world, of which Millie Dillmount arrives from rural America so eager to become a part, is brilliantly evoked from the opening moments by **David Gallo**'s shining image of towering sky-scrapers, backlit in crimson, at which **Donna Steele** is staring up as the curtain rises. She is then alone on the stage and turns towards us, to immediately draw us in to her great hymn of aspiration. This is a splendid individual performance, not only in its song and dance but in the wide range of acting evoking its plucky character, a range of grimaces to stress various turns in her fortune but more subtle acting to dress the essential simplicities of a musical character with a degree of depth. The next essential ingredient for creating the musical's world, however, is the dynamic and talented chorus, which now dances on, singing the title song and showing a city constantly on the move, here making its way to work but continuously filled with excitement around the clock. This highly talented dancing and choreography, by **Rob Ashford**, is a core strength of the show.

This splendid artifice at first seems to be being replaced by a rather more dubious one when Millie finds herself cheap accommodation in the Hotel Priscilla, which has the distinctive large wall-sign No Tap In The Lobby, which I took to be not a reference to the plumbing but an injunction to the principal group of residents, - young ladies hoping for a future on the stage – not to rehearse their arts on the tiled floor. Disappointingly, this instruction was never disobeyed but we got plenty of dance, of all kinds in every other setting, so we cannot complain. The artifice which caused concern was that the first entrant was the proprietor, Mrs Meers (**Lesley Roberts**), who was manifestly not Chinese but seeking to suggest that she was in very heavy-handed ways, such as an exaggerated confusion of Ls and Rs. This was not so inappropriate as it seemed, however, as the character was not meant to be Chinese but a former actress who prided herself on her ability to represent herself as one. This would also excuse the rather Fu Manchu representation of Chinese in New York society. – their role seeming to be confined to laundry and high crimes and misdemeanours -, as they were only constrained into such channels by the putative Mrs Meers. The genuinely Chinese characters spoke Cantonese and great fun was had with translating their conversations into blunt vernacular American in projected surtitles. The changes were neatly rung on this when, because the power Mrs Meers had over Ching Ho (**Yo Santhaveesuk**) and Bun Foo (**Unku**) lay in whether they would ever be able to bring their dear old mother from Hong Kong to America, they expressed their affection for her by singing Mammy, in English but now with the words appearing in Chinese ideograms in the surtitles.

This was not the only music from previous sources to be used. When Millie celebrates getting a job by inviting all her friends to a speakeasy, they sing and dance to The Nuttycracker Suite, which is quite properly credited in the programme as "based on the music of **Peter Ilych Tchaikovsky**." To gain this position, however, she has shown herself to be extremely adept at shorthand by triumphing in The Speed Test, sung by Trevor Graydon (**Andrew Kennedy**), the rich boss she is convinced that she will marry. This is an extremely funny patter song, complaining of deficiencies in a tin of polish supplied to his Sincere Trust Insurance Company, although unfortunately the cast were not quite up to making all the words audible in the even more rapid second verse. As all but the first and last lines of this were original, it may be fair enough for this to be credited as "lyrics by **Sammy Cahn**." Quite what **James Van Heusen** had to do to gain the credit for "Music," my musical apprehensions would not be adequate to determine. As was most amusingly indicated by the retained first and final lines, to the untrained ear it seemed to be borrowed directly from the Patter Song in **Ruddigore.**

While the Evil Plans of Mrs Meers were mere plot mechanics in a work aspiring only to be highly talented fun, **Billy Cowan** invoking the whole array of hallmarks of The Troubles in Belfast, - from barricades to hunger strikes, masked paramilitaries, loud-voiced religious leaders and intolerant language -, to tell the tale of a young man's dispute with his mother over his Gay nature, obviously does so with entirely serious intent, whilst creating a most hilarious comedy. Farmers becoming drunken and violent in rural Cheshire when their traditional skills become irrelevant is only in the background of **Tim Firth**'s **The Safari Party** but does provide a valid backbone to a constantly amusing comedy of manners, which is also a very firmly rooted comedy of our times.

The Safari Party is not a quaint rural custom I had come across but does seem a sound representative of the sort of practice that can grow up among prosperous people living in a rural area because they find it a congenial place to be, rather than because it has anything to do with their livelihood or the occupations of their neighbours. I had assumed some sort of guying of social artifice along the lines of **Willy Russell**'s suburban **The Tupperware Party**, which did not seem to me to be likely to be a mine of infinite riches and, whilst I found most of **Tim Firth**'s **Neville's Island** tremendously funny, I had not felt it quite sustained its full length. **The Safari Party** certainly does. The comic invention lasts the whole night through but is enabled to have its full impact because it is built on a thorough knowledge of the society it represents.

The convention of a Safari Party is apparently that a group of close neighbours shall each host a separate course of an evening meal, walking between each other's houses for each phase of the dinner party, an apt way to build relationships between people who do not have much natural connection between them but who wish to be selectively sociable, to have some sort of interaction with their, usually new, environment and often to display the domestic improvements in which they are investing. Much of the comedy but also the serious reflection comes from such people having no natural connection with their new environment but feeling that they ought to, - assuming that it has Traditions, which they wish to learn and if possible share, as a way of making them feel that they have roots. This may well be a preferable attitude to simply electronically isolating oneself beyond fences and an extensive drive way and only taking note of rural activities when they prove to be smelly or noisy in a way which inconveniences them but it does make them a potential prey to gullibility as those who realise that there is a market for Tradition package and fabricate it on issues which may be of no especial interest to those with longer residence and activities more genuinely linked to their environment.

Such ties are withering. Daniel (**Drew Mulligan**) and Adam (**David Partridge**) have inherited their father's farm but it is not what it was. There

THE SAFARI PARTY (67); Adam (DAVID PARTRIDGE, left) and Daniel (DREW MULLIGAN) despair when they learn that the paddock from which they had hoped to earn, by tending it for their prosperous new neighbours, is to be turned into a swimming pool

had been a prize-winning herd upon it but that had gone when compulsory purchase took most of the acres for a landfill waste site. Landscaping this for the Council is now an important income strand for them, if only £60 a month. The hope that they might get £80 from the new neighbours for similarly tending their paddock is their main incentive to take part in the Safari Party. They do have some genuine rural knowledge, - unlike their new neighbours, they do naturally know the difference between a beech and an ash - , but their interests are not primarily local or rural and their skills are often not traditional. Their father's death has been an inconvenience for Daniel because he would rather have been in Ibiza than organising the funeral, Adam's prime aspiration if they get the extra £80 is multi-channel TV and the wonderful smell of lilacs which so entrances their neighbours is what they spray on the landfill site to mask the odour people had complained of. The death had been a drunken accident, rather than the suicide Adam, who had been away, believes it to be and which was believable because farmers are one of the highest risk categories for suicide.

Adam had spun a tale when he realised that the kitchen table he had taken to place goods upon at a car-boot sale was the real focus of a buyer's interests, when selling off his father's property, achieving the £60 he set his mind on but then finding it had been re-sold for forty times as much to their new neighbours (Lol and Esther, **Claude Close** and **Sue Wallace**) by the proprietor of the Antique Furniture shop (Inga, **Jenifer Armitage**) spinning an even more elaborate tale, tailored to their susceptibilities. She is the great inventor of tradition for such incomers as Lol and Esther. These all have a great need for social links, commercial but also personal. Their daughter Bridget (**Lindsay Allen**) has less desperate need but forms more natural contact, - with Daniel and Adam, who are more her own age and have suffered similar pains in their upbringing. They do not need to Invent Tradition in order to do this and whether the play's final image of all colluding to do this was quite the most appropriate ending I was not too sure. Nevertheless, it was a most successful play, constantly finding well-taken opportunities for comic emphasis but delineating an accurate portrait of an evolving aspect of our contemporary society.

A parallel with **Smilin' Through** was that all parts provided splendid opportunities for actors. **Tim Firth** is now a playwright of considerable standing and experience, so it is less surprising that he should have this ability and be granted the cast to realise it. It is very encouraging to see **Billy Cowan**, far newer to the field, achieving the same success. It is also pleasant to see how different it is from his only other performed stage piece, **Heart Is A Lonely Hunter (04: 230)**, whilst remaining equally assured and successful.

This is not only a matter of length, two acts as against one, or elaboration of staging, - **Hunter** was two actors on an essentially bare stage., this has a fully developed set and costuming. There is an overlapping theme, being Gay today, but a completely different artistic approach. In **Hunter** it is very important that we see events from two points of view, so there is a question about what is 'reality.' Nevertheless, the primary mode is realistic. Either version of events that we see or some combination of them could be What Actually Happened. In **Smilin' Through** there would seem to be a significant admixture of Fantasy but it is a real question how much.

At first glance, the set seems to suggest a rather traditional naturalism: a working class sitting room with a realistic representation of brick terraced housing in the background. Closer inspection shows this dual setting to have been achieved with some ingenious sleight of hand: - the brick outside walls of the housing merging into the indoor walls of the sitting room, but that could just be a modern alternative to a once-traditional box.

The first action is that **Gillian Hanna** advances to the forestage in a dark gown, with a shining crimson design, singing the **Jeanette MacDonald** part to a **Nelson Eddy** LP on her record player. Then, the curtains in the upstairs window of one of the houses in the background are drawn and her performance is observed by a Royal Canadian Mounty, one of **Nelson Eddy**'s most famous persona.

Pretty obvious fantasy one assumes and it probably is, apparently marked off clearly as such by **Gillian Hanna**, the song over, then re-entering in her ordinary house-clothes as Peggy, in mid-nag of her long-suffering husband Willy (**Walter McMonagle**), now seated in the armchair, behind his newspaper. This clearly is the day-to-day reality. Eventually, however, after several more appearances, actually intruding into her sitting room to offer her wise words of wisdom, Peggy embraces the Mounty and finds him to be a woman (**Allison Harding**),

SMILIN' THROUGH (68); Is Donal (TERENCE CORRIGAN) the more unwelcome to Peggy (GILLIAN HANNA, back to camera) because he's a Catholic or because he's One of Them?

specifically the old school-friend who, for reasons of economy, used to wear boy's clothing and with whom, - she admits to her son Kyle (**Marty Rea**), when she can at last bring herself to attempt a discussion with him of his declaration that he is Gay -, she used to think herself in love. It is unlikely that this old friend has ever since been living in the house next door, dressing as **Nelson Eddy** and waiting for the chance to renew their relationship but is it more unlikely than that a Cardinal of the Church of Rome (also **Walter McMonagle**) should be able to walk in full fig (with possibly a slightly pink shade of scarlet in his robes) into a house in a Protestant area, when the populace are in active stone-throwing mode, even if accompanied by the most zealous of Presbyterian ministers, the towering Reverend MacMillan (**Sean Kearns**)?

Peggy has appealed to the latter to help her evict her son, who has barricaded himself in his room, rather than obey her orders to leave her house, and is appalled to see him arrive with the Cardinal on his arm. Just as the emerging Gay community has no time for the sectarian divide (Kyle's lover is the Catholic Donal [**Terence Corrigan**]), the one thing that unites the religious leaders is their detestation of Sodomy, so they are shown combining forces to hunt it down.

That what is fantasy and what simply ludicrous should be ambiguous is a good way to emphasise that what is undoubtedly real is ludicrous, in the way that the world outside the theatre, but also faithfully represented within it, reacts to both the supposedly religious divide and to Gays. The nattily clad masked representative of the Irish Queer Liberation Army, who expresses his solidarity with Kyle by climbing through the window of his barricaded bedroom, in his trim black combat trousers and beret and a fetching pink lining to his leather jacket, may spout slogans which are fantastically original but those sprayed on the walls of Peggy's sitting room by his opposite number, the burly figure who breaks in wearing a balaclava, are all too real and familiar: Gays Spread Aids; Kill All Queers.

The flier for the production bears the bold conspectus "When You Live With Hate You Forget How To Love" and the play may, towards its conclusion, point this moral to adorn its tale a shade too overtly, - Willy explaining to Kyle how Peggy, the harridan who now gives both of them such a hard time, could have become this out of the happy, fun-loving young woman he first knew -, but it does establish that there is a valid link between the years of violence which the Good Friday Agreement is desperately trying to end at the moment at which the play is set and the same arsenal of conflict being used against Gays, which it represents in its highly satirical way. That it is able to be so funny about such bitter matters probably makes the point far more effectively than trying to sum it up in more sober exchanges.

There is no serious point behind the **Paperworld** of the **Mim-I-Richi Clowns**, which was just exactly the right show with which **The Lowry** could celebrate its Fifth Birthday. It did not hang any banners on its outward walls and at the far end of the building it was business as usual, with the **Propeller** company continuing their run of **A Winter's Tale.** There was a modest gathering of Press and dignitaries on the upper floor to celebrate the completion of the sequence of mechanical birds which the imagination of **Whalley Range All Stars** had been creating around the building for several months. There was nothing to match the mass popular infestation of the building at the original opening, with period children's games flooding the forecourt, percussionists from the local orchestras making a circuit of the interior to try out the musical potential of the steel supports, all manner of groups on stage and **Walk The Plank** sailing down the canal outside, with climactic fireworks going off in all directions as the new footbridge to Trafford rose to let them pass.

This time, outside the auditorium, you might not know anything special was going on. Inside, however, the massive Lyric was a-buzz with all generations, as a flat five-pound ticket price meant anyone could get in to any part of the theatre and the show we saw could enthuse anyone of any age.

All we could see at first was an enormous curtain of white paper, hanging the full height of the stage. Vigorous loud "Clown" music built up the atmosphere. When the lights went down, all we could see at first were enormous shadow legs stamping about behind, projected onto the paper curtain. We then saw a human-sized clown in silhouette dodging about between the giant boots. At first one might have thought that he was escaping from them but then we saw that he was a doughty cleaner, equipped with brush and pan, bent on cleaning the stage. If the large feet were it his way, he walloped them with his broom and got them to shift. Sometimes one thought he might be squashed like a cockroach in retaliation but he got his way.

PAPERWORLD (66)

Litter control was clearly his obsession. He now appeared in front of the paper curtain, still sweeping away. A second, bespectacled clown entered and seeing the audience, which the cleaner had been far too busy to do, realised that the appropriate thing to do was to deliver an imposing speech. After preening himself, he produced a paper from his pocket but had scarcely begun to unfold it when it was snatched from him by the first clown, who knew only that the proper place for all paper was in the bin. After a vigorous altercation, in which he also relieved the second clown of further papers which he proved to have in his pocket, the latter was driven from the stage.

The first has scarcely master of his domain when a younger, green-nosed and more woe-begone clown entered, whose pressing need was clearly to find the lavatory. The cleaner was as helpful as circumstances permitted, miming to him the route which he should take, lengthy and devious though this was obviously to be. The young clown seemed ready to take his departure but then realised that his intended purpose required a supply from the cleaner's prized stack of paper. He doubled back rapidly to seize a handful. The outraged cleaner leapt to retrieve his sacred trust but was delayed by a hand bursting through the paper wall and striking him in the face. He shoved his own arm through the breach, to try and arrest his assailant, but this resulted in a hand appearing through the paper on the far side of the stage, without his having managed to grasp anything.

This first breach in the wall led to its progressive demolition, as escaping clowns jumped through it, artistic clowns tried to make the shape of the resulting gash more fetching, provocative clowns cast shreds about the place to annoy the cleaner and aggressive clowns pelted the would-be speech-maker. This was where the shows excitement really took off. Some missiles landed in the audience, which vigorously returned them. Now all the Youth of Salford were on Fire, not content with throwing back balls of paper from where they sat but climbing over the seats to get a better shot from the edge of the stage. House staff did make some attempt to limit the advance but it was really the three clowns who deftly established, without making it overt that this was their objective, that this was where the dividing line should be. All the ranks of Tuscany could scare forbear to cheer

The clowns did cross this line themselves at other points, with less mass forms of audience involvement. At one point, when the bespectacled clown got the chance to make slightly greater progress than previously with attempting to read his speech, he realised that his own glasses were not really up to reading his (completely blank) sheet of paper (of which he had an inexhaustible stock of replacements). He got a member of the audience near the front to lend him his spectacles and, when he decided these were not adequate either, descended into the auditorium and borrowed half-a-dozen more, leaving the original owners to sort out how they got back their own pairs, evoking some pleasantly amiable co-operation amongst them. The other clowns also made raids on people's coats and handbags, parading in them and displaying the contents on stage.

The most distinctive achievements, however, were in their particular world of paper. This not only created the bacchanalia of the paper-throwing. Increasingly large sheets of it were passed back through the audience, eventually including one the entire width of the stage and massively long. Some of this was torn off but one felt this was not the destructive daemons continuing to he unleashed but a wish for everyone to share in the collective action throughout the widening auditorium. A few quite large patches of the sheet even somehow managed to reach the circle, which is quite some height above the stalls.

It was certainly a dramatic experience and engaged everyone. The eighteen-month-old next to me was enthralled throughout, enjoyed the paper-throwing and would have joined the climb forward over the seats if his wise papa had not restrained him. The grey-haired raised their thumbs in triumph as they confirmed that they had at last got back the right spectacles. It was a notable triumph for a Ukrainian company to create and control such active involvement from an especially local Salford audience. The spirit they engendered was doubtless of as much "social value" as some of the openly serious themes which some of these highly entertaining works addressed. The range of skills in these half-dozen pieces was impressive, in many ways very different but all of them were tremendous fun.

25 MAY. **LAST TURN OF THE NIGHT (193);** Royal Oak. *27 MAY.* **ABU BEN / ADAM (212);** Coliseum. *1 JUNE.* **EMERGE (213);** Taurus. **214-217: Write 2 Festival** *13 JUNE.* **PICKERS (214);** *14 JUNE.* **LOCUST BEAN GUM (215); PICTURES OF CLAY (216);** *15 JUNE.* **PEACEFULLY, AT HOME (217);** Royal Exchange. **CURRY TALES (257);** Coliseum. *21 JUNE.* **LE STATE (258);** Zion. *24 JUNE.* **SLAVE TO LOVE (218); CATCHING LIGHTNING IN A BOTTLE (219);** Royal Exchange. *6 JULY.* **MUCH ADO ABOUT NOTHING (220);** Wythenshawe Park. *12 JULY.* **IRON (256);** *15 JULY.* **0161 – THE MUSICAL (222);**

Contact. *16 JULY* **CHILDREN OF THE MOORS (223);** Coliseum. *19 JULY.* **THIS IS HOW IT GOES (224);** Lowry. *20 JULY.* **HAMLET (221);** Wythenshawe Park. *21 JULY.* **HOOK, LINE AND SINKER (225);** Green Room. *23 JULY.* **THE BABY AND FLY PIE (226);** Royal Exchange. **227-247: 24:7 Theatre Festival (which also included 12, 22 and 24, - discussed elsewhere -, 193 and 236 [cf 23])**: *24 JULY.* **DRINKS WITH NATALIE (227);** Midland Hotel. **MILK (228);** Late Room; **THE FIRST RULE OF COMEDY (229);** Bedlam; **LAZY DAZE (230);** Life Café; **THE FALLING (231);** Midland Hotel. *25 JULY.* **BOTTLE (232);** Life Café. **THE FRENCH LECTURES (233);** Late Room. *26 JULY.* **VODKA KNICKERS (234); I'M FRANK MORGAN (235); SALAD OLVAY (237);** *27 JULY.* **NOW BREATHE OUT (238);** *28 JULY.* **HERE IN THE NIGHT (239); WHITE WEDDING (240);** *29 JULY.* **LOVESICK (241);** Midland Hotel. *30 JULY.* **THE HANGED MAN (242);** Bedlam; **NOWHERE MAN (243);** Midland Hotel; **THE GHOSTS OF CRIME LAKE (244);** Coliseum. *3 AUGUST.* **THE ROOT OF IT (245);** Contact. **246-255: Blue 3 Festival** *4 AUGUST.* **360° (FALLING) (246); VENT (247); HALF HEAVEN, HALF HEARTACHE (248); JOURNEY TO THE CENTRE OF YOUR MIND (249);** *5 AUGUST.* **PEPPERED MOTH (250); NIGHT PIECES (251); THE**

POETRY OF MATTY P (252); THE THREE LITTLE PIGS (253); *6 AUGUST.* HARRIOT AND I (254); A WAR IN THE MORNING (255); Royal Exchange. *19 AUGUST.* TRANSFORMATIONS (261); Contact.

What unites the greater part of the productions considered here is that they are based on new writing, most of it from the immediate environs of Greater Manchester and most of it of notably high quality in itself and in the standard of performance through which it was presented. Most of what is considered here is from festivals, - **24:7, Write 2** and **Blue 3** -, specifically dedicated to new work, as are the **North West Playwrights Showcase Workshops**, several works from which are also included. However, several other pieces covered are new work which just happened to be being presented at around the same time, showing, as does much of the rest of this book, that new writing, often by local authors, is a major part of the regular theatrical fare in these parts, not just the preserve of special projects.

Shakespeare is, of course, no longer a 'new writer,' although those in the distant metropolis, - where new work seems not to be so deeply ingrained as a natural part of ordinary theatrical life -, who struggle to gain support for such projects as the **Royal Court**, do try to point out that the theatres for which he wrote, such as **The Globe**, were, in their day, hot houses of 'new writing.' He gets in here mainly because the two productions I saw by **Heartbreak Productions** were notably good and it would be a pity to miss them out, although that is true of a great many productions I have seen this year for which there has not been time to include mention in this journal. As summery outdoor pieces they also fit in spirit with the festive celebrations of new writing and included genuine elements of this, both in **Peter Mimmack**'s skilful editing of the texts, to enable each play to be performed by a cast of seven, and in establishing the period for their production of **Much Ado About Nothing**, which, suitably for the sixtieth anniversary, was set at the cessation of hostilities in 1945, by not only putting us In The Mood with Big Band music and songs of the period but having these interspersed amid pre-show anecdotes and recollections of life in the **ARP**, very finely performed by those who were to represent The Watch and scripted as **Brief Encounters** by **Phil Reynolds.**

Heartbreak Productions seem to make regular use of a similar basic pattern of outdoor staging but varied ingeniously to the requirements of each play. There is a raised platform, which is not especially wide but quite deep, with some sort of high feature at the back, not only to add character to the design, - for instance, a backing to the throne room and an arras for the Queen's Bedchamber in **Hamlet** -, but to provide screening for quick costume changes, which the compact cast requires. The platform can include large gaps, too high to be readily visible to the audience, to enable such things as an abrupt appearance by The Ghost (**Thomas Hayler**), helped by this to be impressively spooky, even in broad summer daylight, assisted by a well-designed pallid death's mask and loud

HAMLET (221); Grave Digger (GARETH WYN-JONES).

hissing by the actor, to announce his arrival and his troubled spirit. These apertures had obvious uses at such times as the graveyard scene and had been used in last year's **Midsummer Night's Dream (04:469)** for mysterious appearances and disappearances in fairyland. The comparatively great height of the platform also enabled Under The Stage to be another area for costume changes as well as a useful depository for props and a source of appropriate sound effects.

A variation in **Much Ado** was to have a piano set into the front of the stage, which could be used whenever there was a call for song, which made several lively and well-judged contributions to the proceedings, and the top of which could sometimes be adapted as a bar, for the low tavern in which Don John (**Jonathan Wadey**) forgathered with Borachio (**Laurence Aldridge**) and Conrade (**Dan McGarry**). The character of the platform itself could be varied by such means as having a limited number of corner and side posts with the beginnings of beams projecting from them, effectively suggesting, when turned inward, the enclosed atmosphere of Elsinore, despite the wide open greensward upon which the stage was set, banners being hung upon them when court ceremony was required, turned more like signposts at the time of Hamlet's travels and pointed in all directions when he is seeking to present himself with a disordered mind.

To the side of the main platform adaptable features provided for some variation and additional amenities, for instance shrubbery or a washing line behind which first Benedick (**Laurence Aldridge**) and later Beatrice (**Gemma Kelly**) could hide themselves to hear tales of how much they were beloved. As the audience was kept low, those on rugs or directly on the ground at the front, those on low deck chairs at the back, and in **Hamlet** to the side, the actors could perform directly on the grass, in front of the raised stage, where, especially in **Much Ado**, much of the action took place and could be perfectly well seen.

Good staging is always a help but in **Shakespeare** the key question is "Can they speak the verse?" The answer in both these productions is very much "Yes." The device for lopping the enormous size of **Hamlet** down to something nearer two hours' traffic was to have **James Webster** come on at the beginning and to move directly from the conventional invitation to turn off watch alarms and mobile phones into announcing himself as being called Horatio, whose best friend had recently died in tragic circumstances. The company formed itself into the play's corpse-strewn conclusion, with the dying Hamlet (**Peter Collis**), lying in

Horatio's arms, beseeching him, "If thou didst ever hold me in thy heart, / Absent thee from felicity awhile / … To Tell My Story." This, Horatio now informs us, is what he has applied himself to do and recounts "So I set myself to find the best actors in the country. And I found them! - But I couldn't afford them! So I'm very grateful to **Heartbreak Productions** for helping me to stage this presentation." It would be false praise to suggest that the company scales incomparable heights of Shakespearean performance on all hands but they are very good indeed, everyone succeeding both in speaking the text very effectively as verse, in bringing out meaning clearly and naturally and in being full of character, not only in such matters asfinding natural wit and creating a generally plausible atmosphere but in distinctive characterisation, in most cases for several parts per actor.

Benedick and Beatrice are genuinely funny, where not all actors can escape being unwitty and obscure, and not only become movingly in love themselves but find a persuasive way to integrate this with their sadness and outrage at the treatment of Hero (**Abigail Gallagher**) by Claudio (**Dan McGarry**) and facing what will have to be done about it. Most actors playing Rosencranz (**Mark Plonsky**) and Guildenstern (**James Webster**), - who I thought got rather bogged down here in excessive bowing and scraping -, will try to find some rather obvious way to bring out the anatomical meaning of "Her privates we," but here they do not get the chance because it is Hamlet who makes a sudden grab for the relevant area, thereby injecting not only the liveliness of being brisk but a sense of them all having been rackety students together, the atmosphere Rosencrantz and Guildenstern were doubtless conscripted by Claudius (**Thomas Hayler**) to create but have not the ability to sustain under artifice.

This is a frequently enough signalled meaning but **Hamlet** probably contains more than most will ever discover in a lifetime. **Heartbreak** speak the lines well enough to give meanings perhaps previously unnoticed the chance to emerge. That Hamlet finds the idea of his mother making love to his uncle disgusting is a broadly apparent theme. With **Peter Collis** one could hear him doing this from the viewpoint that it should be impossible: "At your age / The heyday of the blood is tame …" She is too old for sex. This becomes apparent, not because **Peter Collis** belabours it but because he speaks the lines clearly and with understanding, so the meaning stands out.

The occasional brief interventions by Horatio, to speed the story along, make no attempt to seem to be in Shakespearean English, but although there is some fairly major pruning, - not a whiff of Fortinbras or Norway, for instance -, there is by no means a sense of a play cut to the bone, the Players, for example, get plenty of time, both for the Hecuba speech and for **The Murder of Gonzago**, although Hamlet's Advice to the Players is effectively trimmed to rehearsing **James Webster** in various ways to perform Lucianus' lines "Thoughts black, hands apt, drugs fit …" This is typical of the ingenious compressions which seem to characterise **Peter Mimmack**'s editing. The Watch's attempts, immediately before the intended wedding of Hero, to alert Don Pedro (**Antony Marwood**) to their arrest of Borachio and Conrade, to allow for the compact nature of the cast, has to be by letter and The Messenger

MUCH ADO ABOUT NOTHING (220); LAWRENCE ALDRIDGE overhears amazing news: "Benedick, The Married Man."

at the opening of the play proves to be Benedick in disguise but both of these are fully effective dramatically. Apart from a very few brief interpolated allusions to 1945, the text for **Much Ado …** is unremittingly **Shakespeare** and very effectively delivered to do this justice.

Outdoor summer theatre is by no means confined to the classics, although in the same week as the **Hamlet, Chapter House** were presenting their **Romeo and Juliet** at **Dunham Massey. Dracula** is too a classic in its way but the outstandingly successful version by **Feelgood Theatre** in **Heaton Park**, was also 'new writing' in this re-creation. This is described elsewhere by other hands: I could not see it, as it was presented simultaneously with **Blue 3** and the all-new **24:7 Festival.** All-comparatively-new, as I had in fact seen half-a-dozen of its works in previous appearances over the preceding months (and one of them, it proved, a great deal earlier than that). **Write 2, Blue 3** and the rolling roadshow by **North West Playwrights** were all new work, as, it is intended, will be the Drama element in the proposed **Manchester Festival 2007.** This is not, however, the only form that local Festivals can take. In the incredibly diverse **Chorlton Festival** in May, all the work I managed to see was new but **Lip Service**, one of several companies and individual artists of national reputation but resident in Chorlton, chose to make their contribution one of their Golden Oldies, **Withering Looks (194).** All the Arts were represented over a packed eight days by both talented amateurs and noted professionals, with dozens of performances at fifteen venues. I saw **Fantastic Fables (190)**, in which over 200 lively young school children tacked **Aesop,** and **Adopted (192)**, a poetic drama by **Copland Smith**, telling the tale of an adopted child's experiences and of his eventual contact with his birth mother. This is a general theme which has received a lot of treatment in recent years, as more contacts have been facilitated by the **Children's Act, 1989**, but this was the first I had seen focussing on the experiences of a specifically male child growing to adulthood and very distinctive and telling it was.

I also saw **Last Turn of The Night**, which later re-appeared at **24:7.** There were two major omissions from the programme leaflet for this. The first was Make-up Artist. The second character was revealed to be making a posthumous appearance; Bri Burnett (**Matt Alstrup**), a line-dancer, had shot himself through the head with his six-gun and when he raised his gory locks from the bar table at the side, over which he had been slumped throughout the preceding action, they not only made a great impression at first appearance but sustained themselves

throughout the rest of the play as a most plausible representation of the wounds of someone who had met his end in that way, without incapacitating the actor's ability to give a most lively and expressive performance.
The other great omission was the name of the performer who, in the normal course of events, would have been the Last Turn of The Night. The only female name on the programme was that of **Ruth Cleeves**, the director. Whether she also took on this most demanding and superbly executed role, I did not manage to discover. In some ways it reminded me of **Satin and Steel (142),** which I had seen the month before at the **Octagon, Amanda Whittington**'s tribute to the talented singers who, night after night, give a lot of pleasure to audiences in far flung Working Men's Clubs, without ever making it to their longed-for Big Time. The Singer in **Last Turn of The Night** was probably of rather lesser talent, although her performer certainly was not. The character's main aspiration clearly was to get through the evening and to collect her wage packet. She regarded her audience of boozed up males as having a rather narrow range of interest in her performance. She was, therefore, exceptionally vigorous in shaking those bits of her anatomy she saw as being of most interest to them. Most of her interpolated remarks and solicitations of individual members of the audience were in the same vein but sometimes her desperate efforts to keep her show on the move threw up more generally witty lines. As I was wearing a checked shirt, the one that came my way was "I can get 3 Down but I'm not too sure about 7 Across."

Usually, I do not think that singing badly makes for as much entertainment as the number of times the attempt is made to make it so suggests that others think it does. However, it was highly successful in two of the items covered here. In addition to the uncredited singer, desperately by dynamically making her way through the opening of **Last Turn ..., Sarah Ashton** also made a splendid performance out of her appearance as Gina Pitney in her self-penned **Half Heaven, Half Heartache.** She wobbled forward on stiletto heels in a tight black, ankle-length ball gown, with long black gloves, stretching above her elbows. Reaching the microphone, she addressed herself to singing as well as she could the songs of her near namesake, **Gene Pitney**, as a tribute to the father she believed him to be, on the basis of discovering in the caravan of her birth mother what she took to be his letter, ending with his name, explaining, when he was 24 Hours From Tulsa, why he had left her. She remarks how close they must have been by noticing how similar his handwriting was to that of her mother. The tone in which she made these ingenuous revelations and her personal commitment to developing this tribute to him was beautifully conceived and captured. In the songs she dutifully attempted to imitate the body-caresses of a certain style of concert singer. The style of the singer in **Last Turn ...** was completely different: her high heels were the more substantial ones of cowboy boots, the hem of her dress was several feet above her ankles and its skirt disappeared again rapidly after the waist, another foot or so of midriff being exposed before any degree of clothing was resumed. Her body movements and gestures were far more explicit in their intention than those of the supposed decorousness of Gina Pitney but shared with hers the character of being drawn from a well-established canon, made ridiculous by being performed, by the character, with infinitely more dedication than art. The art of the actual performers in representing this was very considerable and the results hilarious.

In **Half Heaven, Half Heartache**, the burlesque tribute act was the whole show, and very funny and skilful it was too. In **Last Turn ...**, it was not so terminal as it seemed. Having made her bow, collected her recalcitrant portable karaoke and departed, the empty glasses were collected, the audience (in Chorlton) having departed and the lights extinguished, the window behind the curtain creaked open and Steve Foxx (**David Raynor**, the author) climbed in. from the fire escape. [He had to devise a different method of ingress for his appearance in the **Late Room** basement club for **24:7**]. The club was the scene of his former triumphs as a **Rod Stewart** tribute act. But now the bookings aren't coming in, his relationship with his partner has moved from bad to disastrous. He has determined that this is where he should end it all. Not so determined in fact, as although he has a bottle of pills, he has not the bottle to swallow them. It later proves that they were only vitamin tablets, so even his preparations had been ineffective. They fly from his hand and scatter as he suddenly realises that he is not alone. The slumped cowboy to the side, who had been there since the audience first came in, so long that any who had ever noticed had probably by now forgotten him, suddenly comes, if not to life, as he is definitely beyond the grave, at least active and Steve recognises his old friend Bri, the line dancer.

The latter upbraids him for his pathetic attempts to take his own life, a field in which Bri has clearly been far more proficient. He claims to be on a last mission from St Peter, before being allowed to pass through the Pearly Gates. This is supposedly to encourage Steve to make a decent job of it and not to mess about with stupid pills, whose inadequacy he demonstrates by retrieving his bottle and reading out the label. The greater part of the play is droll cross-talk between the two of them, disputing the comparative inadequacy of their washed-up lives. Eventually Bri does persuade Steve to adopt his tried and tested method for a really good suicide and lends him his six-gun. When Steve finally does press the trigger, nothing happens. "D'ye think I'd give yer a loaded gun?", Bri asks (the whole dialogue has been conducted in light Geordie). His intention in coming to Steve would seem to have been the reverse of that he originally announced, more to persuade him that trying to kill yourself is bloody stupid. As a sign of restored friendship and perhaps to show that life does have something to offer, they conclude the play by combining in one of Bri's line dances.

The effect of the show was to be lightly ridiculous throughout and its success was in the performers being able to sustain this constantly, with just the right number of spikes at which the pointing of the lines pushed us into outright laughs. Although some of the other new work also voyaged into the fantastical, most of it pursued a much more realistic course. The play which seemed to me to approach **Last Turn ...** most closely in spirit was **Nowhere Man.** It is a nice question how much of the eccentricities apparent to us were as a result of seeing it from the very distinctive viewpoint of Kid (**Andrew Rankin**), although it is likely that, in any reality which may have lain beyond

NOWHERE MAN (243); Kid (ANDREW RANKIN, centre) tries to concentrate on making sense of his story while all around him his family continues on its senseless way: Aunt (HILLY BARBER, above him) tells Uncle (ROBERT LAWRENSON) that he has gone far enough in attacking The Joker (BRONWYN EBDON) for picketing a factory which he has already closed. She is the partner of Cousin (DONNA COLEMAN), who is, none the less, heavily pregnant. The Priest (CELLAN SCOTT, behind, far left) still hopes that this is a household in which he can find sanctuary, after taking too much interest in altar boys.

this, at least some characters were behaving in very unusual ways.

This proved to be the play with the oldest lineage. I had thought that the title seemed vaguely familiar and once it was in performance I recognised it as an altered version of the play of the same name **(94: 115**) which was presented, at **Contact,** script in hand, as part of the **North West Playwrights Summer Festival** during the **City of Drama.** I expressed the hope at the end of my account of that performance that we would get the chance to see a full production but I am not sure that this was really it. In one sense it was certainly less full, as the author, **Ian Karl Moore**, explained to me afterwards that one of the hardest tasks in preparing this version was to trim it down to one-hour, the maximum length allowed in the **24:7** festival.

Certainly substantial details had been stripped out. The great obsession of Kid, - all characters but one in this version having only their familial titles -, is "to complete my story." In the original, this was to "bring together all the pieces of my jigsaw," in which all the pieces were black, so he would never have seen a full picture but he did associate the possibility of its completion with the death of his mother during his infancy. In the new version of the play he is writing his story on the back of the envelopes in which his father had sent copious letters to his mother before he was born and which explained her death. Cutting out one level of symbolism might have seemed a possible strength but I am not sure that it works as well. One might have expected Kid to have treated these letters with the same reverent fear as Christopher in **Mark Haddon**'s **The Curious Incident of the Dog In The Night Time** treats the letters he finds from his mother, after her supposed death, rather than to start writing on them. Even though the letters in this version come into greater prominence an important detail of their contents did not seem to me to have been apparent. We do hear that Kid's Dad (**Bernie Merrick**) wanted him not to be born but the original had made clear the humane grounds upon which he had argued so insistently for this. It had been detected, accurately, that giving birth would trigger in the mother a wasting calcium-deficiency disease which would, inevitably, lead to her early death. This was not therefore a parallel to the wish which the sinister Xavier represented himself as having had in **Alison White**'s formidable **The Hanging Man**, that he should not have to share the love of his girlfriend with a child. Kid's Dad knew he would only be able to share his future life with either his wife or his child and would have preferred to keep the love he already knew. Kid's mother had chosen otherwise.

Naturally this knowledge, in any form, was not easy for Kid to live with but trying to get the pieces of his story in the right order, by shuffling the envelopes, was not only a less clear visual symbol than the black jigsaw puzzle. It also seemed to tie in less well with the way in which he tried to resolve his difficulty by locking up all the other characters in various rooms of his house. Not only, in this version, did he make a less clean sweep of this, the process of getting various of them into their boxes might have seemed to relate more clearly to fitting together the pieces of a puzzle than to shuffling the episodes of a story (of whose content we heard nothing.) In this version his Cousin (**Donna Coleman**), here constantly drifting around in a wedding dress, is still heavily pregnant, although by what process is less clear, as her constant companion, and explicitly her sleeping partner, The Joker, is here female (**Bronwyn Ebdon).** The cries of her baby being born in the room in which she has been imprisoned at the end of the original, not only emphasised how ruthless the actions of Kid were, beneath all the play's frequent humour, but linked in well with these all being driven by the circumstances of his own birth. In this version there were no such cries and it was not so apparent how the play made a dramatic whole.

These reservations should not hide the fact that this remained an absorbing dramatic work, aided by a bold and lively style of performance. Indeed, it should be noted that, after a somewhat mixed beginning last year, every production in **24:7** was a thoroughly interesting piece and well performed (except one which, despite the presence of some good actors, seemed to me a complete mess dramatically, but twenty out of twenty-one ain't bad and doubtless the one of which I thought so little had virtues apparent to other eyes then mine). Also, one may add here, every play in the **Royal Exchange Write 2** season had a notable sureness of touch in construction and, again, excellence of performance, even when these were script-in-hand, a circumstance in which our local actors frequently give performances of remarkably high quality.

The assurance of the writing in **Write 2** was doubtless aided by the writers being the same four who were performed last year (**04: 202-205**), who were not just selected directly from anyone who might have chosen to submit work but were new writers who had been given a year's residency at the **Royal Exchange**, which has now grown to two, in which they have had direct access to anyone in the company, to learn about theatrical possibilities, as well as being attached directly to those who would read and comment on their work.

The result was scripts of impressive rigour, every line being germane and speakable, the shape of the action, moving from scene to scene or issue to issue by natural progression and without delays, creating characters worthy of the steel of the notable casts gathered to portray the pieces. Some stuck to territory noticeably similar to that in which they had been effective last year, **Dominic Corey** in **Pickers**, for instance, concentrating on Men At Work, as he had done in **Plastered (04:204)**. **Sharif Samad**, whose **Pictures of Clear** was this year the work selected for full production, with set, lighting, sound and costume, was the one who wrote something completely different, in a very tricky field, with impressive success. After his very contemporary **Carol** last year (**04:203**), he elected to present episodes from the history of the Lancashire Witches.

The biggest difficulty for a writer today tackling such a topic is to find a convincing language. If he wants the action to appear to be in its own day, he or she is unlikely to be able to facsimilate seventeenth-century speech accurately and fluently. **Samad** chooses what is probably the best solution, to adopt a clear bold simplicity, eschewing all phrases which are recognisably those of some other period. It requires an intelligently applied Historical sense to realise that such terms as "there for me" cannot be included and **Samad**'s application of this principle is very sound.

"History is a dialogue between the past and the present," wrote **E H Carr** in **What Is History?**, a fine perception which he failed to show that he needed a full book to elaborate. In other words, in this context, a playwright selecting an Historical theme must have some reason for doing so but if he allows that reason overtly to dominate his work he may not only distort the History, which in terms of his dramatic purposes may be allowable, but destroy his drama by clearly having something too specific to teach, rather than an absorbing apprehension to provide. **Samad** judges this very well. First and foremost he provides a convincing picture of a time in which people had genuine fears and beliefs. The farmer and landowner (Richard Baldwin, **Jack Lord**) who sees his cattle sickening believes this could be caused by witchcraft. The Widows Demdike and Chattox (**Maggie McCarthy** and **Polly Hemmingway**) believe that they do have the power to cast spells. Both they and Baldwin and the magistrate (Roger Newell, **Des McAleer**) see a connection between this and the practices of Roman Catholicism. Although, as his daughter Clara (**Laura Elphinstone**) points out, this is the faith in which he as well as she grew up, Newell is quite clear of the necessity "We are all Protestants now." This is not only because no dividing line can advisably be drawn between a rosary and a clay figure with pins stuck in it.

Here we move from considerations which may seem to be specific to the times portrayed to concerns which show how they are linked to ours. It is only a few years since a plot was discovered, linked to Catholicism, in which an attempt had been made to blow up the King in Parliament. This means the whole fabric of the nation and the lives of all of them are at risk. When his daughter questions the justice of his methods of interrogation and conviction, to discover and execute those who practice witchcraft, which he barely distinguishes from Catholicism, he replies, "There are two sorts of Justice.: that which is intended to discover the truth and that which is to strike terror into the hearts of the wicked." In the shadow of the Gunpowder Plot, he has no doubt which it is his duty to pursue.

The link between the Plot and present concerns over Terrorism is one which several have made, The **Royal Shakespeare Company** is apparently presenting a whole series of early Seventeenth Century plays which can be seen in that context, **Ben Jonson**'s **Sejanus** apparently coming very much to life when perceived as having been written at that time. The **Chichester Festival** has commissioned **Edward Kemp** to write **5/11**, bringing out all sorts of parallels in fears of covert teaching by 'religious extremists' and of those who have gained military experience fighting against Protestants abroad and then returning to this country. **Samad** however was writing his play before either such productions, or the experience of the London bombing, let alone the Prime Minister pronouncing that "The Rules of the Game have changed," in respect of legal principles which some might have thought fundamental to the 'British Way of Life' he professes to be defending. Any political principles **Samad** may be indicating, however, are made vivid not only in a convincing snapshot of Lancashire way of life in particular circumstances but in realistic and involving individual human portraits: the magistrate who returns from a ruthless day's interrogation and torture to be able to sit reflectively smoking his pipe on his porch in the sunset, the farmer who may have wished stern justice to be called into play to defend himself and his livelihood from heresy and witchcraft but who quakes when he sees the methods used to send aged women off for execution, these same ill-educated and superstitious women, who have rowed furiously with each other as much as they have been neighbourly and equally outraged by the way they are treated by Society, deciding that the only way in which they can face the scaffold is to take each other's hands and walk towards it in silence.

This is not a long play but it is a very strong one, its excellent performances being fuelled by having such a rigorous script from which to work.

All the other plays had serious issues but were lightened by considerable doses of humour. The most numerous of these were in **Pickers**, in which three young warehouse workers (**William Ash, Craig Cheetham** and **Richard Cottier**) plot to disencumber themselves of an odious supervisor (**Roger Morlidge**), an intention which has conveniently also come to the mind of management (**Emma Atkins**), so their drastic methods come to be condoned. It was a somewhat more mechanical, and therefore, in certain respects, less plausible plot than in **Plastered** but **Dominic Corey** still showed a real talent for keeping action moving in sections where there is not much narrative and in keeping desultory workplace conversation highly amusing without displacing reasonable plausibility with clearly contrived 'comic dialogue.'

Locust Bean Gum was also in its way a 'workplace drama', being set on the doorstep and in a bedroom of a brothel. Like many of the new pieces appearing in these various festivals, it was given a very specific local setting, Whalley Range, and it was also set in the context of particular local activities: the August Bank Holiday Gay Village **Mardi Gras** – not that this impinged very much on the action – and a **United** home game. It gave a plausible portrait of its not very successful business although the specifically bad employment practices which eventually cause the mature student Billy (**James Scales**) to lose his job are off-stage, in the restaurant where he endeavours to earn enough money as a waiter, working all hours when he is not studying, to see him through his course and, in particular, to pay his rent for the room which the brothel is unable to fill with its struggling business.

Struggle is the main experience of most of the characters, trying to pursue their chosen path against primarily economic difficulties but all believing that they have found a fundamentally right way to pursue their lives and that they have decent instincts towards any others who deserve it. The one who is under the least economic pressure is Ruth (**Vicky Brazier**), who is from a prosperous family who could afford her to have a full year in Paris, just to learn the language. There she had met Billy, who had managed to get a grant to go there for a study week-end with his class, had liked him a lot, in circumstances in which he could for once relax, but, disappointed that she had been unable to persuade him to go to bed with her, has flown to Manchester the next week-end, which she can easily afford to do, on the impulse that she can achieve a *grande seduction.* As Billy, while getting a grant to go to Paris, had none the less missed the opportunity to actually earn anything that week-end, washing-up in the restaurant kitchen, and consequently is under especial pressure from Lilian (**Joan Kempson**) to pay his rent, he has no time now to spend with Ruth, as it is even more imperative than usual that he go straight off to work. This throws her a lot into the company of Juliette (**Rachel Brogan**), who is the only worker Lilian has available for the busy week-end and, therefore, too tired in the intervals to welcome Ruth's flow of chat and naïve questions. To Ruth the idea of working in a brothel seems rather a lark and when Lilian needs an extra face to sit at the counter during the visit by the writer of a guidebook to Adult Services, a good entry in which she hopes will bring her much-needed extra custom, so she does not wish her resources to seem too exiguous, Ruth is very willing, until the visitor selects her, rather than Juliette, for his free sample and she finds, at the last minute, that she cannot go through with it. This leaves Lilian in no mood to be lenient when Billy returns home without his rent money, having walked out from his desperately needed work on principle, when a colleague who could not get in had been sacked over the telephone by the enraged proprietor, unable to provide for his holiday week-end clientele.

There is, therefore, more significant action going on during the time-span covered by the play than in the same author's **Honesty Bar (04:205)** last year but, as it is all off stage, what we actually see again is the actors sitting around and talking. This is a risky route, though one well-used by the Greeks and one which **Jemma Kennedy** shows herself well able to sustain as, even in a briefly rehearsed, script-in-hand performance, the actors could make the dialogue riveting, the characters being well distinguished and all having strong commitments on issues they thought important: Lilian never again to be dependent on a man, after the battering which had knocked her into a hostel, where she had been able to recruit her first employees from amongst her fellow victims, Juliette to regard her employment simply as a job she can do well and to use her earnings to invest in body enhancements which will extend her period of prime employability, even though Lilian advises her that it is her present young, girlish looks which make her 'naturalness' attractive to customers, Billy committed to the political principles for a fairer society, which he thinks it worth struggling to give himself the chance to study but even more important to hold to in practice. Some of his occasional quotations from the books he reads seem a little over-conscious as do one or two of those by Daisy (**Anne Prendergast**) in **Lazy Days**, one of the contributions by **John Chambers** to **24:7**. She has no problems with finding sufficient time to read, nor any problem that doing so would interfere with her love life, indeed, her great hope had been that it would enable it. In some ways, the play is an **Educating Rita** *de nos jours,* celebrating the joys of learning to study, although with a clear context in the play, if not particularly in the mind of its main protagonist, of deficiencies in the social order which Billy would have recognised.

Daisy is a warehouse worker but without the social opportunities so eagerly seized upon by the lads in **Pickers**. She has a lazy eye and a limp, which her employers regard as making her unfit for human society, but isolating her in a store-room beside a terminal through which she can receive instructions to collect various items from the shelves and dispatch them down the hatch to the show room, enables them to show that they have the requisite number of employees with disabilities. Daisy had never really expected even this much employment or opportunity, having reconciled herself to living alone with her mother and making her way as obscurely as she could to the Job Centre to claim her allowance. Having got this post had not done anything to extend her circle of contacts until the Christmas rush had brought in a student, Steven, to work alongside her. He had not only been willing to make conversation but had pressed her to join him for the occasional drink after work. He not only regarded her withdrawn behaviour as wrong in itself but saw her ability to recognise every item by its code number in a 900-page catalogue ("973-page," she corrected him) as proof of a mental capacity which should be put to better use. He began to recommend books to her from his course and kept in touch in between his occasional seasonal returns to the warehouse. She found some of this reading hard work but had plenty of time during her lonely hours in the warehouse to battle away at it and soon became fascinated. She could afford a computer which came back as a return and found the information available on the internet literally a world of opportunity.

The last episode of the play, however, made it clear why she had first entered to announce "the most shattering day in all my life." There had been a works leaving-do, which no one had expected her to attend but for which she had signed up, partly on principle, as she had become determined no longer to be excluded, but especially because she knew Steven had also decided to come back for the occasion. The idea of sitting beside him all the evening, discussing all the wonderful ideas she had gained from her reading, overwhelmed her and she even had dreams that it might lead to a much closer relationship. He never showed up. She felt profoundly betrayed. She had seen him, as she thought on his way, nipping into the library which had become so important to her, just opposite the catalogue store. She now assumed that he had had no real wish to see her. Then a message came from his family, specifically to her, that he was not there because the beer-swilling drunks on the bench outside the library, who regarded its users as being engaged in an anti-social activity, had selected him as the one to stone as he came out on the way to the party. The message had been accompanied by a book he had bought from the discards tray, which he had though she would like. This was soon followed by another message, announcing he was dead.

It made a gripping one-person performance by **Anne Prendergast**, from the **Northern Quarter Theatre Company**, who also presented **John Chambers**' work last year. As these were all newly-trained actors, if some of them, like **Anne Prendergast**, of mature years, it had seemed an act of some generosity by a playwright of **Chambers**' experience to place his work in their hands. This confidence has been well-repaid. If last year the **Northern Quarter** performances had been a little uneven, this year they were all very strong indeed.

The other **John Chambers** piece in **24:7** this year was a three-hander, **Bottle.** It is set in the late evening in the **Accident and Emergency Department** of **Manchester Royal Infirmary,** rather lightly populated for an area which is usually very busy through most of the night but perhaps the characters are being kept in some isolation, although they seem pretty free to move around, as the patient about whom they are concerned is there as a result of a criminal attack, if none of them initially is thought to be a suspect. A policeman is said to be in the offing, but that is usually the case there, presumably because a high enough percentage of those making their way to **A&E** do so for reasons in which the law might take an interest, for a permanent presence to be worth maintaining. The officer off-stage mainly seems to be approached as a source of change for the drinks machine.

The patient receiving treatment is the mother of the teenage Tom (**Shaun Mears**), who apparently discovered her battered body in their home. He is accompanied by her new husband Clive (**Amir Rahimzadeh**), with whom he is on extremely bad terms. He is meant to be a psychiatrist who was called in to treat Tom after his mother and father split up, then became attracted to his mother during the course of treatment and convinced himself that marrying her would be justified, as it would give both her and Tom a stable home. How frequent such a crossing of professional boundaries may be I would not know but it also seemed to be a factor in **Steve Timms' Lovesick.** If this made one doubtful about Clive's role, it also made one surprised, when one learned of his psychiatric status, that he should have been so clumsy in his early remarks, expressing his own disquiet and being entirely useless at being in anyway comforting. burbling directly to Tom about how tragedies are meant to bring families together. He may be very shaken by the sudden discovery of his wife's beaten body and conscious that his long-standing difficulties with Tom will make his being helpful difficult but he did seem extraordinarily inept for one with supposed professional abilities in the field.

He did realise, however, the importance of promptly advising Paul (**Philip Lightfoot**) that the life of his former wife was hanging in the balance and he soon comes charging in furiously, grasping his car keys. He naturally has little regard for Clive, professes to regard his former wife as history and says he has only come in case he is needed by Tom. It later emerges that Tom does have happy memories of childhood with his dad but as he is at first entirely unwelcoming and aggressive, Paul initially prepares to take his leave, until he notices that the amount of blood on Tom's trousers seems inconsistent with his only having cradled his mother's body. The fuller story of what has happened emerges in persuasive detail and the discussions of what to do about it take very dramatic form. There are a good many layers in the writing revealing the character issues involved and how they led to various actions. Clive's role, I have said, I found a little unpersuasive but the forcefulness of the acting in bringing out the character and the drama of Paul and Tom I found formidable.

The frangibility of family structures was a feature of several plays. Jackie (**Tricia Ashworth**) in **Lovesick** regards herself as a "serial monogamist" but her relationships seem to have been so frequent and short-lived that "–gamy" would rarely seem to have been the appropriate term. It would seem suitably applied to the off-stage former husband of the narrator of **Drinks With Natalie**, who would currently seem to be on his fifth marriage but to have gone through due ceremony to initiate each of them and to have got through at least a year with each. The departure of his first wife seems to have had as disruptive an effect on their sons as Paul's on Tom, but leaving them bruised rather than belligerent. Concern not to let similar disruption affect her daughters is the reason Natalie gives for "that's why I made sure to keep the house," after her severance.

It is one of the later details in her tale which show us how very much she succeeded in looking after Number One in the course of her family dealings which, by her account, still left her so

DRINKS WITH NATALIE (227)

affectionately regarded by one and all. The progressive revelation of this dimension of her account was its core dramatic thread but just as valuable, I thought, was its accurate picture of how family norms have changed over recent decades. "It was 'Mr and Mrs Oglethorpe' until you were engaged; then it was 'Mum and Dad'," Natalie tells of the expectations of her former parents-in-law, which she claims to have handled much more discretely than her predecessor, Maureen. She also claims to have had much more insight into the involvement grandparents would have expected in the care of their children's off-spring, complying more with the degree to which they would wish to see them and, while no more wishing than Maureen to clean off with a soapy flannel, rather than antiseptic cream, when changing nappies, able to sell the policy more effectively by stressing her status and approved knowledge as a hospital nurse. That husbands and wives should split up as readily as is now customary she reminds us was completely contrary to the expectation of the in-laws, thus explaining how she took steps to camouflage the process by which this happened between their son and herself, hiding the final stages under the distraction that the same thing was happening to their second son also.

This seemed to me a far stronger and more insightful piece than the same author's **O'Leary's Daughters (04:224)**, which was her contribution to the festival last year. On this occasion **Elizabeth Baines** played the single-part herself and most effectively. Apparently this was her first on-stage role and she later seemed disproportionately concerned that, in a 45-minute show, she had had to take a single prompt at the opening performance. This certainly should not deter her from taking to the boards again.

"At least it wasn't my lines!" **Colin Carr** and **Alan French** chorused together at the end of the first sketch in **The French Lectures**, as the response of Dame Daphne (**Carr**) to an enquiry from the Stage Manager in Stoke, after their arrival in Bristol on a tour of **Hamlet**, asking if she had forgotten anything, when, demonstrating the spirit of "The Show Must Go On," she had nipped behind a turret whilst playing Ophelia to deliver her first child and returned in time for "How does your honour for this many a day?," subsequently leaving for Bristol without giving the intervention a second thought.

This was a fairly representative ingredient of the actors' representation of themselves as two Grand Old Stalwarts of The English Stage, touring with their reminiscences. They were followed by **Emma Kanis** presenting a character whose commitment to a bevy of Slimming and Fitness classes was somewhat compromised. After her, the boys rushed on again as a young Gay couple, giving advice on how to proceed if one wished to adopt a fashionably Gay Life Style. **Emma**'s next character was as an actress filming a commercial, dilating, while the rest of the crew were on tea-break, to the unseen cameraman, - as she took her to be -, on how she had had a much more distinguished stage career. **Colin Carr** then returned as the *doyenne* of Mrs McGilicuddie;s School of Comedy, keen to give her terminally dim pupil (**French**) a first opportunity to display her skills in public. The whole cast then appeared in their basic black performance outfits to demonstrate how (not) to stage a Comedy Improvisation show.

The most frequent comment that week up and down Peter Street, on which the whole **24:7 Festival** this year took place, was "Have you *seen* **The French Lectures**? Wasn't it *wonderful?* The performances …!" It was indeed very funny and all three are certainly very talented actors. I do rather hope that its main author (he claims; - graffiti in the programme suggest other members of the cast dispute this) will turn his talents back towards something more on the scale of his interesting as well as highly enjoyable **Picture of Doreen Gray (00:79)** but that was not what was on offer on this occasion and what was, was great fun.

The more complete drama of which I suspect that **Alan French** is capable might be somewhat nearer in character to **Andrew Norris**' splendid **Abu Ben / Adam.** (The authorship was shared with **Joanne Street** and **Jane Hollowood**, who also directed, but the performance is entirely **Norris** and one suspects that he was the principal creative force as well). Like **French**, he clearly has a commitment to tackling issues of Gay identity. Like Martin Craigly, the character **French** played in his original version of **Picture …**, Ben, the central character in **Norris**' play, aspires to keep his Gay inclinations secret but, unlikely Craigly, also seeks to suppress them altogether. For Craigly this was a matter of vaulting ambition in the media, seeing that no-one of known Gay orientation rose to the supreme heights of serious programming. To this end he was prepared to be both deceitful and ruthless, not least towards his partner.

Such behaviour would have been completely alien to Ben's gentle and loving nature. He might not have worked out how he would handle being openly Gay in the context of his work as a local newspaper journalist but the issue had never arisen because he had determined to remain entirely inactive and solitary, primarily out of respect for his adored mother, with whom he continued to live, and then, after her death, realising that, while it was just conceivable he might have found a way to tell her, he would never have been able to explain a homosexual commitment to his father. The latter is now extremely difficult to live with. Whilst the loss of his wife has been a severe blow to both of them, the father is totally shattered. The play begins with Ben receiving a telephone call from a neighbour to tell him that his father is (again) up on the roof tiles. He does manage to talk him down but he has the greatest difficulty persuading him to eat anything, either the more interesting dishes he can attempt or the more basic fare his mother knew his father preferred. He seems to have no real will to live without her. Any attempt made by Ben to tidy up the room is regarded as sacrilegious to her memory if it involves moving any item of furniture the slightest degree out of the way she always had it.

Norris is extremely skilful in giving us the effect of seeing both parties simultaneously in these heightening arguments and in showing how they developed into blazing rows. Ben decides it might be better if he moved out, especially when faced with his father's furious accusations that he does not need looking after, gets a room near enough to 'keep an eye,' and begins moving out his things. Being on his own increases his personal tensions and these are heightened when he visits the **Local History** section in **Manchester Central Library** for background information for one of his articles and is introduced to the new Assistant, the exceptionally attractive and approachable Adam. Although it is clearly love at first sight, his years of conditioning himself to restraint means that he keeps their exchanges to the barest formalities, endeavours to read the required records, - although his concentration is shattered -, and departs.

This experience leaves him even more ill at ease and his equilibrium is further disturbed when he visits home to pick up some more of his things and finds his father preparing a surprisingly elaborate meal. The local Community organisation has succeeded where Ben had failed in helping his father to get out of himself. A leaflet through his door had led him to their drop-in centre and to enrol in their Samba classes. These have brought him into contact with a woman to whom he has grown increasingly attracted and whom he is now inviting for dinner. She, Gladys, now arrives and Ben thinks that she is absolutely ghastly, although she is volubly friendly towards him. He is now the one to feel that his mother's memory is being abused. (His father is even changing the position of the furniture). The tensions within him build up and a reciprocal invitation to dinner from his father's new companion, which she insists he attends, prays upon his mind as an occasion to be dreaded.

He somehow instinctively feels that the thing to do is to meet again with Adam but the only way he can attempt to bring this about is to go and sit in a coffee shop behind the library where he hopes that Adam might drop in after work. After ages of waiting, this does indeed happen. Adam immediately recognises him and comes over, the result of which is that Ben bursts into floods of tears, at which Adam takes him by the shoulder, saying that he does not usually have this effect on people, - a very nice example of how the play modulates between emotion and humour and also being a persuasive means by which Adam could be shown establishing an instantly comforting rapport. The intervention at this point from the proprietor, proclaiming his wares from the counter and asking if they were going to place an order, seemed to me less stylistically sure, -

cartoon as against the appearance of realism and unlike the way most establishments conduct their business -, but this did not destroy the sense of emotional relief as Ben and Adam spent an hour or more discussing he knew not what but certainly agreeing to meet again.

After this he attended the dreaded dinner in a far more positive frame of mind and even felt that it went quite well. He now appreciated the affection between his father and his new companion and also felt that she perceived his own nature and was positive towards it.

The day's events, however, were not over. After driving him home, he put on the kettle, while his father went to the bathroom. He heard a bit of a bump but assumed he had just knocked into something. He did call up, "Are you alright, Dad?" but it was a little while before the silence caused him to sprint upstairs. He found him collapsed. He rang everyone he could. The Ambulance, obviously. Gladys' telephone number was written up large beside the phone. Adam. They all met at the hospital, where Adam arrived just after his father had passed away. The end of the play was Ben's overwhelming feeling of confidence that he and Adam would never again be separated.

It was a distinctive romance, sharply written and ably structured, in particular providing a well-taken opportunity for a splendid acting performance by **Andrew Norris.** The staging was simple, just a few items of furniture and hands props, - sufficient to give **Norris** some basic assistance in indicating a change of scene and, especially, to give the impression of two or more people in conversation While primarily telling the story from the point of view of Ben, he represents half a dozen characters, the encounters between Ben and his father being especially vivid.

One slight peculiarity was the title. When the father is first spotted up on the roof, Ben tells us that he seems to be reciting a poem, so one assumes, having little to go on at that stage, that it must be the **Leigh Hunt** piece suggested by playbill. There does not seem any reason why the father should have been concerning himself with that, or any other poem from what one sees of him later in the play, so that seemed a bit of a red herring. The poem's endorsement of one who loved his fellow men is obviously apt, although its concern was probably somewhat wider than that most specific to the play. The flier suggests the emphasis on a guardian angel, discovered in Adam, although the poem takes more note of a recording angel, the two roles, however, often being closely connected in Muslim thought.

Awareness of such matters and some circumspection in the use of names such as Abu is a matter which all Oldham institutions take seriously now. [**Abu Ben / Adam** was not originated at the **Coliseum** but on this occasion was being performed there]. That theatre has recognised the South Asian dimension of its community in its adult and youth programming for many years and has never been more active in this regard than in the current season. Apart from its specific involvement in Asian Arts in the **Kala Festival** last November and the invitation to **Rani Moorthy** to present her **Curry Tales** in June, its most major and valuable contribution was the **Inside Out** project which reached its climax in the performances of **The Ghosts of Crime Lake.**

In **Grange School**, one of the main contributors to the project, 97% of pupils do not have English as their first Language. In other Oldham schools, such as **Kaskenmoor**, also heavily involved and, indeed, inspiring the play's central narrative, that proportion could be less than 1%. What came to be widely recognised after the riots of 2001 was that, while there might be many opportunities for the various peoples of Oldham to pursue their own cultures, there were surprisingly few in which they could share these and naturally work and play together. Much of the inspiration for the **Inside Out** project was to meet this need.

120 young people were involved, not only from schools but also from other groups designed to support young people in various ways. Although the **Coliseum**'s ability to offer development in theatre skills was the core activity of the project, it was not addressed primarily to those with especial theatrical interests or aspirations in that direction. Most had never acted before, certainly not on so major a stage, but all who appeared in the final production gave a notably good account of themselves.

Acting was not the only skill involved. Not least, everyone had the chance to contribute from the first in deciding what the play was to be about. The binding theme decided upon was "What really scares you?" Quite a number of separate strands emerged which playwright **Kevin Fegan** them most skilfully wove together. **Kaskenmoor** had a good local ghost story to offer, which provided a framework, but others had put forward issues which were a lot more immediate, such as bullying and serious family divisions.

The Kaskenmoor story related to the Eighteenth Century Farmer Kasken who used to invite everyone to his fields once a year for a day of feasting, sports and merrymaking. This was an exceedingly popular event but always seemed to coincide with some member of the community disappearing shortly beforehand and the belief grew up that the excellent pies which were always a feature of the generous provision were not made from a member of Farmer Kasken's extensive herd but by his applying the principles of Mrs Lovett's cookbook. The bottom of the lake is where he was believed to dispose of unneeded parts his carcases and it was perhaps while performing this action one year after the feast that he himself met his end, falling through the ice.

The play began with the **Kaskenmoor** contingent, in Eighteenth Century costume, introducing us to the basic outline of this story in ballad form, ending with the warning "Never eat pies in Hollinwood," illustrating nicely the show's ability to keep a generally amusing tone to its proceedings amongst its more scarey and serious elements.

Today, the farm is a rural leisure centre and the action now moved to a modern group of young people who have agreed to a sponsored sleep-over there for a night in their sleeping-bags, to raise money to develop the facilities. The one regulation from their supervising teachers is that the boys and the girls are meant to stay in separate rooms but it is not the boys' randy suggestions which lead to this being abrogated but their ghostly apprehension of the earlier blood-thirsty deeds associated with

Farmer Kasken. (**Alison Heffernan** had designed a splendidly Gothic set). This experience not only provides occasion to move back to episodes in the Eighteenth Century events but to insert other items as the pupils try to find things to do or to talk about, to keep their minds off the ghostly sensations which impel themselves upon them from time to time.

One girl suggests that ghosts are not necessarily frightening. She does not use this term or concept to express her awareness of her Grandmother still being with her after her death. They chat and play pool together and share their amusement when the girl's mother comes in and cannot see who she is talking to. One main point on which her grandmother is keen to assure her is that she has friends all over the world. This is as a result of her own grandmother and her sisters having had so many children and these, over the years, travelling to establish new branches of the family in such countries as Canada and Australia.

I suspect that this episode was presented by the group from **Our Lady's RC High School.** It included a very jolly quartet who spread themselves about in happily waving groups to give the impression of each of the great-great-grandmothers having had ten to a dozen children and then giving up in most amusing exasperation when it was announced that the fourth sister had had seventeen children.

The same group also provided a very jolly little scene later of Farmer Kasken's cows relaxing happily in the field, secure in the knowledge that his catering arrangements removed any danger of their having to make a contribution to the feast. One of them still thinks that they are being exploited, in having to surrender all their milk, but her companion tries to persuade her that they have got a good deal: they are waited on horn and hoof and every so often get to enjoy the attentions of the Bull.

The less cartoon-like part of the Eighteenth Century narrative began with four boys, on the eve of the feast, making their way out to Kasken Farm, with the intention of spying on the farmer in his slaughterhouse to see if the rumours about how he prepares the pies is true. On their rather meandering way, the bonnet of one of them, Noodle, is thrown onto the ice of the lake. He spreads himself out on the surface to try and retrieve it, in which he succeeds but not before the fear has been very successfully communicated not only of the cracking ice but also of the terrible remains of which he catches a glimpse below.

They do reach their objective and look through the window to see the huge, black silhouette of Farmer Kasken wielding his cleaver. He then disappears and they look round to see that he has appeared behind them. They leg it and scatter but Act I ended with the farmer coming upon Noodle messing about by himself, fascinated by some gory cow's eyeballs among Farmer Kasken's slaughterhouse waste. Kasken is able to creep up behind him and to throw a sack over his head.

Although his friends are asking next day "Where's Noodle?", this does not prevent everybody enjoying themselves, not least in the sack-race. The transition to this had come after the suggestion from the Bangladeshi girl among the sleepers-over as to how they should keep themselves awake and avoid having ghostly thoughts is to have a sack-race, using their sleeping

THE GHOSTS OF CRIME LAKE (224); A sudden clap of thunder destroys the pupils' attempts to take their minds off their spooky surroundings by sack-racing in their sleeping bags.

bags. Whether by the stimulation of this parallel with past events or co-incidence, a clap of thunder as they are about to start leads them all to bury themselves in their bags with a shriek as the main action on stage is taken over by the race from three hundred years previously.

The Bangladeshi girl and her brother (pupils from various schools had been combined to form the sleeping party) contributed again, once the modern group had emerged from their cocoons, first by telling a creation myth of a giant elephant dividing the once omnipresent waters and then regulating their rise and fall so as to allow the emerging human population to sustain themselves by farming and then telling of a family trip to Bangladesh itself, which they had never seen. The occasion for the trip had been meant to be so that the uncle of the boy, a cricketing enthusiast who has even brought his bat to the sleep-over, could take him to see the first ever Test Match in the country between Bangladesh and England. Unfortunately, the uncle had died just before these things could be accomplished but he had still seen the match, finding himself much confused about which team he should applaud, as at matches in this country he supported England without a second thought.

The **Grange School** contingent presented the Bangladeshi episode most effectively. The mother of those born here has to apologise to their relatives in Bangladesh for their 'Oldham manners.' The trip was also timed to enable them to celebrate Eid-l-Fitri, which entailed being there for the last days of the fasting month of Ramadan. The Oldham boy complains, "I hope we can eat soon. I'm starving!" He is severely told by his Bangladeshi aunt "No you're not! People here are really starving." The festival itself provides scope for a lively display of Bangladeshi dancing and the cast then very well represent the journey on the crowded train to see the Test Match, the Oldham children seeing countryside and dwellings completely unlike those of their previous experience.

Although the **Grange** Bangladeshi pupils appropriately seem to have prepared these scenes on their own, they combined with pupils from other schools to present other episodes. In one a father persuaded his daughter to hide in a sack in the boot of his car, so that he could smuggle her out of the country on a ferry to Holland and she could live with him rather than her mother. A fellow pupil was sufficiently clairvoyant to be able to tell the family that she was safe for the moment, in a sack in a car-boot, and apparently this information was helpful in enabling the Dutch police to return the girl to her mother. Although this might have brought the seer some acclaim, it in fact leads to her being bullied at school by a gang of boys and girls who see her as a weirdy and deprive her of the heirloom which seems to be helpful to her in using her clairvoyant powers, which proves to be a dried up pair of cow's eyes, like those we have seen with Noodle in the earlier episode.

Performances by young people can range between the highly expert and thoroughly trained Youth Theatres, of which we have several notable examples, and the much more faltering school groups, in which one may see flashes of major talent but the primary virtue to be recognised is what has been learnt by taking part. **The Ghosts of Crime Lake** stood somewhere between these two extremes. One was not in the territory of individual brilliance which gripped the audience or splendidly drilled mass choruses. What one had was thoroughly effective performances, not welkin-ringing declamation but effective and audible speaking of well-remembered lines, several times conveying real character and always keeping the show on the move. Expert direction, by **Chris Wright**, building on numerous preceding workshops and the deployment of the **Coliseum**'s full technical facilities, led to an impressive show to which the cast had manifest commitment, not least because they were among its principal creators.

New work especially for young people, to perform in or to see, is a very major strand of what playwrights around Greater Manchester are currently achieving. **0161** and **Le State** both presented pictures of urban gang violence, in both cases drawing the key elements of the characters and the story from the combined contributions of the company members involved, in **Le State** the director **Brian Morgan** being credited with putting these into the form of the final script, in **0161**, no-one being recorded as having such a role. Both were more than plays, **Le State** being described as an "urban multimedia production," making impressive use of video, filmed initially on actual decrepit streets, on the borders of Ancoats and Miles Platting, but then garishly re-coloured, much of the detail between buildings and border fences excised and then graphically enhanced individuals and vehicles progressing past them in sinister stop-motion.. There was a largely bare stage, houses and rooms being suggested by tall and movable irregular blocks, which had been painted by the noted street graffiti artist **Makosa**, and half-a-dozen smaller cubes and wedges for use as furniture. The music in **Le State** was primarily introductory and for scene changing, using established tracks of recorded music. The full title of the other piece was **0161- The Musical** and, while recorded music was also used, there was an on-stage band and singers and extensive choreography. Virtually the whole cast was at some stage involved in the dancing, - a specialism of the **Gorse Hill Youth Arts Centre**, which seems to have been the primary creative force for the piece -, but particular contributions were made by **Nubian KANE** and **Kryptonite.**

A key factor in why violence comes about was portrayed as a general sense of being constantly on a war-footing, the reasons for which protagonists in both plays said that they did not fully understand but which was none the less real for them. In **Le State** this was just recognised as something that was there. In **0161**, a specific reason was built into the plot. This had a slightly complex chronology. We first got a vivid opening video representation of the Trafford waterfront in 2025, with bright lights and futuristic buildings, rather rapidly filmed and evoked in some very stylish words. We then get a fractured impression of some serious misfortune near a bridge. The bulk of the story is then a further twenty years in the future, most of the characters we see having been born in the interval, not having any real idea of what actually happened but knowing that it is a matter of honour, once a year, to dance on the bridge and to keep off rivals who aspire to do the same, each blaming the other for the original tragedy. This is perfectly believable. I have heard **City** supporters who certainly were not born at the time and quite possibly sired by those who weren't alive then either, expressing their antipathy for **United** by singing in praise of the weather conditions at Munich airport. Whether it would be a comparatively simple or a near impossible matter to help them understand what such attitudes entail, I have no idea. **0161** ends with a melodramatic explanation of how the original tragedy took place, - **Marika Spence** impressively throwing herself on her knees and hollering. Whether understanding was able to turn the tide of antagonism in the play's particular context and to what extent it can in the wider society with which we are more immediately familiar, the play did not delay to examine. Some thought it too short but this is to overlook the enormous amount of work to create the play's impressive choreography in particular and its tight structure and universally vivid performance throughout. It was a most striking achievement.

I was unable to compare its quality too exactly with that of **Le State** as, regrettably, other commitments meant that I was only able to see a dress rehearsal, rather than a full performance. The large **Zion** auditorium being tightly packed with young audiences, identifying closely with the action on stage, which I am told was achieved every night, must have been very different from half-a-dozen of us seeing the performances taking place while technicians were still wandering round trying to fix the lights and not all hand props were yet available. Nevertheless, one could see the bones of a very distinctive production. One could sympathise with the desperation of both Donna (**Deanne Lee**) and Bruce (**Leon Talabi**) to keep their younger brothers (Darren and Carnell: **Taurien Lee** and **Jonathan Sutton**) out of trouble, - no parents still being around or alive to do so -, whilst seeing why their efforts to do so would be found irksome by the younger boys. Both the elder ones are seriously overstretched, not only by their 'parental' roles but by having other things they need to be doing, - study, work, getting some social life. The drugs dealer (Bow, **Borhan Mohammed**) is not a malign influence on the boys, who go to sit in his house when they can escape from their own. He tolerates their presence and does not try to recruit them to work in his now mature business. When Carnell gets into the trade, it is through a rival operator, on the far side of the estate. Darren is drawn back from his rebellious behaviour, much of which has probably resulted from the unsettling early loss of his mother, through the helpful intervention of a Social Worker (**Angie O'Donoghue**). The more adult Ray (**Anthony Adesida**) and Caroline (**Mary Sobers**, who finds good opportunities for humour), have been seriously debilitated by various substances, - he drugs, she alcohol -, but make significant progress through their endeavours to lead more balanced and positive lives. The environment in which all the characters live is dangerous and wearing but showing them in some detail and mostly as being of basically decent instincts makes a more enlightening and fuller drama for the audience and a more notable achievement for the creating actors.

An even more frightening Manchester environment was that presented in **The Baby And Fly Pie, Lavinia Murray**'s adaptation of the novel by **Melvin Burgess,** intended for younger readers, staged in the **Royal Exchange Studio.** This was not an attempt to present Manchester, (or London, where **Burgess** originally set the book), as it is but as it could be, though the shooting, the day before I saw the play, of **Jean Charles de Menezes** , did nothing to make the two worlds, actual and imagined, seem further apart. **Le State** had ended with Darren losing his life in the crossfire of a drugs feud. **Fly Pie** ends with the shooting down of the young title character (**Benjamin Warren**) by police.

The play was inspired by **Burgess'** horror at learning of South American street children, who live by scavenging through rubbish dumps to see if they can find anything saleable and who are treated by the police as a vermin-control problem, setting out on organised operations to gun them down.

At first, he thought the situation too unrelievedly ghastly to be usable for a novel but then did find a way, even in a "what if it happened here?" format, in which he felt that he could be true to that basic fact and still write a work which would be satisfying both to himself and to his young readers, whom he has no qualms about challenging with grim material, - and they appreciate this.

He begins with his two young lads, Fly Pie and Sham (**Calum Callaghan**), plunging into the pile of new deliveries to the rubbish dump, to discover, not saleable items, but a very violent man (**Leigh Symonds**), waving a gun and accompanied by a very dirty baby. He has been wounded in a contested kidnapping of the child, promising the boys more money than they have ever seen before, waving an envelope full of it before them, if they go and get food and medicines for himself and the baby but threatening to shoot them if they will not. Fly Pie does go for the items but these are too late to benefit the man, who has died from his wounds. Sham, who has learned the lesson that to stand any chance on the world he must be as cruel and ruthless as it has been to him, wants to take up the chance of collecting a ransom for the baby, which he has learned from the man, should

THE BABY AND FLY PIE (226); the children know they have to fight every inch of the way; left to right, Sham (CALUM CALLAGHAN, on the ground), their latest attacker (LEIGH SYMONDS), Jane (EMMA HARTLEY-MILLER) and Fly Pie (BENJAMIN WARREN).

amount to an unbelievable seventeen million pounds. Fly Pie has another priority. He wants to use the money they have already got to buy out his sister Jane (**Emma Hartley-Miller**) from Mother Shelly (**Sarah Ball**), who has been providing them with basic shelter, in exchange for what they can scavenge from the dump. Jane has not been part of their expedition that day as Mother Shelly has realised that she has now reached the, not very advanced, age at which she has a saleable item without the need to scavenge, - herself - , and has despatched her in a recovered dress and enhancing make-up to the corner of Piccadilly Gardens.

Brought back by Fly Pie from there, she instantly takes charge of the situation. They should not get involved in the complications and dangers of making ransom demands. Parents from whom seventeen million can be demanded should be able to make them a sufficiently generous reward for returning the baby to them without demands. They cannot do this through the police, whom they perceive as just likely to take the reward for themselves, so they need to make contact for themselves.

First, however, they need to find shelter, having dispensed with the services of Mother Shelly but never having had to provide totally for themselves before. They decide to head for a squatter camp they know is in Levenshulme, whose residents they find have established local amenities for themselves and for newcomers. For seventy-five pounds, which they still have from the man's envelope, they are able to buy a starter pack to build a shelter, - some plastic sheeting, a rope and some clothes-pegs -, and for another fifty Jane gets some more suitable clothing. Sham tries to equip them to find the baby's parents by stealing a newspaper from one of the camp's longer-established residents (Scousie, **Leigh Symonds**), which Jane does her best to read, though finding the small print very difficult.

They look up to find themselves confronted by the massively tall Scousie, who has not found them hard to track down as Sham's stealing methods only amount to grabbing the paper and running off in full view. Scousie is a bloody good thief, who knows how to get things far more surreptitiously. He has only contempt for young kids who think that they need such equipment as guns. To this incompetent trio he is more benignly disposed, lending them a battered old radio, which is among his acquisitions and which is a news medium they are better equipped to understand.

They learn from this that the parents of the child are the proprietors of the paper and do manage to make contact from a phone box. They agree to meet the father outside a store on Cheetham Hill the next day, a postponement it seems that Jane decided upon so that she can buy them some really smart new clothing in which they can present themselves respectably, not as supplicants but as none the less deserving. Rather than enhancing their appearance and that of the baby, however, their experiences in the interval, tend in the opposite direction. Their incompetent attempts to build a shelter, as Scousie had warned them, are completely inadequate in the face of the rain storm which blows up during the night. Luckily, he has decided to keep a fatherly eye on them and comes out with his torch to lead them to his much better appointed bivouac.

Arriving for their rendezvous on Cheetham Hill, what they see as they approach is a young woman with a push-chair grabbed by a group of policemen, emerging suddenly from cover. Jane realises she has been mistaken for her and rushes them all down to Piccadilly station, buying tickets for Derby, as the next train to somewhere reasonably distant, where they can reconsider their strategy. When Sham gets off at Stockport to buy them refreshments, however, he sees the newsstands plastered with their photographs. Jane decides that they must get off the train at the next stop, in a remote rural area. Sham promptly disappears but Jane and Fly Pie feel they have to stay with the baby. They realise, however, that they have not the first clue how to get to anywhere along the country lanes. An old countrywoman (**Sarah Ball**) seems very sympathetic and invites them into her cottage to rest and to feed the baby. When she goes into the kitchen to put on the kettle, however, they hear her telephoning the police. Jane says they should run for it, leaving the baby, as even if they are not getting a reward, they have at least got it to a place of safety. Fly Pie, however, feels that he has to stay to make sure that the baby is safe and hides in the bushes where he can watch the house, not so well hidden, however, as the first action of the police on arrival is to spot him and shoot him down.

Obviously a very grim vision but one in which **Melvin Burgess** has succeeded in his objective of introducing positive elements. Although Sham is under constant suspicion from Fly Pie of wanting to make off with the baby on his own and revert to the idea of ransom, Jane, who is very affectionate towards both of them, always insists to Fly Pie that they must be willing to trust Sham to look after the baby on his own on occasion: that if he is never trusted or thought well of he can never become trustworthy or develop other good qualities, and Sham does respond in some measure to this. Although he does indeed think that the maximum financial profit from their endeavours is the only possible way in which they can ever be free from their terrible existence, Fly Pie's aspirations are more humble. He is fascinated by the idea of becoming a baker, a job he believes he could learn to do really well, although his name results from the one time that a baker had allowed him into his kitchen and the results had turned out most unhygenically. Naturally the Baker (**Leigh Symonds**) was not encouraged to allow him future access but what makes him declare that he never wants to see him again, when they show up on his shop doorstep on their flight from Cheetham Hill, is their obvious association with the notorious kidnapping. He gives them shelter until the main police activity has died down and supplies them with enough pies to fortify them for a while but then sends them very firmly on their way.

The adults in the story have very characterful half-face masks, which suggests the way in which they can be especially terrifying to the children. Scousie and the Baker, however, are not without their virtues. That some decent instincts and enhanced capabilities could manage to grow, particularly in the children, even in such horrendous circumstances, does, through our involvement with the characters, make seeing this play a positive experience.

When children could roam freely on sunlit moorsides seems to many like a golden age. In the early 1960's, however, around Ashton and Saddleworth, parents were beginning to have the fears, very familiar today, of what could happen to children out of their sight. In **Children of The Moors** by **Aelish Michael**, Billy (**Howard Chadwick**) and Lorraine (**Maeve Larkin**) are only able to get up onto the hills because it is assumed that they are at their gran's. That Rob (**Adam Sutherland**) is frequently out of the sight of the grandfather he lives with can surprise neither of them, as the latter frequently leathers the life out of him and locks him in the coal cellar. The circumstance which gives events their very particularly setting and edge is that, just down the track from where the children make their den, **Myra Hindley** and **Ian Brady** (not specifically identified) are disposing of their corpses. That this might lead to the children suffering a far worse fate than does befall them is a constant source of tension for the audience. (That Billy comes off much less badly than he might have done from an encounter with such a ruthless pair, is skilfully made plausible).

That these historical circumstances make a very effective setting for the story is complemented by the fact that the story provided a certain sort of context for the history. If **Hindley** and **Brady** were abnormally cruel, what is the degree of continuity with the much more familiar cruelty suffered by Rob from his granddad? If **Hindley** and **Brady** were dominated by formidable sexual passions, at what point did they become something different from the impulses which Rob and Lorraine are just beginning to discover and be led by? The most distinctive strength of the play was its very persuasive portrait of childhood at that time. A member of the audience, who would have been pretty well the exact contemporary of the characters and, like them, had grown up in the area, found that the play presented to him an exact memory of how he had been at their age.

That certain aspects of human behaviour were much less subjects of public discourse, not least among the young, meant that there was a certain sort of innocence, which meant that it was perfectly possible for the play to have a lightness of touch whilst doing full justice to the grim matters which lay underneath, thereby also making it a more sustainable experience for the audience. There are, for instance, two thoroughly "schoolboy" jokes from the simple-minded Billy which in context, rather than being pathetic, seemed naturally funny. In the early scenes, Lorraine is known by the first part of her name. When Billy has discovered that she is his adopted sister, which she has never been told, he finds that the name is explained by hearing his parents say that "she fell off the back of a lorry." When, as part of the great maturation process marked by her going to secondary school, which includes learning to smoke and endeavouring to drink alcohol, she insists that her name is now Raine, he says, "That's a bit wet." That both are still children is emphasised by the ending of the second scene, where Rob is just about to bring into effect his first attempt to have his wicked way with Lorraine's body, and both she and Billy are completely distracted from what he has in mind by the fact that the wind has suddenly picked up enough to enable them to fly their kite.

The play was a great imaginative achievement as a piece of writing, with a very robust dramatic structure, and the actors were notably successful in bringing out these strengths, despite the fact that this was a script-in-hand performance. As a **North West Playwrights** workshop it had had a much fuller immediately preceding rehearsal period than the analogous work in **Script 2** at the **Royal Exchange**, - several days, rather than **Script 2**'s one -, and this allowed much more developed movement, a basic set and use of at least some of the hand props, a select number of which are key elements in the dramatic development of the narrative.

The **Script2** readings could not progress beyond having the actors sitting on basic chairs, sometimes moved slightly into some pattern but even where, as in **Peacefully, At Home**, they just sat throughout in a simple row, regardless of whether they were "on" or "off stage," this did not prevent the actors from giving thoroughly vivid performances.

I do not think there was a single place name in the script but there was certainly a local feel to the piece, very possible set not too far from that in **Children of the Moors**, although in very different circumstances and definitely today, a small community, probably on the fringes of Greater Manchester. The husband of Bridget (**Judith Barker**) is dying, doped up to the eyeballs by the Health Visitor. Her close friend Una (**Eileen O'Brien**) is present and coming in soon is the eldest son, Chris (**James Nickerson**), who is running the local garden centre. That is about the height of local economic opportunity, which has not been high enough for the younger son James, (**Robert Lawrenson**), who departed to the more prosperous south but is now on the way home with his wife Sarah

(**Donna Alexander**), who is also local. Indeed, it had generally been thought that she was much closer to Chris.

The main achievement of the play is a convincing portrait of family relationships, in a particular social setting. Like **Nicola Schofield**'s play last year (**Maybe Tomorrow; 04: 202**), it was not overburdened with plot and covered a similar range of generations, although with the younger one we see here being rather between the two youngest we saw in the earlier work. If that play brought out the differences within generations and between them, this more came to indicate parallels: in neither have people married the one they might have preferred. Sarah might well have been happier to marry Chris and his mother seems to have been Una, rather than Bridget. Neither he nor Una have ever married. Such disappointments are a matter of portraiture, rather than rows or ill feeling, and it made for effective, quiet, drama.

The circumstances of **Slave To Love** by **Ged McKenna** might seem to be a similar situation several years further on. The husband of Mrs Price (**Romy Baskerville**) has been dead for some time. Her unmarried son, Gavin (**Terence Mann**) lives with her and looks after her. That he might sell up the house and move her to Robin Hood's Bay, she is ready to accept. That he may be seeking intimate female company on the nights he is home late, she finds understandable. She cannot envisage that he might actually marry; - he is now 40 and really much more interested in such a prospect, before it is too late, than in any other form of liaison. Ali (**Jane Hogarth**), the woman to whom he is introduced by his best friend, Dave (**Michael Neary**)' is of a similar age and conscious that this limits not only her chances of marriage but of children. She looks after a far more dependent aging father but hides this from Gavin, in case this should scare him off, as he hides his responsibilities to his mother for the same reason. They become very close and when she learns about his mother he says he will sort things out but in the end it is more than either of them can bear. He moves with his mother to Robin Hood's Bay.

Despite the excellent cast and the fuller staging, this was not a play which really grabbed me as a whole but that may be because I was less perceptive about the subject matter. I was much more held by **Nicholas Corder**'s **Lightning In A Bottle.** On reflection, I am not sure there was more to but it was both an outstanding solo performance, by **Julia Rounthwaite** as **Jean Seberg,** and extremely skilful in the way it linked together an account of that actress' life, from her last moments. What I wondered afterwards was whether it got beyond telling a life. There were moments of fascinating detail but was there not more that could have been done to give the tale more significance or to provide deeper insight?

The occasion of **Seberg** seeking to end her own life, by an overdose in her car, which is where we meet her, was the anniversary of the death of her son in childbirth. Obviously a heavy blow but what was it about the nature of this particular event, many years before, which had now become an insupportable burden? We did not seem to hear much more about it.

We had a lively account of the process by which, with great publicity, as a young, very inexperienced actress from a remote part of Iowa, she was selected for the lead role in **Otto Preminger**'s **Saint Joan**. This led to her becoming "a movie star before, I'd ever made a movie," an experience which could have coloured her whole life and probably did but I am not sure that we got that deep an insight into what that meant for her personally.

When filming began in France there was unsympathetic press comment about "A French heroine, to be played by an American Actress, with a script by an Irish playwright" (up to a point, they might have added) "and a German director." The eventual reviews were not overwhelmingly favourable and nor were they, with one outstanding exception, for her second, and final, **Preminger** movie, **Bonjour, Tristesse.** Yet, subsequent to that, she got taken up by **Jean Luc Godard** and the **Nouvelle Vague**, became more or less a French icon and spent most of the rest of her life there. That was some cultural transition but I am not sure that we got too clear a picture of what that must have meant for her and why she abandoned her homeland as comprehensively as she did. She had a fair number of French husbands, let alone other lovers, all of which must have been significant for her, but this is not too different from the pattern of life followed by many other film stars.

What particularly were we meant to learn or understand from her narrative? I am not too sure but certainly while the tale was being told, we did not have much time for such considerations. What we had was a vivid personality before us, telling a tale which was full of lively details. If there was meant to be more to it than that, perhaps this will emerge in the further writing for which the **Workshop** is said to have shown the way. Meanwhile, there was certainly material for an absolutely dazzling solo performance, with **Julia Rounthwaite**, over ninety minutes, finding a natural way to point every line, having only limited scope for movement as, with imaginative exceptions, the whole action was meant to take place within a small Citroen car, but nevertheless finding expressive ways to make use of the four chairs and a blanket with which it was represented and occasions to stand up and move around which served the narrative without distracting through the notional breach of the circumstances.

There were half-a-dozen solo performances in **24:7**, some of them of comparable length, but the **Blue3** pieces at the **Royal Exchange** did not aspire to be of a comparable scale. Even where, for instance in **Harriot and I** and **Vent**, what we saw was from probably complete works of some length, what the season avowedly sets out to do, is to show us samples of promising local work in progress, of a wide variety of types, so we only saw such work in extract. The piece which was most similar in tone to **Catching Lightning In A Bottle** (**Seberg**'s description of the process of acting), was **Pam Leeson**'s **A War in the Morning.** This we probably saw in its entirety, something over fifteen minutes, in poetry, performed by **Vashti MacLachlan.**

The settings for the **Blue3** presentations, of which there were three or four per evening, were, of necessity in such circumstances, simple. That for **A War In The Morning** was just a double bed with a telephone beside it but this was made vivid by a bright scarlet cover. The size of the bed meant that there was considerable scope for **Vashti MacLachlan** to sit or lie in different positions or to move around. It seems likely that the director, **Gerry**

Potter, made a significant contribution to working out with the actor a series of moves which helped to punctuate the narrative, although this did not seem to fall into clearly recognisable segments.

The basic situation seemed to be the emotions of a woman whose lover is away. She hopes that he will phone but suspects that he will not as she thinks what he is up to is having under-age sex with young girls on a holiday in Thailand.. She both envisages what he is doing and describes her own moves to make him more eager to have her. (They do not live together, He has a wife.)

The most distinctive feature of her expositions is that they are interrupted from time to time by a male voice (**James Quinn**), presumably that of her lover. The first of these is "Everybody has the right …," almost making one think that we are about get a rendition of the opening number from **Assassins** and, indeed, it proves that the intention might be equally cynical. In later utterances, the phrase is expanded into full quotations from the **Universal Declaration of Human Rights**, which it might be thought that the lover, in his apparent profession as a soldier, would have it among his primary responsibilities to defend but which are spoken whenever they express principles which are being broken by the activities which the woman imagines the man to be performing in Thailand. It would not be possible at one hearing to grasp the full meaning of the piece but certainly it was performed with an intensity and detail which made it a thoroughly absorbing performance. At the end the telephone does ring.

Far more incomprehensible was the opening piece, **360° (Falling)**, although, if doubtless not without meaning for its creators, it was primarily intended to be experienced rather than understood. A woman (**Stephanie Ridings,** presumably an angel), was discovered at the summit of a great mountain of bottles. Bottles were also used as a primary source of the music by **Phil Sykes**, who moved a small electric fan over the mouths of a selection which had been filled to different heights and thus produced different notes. It may have been a case of not falling but flying as, after standing up on the pinnacle of her mountain, the angel laid herself horizontally across it, almost like a boat's figurehead but presumably being in flight, as a fan below her was set in motion, which ruffled her robes. **Chris Gilligan** then began throwing feathers by the handful into the blast of the fan, which might have suggested that the angel was having **Icarus** problems but, if so, she took it remarkably equably and just swam on, breasting the breeze.

I have seen several pieces of performance art over the years which have impressed me greatly and as many if not more which have said nothing particular to me. Excellence in performance can help, although many seek to give the impression of being studiously pedestrian in this field. At least the sense of it all adding up to something helps me, even if I cannot apprehend very much of what it is. I did not get much of the latter in either of the two most notable examples we have seen recently, although both did contain elements of performance which it was a joy to see in their own right.

Both had an excellent pedigree: **The Root of It** being created by **Newfound Theatre**, who have presented much highly enjoyable work over the past couple of years (**02: 74; 03:14; 04: 493, 494, 495; 05: 13, 213**),

Transformations being the work of **Contact Young Actors Company**, aided and abetted on this occasion by **The People Show**, no less, primarily represented by the presence of **Tyrone Huggins** and **Alit Kreiz** as directors.

Diffuse collections of material, giving a great many individuals an opportunity to create in their preferred style, within a more or less apparent theme, has been the usual feature of the public work of **CYAC** since it began, almost six years ago. **Newfound** have hitherto presented more conventional plays, occasionally established works, such as **Look, No Hans (04: 493)**, more usually new work, often self-penned by the performers, most usually collections of solo pieces.

The most extensive of these had been **Emerge**, a collection of twelve penned by members of **OUTWrite,** a group run by and for members of the Lesbian, Gay, BiSexual and Transgender community, although not keeping to that particular subject matter. Most, though certainly not all, were attempting dramatic form for the first time but all the pieces were very assured. All were essentially solo performances but the director, **Helen Parry**, had devised ingenious means to keep the action in continuous flow and sometimes to have various cast members interacting with each other.

The first piece, **Holding Court**, had not seemed like a solo as it had begun with a group of young women meeting in a bar after work, the natural setting of the room in which the performance took place at **Taurus.** There was essentially one main speaker, however, **Hellen Kirby**, who drew the attention of all, with her tale of how a man had done her mate wrong and her proposal of how they should collaborate to show him up. This plan seemed to be adjudged to be going too far, so those assembled all severally made their excuses, leaving the proponent isolated and with nothing to do but also make her exit.

The bar was not quite deserted, however, as **Louise Twomney** was still manning the pumps, so when **Karen Warbey** entered, from the opposite direction in her full bridal gown, she was there to be addressed in her great tale of woe, **Someone Borrowed, Someone's Blue**, about how her Great Day had come to nought.

The bar setting was not recognised throughout. When a wall cupboard door, which, despite the limited space behind has often been used as a full-blown exit in previous performances at **Taurus**, creaked open, it revealed behind it **Hannah McHugh** in, it emerged, the persona of the pair of **Sensible Shoes** in the title of her piece. She had begun her relationship with her wearer when required to provide her with suitable footwear for a school expedition to the countryside but had managed to keep her position and saw it as her task to guide her wearer through life. In particular, she had tried to steer her towards a male work colleague, whose shoes she had identified as especially desirable under a bar room table. She had been quite overcome when she found that her wearer was far more susceptible to the advances of a female manager. She had managed to get herself redeployed in the second-hand market, as a suitable companion for schoolgirls going on rural expeditions, the role in which she now felt that she had always been happiest.

By the time our attention had been redirected to the main performance area, we were no longer specifically in a bar, although a certain amount of alcohol was being consumed at the young person's party on private premises, at which the character portrayed by **Sabina Arthur** was persuaded by the young man who had convinced her that she was **Special** to go upstairs with him, 'where they could be more private.' He was not there when she woke up, which she saw as very thoughtful of him. She described in the same way his pronouncement, when she later advised him that she was pregnant, that this was not the right time for them to have a baby.

She was not the only character that evening to end her tale in the waiting room of a pregnancy advisory clinic. **Beth Palmer** in **Jesus Loves You** had begun her piece by telling us that this was the name of the Spanish waiter who had straddled her across the bar-top after closing time. This bar did not only appear in its own character, however. **Susi Wrenshaw** climbed onto it as the **Girl On A Rooftop**. She had made this ascent, with a bottle in hand, whilst her friends were partying down below. She wondered about throwing herself off but, after telling us about the experiences which led her to the rehab clinic, decided that she had benefited sufficiently from this to be able to go down and re-join the party.

The Big Issue Seller (Scott Bradley) was also one who had benefited from help. He had been from a perfectly happy home and likely to get decent A Levels and go on to university. The death of his mother and, in particular, his father bringing another woman into the house, however, had disorientated him and, when his father had grown tired of his emotional complaints he had kicked him out. He had slept rough for some time but getting in with the **Big Issue** had really made a difference. He had not only made money from selling the magazine. The organisation had both helped him to get somewhere more regular to live and arranged for him to get computer training, as a step towards better-paid employment. He had even seen his dad doing the same course, after being thrown out by the woman whose incursions he had so much resented. They did not have much time for each other now. The man who did seem to be taking a close interest in him was a council employee who always overpaid rather generously for his **Big Issue**. He suspected that this was because he had designs on his body but this seemed to be something which it would be worth going along with, for the extra income.

As he departed for where he could usually make this sale, **Sinead Douglas** entered and asked if she could buy a copy, as her lead in to her piece, **This Ain't No Party.** This was a companion to **This Ain't No Disco**, also by **Alison Heffernan**, for which **Louise Twomney** re-appeared later , lugging a crate of bottles in her role as the barmaid. She has performed **Alison Heffernan**'s work before, in the earliest version of **Women's Little Christmas (03:14)**, in which it dovetailed in exactly with material she had written for herself, and here the material, reminiscing about a customer who had just come over, fitted her as exactly as a glove.

Its naturalism was a far cry from the refractions of **The Root of It** which she and other core members of **Newfound** wrote and performed. Like many another work of its kind it began by affecting to be entirely natural, to the point of presenting actors sitting about waiting to begin a show. Here they sat and sat and sat, with one ostentatiously empty chair amongst them. Eventually

Hannah McHugh whispered to **Daniel Wallace** "what about some music?" and he called out more loudly to the control booth, "**Julie**, could we have some music while we're waiting." Relatively calming and interesting music was then supplied, during which all four actors continued to sit. Eventually a telephone answering machine sprang into life with a message from **Kate Henry,** apologising for being late. This brought expostulations from **Louise Twomney** about the vengeance she would wreak upon her for letting them down but they continued to sit until further messages made it apparent that **Kate Henry** was extremely unlikely to arrive at all. **Louise Twomney**'s rage grew into desperation: "What are we going to do? We can't go on? Where's **Juliet**?" (**Ellis,** the director). "Not in!" (She was in fact but sitting in a suitably obscure position). "Typical! Ah! You're moving the chairs, **Hellen**" (**Kirby**). "That will really interest the audience. I can't put up with this! I'm going!" and banged out of the Studio.

Hellen and **Hannah** sat behind the desks at either end while **Daniel** began to mark out some lines on the floor. After a while, he turned round and said to **Hellen**, "I didn't know you smoked?", to which the reply, puffing away, was, "I don't." After a further interval, **Daniel** asked, "Can I have one?" "I thought you'd given up?" "I have," lighting up. **Hannah** then joined them, after similar exchanges. **Louise** eventually rejoined the group through the device of rushing in shouting, "Where is it? I've left it behind! I've got to find it!" She turned over the clothing and looked into and under the bags of various members of the audience, searching, it eventually transpired, for her voice. Her occasion for joining the smokers was when she was called upon to sing the song which was allegedly meant to have been sung by **Kate.**

Her dismissive expressions while she deliberately sent this up, claiming it was a piece of rubbish, which only an eejut like **Kate** would have chosen, were very skilful but **Louise Twomney** singing badly is nothing like as much fun as **Louise Twomney** singing well, which she can do to formidably good effect. (It wasn't a patch on the comparable contributions to **Last Turn of The Night** and **Half Heaven, Half Heartache**).

The other material described was well enough done in its way but some aspects were not exactly original, - the infuriated cast member deserting his colleagues was used by both the **National Theatre of Brent** in its **Messiah** and the **People Show** in its **Cabaret** in the season unveiling the **Royal Exchange** touring module more than twenty years ago and although some Variety acts gain stature with venerability that did not seem to be the coin traded here. The possibility that episodes might mean more to the cast than to members of the audience was strengthened when the monitors began to show live action footage of **Hellen Kirby** crawling around in nappies at the age of One. An enormous pile of cards on one of the tables proved to be multiple copies of a portrait of similar vintage. When she tried to carry the pile across the stage, it tipped over and scattered. Watching **Hannah McHugh** trying to arrange them into patterns did not become fascinating theatre for me.

I found the most distinctive item was a news report read out by **Hellen Kirby,** under the heading "P-P-Pick Up A Gay Penguin." At a zoo in North Europe, keepers had tried to introduce females into their colony. The males had proved to be not that way inclined. The keepers had abandoned the attempt and apologised for not Respecting Their Gay Space, saying that they had made the experiment because they were a threatened species but that they now realised the inappropriateness of their actions. What this led on to by way of theatre was **Daniel Wallace** proving to have a large collection of small model penguins, of which he slowly began to lay out a double column across the stage. This was another episode which I found less than riveting and the Penguin thought so too. His beak turned out to be the colourful obscure image which had been showing motionless on the monitors on the tables at either end since the start of the performance. He now burst into action with a loud cry of "Don't look at him, look at me! I know you could watch telly at home but did you come all the way here just to watch a man playing with those things. Don't look at him! Look at me!", and he waddled off in disgust.

It was a lively intervention but for too much of the show, I though he had a point. There were some nice gestures and inflections when the cast were not being too deliberately inexpressive. I know that the chance to do something completely different meant a lot to them. The show had its moments and was clearly the product of a lot of effort. The fact that it did not speak very much to me does not mean that it may not have its audience. I hope that they will find it in the **Soho Theatre** in London, to which they are taking the piece, but, if they do, I hope they will still come back to Manchester, as I certainly look forward to seeing their future work.

Transformations was on a much larger scale, taking over most of the **Contact** building. People met in the foyer, where some members of the cast were clearly identifiable and already in action: **Fisayo Akinade** suspended by ropes, **Greg Foster** (I think) half-metamorphosed into a copy of **The Times, Fiona Maddox** in a Flight Attendant's uniform, standing on the Box Office counter, making very formal announcements into a microphone about the architectural history of the building and the location of the lavatories. Other cast members were less obviously identifiable but were mingling and three of the smartest dressed, which included **Sakinah Maynard** and **Kyle Ballick**, were moving about distributing programmes, which they usually did with such words as "I'm the Director. Thank you for coming." These programmes were of clearly different colours and when **Fiona Maddox** announced that the flight was ready for boarding, she did so by directing those with programmes of each particular colour to gather by particular gates. This led to different groups seeing three preliminary performances in different orders before all gathered in the auditorium of the largest theatre, **Space One**, for the conclusion.

I began in **Space Two**, which was an Arrivals Hall, where the clocks hanging from the ceiling looked as if they had been designed by **Salvador Dali**, initially the colour of newsprint, - a recurring theme in the design -, but capable of being back-lit in various bold hues at opportune moments. We retained the services of **Fiona Maddox**, manning the Information Desk, the main burthen of her announcements now being how lonely she was (not a common fate, I would have thought, for persons at such posts) and begging anyone to come and talk to her.

The possibility of anyone taking her at her word was always deftly headed off by some other strand of action being initiated. The only passenger waiting as we arrived was **Marika Spence**, showing herself, to anyone who had also seen her in **0161**, to be an actress of some considerable range. There she had been consistently bold and loud, as a teacher dominating a roomful of disorderly, mid-twenty-first-century school pupils. Here she was a quiet, confused and uncertain young teenager. "Why am I always waiting?" was her refrain and it was not too clear to us either, but a letter from her mother, which we later heard as she looked at it, related to being about to meet the other person who had always been significant in her life (not, it seemed, her father, as I thought I heard the unidentified individual referred to as 'she').

While she waited, **Kyle Ballick**, entered restlessly and sat for a while, looking repeatedly at his watch and mobile phone. He then left again, the way he came, but reappeared after **Marika Spence** had wandered through more of her tale. His arrival this time was shortly followed by the sound of **John Phiri**, who hip-hopped his way dextrously in, girt about with ear-phones but apparently creating most of his own musical rhythm by making loud sounds like releasing compressed air. **Ballick** greeted him by calling out

"What's Up? How You Bin?
I've been waiting here for 55 min!"

To which **Phiri** danced his reply

"I'm so sorry that I took a long time.
I've been waiting like an idiot in the wrong line."

They continued in similar vein, **Phiri** giving a consistently impressive physical performance, and then made a joint exit.

Other travellers included **Chris Barlow**, whose suitcase, when he dropped it, proved to be filled with stacks of newspapers, of which he clearly did not have enough, however, as, when he sat down he set himself to read the half man – half newspaper, who took the opportunity to remove his watch. This was not the extent of his interest in Time. As well as taking he also gave: playing cards such as the one passed to me, to which had been added the quotation "Time is merely a feature of our memories and experience: **Avicenna**."

Two young ladies (**Nikki Norton** and **Vanessa Silva Pereira**) were very concerned, in different ways, about their appearances. **Nikki** we could see very clearly, - she even had a transparent mackintosh over her stylish dress -, but she knew comments were made, such as "Your nose is too long" **Vanessa** entered with the query, "What are you looking at?", although, in truth at this stage we could see very little of her. When the dangling hair was pushed aside we could see that she had a major scar on her cheek. Her view seemed to be that it was her business what she looked like but what either of these was wanting to say seemed to me very unclear, - probably intentionally.

The other entrant absorbed by a woman's appearance was the juvenile-seeming **Fisayo Akinade.** Showing great uncertainty, both by his manner of speech and the dishevelment of his otherwise rather formal attire, he clasped a picture torn from a newspaper and at his every entrance showed it to members of the audience and at the information desk, asking, "Do you know this woman?" Eventually, he squatted down with a stick of chalk to try and work out on the floor what he knew about her himself. He was no longer certain whether she was dark or fair, tall or short, pretty or otherwise and kept crossing out answers as he decided against them. The question on which he could not reach a decision was "Did I love her?" and he wandered out, pondering on this.

A character who had no doubts about his appearance, although he suggested that we might, was **Bilal Malik**. With a loud burst of music, an exceptionally hairy leg for one extending beneath a skirt made its appearance around the doorway. After waggling around for some time, the dancer burst onto the stage in drag and cavorted around, soliciting members of the audience to songs of Napoli-a. (It was noticeable that, in a theatre which usually prides itself on the 'latest vibes,' most of the music we had heard up to this point, in the entrance hall and in **Space Two**, was familiar fifty years ago).

It was left to **Fisayo Akinade**, rather than the flight attendant, to move us to the next performance area. Entering with his usual diffidence he said, "They say we've got to go to the Fun Fair. I think it's this way." The "we" was not an entire euphemism as some of the characters we had already seen, such as **Greg Foster** and **Fisayo**, still showing his photograph, were from time among us in the activities we found on the upstairs landing, although presumably nipping back, when appropriate to repeat their performances in **Space Two** for the next audience.

The activities down here seemed to be a lot more improvised than those we had already seen, which, - while often apparently casual, - had probably been fairly tightly scripted. The central attraction was an Emotions-Shy, presided over by **Katie Mettam,** at which she tried to encourage us to throw balls of rolled up newspaper at coloured bottles, with labels such as Joy, Shame, Love. If punters specified what they were really after, she would move all other bottles aside, to give them a clear throw. If we were successful, she promised us a fortune. "I don't say it will be a good one, but it will be a fortune," and, indeed, to any victorious contestants she handed down a bowl of strips of papers, from amongst which a fortune could be selected. I think she drew a mixture of genuine audience members and her fellow actors. Her patter was composed of inducements to take part and complaints about the hours and conditions of work to which she was subjected by her boss. This was not all sparkling but she kept it going pretty well over a considerable period.

Also active around the fairground was **Katie Davies,** whose tea-trolley was in fact a low-loader, largely filled with newsprint, on top of which china cups and a tea-pot most unsuitable for mass catering rattled away. **Tom Hughes** had been among those moving around the foyer before the full performance began, the large fury hood of his parka engulfing his head, not in the manner of a hoodie but of one who is as keen to hide the world from himself as himself from the world. He had now secreted himself in the darkened disabled toilets, whose walls he had covered with obscure graffiti, absorbed in the strumming of his battered guitar. **Shanika Dobson**, smartly dressed but a little degraded, moved among the crowd, telling anyone who would listen that she had once been a really successful business woman, a theme upon which she once managed to get a platform beside **Katie Mettam**'s stall to address the crowd, leading **Mettam** to dismiss her and **Fisayo Akinade**, who was still making his peregrinations with his picture, with the words, "You keep getting these nutters."

After it was felt that we had had sufficient time to appreciate these performances, we were invited to progress to **Space One** and to descend down through the auditorium on the stage, half of which appeared to be covered in scrumpled newsprint, and to look back out towards the seating, about 5% of which, at various points, had been sheathed in bin-bags, with the effective intention, I presumed, of giving it a more variegated appearance. A cleaning lady (**Rukaya Megen**) was working her way along the rows and a Security Guard (**Tapiwa Madovi**) was making occasional patrols up and down the aisles with a torch. The largely darkened auditorium and these activities gave the impression that the theatre was closed. On the other hand, **Sakinah Maynard** sat looking at us, as if we were the performance. Nothing much happened for a while, although **Rukaya Megen** did then address us as she worked, I think largely on the theme that we should not make any assumptions about her, just because of her scruffy working clothes. Then **Sakinah Maynard** abandoned the impression that she thought of herself as being the audience and got up to give a lecture: "Let's start with the art." She drew our attention to a large screen above the aisle and began to discuss its qualities, getting some way before she acknowledged that these lay largely in its being completely blank.

This brief address done, she stood aside and a shadowy figure (**Daniella Edwards**) at the pinnacle of the seating in the darkened auditorium, showing herself to be in the scruffy clothing of a squatter, began to speak and then slid much of the way down over the seats as she did so, finally disappearing behind the fifth row. Quite what the main burthen of her remarks was, I did not much assimilate but we then got two much clearer items, the most literary contributions to the evening.

The Security Guard had seated himself to rest and brought out a letter from his father, back in Africa, assuring "Dear Ola Rotimi , - or is it Tim now?, …" how proud they were that all the sacrifices they had made had finally resulted in him being in England to train as a doctor, which their country so sorely needs. There are not many of his family left now, as both his mother and his sisters have succumbed to the new disease. They are confident that he will pursue his studies diligently and not follow the path of many educated Africans into becoming a security guard. "Our country does not need security guards. There is nothing left to secure."

As he was concluding, **Niven Ganner**, in a dark suit, came down through the auditorium and sat immediately next to him. He removed his sun glasses and addressed us in poetry: " I am the man you do not want to meet." Why should we hide ourselves behind our newspapers, mobile phones or lap tops when there was a real human being beside us we could talk to? He then gave an indication of the answer by giving us a specimen of the facets of his sad life on which he could dilate at length if we did talk to him.

These two items had real power and almost everything we had seen had been well performed but would we not have been able to appreciate the skills of the actors whatever they were performing, - some of what we had seen had not provided the most obvious opportunity to be interesting -, and, aside from the qualities of individual items, were they enhanced by being part of the whole production?

For a while I thought that the final phase of the performance might be going to provide a positive answer to this last question. The Security Guard addressed us and said, “Er. Actually, there’s been a mistake. You’re meant to be sitting here. The actors are meant to be on the stage.” We moved to the seating and nothing much happened for a while, I suspect because the performances in the different locations had proved to be of different lengths. It proved that we were waiting for the scattered audiences to show up and join us. I assumed it was an improvisation to cover part of this gap that **John Phiri** and **Kyle Ballick** came down to join **Tom Hughes** on the forestage, where he had been sitting under his hood quietly plucking at his guitar, and said, “Do you want us to sing you a song?” They picked out a rhythm in what had appeared a rather shapeless performance, extemporised, it seemed, a lively little song, encouraged him with the acclamation, “Ace!”, laying a heartening hand on his shoulder, and withdrew.

I did have hopes that something rather telling was going to emerge as all the characters we had seen earlier came in from various directions and began to mingle. **Greg Foster** restored to **Chris Barlow** his watch, after the latter had emptied the newspapers out of his suitcase, decided they were not enough, requisitioned those which had made up the bulk of the load on **Katie Davies**’ tea trolley and began tearing them purposefully into strips. Deprived of her load, **Katie Davies** began reading allowed to those engaged in such occupations from the book we had seen her perusing previously when business was slow. This proved to be an anthology of wittily bizarre aphorisms, which I would like to have been able to remember but all of which, distinctive though they were, have passed from me. The one reprinted in the programme gives a flavour but I am pretty sure it was not the best: “Never buy a Rolex from someone who is out of breath.”

Katie Mettam sat down beside **Chris Barlow** to help him in his task. **Vanessa Silve Pereira** proved to have a paper-shredder in her suitcase. **Fiona Maddocks** began stretching adhesive paper tapes across the stage and others, such as **Marika Spence** and **Niven Ganner** started breaking these into more elaborate patterns. I had supposed that this was going to prove the basis for the various torn strips of paper being collectively assimilated into some grand design. That did not happen. Instead, what had looked like a pile of waste paper at the back of the stage was raised to the vertical and proved to be a massive butterfly, nearly all of the width and much of the height of the large stage. Its colour and structure was similar to the **Dali**esque giant watches we had seen hanging from the roof of the Departure Hall in **Space Two.** I thought that it might have been effective if they had had the same facility to back-light it with bold colours as the whole cast was united in staring up-stage at it in admiration but this was not done. They began to dance, interweaving amongst each other as they continued to stare at the butterfly. They then turned to face us, still dancing slowly, each individual coming to the centre, to announce their name and three or four words identifying their hopes and fears before running off, one by one, eventually leaving the stage empty, before all came rushing back on to receive their applause.

I was not sure that it really came off as a whole but certainly a treasure-house of skill and dedication was demonstrated on all hands.

The production in the **24:7 Festival** which came nearest to these in style was **Here In The Night (Aquie en la Noche).** Its text being partly in Italian is just one of the ways in which its style was not exactly pellucid. The introduction by a grotesque Waiter (**Thomas Ligget**) was a fair example of the verbal side of things: "Senyoras y Senor (Ladies and Gentlemen): I cordially invite you to my song of the night, as dark and deep as a beautiful mind stained with Christ's blood nests in this half like a knife, a picture, a lost scene from **Shakespeare**'s **~A Midsummer Night's Dream.**"

One might get some general mood or intention out of that but not word for word understanding. Some lines were more blunt and striking: Woman (**Kate Gilbert**): Do you remember the first time you told me "I love you?" Man (**Glenn Collier**): Yes. We were … Woman: Nor do I.

Who knows what that meant but it certainly had impact. If a performance is going to rely on impact rather than meaning, the demands to be made on its source and standard of presentation are very high. These were good but not I thought quite good enough to carry them into the first rank of those whose coin is allusiveness or theatrical experience.

It was the only piece in the festival to incorporate a use of dance. After their first sequence of exchanges, at a restaurant table, at which the Waiter occasionally attended to them, they rose to make soulful movements, separately and together, the Waiter sitting down to regard them. All this was good enough to hold the attention and the dark clothing of all, with the subdued light, was certainly consistent in maintaining the atmosphere of **Night.** It could only have been a scene from a very unusual production of **Midsummer**, however, as, apart from a certain wryness, there was no lightness or comedy. I failed to assimilate quite to what aspect of Love, or any other feature of the human condition, the dialogue was seeking to draw one's attention. It was an interesting experiment and I was happy enough to have seen the endeavour. There is no obligation on a work to provide an answer to the question "What's it all about?" but it does then have to be very strong in other ways.

Footfalls (04:207) in **Blue2** last year succeeded in being thoroughly interesting, even though I could not have said anything of what it was about. A full-length version appeared this year in **24:7** as **The Falling.** When I mentioned to one of the technical team, whose contribution to its success proved to be very significant, that I was intending to come and had seen an intriguing work by the same author (**Ailis Ni Riain**) last year, without having a clue what it meant, he said she had asked him when they were setting up if he had understood it and he had replied "It's about a depressed woman, abused by her father in childhood." She had, apparently, responded, "Got it in one."

I think that I would have got that much this time around without this

THE FALLING (231); AMY LIPTROTT

explication but, although it was useful to understand this much, the point was the experience. There are plenty of details in the poetry, let alone the music which I would not assimilate, certainly not at one performance, but the high quality of all strands and the effectiveness with which they are woven together meant that the effect was tremendous, independent of any precise meaning.

As mentioned, contributions to **Blue** are of necessity simply staged. Nevertheless **Keith Broom** and his team do a tremendous job at the **Royal Exchange**, in setting up for each piece in the manner each group requires. They could have provided everything that **The Falling** now had, so the additional features had come through the piece being more evolved rather than through improved facilities, which were in fact more basic: - what the dedicated festival technical team could set up in a medium-sized hotel events room, rather than in the fully-equipped studio theatre at the **Royal Exchange.**

There, the only item of scenery had been the large, orchestral harp and the stool for the player. **Amy Liptrot** has walked on to address it in a gown appropriate to any concert performance. For **The Falling**, we could see from the first, as we entered, that depression was the subject. She sat facing us in a low rocking chair, on the opposite side of the stage to her harp. Between them, on the back wall was a large abstract painting, of somewhat **Munch**-like character, evoking stress. Her face was expressionless, her eyes apparently unseeing but with large, dark shadows extending beneath them.

When she finally forced herself to her feet and made her way to her harp, she spoke clearly and precisely, after she tilted it towards her and prepared it for use: "The first thing I will do is … begin." There was a constant feeling of constraint. "You must keep going at all times" was a general injunction to herself which we heard later but there was a more particular imperative towards music: "I need to produce the sound. The silence will kill me."

The first music, on the harp, began with single notes, slowly developing into more complex patterns. The music most expressive of a mind stressed to breaking point, however, was *concrete,* sounding as if was being ripped out of circular saws. The piercing clarity as well as the impression that it was moving across the back of the room, behind the audience, showed that the festival technical team, here particularly **Peter Ellis** and **Gemma Carter**, were well above providing a bit of intro music and general lighting that did not wobble too much: They were capable of sophisticated effects of real power. The sound here evinced precisely what **Amy Liptrop** declared: "Everything fills me with fear."

Her words were always as simple as that in form, if not always so much so in meaning. The only means by which I assimilated the second half of the technician's summary of the meaning was an invocation of "Father … who does not remember my name." That seemed to be enough, in the absence of other nominees, to convey to me that he was the source of the distress but I did not assimilate anything much more explicit.

There were other words which were much less direct in meaning, indeed, for me, were more part of the general soundscape. These were poetry in the voice of **Ailis Ni Riain** herself and were part of the recorded sound. This could be brought down very quiet. After **Amy Liptrott** had finished playing the harp, she had a considerable struggle to complete the short return to her chair, eventually having to draw herself towards it on her knees, gripping on to it for some considerable time before she could haul herself into it. She spoke further works, at stages on her journey, but sometimes she was left to struggle on in virtual silence. Finally re-seating herself may have suggested that she had made some progress in overcoming her state of mind but it did not look as if she was out of the wood yet.

That this work should grow out of what we saw in **Blue** last year was a vindication of its policy of seeking to give us an early taste of interesting work in progress. It is likely and strongly to be hoped that more will be seen of most of this year's offerings

The thinnest gruel, especially when considered in comparison with her robust **Ammo (04:206)** last year or with her dramatisation of **The Baby and Fly Pie**, seen a few weeks before, was **Lavinia Murray**'s **Journey To The Centre of Your Mind.** This looked rather as if it might have been inspired by an impressively designed length of shiny cloth, with swirling patterns of red and black, in which both characters were dressed and which fitted well, in the manner of a rather cheesy form of science fiction, with presenting them as visitors from another planet.

This was not the first visual impression, as the scene began in the dark with the display of two whizzing and flashing electric hand toys, of the kind one can see being hawked up and down Princess Street after the theatres are closing to groups of merry young drinkers, passing from bar to bar. This was not an inappropriate context for the first line of dialogue, "What does a guy have to do to get a drink around here?" It was uttered by a robot (**Alex Murray**), perceived, as the lights came up, to be holding the toys and to have his rectangular frame covered in the striking cloth. As if in answer to his question, a jolly electric and radio-controlled insect came dashing on, with a squashed drinks tin on top. The robot made several clumsy but ultimately successful attempts to block off the insect and secure the can, then finding that there was precious little liquid to drain from it.

All this was quite amusing but proved not to lead onto anything very substantial. **Lavinia Murray** then entered, dressed in the same cloth but of far more human appearance. She announced them as visitors from a far more advanced civilisation, come to Save The Earth. Their means of doing so was to essay various feeble conjuring tricks: - identifying the colour of playing cards she had had ample opportunity to see, aspiring to make objects disappear, if our view of them was obscured by the robot for a sufficiently lengthy period of time. There can be humour in inept conjuring. usually, as **Tommy Cooper** repeatedly showed, if they can then be followed by something truly impressive. At least the mistakes should be sufficiently disastrous. Neither of these routes was attempted here. Gentleness and quietness were the tone, meant to imply unshakeable confidence by the visitors in their superior culture. To me it just seemed rather faltering. It did not sound as if a script had been written. A more effective, and witty, impression of being casual might have been created if it had. A nice idea for a show looked as if it was underdeveloped.

A far more effective quiet and apparently casual work was **Night Piece**. This was presented by **Hooh Hah Productions**, who appear to be an evolution from the group which presented **One-Eyed Houseguest (04:231)** at **24:7** last year and who have been touring their production of **Ubu** in the interval. I did not manage to see this, so do not know where it would have fitted on the continuum between **One-Eyed** and **Night Piece**, if there is one, both being completely different in style and performers. I am told the link is in the Director, **Tracy Gentles**, who would certainly seem to be capable of most diverse and interesting work. This began with the utmost apparent casualness and ended with effectively focused concentration.

Before any indication had been given to the audience to reconvene, the performer, (**Phillipa Jenkins**), had taken up her position at the side of the performance area. Her thumbs through the belt straps of her loose white trousers, she just stood listening to what we could hear, once we had been good enough to settle, was a quietly playing **Chopin Nocturne**. The general lighting did then slowly lower, to aid our concentration as well as hers. She rocked slightly on the balls of her bare feet and swayed a little. This was not a preliminary to other action, however. It was just an expression of how closely she was listening to the music. When there was a rapid trill, one could see the fingers on her hip quickly reproduce the keyboard movement which must have made it. Otherwise, there was no other movement until the end of the piece.

For the next **Nocturne,** she did become more balletic, both moving around the performance area and making use of a chair, onto which she climbed on occasion, often accompanied by sudden gasps. At the end of this piece, she mimed herself noticing the beginning of light rain. She raised an umbrella but, rather than this becoming occasion to do a **Gene Kelly**, she simply sat low under it on the chair at the side of the stage and watched the raindrops falling onto the surface of a pond, film of which was now beamed directly down onto the smooth, dance-mat, surface of the stage, as the final **Nocturne** was played. It was a simple but highly effective piece. Doubtless, we will have the chance to see future **Hooh Hah** productions and doubtless they will be completely different.

Fertile variety is the expectation which one now has of **Mishimou**, since they first showed themselves at **Arden** three years ago **(02:13)**. That **Rachael Ayres** and **Maria Ratcliffe** are highly talented actresses, as well as most inventive and agile puppeteers, increases the potential of their performances enormously. One might have thought a cast of this size more suited to the **Tamworth Two** than **The Three Little Pigs** but **Mishimou** are no more constrained by such unimaginative mathematics than **Jon Haynes** and **Angus Barr** were, as **Ridiculusmus**, from presenting **Three Men In A Boat ((04: 189)**, let alone that company's current duo taking all the parts in **The Importance of Being Earnest.**

In truth, the **Mishimou** piglets are less differentiated than those who, in better known versions of the tale, have distinct strategies for escaping the Huff and the Puff of the Big Bad Wolf. Here, their eventual predator is more characterised by the wheeze and the gasp. The two puppeteers, in their black costumes, bring on a life-size human puppet, whom they sit on a chair and operate from behind, as if he were an old man, gently if somewhat unevenly suspirating his way through an afternoon nap. The only unusual thing about his appearance is that, in place of a head, there appears to be a large, white conch shell. This situation is maintained for some while, until there is a sudden loud American cry of "Hi there!" from **Rachel Ayres** and the apparent shell leaps into the air, to reveal itself to be the bottom of an enormously long corcertinaed dress (a recurring design motif in the production). Its wearer continues, "Oh My Gard! Am I decent? What the Hell!", and indeed it did become apparent, if one was prurient enough to scrutinise closely, - the rest of the body, above the elongated dress, being comparatively small -, that there was no clothing on the top half of her not especially voluptuous torso. The figure on the chair said nothing and was not greatly responsive but did come to reach out a hand to her exposed chest, an interest she later reciprocated with attentions to other parts of his body. Before that, however, she exclaimed on a deficiency which I had supposed, since her entry into the action, that we were not supposed to notice: "My Gard! You've got no head!"

This was an omission which was, in fact, later made good. When he next appeared, he had a most distinctive physiognomy, which later allowed him to be very recognisable in silhouette, A small handle on his occiput, which she placed in her mouth, assisted **Maria Ratcliffe** in partnering him in a most elegant and affectionate dance, he wearing slippers long enough to accommodate her feet as well as his and her original method of guiding his head not being so unalterable that the embrace could be changed to become cheek-to cheek.

He was the eventual devourer of the Little Pigs. They were first perceived some way into the action, as finger puppets in silhouette, swarming over **Maria Ratcliffe**'s body like kittens. Their end was to be seen ladled into the saucepan of the old man, as he prepared his meal.

There were various other incidents along the way, none of them having an obvious place in a narrative but all of them displaying major talents in imagination, making and performance of which we must hope to see more.

The two performance poets we saw are, I believe, regularly to be heard at the many venues around Greater Manchester which now present such work. .**Matthew Panesh** made great play of coming on with a beer bottle and cigarette and wearing a T-Shirt which was both vulgar and scruffy, although he, in fact, made noticeably little use of his hand props. The title of his first work, I Killed The Fucking Fucker's Son, was a fair specimen of the argot he chose to use but the substance of what he writes is far from exclusively decadent. The conclusion of this piece was "You Can Use The Bible To Prove Anything." The narrator had left his place of work after being irritated by a colleague, gone to his home and killed his child. He then claims that this is exactly comparable with the way God is said to have punished David after his first fling with Bathsheba. He had another Biblical commentary later, which was rather more sympathetic, and, although his pieces were mainly tirades against numerous contemporary prejudices, he did not source many of these to scripture. Vulgar and vernacular though his works may be, they are genuinely poems, using rhythmic language to powerful effect.

Some address matters of no particular general importance. "Who the bloody hell was With?" was his conclusion to an attempt to parse the Anglo-Saxon roots of Withington, his claimed place if residence. Usually, however, his tone was crusading, ending with a piece that was specifically programmatic. He found that even the very young are demanding such interventions as nose jobs. He appealed for the acceptance of naturally-shaped bodies.

Presenting his performance under the title **The Poetry of Matty P**, one might have expected **Matthew Panesh** to come from a particular ethnic background. He does not but one important respect in which **Blue3** was far more representative of Manchester than **24:7** was the fact that the latter seemed almost entirely to be presented by Persons of Pure European Descent. As is shown by this article alone, regardless of the remainder of the contents of this book, in almost any edition, dozens of creators of new work, whether as writers or performers, as well as among our general citizenry, have recent ancestry in other continents. They would be well qualified to take part in **24:7** but seem not, either this year or last, to have successfully chosen to do so. The organisers might wish to ask themselves how this has come about.

The one performer I spotted in **24:7** who fell outside the description I have given had a part which could have been taken by anyone. This is fine. One important characteristic of the way many people from different backgrounds live here is that they do so in the way everybody else does. That said, all of those who contributed to **Blue3** at the **Royal Exchange** made some reference to difference of background and in most cases this was central. [It might also be worth noting that **Sharif Samad**, whose origins are said to be Anglo-Egyptian, in **Write2** made a far better stab in **Pictures of Clay** than most people with a far longer ancestry here could manage of portraying a plausible Seventeenth Century Lancashire and his portrait of contemporary white youth in **Carol (04: 203)** was as persuasive as any, although his particular background may have been of value in **Pictures …** in bringing out the significance for today].

Having different contributors, also made for significantly different audiences. **Sonia Hughes** made one of the shortest contributions to **Blue3**, a single poem of only modest length, introduced by a brief video. I have no doubt, however, that it was on her account that there was a very substantial Black presence in the audience, which had not been present on the previous day. [She has already encouraged such customers to find their way to the **Royal Exchange** with her sold-out major work **Weeding Cane (04:476,** cf **03:20)**, which is to return next January]. **Peppered Moth**, her poem, very specifically addressed the race issue, the finely speckled moth representing for her the experience of growing up in East Anglia when Black faces were very rare, from **The Three Little Golliwogs** being the story naturally read in Nursery School to exchanging the intimate answers with her Best Friend at sixteen to the question "Do I look pretty?", in her case receiving the reply "I suppose so, for a Black." In the Swinging London of 1968, being Black had been the height of *chic* but later experiences had been less positive. It was not been until she visited the Caribbean in 1990 that she found, swimming in the ocean waters, that she just naturally blended into the landscape.

Ike (**Marcus Hercules**) in **Vent,** in many ways is living just like any other student in the local university where the play is set, - there for a good time, comparable *mores* -, although singing distinctively Black music in the lavatory cubicle when we first become aware of him and apparently referring to himself on occasion as "Nigger." We did not hear him do this in the extracts from the play which were shown but learnt of it when Adam (**Jarrod Cooke**), the Fresher whom he has taken under his wing, assumes it would be correct to address him amiably in the same terms.

This is only a side issue in the scenes we saw. What seemed likely to be the central circumstance of the full play, - which has, apparently been written and booked to appear at **Contact** next year - , is that the new academic year is beginning in the context of there having been a significantly vicious date rape the previous term. This is not a focus I would be over enthusiastic to see but certainly the scenes we saw had a well sustained character and wit, which made for very attractive theatre indeed, for realising which qualities a very able cast had been recruited, who performed without scripts, unlike the other major drama items in **Blue3.**

The staging was effectively simple, **Keith Broom** simply being required to run a white diagonal line of tape down the middle of the performance area, to indicate the line of the washbasins in the men's and women's lavatories on either side, beside which the great majority of the scenes took place, sometimes simultaneously. In the odd scene which took place in a tutorial room, the line could simply be ignored.

We saw events both from the student perspective, **Elianne Byrne** and **Claire Beasdale** being the Fresher and the Second Year on the female side of things, and from the staff, where the re-action of Nick (**Jonathon Finlay**) to the events of the previous year has been not only to commission enhanced lighting around halls of residence but to load the Freshers' Handbook with severe advice about female students not leaving social occasions alone or with a single male companion, whereas Connie (**Alexandra Btesh**) regards this as positively Victorian: many female students, like she herself, positively want to be sexually active and it is ridiculous to try and place too many handicaps in the way of their being so. All this was expressed in most lively dialogue and the chance to see the full play, written and directed by **Chris Wright**, is something to be anticipated.

The race issue is well to the fore in **Harriott and I.** From her name, I would guess **Sandra Yaw** to be of Ghanaian origin, although many, such as **Kwame Kwei-Armah**, adopt such names even when their precise genealogy is ambiguous. The chief process by which these came to be obscured is central to this play.

At its opening we meet Harriot (**Laurietta Essien**), clearly in the role of a house slave during the Eighteenth Century, in one of the more southerly British colonies in North America. She is singing, as she sweeps, in what I took to be Ga. Her Owna (**Bill Ward**) enters, oppressed by the fact that another slave has been found to have hanged himself in the woods. He asks Harriott why this should be, which she tells him he ought to know. He is obviously ill at ease with the way he makes his wealth and also, we learn later, with the fact that he is not making enough of it: his losses are not vast but without profits he can never pay off the debts of his plantation.

He is obviously living on intimate terms with Harriot and she does have affection for him. She is ready to comfort him by such means as washing his feet and reading to him from the Bible, probably not meaning to be too pointed in selecting **I Corinthians 13** and using the term Love, rather than Charity, as most available texts would then have done, for the central virtue described. He disregards the depths in these feelings, however, by telling her, without considering these to be an issue, that the way in which he proposes to solve his commercial difficulties is to marry the daughter of a prosperous business associate in Bristol, whose dowry will be more than sufficient to put the plantation back onto a sound economic footing. Harriot is clearly most upset but simply withdraws submissively and we now hear from the intended bride, Frances (**Kate Ford**), who regards the way she is to be treated as most insulting and has no intention of going along with it.

There was then what seemed at first a very strange development. She removed a layer of clothing, so that she now appeared to be dressed trimly for the present day, and began to sing **The Girl From Ipanema.** **Bill Ward** rejoined the action, his costume also adjusted to being a contemporary T-Shirt. He sat attentively at the far side of the stage and then took up the tune on a clarinet. **Kate Ford** concluded the song by modifying the final verse to be the Man from Ipanema.

It became apparent that they were lovers. As he embraced her, the man, now Jack, explained how difficult he had come to find life with his wife: she was always so intense and you couldn't just run your hand freely through her hair, as he now did with Jasmin. He is thinking of leaving his wife for her.

This wife (Sarah, **Laurietta Essien**) now enters abruptly. She scarcely notices how intimately close Jack and Jasmin are standing, as she is totally pre-occupied with just having been dismissed from her work as a teacher. She is convinced that her students need to know about the horrors of The

Middle Passage and has carried out a reconstruction by cramming them into as confined a space as they would have experienced in the hold of a slave ship. The school has deemed this inappropriate but she has emphatically stuck to her guns: that this is something her pupils need to know. Jack (Jasmine has left) is not antagonistic but does not provide much comfort as he takes the same view as the school: these were terrible events but they were a long time ago and we don't need to bother about them any more. Sarah is outraged. Is this really what he thinks? Yes. Then he should go, right now. Without any particular indication that this is what he had been wanting to do anyway. Jack agrees. He will come back for his things later, but as a first instalment he picks up the pair of top boots which the Owna had thrown to the floor at his first entry. Sarah is left alone, emotionally exhausted. A double reason for her sorrow is that what she had been wanting to tell Jack on her arrival was that she was expecting their child. It had been her deliberate choice to conceive a child with a white father. The future nature of that fatherhood had now been thrown into doubt.

It was not all that apparent in performance quite how these scenes from different centuries were meant to be linked together, not that this mattered very much as we were so consistently held by the strength of the performances that we did not have to seek interpretation. The blurb in the programme suggests that we saw a slightly different selection of scenes from those originally planned and that the method of the link, - the thematic ties were multiple, manifest and fruitful -, was that, if not on the same property, at least furnishing from the old plantation house had been bought for the new and this provided a spiritual link which had made Sarah aware of the earlier Harriot. How that would play out in full, I would not know. What is very apparent is that the work is a creation of great perceptiveness and drama, with a freshness of imagining the past and providing very strong acting opportunities for a talented cast.

The subject matter is closely allied to that searingly dealt with by **Neil LaBute** in **This Is How It Goes.** I had not been aware of his existence until **The Distance From Here (02: 495)** came to the **Lowry** three years ago. I was not particularly impressed by that and thought no more of him until this year. Now, having seen a sizeable part of **Bash**, incorporated into **Aspects' When Medea Met Elvis (18),** and the current work, I see him as a very formidable playwright.

This Is How It Goes is not exactly a revenge play but, as with the **Medea**-like conflict of **Bash**, it does show ancient jealousies being pursued by an elaborate plot in the present. If that is the form, the theme is very definitely race. This is not just related to Cody (**Idris Elba**) being Black. Even if he had not been a character, the facility with which The Man (**Ben Chaplin**) introduces terms like "indentured servant" and "playing the race card" into his language would be biting. How deeply this is ingrained is hard to tell. We learn that some of his talk is deliberate and that relations between him and Cody are closer than we might have thought but even as a facsimilation the picture would be deeply disturbing. Even in regard to Race, the Man's apparent attitudes would seem not to be all part of his plot and, taken with the ruthless degree to which he is prepared

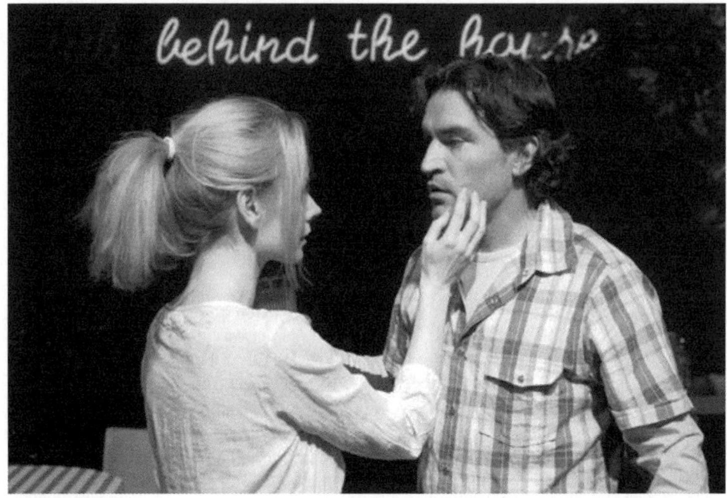

THIS IS HOW IT GOES (224); MEGAN DODDS and BEN CHAPLIN

to manipulate The Woman (**Megan Dodds**), build up a very unpleasant portrait indeed. Even if The Man thinks that his objectives are best for her, as well as himself, the view that this is for him to decide and that her destiny his to be determined by contrivances of which she is to be kept in ignorance is fundamentally as contemptuous as the views implied on race.

It is a very, very fearsome portrait, executed with great skill. As with **Bash**, much of the tale is conveyed through direct narration to the audience but from the first he advises us "I may be An Unreliable Narrator." And some. He gives us two versions of one scene under the guise, "Well, I wasn't there, so I don't know exactly what happened." Later, when a remark is made directly to him, he turns to us and says "Did she really say that? No. I can't believe she really said that." Such distortions are as nothing compared with the fundamental mendacity of his approach. But, if we cannot be certain of any detail, we do know the general terms of discourse and there is plenty of pity and terror just in seeing them worked out, the more so because there is evidence in the programme that the play is presenting a very definite reality. A news report is reprinted of events last April, well after the play was written, in a very similar mid-West small town community. The issues are the same. The deviousness of the plot made in real life was the same. This <u>Is</u> How It Goes.

That Race is an issue in **Iron** is much less explicit. The fact that the daughter, in this splendid production, is played by the magnificent **Rachel Brogan**, who has some Caribbean ancestry, is no

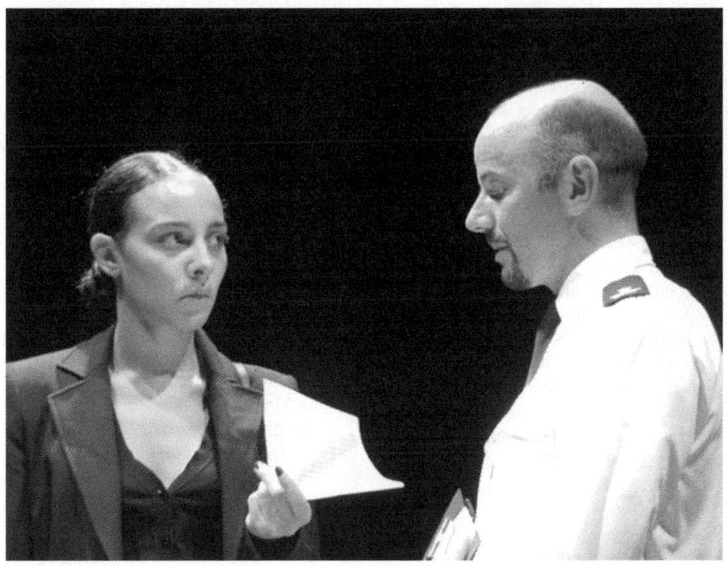

IRON (256); Josie (RACHEL BROGAN) seeks to discover her mother and herself; JAMES LOWEas the Prison Officer.

evidence at all that her character has a Black father. In the current conventions of the British stage, she can properly play anyone. She is not Scots but in her speech in this play gives a formidably accurate impression of being one. I did not pick up any conclusive information, that the character's father, and the Grandmother who had largely brought her up, were Black but what was said of them was entirely consistent with this, - which is, admittedly, a very different matter -, and I had the impression that there were enough indications that they actually were.

Whether or not this was the case, it was good characterisation to make it seem so. The core of the play was the present. It begins with Josie (**Rachel Brogan**) turning up at a prison, wanting to see her mother. This causes some amazement to the staff (**James Lowe** and **Samantha Power**), as never, over the previous fifteen years, has anyone wanted to see this life-sentence prisoner (Fay, / **Joan Kempson**). Most of the following scenes are in the Visitors Room and with the humiliating searches which precede and follow them, with occasional intervening scenes in Fay's cell, - at one end of the basic traverse space used -, the prison garden, - at the other -, or in the staff room.. The main performance space is essentially bare, with just a couple of chairs, whose position is moved between scenes, so that we see the visits from different angles. The lack of privacy was well evoked by the director, **Cheryl Martin**, through having the staff constantly patrolling but without this disrupting our focus on Fay and Josie, by having them often pacing behind the rows of the audience.

Josie's first motivation, after having grown up as a successful professional but now with a short marriage behind her, is to see the mother, of whom she has no real memories and to learn something of the father, of whom she remembers nothing at all. Fay takes some pleasure in helping her to recover these but has a deep manipulative streak. She has no interest in the healthful baskets of fruit which Josie regularly brings. She is far more interested in cigarettes, not primarily to smoke them but because they are good tradable items within the prison walls. Even more so are pills. By the beginning of the second act, Josie is willing to try and smuggle these in to her. What Fay wants even more is for Josie to be able to tell her about the life she would like to be living but can never have again: going to pubs, picking up men, eventually to supply her with grandchildren. Josie finds this distasteful. She would far rather apply herself to getting Fay's sentence reviewed. She is confident that she can achieve this, as she has never failed in anything which she has set herself to do, but Fay is not willing to revisit the painful circumstances in which she killed Josie's father.

All four actors are supremely able and have worked together before. Focussing on them interacting in a confined studio setting made for very intensive drama. Interacting, except, very closely, with the audience, was not a facility open to **Rani Moorthy** in her **Curry Tales**, as this was a solo performance, although one might scarcely have noticed because of the diversity of characters whom she presents. As the seventh of these expresses it: to tell the story of where curry is prepared is a major History and Geography lesson. Its panorama includes situations in which racial divisions are still crucial, from the deadly circumstance of a wife of mixed Indian and Chinese descent being imprisoned in her kitchen and unable to escape during Muslim riots in Malaysia, to the social tensions of the middleclass wife of a white husband in Britain having to improvise an appropriate evening meal for her Methodist in-laws, when they come for their annual dose of multiculturalism, because the husband has failed to carry out the shopping tasks which, in their supposedly egalitarian household, have been entrusted to him.

Some of these countries were evoked with a preliminary burst of film but more often the screen included in the ingenious set was used to show, through a camera placed vertically overhead, how cooking was being conducted on the on-stage stove, in a manner appropriate to the culture being shown, whether this was by a Carnival Demon in Trinidad or Doromi, the Hindu Kitchen God, accompanied by Sita. The product of these preparations was passed around for the audience to sample, but this was not the only occasion for 'their' space to be invaded. A dirt poor Malay street woman climbed all over the seats, searching for any possible sustenance, leading my neighbour to ask me to secrete her handbag, lest she turn her attention to this, which I promptly returned when the housewife in England, improvising her egg-curry was provoked by handling this ingredient to reminisce about how medical examination during her adolescence had revealed that she would always be childless, a tale told so movingly that my neighbour needed the wherewithal to dry her tears. There was thus a tremendous range of mood as well as cultures. The funniest episode had been at the beginning, when the affluent Mrs Dimple swept on in a glittering sari to address a distinguished New Delhi audience on how Curry was a central part of world culture. The predominant tone throughout was jovial but tears and terrors were traversed on the route.

About a third of the plays in **24:7** were solo performances, although, with the partial exception of **Lazy Daze**, none of these presented a range of characters, nor of mood. There weren't many laughs in **I'm Frank Morgan** and there wasn't much pity and terror in **The First Rule of Comedy**, even though its character (Gillian Ferrari, **Sue Jaynes**) spent most of it scared witless.

The lack of wit, in a more specific sense, was deliberate. Gillian Ferrari is making her first appearance as a stand-up and doing it very badly. The action alternates between her performance and expressions of desperation at how it is going and that she had ever attempted it. The plus point is that this provides scope for an absolutely tremendous performance by **Sue Jaynes.** Apparently the first section of this

THE FIRST RULE OF COMEDY (229); SUE JAYNES.

was an improvisation, as she unexpectedly had to fight with the microphone-stand, to reduce it to a height more appropriate to her stature. This was as good a part of the show as any other, in fact, in some ways rather better.

The big risk which was associated with the production was that the greater part of the script had to be made up of very unfunny jokes. That is pretty barren territory for an audience. I wondered why one of those associated with the production confided to me afterwards that, as I heard it, “She missed out two jokes”. I thought “What is two among so many, especially jokes like that?” A later visitor to the show told me that he was still going on about this the next day, saying, in her version “She missed out two pages on the first night.” This might have made a bigger difference but I rather doubt if it did.

There was obvious occasion for there to be more variation in the play but I did not find that there was. After her first, - disastrous -, set, Gillian Ferrari reappeared, quite differently dressed, apparently now some twenty years later, as a patient in a clinic. She told us that after her first attempt to be a comedian “at some scruffy pub in Salford” (were they originally thinking of presenting this at **The King’s Arms**?), she had not given up, as she has intended, but struggled on, usually with an appalling lack of success and a fair amount of alcohol. She had eventually ended up in her secure institution after a widely seen attack, brilliantly mimed, on a distinguished television presenter, with a three-inch-pronged kitchen fork, which she had just happened to have in her handbag.

Before this she had tried to improve her act by establishing a couple of comedy characters, of which we only saw one; (was this the omission?). This was a Blodwen Evans, splendidly established with an archetypal ‘Welsh’ look, whose act was to describe how the numerous Blodwens Evans in her village distinguished themselves by additional soubriquets, denoting their stereotypical Welsh activities.. This was not any more funny than the material with which she began her career, nor could it be, as this had apparently continued as consistently unsuccessful as it had begun.

There could be a good drama, exploring the character of a consistently poor performer. This was not it; we saw too little of the off-stage life and feelings. The overture to **Last Turn of the Night** and **Half Heaven, Half Heartache** showed that it is even possible to get good fun out of a poor ‘performance’ but we did not really get that here. There was a lot that was impressive about the way that **Sue Jaynes** showed her character battling on but there is more scope for finding amusement in a failing singer than in failing jokes and the stream of these here had to be kept going far longer than the songs in the contrasting examples given. It was a play that gave a certain amount of amusement and the performance was well worth seeing but the contents, in some way, needed to be made far more robust to turn it into a real drama.

No lack of drama in **I’m Frank Morgan.** I failed to assimilate quite why he found his final evil deed far harder to live with than the many he had done before. The fact that it increased his ill repute would scarcely signify. One of his first lines is “The people round here hate me.” The rider to this, however, is “But in the end, they always need me.”

He is a loan shark on a fearsome estate, brilliantly evoked in **Jo Carlon**’s backdrop, showing two tall, grey, irregular tower blocks, collapsing towards each other, separated by a jagged, blood-red

I'M FRANK MORGAN (235); JOE O'BYRNE

fissure through the grey sky. The title he likes, suggesting to him the gallant and powerful self-sufficiency of such as the Lone Ranger.

In the first part of his performance he tells of the circumstances in which his ability to supply large sums at short notice is in recurrent demand and how providing this service is absolutely dependent on rigorous enforcement of the agreed timetable of repayment and interest. After stepping aside to relieve himself in the Gents, again represented by a distinctive piece of **Jo Carlon** art work, he tells us of the scientific principles upon which he can always determine if anyone is attempting to deceive him: he knows the fraction of a second in different speeds at which the separate halves of the brain work and so can always detect any discrepancy between them in the face.

Despite this he had failed to enforce a critical repayment exactly enough to enable him to go to a critical poker session with enough thousands in his pocket to triumph in a game against a critical opponent: a rival shark from the opposite side of the estate. That, I would have thought, would have been a more unprecedented blow to his standing than the unanticipated severity of the outcome to his revenge against his defaulter. However that may be, **Joe O'Byrne**, certainly gave a riveting performance in his own composition. It was a strong drama and all the more so because the mean streets in which it was set were persuasively portrayed as a part of our reality.

The other solo performance was **Salad Olvay** (a concoction which seems to be unknown to the dictionary or to the internet, except in the context of advertising this production). It is the solace of Miriam (**Mary-Ann Coburn**), who finds that, despite the intricacy of its ingredients, she can buy it extremely cheaply on Stockport Road. It is not that she lacks for exotic food, as her husband Gareth delights in all

SALAD OLVAY (237); MARY-ANN COBURN

manner of preparations: the one activity to which he devotes an extensive amount of time at home between the employment he so ardently embraces, at a call centre dedicated to giving after-sales advice to purchasers of kitchen equipment, on varied recipes with which they can get full value out of their new apparatus. Once he is done in the kitchen, he then collapses in front of the television. The Salad Olvay is Miriam's one chance to eat something not from his cuisine. She does this on the night he goes for his interminably long series of computer training classes.

She does not strictly need to buy food economically as, although she only works on a supermarket check-out, which also gives her staff discounts, they not only have enough spare household income for her to buy quite extensively from her friend Winsome's catalogue items which she does not strictly need, - but who else has she to talk to? -, and they could have bought a computer, which would have helped him get through his course long ago, but he, having internalised the values of his employers, on the importance of incentives to complete units of work, has decided to make this purchase his reward for passing.

Once that day has come, she sees even less of him, as his acquisition from **PC World** goes straight into the spare bedroom and he with it, never to emerge thereafter, save to go to work. Miriam is not convinced, however, that its sacred mysteries are such that she would need as long as he to master them and a little application in his absence leads her to gain access to the internet. Through a chat room she establishes contact with Carl, whom she invites to the house when Gareth's dedication to his work leads to his being selected for a one-week residential course, as a preliminary to promotion. Despite Gareth's frequent telephone calls, providing a running commentary on every aspect of the catering, from breakfast to late night tea and biscuits, they have plenty of time to enjoy themselves.

She also visits him in his bedsit, which he is conscious is infinitely less well appointed than her trim home. He puts it to her directly that this must be a reason why she could never consider leaving to come to live with him and she concedes this to be the case. In an hilariously described scene she discovers that his plan to correct this deficiency is to try to shop-lift the quite bulky items he takes to be the talismans of her superior life-style from the supermarket where she works. This is at the week-end, when she is present in the store as a customer, with Gareth, using her discount but she is called over when Carl is apprehended because, at their first assignation, she had told her colleagues that she was being picked up after work by her cousin. Events lead to Carl behaving so demonstratively that he is carried away to a secure institution and to Gareth, having become aware of the situation, carrying away his computer to his mother's. [A recent **Abbey National** survey, - they having an interest in our domestic arrangements -, has shown that when marriages break up, the man typically lays claim to the computer and the woman the house, so this and **Cocktails With Natalie**, presented as a sister piece, - both, though by different authors, being directed by **SusanTwist -**, would seem in this respect to be socially accurate.]

Miriam has presented her tale in a comparatively light-hearted fashion. It ends with a sudden expression of despair but not of such a nature as to provide a keenness which might have been dramatically strong. She has found that the shop where she used to buy her Salad Olvay has closed down and that the new proprietors have no intention of continuing supply. She has purchased what she takes to be the ingredients and is endeavouring to formulate them while she tells us the final elements of her story. Then, she abruptly breaks off and inverts her cooking bowl over her head.

Outright slapstick did not seem an appropriate ending and it did not come over as just that. Taking the edge off a sharp act of desperation might have seemed more in tune with the generally jolly tone but in that case why bother with it at all? There had been enough included to show that more painful elements were present than a Chauccrian tale of a housewife finding the A Little of What She Fancied had not Done Her as much Good as she expected. In particular, one of the main things Miriam had not been able to discuss with Gareth as much as she would have wished had been the possibility of their having children. She had assumed, during their not especially hasty courtship that these would be a natural consequence of marriage. He had not. The stratagem of surreptitiously ceasing to take the pill was not open to her because she was not on it: Gareth always insisted on donning his own protection. This practice had continued during most of her sessions with Carl but she had then told us in some detail of how, when he had been leaving in some disappointment at having to be out of the house before Gareth returned from his residential course, they had suddenly been overcome by passion and this had led to unprotected sex in the front porch. This could have led to a pregnancy which might have been an acerbic, and very appropriate, element in the final circumstances. Instead, it just seemed to be a plot element that led nowhere. The play was an entertainingly performed little narrative, with several enjoyable perceptions. I felt that it could have been built into a stronger drama but the author chose otherwise.

Several plays in the festival addressed marriage relationships. **Lovesick** was even set as much among guidance counsellors as anywhere else but, after a lively opening address by **Tracy Daly** from a flipchart, on the diverse meanings of Love, the whole thing seemed to me to be knocked completely widdershins. I could not perceive any consistent way to view its various elements. I don't know where it was going or where it got to.

White Wedding dwelt among untrodden ways to much greater effect. It was set in a remote rural farmhouse as a party arrived because they hoped the priest in the local church could conduct a somewhat unorthodox wedding in decent obscurity. This is not, however, because the intended marriage is of little importance to those involved or of no social significance to those who will be present. Katie (**Helena Coates**) has religious beliefs and is strongly committed to marrying Al, because she believes his declaration that he wants to spend the rest of his life with her. She finds this compatible with frequently having sexual involvements with innumerable other men and knowing that Al does the same. She believes that this is fundamental human nature which it is folly to deny or resist. Resisting inclinations is not in her book. She already has teenage children. Her son Tom (**Darren Beaumont**) has been promised that he can attend as her bridesmaid and her youngest daughter (Jo-Jo, **Karen McDonagh**) refuses to attend unless she can do so not only in a suit but also in a moustache. Katie thinks it would be wrong to repress either aspiration.

Her best friend Gemma (**Kiney Bailes**) is of entirely contrary opinion. She believes that social conventions should be observed because we need them. When Katie asks her what she would do if she found her husband unfaithful she first of all makes the reply which is conventional in many female circles today: "Cut his balls off." When Katie asks her for a little more reality, she replies that she would leave him: there is no point in marriage if we do not play by the rules. Nevertheless, she is there not only as a friend but for her skills a s a beautician, not only to prepare Katie as a bride adorned for her husband but to convert Tom into a bridesmaid. (The actual work on this was done off-stage by **Julie Becque**, for which she receives a special programme credit, the second make-up team in this group of works to do so, **Fiona Shaw** and **Sean at Pee Wees**, also being appropriately acknowledged for creating the looks and hairstyle of Gina Pitney in **Half Heaven, Half Heartache.**)

The central dialectic on the relationship of fidelity to marriage is scarcely new but presumably will always need to be re-argued. What was really fresh was some of the wit. When Katie dilates at some length on how, at her last meeting with Al, they used the various contents of the

WHITE WEDDING (240); That's the Bridesmaid in the centre(Tom, DARREN BEAUMONT), made up to look the part by Gemma (KINEY BAILES, right, above); the bride is his mum (Katie, HELENA COATES, left above); her other two children are Jo-Jo and Cas (KAREN McDONAGH and DEBBIE SALOMAN, front, left and right).

supper table for Enhanced Sexual Pleasure, Gemma replies "I'm not coming to tea at your house!" When Jo-Jo is cutting up, demanding a moustache in which to go to the wedding, she tells her "You can borrow mine." I am not sure that the bizarre aspects of these relationships could not have been heightened in action to greater comic effect but presumably there was not a wish to remove them too far from either real emotional commitments or the way that some people actually do live.

More widely observed marital customs are behind **Hook, Line and Sinker.** It may be that Carl (**Scott Bradley**) has found it very difficult to sustain a stable relationship, - never formalised as a marriage -, or to hold down a regular job partly as a result of never feeling he was in his own home. His father had died when he was young and when his mother re-married he felt that he was not treated as so central to the family as her child by her new husband. Trevor (**Mike Woodhead**, the author) insists that his dad always made every effort to be a true father to Carl but Carl has never felt it to be this way. This may be because he never found fishing to be anything other than utterly boring whereas Trevor had taken to it with great enthusiasm, not only joining his father on his numerous fishing trips but naturally stepping into his shoes in running his tackle shop,

The main reason Carl is with him this evening on the canal bank is that he regards it as his duty to be with him on what he regards as his stag night, although he finds it hard to identify this as the real thing, saying there is still time for them to go out to the airport and buy tickets to Amsterdam, although this would clearly be at Trevor's expense, as Carl is on the dole.

The impending wedding is not the only occasion for Carl's return home from his unsuccessful life in Leeds. Although this is still to go ahead, it has been abruptly preceded by the sudden death of Trevor's father and they have both just been to the funeral. What drives Trevor to dementia, however, is the discovery that Carl has persuaded their Mum

HOOK, LINE AND SINKER (225); Bait, and all other aspects of fishing are a fascination for Trevor (MIKE WOODHEAD, left); not so for Carl (SCOTT BRADLEY0.

that the management of the tackle business, now in her name, should be shared between her two sons. Carl does not know the first thing about it but does desperately need a steady job.

This summary has endeavoured to give a reasonably coherent picture of the family relationships. A major factor in making this very skilfully constructed play fascinating to watch was the way this general picture emerged naturally, piece by piece in the course of events. It did not find that it had to fill everything in and it was entirely successful in holding us with the credible experience of watching two people who obviously had particular concerns and reasons for acting as they did, although we, for long enough, did not know much about what these might be.

The heart of it all, however, was family. This play was outside the **24:7** umbrella, having its main sights on **Edinburgh.** The close relationships in various of the other **24:7** works, however , were outside such formal bounds. Neither **Milk** nor **Vodka Knickers** were realistic works, although they would probably both claim that they are by no means divorced from the way we love now. **Milk** was predominantly comic, **Vodka** mysterious. Neither title was especially central to the action, although linked to it. As a result of a dodgy takeaway meal, milk had been the only drink **Rob Clyne**'s character had been able to stomach the second time he had met that played by **Anna Baatz:** the beginning of the love affair which is just breaking up as the play commences. Vodka Knickers was the name of the preferred beverage of the two lovers (Orla, **Sarah Ibbotson** and Jax **Cat Murphy**) whose relationship seemed to me as if it was meant to be central to the play.

The reason I express this somewhat uncertainly is that there were two other characters (Debs, **Alyx Tole** and Pete, **Julian Waite**), whose scenes took up a comparable amount of time. I did not really see how their experiences inter-related. Perhaps they were meant to be more of the earth, earthy whilst Orla and Jax were of the life-giving spirit. Water and Air are the elements of which we are most conscious, as the action is set on a windy and wave-dashed Scottish islet, whose basic rock the earthiest character, Debs, does not find at all congenial. She wants to

VODKA KNICKERS (234); Orla (SARAH IBBOTSON, left) dreams of being reunited with the spirit of her dead friend Jaz(CAT MURPHY, right) on the west coast Scottish island. The dream of Debs (ALYX TOLE, centre) is to get to a good warm pub.

head for the shelter and company of a good warm pub as quickly as possible. Pete, an accountant, who is only just returning to work after months at home with nervous stress, is far happier to be out alone but does not have the head for heights to handle the situation when he finds that he has trapped himself on an exposed cliff-face. He is at least equipped with an electric torch but this, despite a surprisingly strong closing speech, scarcely makes him a fiery character.

The reason they are all on Port Barry is that Orla, now a hospital cleaner but formerly a nurse, has suggested it as a destination for a staff weekend outing. Her motive for this is that she hopes to be able to recapture her relationship with Jax, whose life she had used her medical skills to end there in a cave, when Jax had begged for this conclusion to her incurable disease. She had fallen in love with her at her bedside when a patient and the trauma of killing her had ended her medical career. She does re-experience the spirit of Jax but is uncertain whether recapturing the memories was something it had been wise to attempt.

There was a lot which I found was intriguing about this strange tale although the Debs / Pete elements seemed to me more of a distraction than a complement.

Unusualness was more a source of comedy than mystery in **Milk** and I enjoyed its peculiar wit. It began with its four characters singing a single tone but then **Rob Clyne**, at the keyboards, burst into a finely voiced solo addressed to **Anna Baatz**, running through all the clichés about how much her love had meant to him and how he would be lost without her. It looked like she was leaving him anyway and was not particularly perturbed about it. The principle of item of scenery was a double bed, not to indicate that everybody who co-habited slept together but primarily to show that we were in a world of shared bedsits, while, turned about, it could be converted into such locales as a canoe in Platt Fields Boating Lake.

The first residence we saw was that shared by **Anna Baatz** and **Cathy Shiel** (the co-authors). **Anna**'s dose of retail therapy (she has a penchant for anything pink, dressed in it from cap to toe) has not been to ease her departure from **Rob**, which she takes very much in her stride. The one who is discomposed is **Cathy**, who sees problems in that the direction in which **Anna** has turned her affections is not only a mutual friend of all of them but actually the room-mate of **Rob, James Shakeshaft.** He is quite frank that his interest in **Anna** is minimal. He regards her as a good lay, an occasional interval in his real pre-occupations as an artist, dabbing paint onto canvasses, but no more. This made it very odd that, in a play punctuated by musical interludes which usually seemed extremely apt, the final one of these should have been **Shakeshaft** guying I Can't Get No Satisfaction. His appearances had generally shown him to be a man who knew what he wanted and usually got it.

While they were enjoying their liaisons, **Rob** and **Cathy** were sharing their sorrows on the Boating Lake, he still disconsolate at the loss of **Anna**, she more or less resigned to her dumpy appearance putting her outside the mating game, seeing the ducks on the lake, - who are in fact most elegant creatures -, as expressive of her ungainly waddle. In fact, the play ends with **Rob** bringing her a present which, when unwrapped, proves to be a plastic bathroom duck, presumably signifying his readiness to be her soul mate. When **Anna** had come to him slightly before, declaring magnanimously that she had decided to take him back, he had to tell her that, despite his earlier declarations of undying love, in the time they had been apart he had found his feelings had moved on.

His profession was that of a stand-up comic and although the couple of excerpts we saw of him plying his trade had not been much funnier than those in **The First Rule of Comedy** they had been more dramatically interesting as

MILK (228); ROB CLYNE got the show off to a strong start with his skills as a singer as well as on the keyboards.

they had seemed to show him reworking his experiences with **Anna.** As the first of these was while he was still apparently cut to the quick, I was not too sure how to take these. Were they part of the process by which he came to realise that he could live without her or were they an example of the often remarked symbiosis between the Clown and Hamlet?

I suspect that the play was not really aspiring to address such questions rigorously and was just having fun by looking aslant at contemporary forms of young love. As such I thought that it had a very pleasant zany humour , ably realised in performances which let its quiet wit shine through..

A sometimes similar humour was used to much more serious effect in **Now Breathe Out** by **Rob Johnston.** It begins with a GP (**Adam Lacy**) staring at the groin of a young man (**Lane Paul Stewart**). He does so for quite some time and then pronounces that he thinks it is just a cyst. Nevertheless, he judges that it is best for the young man to see an expert. "I thought you were an expert." "I'm a GP. I see the broad picture. A specialist sees the fine detail." "Irrelevant detail." "No. Never irrelevant." The specialist (also **Adam Lacy**) finds there is cancer in his testicle and wants to operate. He shouldn't worry: "The survival rates are quite high." He does worry. He is operated upon, - successfully. He needs to go for some more tests, scans, … "But I thought that was it?" "No. We need to make sure it hasn't spread, no secondary infections."

The round from clinic to clinic and inspection to inspection did convey a reality but it was not presented realistically. His antagonism towards the doctor for bringing this upon him was expressed by his drawing a sword from the umbrella stand and fencing with him, the fear at his prospects increased by his encounters with the young woman of his own age (**Nicola Gaskell**) whom he meets in the queues at clinics, who knows she definitely has only three months to live. Sometimes she faces this quite cheerfully, sometimes not. Her appearance certainly deteriorates as she undergoes therapy. She dons a death mask and becomes a figure playing poker with the similarly masked surgeon at his bedside.

Eventually, he is told he is completely in the clear and will live as long as anyone else. He does not know how to express his gratitude to the surgeon, to whom he knows he has often been abrupt. He shakes him by the hand,

NOW BREATHE OUT (238); That his doctor (ADAM LACY) has referred him to a specialist who has diagnosed cancer, makes the patient (LASNE PAUL STEWART) feel like killing him.

although this is not a form of courtesy he is used to performing and he feels awkward about it. Of course he will not live forever. He is still falling towards his grave as much as he ever was. The difference is that now he is conscious of it.

The play very skilfully created a persuasive portrait in a stylised manner, conveying a frightening experience through a frequently comic touch. If some of the encounters seemed somewhat harsher than those I experience treading some of the same paths, doubtless things are sometimes different and certainly must seem so to someone with the greater part of a happy life behind him and to a young man expecting that this is still ahead of him. It was a fine piece, finely acted.

(The make-up artist responsible for tingeing with a senior grey the extremities of the hair of **Adam Lacy**, a young actor, for his role as the surgeon, should have joined the list of hairdressers given special credit for giving skilful assistance to the actors in other programmes in the festival).

This undoubtedly plumbed serious territory, even if often giving it a light-hearted guise. So did **The Hanged Man**, although the mood here was increasingly terrifying. This was another play which had been reduced in length for the festival. There may have been one or two plot- and character-points which thus became slightly over-compressed but in general not only was the overall effect still outstanding but I would have thought the better able to be so by being more compact. If you are going to scare the life out of an audience, this is more sustainable over an hour than over ninety minutes.

It portrays a real marriage, no mere 'relationship' here, - well-established if comparatively young -, the play beginning with the wife , Megan **(Laura Harper**) announcing to Ray (**Dean Ashton**, the co-author) that their first child is due. The terror is in what way the sinister Xavier (**Thomas Aldersley**) may insinuate himself between them

We first meet him at a squash court near, possibly in, a hospital, where both Megan and Ray work, she in Psychiatrics, he in X-Ray. Xavier has put himself down for a match with Ray, whom he knows is the husband of his therapist, although Ray has no idea who he is. He thinks him mildly nutty, because he finds that Xavier takes astrology and other means of divination seriously, but does not realise he is a Mental Health Out Patient. He becomes progressively less 'Out' as he manages to get himself work on the Hospital Radio. In **Vodka Knickers**, Orla had found her love for Jax growing through hearing her sweet voice over the loud speakers. Here, as Ray becomes progressively more disturbed by Xavier, his unease is increased by hearing him broadcast his divinations to patients.

Quite what Xavier's 'real' motivation or state of mind may be we cannot know, and this uncertainty does not to weaken the drama. We know that he is extremely devious, so we cannot rely on anything we hear him say. We know that some of his professions of clairvoyance are supported by knowledge he has obtained earlier by covert means. This probably means that he has no praeternatural abilities, but can we be sure that he has none at all? His tale to Megan in counselling is that he has been made subject to panic attacks by losing his former partner through perceiving that she was to have a stillborn child and being conscious that this was what he had really wanted, as he had not wanted to have to share her love for him with a baby. Is he by this or some similar experience really especially prone to place exceptionally high reliance on Megan when, after he talks of how alone and isolated he feels, she seeks to reassure him by saying, "You have always got me," "You can always trust me"? If he is one especially subject to the wish not to be loved but to be loved alone, no wonder he tries to drive a wedge between her and Ray, no wonder we fear the possibility that he could ever get his hands on the baby. Amazing show of courage by Megan, presumably being professionally attuned to all these possibilities, that, to give him the sense

THE HANGED MAN (242); by the time of their second squash match, the relationship between Xavier (THOMAS ALDERSLEY, left) and Ray (DEAN ASHTON) has become very intense; LAURA HARPER is not only central as Megan to the concerns of both of them but here making an important ensemble contribution to the atmosphere of the match.

of being trusted, she is ready to let him hold her child. No wonder that Ray is prepared to countenance no such thing and, indeed, responds to such advances with especial asperity. Megan might, having seen what she had risked so much to build up being so quickly kicked down, have shouted at Ray about Xavier's right to be treated with respect but, if she felt so strongly about Xavier's due in this regard, would she not have recognised this as being at least equally due to Ray? Would she have left him on the strength of this single incident, as, at the play's conclusion, it seemed that she had?

This was the point at which it is possible that the pruning of the play might have left its developments over abbreviated. Nevertheless, seeing it was a formidable experience. The characters were vivid and full, the staging bone-simple but powerful. All the set was three benches, one on each side of the performance area. This well suggested the locker room for many of the scenes at the squash court. Players could sit on them when out of the action but also sometimes play a part from there. At the second encounter at the squash court we actually saw the game. By then considerable antagonism had built up, so it was played fiercely, This was emphasised by having **Laura Harper** on the bench at the back, in sight but not in role as Megan, clapping her hands vigorously each time the ball was struck. The final encounters, with the baby, took place in an annex to the hospital near its multi-storey car-park. Police were requiring patients and staff to wait there because a bomb had just gone off. [The play was written before the London bombings but performed just after them. The authors know the times in which we live]. The situation was evinced by taking all the benches and stacking them in a lopsided pile at the back, with a strip of Police tape around them. It was a quick and simple way to show not only the scene but the fractured emotions of the characters, whose conflicts were reaching their peak.

The whole work, in writing performance and stagecraft, was a gripping experience. It was dealing with issues of substance, making the audience both fearful at their nature and elated by witnessing the skill with which they were presented. This I thought was the pinnacle of **24:7**'s achievements but every item in the festival showed all manner of theatre arts to be thriving creatively in every way. The rest of this article and most of this book show this only to be a part of a most impressive wider picture. Theatre is a very ancient art, probably going back to the cave dwellers. Other sections show that we can still bring the oldest plays we know imaginatively to life. Some of those will never be bettered but **24:7** and all else described here show that we can still create new work which can rightly stand beside them. Praise be!

7 JULY. **THE IMPORTANCE OF BEING EARNEST (260);** Wythenshawe Park

BREN PATRICK writes: **Oscar Wilde**'s brilliant satire on the hypocrisy of the British aristocracy was as delightful and fresh as ever in the capable hands of **Heartbreak Productions** at **Wythenshawe Park**'s outdoor production of the play.

The drama began with an empty stage, popular music blaring out on the radio, interrupted by news broadcasts alluding to imminent wars in Europe and Russia. Although not in the original stage directions, this gave a good backcloth for the play, providing a contrast between world affairs and the world of the privileged, who have time to worry about such things as cucumber sandwiches and the importance of birth place in assessing suitability for marriage. However, useful though this was, it went on far too long. Members of the audience, attentive at the start, lost interest and dissolved into conversation long before the opening lines of the play. This is the only criticism in an otherwise excellent production.

The scenery and props were minimal and well-designed, unobtrusive and serving the purpose. The actors took the play at a fast pace, delivering the

THE IMPORTANCE OF BEING EARNEST (260); Algy (ALAN ATKINS) and Jack (LAWRENCE STUBBING).

lines clearly and with good timing, and doing justice to **Wilde**'s wonderful script.

The play ended, as it began, with a contrast; sound effects of a war torn Europe, and a series of effective dance 'freeze frames' from the happy couples whose lives are made perfect by the importance of having sorted out names.

A thoroughly entertaining experience.

7 AUGUST. **DRACULA – THE BLOOD COUNT (259);** Heaton Park

.

ALAN KELSEY writes: For those who have never seen a production in the Park, the acting initially appears disconcertingly stagey, the actors shouting their lines and throwing out exaggerated gestures. It quickly becomes apparent that this is a necessity in order that all the audience ringed around each scene can follow the plot. (It also helps in their battle with the other denizens of the evening skies – charter airlines.)

The first half of the show proceeds at a leisurely pace, setting the scene for the confrontations that are to come with the Count (**Peter Clifford**) and introducing the characters. **Bibi Nerheim** deserves particular mention: she is notably effective as the flighty, easily led (and doomed) Lucy.

The park scenery and the hall come into their own in the second half. The action switches to Transylvania and the fading light invests the play with a genuinely creepy air. With bodies hanging from trees, spectres flitting in and out of the surrounding bushes and screaming

DRACULA (259); Mina (JILL KEMP) rushes to the aid of Jonathan Harker (DAN WILLIS), who is in the grip of The Count (PETER CLIFFORD).

apparitions, a nervous air quickly spread through the audience.

The Count's lair, in a dimly lit piece of woodland, and the use of the hall, featuring a backlit Count in red cape on a wall, provided an exciting spectacle.

The script is witty as are the asides from those cast members who, as local gypsies, offer garlic as protection to the audience whilst they are led by the director, **Caroline Clegg**, between scenes. References to contemporary popular culture are used to create light relief and the play walks the line between humour and horror in an engaging manner.

The production provided a highly entertaining evening. The company, **Feelgood Productions**, should be congratulated on their efforts.

Section 3

PROGRAMME DETAILS

ABBREVIATIONS

ACCESS

D: Regular **D**escribed Performances, for Blind / Partially Sighted

G: Provision for **G**uide Dogs

H: **H**earing Loop Installed

S: Regular **S**ign Language Interpreted Performances

W: Wheelchair Access and Adapted Toilet

MAP REFERENCES

CAZ: Current Colour **A-Z Manchester Street Atlas,** published by Geographers' A-Z Map Company , Fairfield Road, Borough Green, SEVENOAKS, Kent TN15 8PP; 01732 781000; 1997 edition

WAZ: Wigan A-Z Street Plan; published by Geographers' A-Z Map Company , Fairfield Road, Borough Green, SEVENOAKS, Kent TN15 8PP; 01732 781000; 1993 edition

BOLTON

BEAUTIFUL THING (141) at OCTAGON; OLIVER LEE and KERRY STACEY

THE ALBERT HALLS, Victoria Square BL1 1RU; 01204 364333; **CAZ:** 32, B6 **G, H, W**

. **83. OKLAHOMA;** Music by Richard Rodgers; Book and Lyrics by Oscar Hammerstein II; BOLTON CATHOLIC M&CS; *26 – 30 October 2005.*

79. HELLO, DOLLY; Book by Michael Stewart; Music and Lyrics by Jerry Herman; based on **The Matchmaker** by Thornton Wilder, based, in its turn, on **Einen Jux Will Er Sich Machen** by Johann Nestroy; FARNWORTH PERFORMING ARTS COMPANY; *12-16 April 2005*

122. THE HOT MIKADO; Lyrics by David H Bell; Musicis by Bob Bowman, based on th opera by W S Gilbert and Arthur Sullivan; BOLTON CATHOLIC MCS YOUTH THEATRE; *28-30 April.2005;*

123. THE ARMED MAN by Karl Jenkins; BOLTON CATHOLIC MCS YOUTH THEATRE; *14 May 2005.*

THE ARTS CENTRE; Bolton School, Chorley New Road BL1 4PA; 01204 849474; CAZ: 31, G6. **G W**

BEAUMONT PRIMARY SCHOOL; Wendover Drive BL3 4RX; 01204 652 149; **CAZ:** 44, C2

BISHOP BRIDGEMAN CHURCH OF ENGLAND SCHOOL; Rupert Street BL3 6PY; 01204 333 466

BLACKSHAW PRIMARY SCHOOL; Bideford Drive BL2 6TE; 01204 386920; CAZ: 48, A1

BOLTON UNIVERSITY PAVILION THEATRE; Chadwick Street Campus BL2 1JN; 01204 531411 / 659950; **CAZ:** 46, C

14. DANNY, KING OF THE BASEMENT by David S Craig; M6 THEATRE COMPANY; SHEFFIELD THEATRES; *13 Arpil 2005.*

GHOST TRAIN (86); left to right: ANDREW CLOSE (Teddie), MICHAEL HAWORTH (Saul), VINCENT BRADLEY (Charles), CHERYL HARDISTRY (Peggy), MARK LEIGH (Richard)

BOLTON LITTLE THEATRE: Hanover Street BL1 4TG; 01204 524469; **CAZ:** 32,A6. **G, H, W**

80. HOME AND BEAUTY by W Somerset Maugham; *11-18 September 2004. William:* Paul WALKER; *Frederick:* Connor O'BEIRNE; *Victoria:* Helen Price AINDOW; *Leicester Paton:* Ernest DAWSON; *A B Raham:* Michael TATMAN; *Miss Montmorency:* Nina FAULKNER; *Mrs Shuutleworth:* Rita MAYOH; *Miss Dennis / Nannie:* Donna NEALON; *Mrs Pogson:* Susan COUTTS; *Taylor:* John TOWERS. *Director / Designer:* Barry HALL; *Production Secretary:* Viv BLOOMFIELD; *Stage Manager:* Kevin SHIPLEY; *Electrical Illumination:* Jeffrey LUNT, Neil DWYER; *Auditory Enhancement:* Ian BEEBY, Peter HARRISON; *Apparel:* Elizabeth TATMAN, Ernest DAWSON;

Properties: Dorothy GREEN, Cecilia UNSWORTH.

86. **THE GHOST TRAIN** by Arnold Ridley; *16-23 October 2004. Elsie:* Jennifer LEE; *Richard:* Mark LEIGH; *Saul:* Mike HAWORTH; *Charles:* Vincent BRADLEY; *Peggy:* Cheryl HARDISTY; *Miss Bourne:* Nina FAULKNER; *Teddie:* Andrew CLOSE; *Julia:* Helen Pierce JONES; *Price:* Steven GILL; *Sterling:* Mark BLOOMFIELD; *Jackson:* Stuart O'HARA. *Director:* Stephen STUBBS; *Set Design:* Helen Pierce JONES; *Set Realisation / Construction / Construction:* Michael TATMAN, Jeff LUNT et al; *Set Painting:* Jo YATES et al; *Lighting:* Neil DWYER, Aaron DOOTSON, Stuart TREMAYNE; *Sound:* Ian BEEBY et al; *Costumes:* Elizabeth TATMAN; *Properties:* Cecilia UNSWORTH, Christine Pierce JONES et al; *Rehearsal Prompts:* Dorothy GREEN, Christine Piearce JONES; *Stage Manager:* Mark REID; *Assistant Stage Manager:* Kelly JOHNSTONE.

89. **ALICE IN WONDERLAND**, adapted from Lewis Carroll by Sandra Simpson; *27 November – 4 December 2004. Charles Dodgson / March Hare:* Andrew CLOSE; *Lorina Liddell:* Kellie JOHNSTONE; *Edith Liddell;* Carmen DOOLEY; *Alice:* Emma POLLARD; *White Rabbit / Tweedledee:* Stuart O'HARA; *Little Alice / Dormouse:* Kayleigh LUNT; *Dodo / Red King:* Gary CUBBAGE; *Bird / Knave of Hearts:* Jordan CROOK; *Mice:* Kellie JOHNSTONE, Carmen DOOLEY; *Duck / Executioner / Footman Messenger* Donna NEALON; *Cheshire Cat:* Mark LEIGH; *Footman / Executioner:* Derek FRAZER; *Cook:* Pat HILL; *Caterpilla Unicornr:* Adam WALTON; *Duchess:* Jo YATES; *Mad Hatter:* Ernest DAWSON; *Tweedledum:* Jeff LUNT; *Red Queen:* Christine FLANIGAN; *Humpty Dumpty:* Dave POLLARD; *White King:* Harvey WALTON; *Lion:* Mark TURNBULL; *White Queen:* Rita MAYOH; *Gryphon:* Julia ROWE; *Mock*

Turtle: Charlotte CARLIN; *Georgie Porgie:* William ROWE. *DANCEWORKS: Cards:* Olivia MOSS, Bethany HARVEY, Lauren TIERNEY, Lana JORDAN, Brogan MOSS, Sarah MAXWELL, Sarah GIBSON, Rachael WHITTLE, Katie BROMILOW; *Princesses (Group 1):* Stephanie ASHWORTH; Natalie ASHWORTH, Charlott GILBERTSON, Gemma MURRAY; *(Group 2):* Chloe FORD, Lucy MOSS, Natalie HOUGH, Stephanie ASHWORTH, Natalie ASHWORTH, Gemma MURRAY; *Princes (Group 1):* Victoria TAYLOR, Felicity ECCLES, Amelia HARVEY, Faya BUTTERFIELD; (*Group 2:* Francesca O'REILLY, Sophie ELLIOT, Aimee GAVIN, Emma HALLIWELL, Emma GIBSON. *Director:* Sandra SIMPSON; *Lyrics / Music:* Stephen KNOWLES; *Pianist / Arrangements:* Ed LOMAX; *Lighting Designer:* Aaron DOOTSON; *Lighting Crew:* Neil DWYER, Stuart TREMAYNE, Dave MERCER; *Sounr Effects:*Ian BEEBY; *Stage Manager:* Eric CHEETHAM; *Set Design:* Jo YATES, Peter PEMRICK; *Set Construction:* Michael TATMAN, Jeff LUNT et al; *Props:* Kate CHEETHAM et al; *Costumes:* Mair HOWELL-BENNETT, Frances CLEMMITT, Sandra SIMPSON, Ernest DAWSON, Elizabeth TATMAN,.

92. SKYLIGHT by David Hare; *15 – 22 January 2005. Cast:* Bob HOWELL, Helen Price AINDOW, George CRITCHLEY. *Directors:* Audrey LIAS, Jim LIAS; *Stage Manager:* Michael HAWORTH; *Set Construction:* Michael TATMAN, Jeff LUNT, Len PRICE, Jim LIAS; *Lighting Design:* Aaron DOOTSON; *Lighting Team:* Aaron DOOTSON, Neil DWYER; *Properties:* Viv BLOOMFIELD, Dorothy GREEN et al; *Sound Design:* Ian BEEBY; *Wardrobe:* Elizabeth TATMAN.

95. DICK BARTON – SPECIAL AGENT by Phil Willmott; *19 – 26 February 2005. BBC Announcer / Sir Stanley Fritters:* Stephen STUBBS; *Dick Barton / Snowy:* Mark LEIGH; *Baron Scarheart:* David POLLARD; *Marta Heartburn:* Heliene GODDING; *Jock Anderson:* Vincent BRADLEY; *Newspaper Reporter:* Jeff LUNT; *Colonel Gardener:* Ernest DAWSON; *Daphne Fritters:* Beverley CUTLER; *Lady Laxington:* Helen Pierce JONES; *Marta's Sidekick:* Ian PHILLIPS. *Director / Choreographer:* Andrew CLOSE; *Additional Choreography:* Mark LEIGH; *Stage Managers:* Ian PHILLIPS, Mark TURNBULL; *Set Builders:* Michael TATMAN, Jeff LUNT et al; *Set Painting:* Jo YATES; *Properties:* Christine Pierce JONES; *Costumes:* Elizabeth TATMAN; *Lighting:* David LODMORE, Peter HARDMAN; *Sound:* Fergus WATT Ian BEEBY; *Original Music:* Stephen

KNOWLES; *Music Preparation:* Stephen KNOWLES, Ed LOMAX.

100. **KES;** adapted by Lawrence Till from the book **A Kestrel For A Knave** by Barry Hines; *2- 9 April 2005.Billy Casper:* sam DOOTSON; *Jud:* Stewart TREMAYNE; *Mrs Casper:* Christine FLANAGAN; *Mr Porter / Mr Sugden . YEO:* Robin THOMPSON; *Customer / Farmer / Mr Beal:* Stuart O'HARA; *Mr Farthing:* Matthew JAMES; *Mrs McDowell / Librarian / Mrs Rose:* Susannah NIGHTINGALE; *Mr Gryce:* Stave KNOWLES; *Mr Crossley / Milkman / Gambler:* Nigel CARTER; *MacDowell:* Alex PARKINSON; *Delamore:* Hedley HILL; *Fisher:* Danny BOLTON; *Anderson:* Adam WALTON; *Gibbs:* Michaela WILKINSON; *Whitbread:* Emma VENABLES. *Directors:* Sue BOLUS, Steve GILL; *Set Design and Building:* Steve GILL; *Stage Manager:* Paul WALKER; *Lighting design:* Steve GILL, Neil DWYER; *Sound Design:* Ian BEEBYM Steve GILL, Sue BOLUS; *Guitar:* Tom GREENHALGH; *Technical Operators:* Neil DWYER, Krissy SAINSBURY, Jed LECK, Aaron DOOTSON; *Wardrobe:* Sue BOLUS, Elizabeth TATMAN; *Props:* Kath CHEETHAM et al; *Fight Arrangements:* Barry HALL

103. **BRASSED OFF;** adapted from the filmscript by Mark Herman and Paul Allen; *7-14 May 2005. Shane:* Chris KEMPSTER; *Phil:* Dave EYRE; *Vera* Sue BAMFORD; *Rita:* Cecilia UNSWORTH; *Sandra:* Helen Price AINDOW; *Gloria:* Caroline WEEKES; *Danny:* Harold SMITH; *Harry:* Mike LEIGH; *Jim* John HAWORTH; *Andy:* Jason DUNK; *Nurse:* Charlotte CARLIN; *Bailiff:* Mark TURNBULL; *THE BAND: Cornets:* Roger FORD, Martin AINSWORTH, Stephen NEWCOMBE, Graham JACKSON, Julia OWENS, Roy FARNWORTH, John ISON, Vivien WILD, Jack HOLT; *Horns:* Jill BRIGHOUSE, Steven McGUIRE. Trevor CLARKE, Michelle ROSCOE; *Euphoniums*: Jim OWEN, Alan HOBSON, Ian ROSCOE, Chris SIMMS; *Trombones:* Chris BARRETT, Frank PARTINGTON, Bill ROSCOE;

MARK LEIGH (Harry); JOHN HOWARTH (Jim)

Basses: Matt WALKER, Neil MAYOH, Bill ROBSON, Mike HURST; *Percussion:* George WHITTLE, Gary BRANAGAN. *Director:* Andrew CLOSE; *Musical Director:* Peter ASHLEY; *Stage Manager:* Mark TURNBULL; *Set Building:* Michael TATMAN, Jeff LUNT; *Lighting:* Jeff LUNT, Steve GILL, Neil DWYER et al; *Sound* :Fergus WATT, Ian BEEBY; *Set Painting:* Jo YATES; *Production Assistant:* Adam WILDER; *Props:* Kath CHEETHAM et al

107. **SUMMERTIME VARIETY SHOW;** *22-28 August 2005. Producer:* Kevin SHIPLEY.

BOLTON MUSLIM GIRLS SCHOOL; High Street BL3 6TA; 01204 361103; CAZ: 46, A3

BOLTON SCHOOL (BOYS); Chorley New Road BL1 4PB; 01204 822669; **CAZ:** 31, F6

271. **ROMEO AND JULIET** by William Shakespeare; MANCHESTER ACTORS COMPANY; *25 November 2004*

268. **MACBETH** by William Shakespeare; MANCHESTER ACTORS COMPANY; *3 February 2005.*

BOLTON SCHOOL (GIRLS); Chorley New Road BL1 4PB; 01204 840201; CAZ: 31, F6

BOLTON SOCIALIST CLUB; 16 Wood Street BL1 1DY; **CAZ:** 32, B6

BRANDWOOD COUNTY PRIMARY SCHOOL; Brandwood Street BL3 4BG; 01204 333444; **CAZ:** 45. G3

CANON SLADE CHURCH OF ENGLAND HIGH SCHOOL; Bradshaw Brow BL2 3DB; 01204 591 441; **CAZ:** 33, E1

CASTLE HILL PRIMARY SCHOOL; Castle Hill Street BL2 2JT; 01204 520290; **CAZ:** 32, D3

269. **PINOCCHIO** by Stephen Boyes, based on the original story by

Carlo Collodi; MANCHESTER ACTORS COMPANY; *28 February 2005.*

CENTRAL LIBRARY; Le Mans Crescent OL1;

CHORLEY OLD ROAD METHODIST CHURCH; BL1 3AA; 01204 840824 / 848935; **CAZ:** 31, F4

132. **OH WHAT A LOVELY** by Charles Chilton, Gerry Raffles, original Theatre Workshop cast; THE MARCO PLAYERS; *9-13 November 2004* *Director:* Alan MacPHERSON; *Choreographer:* Natalie CROMPTON.

.93. **SEE HOW THEY RUN** by Philip King; THE MARCO PLAYERS; *16-19 February 2005.*

133. **COMMUNICATING DOORS** by Alan Ayckbourn; THE MARCO PLAYERS; *1-4 June 2005. Phoebe* :Natalie CROMPTON; *Reece Wells:* Jason CROMPTON; *Julian Goodman:* Mark WEATHERALL; *Buella Wells:* Irene SMITH; *Jessica Wells:* Gail COSTELLO; *Harold Paslmer:* David HOLT. *Director:* Peter HASLAM.

CORPORATION STREET BL1 2AN; CAZ: 32, A6

CROWN AND CUSHION; Mealhouse Lane BL1 1DD; CAZ: 32, B6

THE DEANE SCHOOL. New York BL3 4NG; 01204 564521; **CAZ:** 45, D3

DEANSGATE; CAZ: 32, B6

DEVONSHIRE ROAD PRIMARY SCHOOL; BL1 4ND; 01204 843556; **CAZ:** 31. F5

EAGLEY JUNIOR SCHOOL; Chapeltown Road, BROMLEY CROSS BL7 9AT; 01204 303 125; **CAZ:** 19, F3

EATOCK COUNTY PRIMARY SCHOOL; St George's Avenue,

WESTHOUGHTON BL52EU; 01942 812874

FARNWORTH LITTLE THEATRE; Cross Street, FARNWORTH BL4 7AG; 01204 792599/ 303808 **CAZ:** 47, F6. **G, W**

108. DIAL M FOR MURDER by Frederick Knott; FARNWORTH LITTLE THEATRE; *18-25 2004*

109. THE IMPORTANCE OF BEING EARNEST by Oscar Wilde; FARNWORTH LITTLE THEATRE; *13 –20 November 2004.*

110. HANS, THE WITCH AND THE GOBBIN by Alan Cullen; FARNWORTH LITTLE THEATRE; *22 – 29 January 2005.*

111. RUMOURS BY Neil Simon; FARNWORTH LITTLE THEATRE; *12 – 19 March 2005.*

112. SHADOWLANDS by William Nicholson; FARNWORTH LITTLE THEATRE; *14 – 21 May 2005.*

113-131: Greater Manchester Drama Federation One-Act Play Festival

113. GIZMO by Alan Ayckbourn; ROMILEY LITTLE THEATRE; *6 June 2005. Ben Mason:* Jack CUMSTON; *Prof Ruth Barth / Dazer:* Jordan HARMSTON; *Dr Bernice Mallow:* Molly WHEELDON; *David Best:* Simon PLAYLE; *Nerys Potter:* Holly MAUDSLEY; *Ted Wilkins / Rust:* Callum MAUDSLEY; *Fritzo:* Joanna RUSHTON; *Hezza:* Eleshi OAKES; *Dart:* Aimee WHEELDON; *Tiz:* Helena GORDON; *Rikki:* Rachel KEENAN; *Manny Rice:* Ben COOKSON; *Rudi:* Willaim PARRY; *Keith:* Gavin ORVIS; *Cevril Teese:* Emma BYERS; *Sir Trevor Perkins:* George CUMSON. *Director:* Roy H VERNON.

114. FLATMATES by Ellen Dryden; ROMILEY LITTLE THEATRE; *6 June 2005. Steve:* Chris PRIESTLEY; *Lyn:* Bex WICKENS; *Tom:* Mark SCHOFIELD; *Tony:* Catherine VERNON; *Coralie:* Nat MARSOM. *Director:* Liz VERNON.

115. SAY SOMETHING HAPPENED by Alan Bennett; ST JOSEPH'S PLAYERS; *6 June 2005. Mum:* Betty HARDMAN; *Dad:* Charles SERVICE; *June Potter:* Kim GRIFFITHS. *Director:* Maureen SERVICE.

116. **TOO LONG AN AUTUMN**by Jimmy Chinn; BROOKDALE THEATRE; *8 June 2005. Maisie May:* Brenda brooks; *Arnold Windrush:* Alan BUXTON; *Ursula Windrush:*Barbara DICKINSON; *Miss Tate:* Sally JOLLY; *Dad:* Harvey DICKINSON; *Dora Coxham:* Sheila SHARP; *Chris:* Neil LINGWOOD. *Director:* Ian McEWEN.

117. **ALBERT** by Richard Harris; PARTINGTON THEATRE; *8 June 2005. Karin:* Monica VANESS; *Nico:* Cliff PRICE; *Albert:* Chris STURMEY. *Director:* Melvin WARHURST.

118. **GOSFORTH'S FETE** by Alan Ayckbourn; PLAYERS DRAMATIC SOCIETY; *8 June 2005. Mrs Pearce:* Margaret WILLIAMS; *Milly:* Anne WINT; *Gosforth:* Ray GIDLEY; *Vicar:* Ian PEARSON; *Stewart:* Ian PEARSON. *Director:* Jenny GIBSON.

119. **LAST TANGO IN LITTLE GRIMLEY** by David Tristram; HYDE LITTLE THEATRE; *9 June 2005. Gordon:* Tony THOMPSON; *Bernard:* Roger BOARDMAN; *Joyce:* Alison BOWERS; *Margaret:* Stephanie MORRIS. *Director:* Janice C HAUGHTON.

120. **SOAP IN MY EYE** by Vin Kenny; UPPERMILL STAGE SOCIETY; *9 June 2005. Jack Duxbury:* Phil COOME; *Dennis Duxbury:* Vin KENNY. *Director:* Vin KENNY.

121. **THE LOVER** by Harold Pinter; SALE NOMADS THEATRE CLUB; *9 June 2005. Richard:* Ross DOUGLAS; *Sarah:* Natasha WILDE; *Milkman:* Stuart HARDING. *Director:* Barbara TURNER.

123. **WITH MY LITTLE EYE** by Elaine McCann; EDGEFOLD PLAYERS; *10 June 2005. Cassie:* Casey DAWSON; *Beth:* Sophie RENSOMI; *Emma:* Caroline McGRATH; *Louise:* Jessica JARDINE; *Caroline:* Caroline GRIFFIN; *Tara:* Katie GRIMSHAW; *Ryan:* Alex BANKS. *Director:* Elaine McCANN.

124. **OUR BLITZ** by Elaine McCann; EDGEFOLD PLAYERS; *10 June 2005.Teacher:* Charlotte TITLEY; *Betty:* Abigail CRAVEN; *Annie (young):* Jennifer CRAVEN; *Mary (young):* Frances WARBURTON; *Doris:* Cathy WARBURTON; *Mrs Lipton:* Camilla FRENCH; *May:* Elizabeth TITLEY; *Jack:* Steve BLAKESLEY; *Emily:* Amy BANKS; *Raymond (young):* Alex BANKS; *John:* David WARBURTON; *Lenny:* Joe BURNS; *Alf:* Nick TITLEY; *Raymond (adult):* Ralph ETHERINGTON; *Mary (adult):* Moira CARR; *Annie (adult):* Pat

COTTRELL; *Billy:* Colin TITLEY. *Director:* Elain McCANN.

125. LITTLE BROTHER, LITTLE SISTER by David Campton; SLR THEATRE COMPANY; *10 June 2005. Madam:* Rachel GODIFF; *Sir:* Daniel KENNEDY; *Cook:* Mark LYTH. *Director:* Mark LYTH.

126. SCHOOL JOURNEY TO THE CENTRE OF THE EARTH by Ken and Daisy Campbell; ST PHILIPS AODS; *11 June 2005. Georgia:* Kimberly RIGBY; *Chrissy:* Charlotte DAVENPORT; *Richard:* James STANLEY; *Hal:* Alex BLACK; *Tricia:* Elisha CHALLENDER; *Sonny:* Adam CRITCHLEY; *Anna:* Rebecca BOLTON; *James:* Rishi KUKAOIA; *Rab:* Nathan BARLOW; *Jonathan:* Zac THORNLEY; *Ben:* Emma FOLEY; *Mathew:* Sam WALKER; *Tom:* Alex CRITCHLEY; *Louis:* Coral EVANS. *Director :*Sarah PILKINGTON

127. GOODBYE IPHIGENIA by George MacKewan Green; KNOW YOUR ONIONS; *11 June 2005. King Agamemnon:* Andrew CONNELLY; *Kalchas:* Geoff RICHARDS; *Andreas:* Gary HANDFORTH; *Queen Clytemnestra:* Catherine CONNELLY; *Iphigenia:* Shona BODE; *Penelope:* Lisa SWINN. *Director:* Malcolm COOPER.

128. RAINDROP FAIRIES by Sherri Phillips; MOSSLEY AODS NEXT GENERATION *11 June 2005; Whiskers:* Kiera BAXTER; *Cashew:* Jessica BUSKLEY; *Slimestool:* Eleanor REYNOLDS; *Rosebud:* Chloe THORPE; *Pomme:* Lauren HOLLAND; *Fairy 2 / Raindrop:* Nicole ASHTON; *Horatio:* Harriet STANFIELD; *Queen Flame:* Katy HOLLAND; *Fairy 3:* Jenny ANDREW; *Fairy 1:* Fatherine FARROW; *Petal:* Laura MOORE; *Servant / P. One / Announcer:* Caerys THOMAS. *Director:* Sherri PHILLIPS.

129. WHO CARES by John Chambers; MOSSLEY AODS NEXT GENERATION; *11 June 2005; Angie:* Jenny CLAYS-JONES; *Jane:* Susan GODDARD; *Chris:* Kim WRIGLEY. *Director:* Andrew RYDER.

130. CAGE BIRDS by David Campton; MOSSLEY AODS; *11 June 2005;Gossip:* Tori BURGESS: *Gazer:* Nicki RE; *Gloom:* Rachel LOLE; *Thump:* Rachel FARROW; *Twitting:* Jess ROYLE; *Guzzler:* Lizzie BROOKE; *The Wild One:* Lizzi RIGBY; *The Mistress:* Emily WILSON. *Director:* Colin WARD.

131. ELERGY FOR A LADY by Arthur Miller; FARNWORTH LITTLE THEATRE; *11 June 2005. Man:* Norman PICKLES; *Woman:* Julia

ROWE. *Diirector:* Christine DARLINGTON.

106. **ONE O'CLOCK FROM THE HOUSE** by Frank Vickery; FARNWORTH PERFORMING ARTS COMPANY; *21-25 June 2005.*

GEORGE TOMLINSON HIGH SCHOOL; Springfield Road, KEARSLEY BL4 8LZ; **CAZ:** 63, G3

268. **MACBETH** by William Shakespeare; MANCHESTER ACTORS COMPANY; *9 February 2005.*

HALLIWELL LIBRARY; Shepherd Cross Street BL1 3EJ; 01204 333 173; **CAZ:** 31, G4

HALLIWELL ROAD METHODIST CHURCH; Harvey Street, HALLIWELL BL1 8BH; 01204 597055 / 847878; **CAZ:** 32, A3

87. **BEDROOM FARCE** by Alan Ayckbourn; HALLIWELL THEATRE COMPANY; *23-27 November 2004*

97. **QUARTET** by Ronald Harwood; HALLIWELL THEATRE COMPANY; *5-9 April 2005.*

HARPER GREEN SCHOOL; Harper Green Road, FARNWORTH BL4 0DH; 01204 577451 / 402052; **CAZ:** 46, D6

HAYWARD SCHOOL; Lever Edge Lane, Morris Green BL3 3HH; 01204 562605; **CAZ:** 45, 5G.

14. **DANNY, KING OF THE BASEMENT** by David S Craig; M6 THEATRE COMPANY; SHEFFIELD THEATRES; *7 Aprily 2005.*

HEATHFIELD COUNTY PRIMARY SCHOOL; Henniker Road BL3 3TP; 01204654423; CAZ: 45,

HORWICH LEISURE CENTRE; Victoria Road BL6 5PY; 01204 692211; G, W

LADYBRIDGE PRIMARY SCHOOL; Broadford Road BL3 4NB; 01204 661784; **CAZ:** 44, D2

MARKLAND HILL COUNTY PRIMARY SCHOOL; BLI 5EJ; 01204 841574; CAZ: 30, DA

MOUNT ST JOSEPH BUSINESS AND ENTERPRISE COLLEGE; Greenland Road, FARNWORTH BL4 0UH; 01204 391800; **CAZ**: 46, C5

268. MACBETH by William Shakespeare; MANCHESTER ACTORS COMPANY; *17 March 2005.*

THE OAKS PRIMARY SCHOOL; Sharples Hall Drive BL1 7HS; 01204 333 171; **CAZ:** 18, D5

270. FIREBIRD by Stephen Boyes; MANCHESTER ACTORS COMPANY; *20 July 2005.*

OCTAGON; Howell Croft South BL1 1SB; 01204 520661; **CAZ:** 32, B6 **D, G, H, S W**

134. VERY LITTLE WOMEN by Maggie Fox and Sue Ryding; LIP SERVICE; CHESTER GATEWAY; *14 – 18 September 2004.All Sisters and Other Characters:* Maggie FOX, Sue RYDING.

135. TWELFTH NIGHT by William Shakespeare; OCTAGON; *23 September – 16 October 2004. Sebastian / Curio:* Giles COOPER; *Antonio / Valentine:* Marshall GRIFFIN; *Orsino:* David GROVES; *Olivia:* Inika Leigh WRIGHT; *Malvolio:* Michael MEARS; *Feste / SeaCaptain:* Michael O'CONNOR; *Maria:* Debra PENNY; *Sir Toby Belch:* Matthew RIXON; *Sir Andrew Aguecheek:* Paul TRUSSELL; *Viola:* Kelly WILLIAMS; *Arresting Officer:* Daniel WALSH. *Director:*Mark BABYCH; *Designer:*

Patrick CONNELLAN; *Lighting Designer:* Richard G JONES; *Sound Designer:* Andy SMITH; *Fight Director:* John WALLER; *Deputy Stage Manager On The Book:* Jen JARVIIS; *Stage Manager:* Scott McDONALD; *Assistant Stage Manager:* Graeme BROWN; *Chief Electrician:* Tom WEIR; *Workshop Manager:* Ian CALLAGHAN; *Construction Assistants:* Harry HEARNE, Kay FOWLER; *Wardrobe Supervisor:* Mary HORAN; *Wardrobe Assistant:* Rosalyn ASPDEN; *Scenic Artist:* Imogen PEERS.

How close did she mean to get? SARAH MOYLE (Marsha) and STEPHEN BECKET (Charlie)

136. DROWNING ON DRY LAND by Alan Ayckbourn; STEPHEN JOSEPH THEATRE; *19 –23 October 2004. Charlie Conrad:* Stephen BECKETT; *Linzi Ellison:* Melanie GUTTERIDGE; *Jason Ratcliffe:* Adrian McLOUGHLIN; *Hugo de Prescourt:* Stuart FOX; *Gale Gilchrist:* Billie-Claire WRIGHT; *Marsha Bates:* Sarah MOYLE; *Simeon Diggs:* Paul KEMP; *Laura* Grace USHER; *Katie:* Lucy USHER. *Director:* Alan AYCKBOURN; *Designer:*roger GLOSSOP; *Lighting Designer:* Mick HUGHES; *Costume Designer:* Christine WALL; *Wigs:* Felicite GILLHAM; *Original Music:* David NEWTON; *Stage Manager:* Fleur Linden BEELEY; *Deputy Stage Manager:* Emily THURLBY; *Assistant Stage Manager:* Mary HELY; *Wardrobe Supervisor:* Christine WALL; *Master Carpenter:* Frank MATTHEWS.

137. FRANKIE AND JOHNNY IN THE CLAIR DE LUNE by Terrence McNally; OCTAGON THEATRE; *28 October – 20 November 2004. Frankie:* Caroline HARDING; *Johnny:* Chris GASCOYNE. *Director:* Mark BABYCH; *Design:* Hannah CLARK; *Stage Manager:* Scott McDONALD; *Assistant Stage Manager:* Graeme BROWN; *Chief Electrician:* Tom WEIR; *Workshop Manager:* Ian CALLAGHAN; *Construction Assistants:* Harry HEARNE, Kay FOWLER; *Wardrobe Supervisor:* Mary HORAN; *Wardrobe Assistant:* Rosalyn

ASPDEN; *Scenic Artist:* Imogen PEERS.

FRANKIE AND JOHNNIE (137): CHRIS GASCOYNE and CAROLINE HARDING

138. GEORGE'S MARVELLOUS MEDICINE by Roald Dahl, adapted by Stuart Patterson; OCTAGON THEATRE; *26 November 2—4 – 8 January 2005. George:* Shane ZAZA; *Grandma:* Maureen PURKIS; *Dad:* Peter HAMILTON-DYER; *Mum:* Jo COWEN; *Various Chickens:* Liam WHITTAKER. *Director:* Lucy PITMAN-WALLACE; *Design:* Jessica CURTIS; *Puppets / Animation Director:* John BARBER; *Sound Design:* Andy SMITH; *Deputy Stage Manager On The Book:* Jen JARVIS; *Stage Manager:* Scott McDONALD; *Assistant Stage Manager:* Graeme BROWN; *Lighting Design:* Tom WEIR; *Workshop Manager:* Ian CALLAGHAN; *Construction Assistants:* Harry HEARNE, Kay FOWLER; *Wardrobe Supervisor:* Mary HORAN; *Wardrobe Assistant:* Rosalyn ASPDEN; *Scenic Artist:* Imogen PEERS.

GEORGE'S MARVELLOUS MEDICINE(138); MAUREEN PURKIS (Grandma) and SHANA ZAZA (George

139. THE BEAUTY QUEEN OF LEENANE by Martin McDonagh; OCTAGON THEATRE; *27 January – 19 February 2005. Ray:* Paul DINNEN; *Mag:* Eileen O'BRIEN; *Maureen:* Maggie O'BRIEN; *Pato:* Ged SIMMONS; *Announcer:* Peter Hamilton DYER. *Director:* Paul HUNTER; *Designer:* Fiona WATT; *Lighting Designer:* Tom WEIR; *Sound Designer* Andy SMITH; *Voice / Dialect Coach:* Mark LANGLEY; *Deputy Stage Manager On The Book:* Graeme BROWN; *Stage Manager:* Scott McDONALD; *Deputy Stage Manager:* Jen JARVIS; *Chief Electrician:* Tom WEIR; *Assistant Electrician:* Jason OSTERMAN; *Workshop Manager:* Ian CALLAGHAN; *Construction Assistants:* Harry HEARNE, Kay FOWLER; *Wardrobe Supervisor:* Mary HORAN; *Wardrobe Assistant:* Rosalyn ASPDEN; *Scenic Artists:* Imogen PEERS, David FANNING, John MINCH.

140. GOING DUTCH by John Godber; HULL TRUCK THEATRE COMPANY; *21-26 February 2005. Sally:* Gemma CRAVEN; *Mark:* James HORNSBY; *Karl:* Rob HUDSON; *Gill:* Jackie LYE. *Director:* John GODBER; *Designer:* Pip LECKENBY; *Lighting Designer:* Graham KIRK; *Costume Designer:* John BODDY; *Compant Stage Manager:* Fran MASKELL; *Stage Manager On The Book / Sound Operator:* Sally LITTLE; *Production Manager:* Richard BIELBY; *Technical Manager:* Dave SMELT; *Production Assistant:* John SIMS

THE BEAUTY QUEEN OF LEENANE (139); EILEEN 'BRIEN (Mag); MAGGIE O'BRIEN (Maureen)

GOING DUTCH (140); JAMES HORNSBY (Mark), ROB HUDSON (Karl), JACKIE LYE (Gill) and GEMMA CRAVEN (Sally)

155. **THE UGLY EAGLE;** MOVING HANDS THEATRE COMPANY; BIRMINGHAM REPERTORY THEATRE COMPANY; *2 –3 March 2005 Director:* Steve JOHNSTONE..

141. **BEAUTIFUL THING** bt Jonathan Harvey; OCTAGON THEATRE; PILOT THEATRE; *10 March –2 April 2005. Cast: Tony:* Adonis ANTHONY; *Sandra:* Maria CRITCHLEY; *Ste:* Jonathan HOWARD; *Jamie:* Oliver LEE, *Leah:* Kerry STACEY. *Director:* Marcus ROMER; *Designer:* Laura McEWEN; *Lighting Designer:* Judith CLOKE; *Sound Designer:* Andy SMITH; *Assistant Director:* Joanna TURNER; *Fight Director:* Richard RYAN; *Deputy Stage Manager on The Book:* Jen JARVIS; *Audio Describer:* Anne HORNSBY; *British Sign Language Interpreter:* Kyra POLLITT; *Stage Manager:* Scott McDONALD; *Assistant Stage Manager:* Graeme BROWN; *Chief Electrician:* Tom WEIR; *Workshop Manager:* Ian CALLAGHAN; *Construction Assistants:* Harry HEARNE, Kay FOWLER; *Wardrobe Supervisor:* Mary HORAN; *Wardrobe Assistant:* Rosalyn ASPDEN; *Scenic Artist:*Nerissa CARGILL-THOMPSON, Tara LOFTHOUSE.

SATIN 'N' STEEL (142); SARA POYSER and NORMAN PACE, a tribute to the hard graft of quality entertainers in local clubs.

142. **SATIN 'N' STEEL** by Amanda Whittington; OCTAGON THEATRE; NOTTINGHAM PLAYHOUSE; THEATRE WRITING PARTNERSHIP; *6- 30 April 2005. Vince Steel:* Norman Pace; *Teena Satin:* Sara POYZER. *Director:* Esther RICHARDSON; *Designer:* Helen DAVIES; *Lighting Designer:* Richard G JONES; *Assistant Lighting designer:* Matthew NEWBURY; *Musical Director / Composer:* Stuart BRINER; *Choreographer:* Claire MAURER; *Deputy Stage Manager On The Book:* Anita DRABWELL; *Audio Describer:* Anne HORNSBY; *Vritish Sign Language Interpreter:* Kyra POLLITT; *Stage Manager:* Scott McDONALD; *Deputy Stage Managers:* Jen JARVIS, Graeme BROWN; *Assistant Stage Manager:* Helen REDCLIFFE; *Chief Electrician:* Tom WEIR; *Workshop Manager:* Ian CALLAGHAN; *Construction Assistants:* Harry HEARNE, Kay FOWLER; *Wardrobe Supervisor:* Mary HORAN; *Wardrobe Assistant:* Rosalyn ASPDEN.

143. **TWO** by Jim Cartwright; OCTAGON THEATRE; *5 – 28 May 2005. Man:* Simeon TRUBY; *Woman:* Emma ATKINS. *Director:* Mark BABYCH; *Design:* Hannah CLARK; *Stage Manager:* Scott McDONALD; *Deputy Stage Manager On The Book:* Graeme BROWN; *Lighting Design:* Tom WEIR; *Sound Design:* Andy

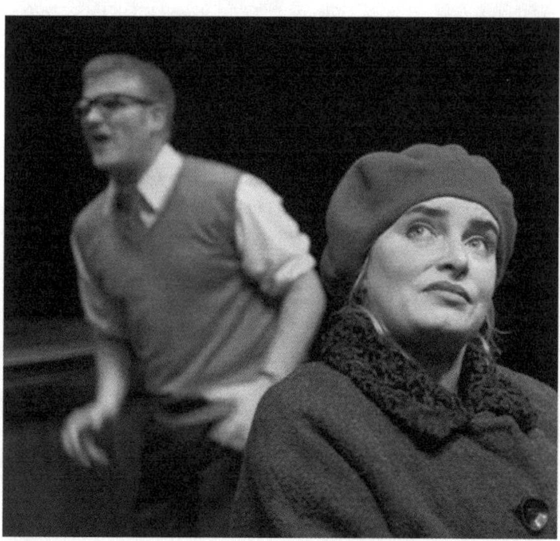

TWO (143); SIMEON TRUBY and EMMA ATKINS

SMITH; *British Sign Language Interpreter:* Kyra POLLITT; *Audio Describer:* Anne HORNSBY; *Workshop Manager:* Ian CALLAGHAN; *Construction Assistants:* Harry HEARNE, Kay FOWLER; *Wardrobe Supervisor:* Mary HORAN; *Wardrobe Assistant:* Rosalyn ASPDEN; *Scenic Artist:* Imogen PEERS.

145. RE:GENERATION OF ROAD by THE BIG ROOM, with some material by Jim Cartwright; ACTIV8; *3 June 2005.* Road, 1982 *Zonya:* Zonya MARSH; *Professor:* Robbie BUCHANAN; *Professor's Voice:* Michael MARSH; *Dor:* Hannah GRUNDY; *Mrs Bald:* Hannah DNISTRIANSKI; *Brink:* Jack LEIGH; *Scullery*: Shabani KILASI; *Skin Lad:* Hayley GAFFNEY; *Louise:Louise 1960's:* Deborah RICHMOND; *Carol's Father 1960's:*Matthew BELL; *Carol:* 1960's: Kate PEARSON; *Louise 1980's:* Pippa CUNNINGHAM; *Louise 2005:* Laura MARGINSON; *Chatmate 2005:* Victoria CUNNINGHAM; *The News People:* Sarah CROW, Gary CUBBAGE; Hannah MIDDLETON, Donna NEALON; *Road 2005: Pippa:* Sarah GARNER; *Shane:* Asg HOUGHTON; *Zoe:* Emma SUTCLIFFE; *Scullery:* Harvey WALTON. *Directors:* Caz BRADER, Ben FAULKS, Sumit SARKAR, Chris SUDWORTH; *Lighting Design:* Jason OSTERMAN; *Sound Design:* Andy SMITH.

ZITA FRITH, JAKE NORTON, ROSIE JENKINS

144. EIGHT MILES HIGH by Jim Cartwright; OCTAGON THEATRE; *9 June – 2 July 2005. Jean / Yogi:* Eithne BROWN; *Hell's Angel / Landowne:* Phil CORBITT; *Celia / Patsy:* Zita FRITH; *Musical Director:* Howard GAY; *Al / Jed:* Bob GOLDING, *Jasmine / Lola:* Rosie JENKINS; *Tod:* Adam KEAST; *Jay:* Jake NORTON; *MC / Traveller:* Andrew SCHOFIELD; *Reporter / John / Yogi:* Simeon TRUBY; *Spangle / Hippie:* Francis TUCKER. *Director:* Mark BABYCH; *Design:* Richard FOXTON; *Musical Director:* Howard GAY; *Sound Designer:* Andy SMITH; *Deputy Stge Manager On The Book:* Jen JARVIS; *British Sign Language Interpreter:* Kyra POLLITT; *Audio Describer:* Anne HORNSBY; *Stage Manager:* Scott McDONALD; *Deputy Stage Manager:* Graeme BROWN; *Assistant Stage Manager:* Helen RADCLIFFE; *Lighting Designer:* Tom WEIR; *Assistant Electrician:* Jason OSTERMAN; *Workshop Manager:* Ian

CALLAGHAN; *Construction Assistants:* Harry HEARNE, Kay FOWLER; *Wardrobe Supervisor:* Mary HORAN; *Wardrobe Assistant:* Rosalyn ASPDEN; *Prop Maker:* Julie Anne HESKIN; *Cutter / Maker:* Anne Marie HUNT; *Scenic Artist:*Dave FANNING, John MINCH

BILL NAUGHTON THEATRE, at the Octagon.

151. THE MAGIC SANDALS; TAM TAM THEATRE COMPANY; *18 September 2004.*

152. THE GOLDEN CROWN, from the **Panchtantra**; TREASURE TROVE PUPPET COMPANY; *2 October 2004.*

146. GARDEN OF THE HEART by Crystal Stewart; BOOJUM; *7 – 9 October 2004.*

147. MEGALOMANIAC by Shamshad Khan; *4 November 2004. Performer:* Shamshad KHAN. *Director:* Mark WHITELAW; *Music:* Basil CLARKE, Jason SINGH; *Movement Input:* Penny COLLINSON.

153. THE FOOL OF THE WORLD; CTC THEATRE COMPANY; *6 November 2004.*

148. ROUGH CUTS; ACTIV8 COMPANY; *9 December 2005.***Death Warmed Up:** *Death* :Mark MILLER; *Gail:* Donna NEALON; *Sue:* Hannah MIDDLETON; *Anchorman:* David HOGAN; **Living Rough:** *Phil:* Gary CUBBAGE; *Susan:* Jenna HICKMAN; *James:* Ben BATES; *Kate:* Priya VORA; **A Question of Time:** *Political Commentator:* Grace SOBEY; *Prime Minister:* Ed BARRY; *Electrician:* Mark ASHCROFT; *Narrator:* Dale HUGHES; **The Waiting Room:** *Jenny:* Jennifer RIDING; *Gemma:* Gemma CARCIONE; *Older Man:* Liam WHITTAKER; *Rachel:* Rachel HIGGINS; *Dan:* Dan WALSH; *Gary:* Gary BENNETT. *Other Performers:* Matt BERRY, Debs RICHMOND, Pooja SITPURA, Harvey WALTON; *Creative Input:* Hayley GAFFNEY, Chris SUDWORTH, Liam WHITTAKER.

154. SONYA'S GARDEN; M6 THEATRE COMPANY; *11 December 2004. Puppeteers:* Lizzy HUGHES, Gillian BASKEYFIELD.

196. THE GARDEN IN WINTER; M6 THEATRE COMPANY; *11 December 2004.*

163. SYD AND FANNY'S CHRISTMAS TURKEY by Terence Mann and Julia Rounthwaite; MOTION

LOCO; *20-23 December 2004. Syd Selby:* Terence MANN; *Fanny:* Julia ROUNTHWAITE.↓↓

156. THE OWL AND THE PUSSYCAT, based on Edward Lear by TALL STORIES; *5 February 2005.*

49. THE LIFE OF MOLIERE by Matthew Cameron Harvey; TALIA THEATRE; *16 February 2005. Mikhail Bulgakov / Older Moliere:* Terence MANN; *Younger Moliere:* Benedict POWER; *Rdtape / Ratabon / Capitano:* Julia ROUNTHWAITE; *Goon / Madeleine / Poquelin / Harlequin:* Carys WILLIAMS. *Director:* Gennadi BOGDANOV; *Producer / Designer:* James BEALE; *Stage & Technical Manager: Set Builder / AdditionalDesign:* Bryan TWEDDLE; *Costume:* Alison PICKLES; *Scenic Artist:* Steve ELLIOTT. **Journal:** 16/2/05

157. DUDE! WHERE'S MY TEDDY BEAR? By Sheridan Humphreys and Jonny Berliner; MODIFY THE VAN; *26 February 2005.*

154. SISTERS, SUCH DEVOTED SISTERS by Russell Barr; OUT OF JOINT; THE DRILL HALL; *28 February 2005. Performer:* Russell BARR. *Associate Director:* Naomi JONES.

Programme Details

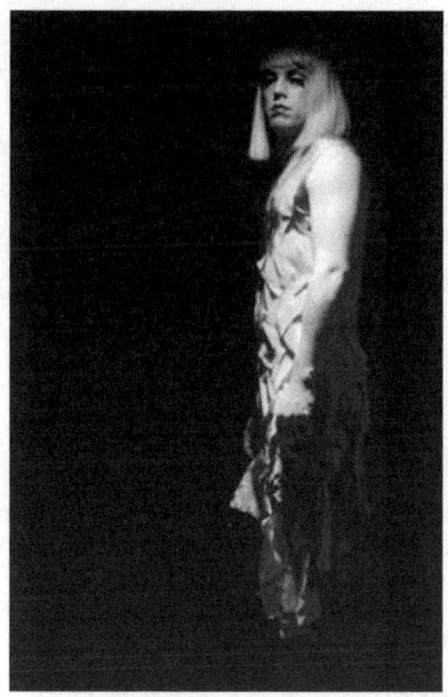

SISTERS, SUCH DEVOTED SISTERS (154); RUSSELL BARR

158. RED RIDING HOOD AND THE WOLVES by Karina Wilson, after Charles Perrault; C THEATRE; *2 April 2005. Traveller / Bully / Own / Yaroslov:* Frances BUCKROYD; *Pashnik:* Ranie DAW; *Skorepa:* Clare HANNAN; *Baryluk:* Jane JEFFERSON; *Kid / Owl / Grandmother:* Judith QUINN. *Director:* Chris SUDWORTH; *Assistant* ***Director:*** Anish PATEL; *Design:* Rachel BAYNTON; *Lighting:* Peter HARRISON; *Original Music:* Nicholas KINGMAN.

58. IN GOD WE TRUST by Avaes Mohammed; PESHKAR PRODUCTIONS; *12-13 April 2005. Hamza / Marine:* Gary STONER; *Sarfraz:* Asif KHAN; *Louise / Tariq:* Roksaneh Ghawam SHAHIDI. *Director:* Sazzadur RAHMAN; *Designer:* Emma M WEE; *Soundtrack Composer:* Jaydev MISTRY; *Lighting Designer / Production Manager:* Chris WHITWOOD; *Dramaturg:* Linda BROGAN. **Journal:** 16/2/05.

159. THE IGNATIUS TRAIL; written and composed by Oliver Birch; EN MASSE THEATRE; *23 April 2005. Director:* Amy LEACH.

160. CARTWRIGHT CABARET; ACTIV8 (COMPANY 0); *17 – 18 June 2005. Director:* Chris SUDWORTH

218. SLAVE OF LOVE by Ged McKenna; NORTHWEST PLAYWRIGHTS; *22 June 2005.*

219. CATCHING LIGHTNING IN A BOTTLE by Nicholas Cordner; NORTHWEST PLAYWRIGHTS.*234 June 2005.*

161. THE BOOTLEGGER'S DAUGHTER by John Forde; NORTHWEST PLAYWIGHTS; *29 June 2005. Red:* James QUINN; *Susan:* Rina MAHONEY; *Tony:* Phil ATKINSON; *Boris:* Graeme HAWLEY. *Director:* Mark BABYCH; *Dramaturg:* Eileen MURPHY.

162. THE BUDDING by Angela Johnson; NORTHWEST PLAYWRIGHTS; *30 June 2005. Nanna Agg Carney:* June BROUGHTON; *Mary-Rose McGrath:* Kate CROSSLEY; *Jacko Byrne:* Ian BLOWER; *Joe Young:* James NICKERSON; *Chad BORG:* Carl CIEKA. *Director:* Bill HOPKINSON; *Dramaturg:* Kaite O'REILLY.

OUR LADY OF LOURDES SOCIAL CENTRE; Plodder Lane, FARNWORTH BL4 0BR; 01204 573728; CAZ: 62, C1

OVER HULTON CONSERVATIVE CLUB; St Helens Road Bolton Lancashire BL5 1AA; 01204 61384

741. LAST TANGO IN LITTLE GRIMLEY by David Tristram; TYLDESLEY LITTLE THEATRE; *4 February 2005.* : Ian TAYLOR, Garth WADDUP, Winnie EVANS, Ingrid FOLKARD-EVANS – *Director:* Lisa TAYLOR.

PHOENIX CENTRE; Bark Street BL1 2AX; 01204 535 861; **CAZ:** 32, A6

308. CROSSING BOUNDARIES; M6 YOUTH THEATRE; OLDHAM THEATRE WORKSHOP; PHOENIX YOUTH THEATRE; *February 2005.*

267. SMASHED by Mike Harris; GW THEATRE COMPANY; *28 June 2005.*

PLODDER LANE PRIMARY SCHOOL; FARNWORTH BL4 0DA; 01204 572582; CAZ: 46, D6

RED LANE PRIMARY SCHOOL; Red Lane; 01204 527925

RIVINGTON AND BLACKROD HIGH SCHOOL; Rivington Lane; HORWICH BL6 7SL; 01204 692511

193. MACBETH by William Shakespeare; MANCHESTER ACTORS COMPANY; *10, 11 February 2004.*

ST JAMES CHURCH OF ENGLAND SCHOOL; Lucas Road, FARNWORTH BL4 9RU; 01204 7000008; CAZ: 62, C1

ST JOHN'S CHURCH OF ENGLAND PRIMARY SCHOOL; Darwen Road, BROMLEY CROSS BL7 9HT; 01204 593988; CAZ: 19, E4

ST JOHN'S CHURCH OF ENGLAND PRIMARY SCHOOL; Church Road, KEARSLEY BL4 8AP; 01204 572341; **CAZ:** 64, B1

.

ST JOSEPH'S PRIMARY SCHOOL; Shepher Cross Street, BROWNLOW FOLD BL1 3EJ; 01204 845128; CAZ: 31, G4

ST JOSEPH'S ROMAN CATHOLIC SECONDARY SCHOOL; Chorley New Road, HORWICH; 01204 697456

ST MARY'S CHURCH OF ENGLAND PRIMARY SCHOOL; Edale Road, DEANE BL3 4QP; 01204 562 406; **CAZ:** 44, D4

270. **FIREBIRD** by Stephen Boyes; MANCHESTER ACTORS COMPANY; *18 July 2005.*

ST MATTHEW'S CHURCH OF ENGLAND PRIMARY SCHOOL; Kentford Road BL1 2JL; 01206 526306; CAZ: 32, A4

ST MICHAEL'S CHURCH OF ENGLAND PRIMARY SCHOOL; Green Lane BL3 2PL; 01204 524740; CAZ: 47, E4

ST OSMUND'S SCHOOL; Blenheim Road BL2 6EL; 01204 532866; CAZ: 33, G6

ST PAUL'S CHURCH OF ENGLAND PRIMARY SCHOOL; Newnham Street, ASTLEY BRIDGE OL1 8QA; 01204 301079; CAZ: 32, B2

ST PETER'S METHODIST CHURCH HALL; St Helens Road BL3 3SE; 01204 302560; CAZ: 45, E5

ST PETER'S CHURCH OF ENGLAND PRIMARY SCHOOL; Alexandra Street, FARNWORTH BL4 9JT; 01204 571554; CAZ: 63, F2

ST PHILIP'S PAROCHIAL HALL; Bridgeman Street BL3 6TH; 01204 559586; **CAZ:** 45, H3 **G**

96. THE PAJAMA GAME; Book by George Abbott and Richard Bissell; Music and Lyrics by Richard Adler and Gerry Rose; based on the book **7 ½ Cents** by Richard Bissell; ST PHILLIPS AODS; *14-19 March 2005.*

Babe Williams: Jenny BOWLING; *Sid Sorokin:* Nick LARKIN; *Hines:* Neville MOSS; *Mabel* Marion HENRYS; *Gladys:* Emily WARREN; *Hasler:* Peter SMITH; *Pop:* Paul STANLEY. *Director:* Kathryn HENRYS; *Producer:* Julie WRIGHT.

ST SIMON AND ST JUDE'S PRIMARY SCHOOL; Newport Road, GREAT LEVER BL3 2DT; 01204 526165 / 520232; **CAZ:** 46, C4

123. JACK AND THE BEANSTALK; SS SIMON AND JUDE ADS; *18-21 February2004.*

ST THOMAS CHURCH OF ENGLAND PRIMARY SCHOOL; Eskrick Street, Halliwell BL1 3BJ; 01204 841509; **CAZ:** 31, H3

269. PINOCCHIO by Stephen Boyes, based on the original story by Carlo Collodi; MANCHESTER ACTORS COMPANY; *2 March 2005.*

ST VINCENT'S; 01204 64049

84. THE LOVE MATCH by Glenn Melvyn; ST VINCENT'S DS; *26 – 30 October 2004. Bill Brown:* Bert HALLIDAY; *Sal Brown:* Maureen CLARE; *Wally Binns:* Howard CLAN; *Emma Binns:* Maureen McMANUS. *Rose Brown:* Julie NAPPIN; *Alf Hall:* Patrick MALONEY; *Arthur Ford:* Giuseppe RUOTOLO; *Percy Brpwn:* Ben KILBURN. *Director:* Mary RILEY

105, LOVE ME SLENDER by Vanessa Brooks; ST VINCENT'S DS; *31 May – 4 June 2005.*

SHARPLES HIGH SCHOOL; Hill Cot Road BL1 8SN; 01204 308421; CAZ: 19, E6

268. MACBETH by William Shakespeare; MANCHESTER ACTORS COMPANY; *7 March2005.*

SMITHILLS HALL; Smithills Dean Road BL1 7NP; 01204 332 337; CAZ: 31, 1F.

SMITHILLS SCHOOL; Smithills Dean Road BL1 6JS; 01204 842382; CAZ: 31, G1

THEATRE CHURCH; Seymour Road, ASTLEY BRIDGE BL1 8PG; 01204 364355. CAZ: 32, B2

81. FISH OUT OF WATER by Derek Benfield; ST PAUL'S AOS; *16-18 September 2004.*

88. JESUS CHRIST SUPERSTAR; Music by Andrew Lloyd Webber; Book and Lyrics by Tim Rice; CATS YOUTH THEATRE; *25-27 November 2005.*

120. WHEN WE ARE MARRIED by J B Priestley; ST PAUL'S AOS; *3-5 December 2003.*

91. ALADDIN by Stephen Duckham; FARNWORTH PERFORMING ARTS COMPANY; *19-22 January 2005.*

94. SOUTH PACIFIC; Music by Richard Rodgers; Book and Lyrics by Oscar Hammerstein II; ST PAUL'S AOS; *22-26 February 2005.*

102. WEST SIDE STORY; based on a conception by Jerome Robbins; Book by Arthur Laurents; Music by Leonard Bernstein; Lyrics by Stephen Sondheim; CHADS (Children's Amateur Dramatic Society); *17-21 May 2005.*

THORNLEIGH SALESIAN COLLEGE, Sharples Park BL1 6PQ; 01204 301351; **CAZ:** 31, H1. **G**

TRINITY CHURCH HALL; Market Street, FARNWORTH BL4 8EZ; 01204 573594 / 793172; **CAZ**: 63, F1

90. **DICK WHITTINGTON** by Eric Fowler; TRINITY PLAYERS; *15 –22 January 2005.*

TURTON HIGH SCHOOL; Bromley Cross Road BL7 6LT; 01204 595888; CAZ: 19, F4

MACBETH(150); DANNY SAPANI and MONICA DOLAN

UNION MILL; Vernon Street BL1 2PT; **CAZ:** 32: 5A

150. **MACBETH** by William Shakespeare; OUT OF JOINT; *28 September – 2 October 2004. Cast:* Kwaku ANKOMAH, Jotham ANNAN, Nicole CHARLES,

Sidney COLE, *Lady MacBeth:* Monica DOLAN, Kevin HARVEY, Chu OMAMBALA, Ben ONWUKWE, Christopher RYMAN, Susan SALMON, *MacBeth:* Danny SAPANI. *Director:* Max STAFFORD-CLARK; *Design:* Es DEVLIN; *Lighting:* Johanna TOWN; *Sound:* Gareth FRY; *Music* Felix CROSS

UNITED REFORMED CHURCH; Chorley Old Road BL1 3BE; 01204 527692; **CAZ:** 31, G4

82. **CAUGHT IN THE NET** by Ray Cooney; PHOENIX THEATRE COMPANY; *22-25 September 2005.*

98. **EDUCATING RITA** by Willy Russell; PHOENIX THEATRE COMPANY; *13 – 16 April 2005.*

104. **AN INSPECTOR CALLS** by J B Priestley; PHOENIX THEATRE COMPANY; *25 – 28 May 2005*

UNITED REFORMED CHURCH; Park Road, WESTHOUGHTON BL5 3H

VICTORIA SQUARE BL1 1RJ; CAZ: 32, B6

WALMSLEY PARISH HALL; Blackburn Road, EGERTON BL7 9RZ; 01204 520334; **CAZ:** 18, B1. **G, W**

85. **THE HOT MIKADO;** Lyrics by David H Bell; Musicis by Bob Bowman, based on th opera by W S Gilbert and Arthur Sullivan; WALMSLEY CHURCH AODS; *8-13 November 2004.*

99, **KISMET;** Book by Charles Lederer and Luther Davies, based on a play by Edward Knoblock; Music and Lyrics by Robert Wright and George Forrest, from the themes of Alexander Borodin; WALMSLEY CHURCH AODS; *25-30 April 2005.*

WASHACRE PRIMARY SCHOOL; Clough Avenue,

WESTHOUGHTON BL5 2NJ; 01942 813318

WESTHOUGHTON HIGH SCHOOL; Bolton Road BL5 3EF; 01942 814122

WESTHOUGHTON PAROCHIAL SCHOOL;
School Street BL5 2BG;
01942 812448

WITHINS SCHOOL;
Newby Road BL2 5JB;
01204 526519; 33, G

BURY

OUT OF THE BLUE (51); REJECTS REVENGE brilliant dramatisation of the sinking of HMS Thetis; Stoker (TIM HIBBERD), gathering the wreckage, finds the spot of paint that blocked the fatal test valve, watched by Kathleen (JULIE WALKER), whose father was among the dead.

ALL SAINTS; Elton; 0161-764 1431

ALL SAINTS CHURCH OF ENGLAND PRIMARY SCHOOL; Stand, Rufford Drive, WHITEFIELD M45 8PL; 0161-796 8005; **CAZ:** 51, E5

BROADOAK HIGH SCHOOL; Hazel Avenue BL9 7QT; 0161-797 6543; **CAZ:** 37, 3F

271. **ROMEO AND JULIET** by William Shakespeare; MANCHESTER ACTORS COMPANY; *25 November 2004*

267. **SMASHED** by Mike Harris; GW THEATRE COMPANY; *21 June 2005*

BURY CHURCH OF ENGLAND HIGH SCHOOL; Haslam Brow BL9 0TS; 0161-797 6236; **CAZ:** 36, C5

268. **MACBETH** by William Shakespeare; MANCHESTER ACTORS COMPANY; *7 February 2005.*

BURY GRAMMAR SCHOOL (BOYS); Tenterden Street BL9 0HN; 0161-797 2700; **CAZ:** 36, B3

BURY HEBREW CONGREGATION HALL; Sunny Bank Road BL9 8EB; 07973 725 683; **CAZ:** 50 D4

209. **YOU DON'T HAVE TO BE JEWISH** by Bob Booker; JEWISH THEATRE GROUP; *31 October 2004.*

BURY LIBRARY; Manchester Road BL9 0DR; 0161 - 705 5873; **CAZ:** 36, C3

BUTTERSTILE COUNTY PRIMARY SCHOOL; School Grove, PRESTWICH M25 9RJ; 0161-773 4211; **CAZ:** 81, E1

270. FIREBIRD by Stephen Boyes; MANCHESTER ACTORS COMPANY; *7 June 2005.*

CAMS LANE COUNTRY PRIMARY SCHOOL; RADCLIFFE M26 3SW; 0161-724 8018; CAZ: 49, F4

CASTLEBROOK HIGH SCHOOL; Parr Lane BL9 8LP; 0161-796 9820; **CAZ:** 51,G4

CHANTLERS COUNTY PRIMARY SCHOOL; Foulds Avenue BL8 2SF; 0161-761 1074; **CAZ:** 35, G3

270. FIREBIRD by Stephen Boyes; MANCHESTER ACTORS COMPANY; *14 July 2005.*

CHESHAM COUNTRY PRIMARY SCHOOL; Talbot Grove BL9 8PH; 0161-764 4927; CAZ: 23, G5 .

CONEY GREEN HIGH SCHOOL, Spring Lane, RADCLIFFE M26 9SZ; 0161-724 8704; **CAZ:** 49, G4

DERBY HIGH SCHOOL; Radcliffe Road BL9 9LH; 0161-764 1819; **CAZ:** B36, B5

ELIZABETHAN SUITE; Town Hall, 60 Knowsley Street BL9 0SW; 0161-253 6196; **CAZ:** 36, C4

ELTON HIGH SCHOOL, Walshaw Road BURY BL8 1RD; 0161-763 1434; **CAZ:** 35, G1

GORSEFIELD PRIMARY SCHOOL; Robertson Street, RADCLIFFE M26 4DW; 0161-733 5361; **CAZ:** 49, G3

GREENMOUNT PRIMARY SCHOOL; Holhouse Lane BL8 4HD; 01204 884031; CAZ: 21,

HEATON PARK PRIMARY SCHOOL; Cuckoo Lane WHITEFIELD M45 6TE; 0161-773 9554; CAZ: 67, F3

LANCASHIRE RAQUETS CLUB; Bury New Road, WHITEFIELD

LOWERCROFT COUNTY PRIMARY SCHOOL; Ashington Drive BL8 2TS; 0161-761 2798; **CAZ:** 35, F3

MARKET PLACE; CAZ 36, C3

MARKET STREET BL9 0AH; CAZ: 36, C3

THE MET ARTS CENTRE; Market Street, BURY BL9 0YZ; 0161-761 2216; **CAZ:** 36, C3; **G, H, S,W**

164. TOP BANANA; QUONDAM THEATRE; *12 October 2004.*

165. THE PUGILIST; BREAKING CYCLES; BENJI REID; *20 October 2004.*

166. THE HOLIDAY; BREAKING CYCLES;BENJI REID; *20 October 2004.*

167. STYLE 4 FREE; BREAKING CYCLES;BENJI REID; *20 October 2004.*

168. THE MAGIC CIRCUS; MAGIC CARPET THEATRE; *29 October 2004.*

180. MIND YOU ... WE'RE OFF TO SEE THE WIZARD; GET ON! THEATRE COMPANY; *3-4 November 2004.*

170. MACBETH 2004; by William Shakespeare; ITHAKA THEATRE

COMPANY; *16 November 2004.*

169. THE SNOW QUEEN, based on Hans Christian Anderson; ROCIAN PRODUCTION COMPANY; THE MET; *4 December 2004 – 3 January 2005.*

51. OUT OF THE BLUE by Andrea Earl and REJECTS REVENGE; *5 March 2005. Captain Bolus / Mr Bradshaw / Nun / Minister / Secretary:* Nicholas COLLETT; *Mrs Bolus / Mary Kelly / Rose / Maria / Woman In Bar:* Fionnuala DORRITTY; *Stoker Arnold / Priest / Navy Man:* Tim HIBBERD; *Jack Kelly / Navy Man / Nun / Tug Boat Crew:* Sean KEARNEY; *Lieutenant WOODS / Billy Kelly / Judge:* Ben O'SULLIVAN; *Trevor / William / Tug Boat Skipper / Pilot:* Matthew STEER; *Kathleen Kelly / Elsie / Barmaid / Mother:* Julie WALKER. *Director:* John WRIGHT; *Musical Director / Composer:* Simon JAMES; *Lighting Design / Video Design / Production Manager:* Mike WIGHT; *Set and Costume Design:* Michael BREAKEY; *Stage Manager:* Jo TOPPING; *Musician:* Carl BOWRY; *Costume Supervisor:* Amanda BRACEBRIDGE; *Assistant Multimedia Designer:* Danny WILLIAMS; *Assistant Technical Designer / Touring Technician:*Justin BREMAN; *Touring Technician:* Stacey POTTER; *Costume Maker:* Maureen SAUNDERS; *Music Programmer:* Pete FRANKS; *Technical Consultant:* Jon BURKE; *Additional Devising:* Russell EDWARDS, Ann FARRAR, Liam TOBIN; *Producer:* Ann FARRAR. **Journal: *16/2/05***

265. ACTING YOUR AGE by Mike Harris; GW THEATRE; *11 March 2005.*

52. THE GOSPEL OF MATTHEW, performed by George Dillon; VITAL THEATRE; *17 March 2005.* **Journal: *16/2/05***

171. STONE SOUP; MAC PRODUCTIONS; *22 March 2005.*

172. STIG OF THE DUMP by Clive King, adapted by IMAGE MUSICAL THEATRE; *26 March 2005. Director:* Brian THRESH; *Composer:* Roger HYMAN.

173. TWO by Jim Cartwright; STAGEWORKS; *7 April 2005.*

174. FIDDLER ON THE ROOF; based on the stories of Sholem Aleichem; Book by Joseph Stein; Music by Jerry Bock; Lyrics by

Sheldon Harnick; PADOS; *17 –21 May 2005.*

175. THE GOOD, THE BAD AND THE BOTOXED; MsFITS THEATRE COMPANY; *19 May 2005.*

176. THE SORCERER'S APPRENTICE; devised by Mark Pitman and Iklooshar; GARLIC THEATRE; *1 June 2005. Director:* Bob PEARCE; *Puppetry Director:* Iklooshar MALARA; *Music Composition:* Jonathan LAMBERT, Iklooshar MALARA; *Design:* M BARTONOVA.

177. AN INSPECTOR CALLS by J B Priestley; JEWISH THEATRE GROUP; *6-9 June 2005.*

178. STAND; REFORM THEATRE; *22 June 2005.*

179. FREEFALLING; RED LADDER; *23 June 2005.*

MOSSES CENTRE; Cecil Street

PADOS HOUSE; St Mary's Road, PRESTWICH M25 5AQ; 0161-766 4510; **CAZ**: 67, F5

PARRENTHORN HIGH SCHOOL; Heywood Road, PRESTWICH M25 2GR; 0161-773 1506; **CAZ:** 67, H2

PEEL CENTRE; Bury College, Parliament Street; 0161-763 1505 / 761 2216; **CAZ:** 36, C4

PHILIPS HIGH SCHOOL; Higher Lane, WHITEFIELD M45 7EZ; 0161-766 2720; **CAZ:** 66, C1

PRESTWICH HIGH SCHOOL; Heys Road M25 1JZ; 0161-773 2052; **CAZ:** 67, F4

SCROOGE (181); HOWARD RAW (centre), -a much praised performance – sees the hardships he has neglected

RADCLIFFE CIVIC HALL; Thomas Street M26 2UH; 0161-723 2917 / 705 5919 / 705 5111; **CAZ** 49,H4 **H**

181. **SCROOGE;** Book, Lyrics and Music by Leslie Bricusse, owing something to Charles Dickens; WHITEFIELD AODS; *19 – 23 October 2004.Tom Jenkins:* Keith McEVOY; *Fezziwig:* Neil COE; *Ebenezer Scrooge:* Howard CARTER; *Bob Cratchit:* Martin OGDEN; *Mrs Cratchit:* Hilary EASTWOOD; *Tint Tim:* Travis YATES; *Jacob Marley:* Mige DONOHUE; *Ghost of Christmas Past:* Una EVANS-O'CONNELL; *Ghost of Christmas Present:* Mike SAMMON; *Isabel / Helen:* Emma SAVAGE; *Nephew / Young Scrooge:* Jason CAIN. *Director:* Carol McCORMACK; *Musical Director:* Sarah DAY.

RADCLIFFE HALL METHODIST PRIMARY SCHOOL; Bury Street, RADCLIFFE

M26 2GB; 0161-723 2233; **CAZ:** 50, A2

RADCLIFF RIVERSIDE SCHOOL; Abden Street M26 3AT; 0161-723 3110; **CAZ:** 49, G4.

267. SMASHED by Mike Harris; GW THEATRE COMPANY; *11 July*

RADCLIFF RIVERSIDE SCHOOL; East Campus, Spring Lane M26 2SZ; 0161-723 3110; **CAZ:** 49, G4.

267. SMASHED by Mike Harris; GW THEATRE COMPANY; *11 July*

RIBBLE DRIVE PRIMARY SCHOOL; Whitefield M45 8NJ; 0161-766 6625; CAZ: 51, E6

THE ROCK; CAZ: 36, C3

ST ANNE'S; Chapel Street, TOTTINGTON BL8 4AP; CAZ: 21, H4

ST GABRIEL'S ROMAN CATHOLIC HIGH SCHOOL; Bridge Road BL9 0TZ; 0161 - 764 3186; **CAZ:** 36, B4

267. SMASHED by Mike Harris; GW THEATRE COMPANY; *24 June2005*

ST MARY'S CHURCH OF ENGLAND PRIMARY SCHOOL; Rectory Lane, PRESTWICH M25 1BP; 0161-733 3794; **CAZ:** 67, E5.

ST MONICA'S HIGH SCHOOL; Bury Old Road, PRESTWICH M25 0FG; 0161 - 773 6436; **CAZ:** 67, G6

3. SPARK by Mary Cooper; M6 THEATRE COMPANY; *1 December 2004.*

14. DANNY, KING OF THE BASEMENT by David S Craig; M6 THEATRE COMPANY; SHEFFIELD THEATRES; *5 April 2005.*

SEDGLEY PARK COUNTY PRIMARY SCHOOL; Bishops Road, PRESTWICH M25 0HT; 0161-773 3146; **CAZ:** 67, G6

STUBBINS COUNTY PRIMARY SCHOOL; Bolton Road North, Stubbins, RAMSBOTTOM BL0 0NA; 01706 822063; **CAZ:** 12, A4

THEATRE ROYAL; Smith Street, RAMSBOTTOM BL0 9AT; 01706 826760; **CAZ:** 12, 4D

TOTTINGTON HIGH SCHOOL, Laurel Street BL8 3LY; 01204 882327/ 885913; **CAZ:** 21, H5

TOTTINGTON SOUTH PRIMARY SCHOOL; Moorside Road BL8 3HR; 01204 886169; **CAZ**: 21, H6

WHITEFIELD GARRICK; Bank Street M45 7JF; 01204 591131; AZ: 29, E1

WOODHEY HIGH SCHOOL; Bolton Road, RAMSBOTTOM BL0 9QZ; 01706 825215; **CAZ:** 12, C6

268. **MACBETH** by William Shakespeare; MANCHESTER ACTORS COMPANY; *3 March 2005.*

THE WYLDE; CAZ: 36, C3

MANCHESTER

KES(435, previous page); ANDREW GARFIELD as Billy Casper wins Manchester Evening News Best Newcomer Award

163 PALATINE ROAD; DIDSBURY M20 2GH; **CAZ:** 125, E5

60/40 BAR; 448 Wilmslow Road, WITHINGTON M20 3BW; 0161-282 6040

ABBEY HEY INFANT SCHOOL; Abbey Hey Lane M18 8PF; 0161 - 223 1592; **CAZ:** 111, G2

ABBOT PRIMARY SCHOOL; Sudell Street, COLLYHURST M40 7PR; 0161-834 9529; CAZ: 7, E1

ABRAHAM MOSS CENTRE THEATRE; Crescent Road, CRUMPSALL M8 6UF; 0161-795 4186; **CAZ:** 82, C3; **G, H, W**

ABRAHAM MOSS HIGH SCHOOL; Crescent Road, CRUMPSALL M8 5UF; 0161-740 5141; **CAZ:** 82, C3

193. **MACBETH** by William Shakespeare; MANCHESTER ACTORS COMPANY; *25 March 2004*

A FE WE; Royce Road, HULME M15 5BP; **CAZ:** 9, G5

28. **FROM YARD 2 ABROAD** by Destiny Thomas; JAM DOWN THEATRE COMPANY; *5-6 February 2005. Performer:* Destiny THOMAS. **Journal:** 18/1/05

ALBERT SQUARE; CAZ: 5, H6

ALMA PARK PRIMARY SCHOOL; Errwood Road, LEVENSHULME M19 2PF; 0161 - 224 8789; CAZ: 126, C1

APOLLO; Stockport Road, ARDWICK M12 6AP; 0870 401 8000; **CAZ:** 11, F4

ARDEN COLLEGE; Sale Road, NORTHENDEN M23 0DD; 0161-957 1715. **CAZ:** 136, A2.

ARDWICK YOUTH CENTRE; 100 Palmerston Street M12; 0161- 273 1763

ARNDALE CENTRE; CAZ: 6,A4

ASHES SOCIAL CLUB; Zeta Street, MOSTON M9 4ZA; 0161-681 0558; **CAZ:** 83, H4.

ATTIC; THE THIRSTY SCHOLAR; Archway 50, New Wakefield Street M1 5NP; 0161-236 6071; **CAZ:** 10, A3

22. TWISTED TRAILS or MOULDILOCKS AND THE THREE BEARS; created and performed by Nicola Hayes, Amy Hiscocks, Richard Sails and Maggie Walker; NOT ANOTHER THEATRE COMPANY; *1-2 February 2005.* **Journal:** 18/1/05

23. CABBAGES by Mark Winstanley and Lawremce Ghorre; GREEN LIGHT PRODUCTIONS; *1-2 February 2005.. Geoffrey:* Alan DICKIE; *Audrey / Nurse Hart:* Trees MAESSEN; *Warren / Orderly:* Mark WINSTANLEY; *Dr Spinoza:/ Noel / Policeman:* Steve BEZZINA; *Eric / Detective / Orderly:* Lawrence GHORRA. *Director:* Lawrence GHORRA; *Assistant Director:* Mark WINSTANLEY; *Lights / Sound / Set Production / Denouements:* Jonathon WINSTANLEY; *Costumes / Design:* Trees MAESSEN. **Journal:** 18/1/05

BABUSHKA; 2a The Printworks M4 2BS; 0161-832 1234; **CAZ:** 6,A3

BARCA; Arch 8, Catalan Square, Castle Street M3 4LZ; 0161-834 9957; **CAZ:** 9. E2

26. MARBLES Kate Hazlewood and Kathryn Haycock; K8 THEATRE COMPANY; *3-4 February 2005. Carol:* Kate HAZLEWOOD; *Myfanwy:* Kathryn HAYCOCK. **Journal:** 18/1/05

27. CHICKEN TIKKA MASALA; devised by Christian Knott, Laura

Bestley and Emanuela Greco; NEVER AGAIN PRODUCTIONS; *3-4 February 2005. Roy / Tom / Colin / Man:* Christian KNOTT; *Brittany:* Laura BESTLEY; *Paris:* Emanuela GRECO **Journal:** 18/1/05

BARLOW HALL PRIMARY SCHOOL; Darley Avenue M21 7JG; 0161-881 2158 / 1934; CAZ: 124, A4

BAR RISA; 40 Chorlton Street, M1 3HW; 0161-236 5663; **CAZ:** 10, B1

BARLOW HIGH SCHOOL; School Lane DIDSBURY M20 6JP; 0161-445 8053; CAZ: **137, G1**

BEAVER ROAD JUNIOR SCHOOL; DIDSBURY M20 6SX; 0161-445 5068; **CAZ:** 125, F6

270. FIREBIRD by Stephen Boyes; MANCHESTER ACTORS COMPANY; *6 June 2005. Babooshka / Mrs Kopek:* Susi WRENSHAW; *Diaghilev / Singer / Baba Yaga:* Stephen BOYES; *Stravinsky / Prince Ivan:* Gareth McCANN. *Director / Designer:* Stephen BOYES; *Vocal Arrangements:* Kerry HENDRY.

BEDLAM; 33 Peter Street M2 5BG; **CAZ:** 9, G1

22, 24, 229, 242; 24:7 THEATRE FESTIVAL

229. THE FIRST RULE OF COMEDY by Trevor Suthers; REALLIFE THEATRE; *24-29 July 2005. Gillian Ferrari:* Sue JAYNES. *Director:* Alan ROTHWELL; *Stage Manager:* Toby ROTHWELL. **Journal:** ***25/5/05***

242. THE HANGED MAN bt Alison White and Dean Ashton; RAISE CAIN THEATRE; *24-30 July 2005. Xavier Hardcastle:* Thomas ALDERSLEY; *Megan Constance:* Laura HARPER; *Ray Constance:* Dean ASHTON. *Directors:* Dean ASHTON, Julian WAITE; *Stage Management:* Mick RAWES. **Journal:** ***25/5/05***

22. TWISTED TRAILS or MOULDILOCKS AND THE THREE BEARS; created and performed by Nicola Hayes, Amy Hiscocks, Richard Sails and Maggie Walker; NOT ANOTHER THEATRE COMPANY; *25-30 July 2005.*

24. **ONE BIRD, TWO STONES** by Victoria Scowcroft, Neville Millar and Darren Langford; MIDAS TOUCH THEATRE COMPANY; *25-30 July 2005.*

BENCHILL PRIMARY SCHOOL; Benchill Road M22 8EJ; 0161-998 3075; **CAZ:** 136, A5

269. **PINOCCHIO** by Stephen Boyes, based on the original story by Carlo Collodi; MANCHESTER ACTORS COMPANY; *15 February 2005.*

BIRCH COMMUNITY CENTRE; Brighton Grove M14 5JG; 0161-224 4624; CAZ: 109, H5

BISHOP BILSBORROW MEMORIAL ROMAN CATHOLIC PRIMARY SCHOOL; Princess Road MI4 7LS; 0161-226 3649; **CAZ:**108, D4

269. **PINOCCHIO** by Stephen Boyes, based on the original story by Carlo Collodi; MANCHESTER ACTORS COMPANY; *17 February 2005.*

270. **FIREBIRD** by Stephen Boyes; MANCHESTER ACTORS COMPANY; *22 Julye 2005.*

BLUE BOX THEATRE; Chorlton High School, Nell Lane, CHORLTON-CUM-HARDY M21 7SL; 0161-882 1150; **CAZ:** 124, A2

210. **THE ROSES OF EYAM** by Don Taylor; YELLOW JELLY YOUTH THEATRE; *21 May 2005.*

190. **FANTASTIC FABLES: THE AESOP PROJECT;** BARLOW HALL PRIMARY SCHOOL; BROOKBURN PRIMARY SCHOOL; CHORLTON CHURCH OF ENGLAND PRIMARY SCHOOL; CHORLTON PARK PRIMARY SCHOOL; OSWALD ROAD PRIMARY SCHOOL; ST JOHN'S PRIMARY SCHOOL; *23-24 May 2005.*

200. **CHANGE;** CHORLTON HIGH SCHOOL; CITY COLLEGE MANCHESTER; *24 May 2005.*

197. **THE NET;** NK THEATRE ARTS; *25 May 2005*

WITHERING LOOKS (194); SUE RYDING and MAGGIE FOX bring the Bronte Sisters to he Chorlton Festival.

198. THE GREAT BIG JOURNEY; NK THEATRE ARTS; *26 May 2005.*

199. OUR STREET; NK THEATRE ARTS; *26 May 2005.*

194. WITHERING LOOKS by Maggie Fox and Sue Ryding; LIP SERVICE; *26 May 2005. Cast:* Maggie FOX, Sue RYDING.

154. SONYA'S GARDEN; M6 THEATRE COMPANY; *28 May 2005.*

Puppeteers: Sarah HAN, Simon KERRIGAN.

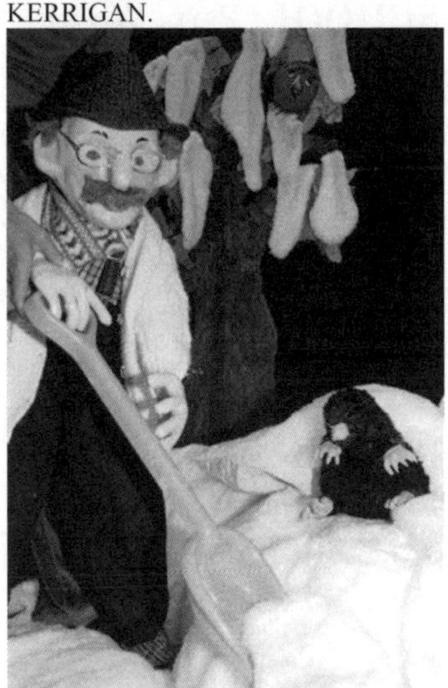

196. THE GARDEN IN WINTER; M6 THEATRE COMPANY; *28 May 2005. Puppeteers:* Sarah HAN, Simon KERRIGAN.

BOAT HOUSE; Platt Fields; CAZ: 109, G6

.BOOTH HALL CHILDREN'S HOSPITAL; Charleston Road M9 7AA; 0161-795 7000; CAZ: 69, H6 .

BOWKER VALE PRIMARY SCHOOL; Middleton Road M8 4NB; 0161 - 740 5993; **CAZ:** 68, B6

270. FIREBIRD by Stephen Boyes; MANCHESTER ACTORS COMPANY; *8 July 2005.*

BRIDGEWATER HALL; Lower Moseley Street M2 3WS; 0161-907 9000; CAZ: 9, H2; G, H, W

BRITON'S PROTECTION; 50 Great Bridgewater Street M1 5LE; 0161-236 5869; **CAZ**: 9, G2

BROAD OAK PRIMARY SCHOOL; Broad Oak Lane, DIDSBURY M20 5QP; 0161-445 6577; CAZ: 137, F3

BROADHURST PRIMARY SCHOOL; Williams Road, MOSTON M40 0AP; 0161-681 4288; **CAZ:** 84, C4

BROOKWAY HIGH SCHOOL; Moor Road.

WYTHENSHAWE M23 9BP; 0161-998 3992; **CAZ:** 135, 4E.

BURLINGTON ROOMS; The University of Manchester M13 9PL; 0161-275 2392; **CAZ**: 109, F2

202. **PUSH UP** by Roland Schimmelfennig; UNIVERSITY OF MANCHESTER DRAMA SOCIETY; *20 –22 February 2005. Directors:* Emily SMERDON, Lee SIMPSON.

204. **MIME PIECE,** devised and directed by Esther Wainwright; UNIVERSITY OF MANCHESTER DRAMA SOCIETY; *26-28 February 2005.*

208. **THE SWEETEST SWING IN BASEBALL** by Rebecca Gilman; UNIVERSITY OF MANCHESTER DRAMA SOCIETY; *11-13 March 2005. Dana:* Louise BAKKA; *Roy / Gary:* Sebastian CHRISPIN; *Erica / Dr Stanton:* Clemence BARTRAM; *Rhoda / Dr Gilbert:* Alannah CHANCE; *Brian / Michael:* Tom YOUNG. *Director:* Liam COOKE; *Lighting:* David JOHNSON; *Sound:* Jeremy SHELDRAKE.

BURNAGE HIGH SCHOOL; Parrs Wood Road M20 6EE; 0161-432 1527; **CAZ:** 125, H3

BURNAGE VILLAGE HALL; West Avenue M19 2NY; 0161-225 3587; CAZ: 126,B2.

BUTTON LANE PRIMARY SCHOOL; Northern Moor M23 0ND; 0161-998 3141 / 2680; CAZ: 135, F1

BUZZ CLUB; Southern Hotel, Mauldeth Road West M21 7SP; 0161-881 7048 / 1917 / 3567; **CAZ:** 124, A2

CAPITOL; Mabel Tylecote Building, Cavendish Street, All Saints M15 6BG; 0161-247 1306; **CAZ:** 10, B4

277. **YOU NEVER CAN TELL** by George Bernard Shaw; MANCHESTER METROPOLITAN UNIVERSITY SCHOOL OF THEATRE; *20-23 October 2004.*

YOU NEVER CAN TELL(277); among many achievements in a splendid production, SCOTT BRADLEY as William (left) and GRAEME BROOKS as Crampton were among several in a young cast who were notably successful in portraying older characters

Gloria: Laura JUSTICE; *Mrs Clandon:* Claire JONES; *Dolly:* Claire DISLEY; *Parlour Maid:* Emily STAVELEY-TAYLOR; *Waiter:* Scott BRADLEY; *Valentine:* Jack ALLEN; *Philip:* Ross GRANT; *Mr Crampton:* Graeme BROOKES; *M'Comas:* Dale CLARK; *Bohun:* Chris HARGREAVES. *Director:* David BYRNE; *Designer:* Louis PRICE; *Lighting / Sound:* Mark THURSTON; *Stage Manager:* James NICKERSON; *Wardrobe Supervisor:* Sheila PAYNE; *Lighting Crew:* Annie WALLACE.

278. **A LAUGHING MATTER** by April de Angelis; MANCHESTER METROPOLITAN UNIVERSITY SCHOOL OF THEATRE; *3-6 November 2004. Samuel Johnson:* Gareth BAYLISS; *Oliver Goldsmith / Duke of Kingston:* Paul MALLON; *James Boswell / Mr Barry:* Paul JOHNS; *Edmund Burke / Bounce:* Marcus J EVANS; *Joshua Reynolds / Cross / Larpent:* Andrew CHAMBERLAIN; *David Garrick:* Robert HARDMAN; *Mrs Eva Garrick:* Catherine GROSE; *Lady Kingston:* Jackie LINDSAY; *Reverend Richard*

THE HOUSE OF POMEGRANATES (279); the whole year combines to create a lively Christmas production; here, left to right: DALE CLARK, HELEN TRAHAR, GARETH BAYLISS, PAULJOHNS, PHILL FORD, SELINA DANIELS and ROSS GRANT.

Cumberland / O'Ryan: Arron JONES; *Sam Cautherlay:* Phill FORD; *Mrs Sussanah Cibber:*Paula WILLIAMSON; *Mrs Butler:* Helen TRAHAR; *Mrs Lavinia Barry / Master Barry:* Ruth E COCKBURN; *Mr Charles Macklin:* Wesley THOMAS; *Hannah More:* Nicole HALL; *Peg Woffington:* Selena DANIELS. *Director:* John GARDYNE; *Assistant Director:* Owain ROSE; *Designer:* Louise RICE; *Lighting / Sound:* Mark THURSTON; *Stage Manager:* James NICKERSON; *Wardrobe Supervisor:* Sheila PAYNE; *Lighting Crew:* Annie WALLACE.

279. A HOUSE OF POMEGRANATES by Oscar Wilde, adapted by MANCHESTER METROPOLITAN UNIVERSITY SCHOOL OF THEATRE; *15 – 18 December 2004.* **The Young King:** Emily STAVELY-TAYLOR, Chris HARGREAVES, Andrew CHAMBERLAIN, Marcus J EVANS, Dale CLARK, Paul MALLON; **The Star Child:** Scott BRADLEY, Nicole HALL, Arron JONES, Claire JONES,

Paula WILLIAMSON, Gaeme BROOKES, Wesley THOMAS; **The Birthday of The Infanta:**Paul JOHNS, Phill FORD, Selena DANIELS, Catherine GROSS, Gareth BAYLISS, Ross GRANT; **The Fisherman and His Soul:** Claire DISLEY, Ruth E COCKBORN, Robert HARDMAN, Jackie LINDSAY, Helen TRAHAR, Colin CONNOR, Jack ALLEN. *Director:* Andy CROOK; *Assistant Director:* Catherine PASKELL; *Designer:* Louise PRICE; *Lighting / Sound:* Mark THURSTON; *Stage Manager:* Owain ROSE; *Wardrobe Supervisor:* Sheila PAYNE; *Wardrobe Assistant:* Laura JUSTICE; *Lighting Crew:* Annie WALLACE.

280. **THE COUNTRY** by Martin Crimp; LIBRARY THEATRE; *23-26 February 2005. Richard:* Martin WENNER; *Corinne:* Meriel SCHOLFIELD; *Rebecca:* Renee WELDON. *Director:* David KENWORTHY; *Designer:* Louis PRICE; *Lighting Designer:* Pradeep DASH; *Sound Designer:* Paul GREGORY; *Company Stage Manager:* Lisa HALL; *Deputy Stage Manager On The Book:* Kirsty RUSSELL; *Assistant Stage Manager:* Pippa SMITH-AITCHISON; *Additional Wardrobe Assistance:* Jeanette PICKWELL.

31. **FURTHER THAN THE FURTHEST THING** by Zinnie Harris; MANCHESTER METROPOLITAN UNIVERSITY SCHOOL OF THEATRE; *2-5 February 2005. Francis:* Gareth BAYLISS; *Bill:* Scott BRADLEY; *Mr Hanson:* Graeme BROOKES; *Rebecca:* Ruth E COCKBURN; *Mill:* Claire JONES. *Director:* Hywel EVANS; *Designer:* Emily PAIN; *Assistant Director:* Andrew ROSSER; *Lights / Sound:* Mark THURSTON; *Costume:* Sheila PAYNE; *Music Composer / Performer:* Iain JACKSON; *Stage Manager:* Owain ROSE; *Set Builder:* Des BIRLEY; *Lighting Crew:* Alice BATE; *Stage Crew:* Karl DOBBY; *Assistant to Designer:* David MEACHAM; *Magic Consultant:* Quentin REYNOLDS. **Journal:** 18/1/05

281. **A CHORUS OF DISAPPROVAL** by Alan Ayckbourn; MANCHESTER METROPOLITAN UNIVERSITY SCHOOL OF THEATRE; *16-19 February 2005. Director:* Claude CLOSE.

282. **SAVED** by Edward Bond; MANCHESTER METROPOLITAN UNIVERSITY SCHOOL OF THEATRE; *9-12 March 2005. Director:* Nick HUTCHINSON

283. **SPRING AWAKENING** by Frank Wederkind; MANCHESTER METROPOLITAN UNIVERSITY

SCHOOL OF THEATRE; *4 – 7 May 2005. Director:* Chris HONER

61. POEMS OF ANTIGONE, developed from Sophocles by MANCHESTER METROPOLITAN SCHOOL OF THEATRE and TEATR PIESN KOZLA MA COURSE; *11 May 2005. Performers:* Sonia BEINROTH, Robert BERGE, Zoe CROWDER, Antonia DGGETT, Ewan DOWNIE, Bryn EVANS, Magdalena KLEPARSKA, Kate LUSH Neil McDONALD, Mark McGURRAN, Kate PERRY, Wilhelm STOYLEN. *Project Leader:* Anna ZUBRZYCKI, *Artistic Director:* Grzegorz BRAL; *Costume Designer:* Bajka TWOREK; *Lighting:* Arkadiusz CHRUSCIEL; *Acting Consultant:* Helene KAUT-HOWSON; *Text Consultant:* Irina BROWN; *Voice Work:* Zygmunt MOLIK; *Greeks Chorus Consultation:* Tomasz RODOWICZ; *MA Course Co-ordinator:* Niamh DOWLING.

286. CHRONICLES – A LAMENTATION; PIESN KOZLA; *13 May 2005.*

284. MARVIN'S ROOM bu Scott McPherson; MANCHESTER METROPOLITAN UNIVERSITY SCHOOL OF THEATRE; *1-4 June 2005. Bessie:* Helen TRAHAR; *Doctor Wally:*Dale CLARK; *Ruth:* Ruth COCKBURN; *Seb:* Andrew EDWARDS; *Lee:* Selena DANIELS; *Dr Charlotte / Retirement Home Director:* Nicole HALL; *Hank:* Paul MALLON; *Charlie:* Ross GRANT; *Marvin:* Paul JOHNS.

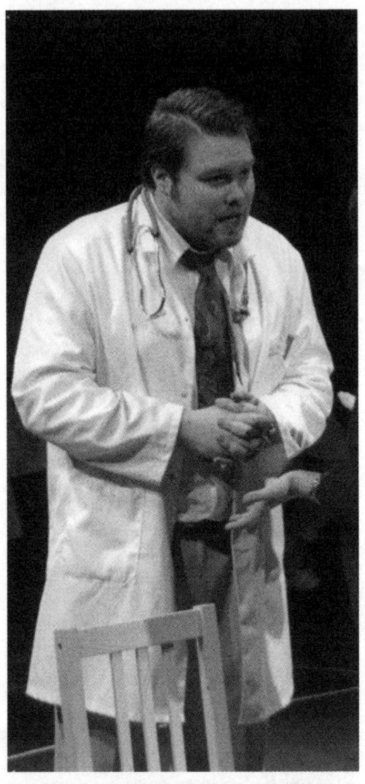

MARVIN'S ROOM (284); if "Wally" means the same in American as it does in local English, DALE CLARK proved able to be the perfect embodiment of a doctor of that name; an hilarious start to a play which dealt distinctively with death and suffering

285. **BREEZEBLOCK PARK** by Willy Russell; MANCHESTER METROPOLITAN UNIVERSITY SCHOOL OF THEATRE; *15-18 June 2005.*

CASTLEFIELD ARENA; off Liverpool Road M60 3DQ; **CAZ:** 9, E2

ex CASTLEFIELD GALLERY; Campfield Avenue Arcade, off Liverpool Road M3 4FH; **CAZ:** 9, E2

CATHEDRAL; M3 1SX; **CAZ:** 5, H4

CAVENDISH ROAD PRIMARY SCHOOL; M20 1JG; 0161-445 4891; **CAZ:** 124, D4

CEDAR MOUNT HIGH SCHOOL; Mount Road M18 7GR;0161-248 7009; **CAZ:** 111, E4

THE CELLAR; Union Building, Manchester University M13 9PL; 0161-275 2930; **CAZ:** 109, F2.

203. **THE GOAT, OR WHO IS SYLVIA?** by Edward Albee; UNIVERSITY OF MANCHESTER DRAMA SOCIETY; *23-25 February 2005. Directors:* Tom COPESTAKE, Oli LYTTELTON.

205. **GAGARIN WAY** by Gregory Burke; UNIVERSITY OF MANCHESTER DRAMA SOCIETY; *1-3 March 2005. Director:* Poppy MERTON,

207. **A DAY IN THE DEATH OF JOE EGG** by Peter Nichols; UNIVERSITY OF MANCHESTER DRAMA SOCIETY; *8-10 March 2005. Director:* Alex BARSON.

262. **A REVENGE TRAGEDY;** based on the film of the same name; UNIVERSITY OF MANCHESTER DRAMA SOCIETY; *26 – 28 May 2005. Albert Spica:* Adam HARPER; *Georgina Spica:* Lily LOWE-MYERS; *Richard Borst:* James MATTHEWS-PAUL; *Michael:* Nicolas THOMPSON; *Mews:* Joel H SWANN; *Cory:* Ed BOWMAN; *Pup:* Sophie WEBBER; *Patricia:* Katherine LITTLER; *Alica:* Gabrielle RITCHIE; *Roy:* Rob HAYES; *STRING QUARTET: 1st Violin:* Dewi TUDOR-JONES; 2nd Ryuko REED;

Viola: William YOUNG; *Cello:* Louise COWLEY. *Directors:* Melissa SMITH, Johny MILLER; *Stage Manager:* Sam CHESTER; *Producer:* Laura FISHER; *Costume / Lighting:* Rachel PINNOCK; *Design:* Emily JORDAN; *Stage Hands:* Jessica DAVIES, Clare QUINN.

CENTRAL LIBRARY; St Peter's Square M2 5PD; 0161-234 1974. CAZ: 9, H1. W

CHAPEL WALKS; M2 1HN; CAZ: 5, H5

CHRIST CHURCH; Parrs Wood Road M20; 0161-225 5070; **CAZ:** 125, H5

CHORLTON PARK; CAZ: 124, A2

CHORLTON PARK PRIMARY SCHOOL ; Barlow Moor Road M21 7HH; 0161-881 1621; CAZ: 124, A2

CITY COLLEGE MANCHESTER; City Campus, Whitworth Street M1 3HB; 0161-236 3418; **CAZ:** 10, B1

182. THE WITCHES OF LANCASHIRE by Richard Brome and Thomas Heywood; ARDEN SCHOOL OF THEATRE; *2-4 December 2004.* *Mistress Generous:* Kate HAZELWOOD; *Joan Seely:* Sarah JONES; *Winnie Seely / Girl:* Amy HISCOCKS; *Parnell:* Emanuela GRECO; *Moll:* Nicola HAYES; *Doughty:* Kathryn HAYCOCK; *Gillian:* Francesca LARKIN; *Meg:* Trees MAESSEN; *Mawd:* Ann-Marie THOMAS; *Shakestone / Millar / Witch:* Rebecca BLACKSHAW; *Generous:* Lawrence GHORRA; *Seely / Soldier / Bantam:* Tom HARVEY; *Gregory Seely:* Richard Lee KIRKBRIDE; *Lawrence / Robert / Arthur:* Neville MILLAR. *Director:* Alan PATTISON; *Designer:* David MILLARD; *Production Manager:* Sharon STONEHAM; *Theatre Technicians:* Greg AKEHURST / Phil BUCKLEY; *Costumes:* Jacquie DAVIES; *Wardrobe:* Nicky RANSOM; *Lighting Design:* Chris WHITWOOD; *Sound Design:* Louis GILBERT; *Sound Operator:* Karen HATHERLY; *Lighting Operator* :Emily SCALE; *Stage Manager:* Andy OWEN; *Deputy Stage Manager:* Jo GREENWOOD;

THE WITCHES OF LANCASHIRE (182): a notable and enterprising production; here, left to right, DESTINY THOMAS, TREES MAESSEN (lying), KATE HAZELWOOD (in mask),NICOLA HAYES, FRANCESCA LARKIN

Assistant Stage Manager: Louise LAING; *Painter:* Richard FOXTON

183. PERICLES by William Shakespeare; ARDEN SCHOOL OF THEATRE; *9-11 December 2004. Gower:* Victoria SCOWCROFT; *Marina:* Margaret WALKER; *Thaisa:* Victoria BROWN; *Diana:* Lowri SHIMMIN; *Dionyza / Daughter of Antiochus:* Laura BESTLEY; *Bawd / Lychorida:* Catia SOEIRO; *Pericles:* Darren LANGFORD; *Lysimachus:* Geoff MORTON; *Helicanus:* Christian KNOTT; *Antiochus / Cerimon:* Richard SAILS; *Simonides / Leonine:* Alan

MARGARET WALKER as Marina

DICKIE; *Boult / Thaliard:* Stephen BEZZINA; *Cleon / Pander:* Stephen BLOWER. *Director:* Julia NORTH; *Designer:* Heather SHAW; *Production Manager:* Sharon STONEHAM; *Theatre Technicians:* Greg AKEHURST / Phil BUCKLEY; *Costumes:* Jacquie DAVIES; *Wardrobe:* Nicky RANSOM; *Lighting Design:* Alice BATE; *Sound Design:* Claire MacLEA; *Sound Operator:* Julie NAYLOR; *Lighting Operator :*Stephen BEASLEY; *Stage Manager:* Camilla O'NEILL; *Deputy Stage Manager:* Toby LARNER; *Assistant Stage Manager :*Ellie MOGG; *Painter:* Richard FOXTON

271. **ROMEO AND JULIET** by William Shakespeare; MANCHESTER ACTORS COMPANY; *17 December 2004*

184. **THE HOUSE OF BERNADA ALBA** by Federico Garcia Lorca; ARDEN SCHOOL OF THEATRE; *3-5 March 2005. Maria Josepha / Second Mourner:* Victoria BROWN; *Bernada Alba:* Vicki SCOWCROFT; *Angustias:* Lowri SHIMMIN; *Magdalena:* Sarah JONES; *Amelia:* Emanuela GRECO; *Martirio:* Maggie WALKER; *Adela:* Francesca LARKIN; *Prudencia / First Mourner:* Laura BESTLEY; *Poncia:* Catia SOEIRO; *Maid:* Trees MAESSEN; *Beggar Woman / Girl:* Amy HISCOCKS. *Director:* Robert

CATIA SOEIRO as Poncia

MARSDEN; *Designer:* David MILLARD; *Production Manager:* Sharon STONEHAM; *Theatre Technicians:* Greg AKEHURST / Phil BUCKLEY; *Costumes:* Jacquie DAVIES; *Wardrobe:* Nicky RANSOM; *Lighting Design:* Robin WATKINSON; *Sound Design:* Clare McALEA; *Sound Operator:*Lynsey HICKS; *Lighting Operator :*Stephen BEASLEY; *Stage Manager:* Caroline WEAVIS; *Deputy Stage Manager:* Rachel REEVE; *Props:* Camilla O'NEILL; *Painter:* Alison EYERS.

48. **MOUNTAIN LANGUAGE; SILENCE; PARTY TIME** by Harold Pinter; ARDEN SCHOOL OF THEATRE; *10-12 March 2005.* **Mountain Language:** *Young Woman:*

Programme Details

TOUCHED (185); VE Day;. CATIA SOEIRO (Mary), DARREN LANGFORD (Johnny), VICKY BROWN (Betty), AMY HISCOCKS (Sandra) , left to right, with NICOLA HAYES in front celebrate the announcement

Nicola HAYES; *Elderly Woman:* Kathryn HAYCOCK; *Sergeant:* Alan DICKIE; *Officer:* Stephen BEZZINA; *Guard:* Christian KNOTT; *Prisoner:* Steven BLOWER; *Hooded Man:* Darren LANGFORD; *Second Guard:* Richard Lee KIRKBRIDE; **Silence:** *Ellen:* Rebecca BRADSHAW; *Rumsey:* Richard SAILS; *Bates:* Neville MILLAR; **Party Time:** *Terry:* Geoff MORTON; *Gavin:* Darren LANGFORD; *Dusty:* Nicola HAYES; *Melissa:* Kathryn HAYCOCK; *Liz:* Kate HAZLEWOOD; *Charlotte:* Destiny THOMAS; *Fred:* Richard Lee KIRKBRIDE; *Douglas:* Lawrence GHORRA; *Jimmy:* Steven BLOWER. *Director:* Helen PARRY; *Designer:* Julieann HESKIN; *Production Manager:* Sharon STONEHAM; *Theatre Technicians:* Greg AKEHURST / Phil BUCKLEY; *Costumes:* Jacquie DAVIES; *Wardrobe:* Nicky RANSON; *Lighting Design:* Mary-Alice BATE; *Sound Design:* Louis GILBERT; *Sound Operator:* Julie NAYLOR; *Lighting Operator:*James WAKE; *Stage*

Managers: Rachel GARRETT, Caroline WEAVIS; *Deputy Stage Manager:* Gemma AKSIUK; *Assistant Stage Manager:* Sally ROBETS; *Painter:* Richard FOXTON. **Journal:** 7/3/05.

185. **TOUCHED** by Stephen Lowe; ARDEN SCHOOL OF THEATRE; *2-4 June 2005. Sandra:* Amy HISCOCKS; *Mary:* Catia SOEIRO; *Betty:* Victoria BROWN; *Johnny:* Darren LANGFORD; *Joan:* Nicola HAYES; *Pauline:* Delphi MacPHERSON; *Bridie:* Francesca LARKIN; *Keith:* Geoff MORTON; *Harry:* Richard Lee KIRKBRIDE; *Mother:* Kathryn HAYCOCK. *Director:* David O'SHEA; *Designer:* David MILLARD; *Design Assistants:* Vicki MacKENZIE, Holly RICHMOND, Steven ROGAN; *Design Supervisor:* Mark HINTON; *Production Manager Stage Manager Supervisor: :* Sharon STONEHAM; *Theatre Technician:* Phil BUCKLEY; *Costumes:* Jacquie DAVIES; *Wardrobe:* Michelle HUITSON; *Lighting Design:*Robin WATKINSON; *Sound Design:* Dan STEELE; *Sound Assistant :*Lynsey HICKS; *Sound Supervisor:* Christopher BRIDE; *Lighting Operator :* James WAKE; *Stage Managers:* Nikk STOREY, Julieann HESKIN; *Deputy Stage Manager:* Ellie MOGG; *Assistant Stage Manager:* Gemma AKSIUK.

DESTINY THOMAS (Doreen) and STEPHEN BLOWER (Ernest) Talk In The Park.

186. **CONFUSIONS** by Alan Ayckbourn; ARDEN SCHOOL OF THEATRE; *9-11 June 2005.* **Mother Figure:** *Lucy:* Maggie WALKER; *Terry:* Steven BLOWER; *Rosemary:* Lowri SHIMMIN; **Drinking Companions:** *Harry:* Lawrence GHORRA; *Paula:* Sarah JONES; *Bernice:* Emanuela GRECO; *Waiter:* Neville MILLAR; **Between Mouthfuls:** *Pearce:* Richard SAILS; *Mrs Pearce:* Laura BESTLEY; *Polly:* Rebecca BLACKSHAW; *Martin:* Christian KNOTTS; *Waiter:* Neville MILLAR; **Gosforth's Fete:** *Gosforth:* Tom BELL; *Stewart:* Stephen BEZZINA; *Vicar:* Alan DICKIE; *Mrs Pearce:* Trees MAESSEN; *Milly:* Kate

HAZELWOOD; **A Talk In The Park:** *Beryl:* Victoria SCOWCROFT; *Doreen:* Destiny THOMAS; *Charles:* Stephen BEZZINA; *Ernest:* Steven BLOWER; *Arthur:* Neville MILLAR. *Director:* Paul JAYNES; *Design:* David MILLARD; *Design Assistand:* Emily CAMPBELL; *Production Manager:* Sharon STONEHAM; *Theatre Technician:* Phil BUCKLEY; *Costumes:* Jacquie DAVIES; *Wardrobe:* Michelle HUITSON; *Lighting Design:* Robin WATKINSON; *Sound Design:* Greg AKEHURST; *Sound Assistant:* Karen HATHERLY; *Lighting Operator :*Steven BEASLEY; *Stage Manager :*Caroline WEAVIS; *Deputy Stage Manager:* Louise LAING; *Assistant Stage Manager:* David WHITE

187. **THE THREE MUSKETEERS** by Alexandre Dumas, adapted by the cast; ARDEN SCHOOL OF THEATRE; *23-25 June 2005.* *D'Artagnan:* Graham ATKIN; *Treville:* James ARKINSON; *Tula / Sister Danielle / Page / Sister Agatha:* Dominique BELLAS; *Estaniania:* Hannah BINNS; *Chevreause:* Jane BRACHANIAC; *Bonacieux:* Marvin BROWN; *Pere:* Joe CRITCHLEY; *Athos:* Andrew CULLIMORE; *Anne:* Laura DONOUGHUE; *Kitty:* Kimberley DOOLEY; *Rochefort:* Dominic DOUGHTY; *Margaret:* Hazel EARLE; *Buckingham:* Tim FALLOWS; *Flora / Apprentice / Page:* Sian HASLOCK; *Jussac / O'Reilly:* Stephen GILROY; *Louis:* Karl JONES; *Constance:* Jennifer KAY; *Man 2 / Keeper / Auguste:* Aston KELLY; *Daughter 3/ Sister Veronique / Totturer:* Emma LAIDLAW; *Porthos:* Matthew LANNIGAN; *Daughter 1 / Chloe:* Jenny MORGAN; *Richlieu:* Joseph MORRIS; *Milady:* Karen OAKES; *Mere / Lady 2:* Louise O'LEARY; *Aramis:* John REEVEL; *Amelie / Lady 1 / Mother Superior:* Clair ROBINSON; *Innkeeper:* Rhian ROGERS; *Man 3 / Guard / Felton:* Mark SHAW; *Daughter 2 / Sister Angelica:* Laura SHARP; *Planchet:* Carl SZYMANEK; *Man 1 / Physician / Louise / Hostess:* Laura WILKINSON. *Director:* Mark LANGLEY; *Fight Director:* Andy QUINE; *Designer:* Emily CAMPBELL; *Production Manager:* Sharon STONEHAM; *Theatre Technician:* Phil BUCKLEY; *Costumes:* Jacquie DAVIES;; *Lighting Design:* Mary Alice BATE; *Sound Design:* Greg AKEHURST; *Sound Operator:* Lynsey HICKS; *Lighting Operator :*Mary Alice BATE; *Stage Managers:* Camilla O'NEILL, Caroline WEAVIS; *Assistant Stage Managers:* Gemma AKSUIK, Ellie MOGG; *Painter:* Julieann HESKIN

CLAREMONT INFANTS SCHOOL; Claremont Road, MOSS

SIDE M14 7NA; 0161-226 2066; **CAZ**: 109, E4

CLAYTON YOUTH CENTRE; Clayton Street M11; 0161 - 223 3321

CHORLTON PARK PRIMARY SCHOOL ; Barlow Moor Road M21 7HH; 0161-881 1621; CAZ: 124, A2

CLAREMONT JUNIOR SCHOOL; Claremont Road, MOSS SIDE M14 7NA; 0161-226 2066; CAZ: 109, E4

CLAYTON YOUTH CENTRE; Clayton Street M11; 0161 - 223 3321

THE COMEDY STORE; Deansgate Locks, Whitworth Street West M1 5WZ; 0161-839 9595 /0870 593 2932; comedy-store.net ; **CAZ:** 9, H2

CONTACT; Oxford Road M15 6JA; 0161-274 0600; **CAZ:** 109, F2 **D,G,H,S,W**

288. **TAGGED** by Louise Wallwein; RED LADDER THEATRE COMPANY; *21-25 September 2004.*

287. **SILENT CRY** by Madani Younis; ASIAN THEATRE SCHOOL; RED LADDER THEATRE COMPANY; *22-23 September 2004. Safia Ahmed:* Nasreen HUSSAIN; *Bashir Ahmed:* Sanjiv HATRE; *Nadeem Ahmed:* Kashif KHAN; *Noreen Ahmed:* Bhavini RAVAL; *Shahid Khan:* Dharmesh PATEL; *Nina Desai:* Amelia SABERWAL; *PC1:* Mohammed IRFAN; *PC2:* Ivan STOTT. *Directors:* Madani YOUNIS, Sarah BRIGHAM; *Assistant Director:* Wakas ZAMURAD; *Dramaturg:* Seamus FINNEGAN; *Set Design:* Leslie TRAVERS; *Composer:* Ovan STOTT; *Additional Vocals:* Nursrat BHATTI; *Lighting Design / Visuals Director:* Jeremy NICHOLLS; *Set Build:* Marcus RSAPLEY; *Stage Manager:* Martin TOOMER.

289. **SKITTISH** by Jonathan McGrath; IKEBANA PRODUCTIONS; *30 September – 2 October 2004.*

290. **COMPACT FAILURE** by Jennifer Farmer; CLEAN BREAK; *6-9 October 2004. Ruthie:* Claire-Louise CORDWELL; *Chelle:* Lorna GAYLE; *Maya:* Sharlene EHYTE. *Director:* Sarah ESDAILE; *Designer:* Ti GREEN; *Lighting Designer:* Natasha CHIVERS; *Sound Designer:* Ilona SEKACZ.

9. **OFFLINE** by Melanie Hughes, Dominic Berry and Carly Henderson; LIGHT ENSEMBLE; *12-16 October 2004. Mel:* Melanie HUGHES**;** *Dom / Nick:* Dominic BERRY**;** *Carly* Carly HENDERSON**;** ***Antony:*** Antony POWELL. *Sound**:*** Justine FLYNN; *Lighting / Stage Design:* Pete O'HAGAN. **Journal:** 13/10/04

291. **MANDRAGORA – KING OF INDIA** by Nirjay Mahindru; TARA ARTS; *14 – 16 October 2004. Jasper / Lord Hastings :*Shaun CHAWDHARY; *King Mandragora / Spade:* Avin SHAH; *Thatch / Lord Munshi:* Tim BRUCE; *Bindio / Lord Susna:* Arif JAVID; *Narrator / Sunita:* Anushka DAHSSII; *Lady Catherine / Psychic:* Emma BROWN. *Director:* Jatinder VERMA; *Designer:* Claudia MAYER; *Lighting Designer:* Jonathan CLARK; *Music:* Chandran VEYATTUMMAL; *Production and Stage Manager:* John PAGE; *Costume Supervisor:* Claire HARDACRE.

293. **58** by Philippe Cherbonnier; YELLOW EARTH THEATRE; *21-22 October 2004. Kate:* Terri-Ann BRUMBY; *Dave / Chen Min:* Tim McCLUSKEY; *Zhaodi:* Nina KWOK; *Xiu Xiu / Meng Xing:* Liz SUTHERLAND; *Granny / Lan:* Bronwyn

SKINNER-LIM. *Director:* David K S TSE; *Set & Costume Design:* Sigyn

58: - the number of Chinese found suffocated in a lorry trying to enter Britain;

STENQVIST; *Lighting Designer:* Douglas KUHRT; *Videomaker:* Shan Pui NG; *Sound Designer:* Roger DOUEK; *Movement Consultant:* Caroline PARKER; *Production Manager:* Jo RAWLINSON; *Company Stage Manager:* Mark B HENDERSON; *Deputy Stage Manager:* Jen WALSH.

MANIA (292) demonstrated observed a society we live by MIKE MAYHEW and GERRY POTTER conduction part of their performance in a rainstorm on Oxford Road while those inside Contact Theatre could see and hear not only their every act and word but those whom they encountered.

292. MANIA; MAYHEW & Co.LLABORATORS; *22-23 October 2004. Performer/ Clyde Tolson:* Michael MAYHEW; *Performer / J Edgar Hoover:* Gerry POTTER; *Performer / Helen Grady:* Sadie MADDOCKS; *Chat Room Host / Undercurrent:* Mick FUZZ; *Voices of History:* Sara MAGUIRE, Jo LEDWIDGE, Kelly ROBBERTS, Sonia HUGHES, Anna CAHILL. *Director / Writer:* Michael MAYHEW; *Digital Artist / Lifeliner:* Sara MAGUIRE; *Sound Artist:* Dan STEELE; *Production / Light Artist:* Mark RITCHIE; *Software / Web Developer:* Asa CALOW; *Documentors / Surveyors / Archivists / Witnesses:* Stacey POTTER, Paula HATELY, Sophia Di MARTINO, Andrea POPOVER; *Lifeliner:* Roshana RUBIN-MAYHEW; *Wardrobe:* Keith RIDING.

294. ZERO DEGREES (AND DRIFTING) by Claire Duffy, Liz Margree, Jon Spooner and Chris Thorpe; UNLIMITED THEATRE; ***26 –*** *27 October 2004. Cast:* Elizabeth BESBRODE, Sarah BELCHER,

Nathan RIMMEL, Theron SCHMIDT, Chris THORPE. *Director:* Jon SPOONER, *Designer:* Davis FARLEY; *Lighting Design:*Guy HOARE*; Sound Design*: Gareth FRY; *Artictic Associate:* Chris GOODE.

295. SOMETHING DARK; written and performed by Lemn Sissay; CONTACT; APPLES AND SNAKES; *29 – 30 October 2005. Director:* John E McGRATH; *Musical Director:* Jim PARRIS; *Designer:* Emma WEE; *Lighting Designer:* Anne MEEUSSEN; *Assistant Producer:* Mike KIRCHNER; *Producer:* Geraldine COLLINGE.

LEMN SISSAY

296-301 WORD UP! New Writing Festival:

296. DEAR JESUS by Hannah Salt; CONTACT; BBC NORTHERN EXPOSURE; *28 October 2004. Cast:* Andrew GROSE, Rachel BROGAN, Leyland O'BRIAN, Jaheda CHOUDHURY. *Director:* Cheryl MARTIN; *Writing Tutor:* Linda BROGAN

297. CRISPS by Claire Dean; CONTACT; BBC NORTHERN EXPOSURE; *28 October 2004. Cast:* Andrew GROSE, Rachel BROGAN, Leyland O'BRIAN, Jaheda

CHOUDHURY. *Director:* Cheryl MARTIN; *Writing Tutor:* Linda BROGAN

298. ROUGE by Neil Virani; CONTACT; BBC NORTHERN EXPOSURE; *29 October 2004. Cast:* Andrew GROSE, Rachel BROGAN, Leyland O'BRIAN, Jaheda CHOUDHURY. *Director:* Cheryl MARTIN; *Writing Tutor:* Linda BROGAN

299. HELP by Jackie Hagan; CONTACT; BBC NORTHERN EXPOSURE; *29 October 2004. Cast:* Andrew GROSE, Rachel BROGAN, Leyland O'BRIAN, Jaheda CHOUDHURY. *Director:* Cheryl MARTIN; *Writing Tutor:* Linda BROGAN

300. F* BUDDHA** by Kelly Roberts; CONTACT; BBC NORTHERN EXPOSURE; *30 October 2004. Cast:* Andrew GROSE, Rachel BROGAN, Leyland O'BRIAN, Jaheda CHOUDHURY. *Director:* Cheryl MARTIN; *Writing Tutor:* Linda BROGAN

301. SPIKED by Martin Stannage; CONTACT; BBC NORTHERN EXPOSURE; *30 October 2004. Cast:* Andrew GROSE, Rachel BROGAN, Leyland O'BRIAN, Jaheda CHOUDHURY. *Director:* Cheryl MARTIN; *Writing Tutor:* Linda BROGAN

11. CRAZY LADY by Nona Shephard; TAAL PROJECT; CONTACT THEATRE; *10-20 November 2004. Cellist:* Nikki-Kate HEYES; *Claudia:* Heather PEACE; *Jaz:* Shobna GULATI. *Director:* Nona SHEPPARD; *Composer:* Nikki-Kate HEYES; *Design:* takis; *Production Managers:* Sharon STONEHAM, Nikk STOREY; *Board Operator:* Mark DISTIN **Journal:** 13/10/04

302. SINNER by Ben Payne; STAN WON'T DANCE; *16 November 2005. Performers and Directors:* Liam STEEL, Rob TANNION; *Design:* Ruth FINN; *Lighting Design:* Ian SCOTT.

303. BLOODY MESS; FORCED ENTERTAINMENT; *23-24 November 2005.*

13. THREE GOBBY COWS by Louise Twomey, Kate Henry and Deborah Brian; NEWFOUND THEATRE COMPANY; *19-22 January 2005.* **Women's Little Christmas:** *Kate:* Louise TWOMEY; **Monday Morning:** *Carla:* Kate HENRY; **Video Dating:** *Sandra:* Deborah BRIAN. *Director:* Chris SUDWORTH; *Producers:* Hellen

KIRBY, Iain SCOTT; *Stage Manager:* Julie PARKER. **Journal:** 13/10/04

304. BUBBYSAURUS by Catherine Kay; HAPPY THEATRE COLLECTIVE; *25 –29 January 2005. Vanda:* Catherine Kay; *Worm:* Sorrel ALEXANDER; *Sharna:* Lorna LEWIS; *Kile:* Justin GREGG. *Director:* David SPENCER; *Stage Manager:* Sorrel ALEXANDER.

305. LOVE, SEX AND CIDER by Paul Charlton; JACUZZI THEATRE; *3-4 February 2005. Director:* Stephen ELLIOTT.

306. ON THE VERGE by Mike Kenny; MIND THE … GAP; *15 February 2005. Cast:* Jez COLBORNE. *Director:* Tim WHEELER; *Film Maker:* Jonathan BENTLEY; *Tour Company Managers:* Philippa D'NETTO, Maria THELWELL; *Production Manager:* Ben PUGH; *Project Manager:* Rachel PORTER; *Music:* Jel CLOBORNE; *British Sigh Language Interpreter:* Tony EVANS.

307. HYMNS by Chris O'Connell; FRANTIC ASSEMBLR; *22-26 February 2005. Cast:* Steven HOGGETT, Karl SULLIVAN, Joseph TRAYNOR, Eddie KAY. *Director:* Liam STEEL; *Co-Directors:* Scott GRAHAM, Steven HOGGETT; *Lighting Design:* Natasha CHIVERS; *Production Manager:* Richard EUSTACE; *Company Stage Manager:* Joni CARTER; *Technical Stage Manager:* Paul LIM; *Soundtrack:* Steven HOGGETT, DJ Andy CLEETON, Liam STEEL.

HYMNS (307)

308. **CROSSING BOUNDARIES;** M6 YOUTH THEATRE; OLDHAM THEATRE WORKSHOP; PHOENIX YOUTH THEATRE; *24 February 2005. Cast:* Charles TOMLIN, Kim WHITE, Tony GROGAN, Sammie HULSE, Harooj SONIA, Kirsty Lee LORIMER, David LONGHURST, Abbie McGRATH.

309. SWEET LITTLE THING by Roy Williams; ECLIPSE THEATRE; *28 February –5 March 2005. Tash:* Seroca DAVIS; *Zoe:* Lauren TAYLOR; *Nathan:* Ben BROOKS; *Miss Brooks:* Kay BRIDGEMAN; *Ryan:* Glenn HODGE; *Jamal:* Richie CAMPBELL; *Kev:* Marcel McCALLA; *Angela:* Ashley MADEKWE. *Director:* Michael BUFFONG; *Designer:* Ruari MURCHISON; *Choreographer:* KAT; *Fight Director:* Renny KRUPINSKI; *Lighting Designer:* Malcolm RIPPETH; *Sound Designer:* Al ASHFORD; *Voice Coach:* Claudette WILLIAMS; *Assistant Director:* Steve MARMION; *Production Manager:* Dennis CHARLES; *Technical Manager:* Nikk TURNHAM; *Company Stage Manager:* Tracey J COOPER; *Technical Stage Manager:* Gary WRIGHT; *Deputy Stage Manager:* Nina SCHOLAR; *Assistant Stage Manager:* Michelle DAWKINS; *Technical Assistant Stage Manager:* Mark RICHARDS; *Costume Supervisor:* Yvonne MILNES; *Re-Lights On Tour:* Matt BRITTEN.

35-45: Palaver Festival

35. WORDS LEAVE US; CADMIUM COMPAGNIE; *7 March 2005. Performers:* Angela BAUBUIN, Irenee BLIN. **Journal:** 7/3/05.

36. FACE by Veronica Needa; YELLOW EARTH THEATRE; *7 March 2005. Performer:* Veronica NEEDA. *Director / Designer:* Shu-Wing TANG; *Original Lighting:* Virginia KAM; *Lighting On Tour:* Paul St John SHAW. **Journal:** 7/3/05.

37. 10% by Ted Moore; SYNTHESIS-PROJECT; *8 March 2005. Beni:* Alessandro MAURO. *Director:* William NEWELL

38/ RHINOCEROS by Eugene Ionesco; MANCHESTER UNIVERSITY FRENCH DEPARTMENT; *10-12 March 2005.*

39. HOTEL BABELE; PETIT SOLEIL' *10 March 2005.I BUFFONI (The Clowns): Peter, doorman:* Aldo VIVODA; *Martha, cook:* Lucua GADOLINI; *Magdaleine, waitress:* Silvia MELOTTI; *Gabriel, waiter:* Sergio PANCALDI; *Mary, director:* Susannah TRESILIAN; *Matthew, liftman:* Andrea NEAMI; *I PERSONAGGI (The Characters): Shirley Weiseman (Public Relations):* Susannah TRESILIAN; *Vasilj Stepanov (Professor):* Sergio PANCALDI; *Adrian Amen (Business Man):* Andrea NEAMI; *Elke Schiltz (Teacher):* Silvia MELOTTI; *Rosa Lespinas (Revolutionary):* Lucia GADOLINI. **Journal:** 7/3/05.

40. **HOMESICK;** SERVI DI SCENA;*14 March 2005.* **Waiting:**: Jacopo LANTERI; **Supper At Eight:** Lucia GADOLINI, Susanna TRESILIAN, Jacopo LANTERI; **Sunday Morning:** Davide PASSERA. **Journal:** 7/3/05.

41. **NUNCA NADA DE NINGUEM;** adapted from Luisa Costa Gomes; MANCHESTER UNIVERSITY PORTUGUESE DEPARTMENT; *15 March 2005*

42. **A CRIME AGAINST THE LAMBS** by Carlos Prieto; ENVISION THEATRE; *15 March 2005. Performers:* Jonathan BLAKE, Jim BRADSHAW, Andrea DORAN, Tom GUEST, Helen SPENCER, Lee THORBURN. *Director:* Susannah TRESILIAN. **Journal:** 7/3/05.

43. **FRUHLINGS ERWAKEN (SPRING AWAKENING)** by Frank Wederkind; MANCHESTER UNIVERSITY GERMAN DEPARMENT; *16-19 March 2005.*

45. **DISEMBODIED** by David Glass, with music composed by Jonathan Cooper; THE DAVID GLASS ENSEMBLE; *16-19 March 2005. Performers:* David GLASS, Jonathan COOPER. *Directors:* David GLASS, Tom MORRIS; *Design:* Ruth FINN; *Video Design:* Matt SPENCER; *Lighting Design:* Alex GUEMBEL; *Assistant Director:* Mark ESPINER; *Poducer:* Matthew JONES; *Sound Operator:* Mim SPENCER; *Builder:* Rom ROBERTS; *Recorded Accompanists – Cello:* Thangam DEBBONAIRE; *Oboe:* Belinda SYKES; *Viola:* Rebecca BROWN. **Journal:** 7/3/05.

310. **LaLa#2: CAROLINE AND ROSIE;** conceived, choreographed and performed by Laure Dever and Laura Vanborm; VICTORIA; *2 April 2005. Coaching:* Einat TUCHMAN; *Video:* Michiel De JAGER; *Costumes:* An BREUGELMANS; *Musical Advice:* Arthur VAN DER KUIP, Lies VANBORM; *Technical Crew:* Philippe DIGNEFFE; *Set:* Herman DE ROOVER.

318. **SPEECH** by Peter Vekeman; VICTORIA; *2 April 2005. Performer:* Martin STANNAGE.

311. **EVERYBODY WATCHES TV;** CONTACT YOUTH THEATRE; VICTORIA; *2 April 2005. Cast:* Fisayo AKINABE, Georgie BARRATT, Chris BARLOW, Simon CRABB, Katie DAVIES, Lowri EVANS, Nicole GASKELL, Tochino CORNWELL, Tuheen HUDA, Tom HUGHES, Edward KEANE, Jessica LAU, Fiona MADDOCKS, Ben

MOORES, Marika SPENCE, Rebecca TAYLOR, David TROWBRIDGE, Yursa WARSAMA, Martin STANNAGE. *Directors:* Tanya HERMSEN, Ben BENAOUISSES; *Set Design:* Emily CAMPBELL; *Lighting Design:* Anne MEEUSSEN; *Sound Design:* Greg AKEHURST; *Producer:* Sarah SANSOM; *Project Manager:* Jennie SUTTON; *Production Manager:* Chris WHITWOOD; *Stage Manager:* Veronica MacDONALD; *Technical Support:* Mark DISTIN; *Production Support:* Jo KELLY, Julie NAYLOR; *Workshop Leaders:* Jonathan McGRATH, Summit SARKAR.

57. CHAOS by Azma Dar; KALI; *5-6 April 2005. Salim:* Damian ASHER; *Babar:* Marc ELLIOTT; *Mr Rizvi:* Nicholas KHAN; *Mrs Rizvi:* Shelley KING; *Aunty Moona:* Jamila MASSEY. *Director:* Janet STEEL; *Designer:* Matthew WRIGHT; *Lighting:* Chris CORNER; *Composer:* Sayan KENT; *AssistantDirector:* Sophie AUSTIN; *Dramaturgy:* Penny GOLD; *Stage Manager:* Sarah PEARCE. **Journal:** 16/2/05

56. BELLS by Yasmin Whittaker Khan; KALI; *7-9 April 2005. Charles:* Damian ASHER; *Pepsi:* Marc ELLIOTT; *Aiesha:* Shivan GHAI; *Ashraf:* Nicholas KHAN; *Madam:* Sharona SASSOON. *Director:* Poonam BRAH; *Designer:* Matthew WRIGHT; *Lighting:* Chris CORNER; *Composer:* Sayan KENT; *Choreography:* Kella PANAY; *Assistant Director:* Pia FURTADO; *Dramaturgy:* Penny GOLD; *Stage Manager:* Sarah PEARCE. **Journal:** 16/2/05

53. RESISTANCE by Maria Oshodi; EXTANT THEATRE; *6-7 April 2005. Younger Jacques:* Mark SCALES; *Older Jacques:* John Wilson GODDARD; *Major:* Gerard McDERMOTT; *Jean / Denis:* Paul COLDRICK; *Professor / Phillipe:* Iain CHARLES; *Francoise / Eliot:* James O'DRISCOLL; *Official:* Brian SANDFORD. *Director / Script Consultant:* Eileen DILLON; *Producer:* Maria OSHODI; *Choreographer:* Aidan TREAYS; *Composer:* Aidan TREAYS; *Set Design:* Andrea CARR; *Lighting:* Phil SUPPLE; *Costume Design:* Tina BICAT; *Production Manager:* Alison KING; *Stage Manager:* Jo HOLT; *Technical Manager:* Justin FARNDALE; *Company Manager:* Brian SANDFORD; *Set Builder:* Neil ROBSON; *Production Assistant:* Olly PRICE; *Voice Coach:* Ollie Campbell SMITH: *British Sign Language Interpreter:* Jeni DRAPER. **Journal:** 16/2/05

317. DRACULA; developed from Bram Stoker by ULLALOOM

THEATRE COMPANY; *11-14 April 2005. Director:* Clive MENDUS.

58. IN GOD WE TRUST by Avaes Mohammed; PESHKAR PRODUCTIONS; *18-21 April 2005.*

313. FLIP THE SCRIPT; CONTACT; *4 May 2005.* **Banshee** by Joe O'Byrne: *Kieron:* Jarrod COOKE; *Liz:* Mary SOBERS; **Hen Night** by Debi Dixon: *Marcie:* Mary SOBERS; *Cleo:* Rachel YOUNG; *Ruby:* Leyland O'BRIEN; *Mercedes:* Jarrod COOKE; **Mischief Night** by Ian Bell: *Verity:* Jarrod COOKE; *Rachel:* Rachel YOUNG; *Megan:* Mary SOBERS; *Rickie Stone:* Leyland O'BRIEN; **How Sweet It Is** by Andrew Pollard; *Hansel; Gretel;* **Reverse Psychiatry** by Rob Hayes: *Psychiatrist:* Leyland O'BRIEN; *Patients:* Jarrod COOKE, Mary SOBERS; **Forget-Me-Not And Angels** by Jane Hamer. *Director:* Chris WRIGHT; *Technician:* Anna MEEUSSEN; *Compere:* Jonathan MEYER.

68. SMILIN' THROUGH by Billy Cowan; BIRMINGHAM REPERTORY THEATRE COMPANY; CONTACT; TRUANT COMPANY; QUEER UP NORTH; *5-14 May 2005. Peggy:* Gillian HANNA; *Kyle:* Marty REA; *Willy / Cardinal Dainty:* Walter McMONAGLE; *Donal:* Terence CORRIGAN; *Officer Kildare / Jim Robinson / Rev Macmillan:* Sean KEARNS; *Nelson Eddy:* Allison HARDING. *Director:* Natelie WILSON; *Designer:* Emma DONOVAN; *Lighting Designer* :Emma CHAPMAN; *Sound Designer:* Dan STEELE; *Musical Director:* Peter ENGLAND; *Assistant Director:* David OAKES; *Stage Manager:* Richard Greville WATSON; *Deputy Stage Manager:* Sara CRATHORNE. **Journal:** 25/4/05

314. MYTH, PROPAGANDA AND DISASTER IN NAZI GERMANY AND CONTEMPORARY AMERICA by Stephen Sewell; UNIVERSITY OF MANCHESTER DRAMA SOCIETY; *19-21 May 2005. Talbot:* Sebastian CHRISPIN; *Eve:* Samantha KISSIN; *Marguerite:* Rosia HOLT; *Amy:* Sally CRAWSHAW; *Jack:* Alex BOND; *Stan:* Josh AZOUZ; *Jill:* Vikki MURPHY; *Max:* Ben KNIGHT; *Therapist:* Roxy BOURDILLON; *Security Guard:* Danny EASTON; *The Man:* Alex MAURO. *Director:* Alex SUMMERS; *Producer / Stage Manager:* Diccon RAMSAY; *Production Design:* Grant NAHORNIAK; *Lighting Design:* Morgan OLIVER; *Sound Design:*Phil DICKSON; *Audiovisual Design:* Dave HUGHES; *Assistant Stage Manager / Props:* Jess DRADER; *Associate*

Producer: Felicity Theobald; *Stage Technician:* Anne MEEUSSEN; *Wardrobe Madame:* Issie GIBBONS.

275. UNDO; created and performed by Mem Morrison; *20-21 May 2005.*

315. SPIKE ISLANDS; created and performed by Flick Ferdinando and John-Paul Zaccarini; COMPANY F/Z; *9-10, 17-18 June 2005.*

316. DIFFERENT PERSPECTIVES; written and performed by MARCUS HERCULES; *25 June 2005*

256. IRON by Rona Munro; WORKING GIRLS; *12-16 July 2005. Fay:* Joan KEMPSON; *Josie:* Rachel BROGAN; *Prison Officers:* James LOWE. Samantha POWER. *Director:* Cheryl MARTIN; *Set Designer:* Emma M WEE; *Lighting / Sound Engineer:* Mark DISTIN; *Stage Manager:* Martin FULLER; *Assistant Stage Manager:* Niven GANNER. **Journal:** 25/5/05

222. 0161-THE MUSICAL; GORSE HILL YOUTH ARTS CENTRE; CONTACT; *15 July 2005.Lyon:* Lyon TALABI OLA; *Johnathan:*Johnathan SUTTON; *Miss Barton:* Marika SPENCE; *Melissa:* Sarah-Jane DUFFY; *NUBIAN KANE DANCE TROOP:* Kelly MORGAN, Nicole BLISSETT, Elizabeth BEPASOIS; *KRYPTONITE DANCE CREW:* Kerin MORRIS, Leonie HAWKSHAW, Christina TAYLOR, Naomi MORRIS; *Ensemble:* Natasha PITTERSON, Cherelle TARRY, James ANDREW, Daniella BALL, Louise MULDOON, Lydia COLLETON, Roshane WILLIAMS, Kyle KALLONAGH, Keyshe BELL, Rechelle SMITH, Sophia READ, Naomi READ; *THE BAND:* Simon SHERRAT, Joseph HOSKER, Daniel KAKONGE, Mark EDWARDS, Chris COLLINS, Daryl HOSKER. *Director:* Johnathan McGRATH; *Musical Direction:* Simon HERRATT, Richard SILWA, DELLANO (DT); *Choreography:* NUBIAN KANE, KRYPTONITE; *Visual @ Set Design:* HEMA & JEN; *Production Manager / Lighting Design:* Veronica McDONALD; *Stage Manager:* Anthony YATES; *Youth Arts Manager:* Caroline GLEAVES; Sally MARGETTS, Tamzin ALLAN, Kendra BROWN, Andrew BENNETT. **Journal:** 25/5/05

312. EAST; Chinese Arts Centre; *22 July 2005.*

245, THE ROOT OF IT; NEWFOUND THEATRE; *3-6 August 2005. Performers:* Louise TWOMEY, Hellen KIRBY, Daniel WALLACE, Hannah McHUGH (*and, in absentia*)

Kate HENRY. *Director:* Juliet ELLIS; *Technical Manager / Stage Manager:* Julie PARKER. **Journal:** 25/5/05

261. TRANSFORMATIONS; CONTACT YOUNG ACTORS COMPANY; THE PEOPLE SHOW; *19-20 August 2005. Do You Know This Woman?:* Fisayo AKINADE; *It's good to talk, especially if you have someone to talk to:* Fiona MADDOCKS; *I'm not a stalker:* Tom HUGHES; *Where'd me watch go?:* Chris BARLOW; *Why am I always waiting?* :Marika SPENCE; *Fashion is dirty business of beauty:* Shanika DOBSON; *Appearances can be deceptive:* Rukaya MEGEN; *Roll up, Roll up:* Katie METTAM; *Curiously out of time:* Greg FOSTER; *The thing about me is you never know what you're seeing:* Nikky NORTON; *There's no dogs and no Irish here either:* Tapiwa MADOVI; *Let's start with the art:* Sakina MAYNARD; *A girl went to Napoli:* Bilal MALIK; *Happiness is a sad song and my radio is out of tune:* Vanessa Silva PEREIRA; *Never buy a Rolex from someone who is out of breath:* Katie DAVIES; *Excuse me, but there is supposed to be a performance taking place here:* Daniella EDWARDS; *More than your average Mr Commuter:* Niven GANNER; *I'm so sorry that I took a long time:* John PHIRI; *What's up, how you bin?:* Kyle BALLICK. *Directors:* Tyrone HUGGINS, Alit KREIZ; *Producer:* Sarah SANSOM; *Assistant Directors:* Catherine PASKELL, Nicola BAYES; *Dramaturgy:* Louise WALLWEIN; *Designer:* Emma M WEE; *Design Team:* Alke GROPPEL-WEGENER, Jackie BROWN, Liam CASEY, Tom WATSON; *Lighting Design:* Mark DISTIN; *Sound Design:* Dan STELL; *Sound Design Assistant:* Anna JEWITT; *Video Creation:* Ricardo VILELA; *Technical Manager:* Patrick COLLINS; *Technicians:* Barkery JAMMEH, Dave MITCHELL; *Stage Manager:* Jen JARVIS; *Deputy Stage Manager:* Sunny WRAY; *Assistant Stage Managers:* George BUTCHARI, Joshua CALLARD; *Project Managers:* Louise WALLWEIN, Tony PACE. **Journal:** 25/5/05

CO-OPERATIVE HALL; Hollyhedge Road, WYTHENSHAWE M22 4NQ; **CAZ:** 136, B6

CORNERHOUSE; 70 Oxford Street; MI 5NH; 0161-236 6184; **CAZ:** 10, A2; **W**

COSMO RODEWALD CONCERT HALL; University of Manchester Department of Music and

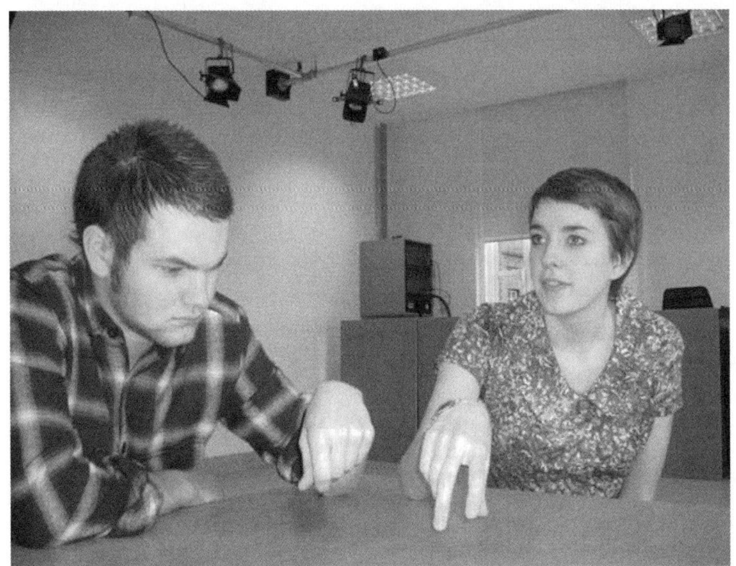

A VIEW FROM THE BRIDGE (370)

Drama, Bridgeford Street M13 9PL; 0161-275 3347; **CAZ:** 10, B6

COUNCIL CHAMBER;
Union Building, Manchester University M13 9PL; 0161-275 2930; **CAZ:** 109, F2

370. A VIEW FROM THE BRIDGE by Arthur Miller; UNIVERSITY OF MANCHESTER DRAMA SOCIETY; *25-27 November 2004. Director:* Tom COPESTAKE.

206. EQUUS by Peter Schaffer; UNIVERSITY OF MANCHESTER DRAMA SOCIETY; *5-7 March 2005. Directors:* Bryony METEYARD, Fay BENSON.

201. THE INSTALLATION by James Matthews-Paul and Emma Swift; UNIVERSITY OF MANCHESTER DRAMA SOCIETY; *14-16 March 2005.Directors:* James MATTHEWS-PAUL, Emma SWIFT.

CRAB LANE PRIMARY SCHOOL; M9 8NB; 0161-740 2851; CAZ: 68, D5

CROSS ACRES JUNIOR SCHOOL; WYTHENSHAWE M22 5AD; 0161-437 1272; CAZ: 148, D1

CROWCROFT PARK PRIMARY SCHOOL; Stovell Avenue, LONGSIGHT M12 5SY; 0161-224 5914; CAZ: 110, C5

DADI BUILDING; 135 Grosvenor Street MI 7HE; CAZ: 10, C4

DANCEHOUSE THEATRE; 10 Oxford Road M1 5AQ; 0161-237 9753; **CAZ:** 10, A3. **G, W.**

DIDSBURY CAMPUS STUDIO; Wilmslow Road M20 2RR; 0161-247 2086; **CAZ:** 137, F1

319. THE CHAINSAW MANICURE by Thomas Kett; URBAN THEATRE COMPANY; *15 April 2005. Cast:* Laura CAINE.

320. I LOVE ME JUST THE WAY I AM by Caroline Mentiplay; MEANT-2.-PLAY PRODUCTIONS; *9-10 August 2005. Lorraine:* Caroline MENTIPLAY; *Also:* Elizabeth THOMPSON, Paul KISSACK.

DIDSBURY CHURCH OF ENGLAND PRIMARY SCHOOL; Elm Grove M20 6RL; 0161-445 7144; **CAZ:** 125, F6

DUCIE HIGH SCHOOL; Lloyd Street North MI4 4GA; 0161-226 8135; **CAZ:** 109, E3

DUKES 92; Castle Street, M3 4LZ; 0161-838 8646; **CAZ:** 9, E2

EAST DIDSBURY METHODIST HALL; Parrs Wood Road M20 0QQ; 0161-427 2441; 061-445 3199; **CAZ:** 137, F3

ENGLISH MARTYRS ROMAN CATHOLIC

PRIMARY SCHOOL; Brantingham Road, WHALLEY RANGE M16 8QH; 0161-226 1524; **CAZ:** 108, C6

EXCHANGE SQUARE; CAZ: 5,H4

FLETCHER MOSS; off Millgate Lane, M20 2SW; 0262-881 9014; **CAZ:** 137, F2

221. **HAMLET** by William Shakespeare; HEARTBREAK PRODUCTIONS; *21 July 2005.*

FOOTAGE PUB; 137 Grosvenor Street, ALL SAINTS M1 7DZ; O161-275-9164; **CAZ:** 10, B4

FORUM THEATRE, Civic Centre, Leningrad Square, WYTHENSHAWE M22 5RT; 0161-437 9663. **CAZ:** 148, A2

GAIA; 46 Sackville Street M1 3WF; 0161-228 1002; **CAZ:** 10,B1

GAY AND LESBIAN CENTRE; Pritchard Street M1 7DA; 0161-235 8035; **CAZ:** 10, B3

GREEN ROOM; 54/56 Whitworth Street West M1 5WW; 0161-615 0500; **CAZ**: 9, H2; **G, H, W**

321. **CREATING CHAOS;** written and performed by CLAIRE DOWIE; *17 September 2004.*

322. **THE LAST SUPPER;** RECKLESS SLEEPERS; *23-24 September 2004.*

323. **CRIKEY MIKEY'S VOLTA VENTURE;** written and performed by ROBIN GRAHAM; *10 October 2004.*

324. **SCHLOCK;** UNINVITED GUESTS; *15 October 2005.*

325. **ALAN CARR IS NO SUBSTITUTE;** written and performed by Alan Carr; ASHLEY BORODA; *24 October 2004*

326. ICE CREAM SUNDAY; written and performed by Alan Carr; ASHLEY BORODA; *24 October 2004*

327. ONLY THE MOON TO PLAY WITH; created and performed by Qasim Riza Shaheen; ANOKHA LAADLA; *5 November 2005.*

328. THE FISH'S WISHES; developed from the original by Marcello Chiarenza; LYNGO THEATRE; HALF MOON THEATRE; *14 November 2005. Performer:* Patrick LYNCH

329. ON/OFF; developed and performed by Ben Faulks; JONATHON PRAM

330. AUTOBIOGRAPHY IN FIVE CHAPTERS; created and performed by JULIET ELLIS; *26 November 2004.*

331. HURRYSICKNESS; THIRD ANGEL; *3 December 2004*

332. UNDERNEATH ALL THE NOISE SOMEBODY WAS SINGING; THE SPECIAL GUESTS; *10 December 2004.*

333. WONDERFULLY GRIMM; SEAN TUAN JOHN; *5 March 2005.* *Performers:* Sean Tuan JOHN, Bert van GORP

334. IAGGI BODDARI – THE STORY BUNDLE; written by Peter Wynne-Willson; Music by Mira Yugai; MOBY DUCK; *10 April 2005.* *Puppetry:* Yang Hye JUNG.

272. FAMILY HOLD BACK; created and performed by Helen Paris; *10-11 May 2005.*

273. SMOKING GUN; created and performed by Leslie Hill; *10-11 May 2005.*

274. CUL-DE-SAC; created and performed by Daniel McIvor; *13-14 May 2005.*

CUL-DE-SAC 9274); DANIEL McIVOR

336. OBJECTS FOR MEDITATION; created and presented by WILLIAM YANG; *24-25 May 2005.*

337. FOLD YOUR OWN; conceived by Rachel Field; DOO COT; *9-10 June 2005. Performers:* Nenagh WATSON, Yasha ISHIYANA. *Director:* Rachel FIELD; *Stage Manager:* Julie PARKER.

335. THE ENORMOUS TURNIP; Dynamic New Animation (DNA); 12 June 2005.

225. HOOK, LINE AND SINKER by Mike Woodhead; FLYING PIG PRODUCTIONS; *20-21 July 2005. Carl:* Scott BRADLEY; *Trevor:* Mike WOODHEAD. *Director:* Helen PARRY; *Light / Sound:* Steve CURTIS; *Producer:* Mike WOODHEAD. **Journal:** 25/5/05

THE GROVE CLUB;
250 Plymouth Grove M13 0BG; 0161 - 224 7624; **CAZ:** 110, A3

HALLÉ SQUARE; Arndale Centre M2 1NP; **CAZ:** 6, A4

HEALD PLACE PRIMARY SCHOOL; Heald Place M14 4PF; 0161-224 7079; **CAZ:** 109, F4

HEATON PARK; Prestwich M25 5SW; 0161-7732581 / 1321 / 1085 /6500 / 8044; **CAZ:** 68, A4

338. A MIDSUMMER NIGHT'S DREAM by William Shakespeare; CHAPTERHOUSE THEATRE COMPANY; *1 July 2005.*

259. DRACULA – THE BLOOD COUNT; adapted by Peter Clifford and Caroline Clegg from the novel by Bram Stoker; FEELGOOD THEATRE COMPANY; *21 July – 7 August 2005. Count Vlad Dracula:* Peter CLIFFORD; *Professor Abraham Van Helsing:* Richard ASHTON; *Dr John Seward:* Martin HARRIS; *Christina Renfield:* Eve ROBERTSON; *Mina Seward:* Jill KEMP; *Lucy Harker:* Bibi NERHEIM; *Jonathan Harker:* Dan WILLIS; *Inspector Morris:* Paul LEEMING; *Charlotte:* Esther HUDSON; *The Wise Woman:* Megan TRUEBLOOD-SMITH; *Gypsy Children:* Carly MOORHOUSE, Poopy MURRAY; *Postman / Policeman / StationMaster / Tarot Reader / Gypsies / Vampires / Vampire Brides:* Mark GERAGHTY / Danny TOPHAM, Helen SERRIDGE, Natalie Jane McGOVERN, Hazel ROY, Orline V RILEY, Ray SHONE. *Director:* Caroline CLEGG; *Associate Director:* Norren KERSHAW; *Musical Director:* Faith WATSON; *Fight Director:* Peter CLIFFORD; *Designer:* Allison CLARKE; *Costume Designer:* Alison EYRES; *Production &Company Manager:* Lee DRINKWATER; *Stage Manager:* Marcus HOLT; *Assistant Stage Managers:* Miriam GOODALL, Esther HUDSON. **Journal** 7/8/05

HOLLYWOOD SHOW BAR; 100 Bloom Street M1 3LY; 0161 - 236 1676 / 6151 / 6905: **CAZ:** 10, B1

HOP AND GRAPE; Union Building, Manchester University, Oxford Road M13 9PL; 0161-275 2930; **CAZ:** 109, F2

HULME PARK; Royce Road M15; **CAZ:**9, F5

INSTITUTO CERVANTES; 320 Deansgate M3 4FN; 0161-661 4200; **CAZ:** 9,F2

IRISH ASSOCIATION CLUB; 17 High Lane, CHORLTON M21 9DJ; 0161 - 881 2898; **CAZ:** 123, H1

IRISH WORLD HERITAGE CENTRE; 10 Queens Road, CHEETHAM HILL M8 8UR; 0161-205 4007; **CAZ:** 82, C6

IVY COTTAGE EVANGELICAL CHURCH, Barlow Moor Road, DIDSBURY M20 2GP; 0161-434 5505; **CAZ:** 125; E6

JABEZ CLEGG; 2 Portsmouth Street M13 9GB; 0161-272 8612; **CAZ**: 10, D6

Gus (NEVILLE MILLAR, right)has words with Mr T (DARREN LANGFORD)

24. ONE BIRD, TWO STONES by Victoria Scowcroft, Neville Millar and Darren Langford; MIDAS TOUCH THEATRE COMPANY; *1-2 February 2005. Gus:* Neville MILLAR; *Bernie:* Victoria SCOWCROFT; *MrT / James:* Darren LANGFORD. **Journal:** 18/1/05

25. CHAMELEON by Richard Kirkbride and Steve Blower; JERK TO POSITION THEATRE COMPANY; *1-2 February 2005. Krakak Anderson / Strutter / Detective Max Waxman:* Steve BLOWER; *Bengle Bo Thomas / Detective Buck Scorne:* Richard KIRKBRIDE; *On Film: Samantha:* Francesca LARKIN; *Chuck:* Neville MILLAR. **Journal:** 18/1/05

THREE BAR SOLO (342); Krissy (SUSSANAH TRESILLIAN) is having a hard time; Colin (JIM BRADSHAW) wants to be sympathetic.

JOHN THAW STUDIO; University of Manchester Department of Music and Drama, Bridgeford Street M13 9PL; 0161-275 3347; **CAZ:** 10, B6

339. I'M OLDER NOW BUT I STILL HATE YOU; created and performed by SILJEE MARX; *5 October 2004.*

340. EN-SUITE LIES by Rowan Martin; THE ASSEMBLED; *5 October 2004.*

341. MAYBE TOMORROW by Nicola Schofield; *5 October 2004*

342. THREE BAR SOLO; devised by William Newell; songs composed by Tom Guest and Helen Spencer, assisted by Anna Jewitt, Lowri Jones and Graham South; script by Ted Moore; written by ENVISION THEATRE; *8-9 October 2004. Colin:* Jim BRADSHAW; *Luke / Piano:* Tom GUEST; *Richard:* David OAKES; *B:* Helen SPENCER; *Kriss:* Sussannah TRESILIAN; *Trumpet:* Graham SOUTH; *Clarinet:* Anne JEWITT; *Trombone:* Tullis RENNIE; *Double*

Bass: Poppy FAY; *Percussion:* Ted MOORE. *Directors:* William NEWELL, Susannah TRESILIAN; *Musical Director:* Tom GUEST; *Stage Manager:* Lowri JONES; *Technical Director:* Lizzie NURSE; *Lighting / Sound:* William NEWELL, Lowri JONES, Holly CHARD; *Company Manager:* Helen SPENCER.

343. I HAVE BEFORE ME A REMARKABLE DOCUMENT GIVEN TO ME BY A YOUNG LADY FROM RWANDA; by Sonja Linden; ICE AND FIRE THEATRE COMPANY; *26 –27 October 2004.*

344. APRIL IN PARIS by John Godber; ENVISION THEATRE; *18 January 2005. Alf:* Jonathan BLAKE; *Bet:* Helen SPENCER. *Director:* Susannah TRESILIAN; *Lighting:* David OAKES, Lizzie NURSE.

33. PHAEDRA by Jean Racine, translated by Julie Rose; ENVISION THEATRE; *9-11 February 2005. Aricia:* Charlotte GASCOYNE; *Theseus:* Tom GUEST; *Phaedra:* Susanna FIORE; *Hippolytus:* David OAKES; *Oenone:* Helen SPENCER. *Director:* Susannah TRESILIAN; *Music Composer:* Vincent MIGLIORISI; *Set Design:* Vicki WHEELER; *Producer:* Helen SPENCER; *Stage Manager:* Jim BRADSHAW; *Lighting Design:* Lizzie NURSE; *Sound:* Chris STOS-GALE. **Journal:** 18/1/05

44. EVERYWHERE; QUARANTINE; MANCHESTER UNIVERSITY DRAMA DEPARTMENT; *16-18 March 2005. Director:* Richard GREGORY; *Designer:* Simon BANHAM.

345. BLOOD by Sergi Belbel, translated by Marion Peter Holt; THE SYNTHESIS PROJECT; *19-22 April 2005. Man / Timid Man:* Tom GUEST; *Young Woman / Young Messenger:* Charlotte GASCOYNE; *Child / Lost Child:* Emma GORDON; *Woman:* Ellie WHITE; *Boy / Polkiceman / Husband:* Martin TAPLEY; *Girl / Policewoman / Lover:* Hannah CRIGHTON. *Director:* William NEWELL; *Stage Manager:* Holly GRAY; *Sound Designer:* Josh KOPECEK; *Lighting Designer / Artificial Appendages / Electrics Operator:* Lizzie NURSE; *Video Designer:* Martin BEHRMAN; *MAKE-Up /Costume Designer:* Alex WILLIAMS; *Assistant Make-Up / Dresser:* Anna JEWITT; *Production Design / Construction:* William NEWELL, Lizzie NURSE; *Audio Visual and Special Effects Operators:* Martin BEHRMAN, Helen WINDEBANK

346. I LOVE YOU, YOU'RE PERFECT, NOW CHANGE!; Book and Lyrics by Jimmy DiPietro; Music by Jimmy Roberts; ENVISION THEATRE; *16-17 June 2005. Cast:* Tom GUEST, Jack LADENBURGH, Helen SPENCER, Susannah TRESILIAN; *MUSICIANS: Piano:* Susannah WAPSHOT; *Violin:* Anna MOORE. *Director:* Susannah TRESILIAN; *Musical Director:* Anna JEWITT; *Company Manager:* Helen SPENCER; *Stage Manager:* Jim BRADSHAW; *Assistant Stage Manager:* Peter BARDSLEY; *Dresser:* Holly CULLEN-DAVIES; *Lighting:* Will SPENCER, Mark DISTIN; *Vocal Coach:* Helen SPENCER.

JONGLEURS; Chorlton Street M1 3FH; 0161-236 5663; **CAZ:** 10, B1

KARMA; 310 Wilmslow Road, FALLOWFIELD M14 6XQ; **CAZ:** 125,G1

KING DAVID HIGH SCHOOL; Eaton Road,

CRUMPSALL M8 5DY; 0161-740 7248; **CAZ:** 82, B2

KING DAVID JUNIOR SCHOOL; Wilton Polygon, Bury Old Road M8 6DR; 0161-740 3343; **CAZ:** 82, B2

KRO BAR; 325 Oxford Road M13 9PG; 0161 - 274 3100; **CAZ;** 109, F2

LATE ROOM; 23 Peter Street M2 5QR; 0161-833 3000; **CAZ:** 9, G1

193, 228, 333: 24:7 THEATRE FESTIVAL; *Technician:* Paul PHILLIPS.

233. THE FRENCH LECTURES, mostly by Alan French; THOSE ACTORS; *24-27 July 2005, Cast:* Alan FRENCH, Colin CARR, Emma KANIS. *Technician:* Peter ELLIS. **Journal:** 25/5/05

228. MILK by Anna Baatz and Cathy Shiel; JELLYBELLY THEATRE; *24 26 July 2005. Cast:* Anna BAATZ, Cathy SHEIL, Rob CLYNE, James SHAKESHAFT. *Director:* Emma KANIS; *Musical Director:* Craig KEADY; *Technical:* Laura DUFF, BEESLEY, Tim DUNK. **Journal:** 25/5/05

193. THE LAST TURN OF THE NIGHT by David Raynor; PAVEMENT THEATRE; *24-26 July 2005.*

LEES STREET CONGREGATIONAL CHURCH HALL; M11 1NW; **CAZ**: 97, F6

770. THE WIZ; Book by William F Brown, based on **The Wizard of Oz** BY l Frank Baum; Music and Lyrics by Charlie Smalls and Luther Vandross; LEES STREET CONCREGATIONAL CHURCH A M & D S. *Dorothy:* Lucy JOHNSON; *Scarecrow:* Carrie BROWN; *Tinman:*Mark STEVENSON; *Lion:* Tony PETRYKOWSKI; *Wiz:* Karl WARDLOW; *Gatekeeper:* Michael TAYLOR. *Director:L* Linda STEVENSON; *Choreographer:* Aimee MAKINSON; *Musical Director:* Collette AINSCOW.

LEVENSHULME HIGH SCHOOL FOR GIRLS; Crossley Road M19; 0161- 224 4625

LEVENSHULME METHODIST CHURCH; Stockport Road / Woodfold Avenue M19; 0161-224 5618; **CAZ:** 110, C5

LEVENSHULME POOLS; Barlow Road M19 2HE; 0161-224 4370; **CAZ**: 110, D6

LIBRARY THEATRE; St Peter's Square M2 5PD; 0161-236 7110. **CAZ**: 9, H1. **D, G, H, S, W**

RICK PEEBLES

347. THE BALLAD OF JOHNNY 5 STAR by David Hauptshein and David Vlcek; SECRET LIFE THEATER; *31 August – 4 September 2004. Johnny 5 Star:* Michael SHANNON; *Johnny Gandy:* Rick PEEPLES. *Director:* Julio Maria MARTINO.

257. CURRY TALES by Rani Moorthy; RASA; *7-11 September 2004*

.

1. VINCENT IN BRIXTON by Nicholas Wright; LIBRARY THEATRE COMPANY; *17 September – 15 October 2004. Ursula Loyer:* Sheila RUSKIN; *Vincent Van Gogh:* Gus GALLAGHER; *Eugenie Loyer:* Hannah WATKINS; *Sam Plowman:* Christopher PIZZEY; *Anna Van Gogh:* Olivia DARNLEY. *Director:* Roger HAINES; *Designer:* Judith CROFT; *Lighting Designer:* Nick RICHINGS; *Sound:* Paul GREGORY; *Dialect Coach:* William CONNACHER; *Assistant Director:* David KENWORTHY; *Company Stage Manager:* Lisa HALL; *Deputy Stage Manager, On The Book:* Kirsty RUSSELL; *Assistant Stage Manager:* Pippa SMITH-AITCHISON; *Painters:* Hilly McMANUS, Alison EVERS; *Wigs:* Angela CARRADUS, Lindy DAVIES; *Wardrobe Supervisor:* Liz HORRIGAN; *Wardrobe Assistants / Cutters:* Lindsey HANRAHAN , Jeanete PICKWELL; *Wardrobe Maintenance:* Kaeren DOOLEY; *Additional Wardrobe Assistance:* Fiona BUNTING, Cathy ALGER, Jan SMITH; *British Sigh Language Interpreter:* Mavis McCUE; *Production Manager:* Michael WILLIAMS;

Deputy Production Manager: Gareth ROBERTS; *Construction Manager:* Derek JONES; *Construction Assistant:* David DOYLE; *Chief Technician / Captions:* Jake TAYLOR; *Assistant Sound and Lighting Technician:* Daniel STEWART. **Journal:** 4/10/04

5. BEYOND BELIEF; scenes from the Shipman Inquiry, edited by Dennis Woolf; LIBRARY THEATRE COMPANY; *22 October 2004. Dame Janet Smith:* Romy BASKERVILLE; *Caroline Swift QC:* Cate HAMER; *Christopher Melton QC:* Jim MILLEA; *Richard Lissack QC:* Christopher WRIGHT; *Andrew Spink QC: Bruce Stuart:* Stephen MacKENNA: *Philip Gaisford:* Simon MOLLOY; *John Shaw:* Stephen MacKENNA; *Nigel Reynolds:* Christopher WRIGHT; *Dorothy Foley:*Joan KEMPSON; *Ghislaine Brant:* Kate LAYDEN; *Dr Susan Booth:* Eileen O'BRIEN; *Deborah Bambroofe:* Alison BURROWS; *Detective Inspector David Smith:* David CRELLIN; *Chief Superintendent David Sykes:* Simon MOLLOY; *Detective Chief Superintendent Bernard Postles:* Jim MILLEA; *Primrose Shipman:* Joan KEMPSON; *Carol Chapman:* Eileen O'BRIEN; *Gillian Morgan:* Alison BURROWS; *Alison Massey:* Kate LAYDEN; *Robert Gray:* Simon MOLLOY; *Court Officials:* Trish FEARON, Paul STEVENS, Ruth WESTLEY. *Director:* Chrid HONER; *Designer:* Dawn ALLSOPP; *Lighting Designer / Captions:* Jake TAYLOR; *Sound:* Paul GREGORY; *Assistant Director:* David KENWORTHY; *Company Stage Manager:* Lisa HALL; *Deputy Stage Manager, On The Book:*Laura FLOWERS; *Assistant Stage Manager:* Pippa SMITH-AITCHISON; *AV Operator:* Matt LEVER; *Scenic Artists:* Hilly McMANUS, Alison EVERS, Colin PIGGOTT; *Wigs:* Angela CARRADUS, Lindy DAVIES; *Wardrobe Supervisor:* Liz HORRIGAN; *Wardrobe Assistants / Cutters:* Lindseyt HANRAHAN , Jeanete PICKWELL; *Wardrobe Maintenance:* Kaeren DOOLEY; *British Sigh Language Interpreter:* Mavis McCUE; *Audio Description:* Anna HASSAN; *Production Manager:* Michael WILLIAMS; *Deputy Production Manager:* Gareth ROBERTS; *Construction Manager:* Derek JONES; *Construction Assistant:* David DOYLE; *Assistant Sound and Lighting Technician:* Daniel STEWART. **Journal:** 4/10/04

6. MERLIN AND THE CAVE OF DREAMS by Charles Way, with original music by Richard Taylor; LIBRARY THEATRE COMPANY; *27 November 2004 – 22 January 2005. Merlin:* Wyllie LONGMORE; *Arthur:* Alexander CAMPBELL; *Cei:* Patrick

CONNOLLY; *Gwyneth / Washer At The Ford:* Rebecca STEELE; *Ector:/ Rhitta of The Beards:* Duncan HENDERSON; *Igraine:* Helen KIRKPATRICK; *Uther Pendragon:* Christian BRADLEY. *Director::* Roger HAINES; *Designer:* Kate BURNETT; *Lighting:* Nick RICHINGS; *Sound:* Paul GREGORY; *Dialect Assistance:* Paul WARD; *Projection and Video Design:* Roma PATEL; *Fight Director:* Renny KRUPINSKI; *Movement Director:* Niamh DOWLING; *Assistant to the Composer:* Dominic KANE; *Company Stage Manager:* Lisa HALL; *Deputy Stage Manager, On The Book:* Kirsty RUSSELL; *Assistant Stage Manager:* Pippa SMITH-AITCHISON; *Scenic Artists:* Sue ROBSON, Allison CLARKE; *Prop Makers:* Hilly McMANUS, Alison EYERS; *Stage Crew*: Emma COOK, Layton McCARTHY, Jason GODDARD, Matt LEVER; *Wigs:* Angela CARRADUS, Lindy DAVIES; *Wardrobe Supervisor:* Liz HORRIGAN; *Wardrobe Assistants / Cutters:* Lindsey HANRAHAN , Jeanete PICKWELL; *Wardrobe Maintenance:* Kaeren DOOLEY; *Additional Wardrobe Assistance:* Fiona BUNTING, Cathy ALGER, Jan SMITH; *British Sigh Language Interpreter:* Mavis McCUE; *Captions* Janice WONG; *Audio Describer:* Helen PALMER; *Production Manager:* Michael WILLIAMS; *Deputy Production Manager:* Gareth ROBERTS; *Construction Manager:* Derek JONES; *Construction Assistant:* David DOYLE; *Chief Technician :* Jake TAYLOR; *Assistant Sound and Lighting Technician:* Daniel STEWART; *Student Placements:* Lois PENNISTON, Heather MEECHAM, James ROTHERAM, Harry RILEY. **Journal:** 4/10/04

348. CINDY RELISHA AND THE DJ PRINCE by Patrick Brown; BADP; JAMBIZ INTERNATIONAL; *26 January – 5 February 2005. Simple:* Marcus HERCULES; *Drizella Cruff / Addessa / Footman:* Dermot DALY; *Punella Cruff / Footman:* Andy BURKE; *Cindy-Relisha:* Ebony FEARE; *Rufus Cruff:* Trevor DWYER-LYNCH; *Tipsy / Fairy Godmother:* Rrenford FAGAN; *Beggar / DJ Prince:* Gary STONER. *Director / Set Designer:* Trevor NAIRNE; *Company Stage Manager:* Martin FULLER; *Assistant Stage Manager:* Roshaneh JHAWAM-SHAHIDI; *Musical Director:* Akintayo AKINBODE; *Lighting:* Jake TAYLOR; *Sound:* Michael O'SULLIVAN; *Choreographers:* Julia GRIFFIN, Imani JENDAI; *Producers:* Celia DONNELLY (BADP), Lenford SALMON (JAMBIZ).

PETER LINDFORD (Henry) and LUCY TREGEAR (Annie)

74. **THE REAL THING** by Tom Stoppard; LIBRARY THEATRE COMPANY; *11 February – 12 March 2005. Max:* Christopher WRIGHT; *Charlotte:* Caroline HARDING; *Henry:* Peter LINDFORD; *Annie:* Lucy TREGEAR; *Billy:* Justin BRETT; *Debbie:* Katie WIMPENNY; *Brodie:* John MILROY. *Director:* Chris HONER; *Designer:* Judith CROFT; *Lighting:* Nick RICHINGS; *Sound:* Paul GREGORY; *Video Artist:* Roma PATEL; *Company Stage Manager:* Lisa HALL; *Deputy Stage Manager, On The Book:*Jo GREENWOOD; *Assistant Stage Manager:* Pippa SMITH-AITCHISON; *Scenic Artists:* Sue ROBSON, Alison EYERS; *Prop Maker / Scenic Artist:* Hilly McMANUS,; *Stage Crew:*, Layton McCARTHY,; *Wigs:* Angela CARRADUS, Lindy DAVIES; *Wardrobe Supervisor:* Liz HORRIGAN; *Wardrobe Assistants / Cutters:* Lindsey HANRAHAN , Jeanete PICKWELL; *Wardrobe Maintenance / Dresser:* Kaeren DOOLEY; *Additional Wardrobe Assistance:* Jean PICKWELL; *British Sigh Language Interpreter:* Mavis McCUE; *Captions* Janice WONG; *Audio Describer:* Anna HASSAN; *Production Manager:* Michael WILLIAMS; *Deputy Production Manager:* Gareth ROBERTS; *Construction Manager:* Derek JONES; *Construction Assistant:* David DOYLE; *Chief Technician :* Jake TAYLOR; *Assistant Sound and Lighting Technician:* Daniel STEWART.

349. **STREET TRILOGY** by Chris O'Connell; THEATRE ABSOLUTE; *15-19 March 2005.* **Car:** *Jason:* Lee COLLEY; *Nick:* Peter ASH; *Tim:* Dan HARCOURT; *Mark:* Sean CERNOW; *Gary:* Graeme HAWLEY; *Robert:* James LOW. **Raw:** *Lex:* Rachel BROGAN; *Trainers:* Samantha POWER; *Addy:* Peter ASH; *Lorna:* Rebekah MANNING; *Rueben:* Graeme

CAR (349)

HAWLEY; *Shelley:* Belinda EVERETT. **Kid:** *Lee:* Lee COLLEY; *Bradley:* Rebekah MANNING; *K:* Sean CERNOW; *Zoe:* Samantha POWER. *Director:* Mark BABYCH; *Producer:* Julia NEGUS; *Youth Arts Director:* Georgina EGAN; *Trainee Director:* Paul SIMPSON; *Set & Costume Design:* Janet VAUGHAN; *Original Soundscapes:* Andi GARBI; *Stage Manager:* Steve COTTON; *Technician / Relights:* Will EVANS.

RAW (349) Lex (RACHEL BROGAN first beats up Trainers (SAMANTHA POWER) and then nurses her→→→

KID (349); Some may be eager to retire from a life of crime but to the young it mat still seem full of excitement; SEAN CERNOW and REBEKAH MANNING

10. **MOVE OVER, MORIATY** by Maggie Fox and Sue Ryding; LIPSERVICE; *29 March – 2 April 2005.*

350. **THE SEAGULL** by Anton Chekhov, translated by Tom Stoppard; COMPASS THEATRE COMPANY; *5-9 April 2005. Trigorin:* Nicholas ASBURY; *Sorin:* Robert AUSTIN; *Polina:* Steph BRAMWELL; *Shamraev:* Mike BURNSIDE; *Yakov:* David COVEY; *Dorn:* Paul GREENWOOD; *Arkadina:* Jane GURNETT; *Konstantin:* Ben HICKS; **Arkadina infuriates Shamraev→→→**

Medvedenko: Michael ONSLOW; *Nina:* Emma STANSFIELD; *Masha:* Amy Rhiannon WORTH. *Director:* Neil SISSONS; *Designer:* Liam DOONA; *Composer:* Christopher MADIN; *Lighting Designer:* Jason TAYLOR; *Production Manager:* Dan FRANKLIN; *Stage Manager:* Elb HALL; *Design Assistant:* Mike ELLIOT; *Trainee Stage Manager:* Cherry MARSDEN; *Set Construction:* PGH Scenic Workshop Ltd; C*ostume Supervisor:* Juliette BERRY; *Tailor:* Barry THEWLIS; *Costume Makers:* Sally BAXENDALE, Janet CHRISTMAS, Wayne MARTIN; *Costume Assistants:* Jenny DONNELLY; Jane LEVICK.

67. THE SAFARI PARTY by Tim Firth; LIBRARY THEATRE COMPANY; *15 April – 14 May 2005. Daniel:* Drew MULLIGAN; *Adam:* David PARTRIDGE; *Lol:* Claude CLOSE; *Bridget:* Lindsay ALLEN; *Esther:* Sue WALLACE; *Inga:* Jenifer ARMITAGE. *Director::* Roger HAINES; *Designer:* Judith CROFT; *Lighting:* Nick RICHINGS; *Sound:* Paul GREGORY; *Dialect Coach:* Sally HAGUE; *Company Stage Manager:* Lisa HALL; *Deputy Stage Manager, On The Book:* Kirsty RUSSELL; *Assistant Stage Manager:* Pippa SMITH-AITCHISON; *Scenic Artists:* Sue ROBSON, Alison EYRES, Hilly McMANUS; *Stage Crew*: David HOLT, Mike O'SULLIVAN; *Wardrobe Supervisor:* Liz HORRIGAN; *Wardrobe Assistant / Cutter:* Lindsey HANRAHAN; *Wardrobe Maintenance:* Kaeren DOOLEY;; *British Sigh Language Interpreter:* Mavis McCUE; *Captions* Janice WONG; *Production Manager:* Michael WILLIAMS; *Deputy Production Manager:* Gareth ROBERTS; *Construction Manager:* Derek JONES; *Construction Assistant:* David DOYLE; *Chief Technician :* Jake TAYLOR; *Assistant Sound and Lighting Technician:* Daniel STEWART. **Journal:** 18/4/05

351. TALKING TO TERRORISTS by Robin Soans; OUT OF JOINT; ROYAL COURT; *17-21 May 2005. An Ex-Member of the National Resistance Army, Uganda / Nodira / Girl / Ingrid:* Chipo CHUNG; *Aftab / An Ex-Member of the Ulster Volunteer Force / An Ex-Ambassador:* Jonathan CULLEN; *Edward / Another Ex-Secretary of State:/ Michael:* Christopher ETTRIDGE; *John / A British Army Colonel / Jad / An Ex-Member of the Kurdish Workers Party:* Alexander HANSON; *Momsie / An Archbishop's Envoy / An Ex-Member of the IRA / Dermot:* Lloyd HUTCHINSON; *Marjory / Rima / Phoebe:* Catherine RUSSELL; *Faiser / The Ex-Head of the Al Aqsa Martyrs Brigade, Bethlehem / Matthew:* Chris

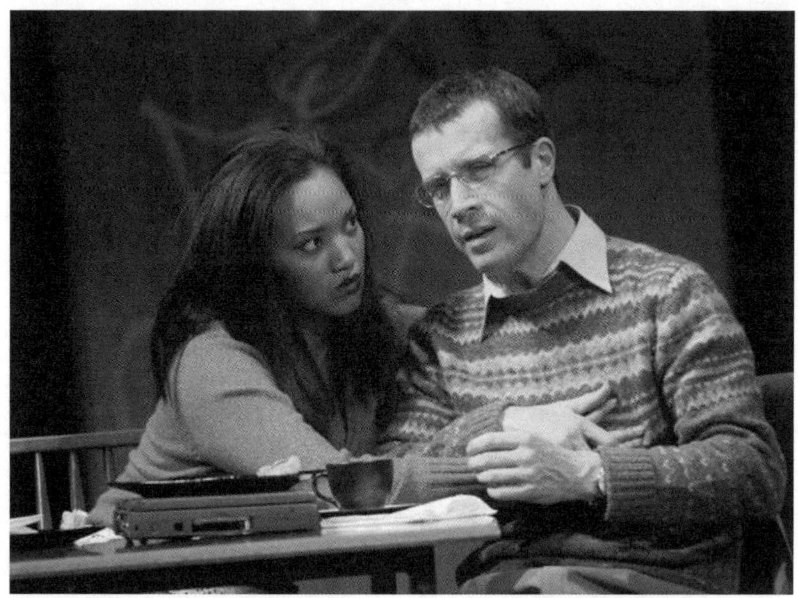

TALKING WITH TERRORISTS (351); The "Ex-Ambassador" (JONATHAN CULLEN) got himself into equally bad odour with his employers for being too open in denouncing the torture practised in a country with which Britain wished to maintain good relations and for expediting a visa for the Uzbek (CHIPO CHUNG) with whom he wished to replace his wife.

RYMAN; *An Ex-Secretary of State / Waitress / Linda / Caroline / Wife:* June WATSON. *Director:* Max STAFFORD-CLARK; *Designer:* Jonathan FENSOM; *Lighting Designer:* Johanna TOWN; *Sound Designer:* Gareth FRY; *Music Arranger:* Felix CROSS; *Assistant Director:* Naomi JONES; *Production Manager:* Gary BEESTONE; *Company Stage Manager:* Terence ELDRIDGE; *Deputy Stage Manager:* Sally McKENNA; *Assistant Stage Manager:* Lizzie DUDLEY; *Dialect Coach:* William CONACHER; *Costume Supervisor:* Frances GAGER; *Associate Lighting Designers:* Tum BRAY, Heidi RILEY; *Associate Sound Designer:* Angela McCLUNEY.

154. SISTERS, SUCH DEVOTED SISTERS by Russell Barr; OUT OF JOINT; THE DRILL HALL; *28 - 28 May 2005.*

One of the shared pleasures of Philip Larkin and Monica (CAMERON STEWART and CATE HAMER) is devising vulgar alternative chapter headings for the works of Iris Murdoch. His honestly adding "- unfortunately" to his answer "No," to her asking if he commits the acts described is her first intimation that she may not be loved alone; a splendidly witty and absorbing production.

352. **LARKIN WITH WOMEN** by Ben Brown; LIBRARY THEATRE COMPANY; RICHARD JORDAN PRODUCTIONS; *10 June – 2 July 2005. Larkin:* Cameron STEWART; *Monica:* Cate HAMER; *Betty:* Meriel SCHOLFIELD; *Maeve:* Sherry BAINES. *Director:* Chris HONER; *Designer:* Sue PLUMMER; *Lighting Designer:* James FARNCOMBE; *Sound Designer:* Paul GREGORY; *Stage Manager:* Kirsty RUSSELL; *Deputy Stage Manager On The Book:* Laura FLOWERS; *Assistant Stage Manager:* Pippa SMITH-AITCHISON; *Scenic Artist:*, Hilly McMANUS; *Stage Crew*: David HOLT, Steve BARRINGTON; *Wardrobe Supervisor:* Liz

HORRIGAN; *Wardrobe Assistant / Cutter:* Lindsey HANRAHAN; *Additional Wardrobe Assistance:* Jeanette PICKWELL; *Hairstyling / Wigs:* Angela CARRADUS, Peter REGAN, Wigs Up North; *Costume Makers:* Fiona BUNTING, Janet CHRISTMAS; *Knitting:* Erica BRIDGEWOOD, Teresa MARTIN; *Wardrobe Maintenance:* Kaeren DOOLEY; *British Sigh Language Interpreter:* Mavis McCUE; *Captions* Jake TAYLOR; *Audio Description:* Anna HASSAN; *Production Manager:* Michael WILLIAMS; *Deputy Production Manager:* Gareth ROBERTS; *Construction Manager:* Derek JONES; *Construction Assistant:* David DOYLE; *Chief Technician :* Jake TAYLOR; *Assistant Sound and Lighting Technician:* Daniel STEWART

LIFE; Jerusalem Place, Peter Street M2; 0161-833 3000; **CAZ:** 9, G1

230, 232; 24:7 THEATRE FESTIVAL; *Technician:* Jonathan HARVEY.

230. LAZY DAZE by John Chambers; NORTHERN QUARTER THEATRE COMPANY; *24-26 July 2005. Daisy :*Anne PRENDERGAST. *Director:* Scott DAVENPORT; *Stage Manager:* Naomi ALBANS. **Journal:** 25/5/05

232. BOTTLE by John Chambers; NORTHERN QUARTER THEATRE COMPANY; *24-26 July 2005. Clive:* Amir RAHIMZADEH; *Tom:* Shaun MEARS; *Paul:* Philip LIGHTFOOT. *Director:* Scott DAVENPORT; *Stage Manager:* Naomi ALBANS. **Journal:** 25/5/05

.

LILY LANE JUNIOR SCHOOL; Kenyon Lane MOSTON M40 9JP; 0161-205 1264; CAZ: 84, A3

LUCID; 11-12 The Printworks M3 2BS; 0161-817 2929; **CAZ:** 6, A3

MANCHESTER GRAMMAR SCHOOL; Old Hall Lane M13 0TH; 0161-224 7201; **CAZ:** 110, A5.

353. THE MORNING AFTER OPTIMISM by Tom Murphy; *10-11 September 2004.*

354. POPCORN by Ben Elton; *23-25 September 2004.*

355. THE BIRD CAGE; *11-13 November 2004.*

356. OLIVER!; Book, Music and Lyrics by Lionel Bart, based on the novel by Charles Dickens; MGS DRAMA SOCIETY; *1-4 December 2004*

357. RICHARD VERGETTE; *3-4 February 2005.*

358. ANTHONY AND CLEOPATRA by William Shakespeare;EVIL BEAN PRODUCTIONS; MGS DRAMA SOCIETY; *23-26 February 2005. Demetrius:* Josh AZOUZ; *Anthony:* Sebastian CHRISPIN; *Proculeius:* Martin CREFFIELD; *Lepidus:* Mark FRITH; *Octavia:* Rosie HOLT; *Enobarbus:* Josh McCRETON; *Philo:* Maeve McKEOWN; *Charmian:* Sian MADDOCK; *Messenger:* Victoria PEACOCK; *Caesar:* Antony RICHARDSON; *Soothsayer / Pompey:* Gabs RODRIGUEZ-CLEARY; *Dolabella:* Annabel SMITH; *Cleopatra:* Emma SWIFT; *Alexas:* Joel SWANN; *Iras:* Raani VIRDEE. *Cellist:* Vicky PEACOCK; *Pianist:* Nathan SHEPHERD. *Director:* James MATTHEWS-PAUL; *Historical Research:* Deborah BAKER, Ilana KARDASIS, Isabel SELFRIDGE; *Composer:* Steve CALVER; *Music Co-ordinator:* Kim SQUIRE; *Make-up:* Liz FOREMAN, Alex WILLIAMS; *Photography:* Charlotte LAMBERT; *Film-Maker:* Amy RUFFELL; *Costumes:* Beth COWEN, Liz FOREMAN; *Upholterer:* Matt FRAME; *Artist:* Kat McPARTIAN; *Designer / Lead Artist:* Abby WARNE; *Props:* Kate PELLETEAU; *Assistant Stage Managers / Non-Speaking Roles:* Sean BROOKS, Pete BULLER, Chris EDDLESTONE, Carl ETON; *Best Boy:* Ben KAY; *Technical Adviser:* Ollie COULOMBEAU; *Sound Operator:* Eytan HALON; *Lighting / Audio Visuals Operator:* Alex KNIGHT; *Lighting Co-ordinator:* Chris TUNNICLIFFE; *MGS Stage Crew:* Charlie BENTLEY, Mike BLANK, Patrick DODDS, Alex GANOSE, Jim GARRARD, Andy GODDARD, Greg HARDING, Mike HOLT, Tristan HONEYBORNE, James NELSON, 'C SHARK.'

359. COPENHAGEN by Michael Frayn; MGS DRAMA SOCIETY; *10-12 March.*

360. ANGELS IN AMERICA, Part I by Tony Kushner;

UNIVERSITY OF MANCHESTER DRAMA SOCIETY; *12-14 May 2005.*

361. **P'TANG YANG KIPPERBANG** by Jack Rosenthal; MGS DRAMA SOCIETY; *30 June – 2 July 2005. Director:* Susan JAMES; *Producer:* Dan FARR.

MANCHESTER HIGH SCHOOL FOR GIRLS; Grangethorpe Road M14 6JA; 0161-224 0447; CAZ: 109, G5

MANCHESTER JEWISH MUSEUM; 190 Cheetham Hill M8 8LW; 0161-832 7353 / 824 9879; CAZ: 95, E1

MANCHESTER METROPOLITAN UNIVERSITY STUDENTS UNION; Oxford Road, All Saints M1 7DY; 0161-273 1162; CAZ: 10, B4

MANCHESTER MUSEUM OF SCIENCE AND INDUSTRY; Liverpool Road, Castlefield M3 4EP; 0161-833 0027. **CAZ:** 9. E1; **W**

MANCHESTER ROAD METHODIST CHURCH; CHORLTON; 0161 - 860 4681; **CAZ**: 123, G1

188. **THE CONSTANT WIFE** by Somerset Maugham ; MANCHESTER ROAD PLAYERS; *19 –21 May 2005.*

MANCHESTER TOWN HALL; Albert Square M60 2LA; 0161-234 3039; **CAZ:** 5, H6

MANLEY PARK JUNIOR SCHOOL; College Road, Whalley Range M16 0AA; 0161-881 3808; **CAZ:** 108, A4

269. **PINOCCHIO** by Stephen Boyes, based on the original story by Carlo Collodi; MANCHESTER

ACTORS COMPANY; *3 March 2005.*

MARKET PLACE CAR PARK; off Blackfriars Street M3 2EQ; CAZ: 5, G4

MARSDEN WAY; Arndale Centre M2 1NP; CAZ: 6, A4

MATT AND PHRED'S JAZZ CLUB; 85 Oldham Street M4 1LF; 0161 - 661 7494; CAZ: 6, B5

M.E.N. ARENA; New Bridge Street M3 1AR; 0161-930 8000; **CAZ:** 5, H2

362. TOY STORY 2, from the screenplay by Andrew Stanton, Rita Hsiao, Doug Chamberlin and Chris Webb; DISNEY ON ICE. *Principals:* Lisa CORNELIUS, Michael GREEN, Kristian RYAN, Josh SPICER, Richard STRINGER; *Other Cast and Crew:* Teryn BARR, Tara BAXTER, Dawn BEFUS, Daniel BOSLTON, Kristyn CARRIERE, Mario CASTRO, Crystal CLARK, Steven DANYLUK, Joel DAVID, James DeANDA, Alice DeLIMA, Tina-Marie Di STEFANO, Alain FILLION, Eduardo GARCIA, Maria GAUDIEL, Jade GOSLING, Angela HIGGINSON, Eri KIKAWA, Megan LAMARRE, Adam LOOSLEY, Alexander MANDRIKOV, Tamara MAPOLES, Rodrigo MENENDEZ, Tim PETERSON, Andy PAULA, Kendra ROBERTS; Lisa ROSE, Brian ROUSH, Dmitryi SAMOHKINE, Elizabeth SHAFFROTH, Steven SHERER, Chantal STRINGER, Bianca SZIJGYARTO, Serguei TCHITALOV, Keiji TSUKAMOTO, Rebecca VANDENBERG, Chrissy WILBEE, Anthony WORGAN. *Director / Music Director:* Jerry BILIK; *Producer:* Kenneth FELD; *Choreographer:* Barry LATHER; *Assistant Choreographer:* Gig SIRUNO; *Lighting Designer:* LeRoy BENNETT; *Costume Designer:*Frank KRENZ; *Scenic Designer:* Loren SHAEMAN; *Assistant Set Designer:* Jim DARDENNE; *Production Performance Director:* Patricia VINCENT; *Pairs Skating Coach:*Tony Paul KUDRNA; *Props Studio Production Manager:* Matthew FREDDES; *Props and Scenery Artistic Lead:* Kevin STANALAND; *Props Production*

Co-ordinator: Rick PAPINEAU; *Props Artistic Supervisor:* William DAHNE; *Props Charge Artist:* Jon SIEROTA; *Scenery and Props Lead Artist:* Tamara SIMMONDS; *Master Electriucian:* David COLSON; *Creative Specialities:* Susan LAHMEYER; *Assistant Creative Costumes:* Janice MATTEN; *Associate to Designer:* Mark HENRY; *Head Sculptor:* Ivan SAXBY; *Head Welder:* Venancio GALVAN; *Head Carpentry:* Gary EVANS; *Associate Costume Designer:* Rachel GRUER; *Director of Costuming:* Todd KAUCHICK; *Head Sound:* Steven SHERER; *Assistant Sound:* Kenra ROBERTS; *Head Wardrobe:* Aaron CARLSON; *Assistant Wardrobe:* Alice DeLIMA; *Company Manager:* Robert STOKER; *Stage Manager:* James DeANDA; *Head Property:* Fabio BORDONI; *Assistant Proiperty:* Eric WIRFEL; *Head Carpaenter:* Paul KRIEGER; *Assistant Carpenters:* Florin ILLIESCU, David JOEL.

METHODIST CENTRAL HALL; Oldham Street M1 1JN; 0161-234 5141; **CAZ:** 6, B5

MIDLAND HOTEL; 16 Peter Street M60 2DS; 0161-236 3333; **CAZ:** 9. H1

227-243; 24:7 THEATRE FESTIVAL; *Co-directors:* David SLACK, Amanda HENNESSY; *Technical Manager:* Paul WEBB.

STANLEY ROOM; *Technical Team from* **Studio Salford:** *Co-ordinator:* James FOSTER; *Lighting:* Ken NORBURY; *Sound:* John SCOTT

234. VODKA KNICKERS by Darren Gallagher; DREAMCATCHER THEATRE COMPANY; *24-30 July 2005. Orla:* Sarah IBBOTSON; *Jax:* Cat MURPHY; *Debs:* Alyx TOLE; *Pete:* Julian WAITE. *Director:* Darren GALLAGHER; *Stage Manager:* Sarah BLANCHARD. **Journal:** 25/5/05

235. I'M FRANK MORGAN by Joe O'Byrne; ALBINO INJUN; *24-30 July 2005. Frank Morgan:* Joe O'BYRNE. *Director:* Jo CARLON; *Lighting:* James FOSTER; *Set Design:* Jo CARLON, Joe O'BYRNE; *Art Work:* Jo CARLON; *Sound:* John SCOTT; *Costume:* Joe O'BYRNE. **Journal:** 25/5/05

239. HERE IN THE NIGHT (AQUI EN LA NOCHE) by Sheryl Clowes; *24-30 July 2005. Man:* Glenn COLLIER; *Woman:* Kate GILBERT; *Waiter:* Thomas LIGGET. *Director / Choreographer:* Sheryl CLOWES; *Lighting Technician:* James SCOTT; *Visuals:* John SCOTT; *Stage Manager:* Megan CLOWES.

240. WHITE WEDDING by Maria Roberts; FINELINE THEATRE COMPANY; *25-30 July 2005. Katie:* Helena COATES; *Gemma:* Kiney BAILES; *Tom:* Darren BEAUMONT; *Cas:* Debbie SALOMAN; *Jo-Jo:* Karen McDONAGH. *Director:* Rhonwen McCORMACK; *Make-up Artist:* Judie BECQUE; *Set Design, Lighting, Film Sound Recording:* Ben SEABY; *Camera Operator, Sound, Film Editing:* Luke BATCHELOR; *Film Creative Director:* Maria ROBERTS; *Sound Operator / Stage Manager:* Ben DAVIES; *Composer:* Dan WATTS; *Lighting:* Andrew ROBINSON. **Journal:** 25/5/05

236. CABBAGES by Mark Winstanley and Lawrence Ghorra; INKY FINGERS; *24-30 July 2005. Geoffrey:* Kenan ALLY; *Audrey:* Hazel EARLE; *Nurse Hart:* Zoe NICHOLAS; *Warren / Policeman:* Mark WINSTANLEY; *Dr Spinoza:* Joe ATACK; *Noel:* John REEVELL; *Eric / Detective:* Lawrence GHORRA. *Director:* Alan PATTISON; *Lights / Sound:* Scott WEST; *Stage Management:* Heather SHAW; *Tomato Squashing:* Laura HARPER. **Journal:** 25/5/05

Courting fatally close to the walls of The Institution; KENAN ALLY and HAZEL EARLE.

241. LOVESICK by Steve Timms; NORTHERN ELASTIC; *24-29 July 2005. Simone:* Tracie DALY; *Michael:* Steve TIMMS; *Jackie:* Tricia ASHWORTH; *John / Terry:* John McELHATTON;

LOVESICK (241) Guidnce Counselling for a very rapid Serial Monogamist. (STEVE TIMMS – also author – and TRICIA ASHWORTH)

Badger: Mike McCORMICK. *Director:* Jason HUDSON.

VICTORIA SUITE;

Technician: Peter ELLIS; *Assistant Technician:* Gemma CARTER.

227. DRINKS WITH NATALIE by Elizabeth Baines; EYE OF THE STORM; *24 – 30 July 2004. Natalie:* Elizabeth BAINES. *Director:* Susan TWIST. **Journal:** 25/5/05

231. THE FALLING by Ailis Ni Riain; EXIT PRODUCTIONS; *24-30*

July 2005. Woman / Harpist: Amy LIPTROTT. *Director / Composer:* Ailis Ni RIAIN. **Journal:** 25/5/05

238. **NOW BREATHE OUT** by Rob Johnston; R J PRODUCTIONS; *24-30 July 2005. Cast:* Lane Paul STEWART, Nicole GASKELL, Adam LACY. *Director: Ian Karl Moore.* **Journal:** 25/5/05

237. **SALAD OLVAY** by David Tucker; DSM THEATRE COMPANY; *24-30 July 2005. Miriam:* Mary-Ann COBURN. *Director:* Susan TWIST. **Journal:** 25/5/05

243. **NOWHERE MAN** by Ian Moore; BLACK BOX THEATRE COMPANY; *25-30 July 2005. Kid:* Andrew RANKIN; *Dad:* Bernie MERRICK; *Uncle:* Robert LAWRENSON; *Aunt:* Hilly BARBER; *Cousin:* Donna COLEMAN; *Joker:* Bronwen EBDON; *Priest:* Cellan SCOTT. *Director:* Christopher NEIL; *Stage Manager / Sound Design / Music Compositon:* Oliver MAWDSLEY; *Sound Adviser:* Bernie MERRICK; *Producers:* Ian Karl MOORE, Gillian STOKES. **Journal:** 25/5/05

MILES PLATTING PRIMARY SCHOOL; Nelson Street M40 8FE; 0161-205 1968; CAZ: 96, A1

MOSS SIDE FIRE STATION; 9 Denhill Road M15 5NR; 0161-608 5203; **CAZ:** 108, D3

MOSTON BROOK HIGH SCHOOL; Northampton Road M40 5BP; 0161-202 2244; CAZ: 83, 5H

MOSTON FIELDS PRIMARY SCHOOL; Brookside Road M40 9GN; **CAZ:** 84, 2A

MOUNT CARMEL CHURCH OF ENGLAND PRIMARY SCHOOL; Wilson Road, BLACKLEY M9 8BG; 0161-740 4696; **CAZ:** 83, F2

269. **PINOCCHIO** by Stephen Boyes, based on the original story by Carlo Collodi; MANCHESTER ACTORS COMPANY; *15 March 2005.*

MUSEUM OF SCIENCE AND INDUSTRY; Liverpool Road, Castlefield M3 4EP; 0161-832 2244; B: 9, E1; **W**

363. **ON THE LINE** by Mike Lucas and Jim Woodland; Music and Lyric by Jim Woodland; MIKRON THEATRE COMPANY; *24 October 2004. Company:* Elizabeth EVES, Marianne McNAMARA, Robert TOOK, Peter TOON;. *Director:* Mike LUCAS; *Musical Arrangers / Directors:* Rebekah HUGHES, Janet RUSSELL; *Costumes / Set / Props:* Michael CAMDEN, Annie DEARDEN; *Tour Manager:* Peter TOON.

364. **PEDAL POWER** by Richard Povall; Music and Lyrics by Rebekah Hughes and Richard Povall; MIKRON THEATRE COMPANY; *25 October 2004* .

365. **WEIRD WAREHOUSE;** *30-31 October 2004.*

366. **WATER, WATER, EVERWHERE;** *13, 14, 27, 28 November 2004.*

367, **MR AND MRS CHADWICK TAKE THE TRAIN;** *27 October 2004,7-11, 16 Februar, 2 May 2005.y*

368. **JAMES WATT;** *5-6, 19-20 March, 9-10, 23-24 April, 7-8, 21-22 May 2005.*

369. **COOKING WITH GAS;** *26-27 March, 2-3, 16 17 April 2004*

MUSIC BOX; 65 Oxford Street M1 6EQ; 0161-236 9971; **CAZ**: 10, A2

NEWALL GREEN HIGH SCHOOL; Greenbrow Road M23 2SX; 0161-499 3878; CAZ: 147, F2

NORTHENDEN METHODIST CHURCH HALL

NORTHENDEN PLAYERS THEATRE CLUB; Boat Lane M22 4HR; 0161-998 9976; **CAZ:** 136; C2

372. **RUMOURS** by Neil Simon; NORTHENDEN PLAYERS; *5-11 September 2004. Chris Bevans:* Jo BOOTH; *Ken Bevans:* Dave McGUIRE; *Claire Cummings:* Deborah GRACE; *Leonard Cummongs:* Bill PLATT; *Ernest Cusack:* Dave HUNT; *Cookie Cusack:* Barbara BOSTOCK;

Glenn Cooper: John WHEATLEY; *Cassie Cooper:* Melanie DAVY; *PC Conklin:* Tom CHINNERY; *WPC Casey:* Nancy BOSTOCK. *Director:* Jo TAYLOR; *Properties:* Barbara LEARY et al; *Wardrobe:* Shirley HANNABUS et al; *Lighting / Sound:* Gary TIMPERLEY, Howard ROSENFELD; *Continuity:* Alma WHEATLEY.

373. **MR WONDERFUL** by James Robson; NORTHENDEN PLAYERS; *October 2004. Norma Green:* Melanie DAVY; *Phoebe Green:* Janet SLADE; *Geoff Lazenby:* Andy FOULKES; *Eric Box:* Howard ROSENFELD; *Lop Wink:* Peter FIRTH. *Director / Stage Manager / Wardrobe:* Brian BUTLER; *Properties:* Barbara LEARY et al; *Lighting / Sound:* Gary TIMPERLEY, Howard ROSENFELD; *On The Book:* Jo BOOTH.

374. **QUARTET** by Ronald Harwood; NORTHENDEN PLAYERS; *12-18 December 2004. Cecily Robson:* Lesley BOWERS; *Reginald Paget:* Peter BOWERS; *Wilfred Bond:* Dave HUNT; *Jean Horton:* Mary DILLON. *Director:* Howard ROSENELD; *Properties:* Barbara LEARY et al; *Lighting / Sound:* Gary TIMPERLEY, Howard ROSENFELD;

375. **SHADOWLANDS** by William Nicholson; NORTHENDEN PLAYERS; *6-12 February 2005. C S Lewis:* John WHEATLEY; *Major Lewis:* Colin BROADY; *Rev Harry Harrington:* Tom CHINNERY; *Professor Chris Riley:* Jack EDMONDS; *Professor Alan Gregg:* Peter FIRTH; *Dr M Oakley:* Joe KNIGHT; *Jo Grasham:* Deborah GRACE; *Douglas:* Jamie KIRK; *Registrar / Doctor:* Rodney HADWEN; *Clerk / Priest:* Andrew CURLEY; *Witness / Waiter:* James ROBINSON; *Nurse:* Jo BOOTH. *Director / Set Design:* Katherine MACHIN; *Properties:* Barbara LEARY et al; *Lighting / Sound:* Gary TIMPERLEY, Howard ROSENFELD; *Prompt:* Jo BOOTH; *Set Building and Finishing:* Nigel MACHIN, Cyril WALKER, Mac WALKER, Rodney HADWEN, Harry STUBBS, Eric MEE, Eric LEARY, Christine BOSTOCK, Barbara BOWES.

376. **THE WINSLOW BOY** by Terence Rattigan; NORTHENDEN PLAYERS; *3-9 April 2005. Ronnie Winslow:* Tim WOOD; *Violet:* Lillian BARLOW; *Grace Winslow:* Lesley BOWERS; *Arthur Winslow:* Peter BOWERS; *Catherine Winslow:* Jo TAYLOR; *Dickie Winslw:* Ian DOGHERTY; *John Watherstone:* Dave McGUIRE; *Desmond Curry:* Tony WILLIAMS; *Miss Barnes:* Pat SAUNDERS; *Fred:* Cyril WALKER; *Sir Robert Morton:* Alasdair KING.

PYGMALION (377); CATHERINE DILLON as Eliza (nominated for Best Actress in the Greater Manchester Drama Federation Awards) and PETER BOWERS as Higgins, after winning the Best Actor Award in Quartet (374); Costumes were also nominated for a GMDF Award.

Director: Mary DILLON; *Stage Manager:* Nigel MACHIN; *Properties:* Barbara LEARY, Jean JONES; *Wardrobe:* Katherine MACHIN, Jean WILSON, Mary DILLON; *Lighting / Sound:* Gary TIMPERLEY; *Continuity:* Tom CHINNERY, Pat SAUNDERS.

377. PYGMALION by George Bernard Shaw; NORTHENDEN PLAYERS; *22-28 May 2005. Mrs Eynsford-Hill:* Barbara BOSTOCK; *Clara Eynsford-Hill:* Alison BILSLAND; *Freddy Eynsford-Hill:* Ross KEEPIng; *Colonel Pickering:* Dave HUNT; *Bystanders:* Tom CHINNERY, Mona LEACH; *Professor Higgins:* Peter BOWERS; *Eliza Doolittle:* Catherine DILLON; *Mrs Pearce:* Alma WHEATLEY; *Alfred Doolittle:* Nigel MACHIN; *Hostess:* Lesley BOWERS; *Nepommuck:* Tom CHINNERY. *Director:* John WHEATLEY; *Properties:* Barbara LEARY et al; *Wardrobe:* Katherine MACHIN; *Lighting / Sound:* Gary TIMPERLEY, Howard ROSENFELD; *Prompt:* Lillian BARLOW.

NORTH MANCHESTER HIGH SCHOOL FOR BOYS; Charlestown Road M10 7BS; 0161 - 681 1526 / 1199; CAZ: 70,B6

NORTH MANCHESTER HIGH SCHOOL FOR GIRLS; Brookside Road M40 9QJ; 0161-947 1858; **CAZ;** 84, A2

THE OLD MONK; 14 Lloyd Street M2 5ND; 0161-832 8311; **CAZ:** 5, G6

ON THE EIGHTH DAY 111 Oxford Road M1 7DU; 0161-273 4878 / 1850; 01422 844786; CAZ: 10, B4

OPENSHAW COMMUNITY CENTRE; 915 Ashton Old Road M11 2NH; 0161-223 3502; CAZ: 97, E6

OPERA HOUSE, Quay Street M3 3JT;0161-834 1787; **CAZ:** 5, F6. **G, W**

378. **CATS;** Poems by TS Elliot, with some additional material by Trevor Nunn and Richard Stilgoe; CLEAR CHANNEL; CAMERON MACKINTOSH; REALLY USEFUL GROUP; *30 August – 11 September 2004. Macavity / Admetus:* Simon ADKINS; *Victoria:* Emily ANDERSON; *Jennyanydots:* Sarah BAYLIS; *Rumpelteazer:*Laura BRYDON; *Carbucketty:* Richard CURTO; *Munkostrap:* Matthew CUTTS; *Bombalurina:*Lisa DONMA; *Bill Bailey:* Alex DURRANT; *Jellyorum:* Karen EVANS; *Grizabella:* Chrissie HAMMOND; *Swings:* Barry HAYWOOD, Lucy HOLLOWAY, Chevaun MARSH, Stuart NEAL, Ian STROUGHAIN, Anthony WHITEMAN, Karen WILLIAMS; *Coricopat:* Lee LOMAS;*Jemima:* Claire PARRISH; *Rumpus / Alonzo:* Richard PEAKMAN; *Demeter:* Leyla PELLIGRINI; *Mungojerrie:* Andrew PRODSSER; *Rum Tum Tugger:* Stuart RAMZEY; *Tantomile:* Kate TYDMAN. *Original Director:* Trevor NUNN; *Associate Director / Choreographer:* Gillian LYNNE; *Designer:* John

Tom and Hatty (Cameron Slater and Jane Riley) explore the Melbourne's house

TOM'S MIDNIGHT GARDEN (380)

NAPIER; *Lighting Designer:* David HERSEY; *Co-Orchestrator:* David CULLEN; *Re-Creator of Original Direction abd Choreography:* Chrissie CARTWRITE; *Production Musical Supervisor:* Daniel DOWLING; *Musical Director:* Stuart CALVERT; *Associate Scenic Designer:* Raymond HUESSY; *Co-Sound Designers:* Simon BAKER, Terry JARDINE; *Resident Director:* Stori JAMES.

379. **GOOD MOURNING, MRS BROWN** by Brendan O'Carroll; THE BRENDAN O'CARROLL GROUP; *14-25 September 2004.*

380. **TOM'S MIDNIGHT GARDEN** by Philippa Pearce, adapted for the stage by David Wood; BIRMINGHAM STAGE COMPANY; *28 September – 2 October 2004. Tom:* Cameron SLATER; *Hatty:* Jane RILEY. *Director:* Graeme MESSER; *Design:* Jackie TROUSDALE; *Lighting:* Jason TAYLOR; *Music:* Matthew SCOTT; *Sound:* Tom LISHMAN.

381. **BLAZEE** by Floyd Knight, adapting Charles Dickens; BLUE MOUNTAIN THEATRE; *4 November 2004. Fanny Fagin:* Lavern ARCHER; *Ms Urchin:* Yolanda HAREWOOD; *Charlie Bates:* Marlon KING; *Nancy :*Olive MILLER; *Bill Sikes:* Ian O'BRIEN; *Lazaris:* Kay OISHI; *Big Bwoy:* Andrew ROACH; *Rude Bwoy Artful Dudger:* Ricky ROWE; *Olver Twist:* Terri SALMON; *Mrs Sorefoot Bosun:* Charles TOMLIN. *Director:* Joseph CHARLES; *Stage Manager:* Paul MICAH; *Assistant Stage Manager:* Andrew ROACH; *Wardrobe Mistress:* Donna ARCHER.

382. **STARLIGHT EXPRESS – THE THIRD DIMENSION;** composed by Andrew Lloyd Webber; REALLY USEFUL THEATRE COMPANY; *1 November – 4 December 2004. Engines:* James GILLIAN, Tom KANAVAN, Anton STEPHENS; Jake SAMUELS, Grant MURPHY, Chris THATCHER, Mykal RAND, Philipps REYNOLD, Adam FLOYD; *Coaches:* Jane HORN, Tanya ROBB, Amy FIELD, Ashley HALL; *Trucks:* Johnny SHENTALL, Tyman BOATRIGHT, Paul CHRISTOPHER, Gavin ASHBARRY; *Electra's Components:* Ruthie STEPHENS, Danielle Leigh MORRIS, Lauren BROOKE, Matthew BOULTON; *Trick Skater:* Matt KING; *Swings:* Andrew MILLAR, Jamie CAPEWELL, Lucinda GILL, Carla PULLEN, Tony ANDRADE, Jason MUSHELL. *Director / Choreographer:* Arlene PHILLIPS; *Designer:* John NAPIER; *Director of 3D Film:* Julian NAPIER.

383. **DICK WHITTINGTON AND HIS CAT;** QDOS ENTERTAINMENT; *11 December 2004 – 9 January 2005. Captain:* Paul CHUCKLE (=ELLIOTT); *Mate:* Barry CHUCKLE (=ELLIOTT); *Sarah The Cook:* Jefferey HOLLAND; *Alice*

Fiztwarren: Helen NOBLE; *Fairy Godmother:* Judy BUXTON.

384. CHICAGO; Lyrics by Fred Ebb; Music by John Kander; Book by Fred Ebb and Bob Fosse; CLEAR CHANNEL ENTERTAINMENT; *11-22 January 2005. Billy Flynn:* Marti PELLOW. *Direct*or: Scott FARIS; *Choreographer:* Gary CHRYST; *Set Design:* John Lee BEATTY.

385. ENJIE BENJY; *7 February 2005.*

386. TELSTAR by Nick Moran, with James Hicks; NEW VIC WORKSHOP; *8-12 March 2005. Cast:* Con O'NEILL, Linda ROBSON, Adam RICKITT. *Director:* Michael BOGDANOV.

387. MRS BROWN RIDES AGAIN by Brendan O'Carroll; THE BRENDAN O'CARROLL GROUP; *22 March – 9 April 2005. Agnes Brown:* Brendan O'CARROLL; *Cathy Brown:* Jennifer GIBNEY; *Maria Brown:* Fiona O'CARROLL; *Rory Brown:* Pat Pepsi SHIELDS; *Dermot Brown:* Paddy HOULIHAN; *Grandad:* Dermot Bugsy O'NEILL; *Winnie:* Clare MULLEN; *Buster Brady:* Danny O'CARROLL; *Dino Doyle:* Clyde CARROLL; *Thomas Clune:* Mike PYATT. *Director:* Brendan O,CARROLL; *Assistant Director:* Jennifer GIBNEY; *Producer:* Martin DELANY; *Wardrobe:* Linda CARTER; *Set Design:* Benni De MARCO; *Production Manager:* Dermot Bugsy O'NEILL; *Stage Manager:* Mervyn RUNDLE; *Assistant Stage Manager:* Danny O'CARROLL; *Hair Styles / Wigs:* Gary KAVANAGH, Emily HANWAY, Peter MARKS; *Lighting:* Julie MATTHEWS.

LINDA NOLAN as Mrs Johnson

388. **BLOOD BROTHERS** by Willy Russell; BILL KENWRIGHT; *2-14 May 2005. Mrs Johnson:* Linda NOLAN; *Narrator:* Keith BURNS; *Mickey:* Stephen PALFREMAN; *Eddie:* Drew ASHTON; *Linda:* Louise CLAYTON; *Mrs Lyons:* Tracy SPENCER; *Sammy:* Danny TAYLOR; *Policeman / Teacher:* Matt SLACK; *Donna Marie:* Katherine DOUGLAS; *Perkins:* Philip MAGGS; *Postman / Bus Conductor:* Rob HUGHES; *Neighbour:* Karl GREENWOOD; *Brenda:* Emma NOWELL. *Directors:* Bill KENWRIGHT, Bob TOMSON; *Musical Director:* Rob EDWARDS; *Design:* Andy WALMSLEY; *Lighting:* Nick RICHINGS; *Sound:* Ben HARRISON.

389. **KEN DODD HAPPINESS SHOW;** *5 June 2005.*

390. **GREASE;** Book, Music and Lyrics by Jim Jacobs and Warren Casey; PAUL NICHOLAS & DAVID IAN; *28 July – 6 August 2005.*

391. **TRACTOR TOM;** PREMIER STAGE PRODUCTIONS; *23 July 2005.*

OUR LADY'S ROMAN CATHOLIC HIGH SCHOOL; Alworth Road, BLACKLEY M9 0RP; 0161-795 0711; **CAZ:** 69, F4

OWENS PARK; 293 Wilmslow Road M14 6HD; 0161-225 5555; CAZ: 109, H6

PALACE SOCIAL CLUB; Farmside Place, LEVENSHULME M19 3AD; 0161-257 3538; CAZ: 110, C6

PALACE THEATRE; Oxford Street M1 6FT; 0161-242 8503/2503; **CAZ:** 10, A2 **G, H, W**

392. **THE VAGINA MONOLOGUES** by Eve Esler; *6-11 September 2004. Cast:* Lesley JOSEPH, Mica PARRIS, Linda ROBSON.

393. **BOOGIE NIGHTS2** by Jon Conway; QDOS; CHURCHILL THEATRE BROMLEY; *20-25*

September 2004. Roddy: Mark JONES; *Terry:* Scott ROBINSON; *Trish:* Emily MASCARENHAS; *Debs:* Sophie LAWRENCE; *Sharon:* Ally HOLMES; *Tracey:* Sarah KITSON; *Spencer:* Joe SPEARE; *Shane:* Sebastian SYKES; *Saint Peter:* David ESSEX; *Angela:* Natasha KHAMANJI; *Bernadette:* Jacqui LEMMENS; *Young Roddy:* Jordan CONWAY; *Eamon:* Don CRANN; *Steve:* Andrew REES; *Rob:* Luke JOHNSON; *Geldof / Thatcher:* Barry HESTER; *Barmaid:* Ildi BALOC; *Arnie:* Laci DINKA. *THE BAND*: *Musical Director:* Simon COLES; *Drums:* Danny COTTRELL; *Bass:* Dave STORER; *Guiter:* Frank DAWKINS. *Director:* Jon CONWAY; *Choreographer:* Alan HARDING; *Musical Arranger / Supervisor:* Olly ASHMORE; *Lighting Designer:* Joe ATKINS; *Set & Costume Designer:* Gary UNDERWOOD.

394. TELL ME ON A SUNDAY; Music by Andrew Lloyd Webber; Lyrics by Don Black; BILL KENWRIGHT; *28 September 2005. Performer:* Marti WEBB.

389. KEN DODD CHRISTMAS HAPPINESS SHOW; *28 November 2004*

JESUS CHRIS SUPERSTAR (395) GLENN CARTER (Jesus) and EMMA DEARS (Mary Magdalen)

395. JESUS CHRIST SUPERSTAR; Music by Andrew Lloyd Webber; Book and Lyrics by Tim Rice; BILL KENWRIGHT' *4-16 October 2004. Jesus:* Glenn CARTER; *Judas:* James FOX; *Mary Magdalen:* Emma DEARS; *Herod:* Martin CALLAGHAN. *Directors:*Bill KENWRIGHT, Bob TOMSON; *Lighting Design:* Nick RICHINGS; *Set & Costumes Design:* Paul · FARNSWORTH; *Sound Design:* Mick POTTER; *Choreography:* Henry METCALFE; *Production Musical Director:* David STEADMAN

396. LONNIE D; LONNIE DONEGAN INC; *17 October 2004. Cast:* Peter DONEGAN, Anthony DONEGAN, David DONEGAN, Tony JOHNSON, Leroy Johnson, Johnny NEWSOME, Kay MILBOURNE, Melissa BELL, Vicky YOUNG, Jason KING, Lynn LARKIN, Jemma MORLAND, Lee PROUD; *THE LONNIE DONEGAN SKIFFLE BANDl Drums:* Chis HUNT; *Percussion:* Alan WICKET; *Guitar:* Paul HENRY; *Harmonica / Saxophone:* Mike PACE; *Bass:* Eddie MASTERS. *Director:* Leah BELL; Producers: Sharon DONEGAN, Leah BELL; *Choreographer:* Lee PROUD.

PAUL NICHOLAS, about to change

397. JEKYLL AND HYDE; conceived for the stage by Steve Cuden and Frank Wildhorn; Book and Lyrics by Leslie Bricusse; Music by Frank Wildhorn; PETER FROSDICK & MARTIN DODD; UK PRODUCTIONS; PAUL NICHOLAS; *19 – 23 October 2005. Dr Henry Jekyll / Edward Hyde:* Paul NICHOLAS; *Lord Savage:* Christopher BLADES; *Lady Beaconsfield:* Winnie CLARKE; *Sir Danvers Carew:* Richard COLSON; *Simon Stride:* Robert IRONS; *Lisa Carew:* Shona LEWIS; *Gabriel John Utterson:* Charles SHIRVELL; *Sir Archibald Proops:* Garry LAKE; *General Lord Glossop:* James HEAD; *The Bishop of Basingstoke:* Phil COLE; *Lucy Harris:* Louise DEARMAN; *Madame:* Gail-Marie SHAPTER; *Spider:* Chris COLEMAN; *Poole:* Peter EDBROOK; *Nellie:* Jennifer HEPBURN; *Newsboy:* Mark POWELL; *Jenny:* Holly GRAHAM; *Mary:* Jessica PUNCH; *Flossie:* Bethan ELDRIDGE; *Rosie:* Natalie WINDSOR; *Nancy:* Nalalie LANGSTON; *Lizzie:* Zoe RAINEY. *Director:* David GILMORE; *Musical Staging:* Chris HOCKING; *Musical Supervisor:* Gareth WILLIAMS; *Production Manager:* Andy BATTY; *Set Designer:* Charles CAMM; *Lighting Designer:* Neil AUSTIN; *Sound Designer:* Glen BECKLEY; *Costume Designer/ Company Manager:* Natalie COLE; *Assistant Costume Designer:* Elizabeth DENNIS; *Stage Manager:* Laura COOPER; *Dance Captain:* Jessica PUNCH; *Fight Co-ordinator:* Mark POWELL; *Production Electrician:* Wingnut; *Stage Electrician:* Vikki STONEBANKS; *Sound:* Leigh DAVIES, Daniel BAILEY; *Production Sound:* Jon HIGSON; *Wardrobe Mistress:* Caroline HANNAN; *Wigs Mistress:* Cheryl HILL; *Wardrobe Assistant:* Donna ISAAC; *Carpenter / Assistant Stage Manager:* Dan CAULWELL; *Assistant Stager Managers:* Natasha WOOD, Samantha BOND, Liam DIXON; *Production Wigs / Milliner:* Barbara ALDERSON; *Jekyll & Hyde Wig:* Brian PETERS; *Production Wardrobe:* Robert PRIESTLEY, Ann BRIGGS,

Rebecca PAMMENT, Pooly LAURENCE, Gina COLE, Beth SPILLER, Lesley BELFIELD, Caroline HANNAM, Donna ISAAC, Kate DAVID.

398. THE COMPLETE WORKS OF WILLIAM SHAKESPEARE (ABRIDGED); THE REDUCED SHAKESPEARE COMPANY; *26 October 2004.*

399. KISS ME KATE; Music and Lyrics by Cole Porter; Book by Sam and Bella Spewack; *16-27 November 2004. Petruchio:* Craig URBANI; *Kate:* Julie-Alanah BRIGHTEN; *Gangsters:* Michael GRECO, Les DENNIS. *Director:* Michael BLAKEMORE; *Musical Supervision* Paul GEMIGNANI; *Choreography:* Kathleen MARSHALL.

400. SCROOGE; Book, Music and Lyrics by Leslie Bricusse; BILL KENWRIGHT; *7 December 2004 – 15 January 2005. Scrooge:* Tommy STEELE. *Director:* Bob TOMSON; *Design:* Paul FARNSWORTH; *Illusions:* Paul KLIEVE;

←TOMMY STEELE as Scrooge.

Choreography: Lisa KENT; *Musical Director:* Stuart PEDLAR; *Lighting Design:* Nick RICKINGS; *Sound Design:* Mick POTTER.

401. HIGH SOCIETY; Music and Lyrics by Cole Porter, adapted by Carolyn Burns from the MGM Motion Picture, based on **The Philadelphia Story** by Philip Barry; CHURCHILL THEATRE BROMLEY; *17 – 22 January 2005. Tracy Lord:* Susie BLAKE.; *Director:* Ian TALBOT.

403. **THE KING AND I;** Music by Richard Rodgers; Book and Lyrics by Oscar Hammerstein, based on the novel **Anna and The King of Siam** by Margaret Landon; CLEAR CHANNEL ENTERTAIMENT;

414. **THE WIND IN THE WILLOWS** by Kenneth Grahame, dramatised by Mike Redwood; SPLATS ENTERTAINMENT *15-19 February 2005.*

404. **LOVE SHACK;** conceived y Kim Gavin and written by Danny Peak; *24 February – 5 March 2005. Cast:* Jon LEE, Faye TOZER, Noel SULLIVAN. *Director / Choreographer:* Kim GAVIN.

405. **JUS' LIKE THAT** by John Fisher; BLUE MAGIC PRODUCTIONS; THEATRE ROYAL PLYMOUTH; *14-19 March 2005. Tommy Cooper:* Jerome FLYNN; *The Cooperettes:* Michelle BISHOP, Lorraine DOUGALL, Claire EVERSON, Kristin KELLY, Amanda PHILLIPS, Kara POOLE; *MUSICIANS: Trumpet:* John BARCLAY; *Trombone:* Pat HARTLEY; *Alto Saxophone / Flute:* John FRANCHI; *Tenor Saxophone / Clarinet:* Jamie TALBOT; *Drums / Percussion:* Mike SMITH; *Double Bass:* Dave OLNEY. *Director:* Simon CALLOW; *Set & Costumes Design:* Christopher WOODS; *Lighting Design:* Nick RICHINGS; *Sound Design:* Mike WALKER; *Musical Supervision / Original Music:* Paul BATEMAN; *Choreography:* Craig Revel HORWOOD; *Associate Choreography:* Heather DOUGLAS; *Magic Direction:* Geoffrey DURHAM; *Company Stage Manager:* John PAGE; *Deputy Stage Manager:* Emma GERRISH; *Assistant Stage Managers:* Andrew GORMAN, Chrissie MALLETT; *Sound Operator:* Dean STEAD; *Costume Supervisor:* Kathy HEMSTOCK; *Magic Props:* David SHAKARIAN; *Production Electrician:* Jim BEAGLEY.

406. **SPACE MAGIC;** MILKSHAKE; *24-26 March 2005. Hi5:* Timothy John HARDING, Nathan Joel FOLEY, Kellie Lynn HOGGART, Kathleen DE LEON, Charli Marie Zeta ROBINSON.

407. **PRIDE AND PREJUDICE** by Jane Austen, adapted by Sue Pomeroy; GOOD COMPANY; *30 March – 2 April 2005. Mrs Bennet:* Jennifer WILSON; *Mr Bennett:* Mark WYNTER; *Lizzy:* Chloe NEWSOME; *Darcy:* Martin Glyn MURRAY; *Mr Wickham:* John LESLIE. *Director:* Sue POMEROY; *Design:* Dennis SAUNDERS.

408. **TOMMY** by THE WHO; Music and Lyrics by Pete Townshend; Book by Pete Townshend and Des McAnuff; Additional Music and Lyrics by John Entwistle and Keith Moon; BILL KENWRIGHT; *4 – 9 April 2005. Mrs Walker:* Vivienne CARLYLE; *Captain Walker:* Damien EDWARDS; *Uncle Ernie:* Tom NEWMAN; *Minister Allied Soldier / Judge / Hawker /News Vendor / DJ:* Andy PELOS; *Minister's Wife Hawker's Girl / Specialist's Assistant:* Rebecca Jo HANBURY; *Nurse / Ladettess / Pinball Lasses:* Rebecca Jo HANBURY, Sophia NORRIS, Landi OSHINOWO, Rachael TUCKER; *1st Officer / Psychiatrist:* Jamie TYLER; *2nd Officer / Lover /. Local Lad:* Lee MEAD; *Allied Soldier / Doctor / Specialist:* David STOLLER; *Allied Solidier / Cousin Kevin:* Alan CRAWFORD; *Tommy Aged 4:* Jacob MILLAR, Keiran WHALEY; *Narrator / Tommy:* Jonathan WILKES; *Tomy Aged 10:* Brian Joseph McCANN; *Lads:* Lee MEAD, Andy PELOS, David STOLLER, Jamie TYLER; *The Acid Queen:* Landi OSHOWI; *Local Lass / Sally Simpson:* Rachel TUCKER; *Reporter:* Sophia NORRIS. *MUSICIANS: Keyboards:* Stuart MORLEY, Ieuan REES; *Guitars:* Tommy EMMERTON, Nick RADCLIFFE; *Bass:* Andy BROWNING; *Drums:* James GAMBOLD; *Directors:* Guy RETALLACK, Keith STRACHAN; *Designer:* Andy WALMSLEY; *Choreographer:* Carole TODD; *Musical Director:* Stuart MORLEY; *Lighting Designer:* Ben P CRACKNELL; *Sound Designer:* Ben HARRISON; *Costume Designer:* Christopher CAHILL; *Assistant Designer:* Jason SOUTHGATE; *Company Stage Manager:* Chris FISHER; *Deputy Stage Manager:* Andy OWEN; *Technical Assistant Stage Manager:* Clair BERESFORD; *Wardrobe Mistress:* Aelish BAUGH; *Sound 1 & 2:* David PREECE, Bob BURROWS; *Touring Electrics:* Gary COOPER; *Production Carpenters:* Phil UMNEY, Maitland WAKEFIELD; *Production Sound:* Marcus WADLAND; *Production Electricians:* Chris CUNNINGHAM, Tim OLIVER; *Lighting Programmer:* David Saddler; *Costume Supervisor:* Brigid GUY; *Deputy Costume Supervisor:* Jules BOTTRILL; *Deputy Wardrobe:* Robin LILL; *Wardrobe Assistants:* Helen Lovett JOHNSON, Melody Tatania WOOD; *Costume Makers:* Elly PARKES, Paddie DICKIE,

Glenn HILLS; *Props Buyer:* Lindah BALFOUR; *Set Building:* Capital Scenery Ltd; *Fight Director:* Terry KING; *Directors' Assistant:* Svanlaug JOHANNSDOTIR.

409. JOSEPH AND THE AMAZING TECHNICOLOR DREAMCOAT; Book and Lyrics by Tim Rice; Music by Andrew Lloyd Webber; BILL KENWRIGHT; *11 – 16 April 2005. Joseph:* Craig ADAMS; *Narrator:* Abigail JAYE; *Jacob:* Henry METCALFE; *Gad / Pharaoh:* Marlon MOORE; *Potiphar:* Christopher JAY; *Mrs Potiphar:* Charlotte HALL; *Naphtali / Baker:* Russell HICKEN; *Simeon / Butler:* David CRANT; *Rueben:* Philip COYLE; *Levi:* Gareth CHART; *Issachar:* John MELVIN; *Asher:* Aaron ROMANO; *Dan:* James MULLER; *Zebulun:* Martin DICKINSON; *Judah:* Stuart KING; *Benjamin:* Geoffrey BRADLEY; *Handmaidens:* Charlotte HALL, Dani McCALLUM, Naomi SLATER; *Swing:* Joshua MARTIN; *ORCHESTRA: Keyboards:* Robert CHALMERS, Gareth WEEDON, Andrew CORCORAN, Colin KING; *Electric / Acoustic Guitars:* Mark WRAITH; *Drums / Percussion:* Neil BROCKLEHURST; *Trumpet / Flugel Horn:* David BROOKE. *Director:* Bill KENWRIGHT; *Choreographer:* Henry METCALFE; *Production Musical Director:* David STAEDMAN; *Musical Director:* Robert CHALMERS; *Designer:* Sean CAVANAGH; *Lighting Designer:* Nick RICHINGS; *Sound Design:* Chris FULL; *Set Design Assistant:* Simon HEAP; *Wardrobe Supervisor:* Brigid GUY; *Assistant Costume Supervisor:* Jules BOTTRILL; *Costume Assistant:* Costume ASSISTANT; *Electrics Programmer:* Jim BEAGLEY

69. THOROUGHLY MODERN MILLIE; Book by Richard Morris and Dick Scanlan; new music by Jeanine Tesori; not so new music by James Van Heusen, Victor Herbert, Jay Thompson, San Lewis, Peter Ilych Tchaikovsky and Arthur Sullivan; new lyrics by DickScanlan; not so new lyrics by Sammy Cahn, Jay Thompson, Rida Johnson Young, Joe Young and Walter Donaldson; PAUL ELLIOTT, DUNCAN C WELDON, PAT MOYLAN; MILLIE PRODUCTIONS LTD; *19 – 30 April 2005. Millie Dillmount:* Donna STEELE; *Jimmy Smith:* Richard REYNARD; *Ruth:* Emma-Gina KING; *Gloria:* Lauren ADAMS; *Rita / New Modern:* Emily SHAW; *Alice:* Laura CLEMENTS; *Ethel Peas / Maid:* Victoria HAY; *Cora / Society Lady:* Nicky WILSON;*Lucille / Dorothy Parker / Daphne* Vanessa BARMBY; *Mrs Meers /* Lesley JOSEPH; *Miss Dorothy Brown:* Robyn NORTH; *Ching Ho;*Yo SANTHEVEESUK; *Bun Foo:* UNKU;

Programme Details

Miss Flannery: Nicola BLACKMAN / Vanessa BARMBY; *Trevor Graydon:* Andrew KENNEDY; *Speed Typists:* Emma-Gina KING, Lauren ADAMS, Emily SHAW, Laura CLEMENTS, Victoria HAY, Nicky WILSON, Vanessa BARMBY, Laura TYRER; *Pearl Lady:* Laura TYRER; *The Letch:* Ian Gareth JONES; *Officer / Prison Guard / Dexter:* Charles DOHERTY; *Muzzy Van Hossmere:* Grace KENNEDY; *Butler:* Brett WATKISS; *Society Lady:* Nicky WILSON; *George Gershwin:* Karl CLARKSON; *Ira Gershwin:* Joseph PROUSE; *Rodney:* Phil HOGAN; *Dishwashers~:* Charles DOHERTY, Brett WATKISS, Laura TYRER, Nicky WILSON; *Muzzy's Boys:* Karl CLARKSON, Ian Gareth JONES, Phil HOGAN, Joseph PROUSE, Daniel SMITH, Karl STEVENS; *Ensemble:* Lauren ADAMS, Vanessa BARMBY, Laura CLEMENTS, Victoria HAY, Emma-Gina KING, Emily SHAW, Laura TYRER, Nicky WILSON, Karl CLARKSON, Charles DOHERTY, Ian Gareth JONES, Phil HOGAN, Joseph PROUSE, Daniel SMITH, Karl STEVENS, Brett WATKISS; *ORCHESTRA: Musical Director:* Keyboards 1: Chris HATT; *Keyboards 2 / Assistant Musical Director:* Ewan ANDERSON; *Guitar / Tenor Banjo:* Derek HARRIS; *Double Bass:* Russell SWIFT; *Drums / Percussion:* Sebastian GUARD; *Lead Trumpet:* Gavin MALLETT; *Second Trumpet:* Adam LINDSEY; *Tenor Trombone:* Chris COLE; *Flute / Piccolo / Bb Clarinet / Alto Saxophone:* Dave WEBB; *Bb Clarinet / Tenor & Soprano Saxophones:* Paul SAUNDERS. *Director:* Michael MAYER; *Tour Director:* Beth EDEN; *Choreographer:* Rob ASHFORD; *Tour Choreographer:* Chris BAILEY; *Set Designer:* David GALLO; *Costume Designer:* Michael PAKLEDINAZ; *Tour Lighting Designer:* Joe ATKINS; *Original Lighting Designer:* Donald HOLDER; *Sound Design:* Gareth OWEN; *Musical Supervisor / Orchestral Management:*Gary HIND; *Orchestrations USA:* Doug BESTERMAN, Ralph BURNS; *Vocal Music Arranger:* Jeanine TESORI; *Dance Music Arranger:* David CHASE; *Music Preparation:* Dave FOSTER, Fraser SKEOGH, Gavin WHITLOCK, Maurice ANELLI; *Keyboard Programme:* Griff JOHNSON, Bruce KNIGHT; *Hair / Wig Designer USA:* Paul HUNTLEY; *Wig / Make-up DesignUK:* Richard MAWBEY; *Wig Makers:* Wig Specialities; *Costume Supervisors UK:* Jackie GALLOWAY, Anna JOSEPHS; *Assistant Lighting Designer:* Alastair GRANT; *General Manager / Executive Producer:* David BOWNES; *Production Manager:* Patrick MOLONY; *Company Manager:* Anthony SAMMUT; *Stage Manager:* Chris HESKETH; *Deputy Stage*

Manager: Lucy WESTNIDGE; *Assistant Stage Managers:* Linda DARBY, Darren McKEOWN; *Electrics Operator:* Adam JONES; *Sound Operators:* Marcus WADLAND *(1),* Ciaron McKENNA *(2); Wardrobe Mistress:* Nikki EDMONDS; *Deputy Wardrobe Mistress :*Rana FOWLER; *Wig Mistress:* Moira O'CONNELL; *Deputy Wig Master:* Rob WILSON; *Costume Alterations:* Sari RUTHERFORD, Christine MANNING; *Costume Making:* Karen CRIGHTON; *Shoe Making:* Gamba, Phil TRENWITH; *Set Building:* Robert Knight – Top of The Bill Ltd, Met Scene Fabrications Ltd, Bowerwood Ltd, Howard Eaton Lighting, Clearwater Scenery Ltd; *Props / Furnitue:* Russell Becck Studio; *Production Carpenters:* Phil LARGE, Eddie CROWTHER; *Production Sound Engineer:* Chris MACE; *Production Sound Crew:* Keith HUTCHINSON *(1),* Jason HATTAMS *(2),* James LOVELESS*(3);* Surtitles: *Michelle HABECK.* **Journal:** 25/4/05

70. SALAD DAYS by Dorothy Reynolds and Julian Slade; Music by Julian Slade; MATTHEW TOWNSHEND PRODUCTIONS LTD; *3-7 May 2005. Jane:* Helen POWER; *Timothy / Nightclub Dancer :*Jamie READ; *Timothy's Mother / Manicurist / Assistant / Fiona:* Sarah SHEPHERD; *Timothy's Father / Inspector:* Neil CLENCH; *Aunt Prue / Heloise / Electrode:* Kate BUXTON; *Adancing Judge / PC Boot / Nightclub Dancer:* Gary O'SULLIVAN; *Nigel:* David RANDALL; *The Tramp / Uncle Baa-Baa / Uncle Zed:* Tony HOWES; *Lady Raeburn / Asphynxia:* Vicki MICHELLE; *Troppo:* Matthew TOWNSEND; *Sir Clamsby Williams / Nightclub Manager / Augustine Williams:* Mark HOLMAN. *Director:* Matthew TOWNSHEN; *Choreography:* Jenny ARNOLD; *Musical Arrangements:* Malcolm BENNETT; *Rehearsal Musical Director:* Michael JEFFREY; *Design / Scenic Artist:* Paul COX; *Lighting:* Bob BUSTANCE; *Costumes:* Ella KIDD; *Assistant Costume Designer /Supervisor:* Cecile DAUBY; *Sound Design:* David HERMON; *Floor Painting:* Peter CLARK; *Company / Stage Manager:* George CRITCHLEY; *Deputy Stage Manager:* Steve WOOLMER; *Assistant Stage Manager:* Kate BUXTON; *Work Experience Costume Assistant:* Rachel CURRY; *Miss Michelle's Costumes:* Claire CHRISTIE, Karen OGBORN, Cecile DAUBY; *Additional Costumiers:* Annalise HARVEY, Lucie KELCHE, Wendy OLVER, Korina ROEDING; *Millinery:* Ella KIDD; *Propeller Carver:* John SPRENTALL **Journal:** 25/4/05

410. THAT'LL BE THE DAY; DEREK BLOCK; TREVOR PAYNE; *19 May 2005. Artistes:* Trevor PAYNE, Gary ANDERSON, Morgan TURNER, Katy SETTLERFIELD, Julia GREENHAM, Iain HAWKINS, Phil HOLLENDER, Mark STREET, Andy HODGE, Clive FISHLOCK. *Director:* Trevor PAYNE; *Sound Engineer:* Neil ATKINSON; *Production Electrician:* Gareth AKEHURST; *Monitor Electrician:* Sam PEREGRINE; *Sound Designer:* Andy FOX.

411. **POSTMAN PAT;** CHILDREN'S SHOWTIME PRODUCTIONS; *28-29 May 2005.*

412. **GUYS AND DOLLS;** Music and Lyrics by Frank Loesser; Book by Jo Swerling and Abe Burrows, based on the stories and characters of Damon Runyon; CLEAR CHANNEL STAGE EXPERIENCE; *25-27 August 2005.*

413. **THE WIZARD OF OZ;**based on the story by L Frank Baum; PAUL HAMMOND; WORTHING PAVILION THEATRE; *31August – 3 September 2005. Scraps :*Dani HARMER; *Tin Man:* Colin WHITE. *Director:* Paul HAMMOND.

PARKLANDS HIGH SCHOOL; Wythenshawe M22 7TH; 0161-499 2726

PARRS WOOD HIGH SCHOOL; Wilmslow Road, DIDSBURY M20 5PG; 0161-445 8786; **CAZ:** 137, H2

PARSONAGE GARDENS; M3 2LF; CAZ: 5, G5

PHOENIX; University Precinct, Oxford Road M13 9PG; 0161-272 5921; CAZ: 10, B5

PICCADILLY GARDENS; CAZ: 6, B5.

PLATT FIELDS; Wilmslow Road; **CAZ:** 109, G5.

415 –430:Garden of Delights; 3-5 July 2005, a small selection of the scores of performances and displays:

415. **BIG BUG BALL;** AVANTI DISPLAY; PRECARIOUS DANCE THEATRE; *4-5 July 2005*

416. **BIRTH OF VENUS;** AVANTI DISPLAY; *4-5July 2005. Venus:* Meera Bell THOMSON. *Producer / Director:* Mike LISTER; *Choreography:* Karla SHACKLOCK; *Costume:* Lynne DURIC; *Original Music:* James ATHERTON; *Design (owing something to* Botticelli*) / Construction:* Bryan TWEDDLE.

417. **FAIRY AND GNOME;** BEE & FOLEY

418. **LOLLIPOP PATROL;** CURIOUS CARGO

419. **THE MIRACLE SHOW;** DESPERATE MEN

420. **PUPPET CAFÉ;** FACELESS

421. **NOW WASH YOUR HANDS;** FAIRLY FAMOUS FAMILY

422. HELLSAPOPPIN; GRAND THEATRE OF LEMMINGS

423. A BUNCH OF ROSES; GUIDE BRIDE YOUTH THEATRE;

424. GASTRONOMIC; HOODWINKL *Performers* Andrew CROMIE, Kate ADAMS, Matthew LAWRENSEN, Josh ELWELL. *Directors:* Stephanie JALLAND, Adam GENT; *Composer:* Kelsey MICHAEL, *Maker:* Neil ROBSON; *Costume:* Karen McKEOWN.

425. BOTANY BEGINS AT HOME; HORSE + BAMBOO

426. EARLY ONE MORNING; HORSE+BAMBOO

427. OPERATION BETA; JOE SATURE ET SES JOYEUX OSSELETS

428. THE SUNFLOWER SHOW; LITTLE BIG TOP

429. COCKTAILS FOR TWO; SWIZZLESHAKER; *Performers:* Dave CHAMELEON, Aila BAILA.

430. TOP SECRET; OPERATION TAPP; *Costumes:* Nerissa CARGILL-THOMPSON

PLATT LANE METHODIST CHURCH; M14 7BU;0161-2486366; CAZ: 109, E5

POWERHOUSE; 140 Raby Street M14 4ST; 0161-227 1939; **CAZ:** 109, E3

PUMP HOUSE PEOPLE'S HISTORY MUSEUM; Left Bank, off Bridge Street M3; 0161-228 7212; **CAZ:** 5, F5.

431. NO BED OF ROSES based on the experiences of Daisy Shortman, Edith Stanley and Dorothy Clark by PEOPLESCAPE THEATRE; 3, *29 Octobre, 7 November 2004. Gabrielle Walker:* PAULETTE LEMARD

433. SHOP FRONT, HOME FRONT by PEOPLESCAPE THEATRE; *2 January 2005. Dolly Salter:* Janet BARRON, Sarah EDGE.

432. THE HARD WAY UP by Eileen Murphy; PEOPLESCAPE THEATRE; *5 December 2004, 6 March 2005. Hannah Mitchell:* Sarah EDGE. *Director:* Eileen MURPHY.

364. PEDAL POWER by Richard Povall; Music and Lyrics by Rebekah Hughes and Richard Povall; MIKRON THEATRE COMPANY; *9 November 2004* .

434. STRIKE A LIGHT!; PEOPLESCAPE THEATRE' *6 February 2005. Maggie McCallow – Match Girl.*

QUEEN'S PARK; Rochdale Road; **CAZ**: 83, F5.

RACKHOUSE PRIMARY SCHOOL; Yarmouth Drive M23 0BT; 0161-998 2544; CAZ: 135, G2

REYNOLDS THEATRE; UMIST; M1 7HS; 0161-306 6000; **CAZ:** 166, C2

371. MY FAIR LADY; Book and Lyrics by Alan Jay Lerner; Music bu Frederick Loewe; adapted from the play **Pygmalion** by George Bernard Shaw and thefilm by Gabriel Pascal; UNIVERSITY OF MANCHESTER DRAMA SOCIETY;*7-10 December 2004. Director:* Ned BENNETT.

RIGHTON BUILDING; Cavendish Street M15 6BG; 0161 - 247 2000; CAZ: 10, A5

ROBINSKI'S; 5 Wilbraham Road, FALLOWFIELD M14 6JS; 0161-248 1930; **CAZ**: 125, G1

ROMAN FORT; Castlefield CAZ: 9, E2

ROUNDWOOD SPECIAL SCHOOL; Roundwood Road, NORTHENDEN M22 4AD; 0161-998 4138; **CAZ:** 136, B4

ROYAL EXCHANGE; St Ann's Square M2 7DH; 0161-833 9833; **CAZ:** 5, H5. **D, G, H, W**

435. KES; adapted by Lawrence Till from **A Kestrel For A Knave** by Barry Hines; ROYAL EXCHANGE THEATRE COMPANY; *8 September – 16 October 2004. Jud:* William BECK; *Billy Casper:* Andrew GARFIELD; *Mr Gryce / Porter:* Ian BARITT; *Mr Farthing / Milkman:* Roger MORLIDGE; *Mrs Casper:* Janet HAZLEGROVE; *Farmer / Youth Employment Officer / Mr Croosley:* Kieran CUNNINGHAM; *MacDowall:* Steven WEBB; *Mr Sugden / Mr Beal:* Gary DUNNINGTON; *Anderson:* Philip McGINLEY; *Delamore:* Steven BLOOMER; *Tibbut:* Thomas MORRISON; *Mrs MacDowall / Mrs Rose / Miss Fenton / Librarian:* Fiona CLARK; *Messenger / Pupil:* Alan NEAL; *Pupils:* Benjamin BOATEN, Sam GRIMWOOD, Sam LINDSAY, Freddie MACHIN. *Director:* Sarah FRANKOM; *Designer:* Becky HURST; *Lighting:* Colin GRENFELL; *Sound:* Peter RICE; *MusicL* Richard ATKINSON; *Dialect Coach:* William CONACHER; *Fights:* Kate WATERS; *Assistant Director:* Cheryl MARTIN; *Stage Manager:* Julia WADE; *Deputy Stage Manager:* Lynn HOWARD; *Assistant Stage Manager:* Ben DONOGHUE; *Audio Describer:* Anne HORNSBY; *Head of Sound:* Steve BROWN; *Deputy Head of Sound:* Peter RICE; *Sound Assistants:* Gerry MARSDEN, Claire WINDSOR; *Head of Props and Settings:* Alan FELL; *Deputy Head Of Props and Settings:* Philip COSTELLO; *Props and Settings:* Andrew BUBBLE; Brian FARRON, Carl HESTON, Stuart MITCHELL, Lee PEARSON, Meriel PYM, Sarah WORRALL*cOSTUME Supervisor:* Ginnie O'BRIEN; *Deputy Costume Supervisor:* Nicola MEREDITH; *Wardrobe Production:* Rachel BAILEY, Jennifer BRIDGES, Rose CALDERBANK, Janet CHRISTMAS, Vanessa PICKFORD; *Wardrobe Mistress:* Kate ELPHICK; *Wardrobe Maintenance:* Sarah ASTBURY; *Wigs Supervisor:* Rowena DEAN; *Wigs Assistance:* Jo SHEPSTONE *Head of Lighting:* Richard OWEN; *Lighting Team:* Thomas SCOTT, Nick SHARP, Mark DISTIN; *Production Manager:* Alan CARRADUS; *Prop Buyers:* Kim FORD, Jackie BELL, John FISHER.

436. VOLPONE by Ben Jonson; ROYAL EXCHANGE THEATRE COMPANY; *20 October –27 November 2004. Volpone:* Gerard MURPHY; *Mosca:* Stephen NOONAN; *Voltore:* Michael CARTER; *Corbaccio:* Gareth THOMAS; *Corvino:* Stephen MARZELLA; *Celia:* Miranda COLCHESTER; *Bonario:* Chris HARPER; *The Dude:* Tom GODWIN; *The Nun:* Dominic BURDESS; *The Nurse:* Sarah DESMOND; *Advocates:* Patrick DRIVER, Ian BLOWER; *Notario:* Sarah DESMOND. *Director:* Greg HERSOV; *Designer:* Lez BROTHERSTON; *Lighting:* Bruno POET; *Sound:* Steve BROWN; *Music:* Arun GHOSH; *Fights:* Renny KRUPINSKI; *Assistant Director:*

VOLPONE (436, GERARD MURPHY) endeavours to have his wicked way with Celia (MIRANDA COLCHESTER)

Philip STORK; *Stage Manager:* Cath BOOTH; *Deputy Stage Manager:* Tamara ALBACHARI; *Assistant Stage Manager:* Kirsten BUCHANAN; *Audio Describer:* Anne HORNSBY; *Head of Sound:* Steve BROWN; *Deputy Head of Sound*: Peter RICE; *Sound Assistants:* Gerry MARSDEN, Claire WINDSOR; *Head of Props and Settings:* Alan FELL; *Deputy Head Of Props and Settings:* Philip COSTELLO; *Props and Settings:* Andrew BUBBLE; Brian FARRON, Carl HESTON, Stuart MITCHELL, Lee PEARSON, Meriel PYM, Sarah WORRALL,*Student Placement:* Amy GOLDMAN *Acting Costume Supervisor:* Nicola MEREDITH; *Wardrobe Production:* Rachel BAILEY, Jennifer BRIDGES, Rose CALDERBANK, Janet CHRISTMAS, Vanessa PICKFORD, Katie BROOKS, Jill FAIRBAIRN, Charlotte HARRISON, David SHORT, Julia Walker, Elizabeth WEBSTER; Sally Winter' *Additional Stage Crew:* Craig PRICE, Pedro SEGURA; *Wardrobe Mistress:* Kate ELPHICK; *Wardrobe Maintenance:* Sarah ASTBURY; *Wigs Supervisor:* Rowena DEAN; *Wigs Assistance:* Jo SHEPSTONE, Georgina GABBIE; *Head of Lighting:* Richard OWEN; *Deputy Head of Lighting:* Kay HARDING; *Lighting Team:* Thomas SCOTT, Nick SHARP; *Production Manager:* Alan CARRADUS; *Prop Buyers:* Kim FORD, Jackie BELL, John FISHER.

7. **LONDON ASSURANCE** by Dion Boucicault; ROYAL EXCHANGE THEATRE COMPANY; *1 December 2004 – 15 January 2005. Cool:* Murray MELVIN; *Martin / James / Solomon Isaacs:* Patrick DRIVER; *Charles Courtley:* Charles AITKEN; *Richard Dazzle:* Andrew

LANGTREE; *Sir Harcourt Courtly:* Garald HARPER; *Max Harkaway:* Jon CARTWRIGHT; *Pert:* Lorna LEWIS; *Grace Harkaway:* Rae HENDRIE; *Mark Meddle:* Jonathan KEEBLE; *Lady Gay Spanker:* Race DAVIES; *Adolphus Spanker*: Peter LINDFORD. *Director:* Jacob MURRAY; *Designer:* Louise Ann WILSON; *Lighting:* Jason TAYLOR; *Music:* Tayo AKINBODE; *Audio Describer:* Anne HORNSBY; *Stage Manager:* Francis LYNCH; *Deputy Stage Manager:* Tracey FLEET; *Assistant Stage Manager:* Alison DANIELS; *Head of Sound:* Steve BROWN; *Deputy Head of Sound*: Peter RICE; *Sound Assistants:* Gerry MARSDEN, Claire WINDSOR; *Head of Props and Settings:* Alan FELL; *Deputy Head Of Props and Settings:* Philip COSTELLO; *Props and Settings:* Andrew BUBBLE; Brian FARRON, Carl HESTON, Stuart MITCHELL, Lee PEARSON, Meriel PYM, Sarah WORRALL, Louise ANDREW, Ben COOK, Graham McHUGH, Susan ROSS; *Acting Costume Supervisor:* Tracy DUNK; *Deputy Costume Supervisor:* Nicola MEREDITH; *Wardrobe Production:* Rachel BAILEY, Jennifer BRIDGES, Rose CALDERBANK, Janet CHRISTMAS, Vanessa PICKFORD, Katie BROOKS, Jill FAIRBAIRN, Charlotte HARRISON, Felicia JAGNE, David SHORT,, Elizabeth WEBSTER; *Wardrobe Mistress:* Kate ELPHICK; *Wardrobe Maintenance:* Sarah ASTBURY; *Wigs Supervisor:* Rowena DEAN; *Wigs Assistance:* Jo SHEPSTONE, Georgina GABBIE; *Head of Lighting:* Richard OWEN; *Deputy Head of Lighting:* Kay HARDING; *Lighting Team:* Thomas SCOTT, Nick SHARP, Cara PLUMMER; *Production Manager:* Alan CARRADUS; *Prop Buyers:* Kim FORD, Jackie BELL, John FISHER. **Journal:** 4/10/04

MAXINE PEAKE addresses the problems of domination by Rutherford

437. RUTHERFORD AND SON by Githa Soerby; ROYAL EXCHANGE THEATRE COMPANY; *19 January – 19 February 2005. Janet:* Maxine PEAKE; *Ann:* Dinah STABB; *Mary:* Christine BOTTOMLEY; *John:* Daniel BROCKLEBANK; *Richard:* Jonas ARMSTRONG; *Rutherford:* Maurice ROEVES; *Martin:* Antony BYRNE; *Mrs Henderson:* Joan KEMPSON. *Director:* Sarah FRANKOM; *Designer:* Simon DAW; *Lighting:* Hartley TA KEMP; *Sound:* Steve BROWN; *Dialects:* Poll MOUSSOULIDES; *Assistant Director:* Cheryl MARTIN; *Stage Manager:* Julia WADE; *Deputy Stage Manager:* Tamara ALBACHARI; *Assistant Stage Manager:* Lynn HOWARD; *Audio Describer:* Anne HORNSBY; *Head of Sound:* Steve BROWN; *Deputy Head of Sound*: Peter RICE; *Sound Assistants:* Gerry MARSDEN, Claire

WINDSOR; *Head of Props and Settings:* Alan FELL; *Deputy Head Of Props and Settings:* Philip COSTELLO; *Props and Settings:* Andrew BUBBLE; Brian FARRON, Carl HESTON, Stuart MITCHELL, Lee PEARSON, Meriel PYM, Sarah WORRALL; *Acting Costume Supervisor:* Nicola MEREDITH; *Wardrobe Production:* Rachel BAILEY, Jennifer BRIDGES, Rose CALDERBANK, Janet CHRISTMAS, Vanessa PICKFORD, Katie BROOKS, Jill FAIRBAIRN, Charlotte HARRISON, Felicia JAGNE, Julia WALKER; *Wardrobe Mistress:* Kate ELPHICK; *Wardrobe Maintenance:* Sarah ASTBURY; *Wigs Supervisor:* Rowena DEAN; *Wigs Assistance:* Jo SHEPSTONE, Georgina GABBIE; *Head of Lighting:* Richard OWEN; *Deputy Head of Lighting:* Kay HARDING; *Lighting Team:* Thomas SCOTT, Nick SHARP; *Production Manager:* Alan CARRADUS; *Prop Buyers:* Kim FORD, Jackie BELL, John FISHER.

JOSETTE BUSHELL-MONGO and TOM MANNION

438. ANTONY AND CLEOPATRA by William Shakespeare; ROYAL EXCHANGE THEATRE COMPANY; *23 February – 9 April 2005. Antony:* Tom MANNION; *Cleopatra:* Josette BUSHELL-MINGO; *Caesar:* Steven ROBERTSON; *Enobarbus:* Terence WILTON; *Charmian:* Sarah PAUL; *Iras / Octavia:* Gugu MBATHA-RAW; *Dercetus:* Fergus O'DONNELL; *Philo / Clown:* Joseph MAWLE; *Alexas / Seleucus:* Chris HANNON; *Soothsayer / Eros:* Everal A WALSH; *Mardian:* Ali SICHILONGO; *Lepidus / Thidias / Watch:* Will TACEY; *Dolabella / Sentry:* Simeon TRUBY; *Scarus:* Glenn CHAPMAN; *Maecenas /Schoolmaster / Diomedes:* Jack LORD; *Agrippa:* James HOWARD. *Director:* Braham MURRAY; *Designer:* Johanna BRYANT; *Battle Choreographer:* Mark BRUCE; *Lighting:* Vince HERBERT; *Sound:* Steve BROWN;

Music: Akintayo AKINBODE; *Fights:* Renny KRUPINSKI; *Musician:* Dan McDONALD; *Stage Manager:* Francis LYNCH; *Deputy Stage Manager:* Tracey FLEET; *Assistant Stage Manager:* Kirsten BUCHANAN; *Audio Describer:* Anne HORNSBY; *Head of Sound:* Steve BROWN; *Deputy Head of Sound*: Peter RICE; *Sound Assistants:* Gerry MARSDEN, Claire WINDSOR; *Head of Props and Settings:* Alan FELL; *Deputy Head Of Props and Settings:* Philip COSTELLO; *Props and Settings:* Andrew BUBBLE; Brian FARRON, Carl HESTON, Stuart MITCHELL, Lee PEARSON, Meriel PYM, Sarah WORRALL, Ben COOK, Simon PEMBERTON; *Student Placement:* Emma GING; *ARMOUR:* Ivo COVENEY; *Swordbelt / Accessories:* Phil O'CONNOR; *Costume Supervisor:* Ginnie O'BRIEN; *Deputy Costume Supervisor:* Nicola MEREDITH; *Wardrobe Production:* Rachel BAILEY, Jennifer BRIDGES, Rose CALDERBANK, Janet CHRISTMAS, Vanessa PICKFORD, Katie BROOKS, Jill FAIRBAIRN, Charlotte HARRISON, Felicia JAGNE, Amy SPEAR, Julia WALKER, Elizabeth WEBSTER; *Wardrobe Mistress:* Kate ELPHICK; *Wardrobe Maintenance:* Sarah ASTBURY; *Wigs Supervisor:* Rowena DEAN; *Wigs Assistance:* Jo SHEPSTONE, Georgina GABBIE; *Stage Crew:* Pedro SEGURA, Liam WHITTAKER; *Head of Lighting:* Richard OWEN; *Deputy Head of Lighting:* Kay HARDING; *Lighting Team:* Thomas SCOTT, Nick SHARP, Cara PLUMMER; *Production Manager:* Alan CARRADUS; *Prop Buyers:* Kim FORD, Jackie BELL, John FISHER.

59/ ON THE SHORE OF THE WIDE WORLD by Simon Stephens; ROYAL EXCHANGE; NATIONAL THEATRE; *13 April – 15 May 2005.* *Alex Holmes:* Thomas MORRISON; *Sarah Black:* Carla HENRY; *Peter Holmes:* Nicholas GLEAVES; *Alice Holmes:* Siobhan FINNERAN; *Ellen Holmes:* Eileen O'BRIEN; *Charlie Holmes:* David HARGREAVES; *Christopher Holmes:* Steven WEBB; *Susan Reynolds:* Susannah HARKER; *Paul Danziger:* Matt SMITH; *John Robinson:* Roger MORLIDGE. *Director:* Sarah FRANCOM; *Designer:* Liz ASHCROFT; *Lighting Designer:* Mick HUGHES; *Music:* Julian SWALES; *Sound Designer:* Peter RICE; *Voice Work:* Wyllie LONGMORE; *Assistant Director:* Tom DALEY; *Audio Describer:* Anne HORNSBY; *Stage Manager:* Julia WADE; *Deputy Stage Manager:* Lynn HOWARD; *Assistant Stage Manager:* Cynthia DUBERRY; *Student Placement:* Beth DIBBLE; *Sound Assistants:* Gerry MARSDEN, Claire WINDSOR; *Head of Props and Settings:* Alan FELL; *Deputy Head Of Props and Settings:* Philip COSTELLO; *Props and Settings:* Andrew BUBBLE; Carl HESTON, Stuart MITCHELL, Lee PEARSON, Meriel PYM, Sarah WORRALL, Louise ANDREW, Ben COOK, Lucy ADAMS, David FANNING, Susan ROSS, Diane SHUFFLEBOTTOM; *Acting Costume Supervisor:* Nicola MEREDITH; *Wardrobe Production:* Rachel BAILEY, Jennifer BRIDGES, Rose CALDERBANK, Janet CHRISTMAS, Vanessa PICKFORD, *Wardrobe Mistress:* Kate ELPHICK; *Wardrobe Maintenance:* Sarah ASTBURY; *Wigs Supervisor:* Rowena DEAN; *Wigs Assistance:* Jo SHEPSTONE; *Head of Lighting:* Richard OWEN; *Deputy Head of*

Lighting: Kay HARDING; *Lighting Team:* Thomas SCOTT, Nick SHARP, Cara PLUMMER; *Production Manager:* Alan CARRADUS; *Prop Buyers:* Kim FORD, Jackie BELL, John FISHER. **Journal:** 16/2/05

ANDREW LANGTREE (Buddy Baker) encounters LUCY CHALKLEY (Peggy)

439. COME BLOW YOUR HORN by Neil Simon; ROYAL EXCHANGE THEATRE COMPANY; *18 May – 25 June 2005. Alan Baker:* Jamie GLOVER; *Peggy Evans:* Lucy CHALKLEY; *Buddy Baker:* Andrew LANGTREE; *Mr Baker:* Malcolm RENNIE; *Connie Dayton:* Sarah-Louise YOUNG; *Mrs Baker:* Amanda BOXER. *Director:* Jacob MURRAY; *Designer:* Di SEYMOUR; *Lighting:* Richard OWEN; *SoundL* Steve BROWN, Gerry MARSDEN; *Dialects:* Lise OLSON; *Assistant to the Director:* Will NEWELL; *Stage Manager:* Jo BRADMAN; *Deputy StageManager:* Clare LOXLEY; *Assistant Stage Manager:* Ruth TAYLOR; *Student Placement:* Tine LUND; *Audio Describer:* Anne HORNSBY; *Head of Sound:* Steve BROWN; *Deputy Head of Sound*: Peter RICE; *Sound Assistants:* Gerry MARSDEN, Claire WINDSOR; *Head of Props and Settings:* Alan FELL; *Deputy Head Of Props and Settings:* Philip COSTELLO; *Props and Settings:* Andrew BUBBLE; Carl HESTON, Stuart MITCHELL, Lee PEARSON, Meriel PYM, Sarah WORRALL *Costume Supervisor:* Ginnie O'BRIEN; *Deputy Costume Supervisor:* Nicola MEREDITH; *Wardrobe Production:* Rachel BAILEY, Jennifer BRIDGES, Rose CALDERBANK, Janet CHRISTMAS, Vanessa PICKFORD; *Wardrobe Mistress:* Kate ELPHICK; *Wardrobe Maintenance:* Sarah ASTBURY; *Wigs Supervisor:* Rowena DEAN; *Wigs Assistance:* Jo SHEPSTONE; *Head of Lighting:* Richard OWEN; *Deputy Head of Lighting:* Kay HARDING; *Lighting Team:* Thomas SCOTT, Cara PLUMMER; *Production Manager:* Alan CARRADUS; *Prop Buyers:* Kim FORD, Jackie BELL, John FISHER.

440. SEX, CHIPS & ROCK 'N' ROLL; Book and Lyrics by Debbie Horsfield and Hereward Kaye; (Lyrics of Right Here, Right Now by Jonathan Moore; Music by Hereward Kaye; ROYAL EXCHANGE THEATRE COMPANY; *29 June – 6 August 2005. The Wolf:* Ben BARNES; *Irma Brookes:* Tracie BENNETT; *Norman Kershawe:* David BIRRELL; *Ensemble / Shane Riordan:* Kevin DOODY; *Arden Brookes:* Elaine GLOVER; *Ensemble / Hayley;* Leanne HARVEY; *Ensemble:* Lindsey LAUER, Lizzie MALLEY, Laura Ann McALPINE, Zara WARREN, Matthew

Programme Details

The 1970's Face of Manchester Music: BEN BARNES (The Wolf), DEAN STOBARD (Dallas), BEN SUTHERLAND (Tex Tunnicliffe)

WOLFENDEN; *Ensemble / Nurse Fido:* Michelle POTTER; *Larry B Cool:* Paul RYAN; *Dallas McCabe:* Dean STOBBART; *Tex Tunnicliffe:* Ben SUTHERLAND; *Ellie Brookes:* Emma WILLIAMS. *BAND: Keyboards:* Dane PREECE, Richard REEDAY; *Alto / Soprano Saxophones:* Norman BROWN; *Accoustic / Electric Guitars:* Hereward KAYE; *Bass Guitar / Double Bass:* Geth GRIFFTHS; *Drums:* Alan BROWN. *Director:* Jonathan MOORE; *Designer:* Conor MURPHY; *Choreographer:* Ann YEE; *Assistant Choreographer:* Matthew WOLFENDEN; *Voice Work:* Mark LANGLEY; *Lighting:* Vince HERBERT; *Sound:* Steve BROWN; *Orchestration:* Neil McARTHUR; *Vocal Arrangements:* Neil McARTHUR, Hereward KAYE; *Musical Director:* Dane PREECE; *Assistant Musical Director:* Richard REEDAY; *Music Preparation:* Colin RAE; *Keyboard Programmer:* Mark DICKMAN; *Stage Manager:* Francis LYNCH; *Deputy Stage Manager:* Tracy FLEET; *Assistant Stage Managers:* Jill DAVEY, Craig PRICE; *Student Placement:* Laura PARKES; *Audio Describer:* Anne HORNSBY; *Head of Sound:* Steve BROWN; *Deputy Head of Sound*: Peter RICE; *Sound Assistants:* Gerry MARSDEN, Claire WINDSOR; *Head of Props and Settings:* Alan FELL; *Deputy Head Of Props and Settings:* Philip COSTELLO; *Props and Settings:* Andrew BUBBLE; Carl HESTON, Stuart MITCHELL, Lee PEARSON, Meriel PYM, Sarah WORRALL *Student Placement:* Helen HALL; *Acting Costume Supervisor:* Nicola MEREDITH; *Wardrobe Production:* Rachel BAILEY, Jennifer BRIDGES, Rose CALDERBANK, Janet CHRISTMAS, Vanessa PICKFORD, Jill FAIRBAIRN, Charlotte HARRISON, Felicia JAGNE, Matthew PAYNE, David SHORT, Julia

WALKER, Elizabeth WEBSTER; *Wardrobe Mistress:* Kate ELPHICK; *Wardrobe Maintenance:* Sarah ASTBURY; *Wigs Supervisor:* Rowena DEAN; *Wigs Assistance:* Jo SHEPSTONE, Lisa DEARNLEY, Charlene ATKINSON; *Head of Lighting:* Richard OWEN; *Deputy Head of Lighting:* Kay HARDING; *Lighting Team:* Thomas SCOTT, Cara PLUMMER; *Follow Spot Operators:* Jen SNAP, Lorraine MARSHALL; *Production Manager:* Alan CARRADUS; *Prop Buyers:* Kim FORD, Jackie BELL, John FISHER.

ROYAL EXCHANGE STUDIO:

441. HARRY AND ME; written and performed by ROBIN DEACON; *16-18 September 2004.*

4. A CONVERSATION by David Williamson; ROYAL EXCHANGE THEATRE COMPANY; *22 September – 9 October 2004. Jack Manning:* Stuart GOODWIN; *Lorin Zemanek:* Cate HAMER; *Derek Milsom:* Martin TURNER; *Barbara Milsom:* Tilly TREMAYNE; *Coral Williams:* Barbara MARTEN; *Bob Shorter:* David STERNE; *Gail Williams:* Sally BRETTON; *Mick Williams:* Andrew LANGTREE. *Director:* Jacob MURRAY; *Designer:* Gemma FRIPP; *Lighting:* Mark DISTIN; *Sound:* Steve BROWN; *Dialects:* Mark LANGLEY; *Assistant Director:* Philip STORK; *Technical Stage Manager:* Keith BROOM; *Stage Manager:* Francis LYNCH; *Deputy Stage Manager:* Francis LYNCH; *Assistant Stage Manager:* Alison DANIELS; *Acting Head Of Props and Settings:* Philip COSTELLO; *Props and Settings:* Andrew BUBBLE; Brian FARRON, Carl HESTON, Stuart MITCHELL, Lee PEARSON, Meriel PYM, Sarah WORRALL; *Acting Costume Supervisor:* Tracy DUNK; *Deputy Costume Supervisor:* Nicola MEREDITH; *Wardrobe Production:* Rachel BAILEY, Jennifer BRIDGES, Rose CALDERBANK, Janet CHRISTMAS, Vanessa PICKFORD.
Journal: 4/10/05

442. LIVING PRETTY by Ray Brown; NORMAL PRODUCTIONS; *14-16 October 2004. Alfred Williams:* Everal A WALSH; *Singer:* Pauline TOMLIN. *Director / Sound Designer:* Ray BROWN; *Stage Manager:* Cat STAYTE.

443. MY ARM; written and performed by Tim Crouch; NEWS FROM NOWHERE; *28-30October 2004. Directors:* Tim CROUCH, Karl JAMES. Hettie MacDONALD; *Digital Material:* Chris DORLEY-BROWN.

444. A STRANGE (AND UNEXPECTED) EVENT; a celebration inspired by J G Posada; HORSE + BAMBOO; *2-6 November 2004. Writer / Director:* Bob FRITH

Susan(PENNY LAYDEN) gets closer to Wesley (SEAN CAMPION) than she expected.

8. MAYHEM by Kelly Stuart; ROYAL EXCHANGE THEATRE COMPANY; *10-27 November 2004. Claire:* Rebecca EGAN; *Susan:* Penny LAYDEN; *David:* Sean GALLAGHER; *Wesley:* Sean CAMPION. *Director:* Tim STARK; *Designer:* Jeremy DAKER; *Lighting:* Richard OWEN; *Sound:* Gerry MARSDEN; *Dialects:* Mark LANGLEY; *Technical Stage Manager:* Keith BROOM; *Stage Manager:* Julia WADE; *Stage Manager:* Julia WADE; *Deputy Stage Manager:* Lynn HOWARD; *Assistant Stage Manager:* Ben DONOGHUE; *Acting Head Of Props and Settings:* Philip COSTELLO; *Props and Settings:* Andrew BUBBLE; Brian FARRON, Carl HESTON, Stuart MITCHELL, Lee PEARSON, Meriel PYM, Sarah WORRALL; *Acting Costume Supervisor:* Tracy DUNK; *Deputy Costume Supervisor:* Nicola MEREDITH; *Wardrobe Production:* Rachel BAILEY, Jennifer BRIDGES, Rose CALDERBANK, Janet CHRISTMAS, Vanessa PICKFORD. **Journal:** 4/10/05

445. MEN IN LOVE; written and performed by Laurence Howarth and Gus Brown; RBM; *9-11 December 2004.*

446. TOO MANY COOKS by Greg Banks; TRAVELLING LIGHT THEATRE COMPANY; *20-31 December 2004. Actors:* Craig EDWARDS, Duncan FOSTER, Cerianne ROBERTS; *Musician:* Ruby ASPINALL. *Director:* Greg BANKS; *Designer:* Katie SYKES; *Composer / Musical Director:* Thomas JOHNSON; *Production Manager/ Lighting Designer:* Jo WOODCOCK; *Stage Manager:* Gemma BROOKS; *Set Builders:* Jeff Cliff Models; *Costume Maker:* Hannah KINHEAD; *Prop Makers:* Marc PARRETT, BiLL TALBOT; *Design Student:* Hannah SUMMERS.

32. THE TRESTLE AT POPE LICK CREEK by Naomi Wallace; ROYAL EXCHANGE THEATRE COMPANY; TENTH PLANET PRODUCTIONS; LIVING PROOF; *31 January –19 February 2005. Dalton Chance:* Stephen WRIGHT; *Pace Creagan:*Hannah STOREY; *Chas Weaver:* Terence FRISCH; *Gin Chance:* DeNica FAIRMAN; *Dray Chance:* Julian PROTHERO. *Director:* Raz SHAW; *Designer:* Jaimie TODD; *Lighting:* David HOLMES; *Sound:* Mike WINSHIP; *Composer / Music Producer:* Andrew GREEN; *Executive Producer:* Mark H SHAW; *Producer:* Alexander HOLT; *Associate Producer:* Nia JANIS; *Artistic Associate:* Elizabeth FREESTONE; *Production Manager:* Bendy ASHFIELD; *Production Consultant:* Cath LONGMAN; *Stage Manager:* Angela WEISS; *Assistant Producer:* Davina SHAH; *Fight Director:* Lewis PENFOLD; *Dialect Coach:* Neil SWAIN; *Fretless and Electric Guitars:* John PARRICELLI; *Accordion:* Mark BOUSIE; *Music Mixing & Recording:* Tony LEWIS. **Journal:** 18/1/05

46. A DIFFERENT LANGUAGE by Renato Gabrielli; SUSPECT CULTURE; *10-12 March 2005. Performers:* Selina Cboyack, Sergio ROMANO. *Director:*

Graham EATOUGH; *Design:* Luigi MATTIAZZI; *Sound Design:* Kenny MacLEOD; *Design Assistant:* Petya MANAHILOVA; *Production Manager:* Fiona FRASER; *Company Stage Manager:* Shona RATTRAY; *Technical Stage Manager:* Paul CLAYDON; *Set building:* Scimitar Scenery. **Journal:** 7/3/05.

265. ACTING YOUR AGE by Mike Harris; GW THEATRE; *18 March 2005.*

TMESIS: The myth of the original human being both male and female; here they are presented as getting along well in that form and finding ingenious ways to co-operate but when then choose to become separate they cease to be such congenial company. In the background, the God Figure usually was shown as taking a benign interest in their activities but here is leaving them alone to work out their own ideas.

447. TMESIS; MOMENTUM; *21-23 April 2005. God's Figure:* Kate CAVE; *Male Half:* Yorgos KARAMALEGOS; *Female Half:* Elinor RANDLE/ *Original Director:* Rowan TOLLEY; *Reworking:* Linda Kerr SCOTT; *Set Design / Construction:* Makis SIDIROPOULOS; *Music:* Patrick DINEEN; *Viola Theme:* Michael DELTA; *Costume Design:* Eilidh BRYAN; *Lighting Design:* Phil SAUNDERS.

159. THE IGNATIUS TRAIL; written and composed by Oliver Birch; EN MASSE THEATRE; *23 April 2005.*

60. ELECTRA by Sophocles, adapted by Jo Combes; ROYAL EXCHANGE THEATRE COMPANY; *23 March – 9 April 2005. Brigid:* Maggie SHEVLIN; *Electra:* Penny LAYDEN; *Chrissy:* Amy HUBERMAN; *Nestra:* Stella McCUSKER; *Restes:* William ASH; *Aengus:* Drew CARTER-CAIN. *Director:* Jo COMBES; *Designer:*Becky HURST; *Lighting:* Tom 'Dexter' SCOTT; *Sound:* Gerry MARSDEN; *Dialects:* Mark LANGLEY; *Technical Stage Manager:* Keith BROOM; *Stage Manager:* Lee DRINKWATER; *Deputy Stage Manager:* Ruth TAYLOR; *Acting Head Of Props and Settings:* Philip COSTELLO; *Props and Settings:* Andrew BUBBLE; Carl HESTON, Stuart MITCHELL, Lee PEARSON, Meriel PYM, Sarah WORRALL; *Acting Costume Supervisor:* Tracy DUNK; *Deputy Costume Supervisor:* Nicola MEREDITH; *Wardrobe Production:* Rachel BAILEY, Jennifer

ELECTRA (PENNY LAYDEN) with Restes (WILLIAM ASH)

BRIDGES, Rose CALDERBANK, Janet CHRISTMAS, Vanessa PICKFORD. **Journal:** 18/1/05

448. **THE LAST FREAKSHOW;** Text by Mike Kenny; Music by Mat Fraser;and Sally Clay; FITTINGS MULTIMEDIA ARTS; *4-7 May 2005. Gustav Drool:* Garry ROBSON; *Hands:* Caroline PARKER; *Aqua:* Karina JONES; *Avia:* Mandy COLLERAN; *Gilbert:* Dave Stickman HIGGINS; *Allegra:* Sally CLAY. *Director:* Jamie BEDDARD

449. **THE MASQUE OF WATER** by Gary Carter; THOMAS CARTER; *11 – 14 May 2005. Natalie:* Gary CARTER; *Himself:* Gidi MEESTERS.

214-217 Write 2 Festival

216. **PICTURES OF CLAY** by Sharif Samad; ROYAL EXCHANGE; *8 – 18 June 2005. Clara / Alizon:* Laura ELPHINSTONE; *Chattox:* Polly HEMINGWAY; *Richard Baldwin:* Jack LORD; *Roger Newell:* Des McALEER; *Demdike:* Maggie McCARTHY. *Director:* Sarah ESDAILE; *Designer:* Becky HURST; *Lighting:* Richard OWEN; *Sound:* Gerry MARSDEN, Clare WINDSOR; Studio Production Manager: Keith BROOM; *Company Manager:* K T VINE; *Stage Manager, On The Book:* Lee DRANKWATER; *Lighting:* Dexter SCOTT.**Journal:** 25/05/05

THE LAST FREAK SHOW (448); DAVE STICKMAN in front; behind, left to right: GARY ROBSON, CAROLINE PARKER, SALLY CLAY, KARINA JONES, MANDY COLLERAN

214, PICKERS by Dominic Corey; ROYAL EXCHANGE; *13 June 2005. Daisy:* Emma ATKINS; *Crump:* William ASH; *Shaun:* Craig CHEETHAM; *The Beard:* Roger MORLIDGE; *Eyrsey:* Richard COTTIER. *Director:* Jo COMBES. **Journal:** 25/05/05

215. LOCUST BEAN GUM by Jemma Kennedy; ROYAL EXCHANGE; *14 June 2005. Juliette:* Rachel BROGAN; *Lilian:* Joan KEMPSON; *Ruth:* Vicky BRAZIER; *Billy:* James SCALES. *Director:* Jo COMBES. **Journal:** 25/05/05

217. PEACEFULLY, AT HOME by Nicola Schofield; ROYAL EXCHANGE; *15 June 2005. Sarah:* Donna ALEXANDER; *Chris:* James NICKERSON; *James:* Robert LAWRENSON; *Bridget:* Judith BARKER; *Una:* Eileen O'BRIEN. *Director:* Jacob MURRAY. **Journal:** 25/05/05

218. SLAVE OF LOVE by Ged McKenna; NORTHWEST PLAYWRIGHTS; *24 June 2005. Mrs Price:* Romy BASKERVILLE; *Gavin:* Terence MANN; *Dave:* Michael NEARY; *Ali:* Jane HOGARTH; *Lin:* Joanne SHERRYDEN. *Director:* Bill HOPKINSON. **Journal:** 25/05/05

219. CATCHING LIGHTNING IN A BOTTLE by Nicholas Cordner; NORTHWEST PLAYWRIGHTS.*24 June 2005. Jean Seberg:* Julia ROUNTHWAITE. *Director:* Eileen MURPHY. **Journal:** 25/05/05

450. LABYRINTH; created and performed by Andy Cannon and David Troughton, with music by David Troughton; WEE STORIES; *5-9 July 2005. Set Design:* Evelyn BARBOUR; *Lighting Design:* Tariq HUSSAIN; *Production ManagerL* Caroline ASTRON.

226. THE BABY AND FLY PIE; adapted by Lavinia Murray from the novel by Melvin Burgess; ROYAL EXCHANGE; *14-30 July.2005. Sham:* Calum CALLAGHAN; *Fly Pie:* Benjamin WARREN; *Man / Luke / Scousie / Tallis / etc:* Leigh SYMONDS; *Jane:* Emma HARTLEY-MILLER; *Mother / Shelly / etc;* Sarah BALL. *Director:* Iqbal KHAN; *Designer:* Angela SIMPSON; *Lighting Designer:* Kay HARDING; *Sound Designer:* Gerry MARSDEN; *Company Manager:* Katie VINE; *Technical Stage Manager:* Keith BROOM; *Stage Manager:* Julia WADE; *Deputy Stage Manager:* Ruth TAYLOR; *Assistant Stage Manager:*Maxine FOO; *Acting Head of Props and Settings:* Phil COSTELLO; *Wardrobe:* Tracy DUNK; *Puppet Maker:* Alison DUDDLE; *Puppet Movement:* Mark WHITAKER; *Props and Settings:* Andrew BUBBLE; Carl HESTON, Stuart MITCHELL, Lee PEARSON, Meriel PYM, Sarah WORRALL; *Wardrobe Production:* Rachel BAILEY, Jennifer BRIDGES, Rose CALDERBANK, Janet CHRISTMAS, Vanessa PICKFORD. **Journal:** 25/05/05

246 –255: BLUE 3 FESTIVAL; *Sound / Audio Visuals:* Gerry MARSDEN; *Lighting:* Cara PLUMMER, Richard OWEN; *Technical Stage Manager:* Keith BROOM; *Producer:* Richard MORGAN; *Associate Producer:* Lela CRIBBIN.

246. 360° (FALLING); GILLIGAN.RIDING.SYKES; *4 August 2005. Woman:* Stephanie RIDINGS; *Voice / Effects:* Chris GILLIGAN; *Music:* Phil SYKES. **Journal:** 25/05/05

247. **VENT** by Christopher Wright; LeKOA; *4 August 2005. Adam:* Jarrod COOKE; *Clarissa:* Eliane BYRNE; *Ike:* Marcus HERCULES; *Jenny:* Claire BLEASDALE; *Nick:* Jonathon FINLAY; *Connie:* Alexandra BTESH, *Director:* Christopher WRIGHT; *Artistic Input:* Mark DISTIN, Niamh DOWLING, George PERRIN. **Journal:** 25/05/05

248. **HALF HEAVEN, HALF HEARTACHE** by Sarah Ashton, with songs by somebody else; *4 August 2005. Gina Pitney:* Sarah ASHTON. *Make-up:* Fiona SHAW; *Hair:* SEAN, at PeeWees. **Journal:** 25/05/05

249. **JOURNEY TO THE CENTRE OF YOUR MIND;** THE GALAXATIVES; *4 August 2005.. Schlumbeck:* Alex MURRAY; *Einekleinestein:* Lavinia MURRAY. **Journal:** 25/05/05

250. **PEPPERED MOTH,** written and performed by Sonia Hughes; *5 August 2005. Outside Eye:* Shamshad KHAN; *Video Filming:* Humbrto VELEZ; *Video Editing:* Darren PRITCHARD. **Journal:** 25/05/05

251. **NIGHT PIECE,** a conjuring of Chopin's Nocturnes. HOOH HAH; *5 August 2005. Performer:* Phillipa JENKINS. *Director:* Tracy GENTLES; *Video Director / Editor:* Teresa McNAMARA; *Music Arrangement and Performance:* Michael J LANGLEY; *Post Production:* Paul WOODWARD. **Journal:** 25/05/05

252. **THE POETRY OF MATTY P**, written and performed by Matthew Pannesh; *5 August 2005.* **Journal:** 25/05/05

253. **THE THREE LITTLE PIGS;** MISHIMOU; *5 August 2005. Makers and Performers:* Maria RATCLIFFE, Rachael AYRES. **Journal:** 25/05/05

254. **HARRIOT AND 1** by Sandra Yaw; *6 August 2005. Harriot / Sarah:* Laurietta ESSIEN; *Frances / Jasmin:* Kate FORD; *Owna / Jack:* Bill WARD. *Director:* Tina GAMBE. **Journal:** 25/05/05

255. **A WAR IN THE MORNING** by Pam Leeson; *6 August 2005. Bridget:* Vashti MacLACHLAN; *Voice:* James QUINN. *Director:* Gerry POTTER. **Journal:** 25/05/05

ROYAL NORTHERN COLLEGE OF MUSIC; 124 Oxford Road M13 9RD; 0161-907 5555; www.rncm.ac.uk ; CAZ: 10, B5; G, H, W

491. **ME AND MARLENE** by Michael Elphick and Patricia Partshorne; GLOVEOFF PRODUCTIONS; *7-9 October 2004.*

146. **GARDEN OF THE HEART** by Crystal Stewart; BOOJUM; *14-15 October 2004. Molly:* Victoria FLEMING; *Ida:* Mary-Ann COBURN; *Eddie:* Tony BROUGHTON; *Ben / Victor:* Patrick BRIDGMAN. *Director:* Chris BRIDGMAN; *Design:* Paul HARFLEET, Juliette ELLIS; *Lighting Design:* Steve BRYANT;

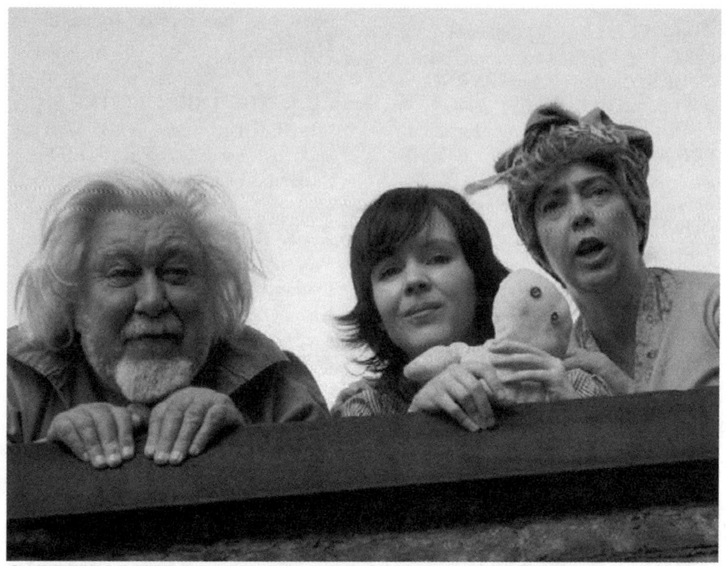

GARDEN OF THE HEART: TONY BROUGHTON, VICTORIA FLEMING, MARY-ANN COBURN

Musical Direction: Patrick BRIDGMAN; *Set Construction:* Joel ROCK; *Opal Construction:* Amy LILLEY; *Stage Managers:* Emma ARMSTRONG, Jessica LUCAS

772. LA CAGE AUX FOLLES; Music and Lyrics by Jerry Herman; Book by Harvey Fierstein, based on the play by Jean Poiret; SOUTH MANCHESTER AOS; *19-23 October 2004/ George:* Martin HULME; *Albin:* Nigel MACHIN; *Jacob*: Tom CHINNERY; *Jean-Michel:* Oliver PUTLAND; *Anne:* Vikki MURPHY; *Edouard Dindon:* Peter BOWERS; *Mme Dindon:* Lesley BOWERS; *Jacqueline:* Juliet BOWERS. *Director:* Katherine MACHIN; *Musical Director:* Ian CHRISTENSEN; *Dance Director:* Kathleen MORETON

55. A TASTE OF HONEY by Shelagh Delaney; NORTHFACE THEATRE COMPANY; *6-9 April 2005. Helen:* Amanda CROSSLEY; *Peter:* Martin GIBBONS; *Jimmie:* David JUDGE; *Jo:* Sarah McDonald HUGHES; *Geof:* Alan NEAL. *Director:* Jason HUDSON; *Stage Managers:* Louise HENRY, Melanie WILLIAMS; *Props:* Phil SKUNDRIC, Debbie SUMNER; *Lighting:* Suzanne PERCIVAL, Daniella EDWARDS; *Sound:* Rachel MATHEWS; *Costume:* Lydia HIRST-MacDONALD, Louise GREGORY. **Journal:** 16/2/05

451. COLD LIGHT SINGINGby Yvonne Pinnington; *30 June- 2 July 2005. Cast:* Damien CHRISTIAN, Mary-Ann COBURN, Chris GARTON, Sarah OLDKNOW, Yvonne

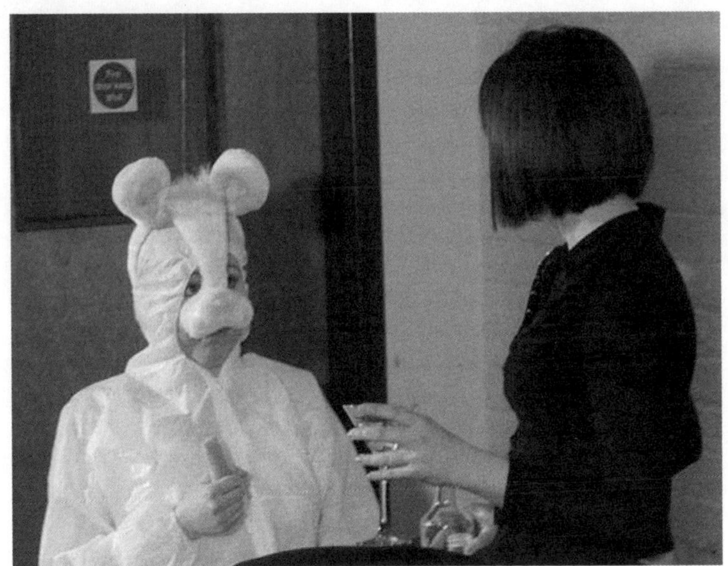

COACH G Expects Interesting Passengers: FRANCESCA WAITE and SARAH McDONALD HUGHES

PINNINGTON. *Director:* Russell TENNANT.

THE ROYAL OAK; 440 Barlow Moor Road, CHORLTON-CUM-HARDY M21 0BQ; CAZ: 107, H6

191. **COACH G** by Stephen Morris; MONKEYWORKS THEATRE; *23-24 May 2005. Matthew / Frank / Eddie:* Martin GIBBONS; *Marlene / Heidi / Waitress:* Sarah McDonald HUGHES; *Susan / Rachel / Janice/Vera:* Francesca WAITE; *Phil / Ticket Collector / Bill:* James HARRIS. *Announcer:* George HOWELL. *Director:* Stephen MORRIS; *Sound / Light:* Alex WADDINGTON; *Props:* George HOWELL, Duncan OAK.

193. **THE LAST TURN OF THE NIGHT** by David Raynor; PAVEMENT THEATRE; *25 May 2005. Steve Foxx:* David RAYNOR; *Bri Burnett:* Matt AISTRUP. *Director:* Ruth CLEEVES. **Journal:** 25/5/05

THE ROYAL OAK; 729 Wilmslow Road M20 6WF;0161-434 4788; CAZ: 125. F6

SACRED HEART ROMAN CATHOLIC JUNIOR SCHOOL; Glencastle Road; M18 7HS; 0161-223 8685; **CAZ:** 111, E3

269. **PINOCCHIO** by Stephen Boyes, based on the original story by Carlo Collodi; MANCHESTER ACTORS COMPANY; *3 March 2005.*

ST ANN'S CHURCH; St Ann's Square M2 7LF; CAZ: 5, H5

ST. ANN'S CHURCHYARD; M2 7LP; CAZ: 5, H5

ST. ANN'S SQUARE; M2 7HG; CAZ: 5, H5

ST. ANN'S STREET; M2 7LF; CAZ: 5, H5

ST ANTHONY'S ROMAN CATHOLIC HIGH SCHOOL; WYTHENSHAWE M22

ST ANTHONY'S ROMAN CATHOLIC PRIMARY SCHOOL; Dunkery Road, WYTHENSHAWE M22 0NT; 0161-437 3029; **CAZ:** 148, B4

269. **PINOCCHIO** by Stephen Boyes, based on the original story by Carlo Collodi; MANCHESTER ACTORS COMPANY; *2 March 2005.*

ST BARNABUS CHURCH OF ENGLAND PRIMARY SCHOOL; South Street, OPENSHAW M11 2EY; CAZ: 96, D5

ST BEDE'S COLLEGE DRAMA STUDIO; Alexandra Park M16 8HX; 0161-226 3323; **CAZ:** 108, C4

ST CLEMENT'S; 6 Edge Lane, CHORLTON M21 9JF; 0161-881 3063; CAZ: 123, G1

211. LIFESPAN; created and performed by Wyllie Longmore; *26 February 2005.*

189. PLAYBACK THEATRE; *23 May 2005.*

192. ADOPTED by Copland Smith; *24 May 2005. Adoptee:* Copland SMITH; *Officialdom / Adopting Mother:* Olivia NELSON; *Birth Mother:* Raquel LOCKE.

ST CUTHBERT'S ROMAN CATHOLIC JUNIOR SCHOOL; Heyescroft Road M20 4UZ; 0161-445 6075; **CAZ:** 125, G3

ST DUNSTAN'S PARISH HALL; Kenyon Lane MOSTON M40 5HS; 0161-683 5919; **CAZ:** 84, A3

ST EDWARD'S ROMAN CATHOLIC PRIMARY SCHOOL; Yew Tree Road, RUSHOLME M14 7WP; 0161-224 6608; CAZ: 109, F4

ST GREGORY'S HIGH SCHOOL; Stopford Street M11 1FG; 0161-370 4143 /3111; CAZ: 97, H5

ST JAMES CHURCH OF ENGLAND PRIMARY SCHOOL; Stelling Street, GORTON M18 8LW; 0161-.223 2423; **CAZ:** 111,F2

270. FIREBIRD by Stephen Boyes; MANCHESTER ACTORS COMPANY; *14 July 2005.*

ST JOHN'S ROMAN CATHOLIC PRIMARY SCHOOL; Chepstow Road, CHORLTON M21 92Q; 0161-881 7754; **CAZ:** 107, G6

ST JOSEPH'S ROMAN CATHOLIC JUNIOR SCHOOL; Plymouth Grove M13 0BT; 0161-224 5347; **CAZ:** 110, A2

269. PINOCCHIO by Stephen Boyes, based on the original story by Carlo Collodi; MANCHESTER

ACTORS COMPANY; *16 February 2005.*

ST LUKE THE PHYSICIAN; Brownley Road, BENCHILL M22 4PT; 0161-998 2071; **CAZ:** 148, C1

ST MARGARET'S; Burnage; CAZ: 126, B3

ST MARK'S CHEETHAM; Tetlow Lane M8 7HF; 0161-740 8600; CAZ: 82, A3

ST MARK'S BLACKLEY; 0161-740 7558

ST MARY'S ROMAN CATHOLIC PRIMARY SCHOOL; Clare Road LEVENSHULME M19 2QW; 0161-224 5995; **CAZ:** 126, C1

269. **PINOCCHIO** by Stephen Boyes, based on the original story by Carlo Collodi; MANCHESTER ACTORS COMPANY; *16 February 2005.*

ST PAUL'S ROMAN CATHOLIC HIGH SCHOOL; Firbank Road M23 2YS; 0161-437 5841; CAZ: 147, 2G

ST PETER'S HOUSE; University Precinct Centre, Oxford Road MI3 9NR; 0161 -273 1465; CAZ: 10, C5

ST ROBERT'S PRIMARY SCHOOL; Montgomery Road, LONGSIGHT M13 0PW; 0161-224 6044; CAZ: 110, B4

ST THOMAS AQUINAS SCHOOL, Nell Lane, CHORLTON-CUM-HARDY M21 7SW; 0161-881 9448; CAZ: 124, 2B

ST VINCENT DE PAUL HIGH SCHOOL; Denison Road, VICTORIA PARK M14 5RX; 0161-224 7138; CAZ: 109, H4

ST WERBURGH'S HALL; St Werburgh's Road, CHORLTON - CUM - HARDY M21 1UE; 0161-445 5829; 0161-374 0231; **CAZ**: 108, A6; **G, H,W**

452. WYRD SISTERS by Stephen Briggs, MANCHESTER ATHENAEUM DRAMATIC SOCIETY; *2-4 December 2005. Magrat Garlick:* Aimee MAKINSON; *Granny Weatherwax:* Pauline WOODCOCK; *Nanny Ogg:* Sue MAHER; *Bowma / Hron / Robber:* Mark PRICE; *Soldier / Hron's Mate / Bedlin / Robber:* Ian HAWTHORNE; *Duke Felmet:* Ray ALDERSON; *Lady Felmet:* Carol SUTCLIFFE; *Chamberlain / Demon / Wimsloe:* Johnson TRUEMAN; *Sergeant / Robber:* Jim RAWCLIFFE; *Fool:* Peter O'TOOLE; *Actor / Witch:* Amy MULLEN; *Olwyn Vitoller / King Verence:* David GARNER; *Mrs Vitoller / Witch:* Rosemary MARK; *Tomjon:* Chris JAMES; *Witch:* Sarala GUNAWARDENA; *Gumridge:* Elizabeth MOONEY. *Director/ Sound / Set Design:* Ian DARKE; *Stage Managers:* Gary BAKER, Don GOULDEN; *Lighting:* Matthew DARKE; *Set Construction / Painting:* Gary BAKER, Steve CONWAY, Sue MAHER, Ian DARKE, Matthew

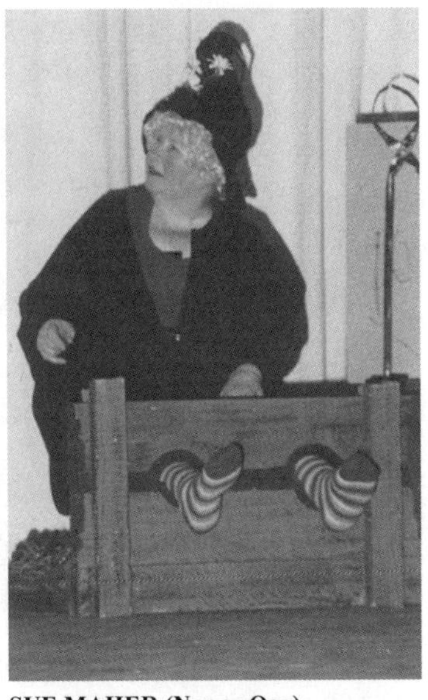

SUE MAHER (Nanny Ogg)

DARKE, Hannah DARKE; *Costumes:* Ina JONES; *Costume Assistants:* Sarala GUNAWARDENA, Johnson TRUEMAN, et al; *Property Mistress:* Sarala GUNAWARDENA; *Property Makers:* Sue MAHER, Gary BAKER.

453. THE MURDER OF MARIA MARTEN IN THE RED BARN; MANCHESTER ATHENAEUM DRAMATIC SOCIETY; *19 February 2005. William Corder:* Peter O'TOOLE; *Dame Marten:* Susan SIDES; *Maria:* Rachel VAN DEN BERGAN; *Anne:* Amy MULLEN; *Tim Bobbin:* Paul EVANS; *Gipsy Lee:* Veronica MARTIN; *Pharos Lee:* Ian SIMMONDS. *Tor:* Sarala GUNAWARDENA.

PETER O'TOOLE and CAROL SUTCLIFFE

454. BRUSH WITH A BODY by Maurice McLoughlin; MANCHESTER ATHENAEUM DRAMATIC SOCIETY; *21-23 February 2005. Sarah Walling:* Amy MULLEN; *Cynthia Walling:* Lara BROUGHTON: *Mr Flaherty:* Peter O'TOOLE; *Mrs Darcy:* Rosemary MARK; *Henry Walling:* Neal WELLS; *Paul Martell:* Paul EVANS; *Sybil Walling:* Carol SUTCLIFFE; *Detective Inspector Hardy:* Robin SHARMAN; *Sergeant Bray:* Ian SIMMONDS; *Rosita Hernandez:* Sarala GUNAWARDENA; *The Hon Pamela Colfax:* Donna KENNEDY. *Director / Set Design:* Sue MAHER; *Stage Manager:* Don GOULDEN; *Assistant Stage Manager:* Barbara MAIDMENT; *Sound:* Ian DARKE; *Lights:* Matthew DARKE, Daniel BURROWS; *Set Construction / Painting:* Sue MAHER, Don GOULDEN, Ian DARKE, Paul EVANS, Barbara MAIDMENT, Katy MAIDMENT; *Cotumes:* Ina JONEs et al; *Props Co-ordinator:* Sarala GUNAWARDENA.

195. COMIC POTENTIAL by Alan Ayckbourn; CHORLTON PLAYERS; *25-28 May 2005.*

ST WILFRED'S CHURCH OF ENGLAND PRIMARY

SCHOOL; Mabel Street, NEWTON HEATH M40 1GB; CAZ: 84, D6

ST WILLIBRORD'S ROMAN CATHOLIC PRIMARY SCHOOL; Vale Street M11 4WR; 0161-223 9345; **CAZ:** 97, E2

269. **PINOCCHIO** by Stephen Boyes, based on the original story by Carlo Collodi; MANCHESTER ACTORS COMPANY; *28 February 2005.*

SCRUFFY MURPHY; 246 Wilmslow Road M14; 0161 - 256 0012; CAZ: 109, G4

SCUBAR

SEYMOUR ROAD INFANT SCHOOL; CLAYTON M11 4PR; 0161-370 3653; CAZ: 97, F3

SLUG AND LETTUCE; 653 Wilmslow Road, DIDSBURY M20 6RA;0161-434 1011; **CAZ:** 125, F6

SOLOMON GRUNDY; Wilmslow Road, WITHINGTON; **CAZ:** 125, G2

21. **GRAZED KNEES;** created and performed by Sarah Jones and Rebecca Blackshaw; PUPPELBOO PRODUCTIONS; *31 January – 1 February 2005.* **Journal:** 18/1/05

SQUIRES; 700 Wilmslow Road, DIDSBURY M20 2DN; 0161-445 1686; CAZ: 125, F6

STARLIGHT THEATRE; Granada Studios, Water Street M3 4JU; 0161-832 9090; CAZ: 9, EI

STEEL MEMORIAL HALL; Wilbraham Road M14 6JS; 0161-224 3744; CAZ: 109, G6

STEPHEN JOSEPH STUDIO; Manchester University Campus, Lime

Grove M13 9PL; 0161-275 3347; **CAZ:** 109, F2

TAURUS (THEATRE DOWNSTAIRS); 1 Canal Street M1 3HE; 0161-236 4593; **CAZ:** 10, B1

13. THREE GOBBY COWS by Louise Twomey, Kate Henry and Deborah Brian; NEWFOUND THEATRE COMPANY; ***7-8 October 2005.***

29. UGLY SISTER BY Joanne Harris; TUCA PRODUCTIONS; *3-5 February 2005. Sister:* Catia SOEIRO. *Directorial Contributions:* Sharon STONEMAN. **Journal:** 18/1/05

30. FARNWORTH PONDLIFE written, devised and performed by Victoria Brown; BROWNMARK PRODUCTIONS; *3-5 February 2005.* **Journal:** 18/1/05

213. EMERGE; NEWFOUND THEATRE; OUTWRITE; *1 June 2005.* **Holding Court** by Hugo Collingridge; *Performer:* Hellen KIRBY;**Someone Borrowed, Someone Blue** by Alasdair Jarvie; *Performer:* Karen WARBY; **Boys and Girls Come Out to Play** by Robin Graham; *Performer:* Bethany

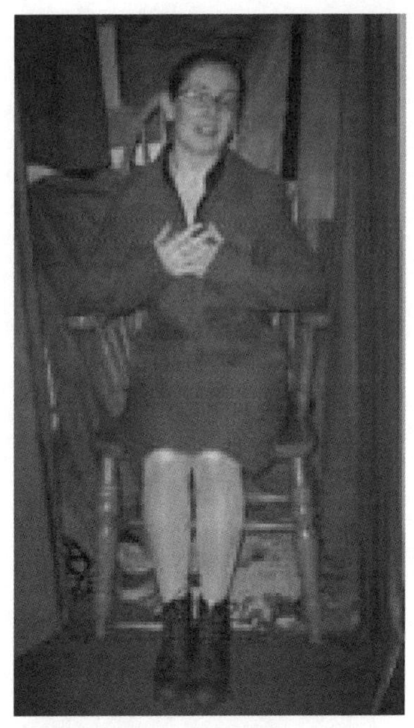

Cupboard Love: HANNAH McHUGH in SENSIBLE SHOES

SHELDON; **Sensible Shoes** by Mark Lucas; *Performer:* Hannah McHUGH;

SPECIAL: SABINA ARTHUR

Special by Philip Watts; *Performer:* Sabina ARTHUR; **Big Issue Seller** by Alan Shenton; *Performer:* Scott BRADLEY; **This Ain't No Party** by Avril Heffernan; *Perfprmer:* Sinead DOUGLAS; **Girl on A Rooftop** BY Cathie Shore; *Performer:* Susi WRENSHAW; **This Ain't No Disco** by Avril Heffernan; *Performer:* Louise TWOMNEY; **Carpe Diem** by Mark Lucas; *Performer:* Elizabeth FISHER; **Jesus Loves You** by Alasdair Jarvie; *Performer:* Beth PALMER; **A Question Too Far** by Neil Green; *Performer:* Daniel WALLACE. *Director:* Helen PARRY; *Technician:* Helen PARRY. **Journal:** 25/05/05

455. **SING-A-LONG-EUROVISION;** *26-29 August 2005. Director:* Andrew NORRIS.

TIGER TIGER; 5-6 The Printworks, Withy Grove M4 2B2; 0161- 385 8080; **CAZ:** 6, A5

TRINITY HIGH SCHOOL; Cambridge Street M15 6BP; 0161-226 2272; **CAZ**: 10, A6

UPPER CAMPFIELD MARKET, Liverpool Road M3 4JG; 0161-833 9833. CAZ: 9, F1

VARNA STREET PRIMARY SCHOOL; M11 1WP; 0161-223 3569; CAZ: 97, F6

VENUE IN THE VILLAGE; Shena Simon College, Whitworth Street M1 3HB; 0161-236 3418; CAZ: 10, B1

VULCAN WORKS; Pollard Street M4 7AN; **CAZ:** 7, G6

150. **MACBETH** by William Shakespeare; OUT OF JOINT; *9 – 13 November 2004.*

WEBSTER JUNIOR SCHOOL; Denmark Road M15 6JU; 0161-226 3928; **CAZ:** 109, E3

269. **PINOCCHIO** by Stephen Boyes, based on the original story by Carlo Collodi; MANCHESTER ACTORS COMPANY; *18 March 2005.*

WEST INDIAN CENTRE, Carmoor Road CHORLTON - ON - MEDLOCK M16 0FB; 0161-257 2092. CAZ: 109, G2

WHALLEY RANGE HIGH SCHOOL FOR GIRLS; Wilbraham Road M16 8GW; 0161-861 9727; **CAZ:** 108, D6

WHITWORTH ART GALLERY; Oxford Road M15 6ER; 0161-275 7450; **CAZ:** 109, F3

WRIGHT ROBINSON HIGH SCHOOL; Falmer Close, ABBEY HEY M18 8XJ; 0161-370 6542; CAZ: 111, H1

WYTHENSHAWE PARK CENTRE; Manchester College, Moor Road, NORTHERN MOOR M23 9BQ; 0161-902 0131; **CAZ:** 135, G3

220. MUCH ADO ABOUT NOTHING by William Shakespeare, with **Brief Encounters** by Phil Reynolds; HEARTBREAK PRODUCTIONS; *6 July 2005. Benedick / Borachio:* Laurence ALDRIDGE; *Beatrice / ARP Watch:* Gemma KELLY; *Don Pedro / Margaret / ARP Watch:* Antony MARWOOD; *Don John / Dogberry / Ursula / Friar:* Jonathan WADEY; *Hero/ Balthasar / Verges:* Abigail GALLAGHER; *Leonato / Sexton/ ARP Watch:* Andrew CALLUM; *Claudio / Conrade:* Dan McGARRY. *Director / Editor:* Peter MIMMACK; *Couturier:* Anna LEWIS; *Technical Composer / Music Arranger:* Andy GUTHRIE; *Movement:* Geoffrey BUCKLEY; *Choreographer:* Michelle CARLTON; *Set / Contruction:* Keith FREDERICK; *Production Co-ordinator:* Nick RIDDIFORD. **Journal:** 25/05/05

221. HAMLET by William Shakespeare; HEARTBREAK PRODUCTIONS; *20 July 2005. Hamlet:* Peter COLLIS; *Claudius / Ghost:* Thomas HAYLER; *Gertrude:* Claire WORBOYS; *Horatio / Guildenstern / Gonzago:* James WEBSTER; *Laertes / Barnado / Player King / Rosencranz:* Mark PLONSKY; *Ophelia / Player Queen / Gravedigger / Courtier:* Emily ROTHON; *Polonius / Marcellus / Gravedigger / Priest:* Gareth WYN-JONES. *Director /*

Editor: Peter MIMMACK; *Designer:* Paul BARRETT; *Composer / Music Arranger:* Matt KATZ; *Artistic Consultant:* Ros WEHNER; *Movement:* Geoffrey BUCKLEY; *Fight Director:* Mark VANCE; *Set / Construction:* Keith FREDERICK; *Production Co-ordinator:* Nick RIDDIFORD; *Producers:* Maddy KERR, Peter MIMMACK. **Journal:** 25/05/05

260. **THE IMPORTANCE OF BEING EARNEST** by Oscar Wilde; HEARBREAK PRODUCTIONS; *8 July 2005. Lady Bracknell:* Maddy KERR; *Algernon:* Alan ATKINS; *Lane / Canon Chasuble / Merriman / Grisby:* Alec WALTERS; *Jack:* Lawrence STUBBING; *Gwendolen::*Pennt Scott ANDREWS; *Miss Prism:* Erika SANDERSON; *Cecily:* Samantha DEW. *Director:* Maddy KERR; *Assistant Director:* Peter MIMMACK; *Set Designer:* Lee CADDEN; *Costume Designer:* Emma IVERY; *Composer/ Music Arranger / Music Consultant:* Andy GUTHRIE; *Movement:* Geoff BUCKLEY; *Dance Choreographer:* Michelle CARLTON; *Couturiers:* Diana LESTER / Anna LEWIS.

XAVERIAN COLLEGE; Lower Park Road, VICTORA PARK M14 5RS; 0161 -224 1781; CAZ: 109, G4

THE YARD, 41 Old Birley Street, HULME M15 5RF; 0161-232 98019, G6. **W**

456. **SCARAMOUCHE JONES** by Justin Butcher; *26-27 April 2005. Performer:* David MILNE. *Director:* Bill HOPKINSON; *Designer:* Nerissa CARGILL-THOMPSON.

457. **MASTER OF FOOLS** adapted by the cast from **The Hour We Knew Nothing Of Each Other** by Peter Handke; SOMETHINK CONCRETE; *Cast:* Naomi BAIRWOOD, Lorna FOLEY, Alice ROBINSON, Emily ROBINSON, Kerry SPILLANE, Rebecca STANTON. *Cellist*: Sarah DALE; *Technician:* Dan ROWLINSON.

458. **SOMEONE WHO'LL WATCH OVER ME** by Frank McGuinness; NORTHFACE THEATRE COMPANY; *20-22 July 2005. Michael:* Michael McKRELL; *Adam:* Simon NORBURY; *Edward:* James SCALES. *Director:* Jason HUDSON.

THE YEW TREE; Yew Tree Lane, NORTHERN MOOR M23 0FF; 0161-998 9883; **CAZ:** 135, H1

SOMEONE WHO'LL WATCH OVER ME (548); EDWARD JAMES SCALES, JAMES NORBURY, MICHAEL McKRELL

YMCA; Castlefield M3 4JR; 0161 - 837 3529; CAZ: 9, E2

ZION ARTS CENTRE; Stretford Road, HULME M15; 0161 - 226 1912; **CAZ:** 9, F6

459. **NOW WE TALKIN'**; CAN; *2-October 2004.***Afrocats:** *Dancers:* Sophie MAKUZA, Shanice MAKUZA, Kiesha THOMPSON, NatashaTURNER, Roshen REGYEMA, Maximinah REGYEMA, Kelly NDIKUMANA, Sophiana RHODEN, Tariro BEMBERE; Nalga MUZA, Joleen LEWIS; *Drummers:* Chess, Papaya; *Trainee:* Joleen LEWIS; *African Dance Costumers:* Shirley THOMPSON, Sophie MAKUZA; *Contemporary & Street Costumes:* Jollen LEWIS; *Choreographer / Co-ordinator:* Magdalen BARTLETT; **Bess Youth Project:** *Cast:* Lauren CORRIS, Danielle TONER, Sinead LEE, Lorna ARROWSMITH, Cleo FEARSON, Loretta WOOLAMS, Rebecca ARMSTRONG, Lauren OLEY, Siobhan LEE; *Poet:* Clair HAYWARD; *Assistant Director:*Roisin CRYAN; *Youth Worker:* Sara JAWANDO; *Writing / Drama Facilitators:* Obi AMAYA, Ben WILTSHIRE; *Dance Facilitators:* Debbie MARGOLIS, Karuna MOHANDAS; *Music:*

Raymond SEWELL; *Film:* Heather JAMES; *Mask Maker:* Cheryl MARNUY; **BOLT – Building Our Lives Together:** *Project Manager:* Sara MAGUIRE; *Video Artists:* Mick CHESTERMAN, Leonie NIMMO; *BOLT Staff:* Steve SHROPSHIRE, Tony WRIGHT; ***Street News-Clash:*** *Participants:* Camille, Merceeeze ROUSE, Daniel; *Editing:* Mitchell; ***Street News-Identity:*** *Participants:* Aaron, Jemma; ***That's A Rap:*** *Participants:* Crumpy, DJ Anwar, Gizzmo, Rector, Skanka, Ruption; *Editing:* Mitchell; ***Street News-Studio:*** *Participants:* Tappa, Rector, Skanka, Ruption; **VJ Crew:** *VJs:* Leonie NIMMO, Brad McDONALD, Richard RAMCHURN; *Video Lead Artist:* Julian TAIT;*VJ Lead Artist:* Adrian BALL; *Live Camera:* Gariel GWIAZDOWSKI; *Protect Manager:* Sara MAGUIRE; **The Bigger Picture Group;** *Street Dance Facilitator:* Carla FARNSWORTH; *Break Dance:* Eddie BRAITHWAITE; *MC & Beatbox:* Jason SINGH; *Co-ordinator:* Rick WALTER;Fac*ilitation:* CARTWHEEL ARTS; **Jubo Shango:** Ali Munirul ISLAM, Ali HAYDAR, Ali AKBAR, Usman ALI, Zaid, Rubel, Ujjal …*Musicians:* Jason SINGH, Crystalize, Robert BUCKNOR; **Hip-Hop Crew:** Bedivalda VINCENT, Rachael GROSSMAN, Ebou MIJE, Chax ANYONNE, Jade INDRISS, Antonio TOMMY, Summer MUGABO, Lairah Sara MUGABO, Wayne JOHNSON, Lewi TODD, Verona DENNIS, Marika OSANGA, Janet DIESA, Mody DENTON, Tendai MOIDZO, NkosanaMAYABA; *Dance Facilitators:* Darran HOLNESS, Wayne EAGLESTONE; *Lyricist:* Avaes MUHAMMAD; **Bennett street youth centre – Small Talk:** *Jade:* Stacie LANCATE; *Morgan:* Gemma EVERS-BUCKLAND; *Rochelle:* Cath Helen RUSK; *Jes:* Emma MURPHY; *Tasha:* Charlotte MURRAY; *Natalie:* Sara SLANN; *Michelle:* Taryn WELSBY; *Rachael:* Michaela CHAMBERS; *Hayley:* Katie DODD; *Katie:* Becki HOWARTH; *Elly:* Kirsty EDWARDS; *PK:* Brendon THOMASON; *Mikey:* Stephen BANNER; *LJ:* Liam GREENHAL;GH; *Tinny:* Mathew MARTONE; *Brad:* Phil DONNELLY; *Step-Dad:* Brad McDONALD; *Dancers:* Ryan VOOTS, Danielle FITZPATRICK, Liam GREENHALGH, Mathew MARTONE, Stephen BANNER, Sara BUCKLEY, Scot PINDER, Amy HOUGH, Krystal GOODARD, Nadia EDAMS, Emma MURPHY, Gemma EVERS-BUCKLAND, Cath RUSK. *Choreography:* Charlene GALLERY; *Youth Workers:* Karen SWINDELLS, Jean PETERS, Charlene GALLERY, Kirsty EDWARDS; *Director / Producer:* Jacqui CARROLL; *Camera/ Editing:* Terry EGAN; *Lighting Director:* Malcolm KEYES; *Sound Director:* Lee PICKERING; *Acting Coaches:* Stella GRUNDY, Claire STRIDE; *Drama Workers:* Paddy WAGON, Jeff CAFFREY, Claire STRIDE, Stella GRUNDY, KerryTUHILL; *Production Manager:* Paddy WAGON; *Runner:* Phil DONNELLY; *Writng:* Stella GRUNDY, Rick STUBBS; *Music:* Rick STUBBS. *TALKIN' PRODUCTION TEAM: Artistic Director / Project Co-ordinator:* Yasmin YAQUB; *Directorial Support:* Joey HATELEY; *Digital Art Co-ordinator:* Sara MAGUIRE; *Digital Support:* Julian TAIT; *Stage Manager:* Melissa IZZO; *Set Design / Set Making Lead Artist:* Gowri SAVOOR; *Technical Manager/ Lighting Design:* Steve BRYAN; *Technical Support:* Curtis LEWIS, Tasos SOTIRIOU; *Hip-Hop Directorial Support:* Tetley B; *Music Support:* Jaydev MISTRY, Chess, Papaye; *Set Making*

Apprentices: Kaiko HIGASHI, Sophie MEDLEY, Louis ENTWISTLE, Gillian PRICE; *Set Making Participants:* Sian THOMAS, Matthew THOMAS, Sabiha BAKHT, Dascalita PETRU, Eleasha GREENHALGH, Laura-May McMILLAN, Kathy M, Rhosyn ADAMS; *Set Making volunteers:* Mercedeeze ROUSE, Cara ROBERTSON, Sara HAMILTON, Sadar MUHAMMADI, Lucas THOMPSONM Peter B

459 – 463 + 231, 465; Part of BRIDGE THE GAP Festival, a change for recently graduated Performing Arts Students in the North West to Show Case their Work; *5-7 November 2004.*

465. LAST IN LINE; IMPRINT THEATRE COMPANY; *5 November 2004*

459. PERSONA; ROGUE PRODUCTIONS; *6 November 2004*

460. 21ST-CENTURY DEMONSTRATION; ESSEN; *6 November 2004*

461. WHERE'S NORMA?; CHIC NEUROSIS; *6 November 2004*

231. THE FALLING by Ailis Ni Riain; EXIT PRODUCTIONS; *6 November 2004*

462. A PUBLIC GATHERING; A4; *7 November 2004*

463. DELIGHT; SOME LADIES MIGHT CARE; *7 November 2004*

464. LADY IN RED by Claire Moore and John Woudberg; *25-27 November 2004. Rose:* Claire MOORE. *Director:* John WOUDBURG.

10. MOVE OVER, MORIATY by Maggie Fox and Sue Ryding; LIPSERVICE; *3 November 2004. Performers:* Maggie FOX, Sue RYDING. *Director:* Gwenda HUGHES; *Designer:* Kate OWEN; *Composer:* Mark VIBRANS; *LyricsL* Malcolm RAEBURN; *Lighting Design:* Jo DAWSON; *Company Stage Manager:* Kellie CLARE; *Technical Manager:* Lorna MUNDEN; *Dresser / Wardrobe:* Bridget FELL. **Journal:** 13/10/04

258. LE STATE by Brian Morgan; ZION ARTS; MANCAT; *22-25 June 2005. Ray:* Anthony ADESIDA; *Asia:* Sarah HAMILTON; *Donna:* Deanne LEE; *Dareen:* Taurien LEE; *Bow:* Borhan MOHAMMADI; *Blaze:* Angie O'DONOHUE; *Caroline:* Mary SOBERS; *Carnell:* Jonathan SUTTON; *Bruce:* Leon TALABI. *Director:* Brian MORGAN; *Video Technician:* Rowan MAY; *Assistant Director:*Linda CLARKE; *Set Design:* Paul COLLEY; *Scene Painter:* MAKOSA; *Music Score:* CRYSTALIZE, Marvin HENDRIQUES; *Sound Engineer Assistant:* Kyle TAYLOR; *Lighting:* Kyle TAYLOR; *Lighting Design:* Steve BRYAN; *Technicians:* Tasos SOTIRIOU, Curtis LEWIS; *Production Assistants:* Shefali KAPOOR, Ailsa McPHEE. **Journal:** 25/05/05.

OLDHAM

THE GHOSTS OF CRIME LAKE (244, previous page); a splendid production in which the OLDHAM COLISEUM gave young people from all Oldham communities the chance to work closely together.

ALBION STREET OL1 3BB; CAZ: 72, 2D

ALEXANDRA PARK JUNIOR SCHOOL; Brook Lane OL8 2BE; 0161-624 4043; **CAZ:** 73, F5

266. **A LIKELY STORY** by Mike Harris; GW THEATRE COMPANY; *21 April 2005.*

ALT PRIMARY SCHOOL; Alt Lane OL8 2EL; 0161-911 3155; **CAZ:** 73, H6

ANCHOR MILL; Daisy Street OL9 6AY; CAZ: 72, B2

BARE TREES INFANT SCHOOL; Holly Grove, CHADDERTON OL9 0DX; 0161-633 0032; **CAZ:** 71, H1

BEAL VALE SCHOOL; Salts Street, SHAW OL2 7SY; 01706 847185; **CAZ**: 43, F6

BEEVER PRIMARY SCHOOL; Moorby Street OL1 3TD; 0161-624 3740; **CAZ:** 73, E1

BLACKSHAW LANE PRIMARY SCHOOL; ROYTON OL2 6NT; 01706 847878; **CAZ:** 57, E3

270. **FIREBIRD** by Stephen Boyes; MANCHESTER ACTORS COMPANY; *16 June 2005.*

BLUECOAT SCHOOL; Edgeton Road OL1 3SQ; 0161-624 1484; **CAZ:** 72, D1

263. **LOVE AND LULLABIES** by Mike Harris; GW THEATRE COMPANY; *23 November 2004.*

BOWER HOTEL; Hollinwood Avenue, CHADDERTON OL9 8DE; 0161-682 7254; **CAZ:** 85, E1

BREEZE HILL SCHOOL. Roxbury Avenue OL4 5JD; 0161-624 6928; **CAZ:** 73, H4

263. **LOVE AND LULLABIES** by Mike Harris; GW THEATRE COMPANY; *3 December 2004.*

265. **ACTING YOUR AGE** by Mike Harris; GW THEATRE; *15 March 2005.*

BROADFIELD PRIMARY SCHOOL; Goddard Street OL8 1LH; 0161 -665 3030; **CAZ:** 72, 5D

196. **THE GARDEN IN WINTER;** M6 THEATRE COMPANY; *7 June 2005.*

BROWNHILL VISITORS CENTRE; Wool Road, DOBCROSS OL3 5PB; 01484 843701; CAZ: 60, A6

BUCKSTONES PRIMARY SCHOOL;

BUCKSTONES JUNIOR SCHOOL; Delamere Avenue, SHAW O**L2 8HN; CAZ:** 43, H5

BURNLEY BROW PRIMARY SCHOOL; Victoria Street, CHADDERTON OL9 0HH; 0161-911 3137; **CAZ:** 56, A6

196. **THE GARDEN IN WINTER;** M6 THEATRE COMPANY; *23 May 2005.*

BYRON STREET INFANTS SCHOOL; ROYTON OL2 6QY; 0161-624 4888; **CAZ:** 56, C3

196. **THE GARDEN IN WINTER;** M6 THEATRE COMPANY; *25 May 2005.*

CENTRE FOR PROFESSIONAL DEVELOPMENT; Fitton Hill OL8 2LU; 0161-621 9400; **CAZ:** 73, E6

CHADDERTON HALL PRIMARY SCHOOL; Chadderton Hall Road, CHADDERTON OL9 0BN; 0161-624 6296; **CAZ:** 55, G5

CHRIST CHURCH PRIMARY SCHOOL; Delph Road, DENSHAW OL3 5RY; 01457 874554

CHRISTIAN CULTURAL CENTRE; Oldham Road, FAILSWORTH; **CAZ:** 85, E4

CITY LEARNING CENTRE; Hollinwood Avenue, CHADDERTON OL9 8EE; **CAZ:** 85, E1

263. LOVE AND LULLABIES by Mike Harris; GW THEATRE COMPANY; *13 December 2004.*

CLARKSFIELD INFANT SCHOOL; Grasmere Road OL4 1NG; 0161-665 1376; **CAZ:** 73, G3

COLISEUM; Fairbottom Street OL1 3SQ; 0161-624 2829; **CAZ:** 72, D2. **D, G, H, S, W**

466. ABSURD PERSON SINCULAR by Alan Ayckbourn; *9 September – 2 October 2004. Marion:* Helen KAY; *Sid:* James NICKERSON; *Jane:* Shuna SNOW; *Eva:* Claire HUMPHREY; *Geoffrey:* Justin GRATTAN; *Ronald:* Martin REEVE. *Director:* Janice DUNN;*Design:* Sarah BURTON; *Lighting Design:* Phil DAVIES; *Sound Design:* Daniel OGDEN; *Deputy Stage Manager On The Book:* Jane JONES; *Wardrobe Supervisor:* Bridget BARTLEY; *Cutter / Deputy Wardrobe Supervisor:* Rebecca GODFREY; *Wardrobe Assistant:* Sarah HOLLAND; *Wardrobe Trainee:* Katherine MEREDITH; *Technical Stage Manager:* Shaun TODD; *Stage Technician:* Adam GENT; *Technical*

ABSURD PERSON SINGULAR; Sid (JAMES NICKERSON) in a very Ayckbourn portrayal of the Festive Season.

Stage Trainee: Caroline SMITH; *Stage Manager:* Marie ROSE; *Assistant Stage Manager:* Sophie HOBDAY; *Stage Management Trainee:* Christopher WILKES; *Audio Describer:* Ann HORNSBY; *British Sign Language Interpreter:* Kyra POLLITT.

467. MAIL ORDER BRIDE by James Robson; OLDHAM COLISEUM; *14 – 30 October 2004. June:* Lorraine BRUCE; *Martin:*Russell DIXON; *Ivy:* Roberta KERR; *Joe:* Richard OLDHAM; *Maria:* Gina RESPALL, *Director:* Kevin SHAW; *Designer:* Alison HEFFERNAN; *Lighting Design:* Phil DAVIES; *Sound Design:* Daniel OGDEN; *Assistant Stage Manager On The Book:* Sophie HOBDAY; *Wardrobe Supervisor:* Bridget BARTLEY; *Cutter / Deputy Wardrobe Supervisor:* Rebecca GODFREY; *Wardrobe Assistant:* Sarah HOLLAND; *Wardrobe Trainee:* Katherine MEREDITH; *Technical Stage Manager :* Shaun TODD; *Stage Technician:* Adam GENT; *Technical Stage Trainee:* Caroline SMITH; *Stage Manager:* Marie ROSE; *Deputy Stage Manager:* Jane JONES; *Stage Management Trainee:* Christopher WILKES; *Audio Describer:* Ann HORNSBY; *British Sign Language Interpreter:* Kyra POLLITT.

287. SILENT CRY by Madani Younis; ASIAN THEATRE SCHOOL; RED LADDER THEATRE COMPANY; *1 November 2004.*

291. MANDRAGORA – KING OF INDIA by Nirjay Mahindru; TARA ARTS; *2 – 6 November 2004.*

468. OUT OF ORDER by Ray Cooney; IAN DICKENS PRODUCTIONS; *9-13 November 2004. Georgwe Pigden:* David CALLISTER; *Also:* Paul SHANE, Vicki MICHELLE, Scoot WRIGHT, Giles WATLING, Tina HALL, Terry O'SULLIVAN, Samantha HUGHES,

MAIL ORDER BRIDE (467); Martin (RUSSELL DIXON, back) has been longing for Maria (GINA RESPALL, centre) to bring life to his remote Yorkshire farm, something to which his hand Joe (RICHARD OLDHAM, right) is very partial; Joe's wife (LORRAINE BRUCE, seated, is very tolerant of his wandering eye; it is Martin's mother (not seen) who objects,

Patrick KEARNS. *Director:* Ian DICKENS: *Lighting Design:* David NORTH; *Production Co-ordinator:* Caroline BURNETT.

475. I AM WHO AM 1; COMPANY GAVIN ROBERTSON; *16 November 2004.*

469. SLEEPING BEAUTY by Eric Potts and Kevin Shaw; OLDHAM COLISEUM; *27 November 2004 – 15 January 2005. Princess Rose / Minnie The Milk Maid:* Gemma BIRD; *King Cuthbert:* John JARDINE; *Lazy Larry:* Andrew NORRIS; *Queen Hermione:* Heather PHOENIX; *Carabosse The Wizard:* Andrew POLLARD; *Nurse Nora Occlesthorpe:* Eric POTTS; *Firy Rainbow:* Neve TAYLOR; *Careless Carrie / Prince Florian:* Kate WILLIAMSON. *CHORUS of Trainee Fairies / Villagers / Royal Pages / Puppeteers and Oscat The Horse:* <u>Red</u>

Programme Details

There Ain't A Nothing Like A Dame; this year ERIC POTTS wrote half the show as well.

Team: Louise McKENDRICK, Bethany PLANT, Patsy CARR, Lauren WALKER, Olivia MAHEED, Natalia KORNYK, Melissa BERNDINO, Amelia CUNLIFFE, Alex PEARSON; Blue Team: Rachel HOLLISTER, Hollie NORMANTON, Nicole BOLTON, Kathryn MASON, Helena FERREIRA, Sally –Jo REILLY, Carla LAALY, Nicola PULFORD. *Director:* Kevin SHAW; *Design:* Dawn ALLSOPP; *Musical Director:* Howard GAY; *Lighting Design:* Phil DAVIES; *Sound Design:* Dave BAXTER; *Chroeographer:* Beverley EDMUNDS; *Assistant Choreographer:* Sarah ASHFORD; *Fight Director:* Renny KRUPINSKI; *Wardrobe Supervisor:* Bridget BARTLEY; *Cutter / Deputy Wardrobe Supervisor:* Rebecca GODFREY; *Wardrobe Assistants:* Sarah HOLLAND, Amy SPEAR; *Wardrobe Trainee:* Katherine MEREDITH; *Technical Stage Manager :* Shaun TODD; *Stage Technician:* Adam GENT; *Technical Stage Trainee:* Caroline SMITH; *Stage Manager:* Marie ROSE; *Deputy Stage Manager:* Jane JONES; *Assiostant Stage Manager:* Sophie HOBDAY; *Stage Management Trainee:* Christopher WILKES; *Audio Describer:* Ann HORNSBY; *British Sign Language Interpreter:* Kyra POLLITT.

WAKE UP LITTLE SUZIE (SUE DEVANEY, centre) with SARAH GROAKE and ANNA BLAKE left and right of her; HOWARD GAY, back left, JEFF MERCHANT, back centre, running the Holiday Camp where it all takes place, and ADAM KEAST, right.

72. WAKE UP LITTLE SUZIE! by Philip Goulding; OLDHAM COLISEUM; HAYMARKET BASINGSTOKE; *3 –26 February 2005. Francesca / Julie-Ann:* Anna BLAKE; *Mick Martin / Chris Peacock / Bradley Bostock / Lucille La Mer / Rocky Sorrento:* Phil CORBITT; *Suzie Bellamy:* Sue DEVANEY; *Andy Cash / Kenny:* Howard GAY; *Beryl / Valeria / Maudie:* Sarah GROARKE; *Ben Tilton:* Matthew HEWITT; *Tony Bell / Derek / Carlos Fandango:* Adam KEAST; *Ted Tilton:* Jeff MERCHANT; *Billy Butler / Pat Gently:* Francis TUCKER. *Director:* Kevin SHAW; *Designer:* Celia PERKINS; *Musical Director:* Howard GAY; *Choreographer:* Beverley EDMUNDS; *Lighting Designer:* Phil DAVIES; *Sound Designer:* Charlie BROWN; *Deputy Stage Manager On The Book:* Jane JONES; *Wardrobe Supervisor:* Bridget BARTLEY; *Cutter*

/ Deputy Wardrobe Supervisor: Rebecca GODFREY; *Wardrobe Assistant:* Sarah HOLLAND; *Wardrobe Trainee:* Katherine MEREDITH; *Technical Stage Manager :* Shaun TODD; *Stage Manager :* Shaun TODD; *Stage Technician:* Adam GENT; *Technical Stage Trainee:* Caroline SMITH; *Stage Manager:* Marie ROSE; *Assistant Stage Manager:* Sophie HOBDAY; *Stage Management Trainee:* Christopher WILKES; *Audio Describer:* Ann HORNSBY; *British Sign Language Interpreter:* Kyra POLLITT.

76. **TURN OF THE SCREW** by Henry James, adapted by Jeffery Hatcher; OLDHAM COLISEUM; *10 March – 2 April 2005. The Woman:* Alexandra MILMAN; *The Man:* Ian TARGETT. *Director:* Robin HERFORD; *Designer:* Michael HOLT; *Lighting Designer:* Phil DAVIES; *Sound Designer:* Daniel OGDEN; *Deputy Stage Manager On The Book:* Jane JONES; *Wardrobe Supervisor:* Bridget BARTLEY; *Cutter / Deputy Wardrobe Supervisor:* Rebecca GODFREY; *Wardrobe Assistant:* Sarah HOLLAND; ***Wardrobe Trainee:*** Katherine MEREDITH; *Stage Technician:* Adam GENT; *Technical Stage Trainee:* Caroline SMITH; *Stage Manager:* Marie ROSE; *Assistant Stage Manager:* Sophie HOBDAY; *Stage Management Trainee:* Christopher WILKES; *Audio Describer:* Ann HORNSBY; *British Sign Language Interpreter:* Kyra POLLITT.

ALEXANDRA MILMAN faces her ghostly predecessors.

58. **IN GOD WE TRUST** by Avaes Mohammed; PESHKAR PRODUCTIONS; *3 November 2004; 7-9 April 2005.*

470. **PERFECT DAYS b**y Liz Lochhead; OLDHAM COLISEUM; *14-30 April 2005. Barbs:* Caroline PATERSON; *Alice:* Emma D'INVERNO; *Sadie:* Anne KIDD; *Brendan:* Andrew POLLARD; *Dave:* Leigh SYMONDS; *Grant:* Michael IMERSON. *Director:* Iqbal KHAN; *Designer:* Dawn ALLSOPP; *Lighting Design:* Phil DAVIES; *Sound Design:* Daniel OGDEN; *Assitant Stage Manager On The Book:* Sophie

Barbs (CAROLINE PATTERSON) has doubts about meeting Dave(MICHAEL IMERSON).

HOBDAY; *Wardrobe* ***Supervisor:***Bridget BARTLEY; *Cutter / Deputy Wardrobe Supervisor:* Rebecca GODFREY; *Wardrobe Assistant:* Sarah HOLLAND; *Wardrobe Trainee:* Katherine MEREDITH; *Technical Stage Manager :* Shaun TODD; *Stage Technician:* Adam GENT; *Technical Stage Trainee:* Caroline SMITH; *Stage Manager:* Marie ROSE; *Deputy Stage Manager:* Jane JONES; *Stage Management Trainee:* Christopher WILKES; *Audio Describer:* Ann HORNSBY; *British Sign Language Interpreter:* Kyra POLLITT.

471. FROZEN by Bryony Lavery; LONDON CLASSIC THEATRE; *3-7 May 2005. Ralph:* Peter CADDEN; *Nancy:* Maggie O'BRIEN; *Agnetha:* Carolyn TOMKINSON. *Director:* Michael CABOT; *Design:* Geraldine BUNZI; *Lighting:* Guy HOARE.

FROZEN 471); MAGGIE O'BRIEN

398. THE COMPLETE WORKS OF WILLIAM SHAKESPEARE (ABRIDGED); THE REDUCED SHAKESPEARE COMPANY; *11 May 2005*

472. THE WIND IN THE WILLOWS by Kenneth Grahame, adapted by Alan Bennett; OLDHAM COLISEUM; *20 May – 11 June 2005. Badger:* Russell DIXON; *Mole:* Rob PARRY; *Ratty:* Martin REEVE; *Mr Toad / Guitar:* Dale SUPERVILLE; *Otter / Albert / Salesman/ Flute / Accordion:* Kieran BUCKERIDGE; *Margaret Mouse / Fox / Gaoler's Daughter / Trumpet / Guitar:* Jacquelyn HYNES; *Portly Otter / Weasel Norm / Ticket Collecto/ Violinr:* Maeve LARKIN; *Rabbit Rose / Squirrel Shirley / Ferret Fiona / Monica / Washerwoman / Bargewoman/ Flute / Saxophone / Clarinet / Piccolo:* Heather PHOENIX; *Chief Weazel / Moise Martin / Policeman / Trumpet / Guiter:* Adam SUTHERLAND; ***Rabbit Roger / Squirrel Sam / Ferret*** *Fred / Rupert / Magistrate / Train Driver* / Gypsy / *Violin:* Andrew WHITEHEAD.

BADGER TAKES COMMAND (RUSSELL DIXON)

Director: Kevin SHAW; *Designer:* Alison HEFFERNAN; *Lighting Designer:* Phil DAVIES; *Sound Designer:* Dave BAXTER; *Choreographer:* Beverley EDMUNDS; *Fight Director:* Renny KRUPINSKI; *Composer:* Jeremy SAMS; *Musical Director:* Kieran BUCKERIDGE; *Wardrobe Supervisor:* Bridget BARTLEY; *Cutter / Deputy Wardrobe Supervisor:* Rebecca GODFREY; *Wardrobe Assistant:* Sarah HOLLAND; *Wardrobe Trainee:* Katherine MEREDITH; *Acting Production Manager :* Shaun TODD; *Stage Technician:* Adam GENT; *Technical Stage Trainee:* Caroline

SUMMER HOLIDAY (473); JOHN WOOD and JOHN MEACHEN get the show on the road.

SMITH; *Stage Manager:* Marie ROSE; *Deputy Stage Manager:* Jane JONES; *Stage Management Trainee:* Christopher WILKES; *Audio Describer:* Ann HORNSBY; *British Sign Language Interpreter:* Kyra POLLITT.

389. KEN DODD HAPPINESS SHOW; *14 June 2005.*

257. CURRY TALES by Rani Moorthy; RASA; *15 June 2005. Performer:* Rani MOORTHY. *Director:* Linda MARLOWE. **Journal:** 25/05/05.

473. SUMMER HOLIDAY; adapted for the stage by Michael Gyngell and Mark Haddigan from the film screenplay by Ronald Cass and Pete Myers, WITH ORCHESTRATIONS BY Keith

Strachan; CONGRESS PLAYERS; *21 – 25 June 2005.*

474. ONE FOR THE ROAD by Willy Russell; OLDHAM COLISEUM; *30 June –23 July 2005. Roger:* Antony BESSICK; *Jane* Helen KAY; *Pauline:* Jessica LLOYD; *Dennis:* Rob PARRY. *Director:* Kevin SHAW; *Designer:*

Keith BAKER; *Lighting:* Phil DAVIES; *Sound Designer:* Dan OGDEN; *Assistant Stage ManagerOn The Book:* Sophie HOBDAY; *Wardrobe Supervisor:* Bridget BARTLEY; *Cutter / Deputy Wardrobe Supervisor:* Rebecca GODFREY; *Wardrobe Assistant:* Sarah HOLLAND; *Wardrobe Trainee:* Katherine MEREDITH; *Chief Stage Technician :* Shaun TODD; *Stage Technician:* Adam GENT; *Technical Stage Trainee:* Caroline SMITH; *Stage Manager:* Marie ROSE; *Deputy Stage Manager:* Jane JONES; *Stage Management Trainee:* Christopher WILKES; *Audio Describer:* Ann HORNSBY; *British Sign Language Interpreter:* Kyra POLLITT.

244. THE GHOSTS OF CRIME LAKE by Kevin Fegan; OLD HAM COLISEUM, GRANGE SCHOOL, GROUNDWORKS – OLDHAM, KASKENMOOR SCHOOL, SMART PROJECT, OUR LADY'S RC HIGH SCHOOL; *28-30 July 2005.* *Performers:* Hazera BEGUM, Nilima BEGUM, Ruhela BEGUM, Shabaz HUSSAIN, Jaheeda KHATUN, RabiaKHATUN, Sahina KHATUN, Dean ASHWORTH, Amy CLOHESSY, Emma KEYLOCK, Dale TAYLOR, Denise WALL, fERN BADDERLEY, Hamish CAMPBELL, Samantha CLARE, Jade CRAWSHAW, Rebecca DEANE, James DICKSON, Jade-Leigh FLOWERS, Natalie GARNER, Amy GOWERS, Andie HAMILTON, Charlotte

The way Farmer Kasken prepares his feasts, his cows do not have to worry about contributing to the menu.

HOLLERAN, Jorden SENIOR, Holly TURNER, Ashleigh WARRINGTON, Callum WILD, Cassie ASPIN, Ria BOOTH, Matthew BOWYER, Danny CREGANHEAP, Amy FAWLEY, Toni JONES, Kellt STANWAY, Rachel CONNOLLY, Leah HARRISON, Catherine McGARRY, Amy OLIVE, Hannah SCOTT, Sarah THEAKER. *Director:* Chris WRIGHT; *Designer:* Alison HEFFERNAN; *Composer:*

MOTLEY; *Project Manager / Workshop Leader:* Jodie LAMB; *Assistant Director / Choreographer:* Karuna MOHANDAS; *Stage Manager:*Andrew WILCOX; *Stage Management Trainee/ Deputy Stage Manager:* Caroline SMITH; *Wardrobe Supervisor:* Bridget BARTLEY; *Lighting Designer:*Phil DAVIES; *Sound Engineer:* Daniel OGDEN. **Journal:** 25/05/05

479. RHYME TO REMEMBER, originally devised by the Central School of Speech and Drama; OLDHAM THEATRE WORKSHOP; *3 August 2005. Director:* James ATHERTON; *Design:* Deena KEARNEY.

COLISEUM STUDIO;

34. INTERVALS, FULL CIRCLE THEATRE COMPANY; *16-17October 2004.* **The Theatre Ghost** by Pam Maddock,*Cast:* Antony CLOWES, Kevin LENNOX **Don't They Know There's A War On** by Peter Connolly, ***Cast:*** Jean ETCHELLS, Mark Stephen Galvin, Michael Sean O'DONNELL, Osman TOSUM; **Jean Alexander** by Pam Maddock, *Dresser:* Alex BRADY; *Jean Alexander:* Joyce BLAKE; **The Audition** by Ken Williams, *Douglas Emery:* Mark Stephen GALVIN; *Mother:* Sarah WHITMORE; *Doughter:* Sarah CROMWELL; **Memoirs of A Wardrobe Mistress** by Pam Maddock, *Cast:* Marie HANSON; **The Baldwin Monkey** by Frank Gibbons, *Cast:* Joyce BLAKE, Natalie GLEDHILL, Sarah CROMWELL, Chris HAYHURST, Norman NEVITT, Carol TALBOT, KevinLENNOX; **Parent In The Bar** by Pam Maddock, *Cast:* Alex BRADY; **Intermission** by Jean Etchells ; *Cast:* Jean BACKHOUSE, Jane CAWDRON, Daniel COULLER, Mary GRAINGER; **By A Local Newspaper Reporter** by Pam Maddock; *Cast:* Chris HAYHURST. *Director:* Justine Potter WILLIAMS; *Script Tutor:* Neil DUFFIELD; *Costume Designer / Wardrobe:* Kat MEREDITH; *Assistant to Director:* Kuruna MOHANDAS; *Technical Stage Manager:* Caroline SMITH; *Deputy Stage Manager:* Christopher WILKES. **Journal:** 16/3/05

170. MACBETH 2004; by William Shakespeare; ITHAKA THEATRE COMPANY; *26-30 October 2004.*

57. CHAOS by Azma Dar; KALI; *4 November 2004.*

56. BELLS by Yasmin Whittaker Khan; KALI; *4 November 2004.*

212. ABU BEN / ADAM by Andrew Norris, Joanne Street and Jane Hollowood; AJN PRODUCTIONS LTD; *27-28 May 2005. Performer:* Andrew NORRIS. *Director:* Jane HOLLOWOOD. **Journal:** 25/05/05

178. STAND; REFORM THEATRE; *1 June 2005.*

476. SPARKLERS by Frank Gibbons; *12 July 2005*

477. MONOLOGUE by Steve Wallis; *12 July 2005.*

478. THE MEN FROM THE BOYS by David Tucker; NORTH WEST PLAYWRIGHTS; *13 July 2005. Gary:* GraemE HAWLEY; *Danny / Keith:* Terence MANN; *Barbara:* Mary CUNNINGHAM; *Karen:* Buffy HALE; *Mark:* Richard OLDHAM. *Director:* Chris HONER; *Dramaturg:* Julie WILKINSON.

223. CHILDREN OF THE MOORS by Aelish Michael; OLDHAM COLIDEUM; NORTHWEST PLAYWRIGHTS; *16 July 2005. Billy:* Howard CHADWICK; *Lorraine:* Maeve LARKIN; *Rob:* Adam SUTHERLAND. *Director:* Justine POTTER. **Journal:** 25/05/05

COPPICE COMMUNITY CENTRE; 61 Werneth Hall Road OL8 4BD; 0161-626 4586; **CAZ:** 72 B4

COPPICE INFANT SCHOOL; Burlington Avenue OL8 1AR; 0161-911 3668; **CAZ:** 72, C5

196. THE GARDEN IN WINTER; M6 THEATRE COMPANY; *27 May 2005.*

COPPICE JUNIOR SCHOOL; Kennedy Street OL8 1BD; 0161-627 5724; **CAZ:** 72, C4

CORPUS CHRISTIE ROMAN CATHOLIC PRIMARY SCHOOL; Old Lane, CHADDERTON OL9 7JB; 0161-652 1275; **CAZ:** 71, H5

266. **A LIKELY STORY** by Mike Harris; GW THEATRE COMPANY; *4 May 2005.*

COUNTHILL HIGH SCHOOL; Counthill Road, MOORSIDE OL4 2PX; 0161-624 6366; CAZ: 57, H5

263. **LOVE AND LULLABIES** by Mike Harris; GW THEATRE COMPANY; *15 November 2004.* *Steve:* Dave JONAS; *Ali:* Qas HAMID; *Donna:* Julie CLAYS; *Rehanna:* Jaheda CHOUDHURY. *Director:* Mike HARRIS; *Sound Technician:* Carol BOROWIAK.

CROMPTON HOUSE SCHOOL; Rochdale Road, SHAW OL2 7HF; 01706 847451 / 291 454; CAZ:42, D6

263. **LOVE AND LULLABIES** by Mike Harris; GW THEATRE COMPANY; *7 December 2004.*

LOVE AND LULLABIES (263); JAHEDA CHOUDHURY, QAS HAMID

CROMPTON PRIMARY SCHOOL; Longfield Road, SHAW OL2 7HD; 01706 844 134; CAZ: 57, E1

DAISY NOOK GARDEN CENTRE; Stannybrook Road, FAILSWORTH M35 9WJ; 0161-681 4245; CAZ: 86, B5

DELPH PRIMARY SCHOOL; Denshaw Road OL3 5HN; 01457 874 400; **CAZ:** 59, G2

EBENEZER CHURCH HALL; School Street, UPPERMILL OL3 6HB; **CAZ:** 61, F1

485. THE HOLLOW by Agatha Christie; UPPERMILL STAGE SOCIETY; *20-23 October 2004. Henrietta Angkatell:* Pauline WHITTAM; *Sir Henry Angkatell KCB:* Vince KENNY; *Lady Angkatell:* Dreda GLENNIE; *Midge Harvey:* Rachell WILD; *Gudgeon:* Phil COOMBES; *Edward Angkatee:* Richard ILES; *Doris* Darrell RE; *Gerda Cristow:* Joan BRADBURY; *John Cristow:* Tony HAMMOND; *Veronica Craye:* Sue STOREY; *Insp Colquhoun:* Gordon CRABTREE; *Det Sgt Penny:* Bill BUTTERWORTH. *Producer:* Colin WATT; *Assistant Producer:* Joyce MALLALIEU; *Stage Managers:* Geoff ILES, Janes ILES; *Continuity:* Nicola JEFFERY-SYKES, Audrey WEST; *Sound / Lighting:* Nigel WINTERS; *Properties / Costumes:* Janet ILES, Joyce MALLALIEU; *Set Design / Construction:* Janet ILES, Geoff ILES, MOSI, Joyce MALLALIEU.

486. LAUGHTER IN THE DARK by Victor Lucas; *25-28 May 2005. Gripe:*Phil COOMBE; *Alathea Budgett:* Pauline WHITTHAM; *Herbert Budgett:* Bill BUTTERWORTH; *Belinda Budgett:* Tracey MOLYNEUX; *Cyril Carraway:* Nigel WINTERS; *Bunny Tucker:* Janet McGRATH; *Thundercloud:* Martin BELL; *Gosforth:* Gordon CRABTREE; *Lydia Prentice:* Zoe DUST; *Alec Ogleby:* Richard ILES; *Aunt Emily Budgett:* Dreda GLENNIE; *Montague Cheyney:* Joyce MALLALIEU. *Producer:* Colin WATT; *Assistant Producer:* Joyce MALLALIEU; *Stage Managers:* Geoff ILES, Janet ILES; *Continuity:* Rose HALL; *Sound / Lighting:* Daniel WINTERS; *Properties: :* Janet ILES, Joyce MALLALIEU; *Set Design / Construction:* Janet ILES, Geoff ILES, MOSI, Joyce MALLALIEU, Colin WATT; *Costumes:* Janet McGRATH.

EUSTACE STREET PRIMARY SCHOOL; CHADDERTON OL9 6LR; 0161 – 624 2516; CAZ: 72, A1

FAILSWORTH HIGH SCHOOL; Brierley Avenue M35 9HA; 0161-681 3763; **CAZ:** 85, G4

271. **ROMEO AND JULIET** by William Shakespeare; MANCHESTER ACTORS COMPANY; *26 November 2004*

263. **LOVE AND LULLABIES** by Mike Harris; GW THEATRE COMPANY; *8 December 2004.*

FIRBANK PRIMARY SCHOOL; Grasmere Road, ROYTON OL2 6SJ; 0161-624 9577; **CAZ:** 42, B6

FITTON HILL JUNIOR SCHOOL; Keswick Avenue OL8 2LD; 0161- 624 7571; **CAZ:** 73, F6

FITTON HILL LIBRARY; Fir Tree Avenue OL8 2SW; 0161 – 633 2011; **CAZ:** 87, E1

FITTON HILL YOUTH CENTRE; Fir Tree Avenue OL8 2SW; 0161 – 624 1775; **CAZ:** 87, E1

FREEHOLD PRIMARY SCHOOL; Sidmouth Street, WERNETH OL9 7RG; 0161-287 2575; **CAZ:** 72, A4

266. **A LIKELY STORY** by Mike Harris; GW THEATRE COMPANY; *27 April 2005.*

FRIEZELAND PRIMARY SCHOOL; Church Road, GREENFIELD OL3 7LQ; 01457 872 601; **CAZ:** 75, G4

266. **A LIKELY STORY** by Mike Harris; GW THEATRE COMPANY; *28 April 2005.*

GALLERY OLDHAM; Greaves Street OL1 1DN; 0161-911 4657; **CAZ:** 72, D3

GRANGE ARTS CENTRE; Rochdale Road OL9 6EA; 0161-785 4239; **CAZ:** 72, C2 **W, H**

3. SPARK by Mary Cooper; M6 THEATRE COMPANY; *9-12 November 2004.*

263. LOVE AND LULLABIES by Mike Harris; GW THEATRE COMPANY; *17 November 2004.*

GRANGE HIGH SCHOOL; Rochdale Road OL9; **CAZ:** 72, C2

263. LOVE AND LULLABIES by Mike Harris; GW THEATRE COMPANY; *29 November 2004.*

GREENFIELD PRIMARY SCHOOL; Shaw Street OL3 7AA; 01457 872831; **CAZ:** 61, 3F

GREENHILL; Harmony Street OL4 1RR; 0161-911 3261; **CAZ:**73, E3

196. THE GARDEN IN WINTER; M6 THEATRE COMPANY; *6 June 2005.*

HATHERSHAW TECHNOLOGY COLLEGE; Bellfield Avenue OL8 3EW; 0161-624 3613; **CAZ:** 86, D1

271. ROMEO AND JULIET by William Shakespeare; MANCHESTER ACTORS COMPANY; *4 November 2004*

263. LOVE AND LULLABIES by Mike Harris; GW THEATRE COMPANY; *25 November 2004.*

HENSHAW STREET OL1 3EN; CAZ: 72, C2

HEY WITH ZION SCHOOL; Rowland Way, LEES OL4 3LQ; 0161-620 3860; **CAZ:** 74, A2

HIGH STREET OL1 1AJ CAZ: 72, D2

HODGE CLOUGH JUNIOR SCHOOL;

Conduit Street, MOORSIDE OL1 4JX; 0161-624 4826; **CAZ**: 57, H4

266. **A LIKELY STORY** by Mike Harris; GW THEATRE COMPANY; *20 April 2005.*

HOLLINWOOD COMMUNITY CENTRE; Whiteley Street OL9 7HY; 0161-625 6597; **CAZ:** 71, H5

HOLY FAMILY PRIMARY SCHOOL; Lime Green Road, LIMESIDE OL8 3NG; 0161-652 2400; **CAZ:** 86, B3

HOLY ROSARY PRIMARY SCHOOL; Fir Tree Avenue, FITTON HILL OL8 2SR; 0161-624 3035; **CAZ:** 86, D1

HOLY TRINITY CHURCH; Woods Lane, DOBCROSS OL3 5AL; CAZ: 60, A5

HOLY TRINITY SCHOOL; Delph New Road, DOBCROSS OL3 5BP; **CAZ:** 59, H6

HORTON MILL PRIMARY SCHOOL; Greengate Street, Glodwick Road OL4 1DJ; 0161-633 1711; **CAZ:** 73, F3

HULME GRAMMAR SCHOOL (BOYS); Chamber Road OL8 4BX; 0161-624 4497. **CAZ:** 72, B5

271. **ROMEO AND JULIET** by William Shakespeare; MANCHESTER ACTORS COMPANY; *8 November 2004*

HULME GRAMMAR SCHOOL (GIRLS); Chamber Road OL8 4BX; 0161-624 2523. **CAZ:** 72, B5

271. **ROMEO AND JULIET** by William Shakespeare; MANCHESTER ACTORS COMPANY; *4 November 2004*

KASKENMOOR HIGH SCHOOL; Roman Road OL8 3PZ; 0161-681 4116; **CAZ:** 85, H2

263. **LOVE AND LULLABIES** by Mike Harris; GW THEATRE COMPANY; *2 December 2004.*

268. **MACBETH** by William Shakespeare; MANCHESTER ACTORS COMPANY; *20 January 2005.*
264. **HIGHS AND LOWS** by Mike Harris; GW THEATRE COMPANY; *27 January 2005. Janice Hopwell:* Julie CLAYS; *Billy / Dad / others:* Dave JONAS. *Director:* Mike HARRIS; *Sound Technician:* Terry COWLEY.

KNOWSLEY PRIMARY SCHOOL; Stoneleigh Road, SPRINGHEAD OL4 4BH; 0161-633 4433; **CAZ:** 74, C2

LIMEHURST PRIMARY SCHOOL; Lime Green Road OL8 3NG; 0161-625 9616; **CAZ:** 86, B3
246. **A LIKELY STORY** by Mike Harris; GW THEATRE COMPANY; *27 May 2004.*

LIMESIDE PRIMARY SCHOOL; Fourth Avenue OL9 3SB; 0161-681 1756; **CAZ:** 86, A2

LITTLEMORE SCHOOL; Littlemore Lane OL4 2RR; 0161-624 4188; 73, G1

LYCEUM; Union Street OL1 1QG; 0161-624 4261; **CAZ:** 72, D3

LYDGATE PARISH HALL; Stockport Road OL4 4JJ; 01457 872897; CAZ: 75, E4

LYNDHURST PRIMARY SCHOOL; Lyndhurst Road OL 8

4JG; 0161-624 2192; **CAZ:** 72, B6

MATHER STREET PRIMARY SCHOOL; FAILSWORTH M35 0DT; 0161 – 911 7020; **CAZ:** 84, D3

MAYFIELD SCHOOL; Mayfield Road DERKER OL1 4LG; 0161-624 6425; **CAZ:** 73, F1

266. **A LIKELY STORY** by Mike Harris; GW THEATRE COMPANY; *29 April 2005.*

MEDLOCK VALLEY PRIMARY SCHOOL; Keswick Avenue OL8 2LQ; 0161-911 3264; **CAZ:** 73, E5

MILLS HILL PRIMARY SCHOOL;

NEW BARN PRIMARY SCHOOL;

NORTH CHADDERTON HIGH SCHOOL; Chadderton Hall Road OL9 0BN; 0161-624 9939; **CAZ:** 55, F5

OLDHAM PARISH CHURCH; Church Terrace OL1 3AT; CAZ: 72, D2

OUR LADY'S ROMAN CATHOLIC HIGH SCHOOL; Vaughan Street, ROYTON OL2 5DL; 0161-624 9974; **CAZ:** 56, C4

PAKISTAN COMMUNITY CENTRE; Oliver Street OL1 1EZ; 0161-628 4800; **CAZ:** 64, D3 **G, W**

264. **HIGHS AND LOWS** by Mike Harris; GW THEATRE COMPANY; *9 February 2005.*

PARK DEAN SPECIAL SCHOOL; St Martin's Road OL8 2PY; 0161 – 620 0231; CAZ: 87, F1

PARISH CHURCH JUNIOR SCHOOL; Horsedge Street OL1 3PU; 0161-624 3924; **CAZ:** 72, D1

270. **FIREBIRD** by Stephen Boyes; MANCHESTER ACTORS COMPANY; *13 Julye 2005*

PLAYHOUSE 2; Newton Street, SHAW OL2 8NX; 01706 846671; **CAZ**: 57, F1; **G, H**

490. **THE DEEP BLUE SEA** by Terence Rattigan; CROMPTON STAGE SOCIETY; *26 February – 5 March 2005.*

491. **ME AND MARLENE** by Michael Elphick and Patricia Partshorne; GLOVEOFF PRODUCTIONS; *9 April 2005. Marlene Dietrich:* Patricia HARTSHORNE. *Directors:* Michael ELPHICK, Patricia HARTSHORNE.

487. **SNAKE IN THE GRASS** by Alan Ayckbourn; CROMPTON STAGE SOCIETY; *23-30 April 2005. Alice:* Molwyn ASHLEY; *Miriam:* Elizabeth BEECH; *Annabel;*Sue WIDDALL. *Director . Designer:* Gwyneth JONES; *Set Construction:* Barry COTTAM, Peter CLABER; *Stage Manager:* Andrew BARNES; *Props:* Helen WYNNE; *Lighting:* Daniel PEARSON; *Sound:* Vincent GILLIBRAND; *Prompt:* Anne WRIGHT.

488. **STAR QUALITY** by Noel Coward; CROMPTON STAGE SOCIETY; *11-18 June 2005.*

502. **THE WIZ** by William L Brown and Charlie Smalls, based on **Thw Wizaed of Oz** by L Frank Baum; NEW MUSIC; *5-7 May 2005.*

505. **70-UP;** CROMPTON STAGE SOCIETY; *21-22 May 2005.*

PATRICIA HARTSHORNE

PLAYERS' THEATRE; Millgate, DELPH OL3 5JG; 01457 874644; CAZ: 59, H3 H,W

480. **BLITHE SPIRIT** by Noel Coward; SADDLEWORTH PLAYERS; *2-9 October 2004. Ruth:* Margaret BLASCZOK; *Edith:* Lianne LEIGH; *Charles:* John TANNER; *Dr Bradman:* Kit THORNE; *Mrs Bradman:* Karen BARTON; *Madame Arcati:* Elizabeth BEECH; *Elvira:* Lisa WALTON; *Child's Voice:* Pat SIM. *Director:* Charles FOSTER; *Production Assistant:* Anne WRIGHT; *Set Design:* Charles FOSTER, Ken WRIGHT; *Construction:* Ken WRIGHT; *Lighting Design:* Brian HILTON; *Sound Design:* Sam AL-HAMDANI; *Make-Up / Hair Design:* Students from Oldham College, supervised by HILARY WINTERS; *Stage Manager:* Julian SMITH; *Wardrobe:* Jean SYKES, Patricia REDSHAW; *Props:* Ian CRICKET, Stacey POGSON, Rachel PICKERING; *Prompt:* Patricia REDSHAW, KatH HODGSON.

481. **LET IT BE ME** by Carey Jane Hardy; SADDLEWORTH PLAYERS; *20-27 November 2004. Amy Flint:* Edwina RIGBY; *Sylvia:* Anne WRIGHT; *Kate:* Sandie BESWICK; *Trixie:* Barbara MICKLETHWAITE; *Colin:* Anthony WRIGHT; *Gregory Roberts:* Kevin GROCOCK. *Director:* Gwyneth JONES; *Production Assistant:* Eillen SOUTHARD; *Set Design:* Sally McKEE; *Lighting Desgn:* Bob CRITCHLEY; *Sound Design:* Chris RICHARDSON-WILLIAMS; *Props:* Gemma RICHARDSON-WILLIAMS; *Stage Manager:* Tom SMITH; *Set Construction:* Sally McKEE, Andrew McCONNELL, Thackrat Family, Ken WRIGHT; *Prompt:* Margaret HILL.

482. **WAIT UNTIL DARK** by Fredrick Knott; SADDLEWORTH PLAYERS; *22-29 January 2005. Mike:* Anthony WRIGHT; *Croker:* Jason SHARP; *Roat:* Julian SMITH; *Susy Henderson:* Jo WEETMAN; *Sam Henderson:* Jonathan KENWORTHY; *Gloria:* Grace WEETMAN; *Policeman:* Frank VOOCOCK; *Policewoman:* Karen BARTON. *Director / Set Design / Construction:* Ken WRIGHT; *Production Assistant:* Anne WRIGHT; *Lighting Design:* Bob CRITCHLEY; *Sound Design:* Ian McCONNELL; *Stage Manager:* Stacey POGSON; *Assistant Stage Manager:* Ruth CREDINGTON; *Properties:* Frank BOOCOCK, Karen BARTON; *Wardrobe:* Jean SYKES, Karen BARTON; *Prompt:* Sandie BESWICK, Anne WRIGHT.

483. **PARDON ME, PRIME MINISTER** by Edward Taylor and John Graham; SADDLEWORTH PLAYERS; *12-19 March 2005. Rt Hon George Venables:* Philip WEETMAN; *Rodney Wilkinson:* Russ LEARMONT; *Rt Hon Hector Crammond:* Vince KENNY; *Miss Frobisher:* Miranda PARKER; *Sybil Venables:* Kathleen HODGSON; *Shirley Springer:* Kathryn SHARP; *Jane Rotherbrook:* Louise BUTTERWORTH; *Dora Springer:* Pat LOWE. *Director / Set Design:* John GILLESPIE; *Set Construction:* Steve HENDREN, Julian SMITH, Andrew McCONNELL, Ken WRIGHT; *Lighting Design:* Herbert MALLALIEU; *Sound Design:* Sam AL-HAMDANI; *Stage Manager:* Frank BOOCOCK; *Properties:* Marion DEIGHTON, Ken DEIGHTON; *Prompt:* Leanne LEIGH; *Production Assistant:* Karen BARTON.

484. **PYGMALION**by George Bernard Shaw; SADDLEWORTH PLAYERS; *7-14 May 2005. Professor Higgins:* John WEETMAN; *Eliza Doolittle:* Kate WESTCOTT; *Colonel Pickering:* Mike LAW; *Mr Doolittle:* John HANKIN*; Mrs Higgins*: Sybil MURRAY; *Mrs Pearce:* Eileen SOUTHARD; *Mrs Eynsford-Hill:* Margaret THOMPSON; *Clara Eynsford-Hill:* Gemma RICHARDSON-WILLIAMS; *Frddy Eynsford-Hill:* Sam AL-HAMDANI; *Ambassador / Bystander 1:* Chris WILLIAMS; *Ambassador's Wife:* Sandie BESWICK; *Nepommuck:* Julian SMITH; *Bysyander 2 / Footman:* Ian McCONNELL; *Young Ruffians:* Patrick SIMS, Joseph WEETMAN; *Older Sister:* Grace WEETMAN; *Fishwife:* Jill Smith; *Woman of the Night:* Joan PERKS; *Parlourmaid:* Selena HARRISON; *Bystander 3 / Footman:* Steven HENDRON; *Cabby:* Simon WILKIES.

QUEEN ELIZABETH HALL; West Street OL1 1UT; 0161-678 4078; CAZ: 72, C2 G, H, W

THE RADCLYFFE SCHOOL; Broadway, CHADDERTON OL9 9QZ; 0161-624 2594; **CAZ:** 71, G3

263. **LOVE AND LULLABIES** by Mike Harris; GW THEATRE COMPANY; *24, 26 November 2004.*

THE RAILWAY; Shaw Hall Bank Road, GREENFIELD OL3 7JZ; 01457 872307; **CAZ**: 61, E3

364. **PEDAL POWER** by Richard Povall; Music and Lyrics by Rebekah Hughes and Richard Povall; MIKRON THEATRE COMPANY; *7 October 2004* .*Company:* Elizabeth EVES, Marianne McNAMARA, Robert TOOK, Peter TOON;. *Director:* Mike LUCAS; *Musical Director:* Rebekah HUGHES; *Costumes / Set / Props:* Michael CAMDEN, Annie DEARDEN; *Tour Manager:* Peter TOON.

363. **ON THE LINE** by Mike Lucas and Jim Wodland; Music and Lyric by Jim Woodland; MIKRON THEATRE COMPANY; *10 Novemberr 2004.*

RICHMOND INFANT SCHOOL; Winterbottom Street, WERNETH OL9 6TS; 0161-624 3593; **CAZ:** 72, B4

RICHMOND JUNIOR SCHOOL; Richmond Street OL9 6HY; 0161-633 1693

ROUNDTHORN PRIMARY SCHOOL; Aspull Street OL4 5LE; 0161 –624 2962; **CAZ:** 73, G4

ROYTON ASSEMBLY HALL; Market Square OL2 5QD; 0161-620 3505; **CAZ:** 56, B3

308. **CROSSING BOUNDARIES;** M6 YOUTH THEATRE; OLDHAM THEATRE WORKSHOP; PHOENIX YOUTH THEATRE; *February 2005.*

ROYTON AND CROMPTON HIGH SCHOOL; Blackshaw Lane, ROYTON OL2 6NT; 01706 846474; **CAZ:** 57, E3

263. **LOVE AND LULLABIES** by Mike Harris; GW THEATRE COMPANY; *16 November 2004.*

SACRED HEART JUNIOR SCHOOL; Whetstone Hill Road, DERKER OL1 4NA; 0161-911 3173; **CAZ:** 57, G5

SADDLEWORTH MUSEUM; High Street,

UPPERMILL OL3 6BU; 01457 874093; **CAZ:** 61, F1

363. ON THE LINE by Mike Lucas and Jim Wodland; Music and Lyric by Jim Woodland; MIKRON THEATRE COMPANY; *11 October 2004.*

SADDLEWORTH SCHOOL; High Street, UPPERMILL OL3 6BU; 01457 873649; **CAZ:** 60, B6

263. LOVE AND LULLABIES by Mike Harris; GW THEATRE COMPANY; *19 November 2004.*

489. ANNIE GET YOUR GUN; Book, Music and Lyrics by Irving Berlin; UPPERMILL STAGE SOCIETY; *15 – 19 February 2005.*

ST AGNES CHURCH OF ENGLAND PRIMARY SCHOOL; Knowles Lane, LEES OL4 5RU; 0161-624 8392; **CAZ:** 74, C5

ST AIDEN AND ST OSWALD'S ROMAN CATHOLIC PRIMARY SCHOOL; Roman Road, ROYTON OL25PQ; 0161-652 2558; **CAZ:** 56, C4

ST ANNE'S CHURCH OF ENGLAND PRIMARY SCHOOL; Cedar Lane, LYDGATE OL4 4DS; 0161-01457 873 777; **CAZ:** 75, E3

ST ANNE'S ROMAN CATHOLIC PRIMARY SCHOOL; Greenacres Road OL4 3EX; 0161 – 624 0179; **CAZ:** 73, G2

ST AUGUSTINE OF CANTERBURY HIGH SCHOOL; Grange Avenue OL8 4EJ; 0161-624 7089; **CAZ:** 72, B5

263. LOVE AND LULLABIES by Mike Harris; GW THEATRE COMPANY; *1 December 2004.*

265. ACTING YOUR AGE by Mike Harris; GW THEATRE; *8 March 2005. Stevie:* Julie CLAYS; *Old Man / Carl / Councillor:* Dave JONAS; *Beth / Amy:* Tracy HIGGINS; *Jeff / Denny:* Qas HAMID. *Director:* Mike HARRIS.

ST CHAD'S PRIMARY SCHOOL; Rhodes Avenue, UPPERMILL OL3 6EE; 01457 875 151; **CAZ:** 60, C6

ST HERBERT'S PARISH CHURCH; Broadway, CHADDERTON OL9 0JY; 0161-633 9059; **CAZ:** 71, G2

769. ALADDIN; ST HERBERT'S AD & ES. *Director:* David WILD; *Musical Director:* Carl McIVER; *Choreographer:* Pauline GEORGE; *Design / Percussion:* Ray MURPHY/

ST HERBERT'S ROMAN CATHOLIC PRIMARY SCHOOL; Middleton Road West, CHADDERTON OL9 9SN; 0161-633 1318; **CAZ:** 71, G2

ST HILDA'S CHURCH OF ENGLAND PRIMARY SCHOOL; Ward Street OL1 2EQ; 0161 – 624 3592; **CAZ:** 72, B1

266. A LIKELY STORY by Mike Harris; GW THEATRE COMPANY; *26April 2005.*

ST HUGH'S PRIMARY SCHOOL; Wildmore Avenue, HOLTS OL4

2BE; 0161-911 3171; **CAZ:** 74, A5

266. **A LIKELY STORY** by Mike Harris; GW THEATRE COMPANY; *6 May 2005.*

ST JAMES' PRIMARY SCHOOL; Castleton Road, East Crompton OL2 7TD;0161-633 1578; **CAZ**: 42, B5

ST JOHN'S CHURCH OF ENGLAND JUNIOR SCHOOL; James Street, FAILSWORTH M35 9PY; 0161-681 5713; **CAZ:** 85, G4

ST JOSEPH'S ROMAN CATHOLIC PRIMARY SCHOOL; Oldham Road SHAW OL2 8SZ; 01706 847 218; **CAZ:** 57, F2

266. **A LIKELY STORY** by Mike Harris; GW THEATRE COMPANY; *5 Mayl 2005.*

ST MARGARET'S CHURCH OF ENGLAND SCHOOL; Hive Street, HOLLINWOOD 0L8 4QS; 0161 – 681 2414; **CAZ**: 85, H1

ST MARK'S PARISH HALL; Waterloo Street, GLODWICK OL4 1ER; 0161-652 3546; CAZ: 73, F4

ST MARTIN'S CHURCH OF ENGLAND PRIMARY SCHOOL; St Martin's Road OL8 2PY; **CAZ:** 87, F1

ST MARY'S CHURCH OF ENGLAND PRIMARY SCHOOL; Rushcroft Road, HIGH CROMPTON OL2 7PP; 01706 847 524; **CAZ:** 42, D5

270. **FIREBIRD** by Stephen Boyes; MANCHESTER ACTORS COMPANY; *7 June 2005.*

ST MARY'S CHURCH OF ENGLAND PRIMARY SCHOOL; Manchester Road, GREENFIELD OL3 7DW; 01457 872264; **CAZ:** 61, G5

ST MARY'S PRIMARY SCHOOL; Ckive Road, FAILSWORTH M35 0NN; 0161-681 6663; **CAZ:** 85, F5

ST MATTHEW'S PRIMARY SCHOOL; Chadderton Hall Road, CHADDERTON OL9 9BN; O161-624 060; **CAZ:** 55,F5

ST THOMAS CHURCH OF ENGLAND SCHOOL; St Thomas Circle, COPPICE 0L8 1SF; 0161 – 287 0097; CAZ: 72, B4

ST THOMAS CHURCH OF ENGLAND PRIMARY SCHOOL; St Thomas Street, LEESFIELD OL1 4RL; **CAZ:** 74, A4

ST THOMAS MOORSIDE; Coleridge Road, SHOLVER OL1 4RL; 0161-624 3035; **CAZ:** 58, A3

SOUTH CHADDERTON HIGH SCHOOL; Butterworth Lane OL9 8EA; 0161-681 4851; **CAZ:** 71, E5

263. **LOVE AND LULLABIES** by Mike Harris; GW THEATRE COMPANY; *9 December 2004.*

SPINDLES SHOPPING CENTRE CAR PARK; CAZ: 73, D3

STANLEY ROAD PRIMARY SCHOOL; Derby Street OL9 7HX; 0161 – 624 6060; **CAZ:** 71, H5

STANSFIELD ROAD PRIMARY SCHOOL; FAILSWORTH M35

9EA; 0161-681 2645; **CAZ:** 85, G3

266. **A LIKELY STORY** by Mike Harris; GW THEATRE COMPANY; *22 April 2005.*

STONELEIGH COUNTY PRIMARY SCHOOL; Vulcan Street, ROYTON OL1 4LJ; 0161-624 9078; **CAZ:** 57, F5

SUMMERVALE PRIMARY SCHOOL; Lee Street OL8 1EF; 0161 - 624 3940; **CAZ:** 72, B3

THE SWAN INN; The Square, DOBCROSS OL3 5AA; 01457 873 451; **CAZ:** 60, A5

364. **PEDAL POWER** by Richard Povall; Music and Lyrics by Rebekah Hughes and Richard Povall; MIKRON THEATRE COMPANY; *7 November 2004* .

TOKYO PROJECT; Roscoe Street OL1 1EA; CAZ: 73, E3

TRANSHIPMENT WAREHOUSE; Wool Road, DOBCROSS OL3 5PN; **CAZ:** 60, B5

WATERSHEDDINGS PRIMARY SCHOOL; Broadbent Road OL1 4HU; 0161-624 1219; **CAZ:** 57, G6

WERNETH COMMUNITY CENTRE

WERNETH JUNIOR SCHOOL; Coppice Street OL8 4BL; 0161-624 3749; **CAZ:** 72, B4

WERNETH INFANT SCHOOL; Coppice Street OL8 4BL; 0161-624 6614; **CAZ:** 72, B4

WESTWOOD PRIMARY SCHOOL, Middleton Road OL9 6BH; 0161-626 4257; **CAZ:** 72, B2

WETHERSPOON'S; High Street OL1; CAZ: 72, D2

WHITEGATE END COMMUNITY PRIMARY SCHOOL; Butterworth Lane, CHADDERTON OL9 8EB; **CAZ:** 0161-682 5067

WOODHOUSES VOLUNTARY SCHOOL; Ashton Road, FAILSWORTH M35 9LW; **CAZ:** 86, A5

YEW TREE INFANT SCHOOL; Alcester Street, CHADDERTON; 0161-284 5464; **CAZ:** 71, G5

YORKSHIRE STREET; CAZ: 72, D2

ROCHDALE

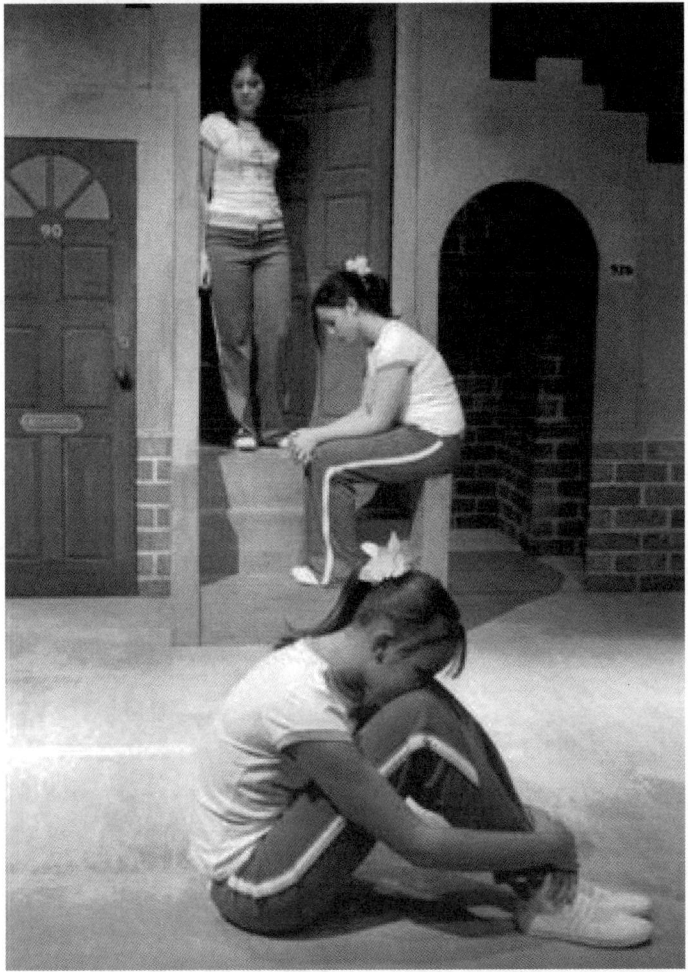

GEMIMA DIAMOND (497); NICOLA PULFORD, LIZZIE HEHIR and KIRSTY WATSON from the M6 YOUTH THEATRE share the title role in their response to the issues raised in DANNY, KING OF THE BASEMENT (140), played on the same set.

ALDERMAN KAY SPECIAL SCHOOL; Tintern Road, MIDDLETON M24 6FQ; 0161 - 643 4917; **CAZ:** 54, A4

496. **THE STREET WHERE I LIVE;** devised and presented by Romy Baskerville; M6; *12 November 2004.*

503. **ODD SOCKS;** devised by Dorothy Wood, Romy Baskerville and Kate Mercer; M6; *1 July 2005*

ALICE INGHAM ROMAN CATHOLIC PRIMARY SCHOOL; Millgate, Halifax Road OL16 2NU; 01706 341 560; **CAZ:** 28, C1

ALKRINGTON COUNTY PRIMARY SCHOOL;Manor Road M24 1JZ; 0161-643 6357; CAZ: 70, A3

ALKRINGTON LIBRARY; Kirkway M24 1LW; 01706 864 972; **CAZ:** 70, A2

ALKRINGTON YOUTH CENTRE; Hardfield Road M24 1TQ; 01706 647474; CAZ: 70, A4

ALL SAINTS CHURCH OF ENGLAND PRIMARY SCHOOL; Maud Street OL12 0EL; 01706 640 728; **CAZ:** 28, A1

APOLLO DAY NURSERY; The Willows, Oldham Road OL11 2HB; 01706 352 861; **CAZ:** 41,G1

ARTS AND HERITAGE CENTRE; The Esplanade OL16 1AQ; CAZ: 27, G4

ASHFIELD VALLEY COUNTY PRIMARY SCHOOL; Valley Road OL11 1TA; 01706 522758; **CAZ:** 41, E1

BALDERSTONE LIBRARY; Platting Lane OL11 2HD; 01706 640 438; **CAZ:** 41, G2

496. **THE STREET WHERE I LIVE;** devised and presented by Romy Baskerville; M6; *26 November 2004.*

503. **ODD SOCKS;** devised by Dorothy Wood, Romy Baskerville and Kate Mercer; M6; *8 July 2005*

BALDERSTONE TECHNOLOGY COLLEGE; Queen Victoria Street OL11 2HF; 01706 649049; **CAZ:** 41, G1

3. **SPARK** by Mary Cooper; M6 THEATRE COMPANY; *29 November 2004.*

14. **DANNY, KING OF THE BASEMENT** by David S Craig; M6 THEATRE COMPANY; SHEFFIELD THEATRES; *11 April 2005.*

BARNADOS; Darlington House, George Street OL16 2DF; 01706 750 076; **CAZ:** 28, A3

BELFIELD COMMUNITY SCHOOL; Samson Street OL16 2LW; 01706 341363; **CAZ:** 28, C3

269. **PINOCCHIO** by Stephen Boyes, based on the original story by Carlo Collodi; MANCHESTER ACTORS COMPANY; *14 February 2005.*

BRIMROD PRIMARY SCHOOL; Holborn Street OL11 4QB; 01706 647146; **CAZ:** 27, F6

BROADFIELD PRIMARY SCHOOL; Sparrow Hill OL16 1QT; 01706 647 4429; **CAZ:** 27, H4

503. **ODD SOCKS;** devised by Dorothy Wood, Romy Baskerville and Kate Mercer; M6; *6 July 2005*

BROWNHILL SCHOOL; Heights Lane OL12 0PZ; 01706 648 990; **CAZ:** 27, G2

BURNSIDE COMMUNITY CENTRE; 36 Burnside Crescent, LANGLEY M24 5NN; 0161-643 5775; **CAZ:** 53, G4

496. **THE STREET WHERE I LIVE;** devised and presented by Romy Baskerville; M6; *18, 25 November 2004.*

503. **ODD SOCKS;** devised by Dorothy Wood, Romy Baskerville and Kate Mercer; M6; *24 June 2005*

THE BUTTS OL16 1ES; **CAZ:** 27, H4

499. **CYBERSTEIN;** PETER JOHNSON ENTERTAINMENTS; *14 May 2005.*

501. **WINGED WONDERS;** SKYLIGHT CIRCUS; *14 May 2005.*

500. **ST JOHN'S AMBULANCE;** STICKLEBACK PLASTICUS; *14 May 2005.*

CALDERSHAW COUNTY PRIMARY SCHOOL; Edenfield Road OL12 7OL; 01706 658623; CAZ: 26, C2

CARDINAL LANGLEY ROMAN CATHOLIC HIGH SCHOOL, Rochdale Road, MIDDLETON M24 2GL; 0161-634 4009; **CAZ**: 54, B4

3. **SPARK** by Mary Cooper; M6 THEATRE COMPANY; *11 October 2004.*

CASTLEMERE CENTRE; Tweedale Street OL11 1HH; 01706 645 200; **CAX:** 27, H5

CASTLETON COUNTY PRIMARY SCHOOL; Hillcrest Road OL11 2QD; 01706 631859; **CAZ:** 40, D3

CHAPELFIELD NURSERY; Platting Lane 0L11 2HD; 01706 640 340; **CAZ:** 41, G1

154. **SONYA'S GARDEN;** M6 THEATRE COMPANY; *8 December 2004.*

503. **ODD SOCKS;** devised by Dorothy Wood, Romy Baskerville and Kate Mercer; M6; *21 June 2005*

CLOVERLEAF CHILDCARE; Bowness Road, LANGLEY M24 5NU; 0161-654 7294; CAZ: 53, F5

496. **THE STREET WHERE I LIVE;** devised and presented by Romy Baskerville; M6; *9, 18 November 2004.*

503. **ODD SOCKS;** devised by Dorothy Wood, Romy Baskerville and Kate Mercer; M6; *14 June 2005*

CURTAIN THEATRE; 47 Milkstone Road OL11 1EB; 01706 642008; CAZ: 27, H5

2. **CHAPTER TWO** by Neil Simon; *27 September 9 October 2004. George Schneider:* John WEETMAN; *Leo Schneider:* Colin SMITH; *Jennie Malone:* Jo WEETMAN; *Faye Medwick:* Rachel MELLOR. *Director:* Rod FITTON; *Designer/ Stage Manager:* Bill NUTTALL; *Sound:* Jon DAVIS; *Lighting:* Robert MONTGOMERY; *Costumes:* Christine GROCOCK; *Props:* Sylvia MASON. **Journal:** 4/10/04

492. **ABELARD AND HELOISE** by Ronald Millar; *14 –26 February 2005. Peter Abelard:* Greg SHERRINGTON; *Heloise:* Sara CINLIFFE; *Alain* Paul DAWSON; *Gerard:* Mick MAGUIRE; *Phillipe:* Peter FITTON; *Robert de Montboissier:* Richard TOLLEY; *Guibert:* Damien KAVANAGH; *Gilles de Vannes:* Des CUNLIFFE; *Jehan:* Tony CRAIG; *Fulbert:* Neil SAMPSON; *Belle Alys:* Judith REDKWA; *Abbess of Argenteuil:* Jackie ASHWORTH; *Sister Laura:* Freda STANLEY; *Sister Godric:* Sybil MURRAY; *Sister Constance:* Annette SLATER; *Other Sisters:* Liz KERSHAW, Maddt BROWN; *Mariella:* Becky SLATER; *Alberic of Rheims:* Jack SUNDERLAND; *Bernard of Clairvaux:* Eric WALTON; *Hugh:* Kevin GROCOCK. *Director:* Brian SEYMOUR; *Stage Management:* Bill NUTTALL, Eric BRIERLEY; *Costumes:* Mirage Costumes; *Lighting:* Adrian MONTGOMERY; *Sound:* Jon DAVIES; *Props:* John SCHOFIELD.

493. **RACING DEMON** by David Hare; CURTAIN THEATRE; *25 April – 7 May 2005. Revd Lionel Espy:* Jerry

KNOX; *Rt Revd Charlie Allen:* Ollie DICKSON; *Revd Tony Ferris:* Paul BODKIN; *Frances Parnell:* Miriam HILL; *Stella Marr:* Judith REDKWA; *Revd Donald Bacon:* Peter FITTON; *Revd Harry Henderson:* Greg SHERRINGTON; *Ewan Gilmour:* Edmund TAYLOR; *Tommy Adair / Head Waite:* Franco PAOLUCCI; *Rt Revd Gilbert Heffernan:* Damien KAVANAGH. *Director:* Jim KNIGHT; *Stage Management:* Bill NUTTALL, Eric BRIERLEY; *Costumes:* Christine GROCOCK, Lynn SHERRIN; *Lighting:* Adrian MONTGOMERY; *Sound:* Jon DAVIES; *Props:* Judith REDKWA / John SCHOFIELD.

504. MOVE OVER, MRS MARKHAM by Ray Cooney and John Chapman; CURTAIN THEATRE; *20 June – 2 July 2005.*

DARNHILL PRIMARY SCHOOL; Sutherland Road, HEYWOOD OL10 3PY; 01706 369756; CAZ: 38, B4

14. DANNY, KING OF THE BASEMENT by David S Craig; M6 THEATRE COMPANY; SHEFFIELD THEATRES; *14 April 2005.*

DARTINGTON HOUSE; George Street; 01706 750 076

DEEPLISH COMMUNITY CENTRE; Hare Street OL11 1JT; 01706 860151; CAZ: 27, H6

DEEPLISH COUNTY PRIMARY SCHOOL; Derby Street OL11 1LT; 01706 347584; CAZ: 28, A6

DEMESNE COMMUNITY CENTRE; Asby Close, LANGLEY M24 2JF; 0161-635 9526; CAZ: 53, F5

496. THE STREET WHERE I LIVE; devised and presented by Romy Baskerville; M6; *22 November 2004.*

503. ODD SOCKS; devised by Dorothy Wood, Romy Baskerville and Kate Mercer; M6; *5 July 2005*

ROMY BASKERVILLE introduces THE STREET WHERE I LIVE (496), one of the M6 THEATRE productions for Nursery Schools

DRAKE STREET; CAZ: 27, H4

EXCHANGE SHOPPING CENTRE;

428. THE SUNFLOWER SHOW; LITTLE BIG TOP; *14 May 2005.*

FALINGE PARK HIGH SCHOOL; Falinge Road OL12 6LD; 01706 631246; **CAZ:** 27, F2

14. DANNY, KING OF THE BASEMENT by David S Craig; M6 THEATRE COMPANY; SHEFFIELD THEATRES;*4 April 2005.*

FURROW COMMUNITY SCHOOL; Windermere Road, LANGLEY M24 5PY; 0161-643 6526; **CAZ**: 53, F5

496. THE STREET WHERE I LIVE; devised and presented by Romy Baskerville; M6; *8 November 2004.*

503. ODD SOCKS; devised by Dorothy Wood, Romy Baskerville and Kate Mercer; M6; *27 June 2005.*

GRACIE FIELDS THEATRE; Oulder Hill Community School, Hudsons Walk OL11 5EF; 01706 341 527; **CAZ:** 26, D4

494. ALADDIN by Colin Meredith; MEREDITH PRODUCTIONS; *20 December 2004 – 3 January 2005. Widow Twankey:* Colin MEREDITH; *Wishee Washee:* Paul OLDHAM; *Aladdin:* Hayley TAMADDON; *Princes So Shi:* Susan McARDLE; *Adanazar:* Russell RICHARDSON; *Ping Pong:* Jason WARD; *Empress:* Sherry ORMEROD. *Directors:* Colin MEREDITH, Paul OLDHAM.

14. DANNY, KING OF THE BASEMENT by David S Craig; M6 THEATRE COMPANY; SHEFFIELD THEATRES; *6 April 2005.*

495. TITANIC; ROCHDALE AMATEUR OPERATIC SOCIETY; *31 May – 4 June 2005. Cast:* Margaret LOGAN, Jon CREBBIN. *Producer:* Jim MASTERS; *Musical Director:* Harry BUTTERWORTH.

ALLADIN (494); PAUL OLDHAM (Wisshee Washee), COLIN MEREDITH (Widow Twankey. = Lord High Everything Else), HAYLEY TAMADDON (The LAD Himself)

TITANIC (495); MARGARET LOGAN and JON CREBBIN

GREENBANK COUNTY PRIMARY SCHOOL; Greenbank Road; OL12 0HZ; 01706 647 923; **CAZ:** 27, H2

HEYBROOK COUNTY PRIMARY SCHOOL; Park Road OL12 9BJ; 01706 647201; **CAZ:** 28, A2

HEYWOOD CIVIC HALL; Wood Street OL10 1LW; 01706 624104 / 368130; **CAZ:** 39, F3

767. CAROUSEL; Music by Richard Rodgers; Book and Lyrics by Oscar Hammerstein II; HEYWOOD AODS. *Billy Bigelow:* Adam BROWN; *Julie:* Sarah DAVEY; *Carrie:* Anne DICKSON; *Enoch Snow:* Alex COCKCROFT; *Nettie:* Eileen TAYLOR; *Jigger:* James EARNSHAW; *Louise:* Charlotte McGRORY; *Heavenly Friend:* Peter DAVEY; *Star Keeper:* Rod FITTON; *Mr Bascombe:* David REEVES. *Producer / Director:* Joanne LORD; *Musical Director:* David ABENDSTERN; *Choreographer:* Jill McINTOSH; *Stage Manager:* Graham SIMPSON.

768. HALF A SIXPENCE; Book by Beverley Cross, from the novel **Kipps** by H G Wells; Music and Lyrics by David Heneker; HEY KIDS. *Kipps:* Martin BRACEWELL; *Ann:* Ruby TURNER; *Chitterlow:* Jack ROBERTSON. *Producer / Director:* Joanne LORD; *Musical Director:* David ABENDSTERN; *Choreographer:* Jill McINTOSH.

HEYWOOD COMMUNITY SCHOOL; Sutherland Road OL10 3PD; 01706 360466; **CAZ:** 38, A4

HEYWOOD LIBRARY; Church Street; 01706 864 497; **CAZ:** 39, F3

HIGH BIRCH SPECIAL SCHOOL; Bolton Road OL11 3NQ; 01706 642 842; **CAZ:** 40, B1

HILLTOP PRIMARY SCHOOL; Hilltop Drive

OL11 2EH; 01706 648019; **CAZ:** 41, G3

154. **SONYA'S GARDEN;** M6 THEATRE COMPANY; *30 November 2004.*

503. **ODD SOCKS;** devised by Dorothy Wood, Romy Baskerville and Kate Mercer; M6; *17 June, 8 July 2005*

HIND HILL CENTRE; OL10 1AQ; CAZ: 38, F3

HOLLINGWORTH HIGH SCHOOL; Cornfield Street, MILNROW OL16 3DR; 01706 641541; **CAZ:** 29, G5

HOLLINS PRIMARY SCHOOL; Waverley Road, MIDDLETON M24 6JG; 0161-643 5148; **CAZ:** 54, A4

496. **THE STREET WHERE I LIVE;** devised and presented by Romy Baskerville; M6; *23 November 2004.*

503. **ODD SOCKS;** devised by Dorothy Wood, Romy Baskerville and Kate Mercer; M6; *20 June 2005*

HOLLINS SOCIAL CENTRE; Tintern Road, MIDDLETON M24 6JQ

503. **ODD SOCKS;** devised by Dorothy Wood, Romy Baskerville and Kate Mercer; M6; *28 June 2005.*

HOLY FAMILY ROMAN CATHOLIC PRIMARY SCHOOL, Great Gates Road, KIRKHOLT OL11 2DN; 01706 640480; **CAZ:** 41, G3

496. **THE STREET WHERE I LIVE;** devised and presented by Romy Baskerville; M6; *7 December 2004.*

503. **ODD SOCKS;** devised by Dorothy Wood, Romy Baskerville and Kate Mercer; M6; *4 July 2005*

HOPWOOD HALL TERTIARY COLLEGE; Rochdale Road, MIDDLETON M24 3XH;

0161-643 7560; CAZ: 54, B2

HOWARD STREET NURSERY; Howard Street OL12 0PP; 01706 646103; **CAZ:** 27, H3

JACOB BRIGHTS CENTRE; Whitworth Road OL12 6EP; 01706 655 709; **CAZ:** 28, C1

KIRKHOLT COMMUNITY CENTRE; Milkstone Road

503. ODD SOCKS; devised by Dorothy Wood, Romy Baskerville and Kate Mercer; M6; *16 June 2005*

LANGLEY LIBRARY; Windermere Road, MIDDLETON M24 5PY; 0161-654 8911; **CAZ:** 53, F5

496. THE STREET WHERE I LIVE; devised and presented by Romy Baskerville; M6; *16, 19 November 2004.*

503. ODD SOCKS; devised by Dorothy Wood, Romy Baskerville and Kate Mercer; M6; *22 June, 7 July 2005*

LANGLEY SCHOOL; Thirlmere Drive; 0161-643 6840; **CAZ:** 53, G5

496. THE STREET WHERE I LIVE; devised and presented by Romy Baskerville; M6; *17 November 2004.*

503. ODD SOCKS; devised by Dorothy Wood, Romy Baskerville and Kate Mercer; M6; *29 June 2005*

LA ROCHE; The Willows, Oldham Road OL11 2HB; 01706 352 861

496. THE STREET WHERE I LIVE; devised and presented by Romy Baskerville; M6; *24 November 2004.*

503. ODD SOCKS; devised by Dorothy Wood, Romy Baskerville and Kate Mercer; M6; *15 June 2005*

LITTLE GEMS NURSERY; 15 Belfield Road OL16 2UP; 01706 630 140; **CAX:**28, B3

LOWERPLACE PRIMARY SCHOOL; Kingsway OL16 4UU; 01706 648174; **CAZ:** 28, C5

496. **THE STREET WHERE I LIVE;** devised and presented by Romy Baskerville; M6; *25 November 2004.*

503. **ODD SOCKS;** devised by Dorothy Wood, Romy Baskerville and Kate Mercer; M6; *28 June 2005. Nina:* Kate MERCER. *Director:* Romy BASKERVILLE; *Design:* Alison HEFFERNAN; *Music:* Jon NICHOLLS.

M6 THEATRE; Hamer County Primary School, Albert Royds Street OL162SU; 01706355898; **CAZ:** 28, B1

3. **SPARK** by Mary Cooper; M6 THEATRE COMPANY; *7 – 8 October 2004. Sakina:* Shahena CHOUDHURY; *Rachel:* Sarah HAN; *Edward:* Marion Lloyd ALLEN; *Ryan:* Jamie A WILSON. *Director:* Greg BANKS; *Composer:* Jon NICHOLLS; *Designer:* Alison HEFFERNAN; *Graffit Artiste:* LIAM; *Set Builders:* John ASHWORTH, Triad Fabrications; *Production Manager:* Joss MATZEN. **Journal:** 4/10.04

14. **DANNY, KING OF THE BASEMENT** by David S Craig; M6 THEATRE COMPANY; SHEFFIELD THEATRES; *25 January 2005. Danny:* Harley BARTLES; *Louise / Callum.'s Mum / Taxi Driver:* Deborah BRIAN; *Callum:* Paul MALLON; *Penelope:* Jo PRIDDING. *Director:* Romy BASKERVILLE; *Designer:* Alison HEFFERNAN; *Sound Designer:* Jon NICHOLLS; *Stage Managers:* Joss MATSEN Camilla O'NEIL .**Journal:** 13/10/04.

308. **CROSSING BOUNDARIES;** M6 YOUTH THEATRE; OLDHAM THEATRE WORKSHOP; PHOENIX YOUTH THEATRE; *February 2005.*

497. **GEMIMA DIAMOND** by Aelish Michael; M6 YOUTH THEATRE; *13-14 April 2005. Cast:* Tom BUTTERWORTH, Hannah CARTWRIGHT, Amy CONNOR, Lizzie COOKE, Gina COOKE, Tony GROGAN, Lizzie HEHIR, Katherine JACKSON, Charlotte JOHNSON, Jodie KING, Nathan LAWRENCE, Kirsty-Lee LORIMAR, Rebecca PHILBIN, Nicola PULFORD, Harooj SONIA, Charles TOMLIN, Jamie-Lee WALER, Kirsty WATSON, Rachel WATSON, Kim WHITE. *Director:* Rowan DAVIES; *Assistant Directors:*

Programme Details

DANNY (HARLEY BARTLES, seated), can make a Best Friend in twenty minutes, - he has to because he is so often on the move -, but when he learns that he is to live at 92B (for Basement) permanently, his new neighbours (JO PRIDDING and PAUL MALLON) have to help him sort his ideas out.

Nikki HEYWOOD, Liz HENSHAW; *Props / Costumes:* Caroline DALY; *Technicians:* Joss MATZEN, Stephen BEASLEY; *Song:* James ATHERTON; *Movement:* Rurh JONES

MARLAND HILL COUNTY PRIMARY SCHOOL; Roch Mills Crescent, Roch Valley Way OL11 4QW; 01706 647147; **CAZ:** 27, E6

14. **DANNY, KING OF THE BASEMENT** by David S Craig; M6 THEATRE COMPANY; SHEFFIELD THEATRES; *8 April 2005.*

MATTHEW MOSS HIGH SCHOOL; Matthew Moss Lane OL11 3LU; 01706 632910; **CAZ:** 40, B1

14. **DANNY, KING OF THE BASEMENT** by David S Craig; M6 THEATRE COMPANY; SHEFFIELD THEATRES; *15 April 2005.*

MEADOWFIELDS COMMUNITY CENTRE; 1 Eafield Road, BELFIELD OL12 2TH; 01706 648 005; **CAZ:**28, C2

MEANWOOD COUNTY PRIMARY SCHOOL; Churchill Street OL12 7DJ; 01706 648197; **CAZ:** 27, E2

MIDDLETON CIVIC HALL; Fountain Street M24 1AF; 0161-643 2389; **CAZ:** 69, 81

MIDDLETON GARDENS; M24 4DF; CAZ: 69, H1

MIDDLETON TECHNOLOGY SCHOOL; Kenyon Lane M24 2DQ; 0161-643 5116; **CAZ:** 70, C1

MOORCLOSE NURSERY SCHOOL; Aspinall Street, MIDDLETON; 0161-643 4602

MOSS FIELD COUNTY PRIMARY SCHOOL; West Starkey Street, HEYWOOD OL10 3PL; 01706 369508; **CAZ:** 39, E2

NEWBOLD BAPTIST CHURCH; Milnrow Road; 01706 359662

NEWHEY PRIMARY SCHOOL; Hawthorne Lane, MILNROW OL16 4JX; 01706 847658; CAZ: 43, E1

NORDEN COMMUNITY PRIMARY SCHOOL; Shawfield Lane OL12 7QR; 01706 657485; **CAZ:** 26, B1

269. PINOCCHIO by Stephen Boyes, based on the original story by Carlo Collodi; MANCHESTER ACTORS COMPANY; *14 February 2005.*

OUR LADY'S AND ST PAUL'S ROMAN CATHOLIC PRIMARY SCHOOL; Sutherland Road, Darnhill, HEYWOOD OL10 3PD; 01706 360827; **CAZ:** 38, A4

PARKFIELD COUNTY PRIMARY SCHOOL; Harold Street, MIDDLETON M24 4AF; 0161-643 2549; CAZ: 53, G6

POLISH CLUB; Westfield, Manchester Road OL11 4LX; 01706 648450; CAZ: 40, C1

PUPIL WELFARE CENTRE

QUEEN ELIZABETH HIGH SCHOOL; Hollin Lane, MIDDLETON M24 1PR; 0161-643 2643; **CAZ:** 70, A4

271. ROMEO AND JULIET by William Shakespeare; MANCHESTER ACTORS COMPANY; *13 December 2004*

QUEENSWAY SCHOOL; Hartley Lane OL11 2LR; 01706 647 743; **CAZ:** 41, E2

154. **SONYA'S GARDEN;** M6 THEATRE COMPANY; *30 November 2004.*

503. **ODD SOCKS;** devised by Dorothy Wood, Romy Baskerville and Kate Mercer; M6; *14, 21 June 2005*

ROCHDALE EXCHANGE MARKET; Newgate, Market Square OL16 1BA; 01706 710400; CAZ: 27, H4

ROYAL TOBY HOTEL; Manchester Road, CASTLETON

RYDINGS SPECIAL SCHOOL; Great Howarth, Wardle Road OL12 9HJ; 01706 657993; **CAZ:** 16, A5

154. **SONYA'S GARDEN;** M6 THEATRE COMPANY *10 December 2004.*

SACRED HEART CHURCH HALL; Kingsway OL16 5BX; 01706 647761; CAZ: B28, B2

SACRED HEART ROMAN CATHOLIC PRIMARY SCHOOL; Kingsway OL16 4AW; 01706 649981

ST CLEMENT'S PAROCHIAL HALL, Sandy Lane, ROCHDALE OL11 5DR; 01706 731353/7351190. CAZ: 27, E3.

ST CUTHBERT'S ROMAN CATHOLIC HIGH SCHOOL; Shaw Road OL16 4RX; **CAZ:** 41, H4

268. **MACBETH** by William Shakespeare; MANCHESTER ACTORS COMPANY; *16 Februuary 2005.*

ST EDWARD'S CHURCH OF ENGLAND PRIMARY SCHOOL; Hanover Street OL11 3AR; 01706 631 755; **CAZ:** 40, C3

ST GABRIEL'S ROMAN CATHOLIC PRIMARY SCHOOL; Vicarage Road South, CASTLETON OL11 2TN; 01706 50280; **CAZ:** 40, D4

ST JAMES CHURCH OF ENGLAND PRIMARY SCHOOL; Hartley Street, LITTLEBOROUGH OL12 9JW; 01706 378 268; **CAZ:** 17, E4

ST JOHN FISHER ROMAN CATHOLIC PRIMARY SCHOOL; Stanycliffe Lane, MIDDLETON M24 2PB; 0161- 643 3271; CAZ 54, B4

ST JOHN'S ROMAN CATHOLIC PRIMARY SCHOOL; Ann Street OL11 1EZ; O1706 647 195

ST JOSEPH'S ROMAN CATHOLIC HIGH SCHOOL; Pot Hall, Wilton Grove, HEYWOOD OL10 2AA; 01706 360607; **CAZ:** 39, E4

3. SPARK by Mary Cooper; M6 THEATRE COMPANY; *30 November 2004.*

ST MARGARET'S CHURCH OF ENGLAND PRIMARY SCHOOL; Heys Lane HEYWOOD OL10 3RD; 01706-369639; **CAZ:** 38, C4

ST MARY'S CHURCH; Queen Victoria Street, BALDERSTONE OL16 2UP; 01706 630 140; **CAZ:** 41, G1

496. THE STREET WHERE I LIVE; devised and presented by Romy Baskerville; M6; *1 December 2004.*

503. ODD SOCKS; devised by Dorothy Wood, Romy Baskerville and Kate Mercer; M6; *22 June 2005*

ST MARY'S CHURCH OF ENGLAND PRIMARY SCHOOL; Oldham Road OL11 2HB; 01706 648 125; CAZ: 41, G1

154. SONYA'S GARDEN; M6 THEATRE COMPANY *10 December 2004.*

503. ODD SOCKS; devised by Dorothy Wood, Romy Baskerville and Kate Mercer; M6; *23 June 2005*

ST MARY'S ROMAN CATHOLIC PRIMARY SCHOOL; Wood Street, LANGLEY M24 5GL; 0161-643 7594; CAZ: 53, G5

496. THE STREET WHERE I LIVE; devised and presented by Romy Baskerville; M6; *10 November 2004.*

154. SONYA'S GARDEN; M6 THEATRE COMPANY; *10 December 2004.*

503. ODD SOCKS; devised by Dorothy Wood, Romy Baskerville and Kate Mercer; M6; *6 July 2005*

ST PATRICK'S PRIMARY SCHOOL; Lomax Street OL12 0DN; 01706 648089; CAZ; 27, H2

ST PETER'S CHURCH OF ENGLAND PRIMARY SCHOOL; Muriel Street; OL16 5JQ; 01706 648195; CAZ: 28, B6

154. SONYA'S GARDEN; M6 THEATRE COMPANY; *29 November 2004.*

503. ODD SOCKS; devised by Dorothy Wood, Romy Baskerville and Kate Mercer; M6; *30 Jun, 7 Julye 2005*

ST THOMAS; Gainsborough Drive OL11 6QU; 01706 343 249; CAZ: 41, ES

496. **THE STREET WHERE I LIVE;** devised and presented by Romy Baskerville; M6; *26 November 2004.*

503. **ODD SOCKS;** devised by Dorothy Wood, Romy Baskerville and Kate Mercer; M6; *1 July 2005*

ST THOMAS MORE; Kirkway, ALKRINGTON M24 1LW; 0161-654 6334; **CAZ:** 70, A3

ST THOMAS MORE ROMAN CATHOLIC HIGH SCHOOL; Evesham Road, MIDDLETON M24 1PY; **CAZ:** 70, A4

ST VINCENT'S CHURCH HALL; Edenfield Road, NORDEN OL12 7QL; 01706 647761; CAZ: 25, H1

SAXON HALL STUDY CENTRE; Smson Street OL16 2XW; **CAZ:** 28, C3

265. **ACTING YOUR AGE** by Mike Harris; GW THEATRE; *16 March 2005.*

SHAWCLOUGH COUNTY PRIMARY SCHOOL; Thrum Hall Lane OL12 6DE; 01706 647991; **CAZ:** 15, E6

196. **THE GARDEN IN WINTER;** M6 THEATRE COMPANY; *7 June 2005.*

SIDDAL MOOR SPORTS COLLEGE; Newhouse Road, HEYWOOD OL10 2NT; 01706 369436; **CAZ:** 39, F5

268. **MACBETH** by William Shakespeare; MANCHESTER ACTORS COMPANY; *26 January 2005.*

SOUTH STREET NURSERY SCHOOL; South Street OL16 2EP; 01706 645435; **CAZ:** 28, A3

SPARROW HILL COUNTY PRIMARY SCHOOL; Coventry Street OL11 1EY; 01706 481194; **CAZ:** 27, H5

SPOTLAND COUNTY PRIMARY SCHOOL; Edmund Street OL12 6QG; 01706 648198; **CAZ:** 27, F3

SPRINGHILL HIGH SCHOOL; Turf Hill Road OL16 4XA; 01706 647474; **CAZ:** 28, B6

SUNNYBROW NURSERY SCHOOL; Sunny Brow Road, Archer Park, MIDDLETON M24 4AD; 0161-643 306; **CAZ:** 69, G1

503. **ODD SOCKS;** devised by Dorothy Wood, Romy Baskerville and Kate Mercer; M6; *14 July 2005*

SYKE METHODIST CHURCH; 01706 672784

THAMES STREET NURSERY; Thames Street OL16 3NY; 01706 649729; **CAZ:** 28, B5

THRUM HALL CHURCH; Thrum Hall Lane, LOWER HEALEY OL12 6NL; 01706 645197; CAZ: 15, E6

TOUCHSTONES; The Esplanade; 01706 864 986 / 928; **CAZ:** 27, G4

498. **A DIFFERENT PLACE** by Robin Graham; AMPERSAND MEDIA, GREENHOUSE NORTHWEST; *18 May 2005. Performer:* Mark STEPHENSON. *Director:* Zoe REASON.

TOWN HALL; The Esplanade OL16 1AH; 01706 864 797; **CAZ:** 27, H4

265. **ACTING YOUR AGE** by Mike Harris; GW THEATRE; *9 March 2005.*

TOWN HALL SQUARE CAR PARK; CAZ: 27, H4

TRINITY METHODIST CHURCH; William Henry Street OL11 1AL; 01706 718 790; **CAZ:** 41, G1

154. **SONYA'S GARDEN;** M6 THEATRE COMPANY *1 December 2004.*

WARDLE HIGH SCHOOL; Birch Road OL11 5EF; 01706 373911; **CAZ:** 16, B4

268. **MACBETH** by William Shakespeare; MANCHESTER ACTORS COMPANY; *17 February 2005.*

WARDLEWORTH COMMUNITY CENTRE; South Street OL16 2EP; 01706 33919; CAZ: 28, A3

WHEATSHEAF LIBRARY;

WHEATSHEAF CENTRE; Baille Street OL16 1JA; 01706861626; **CAZ:** 27, H4

WHITWORTH CIVIC HALL; Market Street OL12 8DP; **CAZ:** 15, H3

WHITWORTH HIGH SCHOOL; Hall Fold OL12 8TS; 01706 343218; CAZ: 14, C1

YORKSHIRE STREET; OL16 1LD; CAZ: 27, H3

SALFORD

ROUND THE HORNE (591) Julian / Kenneth Williams (PAUL RYAN) and Sandy / Hugh Paddick (JONATHAN MOORE) introduce themselves at the Lowry

ACTON SQUARE M5 4NY

ADELPHI STUDIO THEATRE: University College Salford, Peru Street, SALFORD M3 6EQ; 0161-295 6120; **CAZ:** 4: C3

15. **ANTIGONE** by Sophocles, translated by Don Taylor; ASPECTS THEATRE COMPANY; *18-19 January 2005. Antigone:* Jude WILLIAMS; *Creon:* Natalie O'BRIEN; *Ismene / Teireias' Boy:* Emma McCULLAGH; *Haemon:* Daniel BOARER; *Teiresias:* Sue HODGKINSON; *Soldier / Euridica:* Pip HARVEY; *Messenger / Soldier:* Michael H CORBETT; *Chorus:* Donna BASNETT, Sam CRUMP, Rosie GREENHALGH, Beth SPANO. *Director:* Jo HARDING; *Technical Stage Manager:* Gordon ISAACS; *Production Manager:* Ian CURRIE; *Costume:* Eileen CULLEN, Anna LYNTWYN. **Journal:** 18/1/05

17. **STUFF HAPPENS** by David Hare; ASPECTS THEATRE COMPANY; *25-26 January 2005. Codoleeza Rice:* Peregrin TREFFRY; I Dick Cheney / Levitte: Stell Mitchell; *Donald Rumsfeld:* Sarah DAVIES; *Paul Wolfowicz / Narrator:* Crecy YORKE; *George Tenet / Jack Straw / Narrator:* Emily HOLDEN; *Paul O'Neil / David Manning / Narrator:* Andy WRIGHT; *John D Negroponte / Hans Blix / Narrator:* Aaisha MOFFAT; *Tony Blair:*T HENDERSON; *George W Bush:* Gabby SANDERSON; *Colin Powell:* Mackayla CUTHBERT; *De Villepin / Alistair Campbell / Narrator:* Laua CROFT; *Jeremy Greenstock / Sir Richard Dearlove / Narrator:* Charlotte WARD. *Director:* Katy HOWSON; *Stage Manager:* Heather BATSMAN; *Technical Support:* Alice LISTER; *Production Manager:* Ian CURRIE; *Props:* Heather BATSMAN, Peregrine TREFFRY; *Costume:* Laura CROFT, Emily HOLDEN, Charlotte WARD; *Sound* Andy WRIGHT; *Set Design / Construction:* Aaisha MOFFATT, Mackayla CUTHBERT. **Journal:** 18/1/05

18. **WHEN MEDEA MET ELVIS;** merging elements of **Medea** by Euripes, as adapted by Liz Lochhead, **Lives of The Great Poisoners** by Caryl Churchill, **Bash** by Neil Labute and **Cooking with Elvis**with new material written by ASPECTS THEATRE COMPANY; *28-29 January 2005. Chorus:* Nancy BRAY, Louise TARVER, Narinder CHOHAN, Felicity CADDICK; *Medea:* Simone RANDALL; *Jason:* Charles DENTON; *Gluake:* Jennifer COOPER; *Nurse:* Carolyn HOOD; *Debbie:* Jennifer SHARROCKS; *Mam:* Abby SIMMONS; *Dad / Kreon:* Liam GREENFIELD; *Stuart:* Chris BOWLER; *Jill:* Maria BLACKBURN. *Director:* Frances PIPER; *Assistant Director:* Bryony FRYER; *Production Technician:* Alice LISTER. **Journal:** 18/1/05

506. HUSHABYE MOUNTAIN by Jonathan Harvey; ASPECTS THEATRE COMPANY; *21-22 January 2005. /director:* Adam ZANE; *Company Manager:* Gordon ISAACS.

512. WAIT UNTIL DARK by Frederick Knott; ASPECTS THEATRE COMPANY; *6-7 May 2005.*

513. ALAS, POOR GEOFFREY; ASPECTS THEATRE COMPANY; *10-11 May 2005.*

514. ACCIDENTAL DEATH OF AN ANARCHIST by Dario Fo; ASPECTS THEATRE COMPANY; *10-11 May 2005.*

515. GONE by Glyn Cannon, a re-working of **Antigone;** ASPECTS THEATRE COMPANY; *13-14 May 2005.*

516. WAITING; ASPECTS THEATRE COMPANY; *13-14 May 2005.*

ALL SOULS CHURCH HALL; Liverpool Street M5 2HQ; CAZ: 92, D3

ALL SOULS ROMAN CATHOLIC PRIMARY SCHOOL; Kintyre Avenue, Weaste M5 2DP; 0161 - 736 3841; **CAZ:** 92, D4

266. A LIKELY STORY by Mike Harris; GW THEATRE COMPANY; *14 April 2005. George:* Julie CLAYS; *Drado:* Qas HAMID; *Kylie:* Roxanne MOORES; *Narrator / Storyteller / Teacher:* Dave JONAS. *Director:* Mike HARRIS; *Sound Technician:* Carol BOROWIAK

BARTON MOSS PRIMARY SCHOOL; Trippier Road, PEEL GREEN M30 7PT; 0161-707 2421; CAZ: 90, B5

A LIKELY STORY (266, previous page) JULIE CLAYS (George) and ROXANNE MOORES (Kylie), with QAS HAID (Drago) in the background, show 5-year-olds how to tell it.

BEN KINGSLEY THEATRE; Pendleton College, Dronfield Road M6 7FR; 0161-736 5074; CAZ: 92, D1

BLACK HORSE HOTEL; 15 The Crescent M5 4PF; 0161-743 1388; CAZ: 4, B4

BLACK LION; 65 Chapel Street M3 5BZ; 0161-834 9009, 9944; **CAZ:** 5, G4

521. THE MERCHANT OF VENICE by William Shakespeare; POOR TOM; *15-18 June 2005. Laucelot Gobbo / Duke:* Hannah McHUGH; *Portia:* Lorna LEWIS; *Morocco / Bassanio:* Jarrod COOKE; *Arragon / Shylock:* Tobias CHRISTOPHER; *Antonio / Lorenzo / Tubal:* Kenan ALLY; *Jessica:* Sorrell ALEXANDER. *Director:* Charlotte ALLEN; *Designer/ Stage Manager:* Lorna MUNDEN.

BRANWOOD PREPARATORY SCHOOL; Stafford Road, ECCLES M30 9NH; 0161-789 1054; **CAZ:** 91, G2

270. FIREBIRD by Stephen Boyes; MANCHESTER ACTORS COMPANY; *22 June 2005.*

THE MERCHANT OF VENICE (521); "This house, and this same myself are yours; / I give them with this ring/ Which when you part from, lose or give away, / Let it presage the ruin of your love." The success of Bassanio (JARROD COOKE) in winning Portia (LORNA LEWIS) is about to turn to challenge.

BRIDGEWATER SCHOOL; Drywood Hall, Worsley Road, WORSLEY M28 2WQ; CAZ: 78, A5; 0161-794 1463

BUILE HILL HIGH SCHOOL; Eccles Old Road M6 8RD; 0161-736 1773; **CAZ:** 92, D1

268. **MACBETH** by William Shakespeare; MANCHESTER ACTORS COMPANY; *21 February 2005.*

3. **SPARK** by Mary Cooper; M6 THEATRE COMPANY; *7 October 2004.*

CALDERWOOD COMMUNITY CENTRE; 2 Bond Square, Devonshire Street M7

4BH; 0161-708 9757; CAZ:82, A5

CHAPEL STREET; M3

CHRIST CHURCH PRIMARY SCHOOL; Nelson Street, ECCLES M30 OGZ; 0161-789 4531; CAZ: 91, F3

CHURCH STREET; ECCLES M30 0DA; CAZ: 91, G3

DUKE OF YORK; 89 Church Street, ECCLES M30 0DA; 0161-707 5409; CAZ: 91, G3

DUKESGATE PRIMARY SCHOOL; Earlesden Crescent LITTLE HULTON M38 9HF; 0161-799 2210; **CAZ:** 62,C4

269. **PINOCCHIO** by Stephen Boyes, based on the original story by Carlo Collodi; MANCHESTER ACTORS COMPANY; *16February 2005.*

ECCLES CHURCH OF ENGLAND HIGH SCHOOL; Northfleet Road M30 7PQ; 0161-789 5359; CAZ: 90, B4

ECCLES LIBERAL CLUB; 34 Wellington Road M30 0NP; 0161-789 3047; **CAZ:** 91, G3

ECCLES METHODIST CHURCH; 1 Wellington Road M30 0DR; 0161-788 7345; CAZ: 91, 3G

EDGEFOLD HALL; Edgefold Road, WALKDEN M28 7QF; 0161-790 4684; CAZ: 77, F2

ELLESMERE SHOPPING CENTRE; High Street, WALKDEN M28 3NJ; CAZ: 63, F6

FIDDLERS LANE PRIMARY SCHOOL; IRLAM M44 6QE; 0161 - 775 2490; **CAZ:** 103, F4

THE FRIARS COUNTY PRIMARY SCHOOL; Cannon Street M3 7EU; 0161-832 4664; **CAZ:** 4, D2

HARROP FOLD SCHOOL; Worsley; 0161-790 5022

HOLY FAMILY CHURCH SCOUT AND GUIDES HALL; Boothstown; 0161-799 6672

541. **CINBADS: PANTO AT THE OK CORRAL;** *27-30 January 2005.*

HOPE HIGH SCHOOL; Eccles Old Road M6 8FH; 0161 - 736 2637; CAZ: 92, C1

HOPE HOSPITAL; Stott Lane M6 8FJ; 0161-789 7373; **CAZ:** 92, B2

IRLAM AND CADISHEAD HIGH SCHOOL; MacDonald Road M44 5LH; 0161-775 5525; CAZ: 118, C2

IRLAM PRIMARY SCHOOL; Liverpool Road M44; 0161-775 2911; **CAZ:** 103, E6

JAMES BRINDLEY PRIMARY SCHOOL; Parr Fold Avenue, WALKDEN M28 7HE; 0161-790 8050; CAZ: 77, E2

KERSAL HIGH SCHOOL; Mesnefield Road M7 3QD; 0161-792 1748; CAZ: 81, E3

KING'S ARMS – STUDIO SALFORD; 11 Bloom Street M3 6AN; **CAZ:** 5, E4

522. **RELATIVITY** by Claire Berry; DARK PROFIT; *14-18 September 2004.*

523. **GET 'EM IN!** by Stella Grundy; ULTRAVIOLET; *14-18 September 2004. Bet:* Stella

GRUNDY; *Zoe:* Janine CARRINGTON.

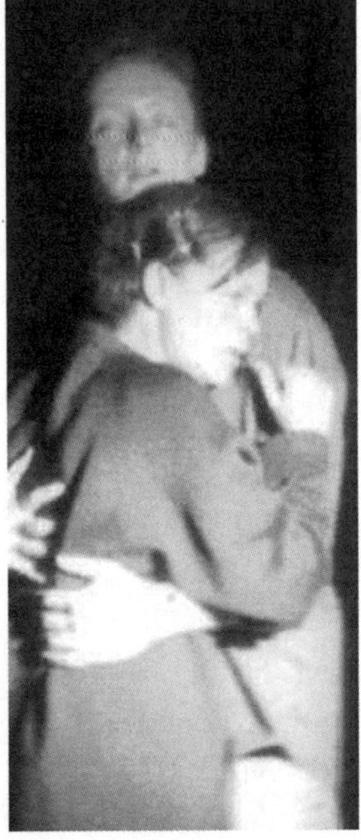

RELATIVITY (522, oreviuos page)

524. CREDITORS by August Strindberg; a new version by Julian Hill and Jenny Forslund; PAPERCUT THEATRE COMPANY; *21-25 September 2004.*

525. 36 HOURS by Neil Bell and John West; EAT THEATRE; *26-30 October 2004. John Cooper Clarke:* Neil BELL; *Eric, et al:* Lynn RODEN; *Nico, et al:* Jo WYNNE-EYTON

12. MOVING PICTURES by Cathy Crabb; MEDIAMEDEA; *23-27 November 2004. Anne:* Denice HOPE; *Tina:* Sue JAYNES. *Director:* James FOSTER; *Stage Manager:* Ken NORBURY; *Lighting:* Ken NORBURY, James FOSTER; *Sound:* John SCOTT; *Props:* Ken NORBURY, Jon COOPER. **Journal:** 13/10/04

319, 526-528 Embryo 9.
work in development:

526. BOB; ROBERT WRIGHT-SMITH; *11 February 2005.*

527. TRINITY by Joe O'Byrne; ALBINO INJUN PRODUCTIONS; *11 February 2005.*

773. PERFECT; written aand performed by Klare Gaulton; RIVERSIDE MEDIA; *11 February 2005.*

528. THE VAGINA MONOLOGUES by Eve Esler; *11-12 February 2005. Performer:* Sue JAYNES.

319. THE CHAINSAW MANICURE by Thomas Kett; URBAN THEATRE COMPANY; *11 February 2005. Cast:* Laura CAINE.

529. FRIDGE MOUNTAIN by Mike Heath; *12 February2005. Cast:* Denice HOPE, Klare GAULTON, Rob COLLIER. (Part of Embryo 10)

534. FIFTEEN MINUTES WITH YOU by Cathy Crabb; MEDIAMEDEA; *22-26 February 2005. Matt:* Neil BELL; *Jane:* Stella GRUNDY. *Directors:* Cathy CRABB, James FOSTER; *Stage Manager:* Ken NORBURY; *Lighting:* Ken NORBURY, James FOSTER; *Sound / Music Arrangement:* John SCOTT; *Props:* Jon COOPER; *Music Compilation:* Laurie REA.

530-531 Embryo 11 work in development:

530. BERT AND ERNIE; *1 April 2005. Cast:* Richard PORTER, Julian KELLY.

531. BRIDE; ***1 April 2005. Cast:*** Julia NELSON, Stella GRANT.

BRIDE (531); STELLA GRANT

532-533 Embryo 12.
work in development:

532. **THE GAME OF TWO HALVES;** *2 April 2005. Cast:* Andrew YATES, Rob COLLIER.

533. **TAM HINTON** *2 April 2005.*

STEVEN MARK as Brian

538. **A HOWARD BRENTON TRILOGY;** VISTA THEATRE; *26 – 30 April 2005.* **Gum & Goo:** *Gum / etc:* Steven MARK; *Goo / etc:* Phil MINNS; *Mary:* Sue JAYNES; **Heads:** *Rock:* Phil MINNS; *Brian:* Steven MARK; *Megan:* Sue JAYNES; **The Education of Skinny Spew:** *Skinny Spew:* Phil MINNS; *Mrs Spew / etc:* Sue JAYNES; *Mr Spew / etc:* Steven MARK. *Lighting:* Ken NORBURY, James FOSTER; *Sound:* John SCOTT.

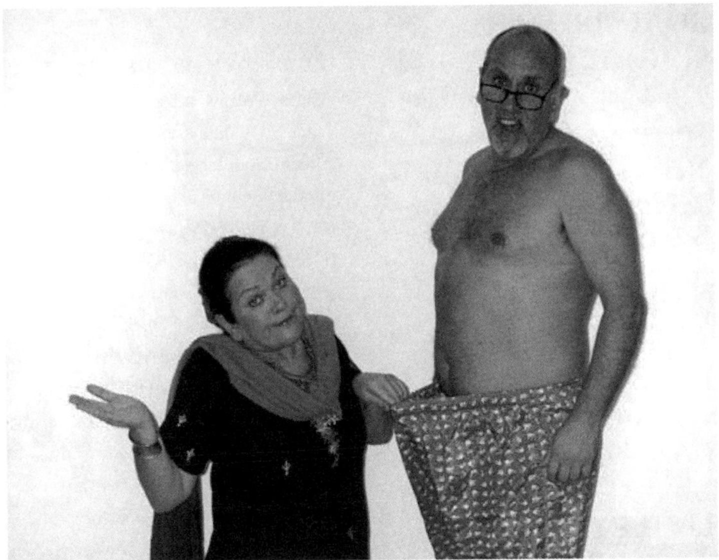

535. KAMA SUTRA by Peter McGarry; EYEWITNESS THEATRE; *2, 4, 7 May 2005. Pamela:* Sue WARHURST; *Tristan:* Peter McGARRY.

536. COACHING by Christine Marshall; JELLYSHOE PRODUCTIONS; *10-14 May 2005. Freda:* Denice HOPE; *Ivy:* Anne Marie GLEESON. *Director:* Christine MARSHALL.

537. CYCLING by Christine Marshall; JELLYSHOE PRODUCTIONS; *10 – 14 May 2005. Sandra:* Rachel PRIEST; *Mary:* Marilyn BAR-ELAN. *Director:* Christine MARSHALL.

276. THE LARAMIE PROJECT by Moises Kaufman and members of the Tectonic Theatre Project; HOPE THEATRE COMPANY; *24 – 28 May 2005. Most of Cast as at* **04:61**; *Director:* Adam ZANE.

191. COACH G by Stephen Morris; MONKEYWORKS THEATRE; *21-25 June 2005.*

539. SALFORD STUFFERS by Christine Marshall; JELLYSHOE PRODUCTIONS; *28 June –2 July 2005.*

LANGWORTHY ROAD PRIMARY SCHOOL M6 5PP; 0161-736 3841; **CAZ:** 93, F2

266. **A LIKELY STORY** by Mike Harris; GW THEATRE COMPANY; *15 April 2005.*

LANCASTRIAN HALL THEATRE; Chorley Road, SWINTON M27 2AE; 0161-794 7466; CAZ: 79, F3

LITTLE HULTON COMMUNITY SCHOOL; Longshaw Drive M28 0AZ; 0161-790 4214; CAZ: 62, C5

LOWER KERSAL PRIMARY SCHOOL; Northallerton Road M7 3TP; 0161-792 2726; **CAZ:** 81, F5

THE LOWRY; Pier 8, Salford Quays M5 2AZ; 0161-876 2000; **CAZ:** 93, E6; G, H. S, W

Lyric Theatre

545. **LOVE ON THE DOLE** by Walter Greenwood, adapted for the stage by Ronald Gow and Walter Greenwood; further adapted for this production by Kevin Fegan; THE LOWRY; *9-18 September 2004. Helen Hawkins:* Suzanne LOUDON; *Harry Hardcastle:* Luke TENNANT; *Larry Meath:* Simon McCOLE; *Sally Hardcastle:* Nicola EAGLETON; *Paul Thornton:* Bill SIMMONDS; *Sam Hardie:* Peter HUGHES; *Jack Lindsay:* Gary CUBBAGE; *Tom Hare:* Edward Vincent ROLAND; *Mrs Hardcastle:* Sam FOX; *Mr Hardcastle:* Raymond Francis SAVAGE; *Ned Larkey:* Harvey WALTON; *Sam Grundy:* John McELHATTON; *Sam Grundy's Women:*Stella Maria Lopez JONES, Aimee GUTRIDGE; *MrS Nattles:* Angela ELPHICK; *Mrs Bull:* Iris SHARPLES; *Insurance Man:* John ADAMIAK; *Mrs Dorbell:* Shirley DRIVER; *Ma Jike:* Marilyn STEVIE; *Delegate 2 / Foreman:* Andrew HOWES; *Kate MOLLOY:* Rachel MANSFIELD; *Clerk 1:* Chris NELSON; *Clerk 2:* Gary CARR; *Clerk 3:* Sandra MAKIN; *Girl With Rose:* Paula MUDD; *Women:* Pauline MURPHY, Jackie HARRISON, Linda MANFREDINI, Jennifer CROWLEY, Sam RHODES; *Delegate 1:* Michael ELPHICK; *Harry'sChorus:* Simon RUSSELL, Abraham TIYAMIYU,

Josh SIMPSON, James HOOLEY, Adam BARLOW, Chris NELSON; *Cotton Girls:* Talitha Thompson, Chloe Anne HILL; Jes PENDLEBURY, Chloe HARRISON, Laura McGREGOR; *Chorus:* Michael ELPHICK, Phillip MAY, Hannah STANDRING, Di CRITCHLEY, Sarah NORDMAN, Jayne MILLER, Sally BROOKS, Denise GARDNER, Bridget WITHYCOMBE-WARTON, Claire GRAY, Victoria HOWES, Jenna DEVENEY, Sheila FAUNCE, Annie O'MALLEY, Cassandra WILFORD, Sarah FIELD, Jenny RANDLE, Anna WARD, Beth NOBLE, Nicky THOMPSON; *THE BAND:* Nigel RUDING, Philip HOWES, Sarah FIELD. *Director:* Andy FARRELL; *Musical Director:* Martin MILNER; *Designer:* Andrew WOOD, *with* Lisa ARNOLD; *Voice Coach / Singing:* Beth ALLEN; *Choreographer:* Lisi PERRY; *Lighting Designer:* David MARTIN; *Producer:* Jane DASILVA; *Project Co-ordinator:* Porl COOPER; *Technical Manager:* Saul HOPWOOD; *Design Team:* Vivien ASHTON, Joanne COATES, Sue PILKINGTON-HANNA, Alan PEASE, *with:* Deborah ASHWORTH, Stephen BILLS, Justin EAGLETON; *Wardrobe Supervisor:* Jacqui DAVIES; *Stage Manager On The Book:* Sally ROBERTS; *Production Manager:* Chris SLEATH; *Stage Manager:* Jo GREENWOOD; *Lighting Operator:* Lizzie MORAN; *Sound:* Andy WILSON; *Stage Technician:* Sacha QUIEROZ; *Flyman:* Neil BOARDMAN.

546. JOURNEY'S END by R C Sherriff; PHIL CAMERON AND MARK GOUCHER; *27 September – 2 October 2004. Captain Hardy / Sergeant Major:* James STADDON; *Lieutenant Osbourne:* Philip FRANKS; *Private Mason:* Stephen CASEY; *2nd Lieutenant Raleigh:* Richard GLAVES; *Captain Stanhope:* Tom WISDOM; *2nd Lieutenant Trotter:* Roger WALKER; *Private Albert Brown / A Private:* Edward FULTON; *2nd Lieutenant Hibbert:* Stephen HUDDSON; *Colonel:* Simon SHACKLETON: *German Soldier:* William GREGORY; *Lance Corporal Broughton:* Christopher KNOTT. *Director:* David GRINDLEY; *Designer:* Jonathan FENSOM; *Lighting Designer:* Jason TAYLOR; *Sound Designer:* Gregory CLARKE; *Associate Director:*Tim ROSEMAN; *Historical Consultant:* Max ARTHUR; *Costume Supervisor:* ChRLOTTE bird; *Company Stage Manager:* Graham MICHAEL; *Deputy Stage Manager:* Helen REYNOLDS; *Assistant Stage Manager:* Martin HOPE; *Wardrobe Manager:* Nina KENDALL; *2nd Assistant Stage Manager / Wardrobe:* Janee ROBINSON; *Costume and Props*

Advisors: Taff GILLINGHAM (at

TOM WILSON (Stanhope)

Khaki Devil Ltd), Richard INGRAM(at Sabre Sales); *Touring Production Manager:* Spencer NEW; *Relights:* Greg GOULD, Jo DAWSON; *Scenic Artist:* Richard NUTBOURNE.

547. THE PLAY WHAT I WROTE by Hamish McColl, Sean Foley and Eddie Braben; DAVID PUGH LTD; *4 – 9 October 2004.*

548. HAMLET by William Shakespeare; THEATRE ROYAL PLYMOUTHL THELMA HOLT; by William Shakespeare; THEATRE ROYAL PLYMOUTH; THELMA HOLT; *2-6 November 2005. Barnardo /Messenger:* James TUCKER; *Francisco:* Graham INGLE; *Horatio:* Bob BARRETT; *Marcellus / Captain/ 2nd Gentleman / Poisoner:* Barry AIRD; *Claudius / Ghost:* Peter EGAN; *Cornelius / 1st Gentleman / 2nd Gravedigger:* Edward CLAYTON; *Voltemand / Priest:* Leon TANNER; *Laertes / Dumb King:* Adam DODD; *Polonius:*Robert DEMENGER; *Hamlet:* Michael MALONEY; *Gertrude:* Frances TOMELTY; *Ophelie:* Laura REES; *Reynaldo / Osric:* Tristram WYMARK; *Rosencrantz:* Brendan O'HEA; *Guildenstern:* Nick BAGNALL; *First Player / 1st Gravedigger:* Jim HOOPER; *Player King:* Daniel RIGBY; *Player Queen:* Takehiro HIRA; *Lucianus / Sailor:* Marc BAYLIS; *Fortinbras:* Mido HAMADA; *Dumb Queen:* Freya DOMINIC. *Director:* Yukio

NINAGAWA; *Set Design:* Tsukasa NAKAGOSHI; *Lighting Designer:* Tamotsu HARADA; *Costume Designer:* Lily KOMINE; *Sound Designer:* Masahiro INOUE; *Assistant Director:* Takaaki INOUE; *Associate Director:* Simon De DENEY; *Associate Lighting Designer:* Nick JONES; *Fight Director:* Terry KING; *Company Manager:* Rob YOUNG; *Stage Manager:* Cal HAWES; *Deputy Stage Manager:* Emma CAMERON; *Assistant Stage Manager:* Rebecca POWNALL; *Company Voice Work:* Mago ANNETT; *Production Manager:* Nick SOPER; *Head of Wardrobe:* Dina HALL; *Workshop Manager:* Tony HARVEY; *Fight Captain:* Tristram WYMARK; *Relights / Production Electrician:* Jonathan CLARK; *Lighting Board Operatpr:* John MANN; *Head Follow-Spot Operator:* James BENTHAM; *Wardrobe Mistress:* Donna RICHARDS; *Wardrobe Assistant:* Alison CROAD; *Sound Operator:* Martin DEWAR; *Wigs / Hair:* Dasnuta BARSZCZEWSKA; *Additional Ladies Costumes:* Carol MOLYNEU; *Addititition Men's Costumes:* Mark COSTELLO, Karm Clothing.

549. THE CRUCIBLE by Arthur Miller; BIRMINGHAM REPERTORY THEATRE; THE TOURING CONSORTIUM; *9-13 November John Proctor:* Malcolm STORRY; *Elizabeth Proctor:* Patricia KERRIGAN; *Danforth:* Tony BROTTON; *Hale:* Paul SHELLEY; *and:* Sara BEHARRELL, Linda BROUGHTON, Bethan CECIL, Pip DONAGHY, John FLITCROFT, Maria GOLLEDGE, James HAYES, Tom MARSHALL, Leah MULLER, Angela PHINNIMORE, Julian PROTHERO, Michelle TAIT, James WALKER, Mary WIMBUSK, Benny YOUNG. *Director:* Jonathan CHURCH; *Designer:* Simon HIGLETTL *Lighting:* Mark JONATHAN; *Music:* Mark TAMS.

550. LORD OF THE FLIES by William Golding, adapted by Nigel Williams; PILOT THEATRE. *23-27 November 2005. Director:* Marcus ROMER.

551. OH! WHAT A NIGHT by Christopher Barr, from idea and story by Stuart Littlewood, Andrew Wake, Tony Gradon; STUART LITTLEWOOD; INTERNATIONAL ARTISTES LTD; *29 November – 4 December 2004. Brutus T Firefly:* Kid CREOLE.

552. THE WIZARD OF OZ by L Frank Baum; PELE PRODUCTIONS; *15 December 2004 – 9 January 2005. Wicked Witch:* Suzie BLAKE.

553. THE WITCHES by Roald Dahl, adapted by David Wood; BIRMINGHAM REPERTORY THEATRE; THE DAVID WOOD COMPANY; THE AMBASSADOR THEATRE GROUP; *25-29 January 2005. Director:* Jonathan CHURCH.

554. SCOOBY-DO IN STAGEFRIGHT! By Jim Millan; WARNER BROS ENTERTAINMENT; *7-12 February 2005..Scooby-Doo:* Rowan TALBOT; *Shaggy Rogers:* Richard LYNSON; *VelmaDinkly:* Clare CORBETT; *Daphne Blake*: Zoe DAWSON; *Fred Jones:* Ryan McCLUSKEY; *Uncle Tim / Blake:* Mark DENHAM; *Belinda Del Monte:* Juliet PREW; *Dracula:* Martin DOYLE; *Crawley / Victor / Red Beard:* Matthew CULLUM; *Kimmi:* Amy ROGERS. *Director:* Jim MILLAN; *Assistant Director / Choreographer:* Jenn RAPP: *Set Design:* Rob BISSINGER; *Original Costume Designer:* Gregg BARNES; *Originasl Sound Designer:* Peter HYLENSKI; *Lighting Designer:* Graham McCLUSKEY; *Associate Lighting Designer:* Adrian J BARNES; *Sound Designer:* Pete COX; *Wardrobe Supervisor:* Anna JOSEPHS; *Production Manager:* Pat MOLONY; *Company Manager:* Nick EARLE; *Stage Manager:* Steve JEFFREYS; *Deputy Stage Manager:* Emma HELE; *Assistant Stage Manager:* Sharon SOOKUR; *Touring Electrician:* Bruno HUNT; *Sound Operators:* James TEBB, Ashley JONES;*Wardrobe Mistress:* Vic CREE; *Deputy Wardrobe Mistress:* Deborah HAMMOND; *Production Carpenters:* Eddie CROWTHER, Graham TAYLOR; *Production Electrician:* Andy FIDGEON; *ProductionSound Engineer:* Steve BRIERLEY; *Electrics Programmer:* Simon SPENCER.

77. ARSENIC AND OLD LACE by Joseph Kesselring; CHURCHILL THEATRE. BROMLEY; *14-19 February 2005. Abby Brewster:* Angela THORNE; *The Rev Dr Harper / Lieutenant Rooney:* David PEART; *Teddy Brewster:* Mark HEENEHAN; *Officer Brophy:* Anthony HOUGHTON; *Officer Klein:* Jon MILLINGTON; *Martha Brewster:* Brigit FORSYTH; *Elain Harper:* Reanne FARLEY; *Mortimer Brewster:* Andrew HAVILL; *Mr Gibbs / Mr Witherspoon:*Peter LAIRD;l *Jonathan Brewster:* Huw HIGGINSON; *Dr Einstein:* Sylvester McCOY. *Director:* Robin HERFORD; *Designer:* Michael HOLT; *Lighting Designer:* Matt DRURY; *Sound:* Ed BRIMLEY; *Production Manager:* Digby ROBINSON; *Assistant Production Manager:* Matt DARBY; *Costume Supervisor:* Janet WHITE; *Company Stage Manager:* Nick MAY; *Deputy Stage Manager:* Claire HENDERS;

BRIGIT FORSYTH and ANGELA THORNE

Assistant Stage Managers: Andrew P STEPHEN, Katie WILLOW; *Wardrobe Mistress:* Judith RAE; *Props Buyer:* David MILLARD; *Dialect Coach:* Julia Wilson DICKSON

75. ONE TOUCH OF VENUS; Music by Kurt Weill; Lyrics by Ogden Nash; Book by S J Perelman and Ogden Nash, based on **The Tinted Venus** by F J Anstey; *1,3,March & 9 April 2005. Whitelaw Savory:* Ron LI-PAZ;*Molly Grant:* Christianne TISDALE; *Taxi Black:* Eric ROBERTS; *Stanley:* Jeffrey LLOYD-ROBERTS; *Venus:* Karen COKER; *Rodney Hatch:* Loreb GEETING; *Gloria Kramer:* Jessica WALKER; *Mrs Kramer:* Carole WILSON; *Zuvetli:* Adrian CLARKE; *Dr Rook:* Eric ROBERTS; *Company Singers:* Vivienne BAILEY; A Galloway BELL, Miranda BEVIN, Peter BODENHAM, Stephem BRIGGS, Anna BRITTAIN, Christine BRYAN, Dominic BURNS, Hazel CROFT, Anthony CUNNINGHAM, Stephen DOWSON, Irene EVANS, Cordelia FISH, Garrick FORBES, Paul GIBSON, Ben KERSLAKE, Susan LEES, Keith MILLS, Rachel MOSLEY, Justin Miles OLDEN, David OWEN-LEWIS, Jeremy PEAKER, Arwel PRICE, Paul RENDALL, Lesley ROBERTS, Victoria SHARP, Harold SHARPLES, Gordon, D SHAW, Angela SORRIGAN, Gladwyn TAYLOR, Shirley THOMAS, Edward THORNTON, Pauline THULBRON, Nicola UNWIN, Claire WILLIAMS; *Dancers:* Alan BURKITT, Paul CHANTRY, Jennifer CHICHEPORTICHE, Josephine

Programme Details

DARVILL-MILLS, Hayley Del SANDERSON, Rebecca JACKSON, Jeffrey RANN, Craiy TURBYFIELD; *ORCHESTRA: First Violins:* David GREED (Leader), Peter MASLIN (Co-Leader), David RILEY, Alison McALISTER, Stephen SHULMAN, Michael ARDRON, Eileen SPENCER, Wendy DYSON, Brian REILLY, Tamsin SYMONS; *Second Violins:* Katherine NEW, Philip CLEGG, Anita CHIDSLEY, Paul UDLOFF, Catherine WHITHAM, Maria VERICONTE, Helen GREIG, Alison DIXON; *Violas:* Howard BREAKSPEAR, Vivienne CAMPBELL, Vince PARSONAGE, Elizabeth WYLY; *Cello:* George KENNAWAY, Andrew FAIRLEY, Miriam ROYCROFT, Judith BURGIN; *Basses:* Paul MILLER, Philip COOPER, Claire SADLER; *Flutes / Piccolos:* David MOSELEY; *Clarinets:* Colin HONOUR, John ROBINSON, Tim REDPATH, Robert BUCKLAND, Simon MURRAY; *Bass Clarinet:* John ROBINSON; *Alto Saxophones:* Colin HONOUR, John ROBINSON; *Tenor / Baritone Saxophones:* Tim REDPATH, Robert BUCKLAND, Simon MURRAY; *Trumpets:* Murray GREIG, Michael WOODHEAD, David HOOPER; *Trombone:* Christopher HOULDING; *Timpani:* Marney O'SULLIVAN; *Percussion:* Christopher BRADLEY, Graham HALL; *Guitar:* Kenneth HEGGIE; *Piano:* John QUERNS. *Conductor:* Martin PICKARD; *Director:* Tim ALBERY; *Choreographer:* William TUCKETT; *Set Designer:* Antony McDONALD; *Costume Designer:* Emma RYOTT; *Lighting Designer:* Adam SILVERMAN; *Assistant Director:* Rob KEARLEY; *Assistant Choreographer:* Jeffrey RANN; *Assistant Designer:* Mauricio ELORRIAGA; *Chief Repetiteur:* John QUERNS; *Dialect Coach:* Robin POLLEY; *Stage Manager:* Peter RESTALL; *Deputy Stage Manager:* Gemma TONGE; *Production Managers:* Ray HAIN, Felix DAVIES; *Costume Supervisor:* Stephen RODWELL; *Acting Costume Supervisors:* Dorothy LAWRENCE, Mary GILLIBRAND; *Wigs and Make-up Supervisor:* Shirley FAIRCLOUGH; *Dyeing / Painting / Breaking-Down:* Chris DUFFELENL *Costume Makers:* Sarah MURGATROYD, Becky GRAHAM, Julie PARTINGTON, Ziang McDOWELL, Barbara FUCHS, Kate EGAN, Karen CRICHTON, Jackie HALLATT, Barry THEWLIS, Alan SELZER, Kay COVENEY, Jamielah LEAK; *Hat Makers:* Chris DUFFELEN, Sean BARRETT, Jenny ADEY; *Costume Props:* Robert ALLSOPP; *Wigs:* Campbell YOUNG, Darren WARE; *Scenery:* Atelier BRIGHELLA; *Props Supervisor:* Many BURNETT; *Production Carpenter:* Jonny HICK.

555. **MARTHA, JOSIE AND THE CHINESE ELVIS**by Charlotte Jones; *7-12 March*

556. **MACBETH** by Julian Chenery (Book and Lyrics), Mark Gimblett (Music and Lyric) and William Shakespeare; SHAKESPEARE 4 KIDZ; *17 March 2005.*

557. **THE TEMPEST** by Julian Chenery (Book and Lyrics), Mark Gimblett (Music and Lyric) and William Shakespeare; SHAKESPEARE 4 KIDZ; *18 March 2005.*

LAURA HOWARD and COLIN BAKER

558. **DRACULA** by Bram Stoker, adapted by Bryony Lavery; JENNY KING; *19- 23 April 2005. Jonathan Harker:* Giles FAGAN; *Carpathian Woman / Mrs Westernra / Air Stewardess:* Jane LUCAS; *Dracula:* Richard BREMMER; *Vampire Woman / Mina:* Laura HOWARD; *Vampire Woman /Lucy:* Katie FOSTER-BARNES; *Vampire Woman:* Eki MARIA; *Dr Seward:* Hywel SIMONS; *Quincey:* James ALBRECHT; *Arthur Homewood:* Damien GOODWIN; *Renfield:* Ben KEATON; *Hospital Attendant:* Paul CHESTERTON; *Hospital Attendant / Coastguard:* Robert CAMERON; *Professor van Helsing:* Colin BAKER; *Boy:* Waldo KEATON; *Little Girl:* Olivia FRANNON , Amy PHILLIPS.. *Director:* Rachel KAVANAUGH; *Design:* Ruari MURCHISON; *Lighting:* Rick FISHER; *Video Designer:* Mic POOL; *Sound:* Fergus O'HARE*; Movement Director:* Struan

LESLIE; *Illusions:* Scott PENROSE; *Associate Director:* Neale BIRCH; *Fight Director:* Terry KING; *Voice Coach:* Charmian HOARE; *General ManagerL* Janet POWELL; *Tour Technical Manager:* Matt COX; *Production Carpenter:* Bill WARDROPER; *Assistant Production Carpenter:* Gareth MORGAN; *Wardrobe Master:* Stuart PEARSON; *Tour Technician:* Cal ROBERTSONS; *Company Stage Manager:* Jane BULLOCK; *Stage Manager On The Book:* Jaci LEATHER; *Acting Assistant Stage Manager:* Eki MARIA; *Production Manager:* Digby ROBINSON; *Costume Supervisor:* Yvonne MILNES; *Lighting Programmer:* Rob HALLIDAY; *Production Sound Engineer:* Karen SZAMEIT.

66. PAPERWORLD; MIM-I-RICHI CLOWN THEATRE; *28 April 2005. Artistic Director:* Andrey GONZALEZ. **Journal:** 25/4/05.

78. WHEN HARRY MET SALLY by Nora Ephron, adapted for the stage by Marcy Kahan; CHURCHILL THEATRE, BROMLEY; *2 – 7 May 2005. Sally:* Gaby ROSLIN; *Harry:* Jonathan WRATHER; *Marie:*Rebecca GETHINS; *Jack:* Qarie MARSHALL; *Ensemble:* Matt WOLF, Polly MABERLY, Ann WENN, Edward HAYES-NEARY; *"How We*

GABY ROSLIN and JONATHAN WRATHER

Met"Couples (on Video): Richard ALLEMAN, Stephen LESTER; John STERLAND, Anita WRIGHT; Liza ROSS, Peter BANKS; Pat STARR, Hugh FUTCHER; Chuck JULIAN, Michelle FINE; Vincent MARZELLO, Kate BESWICK; Maxine HOWE, Johnny MYERS; Michael J REYNOLDS, Valerie COLGAN; Don FELLOWS, Patricia LEVENTON; Richie PITTS, Joan HOOLEY. *Director:* Simon COX; *Set & Costumke Design:* Gemma FRIPP; *Lighting Design:* Tina McHUGH; *Sound Design:* Tom LISHMAN; *Video Artist:* Gabi COWBURN; *Music:* Ben CULLUN, Jamie CULLUM; *Company Stage Manager / Tour Relighting:* David NORRIS; *Deputy Stage*

Manager: Julie SPROULE; *Assitant Stage Manager:* Lorraine KEARIN; *Sound & AV Operator:* Murray AIRLIE; *Wardrobe Mistress:* Lesley BELFIELD; *Costume Supervisor:* Angie BURNS; *Movement:* Lee LYFORD; *Dialect Coach:* Penny DYER.

63. FOREST OF WILD BOARS; NATIONAL BEIJING OPERA COMPANY OF CHINA; *11 May 2005. Fu An:* WANG Ju; *Gao Shide:* ZHENG Yan; *Lin Shou:* WANG Baoli: *Jin Er:* SONG Yi; *Lin Chong:* YU Kuizi; *Lady Lin:* LI Shengsu; *Lu Qian:* CHEN Guosen; *Monk Lu Zhisen:* YANG Chi; *Gao Qiu:* SUN Guiyuan; *Gao Wang:* LIU Kuikui; *Zang Yong:* SONG Feng; *Dong Chao:* CHEN Zhonggjian; *Xue Ba:* SHEN Jianhua. *Company:* CHEN Zhonggjian; GUO Yaoyao, HUANG Xinqing, PAN Yuejiao, SHEN Jinhlin, SONG Feng, SONG Feng, SUN Ke, TAN Yuyang, TUO Zhinguo, WANG Fang, WANG Haoqiang, , WANG Libo, WU Shulin, WU Zhi, XU Teng, YU Zuojung, ZHANG Jing, ZHANG Yi; *MUSICIANS: Qin:* ZHAO Jianhua, LI Yiping, ZHANG Shunxiang; *Drums:* SU Guangzhong, ZHAO Qi; *Erhu:* WANG Yingkui; *Yueqin:* CUI Yukun; *Sanxian:* GAO Xia; *Middle Ruan:* PIE Jie; *Lang Ruan:* ZHAO Xiaoping; *Large Gongs:* YE Tiesen; *Cymbals:* HUO Jianhua. *Artistic Director:* ZHENG Yan; *Tour Director:* LIU Xiaohua; *Tour Vice-Director:* YU Kuizhi; *Surtitle Translation:* Kathy HALL; *Technical Staff:* ZHANG Qingzhu, WEI Yinsheng, JIANG Lianqi, ZHANG Wanqing, QIN Ying, QIN Ying, MA Zhibin; *Company Manager:* LIU Shangya.

62. LEGEND OF THE WHITE SNAKE; NATIONAL BEIJING OPERA COMPANY OF CHINA; *12 & 14 May 2005 Bai Suzhen:* LI Shengsu; *Xu Xian:* ZHANG Wei; *Xiao Qing:* HUANG Hua; *Fa Hai:* YANG Yanyi; *Boat Man:* ZHENG Yan; *Deer Boy:* LI Lei; *Crane Boy:* SUN Liang; *Monk:* LIU Kuikui; *Little Monk:* CHEN Guosen; *Dragon God:* SUN Guiyan; *Company:* CHEN Zhonggjian; GUO Yaoyao, HUANG Xinqing, PAN Yuejiao, SHEN Jinhlin, SONG Feng, SONG Yi, SUN Ke, TAN Yuyang, TUO Zhinguo, WANG Baoli, WANG Fang, WANG Haoqiang, WANG Jue, WANG Libo, WU Shulin, WU Zhi, XU Teng, YU Zuojung, ZHANG Jing, ZHANG Yi; *MUSICIANS: Qin:* ZHAO Jianhua, LI Yiping, ZHANG Shunxiang; *Drums:* SU Guangzhong, ZHAO Qi; *Erhu:* WANG Yingkui; *Yueqin:* CUI Yukun; *Sanxian:* GAO Xia; *Middle Ruan:* PIE Jie; *Lang Ruan:* ZHAO Xiaoping; *Large Gongs:* YE Tiesen; *Cymbals:* HUO Jianhua; *Artistic Director:* ZHENG Yan; *Tour Director:* LIU Xiaohua; *Tour Vice-*

Director: YU Kuizhi; *Surtitles Translation:* Marnix WELLS; *Technical Staff:* ZHANG Qingzhu, WEI Yinsheng, JIANG Lianqi, ZHANG Wanqing, QIN Ying, QIN Ying, MA Zhibin; *Company Manager:* LIU Shangya. **Journal:** 18/1/05

64. AT THE CROSS ROADS; NATIONAL BEIJING OPERA COMPANY OF CHINA; *13 May 2005. Ren Tanghui:* LI Lei; *Innkeeper:*WU Zhi; *Jiao Zan:* CHEN Zhongjian; *Innkeeper's Wife:* HUANG Hua; *Company:* CHEN Zhonggjian; GUO Yaoyao, HUANG Xinqing, PAN Yuejiao, SHEN Jinhlin, SONG Feng, SONG Yi, SUN Ke, TAN Yuyang, TUO Zhinguo, WANG Baoli, WANG Fang, WANG Haoqiang, WANG Jue, WANG Libo, WU Shulin, WU Zhi, XU Teng, YU Zuojung, ZHANG Jing, ZHANG Yi; *MUSICIANS: Qin:* ZHAO Jianhua, LI Yiping, ZHANG Shunxiang; *Drums:* SU Guangzhong, ZHAO Qi; *Erhu:* WANG Yingkui; *Yueqin:* CUI Yukun; *Sanxian:* GAO Xia; *Middle Ruan:* PIE Jie; *Lang Ruan:* ZHAO Xiaoping; *Large Gongs:* YE Tiesen; *Cymbals:* HUO Jianhua; *Artistic Director:* ZHENG Yan; *Tour Director:* LIU Xiaohua; *Tour Vice-Director:* YU Kuizhi; *Surtitles Translator:* Marnix WELLS; *Technical Staff:* ZHANG Qingzhu, WEI Yinsheng, JIANG Lianqi, ZHANG Wanqing, QIN Ying, QIN Ying, MA Zhibin; *Company Manager:* LIU Shangya.

65. SUICIDE WITH A GOLDEN BRICK; NATIONAL BEIJING OPERA COMPANY OF CHINA; *13 May 2005. Guo Rong:* CHEN Zhonggjian; *Yao Gang:* LIU Kuikui; *Yao Qi:* YANG Yanyi; *The Grand Eunuch:* CHEN Guosen; *Liu Xiu:* YU Kuizhi; *Guo Fei:* GUAN Bo; *Deng Yu:*WANG Baoli; *General Ma Wu:* YANG Chi; *Company:* CHEN Zhonggjian; GUO Yaoyao, HUANG Xinqing, PAN Yuejiao, SHEN Jinhlin, SONG Feng, SONG Yi, SUN Ke, TAN Yuyang, TUO Zhinguo, WANG Baoli, WANG Fang, WANG Haoqiang, WANG Jue, WANG Libo, WU Shulin, WU Zhi, XU Teng, YU Zuojung, ZHANG Jing, ZHANG Yi; *MUSICIANS: Qin:* ZHAO Jianhua, LI Yiping, ZHANG Shunxiang; *Drums:* SU Guangzhong, ZHAO Qi; *Erhu:* WANG Yingkui; *Yueqin:* CUI Yukun; *Sanxian:* GAO Xia; *Middle Ruan:* PIE Jie; *Lang Ruan:* ZHAO Xiaoping; *Large Gongs:* YE Tiesen; *Cymbals:* HUO Jianhua; *Artistic Director:* ZHENG Yan; *Tour Director:* LIU Xiaohua; *Tour Vice-Director:* YU Kuizhi; *Surtitles Translator:* Marnix WELLS; *Technical Staff:* ZHANG Qingzhu, WEI Yinsheng, JIANG Lianqi, ZHANG Wanqing, QIN Ying, QIN Ying, MA Zhibin; *Company Manager:* LIU Shangya.

559. AN INSPECTOR CALLS by J B Priestley; NATIONAL THEATRE; *17 –21 May 2005. Cast:* Nick BARBER, Nicholas DAY, Sandra DUNCAN, Mark HEALY, Katie McGUINNESS, David ROPER, Elizabeth ROSS. *Director:* Stephen DALDRY; *Design:* Ian McNEIL; *Lighting:* Rick FISHER; *Music:* Stephen WARBECK; *Associate Director:* Julian WEBBER.

595. THE END OF THE MOON; LAURIE ANDERSON; *24 May 2005.*

560. MIDNIGHT by Jacqueline Wilson, adapted by Vicky Ireland; WATERSHED PRODUCTIONS; *1-5 June 2005. Violet:* Sarah O'LEARY; *Will:* James CAMILLERI; *Mum:* Lynn ARMITAGE; *Dad:* Joe CUSHLEY; *Jasmine:* Rebecca SANTOS; *Jonathan:* Steve DINEEN; *Other Parts:* Rosie ARMSTRONG, Alex Scott FAIRLEY, Samantha NIGHTINGALE. *Director:* Vicky IRELAND; *Designer:* Gemma FRIPP; *Lighting Designer:* Richard G JONES; *Original Music:* Steven MARKWICK; *Puppet-Maker / Adviser:* Lee THREADGOLD; *Choreographer:* Ben REDFERN; *Sound:* Lee QUINN; *Production Manager / Company Stage Manager:*Peter Grant WILLIAMS; *Deputy Stage Manager:* Janette OWEN; *Wardrobe Supervisor:* Angie BURNS; Alex Scott FAIRLEY, Samantha NIGHTINGALE; *Set Building:*

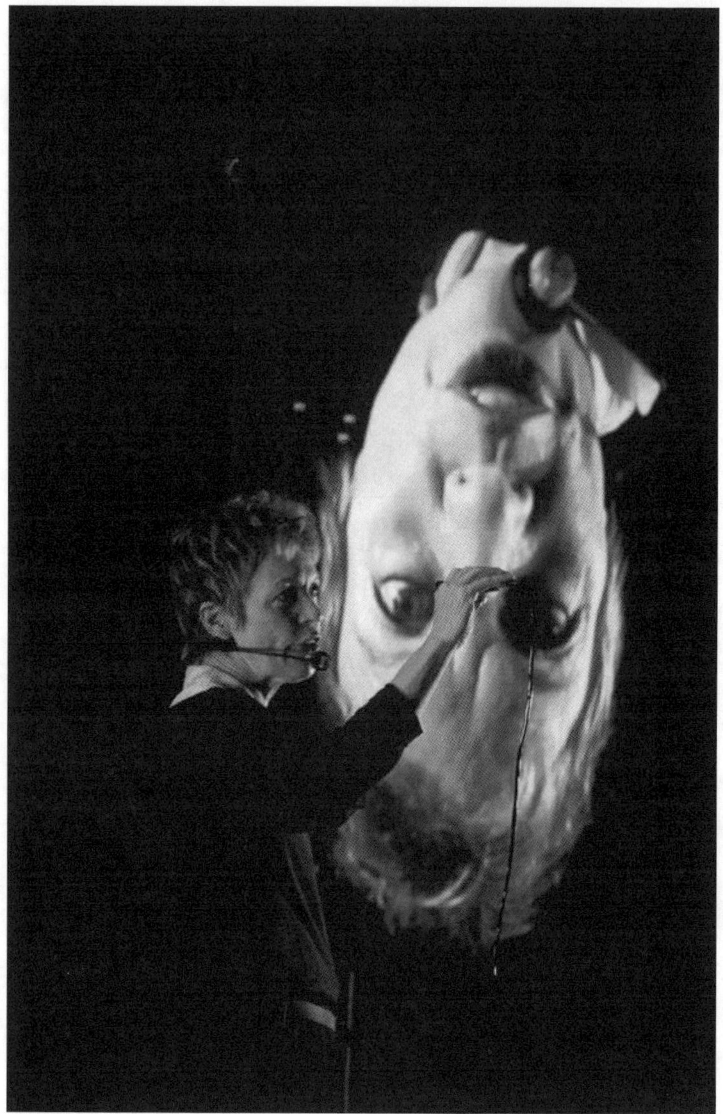

THE END OF THE MOON (595)

MIDNIGHT(560); It might seem a normal family breakfast: *Violet:* Sarah O'LEARY (under Witches arm); *Will:* James CAMILLERI; *Dad:* Joe CUSHLEY and *Mum:* Lynn ARMITAGE; Watershed productions use puppetry to show what other influences may be present.

Johnson Pullen Ltd; *Gauze Painting:* Rod HOLT; *Props Making:* Paula HOPKINS; *Additional Costumes:* Sharon ROGERS; *Sound Programming:* Kevin JAMES.

561. **THE JUNGLE BOOK** by Rudyard Kipling; BIRMINGHAM STAGE COMPANY; *30 August – 3 September 2005. Movement Director:* Peter ELLIOT.

Quays Theatre

562. **DIAL M FOR MURDER** by Frederick Knott; MIDDLE GROUND THEATRE COMPANY; *6-11 September 2004. Tony:* Stephen PINDER; *Sheila:* Joy BROOK; *Max:* Richard GRIEVE; *Lesgate:* Richard WALSH; *Inspector Hubbard:* Michael LUNNEY. *Director / Designer:* Michael LUNNEY.

563. **TWELFTH NIGHT** by William Shakespeare; ENGLISH TOURING THEATRE; *28 September – 2 October 2004. Orsino:* Dugall BRUCE-LOCKHART; *Curio:* Geoffrey LUMB; *Valentine:* Edmund KINGSLEY; *Viola:* Georgina RICH; *Toby Belch:* Michael CRONIN; *Maria:* Susan BROWN; *Andrew Aguecheek:*

Geoffrey BEEVERS; *Feste:* Alan WILLIAMS; *Olivia:* Catherine WALKER; *Malvolio:* Des McALEER; *Antonio:* Patrick DRURY; *Sebastian:* Gareth DAVID-LLOYD; *Fabian:* Robert LISTER. *Director:* Stephen UNWIN; *Set Designer:* Becs ANDREWS; *Costume Designer:* Mark BOUMAN; *Lighting Designer:* Bruno POET; *Original Music:* Olly FOX; *Fight Director:* Terry KING; *Associate Lighting Designer:* Emma CHAPMAN; *Assistant Director:* Bijan SHEIBANI; *Assistant Costume Designer:* Mia FLODQUIST; *Head of Production:* Simon CURTIS; *Technical Manager:* Rupert Barth von WEHRENALP; *Company Stage Manager:* Fiona GREENHILL; *Deputy Stage Manager:* Claire CASBURN; *Assistant Stage Manager:* Maxine FOO; *Technical Stage Manager:* Andy STUBBS; *Tour Technician:* Emily OLIVER; *Wardrobe / Wig Manager:*Susannah THRUSH; *WardrobeAssistant:* Senaria RAOUF; *Props Buyer:* Charlie CRIDLAN; *Technical Placement:* Andy FUREY; *Set Building / Painting:* Rupert BLAKELY; *Costume Maker:* Paddy DICKIE; *Wigs / Hair Design:* Joanna TAYLOR

564. HANNAH AND HANNA by John Retallack; UK ARTS PRODUCTIONS; *4-6 October 2004. Director* John RETALLACK.

565. RICHARD III by William Shakespeare; KAOS THEATRE; *11-13 October 2004. Clarence / King Edward / Buckingham / Richmond:* Jack CORCORAN; *Anne / Margaret / Duchess / Catesby:* Phoebe SOTERIADES; *Richard III:* Ralf HIGGINS; *Hastings / Queen Elizabeth / Tyrrel / Stanley:* Sarah THOM; *Voices of Young Prices In The Tower:* Michael HAHN, Philip CHOWN. *Director / Video / Graphic Design.:* Xavier LERET; *Design:* Fred MELLER; *Costume Design:* Julia PASCOE; *Original Music / Soundscapes:* Jules BUSHELL; *Lighting Design:* Peter HIGTON; *Company Stage Manager:* Sam RENDELL.

566-585: SHAKESPEARE SCHOOLS FESTIVAL;

using the half-hour versions of the text developed by CHANNEL 4 WALES.

566. ROMEO AND JULIET by William Shakespeare; BLESSED THOMAS HOLFORD SCHOOL; *18 October 2004. Romeo:* Connor TUATARA; *Juliet:* Chloe HILL; *Narrator:* Dale GERRARD; *Tybalt:* Joel KELLY; *Benvolio:* Daniel RIDD; *Mercutio:* Daryl HOSKER; *Lord Capulet:* Max DURKIN; *Lady Capulet:* Emily WRAY; *Nurse:* Kelly MORRIS; *Friar:* John Jo MURPHY; *Friar John:*

Sean DWYER; *Servant:* Vicki LEE; *Capulets:* Ana JONES, Faye COOK, Hannah ROFF; *Montague:* Callum MAUDSLEY, Kristi MONAHAN. *Directors:* Cecilia C WALKER, Gerard MURTAGH

567. MACBETH by William Shakespeare; STOCKPORT SCHOOL; *18 October 2004. MacBeth:* James TURNER; *Lady MacBeth:* Claire BARRY; *Duncan:* Zoe THOMAS; *Banquo:* Daniel STOKER; *MacDuff:* Morgan HOUGH; *Witches:* Ashleigh COLLINS, Jordaine HOUGH, Helen BASHAN; *Ross:* Gabrielle WALTON; *Lennox:* Sarah COOMER; *Malcolm:* Scott BROOKES; *Donalbain:* Natalie SOWTER; *Murderer:* Frances MARTLOW; *Apparitions:* Faye WOODFINDEN, Elizabeth EDMONDS, Corina HERRHENTUS; *Noble:* Alexandra HEAVYSIDE; *Narrator:* Roberta WARNE; *Servant / Messenger:* Helen SUNDERLAND; *Stockport Musicians:* Janet COULSON. *Director:* Stephanie GODFREY.

568. TWELFTH NIGHT by William Shakespeare; ST MARY'S CATHOLIC HIGH SCHOOL; *18 October 2004: Narrator / Captain / Officer:* Emma JARDINE; *Duke Orsino:* Christopher BELCHER; *Sir Toby Belch:* Mitchell LLOYD; *Viola:* Amy NEWTON; *Olivia:* Claire GEOGHEGAN; *Maria:* Natalie FIRTH; *Malvolio:* Paul COFFEY; *Feste:* Franchesca BALCHIN; *Sir Andrew Aguecheek:* Joshua HAMPSON; *Sebastian:* Thomas SULLIVAN; *Antonio:* David SAMMON; *Priest:* Robert McLOUGHLIN; *Chorus:* Emma COSTELLO, Kellie TAYLOR, Suzanne SMITH, Rachel OGDEN, Rebecca WORRALL, Samuel LLOYD, Mary DDOTSON, Chelsea PARR, Sarah DOOTSON, Emily MULLERY, Claire WELCH. *Director:* Catherine DOHERTY; *Assistant Director:* Esther HUDSON

569. A MIDSUMMER NIGHT'S DREAM by William Shakespeare; ABRAHAM MOSS HIGH SCHOOL; *18 October 2004. Theseus:* Tom O'KEEFE; *Hippolyta:* Vicki CHADDERTON; *Egeus:* Arfan AZAM; *Hermia:* Samaia SALEEM; *Lysander:* Jamie WALSH; *Demetrius:* Alshafia RAHMAN; *Helena:* Javaira AHMED; *Peter Quince:* Kandeel AKSA; *Nick Bottom:* Bilal HUSSEIN; *Francis Flute:* Yusef AHMED; *Robin Starveling:* Mariam ISLAM; *Oberon:* Abdullah AFZAL; *Titania:* Tessa HEATHCOTE; *Puck:* Tobi ALABI, Demilade AWORINDE; *Chief Fairy:* Danielle MALEY; *Fairy:* Juanita STERLING, Naiyab HUSSAIN, Farah PATHAN, Nehal EZWAM; *Changeling Boy:* Jawad ZAFAR.

Directors: Natalie GRIFFITHS, Jo BELL.

570. A MIDSUMMER NIGHT'S DREAM by William Shakespeare; CHORLTON HIGH SCHOOL; *19 October 2004.*

571. THE TAMING OF THE SHREW by William Shakespeare; CHEADLE HULME SENIOR SCHOOL; *19 October 2004.*

572. THE TEMPEST by William Shakespeare; REDDISH VALE TECHNOLOGY COLLEGE; *19)ctober 2004.*

573. RICHARD III by William Shakespeare; BURNAGE HIGH SCHOOL FOR BOYS; *19 October 2004.*

574. A MIDSUMMER NIGHT'S DREAM by William Shakespeare; ST BEDE'S COLLEGE; *20 October 2004.*

575. AS YOU LIKE IT by William Shakespeare; WALKDEN HIGH SCHOOL; *20 October 2004.*

576. THE TEMPEST by William Shakespeare; EGERTON PARK ARTS COLLEGE; *20 October 2004.*

577. MACBETH by William Shakespeare; HARRYTOWN CATHOLIC HIGH SCHOOL; *20 October 2004.*

578. MACBETH by William Shakespeare; ALL HALLOWS RC HIGH SCHOOL; *21 October 2004.*

579. A MIDSUMMER NIGHT'S DREAM by William Shakespeare; CHEADLE HULME COLLEGE; *21 October 2004*

580. TWELFTH NIGHT by William Shakespeare; POYNTON HIGH SCHOOL & PERFOMING ARTS COLLEGE; *21 October 2004.*

581. THE TEMPEST by William Shakespeare; SWINTON HIGH SCHOOL; *21 October 2004.*

582. THE TEMPEST by William Shakespeare; HOPE HIGH SCHOOL; *22 October 2004.*

583. TWELFTH NIGHT by William Shakespeare; PARK DEAN SCHOOL; *22 October 2004.*

584. A MIDSUMMER NIGHT'S DREAM by William Shakespeare; STOCKPORT GRAMMAR SCHOOL; *22 October 2004.*

585. OTHELLO by William Shakespeare; KASKENMOOR SCHOOL; *22 October 2004.*

586. GIRLS NIGHT; GOODNIGHTS ENTERTAINMENTS by Louise Roche; *23 October 2995.*

587. TEECHERS by John Godber; HULL TRUCK THEATRE COMPANY; *25-30 October 2004. Director:* John Godber.

588. THE BELLS by Leopold Lewis, adapted by Deborah McAndrew; NORTHERN BROADSIDES; *10-13 October 2004. Hans:* Jason FURNIVAL; *Catherine:* Sarah PARKS; *Sozel:* Zoe LAMBERT; *Annette:* Catherine KINSELLA; *Father Walter:* Gerard McDERMOTT; *Christian:* Adam SUTHERLAND; *Mathias:* Sean O'CALLAGHAN; *Dr Zimmer:* Phil CORBITT; *Notary:* Dennis CONLON; *Mesmerist:* Andrew WHITEHEAD. *BAND: Percussion:* Roger BURNETT, Dennis CONLON; *Cliarinet / Guitar:* Phil CORBITT; *Guitar:* Jason FURNIVAL; *Accordion:* Zoe LAMBERT; *Trumpet:* Adam SUNDERLAND; *Violin:* Andrew WHITEHEAD. *Director / Composer:* Conrad NELSON; *Assistant Musical Director:* Andrew WHITEHEAD; *Designer:* Jessica WORRALL; *movement Advisor:* Amit LAHAV; *Company Manager:* Kay PACKWOOD; *Lighrting / Technical Manager:* Antony WILCOCK; *Deputy Stage Manager:* Helen O'REILLY; *Wardrobe:* Hannah CLARK, Susannah THRUSH; *Wind Machine:* Roger BURNETT; *Magic:* Tom SILBURN

589. RUNNING AWAY WITH THE HAIRDRESSER; EARTHFALL; *23 November 2004.*Jessica COHEN, Jim ENNIS

RANJIT KRISHNAMMA, GARY PILLAI, CHRIS NAYAK

590. A PASSAGE TO INDIA by E M Forster, adapted by Martin Sherman; SHARED EXPERIENCE; NOTTINGHAM PLAYHOUSE; *30 November – 4 December 2004. Dr Azix:* Alex CAAN; *Turton / McBryde:*

Maxwell HUTCHEON; *Godbole:* Antony BUNSEE; *Hamidullah:* Ranjit KRISHNAMMA; *Miss Derek / Mrs Turton:* Rina MAHONEY; *Mrs Moore:* Susan TRACY; *Fielding:* William OSBORNE; *Rafi / Das:* Chris NAYAK; *Mahmoud Ali:* Gary PILLAU; *Ronny / Ralph:* Simon SCARDIFIELD; *Adela Quested:* Fenella WOOLGAR. *Musicians:* CHANDRU, SIRISHKUMAR. *Director:* Nancy MECKLER; *Designer:* Niki TURNER; *Composer* Peter SALEM; *Company Movement:* Liz RANKEN; *Lighting:* Chris DAVEY; *Indian Dance:*Sowmya GOPALAN; *Indian Music Advisors:* CHANDRU, SIRISHKUMAR, Ambika JOIS; *Assistant Director:* Aoife SMITH; *Production Manager:* Alison RITCHIE; *Company Stage Manager:* Annabel INGRAM; *Deputy Stage Manager:* Charlotte E PADGHAM; *Sound Operator:* David McSEVENEY; *Costume Supervisor:* Yvonne MILNES; *Tour Lighting:* Jonathan CLARK; *Wardrobe Master:* Stuart PEARSON.

591. ROUND THE HORNE – REVISITED; CHRISTMAS SPECIAL; adapted by Brian Cooke from the Radio Scripts by Barry Took, Marty Feldman, Brian Cooke and Johnny Mortimer; DAVID PUGH; *7-23 December 2004. KennethHorne:* Stephen CRITCHLOW; *Kenneth Williams:* Paul RYAN; *Hugh Paddick:* Jonathan MOORE; *Betty Marsden:* Sherry BAINES; *Douglas Smith:* Stephen BOSWELL. *Director:* Michael KINGSBURY.

592. THE HOLLY AND THE IVY by Wynyard Browne; MIDDLE GROUND THEATRE COMPANY; *10-15 January 2005. Revd Martin Gregory:* Tony BRITTON. *Director:* Michael LUNNEY; *Design / Costumes:* Ali GORTON.

593. GIRLS BEHIND by Louise Roche; GOODNIGHTS ENTERTAINMENT; *29 January 2005.*

594. STONES IN HIS POCKETS by Marie Jones; MARK GOUCHER; PAUL ELLIOTT; *10-12 February 2005.*

73. STRICTLY DANDIA by by Sudha Bhuchar and Kristine Landon-Smith; TAMASHA THEATRE COMPANY; LYRIC, HAMMERSMITH; *15-19 February 2005. Prema Datani:* Sudha BHUCHAR; *PreethiDatani:* Karen DAVID; *Roopa Kotecha:* Susan CRUSE; *Raza Khan:* Wayne PERREY; *Shanti Patel:* Charubala CHOKSHI; *Anant Patel:* Prashant KAPOOR; *Shrenek Patet:* Amarjit BASSAN; *Sonya Patel:* Davina HEMLALL; *Bharat Shah/ Keran Datani:* Simon

NAGRA; *Hina Shah:* Ambur KHAN; *Popatlal Shah / Mohan Patel:* Shiv GREWAL; *Pushpa Shah:* Rina FATANIA; *Dinesh Shah:* Divian LADWA; *Jaz:* Rupi LAL. *Director:* Kristine LANDON-SMITH; *Designer:* Sue MAYES; *Choreographer:* Liam Steel; *Deputy Choreographer:* Iain WOODHOUSE; *Lighting Designer:* Chris DAVEY; *Composer:* SHRI (Shrikanth SRIRAM); *Additional Music:* Felix CROSS; *Sound Designer:* Mike FURNESS; *Sound Operator:* Murray AIRLIE; *Dramaturg:* Graham DEVLIN; *Costume Supervisor:* Alison CARTLEDGE; *Production Manager:* Richard EUSTACE; *Company Stage Manager:* Patricia DAVENPORT; *Deputy Stage Manager:* Charlie PARKIN; *Wardrobe Mistress:* Karen MONTGOMERY

50. THE FIREWORK-MAKER'S DAUGHTER by Philip Pullman, adapted for the stage by Stephen Russlell and TOLD BY AN IDIOT; LYRIC HAMMERSMITH; *1 – 5 March 2005. Lila:* Ayesha ANTOINE; *Hungry Pirate / Villager / Lord Parakit:* Tom ESPINER; *Lalchand / Razvani:* Johannes FLASCHBERGER; *Chang / Villager:* Charlie FOLORUNSHO; *Puffenflasch / Elephan Master:* Gregory GUDGEON; *King / Goddess of The Lake / Ghost:* Joanne HOWARTH; *Little Man / Special and Particular Body Guard / Fuse:* Amanda LAWRENCE; *Rambashi:* Lucian MSAMATI; *Hamlet:* Malcolm RIDLEY; *Sparkington / High Priest:* Jason WEBB; *Chulak:* Mo ZAINAL. *Director:* Paul HUNTER; *Composer / Musical Director:* Iain JOHNSTONE; *Designer:* Naomi WILKINSON; *Lighting Designer:* Jon LINSTRUM; *Sound Designer:* Nick MANNING; *Pyrotechnics Designer:* Mike ROBERTS; *Associate Director:* Hayley CARMICHAEL; *Assistant Director:* Rachel MARS; *Company Stage Manager:* Claire BRYAN; *Deputy Stage Manager:* Ali BEALE; *Assistant Stage Managers:* Helen KING, Bella LAGNADO; *Scenic Artwork:* Nigel DAWS. **Journal:** 16/2/05

47. THE PILLOWMAN by Martin McDonagh; NATIONAL THEATRE; *8-12 March 2005. Tupoilski:* Jim NORTON; *Katurian:* Lee INGLEBY; *Ariel:* Ewan STEWART; *Mother:* Victoria PEMBROKE; *Father:* Mike SHERMAN; *Girl:* Bryony HANNAN; *Boy:* Jordan METCALFE; *Michal:* Edward HOGG: *Recorded Music:* Keyboard: *Paul HIGGS; Saw / Hammer Dulcimer:* Simon ALLEN; *Violin / Cimbalom:* Joe TOWNSEND. *Original Director:* John CROWLEY; *Tour Director:* Toby FROW; *Musical Director:* Paul HIGGS; *Designer:* Scott PASK; *Lighting Designer:* Hugh VANSTONE; *Associate Lighting Designer:* Catriona SILVER; *Music:* Paddy CUNNEEN; *Sound Designer:* Paul ARDITTI; *Fight Director:* Terry KING; *Company Voice Work:* Kate GODFREY; *Production Manager:* Karina GILROY; *Company & Stage Manager:* Jane SUFFLING; *Depuity Stage Manager:* Janice HEYES; *Assistant Stage Manager:* Cynthia DUBERRY; *Costume Supervisor:*Froo GAGER; *Assistant Production Manager:* James MANLEY; *Additional Scenic Painting:* Andy GREENFIELD; *Additional Costume Making:* Kevin MATHIAS. **Journal:** 7/3/05

596. ALL OF ME; LEGS ON THE WALL; *17-19 March 2005. Director:* Nigel JAMIESON.

DON WARRINGTON

597. ELMINA'S KITCHEN by Kwame Kwei-Armah; BIRMINGHAM REPERTORY COMPANY; NATIONAL THEATRE; *22 – 26 March 2005. Digger:* Shaun PARKES; *Deli:* Kwame KWEI-ARMAH; *Ashley:* Michael OBIORA; *Baygee:* Oscar JAMES; *Clifton:* Don WARRINGTON; *Anastasia:* Dona CROLL; *Musicians:* Juldeh CAMARA, Atongo ZIMBA. *Director:* Angus JACKSON; *Musical Director:* Rory McFARLANE; *Designer:* Bunny CHRISTIE; *Lighting Designer:* Hartley T A KEMP; *Music Supervisor:* Neil McARTHUR; *Sound Designer:* Neil ALEXANDER; *Incidental Music:* Juldeh CAMARA, Atongo ZIMBA; *Staff Director:* Kate VARNEY; *Assistant Lighting Designer:* Richard WILLIAMSON; *Fight Director:* Terry KING; *Production Manager:* Milorad ZAKULA; *Company Stage Manager:* Graeme BRAIDWOOD; *Deputy Stage*

PUNCH-A-TANTRA (598); This rich collection of ancient Hindu tales was here hung on the peg of Monkey teaching a modern father the value of telling bed-time stories, rather than the original framework of embodying political principles in a form which even some lackadaisical princes could understand.

Manager: Anne BAXTER; *Assistant Stage Manager:* Tamsin PALMER; *Sound Engineer:* Clive MELDRUM; *Production Electrician:* Simon BOND; *Production Carpenter:* Adrian BRADLEY; *Wardrobe on Tour:* Angie HARRISON

598. PUNCH-A-TANTRA, dramatized by Ayeesha Menon; Music by Merlin D'Sousa; DESTIN ASIAN ARTS; *29-30 March 2005. Cast:* Amogh PANT, Anand TIWARI, Digvijay SAVANT

54. A RAISIN IN THE SUN by Lorraine Hansberry; YOUNG VIC; *6 – 9 April 2005. Ruth Younger:* Noma DUMEZWENI; *Travis Younger:* Matthew HODGE, Anton RICE, Aaron SHOSANYA; *Walter Lee Younger:* Lennie JAMES; *Beneather Younger:* Nicole CHARLES; *Lena Younger:* Novella NELSON; *Joseph Asagai:* Javone PRINCE; *George Murchison / Bobo:* Mark THEODORE; *Karl Lindler:* Jim DUNK. *Director:* David LAN; *Design:* Francis O'COMMOR; *Lighting:* Tim MITCHELL; *Sound:* Crispian COVELL; *Choreography:*

COMEDY OF ERRORS (599); Antipholus of Syracuse (ANDREW CRYER) encounters Adriana (ZOE LAMBERT).

Jeanefer JEAN-CHARLES; *Dialect Coach:* Jeannette NELSON; *Projection Technical Manager:* Philip GLADWELL; *Costume Supervisor:* Sara BOWEN; *Original Music:* Richard HAMMARTON; *Associate Director:* Dawn WALTON; *Assistant Director:* Sara POWELL; *Deputy Stage Manager:* Kim LEWIS; *Assistant Stage Manager:* Bella LAGNADO; *Production Sound & Operator / Deputy Technical Manager:* Sarah WELTMAN; *Lighting Programmer / Tour Relights:* Rachel BOWEN; *Wardrobe Manager:* Miriam KINGSLEY; *Production Manager:* Paul RUSSELL; *Company Stage Manager:* Charlotte GEEVES; *Wardrobe Mistress:* Alison POYNTER; *Electrician:* Graham PARKER; *Set Construction:* Paul RUSSELL, James BUXTON, Simeon TACHEV, Richie TARR, Sean MOONEY, Dave DENBY, Adriano AUGUSTINO, Simon PLUMRIDGE; *Technical Apprentice:* Chris BROWN; *Scenic Painters:* Charlotte GAINEY, Tasha SHEPHERD; *Costume Makers:* Judith WARD, Chloe SIM COX. **Journal:** 16/2/05

398. THE COMPLETE WORKS OF WILLIAM SHAKESPEARE (ABRIDGED); THE REDUCED SHAKESPEARE COMPANY; *14-16 April 2005.*

599. **COMEDY OF ERRORS** by William Shakespeare; NORTHERN BRAODSIDES; *19-23 April 2005. Duke Solinus:* Richard STANDING; *Egeon:* Barrie RUTTER; *Antipholus of Syracuse:* Andrew CRYER; *Antipholus of Ephesus:* Conor RYAN; *Dromio of Syracuse:* Conrad NELSON; *Dromio of Ephesus:* Simon Holland ROBERTS; *Merchant:* Max RUBIN; *Adriana:* Zoe LAMBERT; *Luciana:* Claire STOREY; *Angelo:* Guy PARRY; *Luce / Courtesan:* Ruth ALEXANDER-RUBIN; *Dr Pinch:* Andrew VINCENT; *Abbess:* Sarah PARKS. *Director:* Barrie RUTTER; *Composer:* Conrad NELSON; *Designers:* Giuseppe BELLI, Emma BARRINGTON-BINNS; *Company Manager:* Kay PACKWOOD; *Lighting Designer / Technical Manager:* Antony WILCOCK; *Deputy Stage Manager:* Helen O'REILLY; *Musical Assistant Stage Manager:* Roger BURNETT; *Wardrobe Supervisor:* Hannah GIVERTZ.

600. **SWEET WILLIAM** by Alan Plater; NORTHERN BROADSIDES; *21 April 2005. Jack:* Barrie RUTTER; *Nell:* Sarah PARKS; *Simon:* Max RUBIN; *Peter:* Richard STANDING; *Jane:* Claire STOREY; *Mac:* Andrew VINCENT; *Matthew:* Andrew CRYER; *Mark:* Conor RYAN; *Bella:* Ruth ALEXANDER-RUBIN; *Nicholas:* Simon HOLLAND-ROBERTS; *Will:* Conrad NELSON; *Kate:* Zoe LAMBERT; *Thomas:* Guy PARRY; *Ralph:* Gary SKELTON. *Director:* Barrie RUTTER; *Composer:* Conrad NELSON; *Designers:* Giuseppe BELLI, Emma BARRINGTON-BINNS; *Company Manager:* Kay PACKWOOD; *Lighting Designer / Technical Manager:* Antony WILCOCK; *Deputy Stage Manager:* Helen O'REILLY; *Musical Assistant Stage Manager:* Roger BURNETT; *Wardrobe Supervisor:* Hannah GIVERTZ.

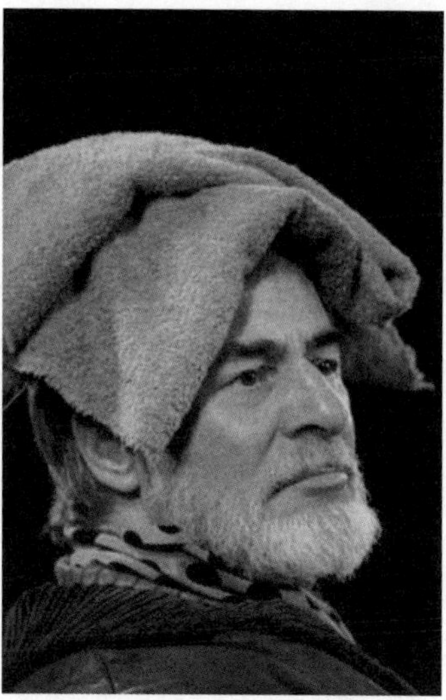

BARRIE RUTTER as Fat Jack; the play was inspired by his telling ALAN PLATER "That could make a play," after the latter remarked that he saw Shakespeare as spending most of his time down the pub with the likes of Falstaff.

Leontes (RICHARD CLOTHIER) kicks off; Hermione (SIMON SCARDIFIELD) on the flor.

601. THE WINTER'S TALE by William Shakespeare; PROPELLOR; *26-30 April 2005/ Polixenes:* Vince LEIGH; *Leontes:* Richard CLOTHIER; *Hermione / Dorcas:* Simon SCARDIFIELD; *Mamilius / Time / Perdita:* Tam WILLIAMS; *Camillo:* Bob BARRETT; *Antigonus / Florizel:* Dugald Bruce LOCKHART; *1st Lord / Mopsa:* Jules WERNER; *Officer / Autolycus:* Tony BELL; *Emilia / Young Shepherd:* James TUCKER; *1st Lady / Cleomenes / Mariner* Alasdair CRAIG; *Paulina:*Adam LEVY; *Dion / Old Shepherd:* Chris MYLES. *Director:* Edward HALL; *Designer:* Michael PAVELKA; *Lighting Designer:* Ben ORMEROD; *Music:* Tony BELL, Dugald Bruce LOCKHART, Jules WERNER, Richard CLOTHIER; *Movement:* Adam LEVY; *Assistant Director:* Adam PENFORD; *Text EditorS:* Edward HALL, Roger WARREN; *Tour Relights:* Mark HOWLAND; *Tour Associate Director:* Heather DAVIES; *Production Manager:* Lawrence T DOYLE;

Assitant Production Manager: Jen SHEPHERD; *Company Stage Manager:* Antony FIELD; *Deputy Stage Manager:* Jenefer TAIT; *Assistant Stage Manager:* Catherine HARPER; *Acting Assistant Stage Managers:* Tim DAISH, Terry O'DONOVAN; *Wardrobe Supervisor:* Carley MARSH; *Set Construction:* Matt STEELE-CHILDE; *Scenic Artist:* Jules FULCHER; *Assistant Carpenter:* Ed GREEN; *Metal Work:* Ray DONCASTER; *Additional Metal Work:* Elena CHILDS;

602. ONCE UPON A TIME IN WIGAN by Mick Martin; URBAN EXPENSION; *4-7 May 2005. Director:* Paul SADOT; *Design:* Guiseppe BELLI, Emma BARRINGTON-BINNS.

THEATRE O's brilliant mime utilises the aperture in the kitchen door to frame an image of the husband undergoing training for space flight.

603. ASTRONAUT – A DOMESTIC ODYSSEY; based on a short story by Andrea Valdes; THEATRE O; *13 May 2005*

604. ME AND MY GIRL; Book and Lyrics by L Arthur Rose and Douglas Furber; Music by Noel Gay; Book REVISED BY Stephen Fry, with contributions by Michael Ockrent; SALFORD MUSICAL THEATRE COMPANY; *17-21 May 2005. Director:* Howard G RAW; *Musical Director:* Karen MASSEY.

605. UNCLE VANYA by Anton Chekhov; MALY DRAMA THEATRE OF ST PETERSBURG; *31 May –4 June 2005. Professor Serebryakov:* Igor IVANOV; *Elena:* Ksenia RAPPOPORT; *Sonya:* Elena KALINA; *Madame Voinitskaya:* Tatiana

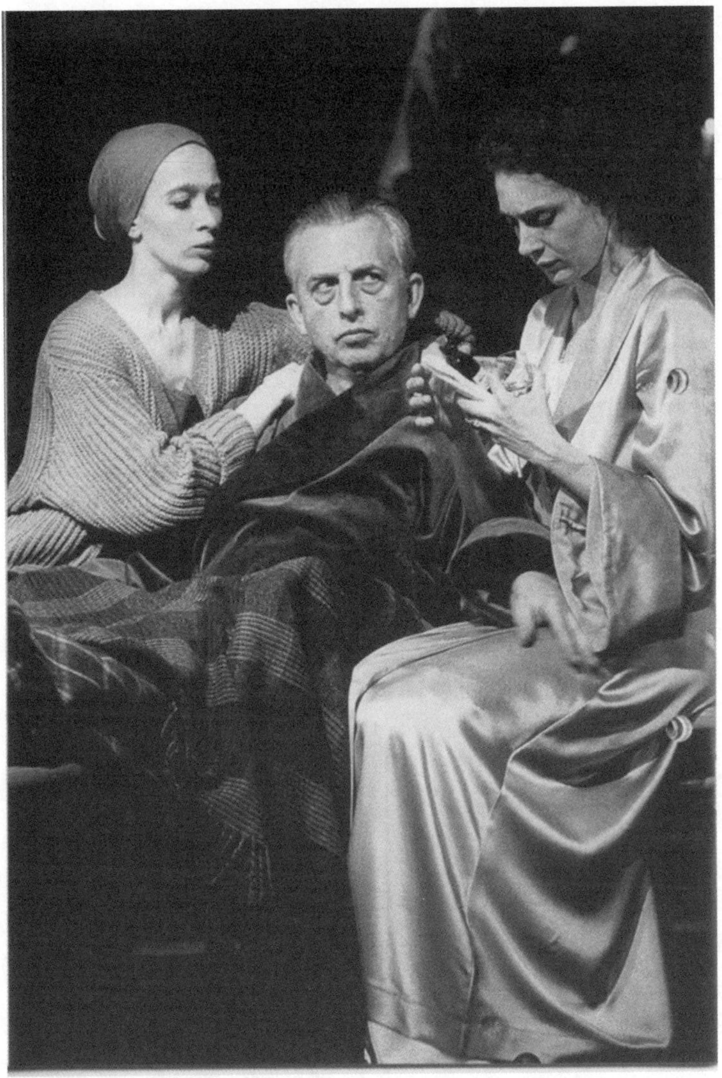

The Professor (IGOR IVANOV) expects his daughter (ELENA KALININA, left) and young second wife (KSENIA RAPPOPORT0, as all others, to entirely dedicate themselves to ministering to him.

SCHUKO; *Vanya:* Sergey KURYSHEV; *Dr Astrov:* Petr SEMAK; *Waffles:* Alexandr ZAVIALOV; *Marina:* Nina SEMENOVA; *Servant:* Vitaly PICHIK. *Director:* LevDODIN; *Set Designer:* David BOROVSKY; *Stage Manager:* Olga DAZIDENKO; *Technical Director:* Vladimir GLADCHENKO; *Set Construction:* Nikolai MURMANOV; *Set Erection Supervisor:* Evgeniy NIKIFOROV; *Lighting:* Ekaterina DOROFEEVA, Vitaliy SKORODUMOV; *Sound:* Vladimir TROYAN; *Props:* Ulia ZVERLINA; *Costumes:* Irina TSVETKOVA, Maria FOMINA; *Make-up:* Galina VARUCHINA; *Props Maker:* Lubov BETECHTINA; *Surtitle Translation:* Fran YORKE

Stoppard's portrait of a lifetime waiting in the wings; here ED BROWNING (on the floor) and, left to right, CHARLIE ROE, LEON TANNER, ROSS WAITON.

606.ROSENCRANTZ AND GUILDENSTREN ARE DEAD by Tom Stoppard; ENGLISH TOURING THEATRE; *14 –18 June 2005. Rosencrantz:* Nicholas

ROWE; *Guildenstern:* James WALLACE; *The Player:* James FAULKNER; *Players:* Ed BROWNING, Grant GILLESPIE, Richard HANSELL, Edmund KINGSLEY, Charlic ROE, Leon TANNER, Ross WALTON. *Director:* Stephen UNWIN; *Set Designer:*Michael VALE; *Costume Designer:* Mark BOUMAN; *Lighting Designer:* Ben ORMEROD; *Original Music:* Olly FOX; *Fight Director:* Terry KING; *Associate Designer:* Charlie CRIDLAN; *Assistant Director:* Katie McALEESE; *Head of Production:* Simon CURTIS; *Technical Manager:* Rupert Barth von WEHRENALP; *Company Stage Manager:*Maria SPON; *Deputy Stage Manager:* Claire CASBURN; *Assistant Stage Manager:* Sarah LYNDON; *Technical Stage Manager:* Andy STUBBS; *Tour Technician:*David MITCHELL; *Sound System Designer:* Dan STEELE; *Audio Descriptiom:* Jonathan NASH, Margaret WICKETTS; *Wardrobe / Wig Manager:*Susannah THRUSH; *WardrobeAssistant:* Senaria RAOUF; *Set Building* Rupert BLAKELY; */ Set Painting:*Mike BECKETT; *Wigs / Hair Design:* Joanna TAYLOR

140. **GOING DUTCH** by John Godber; HULL TRUCK THEATRE COMPANY; *21-26 June 2005.*

607. **ONE NIGHT OF SHAKESPEARE;** BBC SHAKESPEARE SCHOOL FESTIVAL; *3 July 2005.* Simultaneous performances by 400 Schools in 100 Theatres Nationwide.

608. **I SEE NO SHIPS;** The Nelson Projrct – SALFORD MUSIC AND PERFORMING ARTS SERVICE; *4-7 July 2005*

224. **THIS IS HOW IT GOES** by Neil LaBute; DONMAR; *19-23 July 2005. Man:* Ben CHAPLIN; *Woman:* Megan DODDS; *Cody:* Idris ELBA. *Director:* Moises KAUFMAN; *Designer:* Tim HATLEY; *Original Lighting Designer:* Paul PYANT; *Lighting Recreation:* James WHITESIDE; *Sound Designer:* Fergus O'HARE; *Production Manager:* Dominic FRASER; *Company Stage Manager:* Lorna COBBOLD; *Deputy Stage Manager:* Annabel BOLTON; *Assistant Stage Manager:* Vicky BERRY; *Assistant Director:* Christopher ROLLS; *Associate Scenic Designer:* Andrew EDWARDS; *Associate Costume Designer:* Ilona SOMOGYI; *Wardrobe Mistress:* Lisa AITKEN; *Voice & Dialect Coaches:* Julia WILSON-DIXON; Kate GODFREY; *Follow Spot Operator:* Vivienne CLAVERING. **Journal:** 25/5/05

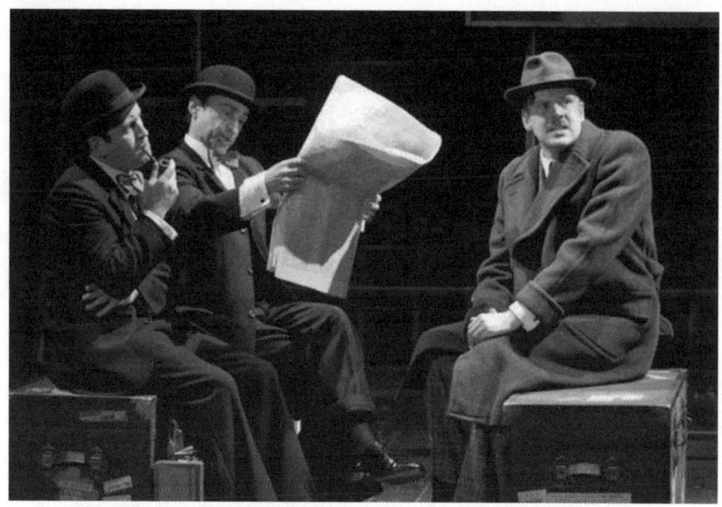

Hannay (ROBERT WHITELOCK) on the train; also travelling: MARK HADFIELD (left) and SIMON GREGSON.

612. THE 39 STEPS by John Buchan, adapted by Simon Corble, Nobby Dimon and Patrick Barlow; FIERY ANGEL; WEST YORKSHIRE PLAYHOUSE; *25 – 30 July 2005.Cast:* Mark HADFIELD, Simon GREGSON, Robert WHITELOCK.

Lowry Studio:

609. FALIRAKI; devised by Paul Roseby and the NATIONAL YOUTH THEATRE; *28-30 October 2004. Carling:* Robbie JARVIS; *Chardonnay:* Crystal CONDIE; *Ditie:* Rebecca CLARKE; *Dawn:* Lizzie PYLE; *The Greek Chorus:* Laura HARDING, Mike DAVIS, Kirsty WOODWARD; *The Lasses:* Eleanor LAWRENCE, Rebecca FLINT, Stacey BLAND, Georgia CHRISTOU, Joanna CASSIDY; *The Lads:* Grant BLACK, Matthew HARRISON, Matthew YOUNG, Gareth JONES, Daniel KIRRANE, Robert OSTLERE, Will PALMER. *Director:* Paul ROSEBY; *Set Designer:* Cath PATER-LANCUCKI; *Costume Designer:* Peter BREEN; *Original Lighting:* Mark DOUBLEDAY; *Reproduction of Lighting:*Aaron McPEAKE; *Script Consultant:* Lucy BRIERS; *Production Manager:* Fred BEAUFORT; *Assistant Director:* Paul CHARLTON; *Stage Management:* James STOREY, Fiona AGAR, Catherine JENNINGS, Daisy GLADSTONE, Lian BRACEWELL; *Lighting / Sound:* Simon FULFORD, Paul GREEN, Miranda HOWARD-

WILLIAMS, Emma St-JOSEPH; *Costume:* Tom ALLEN, Klaudia BACINSTA, Laura BAKER, Kim BURTON, Siofra CAHERTY, Ursula CROCKER, Maya JAUSLIN, Louise JONES, Hollt MORSE, Eleanor MOTTRAM, Sussannah PAL, Louisa THOMAS, Kate WALLIS; *Scenery / Props:* Stephanie ALDEN, Parveen GHIR, Isabel GREENBERG, David HARRIS, Derk IRWIN, Eleanor JACKSON, Kenneth PETRIE, Miranda STENHOUSE, Ruth SUTCLIFFE.

610. ME AND MY MONSTERS by Michael Dalton; POP-UP THEATRE; *22 January 2005.*

611. THREE BILLYGOATS GRUFF; THEATRE OF WIDDERSHINS; *14 February 2005*

328. –THE FISH'S WISHES; LYNGO THEATRE; HALF MOON THEATRE; *5 March 205. Director / Designer:* Marcello CHIARENZA.

614. NATIONAL YOUTH THEATRE SHORTS; *31 March – 2 April 2005, including:* **Roses and Lilies** by Andrew Kaye; *Performers:* Andrew KAYE, Victoria HARGREAVES; *Director:* Ria PARRY; *Assistant Director:* Ben ALDRIDGE; **Skippnig Rope** by David Judge: *Performers:* Joseph APPIAH-DANQUAH, Chris GREEN, Nadine MILNER-EDWARDS, Jasmine QUINLAN, Aman RAKKAR; *Director:* Gbolahan OBISESAN; **Face On The Rye** by Gbolahan Obisesan; *Performers:* Louis BROOKE, Kola GBADAMASI, Mbugah GORO, Chris GREEN, Geu MacBULLEN; *Director:* Gbolahan OBISESAN; **Inspector Dopey** by Graeme Haigh; *Performers:* Christopher ASHMAN, Ben ALDRIDGE, Graeme BRAMWELL, Camilla BURTON-BADDELY, Joe MORRIS, Christpher VINCENT; *Director:* Ria PARRY; *Assistant Director:* Ben ALDRIDGE; **Beans On Toast** by Christopher Langley; *Performers:* Christopher ASHMAN, Ben ALDRIDGE, Graeme BRAMWELL, Camilla BURTON-BADDELY, Andrew KAYE, Joe MORRIS,Christopher VINCENT; *Director:* Ria PARRY; *Assistant Director:* Ben ALDRIDGE. *Writing Course Directors:* Maya CHOWDRY, Ria PARRY; *Development Adviser:* Matthew DUNSTER; *Technical:* Anna ANDERSON, Miranda HOWARD-

WILLIAMS, Jenny ROGERS, Roberto RASKOVSKY; *Designer:* Sid HIGGINS; *Set Painter:* Mike OZOUF; *Lowry Performing Arts Educator:* Jane DaSILVA; *nyt Manchester Project Co-ordinator:* Ria PARRY; *Assistant Company Managers:* Ben ALDRIDGE, Gbolan OBIESAN.

615. CHICKEN LICKEN; DYNAMIC NEW ANIMATION; *9 April 2005*

616. JAZZ MOUSE; *14 May 2005.*

617. DOORMAN by Geoff Thompson; CREWES GALE PRODUCTIONS; *18 –21 May 2005. Tony:* Craig CONWAY. *Director / Designer:* Michael VALE; *Lighting Design:* Tim SKELLY; *Music:* Phela LANE, Steve HOPWOOD; *Producer:* Paul CREWES, accompanied by showing of the film **Bouncer:** Screenplay by Geoff THOMPSON; *Performers:* Ray WINSTONE, Paddy CONSTANTINE; *Director:* Michael Baig CLIFFORD; *Producer:* Natasha CARLISH.

618. FINDERS KEEPERS; CLYDEBUILT PUPPET THEATRE; *4 June 2005.*

619. SHELL CONNECTIONS; plays commissioned by the NATIONAL THEATRE; performed by local Youth Theatres and Schools; *14-18 June 2005*

620. THE SHAPE CHANGER; LEMPEN PUPPET THEATRE COMPANY; *9 July 2005.*

621. PRECIOUS BAZAAR; PHIZZICAL PRODUCTIONS; *14-17 July 2005.*

622. UNDER THE CARPET; WAGGISH RADISH PUPPET THEATRE; *6August 2005.*

Lowry Compass Room

623. **C'EST VAUXHALL;** DUCKIE; *4-14 May 2005*

The Lowry Waterfront

624. **CABARET OF SMILES;** LADYBOYS OF BANGKOK; GANDEY WORLD CLASS PRODUCTIONS; *17 June-30 July 2005.*

LOWRY HIGH SCHOOL; Camp Street M7 1LF; 0161-792 1368; CAZ: 81, H6

LOWRY HOTEL (Forecourt); 97 Chapel Street M3 9DF; **CAZ:** 5, G4

THE MALL; ECCLES M30 0EA; CAZ: 91, H3

MAXWELL HALL THEATRE; Peel Campus, Salford University M5 4WT; **CAZ:** 4, A3

517. **PAST, PRESENT, PRETENCE;** ASPECTS THEATRE COMPANY; *12 May 2005.*

MEMORIAL HALL; Moorside Road, SWINTON M27 0EW; CAZ: 78, D3 G

METHODIST CHURCH HALL; Worsley Road, SWINTON M27 5SF; 0161-794 8266; **CAZ:** 78, D5

542. **THEFT** by Eric Chappell; PRIESTLEY PLAYERS; *27-30 October 2004.*

543. **LOOK, NO HANS!** by John Chapman and Michael Pertwee; PRIESTLEY PLAYERS; *26-29 January 2005.*

544. **THE HAUNTING OF HILL HOUSE** by F Andrew Leslie; PRIESTLEY PLAYERS; *21-24 April 2005.*

MONTON GREEN COUNTY PRIMARY SCHOOL; Monton Green M30 9JO; 0161-707 2287; **CAZ;** 91, F1

MONTON METHODIST CHURCH; Park Road M30 9JJ; 0161-789 1869; CAZ: 91, F1

MOORSIDE HIGH SCHOOL; East Lancashire Road, SWINTON M27 5LX;0161-794 1045 / 1296; CAZ: 78, D4

MOORSIDE PRIMARY SCHOOL; Holdsworth Street, SWINTON M27 0LN; 0161-794B6715; **CAZ:** 78, D4

PEEL GREEN COMMUNITY CENTRE (St Michael's); Liverpool Road, ECCLES M30 7LP; 0161-793 8859; CAZ: 90, C5

PEMBROKE HALL; Victoria Square, WALKDEN M28 3AX; 0161 - 790 4585; CAZ 62, F6

PENDLEBURY (ROYAL MANCHESTER) CHILDREN'S HOSPITAL; Hospital Road M27 4HA; 0161-794 4696; CAZ: 80, A4.

ROBERT POWELL THEATRE; The Allerton Building, University of Salford, Frederick Road Campus M6 6PU; 0161-295 6120 / 3248; **CAZ:** 93: H2

519. **FRANKENSTEIN – THE PANTO** by David Swan; BARTON THEATRE COMPANY; *25-27 November 2004.*

16. ELECTRA by Sophocles, translated by David Gray; ASPECTS THEATRE COMPANY; *18-19 January 2005. Chorus:* Jennifer O'CALLAGHAN, Caroline ANDREW, Natalie SINGH, Christina HENRIKSON, Jessie MACKEY, Kirsten WILLIAMS, Christine MARTIN, Katie MULGREW, Anna PAVLOU; *Clytemnestra:* Rachel FORREST; *Orestes:* Johnny BECK; *Aegisthus:* Chris GELDERD; *Chrysothemis:* Liz MOLLISON; *Electra:* Jo HIGSON; *Pylades:* Nic JAMES. ***Director:*** Collette MURRAY; *Assistant Director:* Caroline ANDREW; *Company Manager:* Alise LISTER. **Journal:** 18/1/05

507. A SNAKE IN THE FRIDGE by Brad Fraser; ASPECTS THEATRE COMPANY; *21-22 January 2005.*

19. HOUSE OF ILLUSIONS (= The Balcony) by Jean Genet; ASPECTS THEATRE COMPANY; *28-29 January 2005. Director:* Tracy CROSSLAND; *Company Manager:* Gordon ISAACS. **Journal:** 18/1/05

508. BANG, BANG, YOU'RE DEAD; ASPECTS THEATRE COMPANY; *3-5 May 2005.*

509. SALIVA MILKSHAKE by Howard Brenton; ASPECTS THEATRE COMPANY; *6-7 May 2005.*

510. THE WOMAN WHO COOKED HER HUSBAND by Debbie Isitt; ASPECTS THEATRE COMPANY; *6-7 May 2005*

511. BAZAAR AND RUMMAGE by Sue Townsend; ASPECTS THEATRE COMPANY; *10-11 May 2005.*

71. LOOT by Joe Orton; ASPECTS THEATRE COMPANY; *13-14 May 2005. McLeavy:* Matthew GANLEY; *HaL:* Adil Mohammed JAVAID; *Fay:* Sarah BURKE; *Dennis:* John GARFIELD-ROBERTS; *Truscott:* Luisa OMIELAN; *Meadows:* Leigh PRICE. *Director:* John GARFIELD-ROBERTS.. **Journal:** 25/4/05.

520. KINDERTRANSPORT by Diane Samuels; BARTON THEATRE COMPANY; *22-25 June 2005.*

SALFORD CATHEDRAL (Forecourt); Chapel Street M3; 0161-834 0333; **CAZ:** 4, D4

SALFORD MUSEUM AND ART GALLERY;

Peel Park M5; 0161-736 2649; CAZ: 4, A4

SALFORD MUSEUM AND ART GALLERY; Peel Park M5; 0161-736 2649; **CAZ:** 4, A4

498. A DIFFERENT PLACE by Robin Graham; AMPERSAND MEDIA, GREENHOUSE NORTHWEST; *25 May 2005.*

SALFORD PLAYHOUSE; Westerham Avenue, Liverpool Street M5 4LG; 0161-736 1556; **CAZ:** 93, G4

SALFORD QUAYS, aboard **M/S Fitzcarraldo;** next to Lowry;. **CAZ:** 93, E6.

ST ANDREW'S CHURCH OF ENGLAND PRIMARY SCHOOL; Barton Lane, ECCLES M30 0FL; 0161-789 4853; **CAZ:** 91, G4

ST GEORGE'S ROMAN CATHOLIC HIGH SCHOOL; Parsonage Drive, LITTLE HULTON M26 3SH; 0161 - 790 4420 / 5156; CAZ: 77, E1

ST GILBERT'S ROMAN CATHOLIC PRIMARY SCHOOL; Campbell Road, ECCLES M30 8LZ; 0161-789 5035; **CAZ:** 79, E5

ST JOHN'S SCHOOL; St John's Road, MOSLEY COMMON M28 1AR; 0161-790 2957; **CAZ:** 76, B4

ST JOSEPH'S PRIMARY SCHOOL; Old Lane, LITTLE HULTON M38 9RU; 0161-790 5278; CAZ: 62, C4

ST LUKE'S PARISH HALL; Derby Road M6 5RA; 0161-737 7034; **CAZ:** 93, E3

ST LUKE'S with ALL SAINTS CE PRIMARY SCHOOL; Eccles New Road M5 2RU; 0161-736 3455

ST MARK'S CHURCH OF ENGLAND PRIMARY SCHOOL; Aviary Road, WORSLEY M28 2WF; 0161-790 3423; **CAZ:** 77, H5

ST PATRICK'S ROMAN CATHOLIC HIGH SCHOOL; Guildford Road ECCLES M30 7JF; 0161-789 1580; **CAZ:** 0161-789 4678

268. **MACBETH** by William Shakespeare; MANCHESTER ACTORS COMPANY; *10 March 2005.*

ST PAUL'S CHURCH OF ENGLAND PRIMARY SCHOOL; Neville Road, KERSAL M7 3PT; 0161 - 792 9474; CAZ: 81, F3

ST PETER AND ST PAUL'S PRESBYTERY; Park Road, MONTON M30 9JQ; 0161-789 4555; **CAZ:** 92, A1.

363. **ON THE LINE** by Mike Lucas and Jim Woodland; Music and Lyric by Jim Woodland; MIKRON THEATRE COMPANY; *3 November 2004.*

ST PETER'S CHURCH OF ENGLAND PRIMARY SCHOOL; Vicarage Road, SWINTON M27 0WA; 0161 - 794 2616; CAZ: 79, E3

ST PHILLIP'S RC PRIMARY SCHOOL; Cavendish Road M7 4WP; 0161-792 4595; CAZ: 81, G2

SEEDLEY PRIMARY SCHOOL; Liverpool Street M6 5GY; 0161-736 3700; **CAZ:** 93, E3

270. FIREBIRD by Stephen Boyes; MANCHESTER ACTORS COMPANY; *24 June 2005.*

SPRINGWOOD SCHOOL; Barton Road, SWINTON M27 5LP; 0161-728 5767**; CAZ:** 79, G5

SWINTON HIGH SCHOOL; Sefton Road M27 6DU; 0161-794 6215; **CAZ:** 79, E2

3. SPARK by Mary Cooper; M6 THEATRE COMPANY; *4 Novemober 2004.*

THEATRE UPSTAIRS; 500 Manchester Road East, LITTLE HULTON M38 9NS; 0161-790 2727; CAZ: 62, C5

UNITED REFORMED CHURCH; 310-312 Worsley Road, SWINTON M27 0EF; 0161-794 1398; **CAZ:** 79, E4

UNIVERSITY HOUSE; off Salford Crescent; **CAZ:** 4, A2

518. THE IMPORTANCE OF BEING EARNEST by Oscar Wilde; ASPECTS THEATRE COMPANY; *12 May 2005.*

WALKDEN HIGH SCHOOL; Birch Road M28 7FJ; 0161-790 4244; **CAZ:** 77, G2

WALKDEN METHODIST COMMUNITY MEMORIAL HALL; M28; 0161-702 8708

540. PUSS IN BOOTS; EDGEFOLD PLAYERS; *24-29 January 2005.*

WENTWORTH HIGH SCHOOL, Wentworth Road, ECCLES M30 6BP; **CAZ;** 91, HI

268. MACBETH by William Shakespeare; MANCHESTER ACTORS COMPANY; *15 February 2005.*

WHARTON COUNTY PRIMARY SCHOOL; Rothwell Lane LITTLE HULTON M38 9XA; **CAZ:** 62, A3

WINDSOR HIGH SCHOOL; Churchill Way M6 6BU; 0161-736 4296 / 4757; CAZ: 93, G3

WORKING CLASS MOVEMENT LIBRARY; 51 The Crescent M5 4NW; 0161-736 3601; **CAZ:** 4, A4

363. **ON THE LINE** by Mike Lucas and Jim Woodland; Music and Lyric by Jim Woodland; MIKRON THEATRE COMPANY; *31 October 2004.*

WORSLEY COURT HOUSE; 0161 - 794 5760

WORSLEY OLD HALL; Walkden Road M28 2NH; 0161 - 799 5015; CAZ 77, G4

STOCKPORT

42ND STREET (604); Peggy Sawyer (JENNIFER TAYLOR, nominee for Best All-Round Performance in the Manchester Musical Awards) gets a crash course from Julian Marsh (ANDREW SUMMERS)

ALL SAINTS PRIMARY SCHOOL; Brickbridge Road, MARPLE SK6 7BQ; 0161-427 3008; **CAZ:** 143, E6

AQUINAS SIXTH FORM COLLEGE; Nangreave Road SK2 6TH; 0161-483 3237; CAZ: 140, A5

AVONDALE HIGH SCHOOL; Heathbank Building, Heathbank Road, CHEADLE HEATH SK8 6HT ; 0161-477 2382; CAZ: 150, C5

BANKS LANE INFANT SCHOOL; Hulme Street, Hempshaw Lane, OFFERTON SK1 4PR; 0161-480 9252; **CAZ:** 140, B3

270. **FIREBIRD** by Stephen Boyes; MANCHESTER ACTORS COMPANY; *20 July 2005.*

BRAMALL HALL; Hall Road SK7 3NX; 0161-485 3708; **CAZ:** 151, F4

BRAMALL HIGH SCHOOL; Seal Road SK7 2JT; 0161-439 8045; **CAZ:** 151, H5

BREDBURY GREEN PRIMARY SCHOOL; Clapgate, ROMILEY SK6 3DG; 0161-430 3078; **CAZ:** 141, F2

BROOKDALE SOCIAL CLUB; Bridge Lane, BRAMALL SK7 3AB; 0161-439 2782; **CAZ:** 151, H4

613. **THE SUNSHINE BOYS;** Neil Simon; BROOKDALE THEATRE; *13-16 October 2004.*

625. **HONK!** Music by George Stiles; Book and Lyrics by Anthony Drewe; BROOKDALE THEATRE; *29 November – 4 December 2004.*

626. **KINDLY LEAVE THE STAGE** by Eric Chapman; BROOKDALE THEATRE; *26-29 January 2005*

627. **ARSENIC AND OLD LACE** by Joseph Kesselring; BROOKDALE THEATRE; *9-12 March 2005.*

628. **THE BOY FRIEND** by Sandy Wilson; BROOKDALE THEATRE; *25-30 April 2005.*

BROOKHEAD PRIMARY SCHOOL; Councillor Lane, CHEADLE SK8 2LE; 0161 - 428 6286; **CAZ:** 138, C6

BRUNTWOOD PRIMARY SCHOOL; Conway Road, CHEADLE HULME SK8 6DB; 0161-485 2101; **CAZ:** 150, A3

CARVER THEATRE; Church Lane, MARPLE SK6 7AW; **CAZ:** 134, D6.

CHADKIRK CHAPEL; off A627; CAZ: 141, A3

CHADS THEATRE; Mellor Road, CHEADLE HULME SK8 5AU; 0161-486 1788; **CAZ:** 150, D4

649. **ONE FOR THE ROAD** by Willy Russell; CHADS; *4-11 September 2004.*

629. **STRANGERS ON A TRAIN** by Craig Warne, adapted from the novel by Patricia Highsmith; CHADS; *16-23 October 2004*

630. **THE RAILWAY CHILDREN** by Dave Simpson, adapted from the novel by E Nesbit; CHADS; *4-11 December 2004.*

631. **BREAKING THE SILENCE** by Stephen Poliakoff; CHADS; *29 January – 5 February 2005.*

632. **THERESE RAQUIN** by Leslie Sands, adapted from the novel by Emile Zola; CHADS; *12-19 March 2005.*

633. **PROOF** by David Auburd; CHADS; *4-11 June 2005.*

CHEADLE HULME CAMPUS, RIDGE DANYERS COLLEGE; Cheadle Road SK8 6BB; 0161-485 4372; CAZ: 150, B2

CHEADLE HULME METHODIST CHURCH; Ramillies Avenue SK8 7AL; 0161 - 485 1606; CAZ: 150, D4

CHEADLE HULME SCHOOL; Claremont Road SK8 6EG; 0161-485 7201; CAZ: 150, C5

CHRIST CHURCH GREEN; Lillian Grove, REDDISH SK5 6EQ; 0161-480 8147

DEANERY SQUARE SK1 1PP; CAZ: 139, G2

DIAL PARK PRIMARY SCHOOL; Blackstone Road, OFFERTON SK2 5NE; 0161-483 9554; CAZ: 152, D1

DIALSTONE YOUTH CENTRE; Lisburn Lane, OFFERTON SK2 7LJ; 0161-474 2241; CAZ: 140, D5

FAIRWAY PRIMARY SCHOOL; OFFERTON SK2 5DR; 0161-483 1873; CAZ: 141, E3

FIR TREE PRIMARY SCHOOL; Browning Road, NORTH REDDISH SK5 6JN; 0161-432 2423; CAZ: 111, G5

GARRICK THEATRE, Exchange Street, Wellington Road South, STOCKPORT SK3 0EJ; 0161-480 5866. **CAZ:** 139, G2

GREAT MOOR JUNIOR SCHOOL; Southwood Road SK2 7DG; 0161-483 4987; **CAZ:** 152, B1

269. PINOCCHIO by Stephen Boyes, based on the original story by

Carlo Collodi; MANCHESTER ACTORS COMPANY; *11 March 2005.*

HATHERLOW UNITED REFORMED CHURCH; ROMILEY SK6 3DR; CAZ: 141, G1

HAZEL GROVE JUNIOR SCHOOL; Chapel Street SK7 4HJ; 0161-483 3699; **CAZ:** 153, E2

HAZEL GROVE YOUTH CENTRE; Jacksons Lane SK7 5JY; 0161-483 9895; CAZ: 152, C4

HEALD GREEN THEATRE; Motcombe Grove SK8 3TL; 0161 - 437 3383; **CAZ:** 149, E2

634. **NOISES OFF** by Michael Frayn; HEALD GREEN THEATRE COMPANY; *18-25 September 2004.*

635. **AND THEN THERE WERE NONE** by Agatha Christie; HEALD GREEN THEATRE COMPANY; *6-13 November 2005*

636. **THERE GOES THE BRIDE** by Ray Cooney and John Chapman; HEALD GREEN THEATRE COMPANY; *8-15 January 2005.*

637. **HAY FEVER** by Noel Coward; HEALD GREEN THEATRE COMPANY; *26 February –5 March 2005.*

638. **I'LL BE BACK BEFORE MIDNIGHT** by Peter Colley; HEALD GREEN THEATRE COMPANY; *4- 11 June2005.*

HEATON MOOR METHODIST CHURCH; Mauldeth Road SK4 3NG; 0161-431 0262; CAZ: 138, B1

HEATON NORRIS PARK; Wellington Road North. CAZ: 139, G1

HEATONS UNITED REFORMED CHURCH; Heaton Moor Road SK4 4LB; 01625 585562; **CAZ:** 126, D5

HIGH LANE PRIMARY SCHOOL; Fairacres Road SK6 8JQ; 01663 762378; CAZ: 154, D5

KINGSWAY HIGH SCHOOL; Foxland Road, GATLEY SK8 4QA;0161-428 7706; **CAZ:** 149, G1

3. SPARK by Mary Cooper; M6 THEATRE COMPANY; *16 November 2004.*

MARPLE HALL HIGH SCHOOL; Hill Top Drive SK6 6JZ; 0161-427 7966; **CAZ** 142, A4

3. SPARK by Mary Cooper; M6 THEATRE COMPANY; *15 Novemober 2004.*

MARPLE UNITED REFORMED CHURCH; 0161-484 5965

MEMORIAL HALL; 0161- 477 2441

METHODIST CHURCH HALL; Hyde Road, WOODLEY SK6 1QG; CAZ: 129, H4

NORRIS BANK PRIMARY SCHOOL; Green Lane, HEATON NORRIS SK4 2NF; 0161-432 3944; CAZ: 126, D6

OFFERTON HIGH SCHOOL; The Fairway SK2 5DS; 0161-483 9335; **CAZ**: 141, E3

271. ROMEO AND JULIET by William Shakespeare; MANCHESTER ACTORS COMPANY; *8 November 2004*

OUR LADY'S PRIMARY SCHOOL; Old chapel Street SK3 9HX; 0161-480 5345; **CAZ:** 139, G3

PERFORMANCE CENTRE MARPLE; Ridge Danyers College, Hibbert Lane, MARPLE

SK6 7PA; 0161-484 6700; **CAZ:** 142, C6.

146. GARDEN OF THE HEART by Crystal Stewart; BOOJUM; *19 October 2004.*

THE PLAYHOUSE; Anfield Road, CHEADLE HULME SK8 5EX; 0161-485 1441; **CAZ:** 150, B2

PLAZA; Mersey Square SK1 1SP; 0161 - 477 7779; **CAZ:** 139, G2

640. 42ND STREET; Book by Michael Stewart and Mark Bramble; STOCKPORT OPERATIC SOCIETY; *11-16 October 2004. Dorothy Brock:* Liz KOLODZIEJ; *Julian Marsh:* Andrew SUMMERS; *Peggy Sawyer:* Jennifer TAYLOR; *Billy Lawlor:* Adam McDIARMID; *Maggie Jones:* Nicky MEAD; *Bert Barry:* Ron SUGDEN; *Ann Reilly:* Janice JACKSON; *Phyllis Dale:* Catherine HARRISON; *Lorraine Flemming:* Lucia COLE; *Oscar:* Alan HADFIELD; *Sandy Lee:* Jenny SAVILL; *Pat Denning:* Peter PHILLIPSON; *Abner Dillon:* Roy ELLISON; *Gladys:* Dawn WILDE; *Diane Lorimer:* Hayley-Louise REILLY; *Ethel:* Heather SCASE; *Mac:* Alan MERCER; *Thugs:* Malcolm MOSS, Alan GIBSON; *Dancers:* Naomi ETCHELLS, Colette HOLT, Paige JACKSON, Jemma PRESCOTT, Hayley-Louise REILLY, Heather SCASE, Faith TAYLOR, Claire WARD, Dawn WILD; *Female Chorus:*Carol ACKERS, Anne ADSHEAD, Kay BAILEY, Pauline BROWNE, Kay GLAZIER, Pat HELICON, Claire KEEGAN, Debbie KELLY, Pat MARNEY, Ann OLDFIELD, Jade QUAYLE, Amelie WOODALL; *Male Chorus:* Alan GIBSON, William HAZELL, Bill JENKINS, Terry JORDAN, Malcolm MOSS, Brian PRICE, Ben SWEENEY, Fred WORRALL. *Director:* John HARRISON; *Musical Director:*Claire SWEENEY; *Choreographer:* Shellie-Beth SINCLAIR; *Assistant Choreographer:* Jemma PRESCOTT; *Stage Manager:*John GRAY; *Deputy Stage Manager:* Beryl GRESTY; *Lighting:* Nigel GRIFFITHS; *Sound:* Graham SYKES; *Props Team:* George WOOD, Mary WOOD; *Properties:* Howorth Wrightson Ltd, George WOOD; *Wardrobe Mistress:* Joyce MOSS; *Costume supply:* Perceptions Theatre Costumes Ltd;; *Make-up:* Sylvia STOPFORD, Alexandra STOPFORD, Pauline CUNNINGHAM; *Scenery Design:* Ian WILSON; *Scenery supply:* Albermarle Scenic Studios.

641. **TALES FROM THE JUNGLE BOOK;** *24 October2004.*

642. **MEMORY LANE;** TIMELESS THEATRE PRODUCTIONS; *18 November 2004*

643. **JIMMY CRICKET AND FRIENDS;** DEREK GRANT; *20 November 2004.*

644. **SNOW WHITE AND THE SEVEN DWARFS;** EXTRAVAGANZA PRODUCTIONS; *10 December 2004 – 9 January 2005. Wicked Queen:* Denise WELCH; *Prince Rupert:* Daniel COLLOPY.

645. **GODSPELL** by Stephen Schwartz; YOUTH UNLIMITED THEATRE COMPANY; *8 – 12 February 2005. Arrangements and Orchestration:* Alex LACAMOIRE.

646. **THE KOSMIC KREW;** *20 February 2005.*

647. **WEST SIDE STORY;** Music by Leonard Bernstein; original concept by Jerome Robbins; Lyrics by Stephen Sondheim; Book by Arthur Laurents; ROMILEY OPERATIC SOCIETY; *8-12 March 2005.*

PRIESTNALL SCHOOL; Priesnall Road, HEATON MERSEY SK4 3HW; 0161-442 8850; CAZ: 126, B6

PROSPECT VALE PRIMARY SCHOOL; Prospect Vale, HEALD GREEN SK8 3RJ; 0161-437 4226; **CAZ;** 149, F4

QUEEN'S ROAD PRIMARY SCHOOL; Buckingham Road, CHEADLE HULME SK8 5NA; 0161-485 1453; **CAZ:** 150, C2

REDDISH VALE HIGH SCHOOL; Reddish Vale Road SK5 7HD; 0161 - 447 3544; **CAZ:** 127, H2

ROMILEY FORUM; Compstall Road SK6 4EA; 0161-430 6570. **CAZ:** 142, A1. **G,W.**

ROMILEY PRIMARY SCHOOL; Sandy Lane

SK8 4NE; 0161-430 3101; **CAZ:** 142, B1

269. **PINOCCHIO** by Stephen Boyes, based on the original story by Carlo Collodi; MANCHESTER ACTORS COMPANY; *17 February 2005.*

ST ANNE'S ROMAN CATHOLIC HIGH SCHOOL; Glenfield Road, HEATON CHAPEL SK4 2QP; 0161 - 432 8162; **CAZ:** 127, F5

ST GEORGE'S CHURCH OF ENGLAND INFANTS SCHOOL; Bramhall Lane SK2 6NX; 0161-480 0729; **CAZ:** 139, H5

ST JAMES' ROMAN CATHOLIC HIGH SCHOOL; St James' Way, off Stanley Street, CHEADLE HULME SK8 6PZ; 0161-486 9211; **CAZ:** 160, BI

268. **MACBETH** by William Shakespeare; MANCHESTER ACTORS COMPANY; *28 January 2005.*

ST MARK'S CHURCH OF ENGLAND PRIMARY SCHOOL; Redhouse Lane BREDBURY SK6 1BX; 0161-430 3418; **CAZ:** 129, G5

ST MARY'S; MARPLE

ST MATTHEW'S CHURCH OF ENGLAND PRIMARY SCHOOL; Bowdon Street SK3 4JL; 0161 - 474 7110; **CAZ:** 139, G3

STOCKPORT COLLEGE; Wellington Road South SK1 3UQ; 0161-480 7331; CAZ: 139, H3

T-BIRDS: MORGAN HOUGH (Sonny), JOE MALLALIEU (Kenickie), ADAM THORBURN (Roger), JAMES GREEN (Doody), DANNY STOKER (Danny)

STOCKPORT GRAMMAR SCHOOL; Buxton Road SK2 7AF; 0161-456 9000; **CAZ:** 140, B6

648. **GREASE;** Book, Music and Lyrics by Jim Jacobs and Warren Casey, with additional songs by B Gibb, J Farrar, L St Louis and S Simon; PAUL NICHOLAS & DAVID IAN; *Danny:* Danny STOKER; *Sandy:* Alex BURTON; *Rizzo:* Ashleigh COLLINS; *Frenchy:* Heather MacKAY; *Marty:* Zoe THOMAS; *Jan:* Heather O'HARA; *Kenickie:* Joe MALLALIEU; *Doody:* James GREN; *Roger:* Adam THORBURN; *Sonny:* Morgan HOUGH; *Patty:* Natalia SOWTER; *Cha Cha:* Fay WOOLFINDENL *Eugene:* Jonathan HINSLEY; *Vince Fontaine / Teen Angel: :* James TURNER; *Johnny Casino /:* Matthew CHAPPELL; *Miss Lynch:* Sarah CROOMER; *Dancers / Chorus:* Sarah HERRINGTON, Fay WOOLFINDEN, Naomi CLAYTON, Elizabeth EDMONDS, Amy WALKER, Hannash WINTER,

Ashleigh DEANE, Jayne ARUNDALE, Morgan BRAMMALL, Amy LYONS, Fay HUDSON, Alison WELSH, Emma HODGKISS, Chloe BANNER, Sophie BIRTWHISTLE, Kaylie KELLY, Danieele MORGAN; *ORCHESTRA: Keyboard:* Nicola LYONS; *Flute:* Amy SEDDON, Katie SCANLON; *Tenor Saxophone:* Joe COWELL; *Guitars:* Darren MATTHEWS, Jason ALLEN, Stuart SMITH; *Bass:* David LUCKHURST, Peter STRUGGLES; *Kit:* Dave Bri WYCHERLEY. *Producer:* S GODFREY; *Musical Director / Arranger / Conductor:* J COULSON; *Stage Manager:* S GODFREY; *Choreography:* J HOWARTH, S MILLINGTON; *Lighting Design:* R BALFOUR, Neil TRENELL; *Sound / Stage Designer:* Jack FIELD; *Make-up:* M O'NEILL; *Paint / Matte Designer:* C FLETCHER; *Costume Supervisor:* E TRENELL.

TOWN SQUARE; Merseyway SK4 2NW; CAZ: 139, G2

TURNING CIRCLE; Merseyway SK11PN; CAZ: 139, G2

VERNON PARK PRIMARY SCHOOL; Peak Street; 0161 - 480 4378; **CAZ:** 140, A2

WERNETH SCHOOL; Harrytown, ROMILEY SK6 3BX; 0161-494 1222; **CAZ:** 141, G1

WHITEHILL PRIMARY SCHOOL; Whitehill Street West, HEATON NORRIS SK5 7LW; 0161 - 480 2142; **CAZ:** 127, G5

WHITE LION; Great Underbank SKI ILF; CAZ: 139, 29

WOMEN'S INSTITUTE; Marple Bridge

363. **ON THE LINE** by Mike Lucas and Jim Wodland; Music and Lyric by Jim Woodland; MIKRON THEATRE COMPANY; *28 October 2004.*

WOODBANK MEMORIAL PARK; CAZ: 140, C2

TAMESIDE

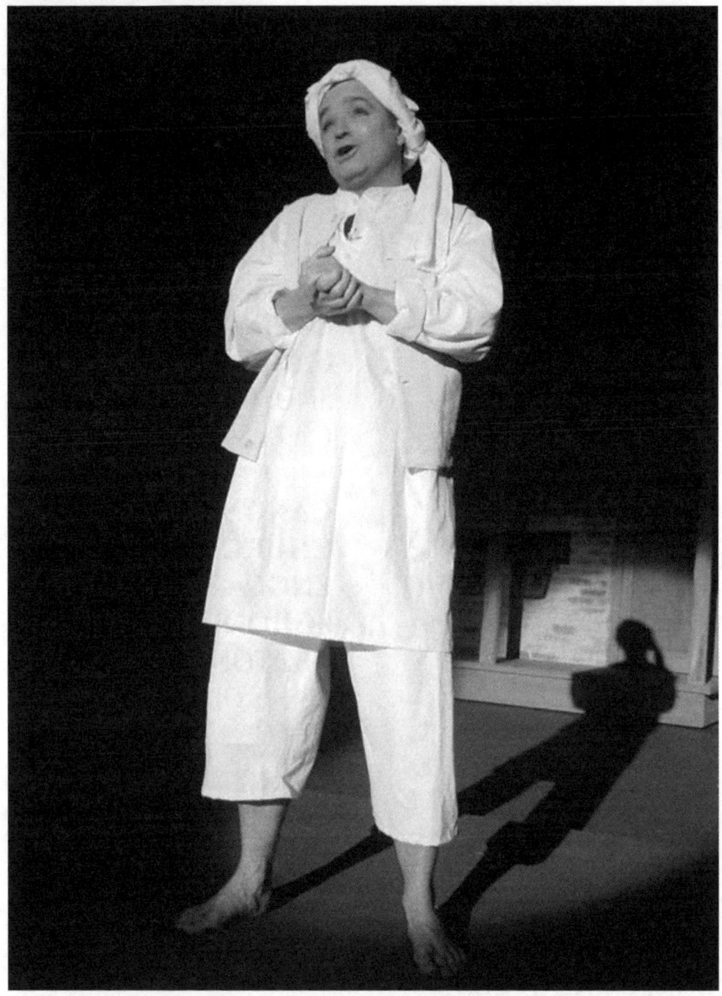

IT AIN'T HALF HOT MUM (667); CARL MORGAN as Char Wallah and nominee for Best Supporting Actor in All-England Theatre Festival

ALBERT STREET; Denton M34 6LB; CAZ: 113, 4F

.

ALDER HIGH SCHOOL; Mottram Old Road, GEE CROSS SK14 5NJ; 0161-368 5132; **CAZ:** 130, D1

265. **ACTING YOUR AGE** by Mike Harris; GW THEATRE; *10 March 2005.*

ARUNDALE COUNTY PRIMARY SCHOOL; Arundale Grove, MOTTRAM SK14 6PF; 01457 762 328; **CAZ:** 116, B4

ASHTON TOWN HALL STEPS; CAZ: 99, H2

ASTLEY HIGH SCHOOL; Yew Tree Lane, DUKINFIELD SK16 5BJ; 0161-338 2374; CAZ: 114, C1

AUDENSHAW PRIMARY SCHOOL; Ash Street M34 5WD; 0161 - 370 2504; **CAZ:** 98, D6

BUCKTON VALE PRIMARY SCHOOL; Swallow Lane, CARRBROOK SK15 3NU; 01457 833 102; **CAZ:** 89, H4

CANON JOHNSON CHURCH OF ENGLAND PRIMARY SCHOOL; Elgin Street, ASHTON-UNDER-LYNE OL7 9DD; **CAZ:** 99, H1

270. **FIREBIRD** by Stephen Boyes; MANCHESTER ACTORS COMPANY; *19 July 2005.*

COPLEY HIGH SCHOOL; Huddersfield Road, STALYBRIDGE SK5 2QA; 0161-338 6684 /6841; **CAZ:** 101, H3.

267. **SMASHED** by Mike Harris; GW THEATRE COMPANY; *30 June 2005.*

COURTYARD THEATRE; Beaufort Road, ASHTON-UNDER-LYNE OL6 6NX; 0161-33O 6911 Ext 2207; CAZ: 100, B2

DENTON WEST COMMUNITY CENTRE; Hulme Road M34 2WZ; 0161-336 3897; **CAZ:** 112, B4

DOWSON COUNTY PRIMARY SCHOOL; Marlborough Road, HYDE SK14 5HU; 0161-366 0177; **CAZ:** 130, C1

DROYLSDEN LITTLE THEATRE; Market Street M35 7AY; 0161-370 7713; **CAZ:** 98, B4

650. **WHY ME?** by Stanley Price; *4-9 October 2004. John Bailey:* Peter LARKIN; *Mary Ferguson:* Dorothy WILKINSON; *Helen Bailey:* Jean NICHOLSON; *Gwen Hollis:* Claire WHITE; *Arthur Hollis:* Paul COOPER; *Tom Bailey:* Nicholas WORTHINGTON. *Director:* Constance M SMITH; *Design:* Steven HYDE; *Lighting Operative:* Giles HEPWORTH; *Sound Opearative:* Andre BELLEMARRE; *Continuity / Stage Manager:* Norma RAIF; *Properties:* Lynn HENRY; *Theatre Artist:* Tracy IRELAND.

651. **COMFORT AND JOY** by Mike Harding; *22 – 27 November 2004. Goff:* Andre BELLEMARRE; *Margaret:* Pat HATTON; *Helen:* Nicky BERRY; *Martin:* Eddie BRADBURY; *Fiona:* Lynn HENRY; *Jimmy:* Jim EDMUND; *Chapman:* Jon COMYN-PLATT; *Monica:* Hazel PHILLIPS; *Kathy:* Joanne BELL; *Crispin:* Mat HEPPLESTONE; *Pat:* Norma RAIF; *Hughie:* Anthony DUNNE. *Director:* David FIELDING; *Lighting Design:* Tony BIRCH; *Lighting Operative:*Giles HEPWORTH; *Sound Operative:* Connie BROOKSBANK; *Continuity / Stage Manager:* Dot HYNES; *Properties:* Peter KEELING, Irene PARKER; *Theatre Artist:* Tracy IRELAND, *Production Co-ordinator:* Peter KEELING.

652. **THE EXORCISM** by Don Taylor; *24-29 January 2005. Dan:* Garry LAWRENCE; *Edmund:* Steven HYDE; *Margaret:* Rachael HAYES; *Rachel:* Claire WHITE. *Director:* Pat

Hatton; *Designer:* Steven HYDE; *Lighting Design:* Tony BIRCH, Steven HYDE; *Lighting: Operative*: Sue THORP; *Sound Operative*: Norma RAIF; *Continuity:* Dorothy WILKINSON; *Stage Manager:* John CARROLL; *Properties:* Amanda HYDE, Jane GREGORY; *Theatre Artist:* Tracy IRELAND; *Production Co-ordinator:* Peter LARKIN.

653. THERE GOES THE BRIDE by Ray Cooney and John Chapman; *14-19 March 2005. Ursula Westerby:* Hazel PHILLIPS; *Judy Westerby:* Shelley RIDLER; *Dr Gerald Drimmond:* Eddie HYNES; *Bill Shorter:* Andre BELLEMARRE; *Timothy Westerby:* David WILD; *Polly Perkins:* Lisa SLATTERY; *Daphne Drimmond:* Dorothy WILKINSON; *Charles Babcock:* Ernie PHILLIPS. *Director:* Johnny BARLOW; *Design:* Steven HYDE; *Lighting Design:* Tony BIRCH; *Lighting Operative:* Anthony DUNNE; *Sound Operative:* Claire WHITE; *Continuity / Stage Manager:* Jean NICHOLSON; *Properties:* Peter Larkin, Lynn HENRY; *Choreography:* Nicky MEAD; *Theatre Artist:* Tracy IRELAND; *ProductionCo-ordinator:* Peter LARKIN.

654. FIND THE LADY by Michael Pertwee; *9-14 May 2005. The Lady:* Jean NICHOLSON; *Mrs Pratt:* Dot HYNES; *Desiree Pratt:* Gwen MONTE; *Dr Ali:* Matt HANKIN:*Rosie Lake:* Lynn HENRY; *Mark Anderson:* Anthony DUNNE; *Tim Cantel:* Peter LARKIN; *Miss Daintee:* Beverley WHEATCROFT; *Jean Smith:* Jayne SKUDDER. *Director:* Norma RAIF; *Design:* Steven HYDE; *Lighting Design:* Tony BIRCH; *Lighting Operative:* Sue THORP; *Sound Operative:* Andre BELLEMARE; *Stage Manager:* Pat HATTON; *Properties:* Sue LEARY, Janet CROZIER; *Continuity:* Dorothy WILKINSON; *Theatre Artist:* Tracy IRELAND; *Production Co-ordinator:* Peter LARKIN.

655. THE HAUNTED THROUGH-LOUNGE AND RECESSED DINING-NOOK AT FARNDALE CASTLE by David McGillivray and Walter Zerlin Jnr; *4-9 July 2005. Thelma:* Dot HYNES; *Lottie:* Rachael HAYES; *Mrs Reece:* Pat HATTON; *Felicity:* Claire WHITE; *Jasmine:* Jayne SKUDDER; *Melody:* Jean NICHOLSON; *Producer:* Eddie BRADBURY. *Director:* Eddie HYNES; *Design:* Steven HYDE; *Lighting Design:* Tony BIRCH; *Lighting Operative:* Giles HEPWORTH; *Sound Operative:* Norma RAIF; *Stage Manager:* John CARROLL; *Properties:*Hazel PHILLIPS, Andre BELLEMARRE, Hilary FLINT; *Continuity:* Gwen MONTE; *Theatre Artist:* Tracy

IRELAND; *Production Co-ordinator:* Peter LARKIN.

EGERTON PARK ARTS COLLEGE;
Egerton Street, DENTON M34 3PD; 0161-320 1127; **CAZ:** 113, E3

268. **MACBETH** by William Shakespeare; MANCHESTER ACTORS COMPANY; *21, 23 February 2005.*

267. **SMASHED** by Mike Harris; GW THEATRE COMPANY;*5 July*

EMMAUS PROJECT; Longlands Mill, Queen Street, MOSSLEY OL5 9AQ; 01457 838608

FAIRFIELD SCIENCE COLLEGE;
Fairfield Avenue, DROYLSDEN M43 6AB; 0161-370 1488; **CAZ:** 98, A5

267. **SMASHED** by Mike Harris; GW THEATRE COMPANY; *8 July*

FESTIVAL THEATRE;
Corporation Street, HYDE SK14 1AB; 0161-320 0542 / 336 8840. **CAZ:** 114, B5

656. **OLD DOG, NEW TRICKS** by Sylvia Walker; SYLVIA WALKER PLAYERS; *22-25 September 2004.*

657. **THE RISE AND FALL OF LITTLE VOICE** by Jim Cartwright; ROMILEY LITTLE THEATRE; *7-9 October 2004.*

658. **BLUEBEARD** by Paul Reakes; HYDE LITTLE THEATRE; *29 November – 4 December 2004.*

659. **GOLDILOCKS AND THE THREE BEARS** by Sandra Lee, Annie Monkman and Tim Senior. TAMESIDE YOUTH DRAMA GROUP; *13-17 January 2005.*

660. **PETER PAN** by J M Barrie, as adapted by Trevor Nunn and John Caird; ROMILEY LITTLE THEATRE; *29-31 January 2005.*

661. **HAPPY FAMILIES** by John Godber; HYDE LITTLE THEATRE; *23-26 February 2005.*

662. SUGAR; Book by Peter Stone, based on the Screenplay **Some Like It Hot** by Billy Wilder and IAL Diamond, based, in its turn, on a story by Robert Thoeren; Music by Jule Styne; Lyrics by Bob Merrill; HYDE MUSICAL SOCIETY; *14-19 March 2005. Sugar Kane:* Wendy FORAN; *Joe:* Michael MILLS; *Jerry:* Scott LEES; *Sweet Sue:* Louise MEACHEN; *Osgood Fielding Jr:* John HARRISON; *Bienstock:* Andy GIBSON; *Spats Palazzo:* Rodney CADD; *Dude:* Terry DOCTOR; *Knuckles Norton:* Roy ELLISON; *Olga:* Janine ROYLE; *Bell Boy:* Daniel LOWERY; *Stage Manager / Contractor:* George E WOOD; *Nurse:* Mary T WOOD; *The Society Syncopators/ 'Chigago' Singers / Dancers:* Jean GRIFFITHS, Kerry WILLIAMS, Rebekah TRAVIS, Joanne MAYALL, Kerry BUCKLEY, Katie-Jo SCHOFIELD, Rachael EDWARDS, Kirsty SMITH, Louise ELLIOTT, Janine ROYLE; *Gangs / Millionaires:* Terry DOCTOR, Roy BELCHER, Roy ELLISON, Robert McCUNE, David OWEN, Alasn MERCER.

663. OFF THE RAILS by John Waterhouse; HYDE LITTLE THEATRE; *20-23 April 2005.*

664. A LITTLE LOCAL DIFFICULTY by Philip Goulding, an adaptation of **The Inspector General** by Nikolai Gogol; ROMILEY LITTLE THEATRE; *12-14 May 2005.*

665. OUR DAY OUT by Willy Russell; HYDE LITTLE THEATRE; *22-25 June 2005.*

666. WHEN SATURDAY COMES by Darren Vallier; TAMESIDE YOUTH DRAMA GROUP; *13-16 July 2005.*

GEORGE LAWTON CENTRE THEATRE; Stamford Street, MOSSLEY OL5 0HR; 01457 832705; **CAZ:** 89, E2

667. IT AIN'T HALF HOT MUM by Jimmy Perry and David Croft; MOSSLEY AODS; *13-18 September 2004.Sergeant Gregory:* Margaret THOMPSON; *Nobby:* Edward MALLON; *Char Wallah:* Carl MORGAN; *Parky:* Ian NORGATE; *Reynolds: Paderewski:* Rodney CADD; *Captain Ashwood:* Martyn PRESTON; *Williams:* Steve MAXFIELD; *Sugden:* John HANKIN; *Beaumont:* Paul FIRTH; *Atlas:* Mark GALVIN; *Nosher:* Ian CURRAN. *Director:* Nigel MARLAND; *Musical Director / Choreography:* Rodney CADD; *Stage Manager:* TRICIA FURNESS;

Assistant Stage Manager: Sue WHARFE; *Lighting:* Martin ORGEN, Nigel GRIFFITHS, Jack MONAGHAN, Andrew RHYMES; *Sound:* C MARSDEN, S DAVENPORT, Steve MILLINGTON; *Properties:* Diane MELLOR, Susan OGDEN, L RYDER, Kimberley WRIGLEY; *Wardrobe:* Terry PARKER; *Set Design:* John BUCKLEY; *Make-up:* John FLETCHER, Sue STOREY, Hilary WINTERS, Jacqueline FOTHERGILL, Sandie BESWICK; *Production Assistant:* Avis BILLINGTON; *Production Secretary:* John BUCKLEY; *Set Construction:* John BUCKLEY, Andy MELLOR, Richard RYDER, Frank WEBSTER, Clive DARBYSHIRE, Robert GODFREY, J WILLIAMSON, C MILESTONE, Brian WHITTAKER, Wyn WITHAM, A EVERETT, Alan WALLEY.

668. LES MISERABLES, based on the novel by Victor Hugo; Music by Claude-Michel Schonbern; Lyrics by Herbert Kretzmer; Original Book by Alain Boubli and Jean-Marc Natel; Additional Material by James Fenton; Orchestrations by John Cameron; MOSSLEY AODS NEXT GENERATION; *6-11 December 2004. Jean Valjean:* Daniel WINTERS; *Javert:* Ian CURRAN; *Fantine:* Sherri PHILLIPS; *Eponine:* Joanne FARROW; *Cosette:* Alice McGREEVY; *Marius:* Anthony J QUIMBY; *Thernadier / Convict:* Jack MONAGHAN; *Madame Thernadier:* Rebecca FALLON; *Constable / Student Courfreyac:* Adam McDIARMID; *Labourers / Workers / Onlookers:* Alex RE, Mia STENT, Rachel COLLEY, Sophie THOMPSON; *Whores:* Alexandra ROBINSON, Charlotte TAYLOR, Holly Mia SIMPSON; *Young Eponine:* Ashleigh CORRIGAN; *Factory Girls:* Becky CONNOR, Rachel FARROW, Sophie BUTTERS, Sophie HOWARD; *Foreman / Student Feuilly:* Ben SWEENEY; *Farmer / Student Brujon:* Ben TURTON; *Lbourers / Workers / Whores / Onlookers:* Bethany LINSDELL, Claire MORREAL, Emily BENNETT, Jessica ROYLE, Lucy TAYLOR, Natalie COVERLEY, Purvi PARMAR, Rachel BUTTERWORTH, Roxanne MULLINER, Suzanne GODDARD; *Young Cosette:* Catherine HILL; *Old Woman:* Catherine PUGH; *Enjolras / Convict:* Chris HAIGH; *Convict / Pimp / Student Joly:* Dan WILSON; *Montparnasse:* Helen BURKE; *Convict / Sailor / Student Prouvaire:* Jonathan SMEDLEY; *Bamatbois / Student Grantair:* Nick WARD; *Bishop of Digne / Sailor / Student Combferre:* Oliver ASTLEY; *Gavroche:* Sam PEACH; *Babet:* Sophie Jo BENNETT; *Convict / Sailor:* Tim WOOD; *Constable / Student Lesgles:* Tom SENIOR; *Claquesous:* Victoria

Programme Details

REBECCA FALLON and JACK MONOGHAN as theThenardiers

BURGESS. *Artistic Director:* Colin WARD; *Musical Director:* Dave CHAPMAN; *Associate Director:* Maryn C H PRESTON; *Associate Musical Director:* Claire CREBBIN; *Assistant Director:* JonCREBBIN; *Choreographer:* Tracy RONTREE; *Assistant Choreographer:* Jeni HALLAM; *Rehearsal Pianists:* Elaine CHAPMAN, Sarah DAY, Claire CREBBIN; *Production Secretary/ Set Design:* John BUCKLEY; *Stage Manager:* Tricia FURNESS; *Assistant Stage Managers:* Sue WHARFE, Andy MELLOR; *Stage Staff:* Nigel BANKS, John BUCKLEY, Clive DARBYSHIRE, Anne EVERETT, Robert GODFREY, Andy MELLOR, Richard RYDER, Tony THOMPSON, Alan WALLEY, Frank WEBSTER, Brian WHITTAKER, J WILLIAMSON, Wyn WITHAM; *Lighting:* Martin OGDEN, Nigel GRIFFITHS, Andy RHYMES; *Sound:* Lea ROYSE, S DAVENPORT, C MARSDEN; *Properties:* Sue OGDEN, Lyn RYDER, Diane MELLOR, Kim WRIGLEY, Emma HILL, Diane OGDEN; *Wardrobe Mistress:* Terri PARKER; *Wardrobe Assistants:* Claire HAWORTH, Jean RYDER, Malcolm PARKES, Lisa KAY; *Make-up Team:* Sandie BESWICK, Sue STOREY, Darryl RE, Diane HOWARD, Hilary WINTERS, Staff and Students of Oldham College.

STEVE MAXFIELD as Captain Tempest

669. RETURN TO THE FORBIDDEN PLANET by Bob Carlton; MOSSLEY AODS; *18 –23 April 2005. Navigation Officer:* Lisa KAY; *Science Officer:* Kerry NEWTON; *Bosun:* Phil COOPER; *Captain Tempest:* Stave MAXFIELD; *Ariel:* John MEACHEN; *Dr Prospero:* Rodney CADD; *Cookie:* Carl MORGAN; *Miranda:* Catherine PUGH; *Backing Crew:* Holly Mia SIMPSON, Sarah THEWLIS; *Dancers:* Sarah BOJANOWSKI, Jeni HALLAM, Daryl COWARD, Zoe FOGG, Katie-Jo SCHOFIELD, Nick WARD, Ben TURTON. *Director:* Colin WARD; *Musical Director:* Paul FIRTH; *Choreography:* Janice HUGHES; *Assistant Musical Director:* Jacqui DAWBER; *Stage Manager:* Tricia FURNESS; *Lighting:* Martin OGDEN, Nigel GRIFFITHS; *Sound:* Lea ROYSE; *Properties:* Sue OGDEN, Lyn RYDER, Diane MELLOR, Kim WRIGLEY; *Wardrobe* Terri PARKER, Jean RYDER; *Set Design:* John BUCKLEY; *Make-up:* John FLETCHER, Sandie BESWICK, Hilary WINTERS; Staff and Students of Oldham College; *Production Secretaries:* John BUCKLEY, JoN CREBBIN, Tricia FURNESS.

GRESWELL PRIMARY SCHOOL; **Percy Road, DENTON M34 2DH**; 0161-336 6854; **CAZ**: 113, E5

GUIDE BRIDGE THEATRE; Audenshaw Road AUDENSHAW M34 5HJ; 0161-330 8078; **CAZ:** 98, D6 **H**

670. BOSTON MARRIAGE by David Mamet; *9-16 October 2004. Anna:* Joan DUFFIN; *Claire:* Julie MANIFOLD; *Maid:* Joan BERESFORD. *Director:* Johnny BARLOW.

671. TOM, THE PIPER'S SON by Norman Robbins; *2-11 December 2004. The Knave of Hearts:* Jason DYSON; *Fairy Harmony:* Joan BERESFORD; *Kitty Fisher:* Jenni HANDS; *Jack Horner:* Sue BORG; *Tom Sprightly:* Sue HOLDEN; *Dame Sprightly:* Bobby CONNOLLY; *Princess Marigold:* Amy GREEN; *The Lord Chamberlain:* Caven SLATE; *Georgie Porgie:* Cliff MYATT; *Buckett*: Callum BAKER*;* *Spade:* Matthew SWIFT; *Herald:* Joella ANDREW; *Old King Cole:* Jason JAMES; *Queen Mattiwilda:* Jean RATCLIFFE; *Pieman / Ship's Captain:* Geoff RICHARDSON; *Grendlegorm:* Jean BROBIN; *Juniors:* Micaela BOYCE, Harriet TAYLOR, Alisha ELLWOOD, Lucy BROADBENT, Alice HANDFORTH, Dignity HUGHES, Shannah WATKISS, Megan RILEY; *Intermediates:* Yasmin CHAMBERS; Ann PRTINA, Olivia LINDLEY, Nicole RICHARDSON, Olivia POWNALL, Leye LINSELL; *Seniors:* Emma PARKER, Carmen THOMPSONE-PASCOE, Joella ANDREW, Rebecca HINCHCLIFFE, Francesca POWNALL. *Director:* Stuart NEEDHAM; *Choreographer:* Julie Ann MAYNE; *Musical Director:* Carol; *Percussion:* Les

672. THE NOBLE SPANIARD by W Somerset Maugham, adapted from the play by Grenet Dancourt; *15-22 January 2005. Lady Proadfoot:* Dot HYNES; *Mr Justice Proudfoot:* Peter BOLGER; *Marion Nairne:* Sue BORG; *Lucy:* Amy GREEN; *Mary Jane:* Alice HAYES; *Captain Chalford:* Jason DYSON; *Count de Moret:* Bill KLIEVE; *Countess de Moret:* Sheila CASEY; *The Duke of Hermanos:* Cliff MYATT. *Director:* Joan SARGENT.

673. THE HERBAL BED by Peter Whelan; *19-26 February 2005. Rafe Smith:* Colin GREEN; *Hester:* Jenni HAND; *Jack Lane:* Cliff MYATT; *Bishop Parry:* Andy CLARKE; *Barnabus Goche:* Stephen KING; *Susannah Hall:* Rachell HARRISON; *Dr John Hall:* Stuart VAUGHAN; *ElizabethHall:* Goergina EDWARDS. *Director:* Louise PLATT.

674. HAMP by John Wilson; *2-9 April 2005. Private Arthur Hamp:* Cliff MYATT; *Corporal of The Guard:* Jason DYSON; *Guard Private:* David NOBLE; *Lieutenant William Hargreaves:* Peter BOLGER; *Lieutenant Tom Webb:* Ian TOWNSEND; *President of the Court:* Alan KENWORTHY: *Members of The Court:* Ken VARE, Tony STALLARD; *Captain Prescott:* Andrew CLARKE; *Captain Midgeley:* Alan GAWLER; *Padre:* David PLATT; *Captain O'Sullivan:* Mike SMITH. *Director:* Bill KLIEVE.

675. **STRANGERS ON A TRAIN** by Craig Warner, based on the book by Patricia Highsmith; *7-14 May 2005. Guy Haines:* Vince BOWER; *Charles Bruno:* Stephen KING; *Elsie Bruno:* Carla STOKES; *Anne Faulkner:* Sue BORG; *Frank Myers:* Andrew CLARKE; *Robert Treacher:* Colin GREEN; *Arthur Gerrard:* David PLATT. *Director:* Jane TONGE.

676. **KISS ME LIKE YOU MEAN IT** by Chris Chibnall; *11-18 June 2005. Tony:* Cliff MYATT; *Ruth:* Ruth BLASZCZOK; *Edie:* Betty WADE; *Don:* Peter BOLGER. *Director:* Ian TOWNSEND.

677. **PYGMALION** by George Bernard Shaw; *23-30 July 2005. Director:* Carla STOKES.

HARTSHEAD SPORTS COLLEGE; Greenhurst Road;ASHTON-UNDER-LYNE OL6 9DX; 0161-330 1651/ 4965; **CAZ**: 87, H4

268. **MACBETH** by William Shakespeare; MANCHESTER ACTORS COMPANY; *17 March 2005.*

267. **SMASHED** by Mike Harris; GW THEATRE COMPANY; *28 June 2005.*

HATTERSLEY COMMUNITY CENTRE; Hattersley Road East, HYDE SK14 3EQ; 0161-368 8513; CAZ: 116, A5

HATTERSLEY HIGH SCHOOL; Fields Farm Road, HYDE SK14 3NP; 0161-368 8513; CAZ: 115, H5

HAWTHORNS SPECIAL NEEDS SCHOOL; Corporation Road, AUDENSHAW M34 5LZ; 0161 - 336 3389; CAZ: 113, D2

HOLLINS MOSSLEY HIGH SCHOOL; Huddersfield Road, MOSSLEY OL5 9PD; 01457 832491; **CAZ:** 89, G2

265. **ACTING YOUR AGE** by Mike Harris; GW THEATRE; *14 March 2005.*

267. **SMASHED** by Mike Harris; GW THEATRE COMPANY; *12 July*

HURST KNOLL CHURCH OF ENGLAND PRIMARY SCHOOL; Ladbrooke Road, ASHTON - UNDER-LYNE OL6 8JS; 0161-330 4049; **CAZ:** 100, A1

HYDE MARKET PLACE; CAZ: 114, B5

HYDE TECHNOLOGY HIGH SCHOOL; Old Road SK14 4SP; 0161-368 1358; **CAZ:** 114, B2

268. **MACBETH** by William Shakespeare; MANCHESTER ACTORS COMPANY; *17 January 2005. MacBeth:* Simon HENSON; *Lady MacBeth:* Hilly BARBER; *MacDuff ' Ensemble:* Gareth McCANN; *First Witch / Ensemble:* Nicola INGRAM. *Director:* Stephen BOYES; *Designer:* Daniel WEST.

267. **SMASHED** by Mike Harris; GW THEATRE COMPANY; *23 June 2005.*

HYDE TOWN HALL; Reynold Street SK14 1LU; CAZ: 114, B5

LEIGH STREET PRIMARY SCHOOL; HYDE SK14 2RP; 0161-368 3259; **CAZ:** 114, C5

LITTLEMOSS HIGH SCHOOL; Cryer Street, DROYLSDEN M35 7LF; 0161-370 2010; **CAZ**: 98, C1

268. **MACBETH** by William Shakespeare; MANCHESTER ACTORS COMPANY; *20 January 2005.*

LIVINGSTONE PRIMARY SCHOOL; Vale Side, MOSSLEY OL5 0AP; 01457 932 495; **CAZ:** 89, E3

LONGDENDALE COMMUNITY

COMMERCIAL LANGUAGES COLLEGE; Spring Street, off Market Street, Hollingworth, HYDE SK14 8LW 01457-764006 /764007. **CAZ:** 114, B5

267. **SMASHED** by Mike Harris; GW THEATRE COMPANY; *6 July*

LYNDHURST PRIMARY SCHOOL; Hill Street, DUKINFIELD SK16 4JS; 0161-330 7220; CAZ: 100, A4

MASONIC HALL; Stamford Street, STALYBRIDGE SK15 1QZ; CAZ: 101, E3

MARKET PLACE; HYDE SK14 2LX; CAZ: 114, B5

MARKET STREET; Ashton OL6 6BP; CAZ: 99, H2

MARKET STREET; DROYLSDEN M43 6DD

MELBOURNE STREET; Stalybridge SK15 2JE; CAZ: 101, E3

OLD STREET; Ashton OL6 7RS; CAZ: 99, H2

PARK BRIDGE; Medlock Valley Visitors Centre OL6 8AQ; 0161-678 4072; CAZ: 87, G1

PORTLAND BASIN MUSEUM; Heritage Wharf, Portland Place; ASHTON - UNDER - LYNE OL6 7SY; 0161 - 308 3374; CAZ: 99, G3

RIDGE HILL PRIMARY SCHOOL; School Crescent, STALYBRIDGE SK15 1EA; 0161-338 2475 / 3157; **CAZ:** 100, D2

ST ANNE'S PRIMARY SCHOOL; Clarendon Road, AUDENSHAW M34 5PP; 0161-370 8698; CAZ: 98, A6

ST DAMIAN'S RC SCIENCE COLLEGE; Lees Road, ASHTON - UNDER - LYNE OL6 8BH; 0161-330 5974; **CAZ**: 87, H4

267. **SMASHED** by Mike Harris; GW THEATRE COMPANY; *4 July*

ST GEORGE'S CHURCH OF ENGLAND PRIMARY SCHOOL; Church Street, HYDE SK14 1JZ; 0161-368 2848; **CAZ:** 114, B6

ST JOHN FISHER ROMAN CATHOLIC PRIMARY SCHOOL; Manor Road, DENTON M34 7SW; 0161-336 5308; **CAZ**: 113, H6

270. **FIREBIRD** by Stephen Boyes; MANCHESTER ACTORS COMPANY; *22 June 2005.*

ST PAUL'S CHURCH OF ENGLAND PRIMARY SCHOOL; Huddersfield Road, STALYBRIDGE SK15 2PT; 0161-338 2060; **CAZ:** 101, F3

ST PAUL'S ROMAN CATHOLIC PRIMARY SCHOOL;Turner Lane, HYDE SK14 4AG; 0161-368 2934; CAZ: 114, D3

ST PETER'S ROMAN CATHOLIC PRIMARY SCHOOL; Hough Hill Road, STALYBRIDGE SK15 2HB; 0161-338 3303; **CAZ:** 101, E4

ST RAPHAEL'S ROMAN CATHOLIC PRIMARY SCHOOL; Huddersfield Road, MILLBROOK SK15 3JL; 0161-338 4095; CAZ: 101, H1

ST THOMAS MORE RC HIGH SCHOOL; Town Lane, DENTON M34 6AF; 0161-336 2743; **CAZ**: 113, E5

SCOTT MEMORIAL HALL; DENTON; 01663 741691

STALYBRIDGE LABOUR CLUB; Acres Lane SK15 2JR; 0161-338 4796; CAZ: 101, F4

STALYHILL INFANT SCHOOL; Stalyhill Drive, STALYBRIDGE SK15 2TR; 01457 763 598; **CAZ:** 116, A1

STAMFORD HIGH SCHOOL; Mossley Road, ASHTON-UNDER-LYNE OL6 6NA; 0161-330 7437; **CAZ:** 100, C1

268. MACBETH by William Shakespeare; MANCHESTER ACTORS COMPANY; *3 February 2005.*

TAMESIDE CONFERENCE CENTRE; Windmill Lane, DENTON M34 3LA; 0161-320 4737; CAZ: 112, B5

TAMESIDE HIPPODROME; Oldham Road, ASHTON-UNDER-LYNE OL6 7SE; O161-308 3223; **CAZ:** 99, H2

557. THE TEMPEST by Julian Chenery (Book and Lyrics), Mark Gimblett (Music and Lyric) and William Shakespeare; SHAKESPEARE 4 KIDZ; *29-30 September 2004*

678. GUYS AND DOLLS; Music and Lyrics by Frank Loesser; Book by Jo Swerling and Abe Burrows, based on the stories and characters of Damon Runyon; DUKINFIELD AODS; *18 23 October 2004. Nicely-Nicely Johnson:* Rodney T CADD; *Benny Southstreet:* Scott LEES; *Rusty Charlie:* Andy GIBSON; *Sarah Brown:* Sarah THEWLIS; *Arvind Abernathy:* Mike STYAN; *Agatha:* Ann HILL; *Harry The Horse:* Carl MORGAN; *Lt Brannigan:* Bob WOOD; *Nathan Detroit:* Nigel GRIFFITHS; *Angie The Ox:* Paul HODGKINSON; *Miss Adelaide:* Samantha BATES; *Sky Masterson:* Michael MILLS; *Joey Biltmore:* Bill OWEN; *General Cartwright:* Carole WARD; *Big Jule:*

David PLATT; *MC:* Malcolm PARKES; *Mission Band:* Ann BAKER, Marjorie BROWNHILL, Ann HILL, Glenys HYDE, Heather LEES, Robert MILESTONE, Viv PROFFITT; *New York Tourists:* Stephanie ECKHATDT, Alison FOGG, Jan GRIFFITHS, Judith HILTON; *Hot Box Girls:* Kimberley BATES, Kerry BUCKLEY, Claire FLETCHER, Wendy FORAN, Jean GRIFFITHS, Jo MAYALL, Tracey RONTREE, Katie-Jo SCHOFIELD, Rebeka TRAVIS, Kerry WILLIAMS; *Crap Shooters:* Terry DOCTOR, Andy GIBSON, Paul HODGKINSON, Ben JACKSON, Alan JOHNSON, Neil JOHNSON, Robert McCUNE, David OWEN, Richard THOMAS, Richard UNWIN. *Director:* Melvyn BATES; *Choreographer:* Jean ASHWORTH; *Musical Director:* Paul FIRSTH; *Stage Management:* Peter S MARSHALL; *Lighting Design:* Shaun EVERTON; *Accompanist:* Adam WALKER; *Assistant Stage Manager:* Andrew GREENWOOD; *Stage Assistants:* Chris BYROM, Katherine DAWSON, Michael DICKENS, Brian Hilton, Andrew S MARSHALL, Stuart NEEDHAM, David STRETTON, Adam WALKER; *Lighting Design:* Shaun EVERTON; *Property Manager:* Darren HILL; *Property Assistants:* Linda BURNS, Eric DYSON, Dave HIBBERT, Darren HILL, Emily HILL, Sheila MARSHALL, Gez PEGLER, Karen REES-UNWIN; *Adelaide's Wig:* Showbiz! Southampton, *Continuity:* Avis BILLINGTON, Rosemarie WOOD; *Make-up Team:* Peter DUNCUFT, Jenny PARKER, Maureen SCHOFIELD, Jean WHITWORTH.

679. DR BUNHEAD'S EXPLODING VEGETABLES SHOW; *25 October.*

385. ENJIE BENJY; *30 October 2004.*

389. KEN DOD HAPPINESS SHOW; *30 October 2004.*

402. CIRCUS OF HORRORS; *13 November 2004*

680. CAN I 'AVE A BUDGIE by Buzz Hawkins**:** THE BRADSHAWS; *23 November 2004*

390. GREASE; Book, Music and Lyrics by Jim Jacobs and Warren Casey, with additional songs by B Gibb, J Farrar, L St Louis and S Simon; PAUL NICHOLAS & DAVID IAN; *6-11 December 2004. Danny:* Paul

MANUEL; *Sandy:* Hayley EVETTS; *Kenickie:* Stuart RAMSAY; *Rizzo:* Deborah HATWARD; *Roger:* Angus MacMILLAN; *Jan:* Michelle BISHOP; *Doody:* Gavin Lee REES; *Frenchy:* Michelle FRANCIS; *Sonny:* Mark POWELL; *Marty:* Joanna RAPLEY; *Eugene:* Jamie TYLER; *Patty:* Betty HANKS; *Vince Fontaine / Teen Angel:* JASON CAPEWELL; *Miss Lynch:* Gemma ATKINS; *Cha Cha:* Soeli PARRY; *Chorus:* Wayne FITZSIMMONS, Stuart WINTER, Stuart DAWES, Jack JEFFERSON, Ryan JENKINS, Kristy CULLEN, Nicky GRIFFITHS, Emma GREEN, Nicky MILFORD, Charlotte BULL. *Director:* David GILMORE; *.Musical Staging / Choreography:* Arlene PHILLIPS; *Musical Staging / New Musical Arrangements:* Mike DIXON; *Costume Design:* Andreane NEOFITOU; *Set Design:* Terry PARSONS; *Sound Design:* Booby AITKEN; *Lighting Design:* Mark HENDERSON.

681. **ANNIE;** Book by Thomas Meehan, based on **Little Orphan Annie** by Harrold Gray; Music by Charles Strouse; Lyrics by Martin Charmin; CHRIS MORENO LTD; *13 – 31 December 2004. Annie:* Stacey HUNT; *Miss Hannigan:* Su POLLARD; *Daddy Warbucks:* James SMILLIE; *Grace Farrell:* Louise ENGLISH. *Director:* Chris COLBY; *Choreography:* David KORT; *Lighting:* Graham McLUSKY; *Settings:* Alan Miller BUNFORD

682. **THE CALCULATING MR ONE;** QUANTUM THEATRE; *25-26 January 2005.*

683. **LAUGHIN' ALL OVER THE WORLD;** CIRCUS HILARIOUS; *15 February 2005. Cast:* Clive WEBB, Danny ADAMS, Clown TIMONI.

642. **MEMORY LANE;** TIMELESS THEATRE PRODUCTIONS; *1 March 2005.*

684. **HALFWAY TO PARADISE;** PARADISE PRODUCTIONS; ZE PRODUCTIONS; *4 March 20054. Billy Fury:* Colin GOLD; *The*

Tornados: Chris RAYNOR (*Lead, Rhythn Guitar, Vocals*), John RAYNOR (*Drums, Vocals*); John CMAMBERS (*Bass Guiter, Vocals*); *Narrator:* Paul VINE. *Company Manager / Sound Engineer:* Paul VINE.

391. TRACTOR TOM; PREMIER STAGE PRODUCTIONS; *26 March 2005.*

685. THE PIRATES OF THE RIVER ROTHER; THE CHUCKLE BROTHERS; *27-28 March 2005.*

THORNCLIFFE NURSERY; 10 Taunton Road, ASHTON-UNDER-LYNE OL7 9DR; 0161-339 6931; **CAZ:** 99, G1

TOWN HALL; The Mall, HYDE SK14 2QT; CAZ: 114, B5

TRINITY STREET; STALYBRIDGE SK15 2BN; CAZ: 101, E4

SMASHED (267); Just look as the way those young people are carrying on (JULIE CLAYS).

TWO TREES HIGH SCHOOL; Two Tree Lane; DENTON M34 7QL; 0161-336 2719; **CAZ:** 113, G6

267. SMASHED by Mike Harris; GW THEATRE COMPANY; *16 June 2005. Cast:* Julie CLAYS, Dave JONAS, Roxanne MOORES. *Director:* Mike HARRIS

VICTORIA PARK; Denton; CAZ: 113, E4

WARRINGTON STREET; ASHTON OL6 6AS

WATERFONT THEATRE; Stamford Park, STALYBRIDGE; CAZ: 101, D2

WEST HILL SCIENCE COLLEGE; Thompson Cross, Stamford Street, STALYBRIDGE SK15 1LX; 0161-338 2193; **CAZ:** 100, D3

267. SMASHED by Mike Harris; GW THEATRE COMPANY; *1 July*

WHARF TAVERN; Staley Wharf, Caroline Street, STALEYBRIDGE SK15 1PD; CAZ: 101, E4

WHITE LION; Market Place, HYDE SK14 2LX; 0161-368 2948; CAZ: 114, B5

WILSHAW NURSERY SCHOOL; Store Street, ASHTON - UNDER - LYNE; 0161 - 330 4167

TRAFFORD

THICK AS THIEVES (725); MARK WHITELEY in one of the many interesting productions coming to the new WATERSIDE CENTRE in Sale.

ALTRINCHAM GARRICK PLAYHOUSE; Barrington Road WA14 1HZ; 0161-928 1677; **CAZ:** 133, F5 **H W**

686. A SMALL FAMILY BUSINESS by Alan Ayckbourn ; GARRICK PLAYHOUSE; *6-11 September 2004. Jack McCracken:* Dave midgley; *Poppy:* Helen COWAN; *Ken Ayres:* Roger METCALFE; *Yvonne Doggett:*Ruth METCALFE; *Tina:* Juliette WILSON; *Roy Ruston:* Ian MAIRS; *Samantha:* Becky WRIGHT; *Cliff:* Mike SHAW; *Anita:* Ros GREENWOOD; *Desmond:* Mark EDGAR; *Harriet:* Mary WRIGHT; *Benedict Hough:* Alex WILSON; *Rivetti Brothers:* Hugh EVERETT. *Director:* Maureen CASKET; *Designer:* Margaret NORRIS; *Sound:* Colin WOODs; *Lighting:* Geoff SCULLARD.

687. KAFKA'S DICK by Alan Bennett; GARRICK PLAYHOUSE; *20-25 September 2005. Kafka:* Mark BUTT; *Brod:* Trevor McKIE; *Linda:* Caroline HICKEY; *Father:* Allan TAYLOR; *Sydney:* David BEDDY; *Hermann K:* Martin OLDFIELD. *Director:* Jeryl WHITELOCK; *Designer:* Mike STOCKS.

688. MAME; Book by Jerome Lawrence and Robert E Lee; Music and Lyrics by Jerry Herman; GARRICK PLAYHOUSE; *4-9 October 2004. Mame Dennis:* Patsy ROBERTS; *Vera Charles:* Anne CHANDLER; *Beauregarde:* Alex WILSON; *Patrick Dennis (aged 10):* Daniel SHAW; *Patrick Dennis (adult):* John KEEN; *Agnes Gooch:* Carla WATTS; *Babcocke:* Roger METCALFE; *Ito:* Brian HOWLETT; *M Lindsey Woolsey:* Brian STONER; *Mme Branislowski:* Jane MARSH; *Gregor:* Jon WHITE; *Uncle Jeff:* David WALTON; *Cousin Fan:* Sarah TAYLOR; *Mother Burnside:* Audrey HUGHES; *Junior Babcock:* Matt STEAD; *Mr Upson:* Ian FENSOME; *Mrs Upson:* Ruth METCALFE; *Gloria Upson:* Laura CHANDLER; *Pegeen Ryan:* Stephanie HAWTHORN. *Director:* Terry CHANDLER.

689. PERFECT DAYS by Liz Lochhead; GARRICK PLAYHOUSE; *1-6 November 2004. Barbs Marshall:* Beverley STUART-COLE; *Alice Inglis:* Pam NOLAN; *Sadie Kirkwood:* Maureen CASKETT; *Brendan Boyle:* Stuart HARRISON; *Dave Marshall:* Duncan BATTMAN: *Grant Steel:* Ian MAIRS. *Director:* Angel WETHERILL.

698 MY FAIR LADY; Music by Frederick Loewe; Book AND Lyrics by Alan Jay Lerner, adapted from **Pygmalion** by George Bernard Shaw and the motion picture by Garial Pascal; TRAFFORD MARGARETIANS; *15-20 November 2004.*

690. DAD'S ARMY by Jimmy Perry and David Croft; GARRICK PLAYHOUSE; *29 November – 4 December 2004. Captain Mainwaring:* Allan TAYLOR; *Jones:* Geoff NOAR; *Wilson:* Charles FOSTER; *Fraser:* Terry CHANDLER; *Godfrey:* Brian TICKLE; *Pike:* Andrew HIGSON; *Walker:* Trevor McKIE; *Hodges:* Brian STONES; *Verger:* Frank BOYLAN; *Sponge:* Jon WHITE; *Hancock:* John DIXON; *German Captain:* Bryn THOMAS; *Fiona Grey:* Carole CARR; *Colinel:* Brian MOORE; *Vicar:* Graham SYMONDS; *Mrs Pile:* Val BACON; *Mrs Fox:* Alison DAVID; *Also:* Philippa CAMERON, Linda CRAWFORD, Rachel CAHILL, David LEATHLEAN.

691. BABES IN THE WOOD by Peter Birch; GARRICK PLAYHOUSE; *18 December 2004 – 2 January 2005. Director:* Peter BIRCH.

692. MURDER ON THE NILE by Agatha Christie; GARRICK PLAYHOUSE; *17-22 January 2005.*

693. THE PRICE by Arthur Miller; GARRICK PLAYHOUSE; *31 January – 5 February 2005.*

694. BRASSED OFF by Paul Allen, adapted from the screenplay by Mark Herman; GARRICK PLAYHOUSE; *28 February – 5 March 2005. Director:* Terry CHANDLER.

699. OLIVER; Book, Music and Lyrics by Lionel Bart; based on **Oliver Twist** by Charles Dickens; SALE & ALTRINCHAM MUSIC THEATRE; *14-19 March 2005.The Artful Dodger:* Ben DAVIES; *Oliver:* Harry HANCOCK; *Fagin:* David LEATHAM; *Nancy:* Maria GOOCH. *Director:* Jeff HARPIN; *Musical Director:* Brian GOODWIN; *Dnce Director:* Michelle BAILEY.

695. LES LIASONS DANGEREUSES by Christopher Hampton, adapted from the novel by Chonderlos de Laclos; GARRICK PLAYHOUSE; *4-9 April 2005. Director:* Sonia DYKSTRA.

700. FIDDLER ON THE ROOF; based on the stories by Sholem Aleichem; Book by Joseph Stein;

Music by Jerry Bock; Lyrics by Sheldon Harnick; TRAFFORD MARGARETIANS

696. ABIGAIL'S PARTY by Mike Leigh; GARRICK PLAYHOUSE; *9-14 May 2005. Dirertor:* Mark JEPHCOTT.

697. THE WIND IN THE WILLOWS by Kenneth Grahame, adapted by Alan Bennett; GARRICK PLAYHOUSE; *30 May – 4 June 2005. Director:* Celia BONNER.

733. HONK!; Music by George Stiles; Book and Lyrics by Anthony Drewe, based on **The Ugly Duckling** by Hans Christian Anderson; SOUTH TRAFFORD OPERATIC SOCIETY; *13-18 June 2005.*

ASHTON-ON-MERSEY COUNTY HIGH SCHOOL; Cecil Avenue, SALE M33 5BW; 0161-973 1179; CAZ: 121, G5

THE BARN OWL; Agden Wharf, Warrington Lane, Warrington Lane, Near LYMM WA13 0SW

BLESSED THOMAS HOLFORD HIGH SCHOOL; Urban Road, ALTRINCHAM WA15 8HT; 0161-928 6020; **CAZ:** 145, G1

268. MACBETH by William Shakespeare; MANCHESTER ACTORS COMPANY; *2 March 2005.*

CLUB THEATRE; 17 Oxford Road, ALTRINCHAM WA14 2ED; 0161-928 1113; **CAZ:**145, F2

701. THE IMPORTANCE OF BEING EARNEST by Oscar Wilde; CLUB THEATRE; *10-16 October 2004.*

702. THE SNOW QUEEN by John F Banks; CLUB theatre; *28 November – 4 December 2004.*

703. DEATHTRAP by Ira Levin; CLUB THEATRE;*23-29 January 2005.*

704. NATURAL CAUSES by Eric Chappell; CLUB THEATRE; *13-19 March 2005.*

705. OLIVER TWIST by Charles Dickens; CLUB DRAMA;*1-2 April 2005.*

706. HARVEY by Mary Chase; CLUB THEATRE *8 – 15 May and (*extract) *7 June 2005.*

707 – 716 + 113-14, 119, 128-30: HALE ONE-ACT PLAY FESTIVAL

707. THE WIZARD OF OZ by L Frank Baum, adapted by Julia Whitehead; PORT SUNLIGHT PLAYERS YOUTH GROUP; *6 June 2005. Dorothy:* Leah COPE; *Sorceress of The North:* Francesca FARLAM; *Tin Man:* Tyler RILEY; *Lion:* Josh FINIAN; *Witch of theWest:* Olivia PERRIAM; *Wizard of Oz:* Bradley TAYLOR; *Munchkins:* Caleb RILEY, Kerry LAMB, Caitlin FINIAN, Hannah KELLY, Hannah DOBSON, Hannah DONE, Faye TAYLOR, Isna COPE.

708. CAN YOU HEAR THE MUSIC by David Campton; THE PLAYERS, SKELMERSDALE; *6 June 2005. Tatty Mouse:* Hayley FARRELL; *Prickle Mouse:* Maire TUCKER; *Elder Mouse:* Rita ALLEN; *Fuss Mouse:* Lauren TAYLOR; *Giggle Mouse:* Catherine CAHILL; *House Mouse:* Lauren HALLAM. *Director / Stage Manager:* Mark ASHTON; *Music Director:* Martyn MELLOWDEW; *Costume:* Christine ASHTON.

709. TRACKS by Geoff Graves; SALE NOMADS; *6 June 2005. Felicity:* Charlotte SMITH; *Annabel:* Sam JOHNSON; *Gillian:* Chris HUTSON; *Lucy:* Leila PILKINGTON; *John:* Dave BLACK. *Director:* Geoff GRAVES.

710. DARN IT AND DUST by Mike Folie; HARLEQUIN PLAYERS; *7 June 2005. Greg:* Dylan WHITE; *Cheryl:* Kelly KITCHEN; *Bob:* john SMITH; *Marion:* Sue CURRAN; *Woman:* Sam DREW; *Man:* Matt LAMBERT. *Director:* Jon KERR; *Crew:* Gordon HAMLIN, Dave NORWOOD.

119. LAST TANGO IN LITTLE GRIMLEY by David Tristram; HYDE LITTLE THEATRE; *7 June 2005.*

128. RAINDROP FAIRIES by Sherri Phillips; MOSSLEY AODS NEXT GENERATION *8 June 2005*

129. WHO CARES by John Chambers; MOSSLEY AODS NEXT GENERATION;*8 June 2005*

130. CAGE BIRDS by David Campton; MOSSLEY AODS; *8 June 2005*

711. A GOOD KNIGHT'S WORK by Allan MacKay; CLUB DRAMA; *9 June 2005. Chamberlain:* Laurence TRALATOS; *Servant:* Sammi WARRING; *LORD Lily:* Aaron JONES; *Lady Lily:* Eleanor BATTRICK; *Lord Fitzroy:* Emma UNWIN; *Lady Fitzroy:* Grace FRYER; *King Ferd:* Ian PREST; *Queen Maud:* Natalie BROWN; *Princess Adeline:* Annabel GILMARTIN; *Executioner:* Natasha ROBSON; *Magician:* Rebecca FITCH; *Sir Blufus:* Jessica IRVING; *Sir Angus:* Lucy SPURRELL; *Sir Richard Trueheart:* Clare KEELING, *Directors:* Val HARRIS, Ian BOWEN.

712. OVERTIME By H Connolly; THE PLAYERS, SKELMERSDALE; *9 June 2005. Mrs Sullivan:* Sandi DUFFY; *Julie:* Christine FELTON; *Kevin:* Mark ASHTON; *Frank:* Ian DUFFY; *ALBERT:* Chris DIXON. *Director:* Ian DUFFY.

713. WIT'S END by Neil Rhodes; WILMSLOW GUILD PLAYERS; *9 June 2005. Nigel Phillips:* Tony HUGHES; *Dave:* Alex WILLIAMS. *Director:* Harry LOWE.

113. GIZMO by Alan Ayckbourn; ROMILEY LITTLE THEATRE; *10 June 2005.*

714. FOOL'S ERRAND by Margaret Wood; CLUB DRAMA; *10 June 2005. Hodge:* Will RODDY; *Margery:* Danielle WILSON; *Diccon:* Michael RUFF; *Bet:* Bethany LOXLEY; *Cuddy:* Andrew HILLS; *Alison:* Louise CARSON; *An Old Man:*Martin THELWELL. *Directors:*John BANKS, Colin WILD.

114. FLATMATES by Ellen Dryden; ROMILEY LITTLE THEATRE; *10 June 2005.*

715. WILL HE STILL LOVE ME TOMORROW by Liz Sharp; THE PORT SUNLIGHT PLAYERS; *11 June 2005. Voice One:* Joanne CARR; *Voice Two:* Elayne BEGGS; *Voice Three:* Mary LUNT; *Voice Four:* Averil HUGHES; *Voice Five:* Sarah SHARP; *Voice Six:* Vicky BURR. *Directors:* Liz SHARP, Judith McDADE.

716. WHODIDIT by Neil Harrison; HOMEBREWERS THEATRICAL COMPANY; *11 June 2005. Inspector:* Bud HODGSON; *Tom Darling:* Steven LEWIS; *Mary Darling:* Lowri JONES; *Bonecrusher:* Gwilym ROBERTS; *Uncle~:* Samantha MORGAN-JONES;

Mrs Meals: Janic YOUNG; *Scribbles:* Stacey GARDEN; *Shutters:* John MORGAN-JONES; *Travis :* Dylan JONES; *Stableman:* Christopher HOLLOWAY; *Susan Dageurrotype:* Elaine SMITH; *Skakles:* Michaela LAUDEN; *Professor:* Aidrian; *TomJnr:* Dylan JONES. *Lights:* Suezanne MORGAN-JONES; *Sound:* Sarah MORGAN-JONES.

DUNHAM MASSEY; WA14 4SJ; 0161-941 1025; **CAZ:** 144, A2

717. **ROMEO AND JULIET** by William Shakespeare; CHAPTERHOUSE THEATRE COMPANY; *23 July 2005. Director:* Philip STEVENS.

DUNHAM MASSEY VILLAGE HALL; School Lane WA14 5RN; **CAZ:** 132, A6 D

ELMRIDGE PRIMARY SCHOOL; Wilton Drive, HALEBARNS WA15 0JF; 0161-980 3543; **CAZ:** 146, C5

THE FIRS SCHOOL; Firs Road, SALE M33 5EL; 0161-973 7350; CAZ: 121, F5

FLIXTON GIRLS HIGH SCHOOL; Flixton Road M41 5DR; **CAZ**: 104, C5

271. **ROMEO AND JULIET** by William Shakespeare; MANCHESTER ACTORS COMPANY; *16 November 2004*

FOREST PARK SCHOOL; Oakfield, SALE M33 6NB; **CAZ:** 122, A4

269. **PINOCCHIO** by Stephen Boyes, based on the original story by Carlo Collodi; MANCHESTER ACTORS COMPANY; *17 March 2005.*

GORSE HILL PRIMARY SCHOOL;Burleigh Road; STRETFORD M32 0PF; 0161-865 1209; CAZ: 107, E3

HAYESWATER METHODIST CHURCH HALL; Hayeswater Road

DAVYHULME M41 7BL; 0161-755 3357; CAZ: 105, E4

IMPERIAL WAR MUSEUM NORTH; Trafford Wharf Road, TRAFFORD PARK M17 1TZ; 0161-836 4000; **CAZ:** 107, E1

JEFF JOSEPH TECHNOLOGY COLLEGE; Croft Road, SALE MOOR M33 2TZ; 0161 -973 2713; CAZ: 134, D1

LORETO CONVENT GRAMMAR SCHOOL; Dunham Road, ALTRINCHAM WA14 4AH; 0161-928 8310 / 3703; **CAZ:** 145, E1

LORETO CONVENT PREPARATORY SCHOOL; Dunham Road, ALTRINCHAM WA14 4AH; 0161-928 8310 / 3703; **CAZ:** 145, E1

LOSTOCK HIGH SCHOOL; Selby Road, STRETFORD M32 9PL; 0161-912 5200; **CAZ:** 106, 4A

MARKET HALL: Market Street, Altrincham; CAZ: 145, F1

MOSS PARK INFANTS SCHOOL; Moss Park Road, STRETFORD; **CAZ:** 106, B5

MOSS VIEW PRIMARY SCHOOL; Moss View Road, PARTINGTON M31 4DX; **CAZ:** 119, E6

NOMADS CLUBHOUSE; Friar's Road, SALE M33 7UU; **CAZ:** 122, B5

771. THE STEAMIE by Tony Roper; SALE NOMADS. *Dolly:* Pam SNAPE; *Mrs Culfeathers:* Val BACON; *Margrit:* Diane MACHIN; *Doreen:* Sam JOHNSON; *Andy:* Sam JOHNSON. *Director:* Brian TICKLE.

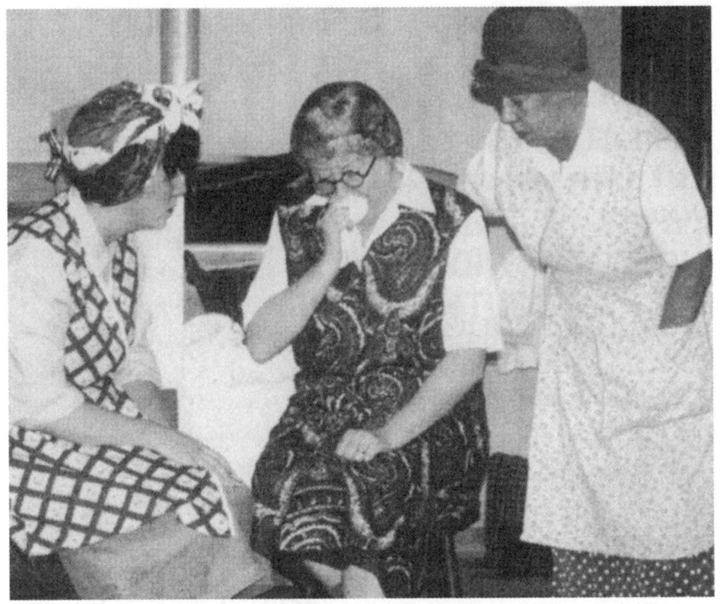

THE STEAMIE (771); SAM JOHNSON (Doreen), VAL BACON (Mrs Culfeathers), PAM SNAPE (Dolly), a trio of Award Winning performances.

PARK ROAD PRIMARY SCHOOL; Abbey Road, SALE M33 6NB; 0161-973 1392; **CAZ:** 122, A3

269. **PINOCCHIO** by Stephen Boyes, based on the original story by Carlo Collodi; MANCHESTER ACTORS COMPANY; *23 March 2005.*

PARTINGTON PRIMARY SCHOOL; Central Road; M31 4FL; 0161-775 2937; **CAZ:** 118, D6

POLISH CLUB; 188 Shrewbury Street M16 7PB; 0161-226 3622; CAZ: 108, B3

POOLSIDE THEATRE; URMSTON LEISURE CENTRE; Bowfell Road

M41 5RR; 0161- 746 8443; **CAZ:** 104, C5

ROBERT BOLT THEATRE; Sale Waterside Arts Complcx

ST ALPHONSUS PRIMARY SCHOOL; Hamilton Street, OLD TRAFFORD M16 7PT; 0161-872 5239; **CAZ:** 108, B2

269. PINOCCHIO by Stephen Boyes, based on the original story by Carlo Collodi; MANCHESTER ACTORS COMPANY; *23 March 2005.*

ST ANTHONY'S ROMAN CATHOLIC HIGH SCHOOL; Bradfield Road, URMSTON M41 9PD; 0161-748 4571; **CAZ:** 105, H5

ST HUGH OF LINCOLN PARISH HALL; Glastonbury Road, STRETFORD M32 9PF; 0161-748 3426; **CAZ:** 105, H4

718. LAST TANGO IN LITTLE GRIMLEY by David Tristram; *25-27 November 2004. Gordon:* Chris SILKE; *Bernard:* Frank OATES; *Joyce:* Barbara WILLIAMSON; *Margaret:* Linda IRISH; *Directo / Promptr:* Thelma ROBERTSON; *Assistant Director:* Tori HAWKER; *Stage Manager:* Garry BLAIR; *Design / Construction:* David BRAMWELL, John ROBERTSON; *Sound:* John ROBERTSON; *Lighting:* Ben TWELVES.

719. LAST PANTO IN LITTLE GRIMLEY by David Tristram; *25-27 November 2004. Gordon:* Alan PEARSON; *Bernard:* Howard ROBERTSON; *Joyce:* Sarah CATLING; *Margaret:* Aoife CAWLEY; *Directo / Promptr:* Thelma ROBERTSON; *Assistant Director:* Tori HAWKER; *Stage Manager:* Garry BLAIR; *Design / Construction:* David BRAMWELL, John ROBERTSON; *Sound:* John ROBERTSON; *Lighting:* Ben TWELVES.

720. THE MEANEST WEAPON by W Casey; HATS; *14-16 April 2005. Philip Jackson:* Chris SILKE; *Edith Carter:* Marjorie READ; *Police*

Sergeant: Frank OATES; *Carol Winters:* Sarah CATLING; *Irene Hunter:* Barbara WILLIAMSON; *Kate Rodman:* Anita PARTRIDGE; *Guy Rodman:* Andrew NEWTON; *Mary Frazer* Linda IRISH; *Inspector Grant:* Mark FINCH. *Director:* Brenda LOGAN; *Stage Manager:* Garry BLAIR; *Design / Construction:* David BRAMWELL, John ROBERTSON; *Sound:* John ROBERTSON; *Lighting:* Ben TWELVES; *Prompt:* Jeanette THORNLEY.

ST JOSEPH'S ROMAN CATHOLIC PRIMARY SCHOOL; Hope Road, SALE M33 3BF; 0161-973 4938; **CAZ:** 122, B5

ST MARY'S CHUCH OF ENGLAND PRIMARY SCHOOL; St Mary's Road SALE M33 6SA; 0161 - 912 3070; CAZ 122, A5

ST MICHAEL'S CHURCH OF ENGLAND PRIMARY SCHOOL; The Grove, FLIXTON M41; **CAZ:** 104, B6

ST PAUL'S CHURCH HALL; Springfield Road, SALE M33 7XS; **CAZ:** 122, B5

SALE MORE TECHNOLOGY COLLEGE; Norris Road M33 3JR; 0161-973 2713; CAZ: 134, D1

SAMUEL PLATTS; Trafford Wharf Road, SALFORD QUAYS M17 1HH; 0161-876 5222; CAZ: 107, F1

SCHOOL ROAD; Sale M33 7YF; CAZ: 122, B4

SHAWS ROAD; Altrincham; CAZ: 145, F1

STAMFORD SQUARE; Altrincham; CAZ: 145, F1

STRETFORD SCHOOL M32 8JB**;** 0161-865 2293.

268. **MACBETH** by William Shakespeare; MANCHESTER ACTORS COMPANY; *23 March 2005.*

TEMPLEMOOR INFANT SCHOOL; Temple Road; SALE; 0161 - 912 3666

TIMPERLEY METHODIST CHURCH; Stockport Road WA15 7UT; 0161-980 7064 / 8799 / 3336; CAZ: 133, G6

TOTTIES; Grafton Mall, ALTRINCHAM WA14 1DF; **CAZ:** 145, F1.

20. **POSSIBLY PORN;** written, directed and performed by Francesca Larkin and Lowri Shimmin; FAKING IT THEATRE COMPANY; *30-31 January 2005.* **Journal:** 18/1/05

TOWN SQUARE; Sale M33 7WW; CAZ: 122, B4

TRAFFORD CENTRE; Barton Dock Road; CAZ: 105, G1

TRAFFORD GENERAL HOSPITAL; Moorside Road, URMSTON M41 5SL; 0161-748 4022; **CAZ:** 104, C4

URMSTON GRAMMAR SCHOOL; Newton Road M41 5AF; 0161-748 2018; **CAZ:** 105, E5.

VICTORIA PARK JUNIOR SCHOOL; Davyhulme Road East, STRETFORD M32 0XZ; **CAZ:** 106, D5

270. **FIREBIRD** by Stephen Boyes; MANCHESTER ACTORS COMPANY; *13 July 2005.*

WAREHOUSE; South Trafford College, Dawson Road, Broadheath WA 14 5JP; 0161-973 7064; **CAZ:** 133, F3

WATERSIDE ARTS CENTRE; 1 Waterside Plaza, SALE M33 7ZF; 0161-912 5616; CAZ: 122, B4

721. THE BORROWERS by Mary Norton, adapted by Andy Graham; SNAP THEATRE COMPANY; *18 November 2004. Pod:* Chris MELLOWS; *Homily:* Elise DAVIDSON; *Boy:* Adam BORZONE; *Ariety:* Sarah Louise KASSELLE. *Director:* Andy GRAHAM; *Puppetry:* Sophia Lovell SMITH; *Lighting:* Bob BUSTANCE; *Design:* Francis GOODHAND.

722. CINDERELLA; SALE NOMADS; *7-15 January 2005.*

257. CURRY TALES by Rani Moorthy; RASA; *15 June 2005.*

155. THE UGLY EAGLE; MOVING HANDS THEATRE COMPANY; BIRMINGHAM REPERTORY THEATRE COMPANY;*10 February 2005 Director:* Steve JOHNSTONE.

724. I'M NOT MAD, I JUST READ DIFFERENT BOOKS; created and performed by Ken Campbell; THE BOOKING OFFICE; *11 February 2005*

723. MY UNCLE ARLY by Shon Dale-Jones and David Farmer, inspired by the life and work of Edward Lear; HOIPOLLOI THEATRE; TIEBREAK; *12 February 2005. Cast:* Ben FRIMSTON, Stephanie MULLER, Jill NORMAN, Andrew PEMBROOKE, Trond-Erik VASSDAL.

156. THE OWL AND THE PUSSYCAT, based on Edward Lear by TALL STORIES; *18-19 February 2005.*

306. ON THE VERGE by Mike Kenny; MIND THE … GAP; *5 March 2005.*

725. THICK AS THIEVES by Mark Whiteley; HARD GRAFT THEATRE COMPANY; *11 March 2005. Barry Ireland:* Daniel HOFFMAN-GILL; *Steph Aston:* Mark WHITELEY. *Director:* Mark WHITELEY; *Technical Director:* G S TODD; *Musical Director:* Jay BLACK.

726. HITTING FUNNYby Philip Ralph; VOLCANO THEATRE COMPANY; *17 March 2005. Chris Rich:* Philip RALPH. *Director:* Paul DAVIES.

WHITELEY. *Director:* Mark WHITELEY; *Technical Director:* G S TODD; *Musical Director:* Jay BLACK.

726. HITTING FUNNYby Philip Ralph; VOLCANO THEATRE COMPANY; *17 March 2005. Chris Rich:* Philip RALPH. *Director:* Paul DAVIES.

PHILIP RALPH, HITTING FUNNY

727. DAUGHTER OF THE WIND by Steve Byrne; INTERPLAY THEATRE; *8-9 April 2005. Director:* Steve BYRNE; *Design:* Barney GEORGE.

729. KISSING MARRIED WOMEN by Gordon Steel; HULL TRUCK THEATRE COMPANY; *5 May 2005. Carole / Other Women:* Emma ASHTON; *Micky:* Jason FURNIVAL; *Daft Dave:* Graham MARTIN. *Director:* Gordon STEEL; *Set / Lighting Design:* Graham KIRK; *Costume Designer:* John BODDY; *Stage Manager:* Jennifer HIRST; *Production Manager:* Richard BIELBY; *Technical Manager:* Dave SMELT; *Production Assistant:* John SIMS

KISSING MARRIED WOMEN (729)); JASON FURNIVAL and GRAHAM MARTIN

730. HOBSON'S CHOICE by Harold Brighouse; SALE NOMADS; *11 – 14 May 2005*

728. CANTERBURY TALES; an adaptation by Phil Woods and Michael Bogdanov; ROCKET THEATRE COMPANY; *18-20 May 2005.*

734 THE SPURTING MAN; AVANTI DISPLAY; *17 June 2005*

735. STALKERS; THE WRONG SIZE; *17 June 2005.*

607. ONE NIGHT OF SHAKESPEARE; BBC SHAKESPEARE SCHOOL FESTIVAL; *3 July 2005.* Simultaneous performances by 400 Schools in 100 Theatres Nationwide.

731. THE SNOW DRAGON by Toby Mitchell, adapted by TALL

STORIES THEATRE COMPANY; *23 July 2005. Billy:* Gareth FARLEY; *Mum:* Ruth HUTCHINSON; *Dad:* Thomas WARWICK. *Director:* Toby MITCHELL; *Creative Producer:* Olivia JACOBS; *Designer:* Polly SULLIVAN; *Puppet Designer:* Yvonne STONE; *Lighting Designer:* James WHITESIDE; *Musical Director:* Jon FIBER; *Music./ Lyrics / Music Production:* Jon FIBER, Andy SHAW.

426. **EARLY ONE MORNING;**
HORSE+BAMBOO; *26 August 2005.*

732. **GOING ...;**
HORSE+BAMBOO; *26 August 2005.*

WELLACRE HIGH SCHOOL FOR BOYS;
Irlam Road, FLIXTON M41 6AP; 0161-748 5011; **CAZ:** 103, F6

WOODHEYS PRIMARY SCHOOL;
Meadway, SALE M334PG; 0161-973 4478; **CAZ:** 133, G1

WIGAN

THE HERBAL BED (745); MARK TALBOT (Jack Lane) and STEPHANIE BAIN (Hester Fletcher); WIGAN LITTLE THEATRE.

ABRAHAM GUEST HIGH SCHOOL; Orrell Mount WN5 8HN; 01942 214 960

ABRAM CHURCH OF ENGLAND PRIMARY SCHOOL; Simpkin Street WN2 5QE; 01942 703 465

270. **FIREBIRD** by Stephen Boyes; MANCHESTER ACTORS COMPANY; *5 July 2005.*

ASPULL COMMUNITY CENTRE

ATHERTON HALL

BEDFORD HIGH SCHOOL; Manchester Road, LEIGH WN7 2AZ; 01942-672682

BRADSHAWGATE; Leigh

BYRCHALL HIGH SCHOOL; Warrington Road, ASHTON-IN-MAKERFIELD WN4 9PQ; 01942 728 221

CANSFIELD COMMUNITY HIGH SCHOOL; Old Road, ASHTON-IN-MAKERFIELD WN4 9TP; 01942 720711

CASTLE HILL ST PHILLIP'S CHURCH OF ENGLAND PRIMARY SCHOOL; Hereford Road, HINDLEY WN2 4DH; 01942 255 578

DEANERY CHURCH OF ENGLAND HIGH SCHOOL; Frog Lane WNI 1HQ; 01942 768 801; **WAZ:** J8

DERBY ROOM; Leigh Library, Town Hall Square, LEIGH; 01942 604131.

DOVER LOCK INN; Warrington Road, ABRAM WN2 5XX

FRED LONGWORTH HIGH SCHOOL, Printshop Lane, TYLDESLEY M29 8JN; 01942 672682 **W**

271. **ROMEO AND JULIET** by William Shakespeare; MANCHESTER ACTORS COMPANY; *16 November 2004*

268. **MACBETH** by William Shakespeare; MANCHESTER ACTORS COMPANY; *8 Febrnuary 2005.*

GARRETT HALL JUNIOR SCHOOL; Garrett Hall Lane, TYLDESLEY M29 7EY; 01942 883340

GOLBOURNE HIGH SCHOOL; Lowton Road

HAGFOLD ESTATE; Atherton

HAIGH HALL, Haigh WN2 1PE; 01942 832895; WAZ: N2

HAWKLEY HALL HIGH SCHOOL;Carr Lane WN3 5NY; 01942 491729 .

HESKETH-FLETCHER CHURCH OF ENGLAND HIGH SCHOOL; Hamilton Street, ATHERTON M46 0AY; 01942 882425

HIGHER FOLDS COMMUNITY CENTRE;4 Carisbrooke Drive, LeighWN7 2XA 01942 703303/704183

736. **A HIGHER VIEW;** HIGHER FOLDS YOUTH THEATRE;WIGAN PIER; GOLDEN YEARS; SCRIPTSHOP; *31 March 2005.*

HINDLEY COMMUNITY HIGH SCHOOL

IMPACT DRAMA STUDIO; Tyldesley; 01925 498829

KILHEY COURT HOTEL; Worthington Lakes, Chorley Road, STANDISH WN1 2XN; 01257 472100

KINGSDOWN HIGH SCHOOL

268. MACBETH by William Shakespeare; MANCHESTER ACTORS COMPANY; *2 February 2005.*

LOW HALL PRIMARY SCHOOL; Dower Street, Platt Bridge, HINDLEY WN2 3TH; 01942 866172

LOWTON CIVIC HALL; Hesketh Meadow Lane WA3 2AJ; 01942 672 971; H, W

LOWTON COMMUNITY HIGH SCHOOL; Newton Road WA3 1DU; 01942 603 419

MABS CROSS PRIMARY SCHOOL; Standishgate WNI IXL; 01942 43340; WAZ: K8

MARKET STREET, WIGAN WN1 IHS; WAZ: 8K NEWTON

MILL AT THE PIER; Wallgate WN3 4EU; 01942 323666; WAZ: J9

MORNINGTON HIGH SCHOOL; Mornington Road, HINDLEY WN2 4LG; 01942 55927

NUGENT HOUSE; Billinge.

OUR LADY IMMACULATE ROMAN CATHOLIC PRIMARY SCHOOL; WN4 0LZ

269. PINOCCHIO by Stephen Boyes, based on the original story by

Carlo Collodi; MANCHESTER ACTORS COMPANY; *9 February 2005. Pinocchio:* Christopher BARLOW; *Gepetto / Catflap / Stromboli:* Richard METCALFE; *Columbine / Foxy / Madam Grimaldi:* Viv WARENTZ. *Director / Designer:* Stephen BOYES; *Commedia Work:* Marcello UNGI.

PROFESSIONAL DEVELOPMENT CENTRE (WIGAN EDUCATION); 01942 254 280

ROSE BRIDGE HIGH SCHOOL, Holt Street, INCE-IN-MAKERFIELD WN1 3HD; 01942 44151

271. **ROMEO AND JULIET** by William Shakespeare; MANCHESTER ACTORS COMPANY; *1 November 2004. Romeo:* Adam BRODY; *Juliet:* Hellen KIRBY; *Capulet / Friar Lawrence:* Paul GUTHRIE; *Nurse / Lady Capulet:* Louise TWOMEY. *Director:* Stephen BOYES; *Designer:* Daniel WEST.

ST CUTHBERT'S ROMAN CATHOLIC PRIMARY SCHOOL; Thornburn Road, Norley Hall WN5 9LW; 01942 222 721; **WAZ:** 10E

269. **PINOCCHIO** by Stephen Boyes, based on the original story by Carlo Collodi; MANCHESTER ACTORS COMPANY; *18 March 2005.*

ST JAMES ROAD JUNIOR AND INFANTS SCHOOLS; ORRELL WN5 7AA; 01695 622659

ST JOHN FISHER HIGH SCHOOL; Baytree Road, SPRINGFIELD WN6 7RH; 01942 510715; **WAZ:** G6

271. **ROMEO AND JULIET** by William Shakespeare; MANCHESTER ACTORS COMPANY; *19 November 2004*

ST JOHN RIGBY COLLEGE; Gathurst Road, ORRELL WN5 0LJ; 01942 214 797; **WAZ:** A6

271. **ROMEO AND JULIET** by William Shakespeare; MANCHESTER ACTORS COMPANY; *19 November 2004*

ST JOSEPH'S HALL; Chapel Street, LEIGH WN7 2DA; 01942 606331

ST MARY'S AND ST JOHN'S ROMAN CATHOLIC PRIMARY SCHOOL; Standishgate WN1 1XL; 01942 824552; **WAZ:** K7

ST MARY'S ROMAN CATHOLIC HIGH SCHOOL, Manchester Road, ASTLEY M29 7EE; 01942 884 144.

ST MICHAEL'S CHURCH; 01942 768801

ST PAUL'S CHURCH OF ENGLAND PRIMARY SCHOOL; Warrington Road, GOOSE GREEN WN3 6SB; 01942 43068; **WAZ:** G13

ST PETER'S CHURCH OF ENGLAND PRIMARY SCHOOL; Leigh Street, LEIGH WN7 4TP; 01942 671442

ST PETER'S ROMAN CATHOLIC HIGH SCHOOL; Howard's Lane, ORRELL POST WN5 8PY; 01942 747 693

3. **SPARK** by Mary Cooper; M6 THEATRE COMPANY; *18 November 2004.*

ST RICHARD'S ROMAN CATHOLIC PRIMARY SCHOOL; Flapper Fold Lane, ATHERTON M46 0HA; 01942 882 980

270. **FIREBIRD** by Stephen Boyes; MANCHESTER ACTORS COMPANY; *8 July 2005.*

ST THOMAS CHURCH OF ENGLAND PRIMARY SCHOOL; Astley Street, LEIGH WN7 2AS; 01942 671442

ST THOMAS MORE ROMAN CATHOLIC HIGH SCHOOL; Wood Street, NEWTON WN5 0QU; 01942 46191; **WAZ:** G9

SACRED HEART JUNIOR SCHOOL; Throstlenest Avenue WN6 7RH; 01942 43013; **WAZ:** H6

SCOT LANE PRIMARY SCHOOL; WN5 0UE; 01942 760013; WAZ: F7

SHEVINGTON HIGH SCHOOL; Shevington Lane WN6 3HD; 01257 422652 / 423030

STANDISH HIGH SCHOOL; Kenyon Road WN6 0NX; 01257 4222265

TYLDESLEY LITTLE THEATRE; Lemon Street M29 8HT; 01204 655619; **W**

738. DAY OF RECKONING by Pam Valentine; *28 September – 2 October 2004. Ethel Swift:* Kaye TAYLOR; *Angela Brownlee:* Karen MORRIS; *Mavis Partridge:* Winnie beatty; *Sally Martin:* Jenny ORMAN; *Gloria Pitt:* Margaret SPEAKES; *Pauline Morris:* Roma ETHERINGTON; *Marjorie Organ:* Andrea PETERS; *Geoffrey Morris:* Denis BEARDSWORTH. *Director:* Ian TAYLOR; *Stage Management:* Wallace TAYLOR; *Continuity:* Hazel RIMMER; *Properties:* Margaret SPEAKES, Kaye TAYLOR, et al; *Wardrobe:* Margaret SPEAKES, Jacqueline COUNSELL; *Lighting Design:* Roger PARR; *Lighting Set-up:* Roger PARR, Paul WHUR; *Lighting Operation:* Ian HUGHES; *Sound:* Paul WHUR; *Set Construction:* Ken BERRY, Charlie SIDLOW, Wallace TAYLOR, Ian TAYLOR, Tony THOMPSON; *Make-up:* Lisa TAYLOR.

739. SINBAD THE SAILOR by John Morley; *4-11 December 2004. Sinbad:* Ingrid FOLKARD-EVANS; *Mrs Semoline Sinbad:* David BEARDSWORTH; *Tinbad the Tailor:*

ANDREA PETERS: Crunchbones, in a production nominated for the GMDF Best Panto Award

Paul BEARDSWORTH; *Mustapha Wee-Wee:* Ian TAYLOR; *The Caliph of Constantinople:* Hazel RIMMER; *The Princess Pearl:* Sara-Jayne ARNOLD; *Sinistro:* Garth WADDUP; *Talida:* Julia HOUGHTON; *Crunchbones:* Andrea PETERS; *The Old Man of The Sea:* Tony THOMPSON; *Bludruncolda:* Winnie BEATTY; *El Hump:* Emily BUTLER, Hannash FLINT; *Audrey:* Lisa TAYLOR; *The Wazir:* Ken BERRY; *Sutra:* Roma ETHERINGTON; *Kama:* Winnie EVANS; *Scrubdeck . Native / Mrs Constance E Nople:* Karen MORRIS; *Mazola:* Kaye TAYLOR; *Radio Voice:* Margaret SPEAKES; *StanT Nople / Native:* Ian HUNTER; *Comical Ali:* Ian HUGHES. *Director:* Ian TAYLOR; *Choreography:* Michaela COURTNEY, *with* Shelley TICKLE; *Musical Director:* Martin TAYLOR; *Stage Management:* Wallace TAYLOR, Val BETTS, Ken BERRY, Paul PETERS, Mike JEFFRIES, Ian HUGHES, Hazel RIMMER; *Properties:* Ken BERRY, Kaye TATLOR et al; *Wardrobe:* Hilda TAYLOR, Margaret SPEAKES, Winnie EVANS, Jacquelie COUNSELL; *Lighting Set-up:* Roger PARR, Paul WHUR; *Lighting Operation:* Jenny ORMAN; *Additional Lighting:*Ian HUGHES, Kaye TAYLOR; *Sound Engineering:* Paul WHUR; *Set Construction:* Wallace TAYLOR, Ian TAYLOR, Charlie SIDLOW, Ken BERRY, Tony THOMPSON; *Set Decoration:* Frank BOWDLER; *Make-up:* Lisa TAYLOR.

740. **SILHOUETTE** by Simon Brett; *25-29 January 2005. Martin Powell:* Tony THOMPSON; *Detective Inspector Bruton:* Mike JEFFRIES; *Celia Wallis:* Kaye TAYLOR; *Detective Sergeant Fisher:* Ian HUNTER; *WPC Leach:* Margaret SPEAKES; *Detectice Constable Wilkins:* Ken BERRY. *Director:* Jenny ORMAN; *Stage Management:* Wallace TAYLOR; *Continuity:* Winnie BEATTY; *Properties / Wardrobe:* Margaret SPEAKES; *Lighting Design:* Roger PARR; *Lighting Set-up:* Roger

PARR, Paul WHUR; *Lighting Operation:* Ian HUGHES, Jenny ORMAN; *Sound Operation:* Paul WHUR; *Set Construction:* Ken BERRY, Charlie SIDLOW, Wallace TAYLOR, Ian TAYLOR, Tony THOMPSON, Denis BEARDSWORTH, Roger PARR; *Set Design:* Paul WHUR; *Set Decoration:* Tony GREEN, Val BETTS; *Make-up:* Lisa TAYLOR;.

742. DON'T DRESS FOR DINNER by Marc Camoletti, adapted by Robin Hawdon; *15 – 19 March 2005.Bernard:* Ian TAYLOR; *Jacqueline:* Andrea PETERS; *Robert:* Jog MAHER; *Suzanne:* Alexandra JONES; *Suzettte:* Lisa GARRISH; *George:* Gary KENNEDY. *Director Set Design:* Mike JEFFRIES; *Stage Management:* Tony THOMPSON; *Continuity:* Winnie BEATTY; *Lighting Operation:* Jenny ORMAN; *Sound Operation:* Paul WHUR; *Set Construction:* Ken BERRY, Charlie SIDLOW, Wallace TAYLOR, Ian HUNTER; Garth WADDUP, Tony THOMPSON, Denis BEARDSWORTH,Paul PETERS, Ben PETERS;*: Make-up:* Lisa TAYLOR.

743. WASHBOARD BLUES by Do Shaw; *20-26 May 2005. Annie:* Winnie BEATTY; *May:* Julia HOUGHTON; *Lily* Ingrid FOLKARD-EVANS; *Edie:* Andrea PETERS; *Jessie:* Roma ETHERINGTON; *Emma:* lisa TAYLOR; *Irene:* Karen MORRIS; *Doris:* Winnie EVANS; *Sandra:* Rachel ELDER; *Marlene:* Hayley WARBURTON; *Maisie:* Kaye TAYLOR; *Eva:* Joyce ELDER; *Gloria:* Hannah SPEAKES; *Joe:* Ian TAYLOR; *Charlie:* Denis BEARDSWORTH; *Kenny:* Paul WARD; *Bert:* Ken BERRY; *Clive:* Garth WADDUP; *Johnny:* Paul BEARDSWORTH; *Tea Lady:* Olive AIRD; *Man In Club:* Ian HUNTER. *Director / Continuit / Set Designy:* Margaret SPEAKES; *Musical Director:* Martin TAYLOR; *Stage Management:* Wallace TAYLOR; *Properties / Wardrobe:* Margaret SPEAKES; *Lighting Design:* Roger PARR' Paul WHUR;; *Lighting Operation:* Jenny ORMAN; *Sound Operation:* Paul WHUR; *Set Construction:* Ken BERRY, Charlie SIDLOW, Wallace TAYLOR, Ian HUNTER, Tony THOMPSON, Val BETTS, Paul PETERS, Ben PETERS, Roger PARR; *Choreography:* Jacqueline COUNSELL

744. DRINKING COMPANION by Alan Ayckbourn; *whenever the company get the opportunity to display their award-winning achievement. Harry:* Tony THOMPSON; *Paula:* Julia HOUGHTON; *Bernice:* Ingrid FOLKARD-EVANS; *Waiter:* Frank BOWDLER. *Director:* Julia

HOUGHTON; *Continuity:* Winnie EVANS; *Stage Management:* Winnie EVANS, Ian TAYLOR.

TURNPIKE CENTRE; Civic Square, LEIGH WN7 1EB; 01942 404469; turnpikegallery@wlct.org

737. PIER ZERO by Stephen M Kelly; SCRIPTSHOP; *6 April 2005.*

UPHOLLAND HIGH SCHOOL, Sandbrook Road, ORRELL WN5 7AL

WATER'S EDGE; Mill Lane, APPLEY BRIDGE WN6 9DA

WESTPARK PRIMARY SCHOOL; Tennyson Avenue, LEIGH WN7 5JY; 01941 606834

WIGAN LITTLE THEATRE; Crompton Street WN1 3SL; 01942 242561; **WAZ:** 8K

745. THE HERBAL BED by Peter Whelan; *22 September – 2 October 2004. John Hall:* Paul DAVIES; *Susannah Hall:* Colette KERWIN; *Elizabeth Hall:* Hannah WORRALL; *Hester Fletcher:* Stephanie BAIN; *Rafe Smith:* Martin GREEN; *Jack Lane:* Mark TALBOT; *Bishop Parry:* Mike DELANEY; *Barnabus Goche:* Stan FELLOWS. *Director / Stage Design:* Bob BARTHOLOMEW; *Stage Manager:* Liam DISLEY; *Set Construction / Painting:* Brian PODMORE, Ivan WILCOCK, Stuart WORTHINGTON, Linda PODMORE, Clare HODKINSON; *Lighting Design:* Rob DELANEY; *Sound Design:* Kenneth TALBOT; *Technical Crew:* Steve UNSWORTH, Stuart WORTHINGTON, et al; *Costumes:* Philip RHODES, Homburgs of Leeds; *Properties:* Pat HALL, Beryl BARTHOLOMEW, Jean DELANEY, Janet HOGAN, Rita ROBY; *Prompts:* Maureen SCHOFIELD, Rita BENSON, Pat JOLLEY.

746. ABSURD PERSON SINGULAR by Alan Ayckbourn; *27 October – 6 November 2004. Sidney Hopcroft:* Frank CULLEN; *Jane Hopcroft:* Debbie NORRIS; *Geoffrey Jackson:* Greg PATMORE; *Eva Jackson:* Kathleen QUINN; *Ronald Brewster-Wright:* John CHURNSIDE; *Marion Brewster-Wright:* June GRICE. *Directors:* Teresa HAMPSON, Tracey

UNSWORTH; *Stage Design:* Brian PODMORE; *Set Construction:* Brian PODMORE, Linda PODMO, Ivan WILCOX, John CHURNSIDE, , Michael VAUGHAN; *Stage Managers:* Linda DonBAVAND, Mauren SCHOFIELD; *Lighting / Sound:* Kentigern QUINLAN, Chris WILCOX, Kenneth TALBOT, Brian HEAP, Stuart WORTHINGTON, Peter HALL; *Properties:* Linda MUSSELL, Mary McKEOWN, Eileen SMALLEY, Edi SPURGEON, Gerald WALKER, Maggie BATE; *Costumes:* Philip RHODES, Rita MAYOH, Rita BENSON.

747. HINDLE WAKES by Stanley Houghton; *1-11 December 2004. Mrs Hawthorn:* Ellen FITTON; *Christopher Hawthorn:* Brian PODMORE; *Fanny Hawthorn:* Victoria ALLEN; *Mrs Jeffcote:* Kath BERRY; *Nathaniel Jeffcote:* Tony WEBB; *Ada:* Mel SHERRIFF; *Alan Jeffcote:* Jamie ROBERTS; *Sir Timothy Farrar:* David SMART; *Beatrice Farrar:* Ruth ROBERTS. *Director:* Paul BUER; *Set Design:* Brain PODMORE; *Set Construction:* Brian PODMORE, Linda PODMORE, Ivan WILCOCK, Stuart WORTHINGTON, John CHURNSIDE, Ellen FITTON, Irene ROBERTS, Rita ROBY; *Stage Manager:* Ian FIELD; *Stage Crew:* Dave JOHNSON, Ivan WILCOCK, Liam DISLEY, Bill COLLINS; *Lighting Design:* Andrew EVERETT, Chris WILCOCK, Kentigern QUINLAN; *Sound Design:* Kenneth TALBOT; *Properties*; Mary McKEOWN, Janet HOGAN, Eileen SMALLEY, Maggie BATE; *Costumes:* Philip RHODES, Clive GREEN, Elsie DANIELS; *Wigs / Hair:* Ellen FITTON; *Promprs:* Margaret DERBYSHIRE, Margaret KINLEY, June WHITTAKER.

748. PUSS IN BOOTS by Bill Collins; *14-29 January 2005. The Crystal Fairy:* Julia WALSH; *Omnivar:* David SMART; *King Septimus:* Ian FIELD; *Princess Mirabelle:* Jessica RICHMOND; *Pickles:* Kevin METCALFE; *Nurse Gertie Grype-Water:* John CHURNSIDE; *Peter:* Kate BLACKLEDGE; *Puss:* Tara HAYWOOD; *Little Puss:* Melissa HIGHAM; *Esmerelda:* Bill COLLINS; *Little Shoddy:* Dave JOHNSON; *Mrs Grubby Bear:* Bill COLLINS; *Loopy Lou:* John CHURNSIDE; *Hanky Panky:* Kevin METCALFE; *Dorothy:* Michaela BENFOLD; *Child:* Anthony WARD; *Dancers:* Holly QUINLAN, Michelle TABERNER, Samantha TABERNER, Katie STOTT, Stephanie HIGHAM, Lauren MOLYNEUX; *Chorus:* Anthony WARD, Lewis RAMSDALE, Keiron BENTHAM, Paul WORRALL, Michaela BENFOLD, Megan WANE, Shannon

METCALFE, Abby KENDRICK, Sandy ARMSTRONG, Eleanor FINCH, Marie GRAHAM, Kelly SILLERY; *MUSICIANS: Keyboard:* Joan BOND; *Drums:* Jas WHITTAKER. *Director:* John CHURNSIDE; *Musical Director:* Joan BOND; *Choreographer:* Jayne QUINLAN; *Set Design:* Brian PODMORE; *Set Construction:* Brian PODMORE, Ivan WILCOCK, John CHURNSIDE; *Set Painting:* Brian PODMORE, Linda PODMORE, Kevin METCALFE, Rot TENNYSON, Tracey UNSWORTH; *Stage Management:* Ivan WILCOCK, George BATE, Roy TENNYSON; *Lighting Design:* Kent QUINLAN, Chris STOTT; *Lighting Operation:* Keny QUINLAN, ChrisSTOTT, Stuart ROWLANDS; *Sound:* Peter HALL, Scott HOWARTH; *Costumes:* Philip RHODES, Elsie DANIELS; *Properties:* Linda MUSSELL, Janet HOGAN.

749. BLITH SPIRIT by Noel Coward; *23 February – 5 March 2005. Edith:* Louise STEGGALS; *Ruth:* Maureen SCHOFIELD; *Charles:* Greg PATMORE; *Dr Bradman:* Paul BUER; *Mrs Bradman:* Jennifer LEE; *Madame Arcati:* Margaret FINCH; *Elvira:* Kathleen QUINN; *Voices of Daphne:* Catrione AITKIN, Aoife AITKIN. *Director:* Jack DEAN; *Stage Management:* Ivan WILCOCK, George BLAKE, Roy TENNYSON, Brian MARSH; *Set Construction / Painting:* Ivan WILCOCK, John CHURNSIDE, Jack DEAN, Liz DODD; *Lighting:* Kent QUINLAN, Paul STOTT, Chris STOTT, Ryan SHAW, Jason SHAW, Stuart ROWLANDS; *Sound Effects:* Kenneth TALBOT, Greg PATMORE; *Sound Operation:* Peter HALL, Scott HOWARTH; *Costumes:* Philip RHODES, Elie DANIELS; *Properties:* Janet HOGAN, Linda MUSSELL, Eileen SMALLEY, Gail BRADBURY, Rita ROBY, Margaret DERBYSHIRE, Kathleen BERRY; *Prompts:* Rita ROBY, Rita MAYOH,Jenny MOKRYSZ.

750. WANTED – ONE BODY by Charles Dyer; *6-16 April 2005.Miss Barraclough:* Linda PODMORE; *Mabel Middy:* Ellen FITTON; *Anne Beale:* Tara HAYWOOD; *Ted Johnson:* Steve UNSWORTH; *Mr Blundell:* Stan FELLOWS; *Mr Mickleby:* Mark TALBOT; *Agnes:* Irene ROBERTS; *Dr Brown:* Tony Webb; *Mr Sorrell:* Kenneth H TALBOT. *Director:* Bill COLLINS; *Set Design:* Brian PODMORE; *Set Construction:/ Painting:* Brian PODMORE,Tony WEBB, Ivan WILCOCK, Beth BUDD, Linda PODMORE, Ellen FITTON, Jayne QUINLAN, Mark TALBOT, Irene ROBERTS, Holly QUINLAN; *Stage Management:* Liam DISLEY, Roy

TENNYSON; *Sound Design:* Kenneth H TALBOT; *Lighting Design:* Kentigern QUINLAN; *Technical Crew:* John CHURNSIDE, Stuart WORTHINGTON, Roy TENNYSON, Brian HEAP; *Properties:* Mary McKEOWN, Ann ROBINSON, Gail BRADBURY, Maggie BATE, Pat STANSBIE; *Wardrobe:* Philip RHODES, Elsie DANIELS, Clive GREEN; *Prompts:* Kathleen BERRY, June WHITTAKER, Cynthia TAYLOR.

751. **DOUBLE DOUBLE** by Eric Elice and Roger Rees; *11-21 May 2005.Duncan McFee:* Peter HALL; *Philipa James:* Linda DonBAVAND. *Director* Pat HALL; *Set Design / Construction:* Brian MARSH, Ivan WILCOCK, Brian PODMORE; *Masks / Specialist Artwork:* Alex SHAW; *Stage Manager:* Linda MUSSELL; *Lighting / Sound:* Kentigern QUINLAN, Ryan SHAW et al; *Prtops:* Marian MYERS, Angela SHAW, Beryl DALLING; *Costume:* Philip RHODES; *Prompts:* Margaret FINCH, Margaret KINLEY, Junr WHITTAKER.

752. **'ALLO 'ALLO!** By Jeremy Lloyd; *22 June – 2 July 2005, Rene:*Bill COLLINS; *Edith:*Jean DELANEY; *Yvette:*Colette KERWIN; *Mimi:*Nicola REYNOLDS; *Michelle:*Tracey UNSWORTH; *Le Clerc:*Bob BARTHOLOMEW; *Pianist:*Joan BOND; *Colonel Von Stromh:* Tony WEBB; *Herr Otto Flick:* Stuart WORTHINGTON; *Helga:* Tara HAYWOOD; *Lt Hubert Gruber:* Clive GREEN; *General Von Schmelling:* Ian FIELD; *German Soldier:* Mark TALBOT; *Capt Alberto Bertorelli:* John CHURNSIDE; *Oficer Crabtree:* Kenneth TALBOT; *Airmen:* Mark TALBOT, David SWIFT; *Also:* Rita BENSON, Margaret KINLEY. *Director:* Mike DELANEY; *Set Design . Construction / Painting:* Mike CRUIKSHANK, Brian MARSH, Eddie WALSH, Tony WEBB, Ivan WILCOCK, Brian PODMORE; *Stage Manager:* Roy TENNYSON; *Lighting Design:* Kentigern QUINLAN; *Lighting:* Andrew EVERETT, Jason SHAW; *Sound Design:* Kenneth TALBOT; *Sound:* Brian HEAP, Ryan SHAW; *Props:* Eileen SMALLEY, Janet HOGAN, Maggie BATE, Mary McKEOWN, Gail BRADBURY, Linda MUSSELL, Ann ROBINSON; *Wardrobe:* Philip RHODES, Elsie DANIELS; *Music:* Joan BOND; *Choreography:* Jane QUINLAN; *Prompts:* Rita BENSON, Margaret KINLEY

753. **GUY 'N' MOLLS;** WIGAN LITTLE THEATRE YOUTH GROUP; *13-16 July 2005. Cast:* Abigale RAMSDALE, Natasha BOLTON, Amber HODGKISS, Paul WORRALL, Keiron BENTHAM, Andrew

LEGGOTT, Amy he, Ben McNALLY, Sam RIGBY, Krista GOODFELLOW, Mel SHERRIFF, Mark CHARLTON, Rebecca BANKS, Tom NOLAN, Nicola ROBINSON, Jessica RICHMOND, Leah JONES, Jessica BIRTWISTLE, Kate LYNCH. *Directors:* Colette KERWIN, Martin GREEN, Mark TALBOT; *Stage Management:* Ian FIELD; *Lighting / Sound:* Kent QUINLAN, Emma ARMSTRONG; *Vocal Coach:* Rick KERSHAW; *Music Production / Arrangement:* Greg PATMORE; *Choreographer:* Jayne QUINLAN; *British Sign language Interpreters:* Co-Sign.

754. WHY ME? by Stanley Price; *17 – 27 August 2005. John Bailey:* Gerald WALKER; *Helen Bailey:* June KIRKBY; *Mary Ferguson:* Kath BERRY; *Arthur Hollis:* John McCABE; *Gwen Hollis:* Jennifer LEE; *Tom Bailey:* Mark CHARLTON. *Director:*Maureen SCHOFIELD; *Set Design:* Brian PODMORE; *Set Construction:* Ivan WILCOCK, Tony WEBB, Brian MARSH, John CHURNSIDE; *Set Painting:* Val MILLER, Brian MILLER, Jayne QUINLAN, Holly QUINLAN; *Stage Manager:* Roy TENNYSON; *Lighting /Sound:* Kentigern QUINLAN, Ryan SHAW; *Properties:* Linda MUSSELL, Janet HOGAN, Ann ROBINSON; *Costume:* Philip RHODES, Elsie DANIELS; *Prompt:* June WHITTAKER, Rita BENSON, Cynthia TAYLOR.

WIGAN PIER; Wallgate WN3 4EU; 01942 323666 / 512994; **WAZ:** J9

755-766: REPLAY CABARET – an evening of script-in-hand performances by WIGAN PIER THEATRE COMPANY of new play-writing, on the theme of Gravity. *Director:* **Stewart Aitken;** *Development Officer:* **Martin Green;** *Dramaturg:* **Kavyasiddhi;** 2 April 2005

755. GRAVE SITUATION by Andrew Hardie; *Cast:* Stewart AITKEN, Will TRAVIS, Vicky FLEMING.

756. THIRTY YEARS OLD, THIRTY YEARS ON by John Clays; *Cast:* Melanie ASH, Martin GREEN, KAVYASIDDHI.

757. BLACK HOLE by Peter Brooks; *Cast:* Will TRAVIS, Vicky FLEMING.

758. **GRAVITY** by Christopher Mumford; *Cast:* Stewart AIUTKEN, Martin GREEN, Melanie ASH.

759. **COOKING FOR ONE** by Lee Kelly; *Cast:* Stewart aitken, Martin GREEN, Will TRAVIS.

760. **KITTY HAD HER MOMENTS** by Frank Gibbons; *Cast:* Melanie ASH, Vicky FLEMING.

761. **GRAVITY** by Rob Roughly; *Cast:* Martin GREEN, Melanie ASH

762. **I WANT TO FLY** by Greg Ritchie; *Cast:* Martin GREEN, Will TRAVIS

763. **FEET OF THE GROUND** by John Darby and Christine Darby; *Cast:* Martin GREEN, Vicky FLEMING, Melanie ASH.

764. **GRAVITY** by Lara Quinn; *Cast:* Will TRAVIS, Melanie ASH, Vicky FLEMING.

765. **STAIRLIFT** by Sue Plover; *Cast:* KAVYASIDDHI, Vicky FLEMING

766. **GRAVITY** by Julie McKiernan; *Cast:* Will TRAVIS, Stewart AITKEN.

WINSTANLEY COLLEGE; Winstanley Road, BILLINGE WN5 7XE; 01942 623006

Section 4

ARTISTS INDEX

Artists Index

A

B

C

CHEN Guosen; 62, 63, 64, 65

CHEN Zhongjian; 62, 63, 64, 65

D

E

F

G

H

Artists Index

T

U

V

W

X

Y

Z

Section 5

PLAYS INDEX

5. PLAYS INDEX

Plays Index; Indexed by PRODUCTION NUMBERS, FROM Section 1

Plays Index; Indexed by PRODUCTION NUMBERS, FROM Section 1

Plays Index; Indexed by PRODUCTION NUMBERS, FROM Section 1

Plays Index; Indexed by PRODUCTION NUMBERS, FROM Section 1

Plays Index; Indexed by PRODUCTION NUMBERS, FROM Section 1

Plays Index; Indexed by PRODUCTION NUMBERS, FROM Section 1

Plays Index; Indexed by PRODUCTION NUMBERS, FROM Section 1

Plays Index; Indexed by PRODUCTION NUMBERS, FROM Section 1

Plays Index; Indexed by PRODUCTION NUMBERS, FROM Section 1

Plays Index; Indexed by PRODUCTION NUMBERS, FROM Section 1

Section 6

C O M.P A N I E S

I N D E X

6. COMPANIES INDEX

2021 Performance; Swansea;

21st Century Demonstration;

2 B' 4;

3D, 15 Higher Calderbrook, LITTLEBOROUGH OL15 9NL; 01706 379164;

50 Dolla Playas;

A&O;

A4; 462

Aakaar Puppet Theatre; Rajastan;

AB Centre of Performing Arts; 22 Greek Street, Stockport SK3 8AB; 0161-429 7413;

Abbey Theatre Dublin; 003531 878 7222; www.abbeytheatre.ie;

Abraham Moss Centre Pantomime Theatre; Crescent Road, CRUMPSALL M8 6UF; 0161-740 1491, Ext 335;

Abraham Moss Centre Theatre; Crescent Road, CRUMPSALL M8 6UF; 0161-740 1491, Ext 335;

Abraham Moss Centre Youth Theatre; Crescent Road, CRUMPSALL M8 6UF; 0161-740 1491, Ext 335;

Abraham Moss High School; Crescent Road, CRUMPSALL M8 6UF; 0161-740 5141; 569

Act I;

Act Productions:

Act Too; 4 Needham Avenue, CHORLTON-CUM-HARDY M21 8AA; 0161-860 6797

ATC - Actors Touring Company; Alford House, Aveline House, LONDON SE11 5DQ; 0207 735 8311;

Action Transport Theatre; EPIC, McGarva Way, ELLESMERE PORT, Cheshire L65 9HH; 0151-357 2120;

Activ8, Octagon Theatre, Howell Croft South, BOLTON BL1 1SB; 01204 529407; 145, 148, 160

Active Performance Society; c/o Manchester University Drama Department M13 9PL; 0161-275 3347;

Action Space Mobile; PO Box 73, BARNSLEY S75 1NE; 01226 384944;

Actors of Dionysus; 44 Old Steine, BRIGHTON BN1 1NH; 01273 320 396; actorsofdionysus.com;

Actors Tourng Company; Alford House, Aveline Street,LONDON SE11 5BR; 0207-735 8311;

Advanced Drama Centre;

Adzido - Pan African Dance Ensemble; Canonbury Centre, 202 New North Road, LONDON N1 7BL; 0207 359 7453;

Aisling Players; 4 Menston Avenue, NEW MOSTON M40 3GE; 0161 - 684 7859;

AJN Productions Ltd; 212

Companies Index; Indexed by PRODUCTION NUMBERS from Section 1

Birchfields Primary School; Lytham Road, MANCHESTER M14 6PL; 0161-224 3548;

Doreen Bird College of Performing Arts; Birkbeck Centre, Birkbeck Road, SIDCUP. Kent DA14 4DE; 0208 -300 6004 / 3031;

Birmingham Hippodrome; Hurst Street B5 4TB; 0121-622 7486;

Birmingham Repertory Theatre; Broad Street B1 2EP; 0121-236 6771; 68, 155, 549, 553, 597

Birmingham Royal Ballet; Birmingham Hippodrome, Thorp Street, BIRMINGHAM B5 4AU; 0121-622 2555;

Birmingham Stage Company; The Old Repertory Theatre, Station Street, BIRMINGHAM B5 4DY; 0121 - 643 9050; 380, 561

Bishop Bilsborrow Memorial Roman Catholic Primary School; Princess Road, MOSS SIDE M14 7LS; 0161-226 3649;

Bitesize Theatre;

Black Arts Alliance; PO Box 86, MANCHESTER M21 7BA; 0161-832 7622; baa@blackartists.org.uk ;

Black Box; www.blackbox,uk.net ; 243

Black Fish Theatre; Karachi, Pakistan; pakimprov@yahoo.com ;

Blessed Thomas Holford College; Urban Road, ALTRINCHAM WA15 8HT; 0161-928 6020; 566

Blinding Image; Manchester Grammar School, Old Hall Lane, MANCHESTER M13 0XT; 01925 755168;

Blind Summit Theatre; info@blimdsummit.com ;

Blue Magic Productions; 405

Blue Mountain Theatre; www.bluemountaintheatre.com ; 381

Boarshaw Primary School; Stanycliffe Lane, MIDDLETON M24 2PB; 0161-653 9536;

Bock & Vincenzi; Toynbee Studios, 28 Commercial Street, LONDON E1 6LS; 0207 247 5102;

Bollington Festival Players; 2 Brampton Avenue, Upton, MACCLESFIELD SK10 3DY; 01625 429872;

Bolton Catholic Musical and Choral Society; 01204 533632; 83, 101

Bolton Catholic Youth Theatre; 122

Bolton Institute;

Bolton Little Theatre; Hanover Street, Bolton BL1 4TG; 01204 394223; 80, 86, 89 , 92, 95, 100, 103, 107

Bolton Multicultural Arts:

Bolton Premier AOS; 20 Carlton Road, Heaton, BOLTON BL1 5HU; 01204 842678;

Booking Office, The; 724

Bootleg Theatre Company: Sherborne House, 20 Greyfriars Close, SALISBURY, Wiltshire SP1 2LR; 01722 421476;

Boojum Theatre Company; 7 Lea Mount, 38 Lea Mount Road, HEATON MOOR SK5 4JU; 07958 285 478 ; boojumtheatrecompany@yahoo.co.uk ; 140

Border Crossings;

Rex Boyd; The Cafe Royal, 68 Regent Street, LONDON W1R 6EL; 0207-734 5300;

Bouge-de-la; Flat 2, Lawn Upton house, Sandford Road, Littlemore, OXFORD OX4 4PU; 01865 749583;

Bowler Hat Productions; info@bowlerhatproductions.co.uk

Brass;

Brassneck Theatre Company; 0161-980 1629;

Breaking Cycles; www.benjireid.com ; 165, 166, 167

Brekete;

The Brendan O'Carroll Group; www.agnesbrowne.com ; 379, 387

Bright Ltd; 10 Macklin Street, Covent Garden, LONDON WC2B 5NF; 0207-242 1882;

Brighton Theatre Events; 01273 821054;

Brilliant Theatre Company; c/o Contact Theatre, Oxford Road, MANCHESTER M15 6JA; www.angelfire.com/celeb2/brillianttheatre

Briscoe Lane Junior School; NEWTON HEATH M40 2TB; 0161-681 1783 / 6465;

Bristol Old Vic; King Street, BRISTOL BS1 4ED; 0117 949 3993;

Broads With Swords; broadswithswords@onetel.net.uk:

Brookdale Theatre; Brookdale Club, Bridge Lane, BRAMHALL SK7 3AB; 0161-483 1441; 116, 613, 625, 626, 627, 628

Nick Brooke Ltd;

Brookside School; Ashbourne Drive, High Lane, DISLEY SK6 8DB; 01663763943;

Brookway High School; Moor Road, Manchester M23 9BP; O161-998 3992;

Brouhaha; Jericho Productions, Toynbee Studios, 28 Commercial Street, LONDON E1 6LS; 0207-377 6010;

Brownmark Productions; c/o Arden School of Theatre, Manchester City College, Chorlton Street, MANCHESTER M1 3HB; 0161-279 7257: 30

Builders Association, The; 453 Broome Street # 4c, New York NY 10013-2669 USA; 001 212 274 1446; www.thebuildersaccociation.org;

Bunion Spring Emporium;

Burnage Garden Village Players; 19 South Avenue M19 2WS; 0161-224 3587;

Burnage High School; Burnage Lane, MANXHESTER M19 1ER; 0161432 1527; 573

Bury Athenaeum AOS;

Bury Theatre Works; The Met, Market Street, BURY BL9 0BW; 0161-761 7107;

Bush Theatre; Shepherds Bush Green, LONDON W12 8QD; 020 8602 3703;

Buzz Stop;

ByPass;

Byte 2 Infinity; Manchester University Drama Department M13 9PL; 0161-275 3347;

C Theatre; 158

Cacahuete;

Cadmium Compagnie; 10 Rue vieille de l'hermitage, 95300 PONTOISE; 033 683 775 229; info@cadmiumcompagnie.com ; 35

Camera:

Cambridge Arts Theatre; 6 St Edwards Passage CB2 3PJ; 01223 578933; smarsh@cambridgeartstheatre.com ;

Cameron MacKintosh; 1 Bedford Square, LONDON WC1B 3RA; 02071-637 8866;

CAN; Community Arts NorthWest; www.can.uk.com ; 459

Canal Studio;

Cardboard Citizens; 26 Hanbury Street, LONDON E1 6QR; www.cardboardcitizens.org.uk ;

Carol Godby Theatre Workshop;

Caribbean Showtime;

Carnesky's Ghost Train Ltd; www.carneskysghosttrain.net ;

Carpe Diem;

Thomas Carter; 449

Cartesian-Welles Co;

Carver Theatre; Church Lane, MARPLE SK6 7AW; 0161-427 3183;

Catapult Theatre;

Caterpillar;

Catherine Wheels Theatre Company; c/o Brunton Theatre, Ladywell Way, MUSSELBURGH, East Lothian EH21 6AF Scotland; 01620 829697;

Celebrating Cultures;

Celebrity Pig Theatre Company; c/o Manchester Mencap Crossacres Resource Centre, 1 Peel Hall Road, MANCHESTER M22 5DG; 0161-437 9465; admin@CelebrityPig.orguk ;

Celesta Players; 13 Moor Park Road, East Didsbury M20 5PF; 0161- 434 7668;

Certain Curtain Theatre Company; Unit 128, Oyston Mill, Strand Road, PRESTON, Lancashire PR1 8RU; 01772 731 024; cctheatre@yahoo.com; 464

C'Est Tout Theatre Company; 01772 431 300;

CHADS, Mellor Road, CHEADLE HULME SK8 5AU; 0161-486 1788: 629, 630, 631, 632, 633, 649

Chad Tadpole; tonybrgss@aol.com;

Champ Productions; 0207-241 6459;

Chaplins Pantos;

Duggie Chapman

Chapterhouse Theatre Company; 8-10 Guildhall Street, LINCOLN LN1 1TT; www.chapterhouse.org ; 338, 717

Charlestown Primary School; Pilkington Road, MANCHESTER M9 7BX; 0161-740 3529;

Cheadle Hulme Campus, Ridge Danyers College; Cheadle Road SK8 6BB; 0161-485 4372; 579

Cheadle Hulme School; Claremont Road SK8 6EG; 0161-485 7201; 571

Cheek By Jowl; www.cheekbyjowl.com ; 581

Chic Neurosis; 461

Chicken Shed Youth Theatre; London; www.chickenshed.org.uk ;

Children's Amateur Theatre Society;02154 671 914 88, 102

Children's Hearing Impaired Charities; 01204 362888;

Children's Showtime; PO Box 127, REDHILL, Surrey RH1 3FE; 01737 642243;

China Here and There; 11 Lansdowne House, Wilmslow Road, DIDSBURY, Manchester M2O 6UJ; 0161-434 6936

Chinese Arts Centre; 36 Charlotte Street, MANCHESTER M1 4FD; 0161-236 9251;

Chipping Norton Theatre; 2 Spring Street, Oxfordshire OX7 5NL; 01608 642 349; admin@chippingnortontheatre.co.uk ;

CHOL Theatre Company; Friends Meeting House, Church Street, Paddock, HUDDERSFIELD HD1 4UB; 01484 424045;

Chorlton High School; Nell Lane M21; 0161-882 1150; 570

Chorlton Players; 27 Clarendon Road, WHALLEY RANGE M16 8LB; 0161 - 860 7605; www.chorltonplayers.co.uk ; 195

Christ Church Green Group; Lillian Grove, REDDISH SK5 6EQ; 0161-480 8147;

Christie Theatre Company;

Chrysalis Theatre Company;

Chuckle Brothers, The; Phil Dale, QDOS Talent, 8 King Street, Covent Garden, KONDON WC2E 8HN; www.thechucklebrothers.co.uk;

Churches Together In Chorlton; Manchester Road Methodist Church M21; 0161 - 860 4681;

Churchill Theatre; High Stree, Bromley, Kent BR1 1HA; 0208-464 7131; 77, 78, 393

CICT;

Cinquefoil Productions;; Arden School of Theatre, Sale Road, NORTHENDEN M23 0DD;

Cirque Baroque;

Circus Hilarious; www.circushilarious.co.uk ; 683

Citizens' Theatre Company; Gorbals, GLASGOW G5 9DS; 0141 429 0022;

City College Performing Arts; Sale Road, NORTHENDEN, Manchester M23 0DD; 0161-957 1719;

City College Performing Arts; Whitworth Street M1 3HB; 0161-236 3418;

Claremont Junior School; Claremont Road, MANCHESTER M147NA; 0161-226 2066;

Classworks Theatre; Cambridge Drama Centre, Covent Garden, CAMBRIDGE CB1 2HR; 01223 461901; www.classworks.org.uk ;

Clean Break Theatre Company; 2 Paithull Road, LONDON NW5 2LB; 020 7482 8600; general@cleanbreak.org.uk ; 290

Clear Channel Entertainment; 35 Grosvenor Street, LONDON W1K 4QX; 020 7529 4300; 405, 412

Cleveland Theatre Company (CTC); Arts Centre; Vane Terrace, DARLINGTON DL3 7AX; 01325 352 004; 153

ClubDrama (Youth); 17 Oxford Road, ALTRINCHAM WA14 2ED; 0161-928 3542; 705, 711, 714

Club Theatre; 17 Oxford Road, ALTRINCHAM WA14 2ED; 0161-928 3542; 701, 702, 703, 704, 706

Clydebuilt Puppet Theatre; 618

Jacqui Coghlan;

Ailie Cohen;

Coliseum Youth Theatre; Fairbottom Street, OLDHAM OL1 3SW; O161-624 1731;

Collaborators Theatre Company; 18 Finkle Street, KENDAL, Cumbria LA9 4AB; O1539 724 684; www.collaboratorstheatre.co.uk ;

Collective Artistes;

Common Ground Sign Dance Theatre;

Community Amateur Theatrical Society; The Co-operative Hall; Holly Hedge Road, WYTHENSHAWE M22 4QN; 0161 - 945 1051, 0161 - 613 1516;

Community Arts NorthWest; 1 Stevenson Square, MANCHESTER M1 1DN; 0161-237 3674;

Company F/Z; www.companyfz.com ; 315

Compact Theatre Company; 30 Sycamore Close, Bolsover, CHESTERFIELD, Derbyshire; S44 6DZ; 01629 534697;

Company:Collisions; PO Box 3357, BRIGHTON BN2 1BB; 01273 710 884; www.company.collisions.com ;

David Glass Ensemble, The; 6 Aberdeen Studios, 55 Brewer Streete, LONDON W1F 9UN; 0207-334 6030; info@davidglassensemble.com ; 45

David Johnson & Richard Temple;

Robin Deacon; 441

DC Entertainment;

Dead Earnest Theatre; 57 Burton Street, SHEFFIELD S6 2HH; 0114 233 4579;

Deceptive Bends Theatre Company;

De La Warr Pavilion; Marina, BEXHILL-ON-SEA, East Sussex TN40 1DP; 01424 787 900; www.de-la-warr-pavilion.org.uk ;

De Musset & Co;

Denton West Amateur Dramatic Society; Comminity Centre, Hulme Road M34 2WZ; 0161-442 6049; 0161-336 3879;

Denver Centre for the Performong Arts; Colorado, USA;

Denys Edwards Players;

Department of Correction; Jo Burgess & Nikki Street, Sentry Farm, EXMINSTER EX6 8DY; 01392 832 268; fools@foolsparadise.co.uk ;

Desperate Measures Theatre Company; c/o Abraham Moss Centre Theatre, Crescent Road, Crumpsall M8 6UF; 0161-795 4186;

Destin-Asian Arts Lyd; 598

Derby Playhouse; Theatre Walk, Eagle Centre, DERBY DE1 2NF; 01332 363 271; derbyplayhouse@demon.co.uk;

Desperate Men; 3 Fairlawn Road, Montpelier, BRISTOL BS6 5JR; 0117 924 0612; 419

Desperate Optimists;

Deus Ex Machina Theatre Company; 18 Elder Mount Road, Blackley, MANCHESTER M9 8BT;

Dewsbury Arts Group;

DGM Productions; Somerset House, Somerset Road, TEDDINGTON, Middlesex TW11 8RT;

Didsbury Church of England Primary School; Elm Grove M20 6RL; 0161-445 7144; 325

Didsbury Studio Theatre Company; 799 Wilmslow Road, MANCHESTER M20 2RR; 0161-247 2086 / 2379;

Disability Action Group; Wigan Youth Service, Gateway House, Standishgate, WIGAN WN1 1XL; 01942 828955;

Disney Theatrical Productions; 6150 Porter Road, Sarasota, FLORIDA FL34240 USA; (813) 349-4848; 362

Dodger Theatrical Holdings; Stage Group, AMSTERDAM, Holland;

Dog Snogger Productions;

Donmar Warehouse; 41 Earlham Street, Seven Dials, LONDON WC2H 9LX; 020 7240 4882; www.donmarwarehouse.com ; 224

Doo Cot; Unit 4, Bentinck Street, MANCHESTER M15 4LN; 0161-835 2546; doo-cot@cssystems.net ; 337

Dood Pard; Spuistraat 226" 1012 VV, Amersterdam, Netherlands; 31 20 4214990;

Double Take Theatre; www.doubletake.org.uk ;

Drama Workshop Youth Theatre; 5 Ventnor Avenue, Astley Bridge, BOLTON BL1 8PY; 01204 307893; 07931 337764;

Dream Theatre Company;

Dreamcatcher Theatre Company; 234

Drill Hall, The; 16 Charles Street, London WC1E 7EX; 029 7307 5060; www.drillhall.co.uk ; 154

Droylsden Little Theatre; 20 Doverdale Road, Offerton, Stockport SK2 5DY; 650, 651, 652, 653, 654, 655

Drum Theatre; Theatre Royal, Royal Parade South, PLYMOUTH, Devon PL1 3LF; 01752 668 282; theatreroyal.com ;

DSM Theatre Company; 237

Dubbeljoint, Belfast;

Ducie Central High School; Lloyd Street North M14 4GA; 0161-2321639;

Duckie; 623

Duende; 25 Hawkes Street. Small Heath, BIRMINGHAM B10 9SA; 0121-773 8542;

Duggie Chapman;

Dukes, The; Moor Lane, LANCASTER LA1 1QE; 01524 67461;

Dukinfield AODS; 27 Ash Street, MIDDLETON M24 2HA; 0161-643 5369; 678

Dunham Thespians; 12 York Street, ALTRINCHAM WA15 9QH; 0161 - 927 7920;

Dynamic New Animation - (DNA Theatre Company); Studio 9, The Watermark, Ribble Lane PRESTON PR2 5EX; 0976 946 003; 335, 615

E&B Productions; Suites 1 & 3, Waldorf Chambers,11 Aldwych, LONDON WC2B 4DA; 0207-836 2795;

earthfall; chapter, Market Road, CARDIFF, Wales CF5 1QE; 029 2022 1314; www.earthfall.org.uk ; 589

East Cheshire Musical Theatre Company;

Eat Theatre; 525

Eclipse Theatre; www.eclipsetheatre.org.uk ; 309

Eclipse Youth Theatre; Phoenix Theatre, Westerham Avenue, off Liverpool Road, SALFORD M5; 0161-736 1566;

Edgefold Players; 17 Walkden Road, WORSLEY M28 3DA; 0161-799 3595; 123, 124, 540

Edinburgh Puppet Theatre; 81 Great Junction Street, LEITH, Edinburgh EH6 5HZ; 0131-554 8923;

Effective Theatrical Productions Ltd;

Fairly Famous Family; Ellerbank, Ellerigg Road, Ambleside, CUMBRIA LA22 9EE; 01539 433 268; 421

Faking It Theatre Company; c/o Arden School of Theatre, Manchester City College, Chorlton Street, MANCHESTER M1 3HB; 0161-279 7257: 20

Fame Factory;

Famos Bramwells;

Famous Music Company Limited;

Fantastic Few Theatre Group; Pendleton College, Dronfield Road, SALFORD M6 7FR; 0161-736 5074;

Farnworth Little Theatre; Cross Street, Farnworth, BOLTON BL4 7AG; 01204 415163; 108, 109, 110, 111, 112 131

Farnworth Performing Arts Company; 20 Glenside Drive, BOLTON BL3 2EL; 01204 654113; 79, 106

Paul Farrah Productions; Strand Theatre, Aldwych, LONDON WC2B 4LD;

Fascinating Aida; www.fascinating-aida.co.uk ;

Fat Cat Theatre;

Fat Bloke Productions;

Faulty Optic; 12 Savile Road, Lindley, HUDDERSFIELD, West Yorkshire HD3 3DH; 01484 536027;

fecund Theatre; 6 Cleland Road, Chalfont St Peter, BUCKINGHAMSHIRE SL9 9BG; 01753 882692 / 01831 770106;

Feelgood Theatre Productions Ltd; 21 Lindum Avenue, WHALLEY RANGE M16 9NQ; 0161-862 9212; caroline.clegg@talk21.com ; 259

Felgates:

Feld Entertainment;

Festival Players; Abraham Moss Centre, Crescent Road, CRUMPSALL M8 5UF; 0161 - 908 8326;

Fiery Angel Ltd; 22-24 Torrington Place, LONDON WC1E 7HJ; 020 7907 7040; www.fiery-angel.com ; 612

Fifth Amendment; Second Floor, 6 Shaw Street, WORCESTER WR1 3QQ; 01905 26424; http: //www.ukarts.com;

Fifth House Productions; 7 Arnesby Avenue, SALE M33 2NJ; 0161-962 3390; fifthouseproductions@hotmail.com;

Filter Theatre; BAC (Battersea Arts Centre): Lavender Hill, BATTERSEA SW11 5TH; O20 7223 0086; www.bac.org.uk;

Fifth Column Theatre; http: www. fithcolumn.org.uk;

Filthy Gibbon Productions; c/o Manchester University Drama Department M13 9PL; 0161-275 3347;

Fineline Theatre Company;

Fink On Theatre Company; 0162-868 0237;

First Cut Drama Group; Hulme Library, Stretford Road, HULME M15 5FQ; 0161-226 1005;

Fittings Multi Media Arts; 44 Bowler Street, LEVENSHULME M19 2TY; 0161-431 5779 / 07887 598219; 448

Five Arts Centre; Malaysia;

The Flying Buttresses; Jo Burgess & Nikki Street, Sentry Farm, EXMINSTER EX6 8DY; 01392 832 268; fools@foolsparadise.co.uk ;

Flying Gorrillas, The; 279a Westbourne Park Road, LONDON W11 1EE; 020 7727 5018; www.flyinggorillas.co.uk ;

Flying Pig Company, The; www.theflyingpigcompany.com ;; 4 West View Cottage, Northwich Road, Higher Whitely, WARRINGTON WA4 4PN; 01925 730 649; 225

Forced Entertainment; Unit 102, The Workstation, 46 Shoreham Street, SHEFFIELD S1 4SP; 01742 798977; fe@forced.co,uk; 303

Forkbeard Fantasy; PO Box 1241, 34 Balmoral Road, BRISTOL BS7 9AZ; 0117 924 8141;

Fortune Youth Theatre;

Forum Company; Romiley Forum, Compstall Road, ROMILEY SK6 4EA; 0161 - 430 6570;

Foundland; Manchester;

Foundry Theatre; New York;

FourPlay;

Foursight Theatre; Newhampton Arts Centre, Dunkley Street, WOLVERHAMPTON WV1 4AN; 01902 714257;

Frantic Assembly; BAC, Old Town Hall, Lavender Hill, Battersea, LONDON SW11 5TF; 0207- 228 8885; 307

Free Expression;

Freehand Theatre; 170

Freehold Theatre Company; 58 Rydal Road, LANCASTER LA1 3HA; 479

Fresco Theatre; 99 Frances Road, Norwood, GUATENG 2191, South Africa; 027 (11) 483 2851; www.frescotheatre.co.za ;

Front Room Theatre Company; flat 6, 120 Daisy Bank Road, VICTORIA PARK M14 5QH; 0161 - 248 8593;

frontROWtheatrecompany

Full Circle Theatre Company; c/o Oldham Coliseum;Fairbottom Street OL1 3SW; 0161-624 1731; 34

Full House Theatre Company;

Fully Functioning Theatre;

Function Factory, The; 01270 505552;

Funjabis, The; www.auntieG.com ;

Fun Song Factory;

Futures Theatre Company; Room 9; The Deptford Albany, London; 0208 865 3;

G&J Productions: 2nd Floor, Piccadilly Mansions, 1 Shaftesbury Avenue, LONDON W1V 7RL; 0207-439 1589;

Galaxatives, The; 249

Gandey World Class Productions; The Arts Exchange, Mill Green, CONGLETON, Cheshire CW12 1JG; 624

Garlic Theatre; 164 Norwich Road, New Costessey, NORWICH NR5 0EW; 01603 741850; www.garlicktheatre.com ; 176

Gecko; BAC (Battersea Arts Centre): Lavender Hill, BATTERSEA SW11 5TH; O20 7223 0086; www.bac.org.uk;

Gekidan Kaitaisha;

Generating Company, The; The Circus Space, Coronet Street, HACKNEY N1 6HD; 0207-613 4141;

Get On! Theatre Company; 180

Gilliganridingssykes; 0775 407 3188; 246

Glej Theatre; Ljubljana, Slovenia;

GlovesOff Productions; 491

Gobi Theatre Company;

Gogmagogs, The; Toynbee Studios, 28 Commercial Street, LONDON E1 6LS; 020 7247 0764;

Golden Years; 736

Good Company; 46 Quebec Street, BRIGHTON BN2 2UZ; 01273 606652; 407

Good Night Out; c/o Department of Drama, University of Manchester M13 9PL;

Goodnights Entertazinment; 586, 593

Gordon Craig Theatre; Lytton Way, Stevenage, Hertfordshire SG1 1LZ;0438 766642;

Gorse Hill Youth Arts Centre; www.gorsehillstudios.com ; 0161-864 1745; 222

Gorton Mount Primary School; Mount Road, MANCHESTER M18 7GR; 0161-224 5524;

Mark Goucher; 546, 594

Grææ Theatre Company; Interchange Studios, Hampstead Town Hall Centre, 213 Havestock Hill, LONDON NW5 4QP; 0207 681 4775;

Grand Theatre of Lemmings; www.lemmings.dircon.co.uk ; 422

Grange Arts Company; Oldham College, Rochdale Road OL9 6EA 0161 - 785 4239;

Derek Grant; 643

Julius Green & Ian Lenaghan;

Green Candle Dance Company; 224 Aberdeen House, 22 Highbury Grove, LONDON N5 2DQ; 0207-359 8776;

Green End Junior School; Burnage Lane M19 1DR; 0161-432 4327;

Green Ginger; 32 The Norton, Tenby, Dyfed, Wales; SA70 8AB; 0117 922 5599;

HATS (Hayeswater Amateur Theatrical Society); 41 Princess Road, URMSTON M41 5ST; 0161-748 5040; 718, 719, 720

Heald Green Theatre Company; 4 St Ann's Road, HAZEL GROVE SK7 5HZ; 0161 - 483 0534; 634, 635, 636, 637, 638, 639

Haymarket Basingstoke; Wole Street, BASINGSTOKE, Hampshire RG21 7NW; 01256 323073; www.haymarkey.org.uk; 72

Heartbeak Productions; The Old Church, Spencer Street, LEAMINGTON SPA, Warwickshire CV31 1NE; 01926 426523; info@heartbreakproductions.co.uk ; 220, 221, 260

Heaton Moor Guild Players; 01625 585562;

Jim Henson Company;

Brian Hewitt-Jones

Heywood Operatic and Dramatic Society; 80 George Street, HEYWOOD OL10 4PW; 767, 768

Higher Folds Youth Theatre; 736

Hindley & Wigan Amateur Operatic Society;

Hiss and Boo Music Hall Company; I Nyes Hill, Wineham Lane, BOLNEY, West Sussex RH17 5SD; 01444 881 707; www.hissboo.co.uk ;

Hit and Run Theatre Company; 550

Hit Entertainment;

Hittite Empire;

HNC Theatre Company; Abraham Moss Centre, Crescent Road, CRUMPSALL M8 5UP; 0161-795 4186;

Hoipolloi; Wysing Arts, Fox Road, CAMBRIDGE CB3 7TX; 01954 718881; 723

Hole In The Ground Theatre Company; c/o Department of Drama, University of Manchester, Oxford Road M13 9PL;

Hollandia;

Hollow Creature; Norway;

Thelma Holt Ltd; Waldorf Chambers, 11 Aldwych, LONDON WC2B 4DG; 020 7379 0438; www.thelmaholt.co.uk ; 548

Holy Rood Church Stage Society;

Homegrown Theatre Company; 2 Dorset Road, MANCHESTER M19 3WA; 07931 568 255;

Hooh Hah Productions; www.hoohhhah.co.uk ; 251

Hoodwink; High Point, Slab Lane, Woodfalls, SALISBURY SP5 2NO; 07816 005 929; info@hoodwinktheatre.co.uk 424

H.O.P.E Theatre Company; 276

Hope High School; Eccles Old Road, SALFORD M6 8FH; 0161-736 2637; 582

Horse + Bamboo; Bacup Road, ROSSENDALE, Lancashire BB4 7HB; 01706 220241; 425, 426, 444, 732

Horwich RMI & District AODS; 58 Merbourne Grove, HORWICH BL6 5LZ; 01204 694643;

HotPot Theatre; http://hotpottheatre.tripod.com;

Hot Wax Theatre Company; 106 Derby Road, STOCKPORT SK4 4NG; 0161-442 9270; HOTWAXTHEATRE@HOTMAIL.COM;

Sonia Hughes;

Hull Truck Theatre Company; Spring Street, HULL HU2 8RW; 01482 224800; 140, 587, 729

Hulme Hall School; 75 Hulme Hall Road. CHEADLE HULME SK8 6JZ; 0161-485 4638;

Hungry Grass Theatre Company; 8 Wolstonbury Road, Hove, East Sussex BN3 6EJ; 01273 202909;

Hyde Festival Association; 1 Springbank Avenue; AUDENSHAW M34 5WG; 0161 - 370 1918;

Hyde Little Theatre; 9 Brooks Avenue, Gee Cross, HYDE SK15 5HP; 0161 - 331 1488; 119, 658,661, 663, 665

Hyde Light Opera Society;

Hyde Musical Society; 662

Ian Dickens Productions; 468

Ice and Fire Theatre Company; www.inplaceofwar.net ;

Iconoclast Foundation, The; c/o Arden Cenre, Sale Road, Northenden M23 0DD; 0161-957 1715

Ilbijerri Aboriginal and Torres Strait Islander Theatre Co-operative; Victoria, AUSTRALIA;

Illyria; Cress Hill Farm, Barton Road, WELFORD - ON - AVON, Warwickshire CV37 8HG; 01789 751017;

ImageMusical Theatre; 23 Sedgeford Road, LONDON W12 0NA; 0208-743 9380; www.imagemusicaltheatre.co.uk ; 173

Imagination Productions; www.imaginationproductions.co.uk ;

Imitating The Dog;

Impact Theatre Company (Oldham);

Impact Theatre Company (Tyldesley); 14 Pennant Close, Oakwood, WARRINGTON WA3 6RR; 01925 498829; info@impact-theatre.co.uk ;

Imperial War Museum North; Trafford Wharf Road, TRAFFORD PARK M17 1TZ; 0161-836 4000;

Imprint Theatre Company; 465

Improbable Theatre; c/o BAC, Lavender Hill, LONDON SW11 5FT; 0207 978 4200;

Inamorata; 2 Clydesdale Tower, Holloway Head, City Cenre, BIRMINGHAM B1 1UG;

In Cahoots;

Kepow Theatre Company;

Kinder Kunst Korporation;

Jenny King; Centreline Productions; www.centrelinenet.com ;558

KipperTIE;

Knockout Theatre Company; 0161-832 9090;

Know Your Onions Theatre Group; 127

Kobal Theatre Company; @bigredartworks.co.uk;

Komedia Entertainment; 11-14 Kensington Stree, BRIGHTON BN1 4AT; 01273 573 711; www.komediaentertainment.com ;

Kompany Malakhi

Kosmic Krew, The; www.thekosmickrew.com ; **646**

KTO; Poland;

Krazy Kat Theatre Company, The; Flat 6, 104 Fentiman Road, LONDON SW8 1QA; 0207 820 0687;

Kushite Theatre; 4 Temple Court, Thorncroft Street, LONDON SW8;

La Fanfarra; Spain;

,
Ladybarn Primary School; Briarfield Road, MANCHESTER M20 4SR; 0161-445 4898;

Laine Johnson Theatre Workshops; Charter Street Ragged School, 142 Danzic Street, MANCHESTER M4 4DN; 07966 449 463;

Lantern Theatre Company;

Larkin About; Martin Long, 1 Buckingham Avenue, West Moseley, SURREY KT8 1TG; 0208878 3018;

Latecomers Theatre Company; 6 Torbay Road, CHORLTON M21 8XD; 0161-881 7066;

Latrinite; Belgium;

Launch Pad; 01270 505552;

Laughing Monsta Theatre Company; 07742 267 416;

Lawnmowers, The; Newcastle Upon Tyne;

Leandre & Claire; Spain;

Lee & Dawes; 13 Percival Road, Sherwood, NOTTINGHAM NG5 2FA; 0115 948 6115 / 962 0783;

Lees Street Congregational Church AMDS; 770

Leicester Haymarket; Belgrave Gate LEI 3YQ; 01533 530021;

Leigh and Atherton Writers;

Leikin Loppu; 3 Roundhay Grove, LEEDS LS8 4DR; leikinlopp@aol.com;

LeKoa; www.lekoe.co.uk ; 07957 3000107; 247

Lempen Puppet Theatre; 620

Lennie & Morris; www.pincusrose.co.uk;

Companies Index; Indexed by Production Numbers; From Section 1

Northern Broadsides; Dean Clough, HALIFAX HX3 5AX; 01422 369704; 588, 599, 600

Northern Elastic; northernfop@aol.com ; 241

Northern International Theatre Projects; c/o Welfare State International, Lanternhouse, The Ellers, ULVERSTON, Cumbria LA12 0AA; 0794 1258485;

Northern Stage Ensemble; Newcastle Playhouse, Haymarket, NEWCASTLE UPON TYNE NE1 7RH; 0191-232 3366;

Northern Quarter Theatre Company; 01625 536069; www.northernquartertheatrecompany.com ; 230, 232

Northern Youth Theatre; c/o Manchester Gr ammar School, Old Hall Lane, MANCHESTER M13 0XT; 0161-224 7201; p.n.a.baylis@mgs.org ;

North Manchesters, The; 74 Medlock Way, LEES, Oldham OL4 3LD; 0161-624 0979;

North West Playwrights; 18 St Margaret's Chamber's, 5 Newton Street, MANCHESTER M1 1HL; 0161-237 1978; 161, 162, 218, 218, 223, 478

Not Another Theatre Company; c/o Arden School of Theatre, Manchester City College, Chorlton Street, MANCHESTER M1 3HB; 0161-279 7257: 22

Not The National Theatre Company; 89 Hargwyne Street, LONDON SW9 9RH; 0207-733 9615;

Nottingham Playhouse; Wellington Circus; East Circus Street, NOTTINGHAM NG1 5AF; 0115 947 4361; www.nottinghamplayhouse.co.uk ; 142

NRG;

NTC Touring Theatre Company; The Playhouse, Bondgate Without, ALNWICK, Northumberland NE66 1PQ; 01665 602 586; ntc-touringtheatre.co.uk;

Nu Century Arts;

Nuffield Theatre; University Road, SOUTHAMPTON, Hampshire SO17 1TR; 023 8031 5500; info@nuffieldtheatre.co.uk ;

Oakwood College of Performing Arts; Darly Avenue, MANCHESTER M217JG; 0161-881 5133;

Octagon Theatre; Howell Croft South, BOLTON BL1 1SB; 01204 529407; 135, 137, 138, 139, 141, 142, 143, 144

Oily Cart; 209 Welsbach House, Broomhill Road, LONDON SW18 4JQ; 0182-877 0743; www.oilycart.org.uk ;

Oldham Coliseum;Fairbottom Street OL1 3SW; 0161-624 1731; 72, 76, 223, 244, 466, 467, 469, 470, 472, 474, 476, 477

Oldham College Performing Arts; Rochdale Road OL9 6EA; 0161-624 8013;

Oldham Metropolitan Amateur Operatic Society; 8

Oldham Sixth Form College; Union Street WestOL3 1XU; 0161-628 8000;

Paines Plough; Fourth Floor, 43 Aldwych, Covent Garden LONDON WC2B 4DA; 0207-240 4533;
Paisley Arts Centre; Abbey Close, PAISLEY, Scotland PA1 1JF; 0141-887 1007; art.els@renfrewshire.gov.uk;

Palace Theatre Watford; Clarendon Road, WATFORD WD1 1JZ; 01923 810307

Palaver Productions; 2b Park Road, Monton M30 7JJ; 0161-789 1869;

Pandies; India;

Panick Puppets & Clowns;

PaperCut Theatre Company; papercuttheatre@yahoo.co.uk ; 524

Parachute Theatre Company; 01392 832268; parachute@parachutetheatre.co.uk ;

Paradise Productions;

Park Dean School; St Martins Road, OLDHAM OL8 2PY; 0161-620 0231; 583

Parm Kaur;

Parrs Wood High School; Wilmslow Road, EAST DIDSBURY M20; 0161-445 8786;

Partisan Theatre;

Partington Players; 65 Sheffield Road, GLOSSOP, Derbyshire SK13 8QX; 01457 861072; 117
+
Sue Passmore Theatre Workshops; Birkbeck Centre, Birkbeck Road, SIDCUP, Kent DA14 4DE; 0208-300 6004;

Patter; BAC (Battersea Arts Centre): Lavender Hill, BATTERSEA SW11 5TH; 020 7223 0086; www.bac.org.uk;

Paul Nicholas & David Ian Associates;

Pavement Theatre; 0161-286 1148; 193

Trevor Payne; 410

Peepolykus Theatre Company; The Croft, Old Church Road, Colwall, Worcestershire WR13 6EZ; 01684 540366;

Pele Productions; 552

Pendleton College Performing Arts, Dronfield Road, SALFORD M6 7FR; 0161-736 5074;

Penny Plain:

Peoplescape Theatre; People's History Museum, The Pump House, Bridge Street, MANCHESTER M3 3ER; 0161-839 6061; 431, 432, 433, 434

People Show, The; People Show Studio, St James The Great Institute; Pollard Row, LONDON E2 6NB; 0207-729 1841; 261

Performance Studio Workshop of Nigeria;

Perth Theatre Company; High Street; 01738 38123;

Peshkar Productions; Oldham Museum, Greaves Street, OLDHAM OL1 1DN; 0161-620 4284; info@peshkar.org.uk ; 58

Peter Frosdick & Martin Dodd;

Presto Puppet Theatre; Greenwood, 13 College Road, BUXTON, Derbyshire SK17 9DZ; 01298 778849;

Priestley Players; 18 Laburnum Avenue, SWINTON M27 0DN; 0161 - 793 0580; 542, 543, 544

Priestnall School; Priestnall Road, HEATON MERSEY SK4 3HW; 0161-442 8850; Priestley Players; 207 Woodsend Road, FLIXTON M41 8QW; 0161-748 9746;

Les Primities; Gordon Wilson, Clos de Ornes 19, Wesembeek Oppem B1970 Belgium; 32/2 215 0217; www.primitives.be ; 445

Primitive Science; Basement Flat, 15 Church Terrace, LONDON SE13 5PT; 0207 247 9745;

Professor Popup's Puppet Theatre; 117 Oakfield Road, Stapleford, NOTTINGHAM NG9 8FE; 0115 939 9027;

Proteus;

Psappa; www.psappha.com ;

AndrÚ Ptaszynski;

David Pugh Ltd; 547, 591

Pump House; Bridge Street, MANCHESTER M3 3ER; 0161 - 839 6061;

Puppelboo Productions; c/o Arden School of Theatre, Manchester City College, Chorlton Street, MANCHESTER M1 3HB; 0161-279 7257: 21

Puppet Lab; 81 Great Junction Street, Leith EDINBURGH EH6 5HZ; 0131-554 8923; info@puppet-lab.com;

Pursued By A Bear; 6 Glenluce Road, LONDON SE3 7SB; 020 8480 9514; pbab@pbab.freeserve.co.uk;

PW Productions; 0207-734 7286;

QuantumSoup; 0161-225 1835;

Quantum Theatre; www.quantumtheatre.co.uk ; 682

Quarantine; 24 Len Cox Walk, MANCHESTER M4 5LA; 0161-839 6520; quarantine.itcuk.net ; 44

Queerupnoth; 5 Oak Street, MANCHESTER M4 5JD; www.queerupnorth.com ;

Quicksilver Theatre for Children; 4 Enfield Road LONDON N1 5AZ; 0207-241 2942;

QDOS Talant; 8 King Street, Covent Garden, LONDON WC2E 8HN; 393

Quondam Touring Theatre; 33 Brunswick Square; PENRITH, Cumbria CAII 7LS; 01768 864307; 164

r2;

Radcliffe St Thomas AODS;

Radcliffe URC Players;

Rainbow Theatre Company;

Raise Cain Theatre; raisecaintheatre@hotmail.co.uk ; 242

raisin the roof;

Royal National Theatre; South Bank LONDON SE1 9PX; 0207 452 3400 ; 47, 559

Royal Shakespeare Company; Stratford-upon-Avon CV37 6BB;01789 205301;

Royce Primary School; Rolls Crescent HULME M15 5FT; 0161-226 3095;

Ruby Tuesday Productions; 8FQ; 0161-226 2271;

Sad Brothers Inc; @ ultramail.co.uk;

Saddleworth Musical Society; Spring Brow Farm, Ladcastle Road, DOBCROSS OL3 5QT;

Saddleworth Players; Players' Theatre, Millgate, DELPH OL35JG; 01457 874644; 480, 481, 482, 483, 484

St Baraabus Church of England Primary School; Parkhouse Street, OPENSHAW M11 2JX;0161-223 3593;

St Bede's College; Alexandra Road, WHALLEY RANGE M16 8HX; 0161-226 3323; 574

St Catherine's Farnworth AMS; 01204 402052;

St Clement's Church of England Primary School; Abbey Hey Lane, MANCHESTER M11 1LR; 0161-301 3268;

St Damian's Roman Catholic High School; Lee Road, ASHTON-UNDER-LYNE OL6 8BH; 0161-330 5974;

St Dunstan's AODS; 10 Kenyon Lane, MOSTON M40 5HS; 0161-683 5919;

St Elizabeth's Roman Catholic Primary School; Calve Croft M22 5EU; 0161-437 3890;

St Francis of Assisi; Newall Green;

St Herbert's AD&ES; 769

St John Fisher and St Thomas More Roman Catholic Primary School; Woodhiuse Lane, BENCHILL M229NW; O161-998 3422;

St Joseph's Academy; Kilmarnock; www.thenanez.com ;

St Joseph's Players; 9 Mancheter Old Road, BURY BL9 0TR; 0161-705 2063; 115

St Joseph's Players; (Wigan); 01942 605981;

St Luke's Church of England Primary School; Langport Avenue , LONGSIGHT M12 4NG; 0161 – 273 3648;

St Luke's Arts and Drama Society (SLADS); Parish Hall, Derby Road, SALFORD M6 5RA; 0161-737 7934; 600,

St Margaret's Primary School; Withington Road, WHALLEY RANGE M16 8FQ; 0161-226 2271;

St Margaret Mary's Roman Catholic Primary School; St Margatet's Road, New Morton, MANCHESTER M40 0JE; 0161- 681 1504;

St Margaret Ward Roman Catholic Primary School; Cherry Lane, SALE M33 4GY; 0161-969 9852;

St Marks, with Christ Church, Glodwick, Stage Society; Waterloo Street GLODWICK OL4 1ER; 0161-652 3546;

St Mary's Primary School; Wilcock Street, Moss Side, MANCHESTER M16 7DA; 0161-226 1773;

St Mary's Roman Catholic Primary School; Wood Street, MIDDLETON M24 5GL; 0161-643 7594;

St Osmund's Amateur Productions; 01204 532866;

St Patrick's RC Primary School; Livesey Street, MANCHESRE M4 5HF; 0161 – 834 9004;

St Paul's (Astley Bridge) AODS; 81, 94

St Paul's Roman Catholic High School; Firbank Road, MANCHESTER M23 2YS; 0161-437 5841:

St Peter's Methodist Church Amateur Dramatic Society; Church Hall St Helens Road, BOLTON BL3 3SE; 01204 520334;

St Peter's Roman Catholic High School; Stopford Street, MANCHESTER M11 1FG; 0161- 370 3111;

St Peter's Roman Catholic Primary School; Firbank Road, MANCHESTER M23 2YS; O161-437 1495:

St Philip's AODS; Parochial Hall, Bridgeman Street, BOLTON BL3 6TH; 01204 595086 /524800: 96, 126

St Philip's Church of England Primary School; Loxford Street, MANCHESTER M15 6BT; 0161-226 2050;

St Simon & St Jude's ADS; 01204 526165 / 520232;

St Thomas More AODS:

St Thomas' AODS, Radcliffe;

St Vincent de Paul High School; Denison Road, Victoria Park MANCHESTER M14 5RX; 0161-224 7138;

St Vincent's ADS; 01204 64049; 84, 105

St Wilfred's Roman Catholic Primary School; Birchvale Close, HULME M15 5BJ; 0161-226 3339;

Sacha Brooks; 020 7437 2900;

Sale NOMADS; 25 Sibson Road, CHORLTON-CUM-HARDY M21 9RH; 0161-881 8416; 121, 722, 730, 771

Sale & Altricham Musical Theatre; Bardslet Hall, Wharf Road, ALTRINCHAM WA14 1ND; 01925 753915; 698

Salford Musical Theatre Company; 604

Salford Charter Players; 58 Moorfield Road, IRLAM O' TH' HEIGHS M6 7QD;

Salford Musical Theatre Company;

Salford Open Theatre Company; 24 Orama Avenue, SALFORD M6 8LL; 0161-789 6644; 0161-792 6735;

Salford University Theatre Department; 0161-295 6118;

Sussanah EK; 471

Martin Sutherland Productions; 430 Merton Road, LONDON SW18 5AE; 020 8875 0220; martin@martinsutherland.co.uk;

Swallow Productions;

Swank;

Swizzleshaker; swizzleshaker.com ; 429

Sydney Theatre Company; Pier 4 Hickson Road, Walsh Bay NSW 2000 PO Box 777, Millers Point 2000, AUSTRALIA; mail@sydneytheatre,com.au;

Sylvia Walker Players; 58 Kenyon Avenue, DUKINFIELD SK16 5AR; 0161-338 4662;

Synthesis-Project, The; www.synthesis-project.co.uk : 37, 345

TAAL Project; 11

Tabs Productions;

tackle owt; tackle.owt@zen.co.uk; 0973 932019;

Taki Rua Productions; Level One, Milbar Building, 85 Victoria Street, PO Box 24 167 WELLINGTON, New Zealand; +64 4 472-7377; takirue@clear.net,nz;

Talawa Theatre Company; the Cochrane Theatre, Southampton Row, LONDON WC1B 4AP; 0207-404 5662;

Talia Theatre; 1 Hoscar Drive, Burnage, MANCHESTER M19 2LS; 0161-249 0564; info@taliatheatre.com ; 49

Tall Stories; www.tallstories.org.uk ;156, 731

Tamasha Theatre Company; Unit E, 11 Ronalds Road, LONDON N5 1XJ; 0207 609 2411; 73

Tameside Arts Education Initiative; based at Egerton Park Arts College, Egerton Street, DENTON M34 3PB; 0161-336 2039; www.egertonpark.u-net.com ;

Tameside College Performing Arts; Beaufort Road, ASHTON – UNDER – LYNE OL6 6NX; 0161-330 6911;

Tameside Youth Drama Group; 31 Woodlands Road, ASHTON – UNDER – LYNE OL6 9DU; 0161-330 3390; 659, 666

Tam Tam; 151

T.A.P.P.; Met Arts Centre, Market Street, BURY BL9 0YZ; O161-761 2216; 430

Tara Arts; 356 Garratt Lane, LONDON SW18 4ES; 0208—333 4459; 291

Tarunya Theatre; Dhaka, Bangladesh;

TaSchen Mullet Theatre Companyc/o Arden School of Theatre, Sale Road, Northenden M23 0DD; 0161-957 1715;

Taud Theatre Company; c/o Arden School of Theatre, Sale Road, Northenden M23 0DD; 0161-957 1715;

Teamwork Films (India); 91 (0) 11 264 67291; www.teamworkfilms.com;

Section 7

AWARDS

7. AWARDS

A STRANGE (AND UNEXPECTED) EVENT (444); HORSE+BAMBOO win the MANCHESTER EVENING NEWS AWARD for Best Special Entertainment.

The following organisations do much to support Theatre in Greater Manchester in many ways. They include the masking of annual Awards, in recognition of outstanding work.

The 'Year' of the various award-givers often does not coincide exactly with that of this volume. Therefore, the work of several persons and productions honoured was detailed in last year's edition. In these cases, the **Production Numbers** given for reference have the prefix **04:**

Where several names are given following an Award, those in plain types were nominees; those in **bold** are the outright winners.

In most cases, only winners, nominees and award categories relevant to Greater Manchester and to the scope of this volume are recorded here, out of the wider range which some Award-givers recognise.

ALL-ENGLAND THEATRE FESTIVAL – West Pennine District;

Hon Secretary: Jeffery Brailsford; Jandowae, Gill Lane, Longton, PRESTON PR4 4SS; 01772 616 092

Full-Length Play Competition 2004-2005; Awarded 25 June 2005:

Holland Enterprise Trophy: GREATER MANCHESTER DRAMA FEDERATION, on its Diamond Jubilee, Sixty meritorious years in support of Amateur Theatre.

Meg StensonAward: for extensive service to a single theatre organisation: PHIILIP DENT, Honorary Secretary, Stockport Garrick

Alan Sanders Trophy (Wardrobe): Mossley AODS – IT AIN'T HALF HOT MUM (667); PADOS – HINDLE WAKES; CHADS – THE RAILWAY CHILDREN (630)

John Palin Trophy (Stagecraft): Mossley – IT AIN'T HALF HOT

MUM (667); **CHADS – THE RAILWAY CHILDREN(630);** CHADS – BREAKING THE SILENCE (631)

Eileen Redfern Trophy (Limited Facilities): PADOS – HINDLE WAKES

Simon Saft Trophy (Adventurous Theatre): CHADS – BREAKING THE SILENCE (631)

Edward Wilson Trophy (Adjudicator's Award) COLIN SNELL, for his outstanding commitment to young actors.

Peter Kennedy Comedy Cup: CHADS – ONE FOR THE ROAD (649); **Stockport Garrick – THE STEAMIE;** ANJI McGREGOR as Dolly in THE STEAMIE, Stockport Garrick

Derek Tipton Award (Best Supporting Actress); DEBBIE LEWIS as Ada in HINDLE WAKES, PADOS.

Peggy Bedford Award (Best Supporting Actor): CARL MORGAN as Char Wallah in IT AIN'T HALF HOT MUM (667), Mossley AODS; ROBIN GRIFFIN as William Tabb in REBECCA, Stockport Garrick; **JOHN PINFIELD as Robert in PROOF (633), CHADS**

David Lane Trophy (Best Actress): HELEN HILL as Norma Green in MR WONDERFUL, Strockport Garrick; ELAIN PRATT as Polya in BREAKING THE SILENCE, CHADS; **RUTH O'HARA as Catherine in PROOF (633), CHADS**

John Langridge Trophy (Best Actor): WILLIAM NOLAN as Dennis Cain in ONE FOR THE ROAD (649), CHADS; HAMISH LAWSON as Geoff Lazenby in MR WONDERFUL, Stockport Garrick; **STEVE HESTER as Lt Barney Greenwald in THE CAINE MUTINY COURT MARTIAL, Stockport Garrick;** DAVID MELLER as Lt Commander Philip Francis Queeg in THE CAINE MUTINY COURT MARTIAL, Stockport Garrick

Vicki Lane Trophy (Best Director): JANE BIRKETT for The Railway Children (630), CHADS; DEREK SLATER for Proof (633), CHADS

McLaughlan Trophy (Best Production): CHADS for Proof (633

<u>BATS:</u> <u>B</u>OLTON EVENING NEWS <u>A</u>MATEUR <u>T</u>HEATRE <u>S</u>TAGE AWARDS 2004/05; Newspaper House, Churchgate, BOLTON BL1 1DE

Made on September 2005

Best Musical: MY FAIR LADY; St Catherine's AMS; Director: PAUL COHEN; THE PAJAMA GAME (96); St Philip's AODS; Director: KATHRYN HENRYS; **OKLAHOMA (83); Volton Catholics Musical & Choral Society; Producer: ROBERT MARGOLIS**

Best Comedy: CAUGHT IN THE NET (82); Phoenix Theatre Company; Director: DAVE EYRE; ONE O'CLOCK FROM THE HOUSE (106); Farnworth Performing Arts Company; Director: ALLAN CHRISTEY; **COMMUNICATING DOORS (133);**

Marco Players; Director: PETER HASLAM

Best Set/ Design/Costume: THE LOVE MATCH (84), St Vincent's Dramatic Society; BEDROOM FARCE (87), Halliwell Theatre Company; **MACBETH, Opera 74**

Reader's Choice of Best Production: HEELO DOLLY (79); Farnworth Performing Arts Company; Director: JEAN HORROCKS; EDUCATING RITE (98); PhoenixTheatre Company; Director: JASON CROMPTON; **LOVE ME SLENDER (105); St Vincent's Dramatic Society; Director: JULIE NAPPIN**

Best Pantomime: CINDERELLA; Victoria Halls ADS, Director: RAY DARBY; LITTLE RED RIDING HOOD; SS Simon & Jude ADS, Director: DAVID CRANK; **DICK WHITTINGTON (90); Trinity SDS, Director: TERRY DODEN**

Best Choreography: MY FAIR LADY; St Catherine's AMS; Choreographer: PAUL COHEN; HOT MIKADO (122), Walmsley AODS, Choreographer: CATHERINE PILKINGTON; **OKLAHOMA (83), Bolton Catholics Musical & Choral Society; Choreographer: BARBARA GRANT**

Best Actor In Comedy: NEIL McMAHON as Ernest in BEDROOM FARCE (87), Halliwell Theatre Company; MARK FORSYTH as Wilf Pearson in BESIDE THE SEA, New Egerton Players; **ROBIN THOMPSON as Stanley in CAUGHT IN THE NET (82), Phoenix Theatre Company.**

Best Actress In A Comedy: JOYCE SMITH as Susannah in BEDROOM FARCE (87), Halliwell Theatre Company; KATH GASKELL as Margaret in ONE O'CLOCK FROM THE HOUSE (106), Farnworth Performing Arts Company; **IRENE SMITH as Ruella Wells in COMMUNICATING DOORS (133), Marco Players**

Best Actress In A Musical: JOANNE HORNBY as Babe Williams in THE PAJAMA GAME (96), St Philip's AODS; IRENE LUNT as Dolly in HELLO DOLLY (79), Farnworth Performing Arts Company; **JENNY BOWLING as Baba Williams in THE PAJAMA GAME (96), St Philip's AODS**

Best Actor In A Musical: TIM SHORTEN as Henry Higgins in MY FAIR LADY, St Catherine's AMS; NICK LARKIN as Sid Sorokin in THE PAJAMA GAME (96), St Philip's AODS; **SCOTT UNSWORTH as Judd Fry in OKLAHOMA (83) in Bolton Catholics Musical & Choral Society**

Best Actress In A Drama: ANDREA PETERS as Marjorie in DAY OF RECKONING (738), Tyldesley Little Theatre; HELEN PRICE AINDOW as Kyra in SKYLIGHT (92), Bolton Little Theatre; **LISA GARRISH as Sheila Wendice inDIAL M FOR MURDER (108), Farnworth Little Theatre**

Best Actor In A Drama: SAM DOOTSON as Billy Casper in KES (100), Bolton Little Theatre; JOHN PRICE as C S Lewis in SHADOWLANDS (112), Farnworth Little Theatre; **JONATHON SIMMONS as Eric Birling in AN INSPECTOR CALLS (104), Phoenix Theatre Company.**

ALICE IN WONDERLAND (89)[MARK LEIGH as Cheshire Cat

Best Drama: DIAL M FOR MURDER (108), Farnworth Little Theatre, Director: CATHERINE JACKSON; SILHOUETTE (740), Tyldesley Little Theatre, Director JENNY ORMAN; **ALICE IN WONDERLAND (89), Bolton Little Theatre, Director: SANDRA SIMPSON**

BUXTON FESTIVAL FRINGE 2005 AWARDS; Announced 25 July

Best Comedy: MOVING PICTURES (12); MediaMedea

Best Drama: SOMEONE WHO'LL WATCH OVER ME (458) Northface Theatre Company

GREATER MANCHESTER DRAMA FEDERATION; Hon Secretary: Sue Mooney, 3 Kingsley Avenue, WILMSLOW, Cheshire SK9 4EN; 01625 531 185; gmdfdrama@aol.com

ONE-ACT PLAY FESTIVAL; 5-11 June 2005; Farnworth Little Theatre (113-131)

Section A (Youth Under 14):

Andrew Winton Trophy (Best Production): CAGE BIRDS (130); Mossley AODS

Certificate of Merit: SCHOOL JOURNEY TO THE CENTRE OF THE EARTH (114); St Philip's AODS

Section B (15-21 Years of Age)

Nan Nuttall Trophy (Best Male Performance): FLATMATES (114); Romiley Little Theatre

Bertram Holland Trophy (Best Female Performance): BEX WICKENS as Karin in FLATMATES (114), Romiley Little THeatre

Awards

Certificate of Merit: WHO CARES (129), Mossley AODS

Section C (Adult)

Settlement PlayersTrophy (Best Production) SAY SOMETHING HAPPENED (115), St Joseph's Players

Stanley Harrower Cup (Runners Up): LAST TANGO IN LITTLE GRIMLEY (119), Hyde Little Theatre

All Sections

Vicki Lane Award (Meritorious Director): MAUREEN SERVICE for SAY SOMETHING HAPPENED (115), St Joseph's Players

Robert L Goodwin Trophy (Outstanding Actor): NORMAN PICKLES as The Man in ELERGY FOR A LADY (131), Farnworth Little Theatre.

Cyril Hines Trophy (Outstanding Actress): MONICA VANESS as Karin in ALBERT (117), Partington Theatre

Julie Emmanuel Award(Best Comedy Performance); SALLY JOLLY as Miss Tate in TOO LONG AN AUTUMN, Brookdale Theatre

Cliff Walker Trophy) Best Presentation): KNOW YOUR ONIONS for Goodbye Iphigenia (127)

Theatre Royal Trophy (Adjudicator's Award):.SHONA BODE as Iphigenia in GOODBYE IPHIGENIA (127), Know Your Onions

NorthWest Playwrights Workshop Award (Best Original Play): VIN KENNY for Soap In My Eye (120), Uppermill Stage Society.

FULL-LENGTH PLAY FESTIVAL 2004-2005

Section A

Best Actress: ROSIE WILSON as Truvy in STEEL MAGNOLIAS, Carver Theatre; **MARIE HOLMES as Shirley Valentine, in SHIRLEY VALENTINE, Summerseat Players;** PAM SNAPE as Dolly in THE STEAMIE (771), Sale Nomads; LINDSAY EAVIS as Joan Maple in MURDERED TO DEATH for Summerseat Players;

Best Supporting Actress:SUE COUTTS as Mag Folan in THE BEAUTY QUEEN OF LEENANE, Whitefield Garrick; **VICKI MYERS as Shelby in STEEL MAGNOLIAS, Carver Theatre;** DORIS MAKIN as Mrs Cullen in KINDLY LEAVE THE STAGE (626), Brookdale Theatre; SARAH BELL as Elizabeth Hartley-Trumpington in MURDERED TO DEATH, Summerseat Players.

Best Actor: BOB HOWELL as Lawrence Garfinkle in OTHER PEOPLE'S MONEY, Whitefield Garrick; **JOHN STILL as Davies in THE CARETAKER, Whitefield Garrick;** PAUL BRACEWELL as Inspector Pratt in MURDERED TO DEATH, Summjerseat Players; TERRY HOLLINSHED as Henry Horatio Hobson in HOBSONSON'S CHOICE (730), Sale Nomada

Best Supporting Actor: BRIAN SEYMOUR as Hravic Zyergefoovc in BODY LANGUAGE, Whitefield Garrick; **STUART SHAW as Mick in THE CARETAKER, Whitefield Garrick;** PETER HASLAM as Rev Arthur Humphrey in SEE HOW THEY

RUN, Marco Players; MARK BLOOMFIELD as William Coles in OTHER PEOPLE'S MONEY, Whitefield Garrick

Cyril Hines Award (Best Actress – Youth): LAUREN LEGG as Annelle in STEEL MAGNOLIAS, Carver Theatre; JESSICA STOTT as Vicki Smith in CAUGHT IN THE NET, Summerseat Players; **ABI FOAN as Nancy in OLIVER TWIST (705), Club Theatre;** LUCY SPURREL as Mrs Corney in OLIVER TWIST (705), Club Theatre

Platt Shield (Best Actor – Youth): DAVID OLIVER as Gavin Smith in CAUGHT IN THE NET, Summerseat Players; **PAUL BRAMMER as Ray Dooley in THE BEAUTY QUEEN OF LEENANE, Whitefield Garrick;** IAIN PREST as Mr Bumble in OLIVER TWIST (707, Club Theatre; MARK DAWSON as Bill Sikes in OLIVER TWIST (705), Club Theatre

Certificates of Promise: JESSICA STOTT as Vicki Smith in CAUGHT IN THE NET, Summerseat Players; MARK DAWSON as Bill Sikes in OLIVER TWIST (705), Club Theatre

John Aldridge Cup (Adventure In Theatre):: SALE NOMADS, The Steamie (771); WHITEFIELD GARRICK, Other People's Money

David Lane Trophy (Front of House Organisation): St Joseph's Players; **Carver Theatre;** Brookdale Theatre; PADOS

Design & Technical Trophy (Technical Presentation): SALE NOMADS, The Steamie (771); WHITEFIELD AODS, Outside Edge; PADOS, Ghost Train; **WHITEFIELD Garrick, Other People's Money**

Harold Onions Trophy (Best Director): HEATHER BAGULEY,Carver Theatre, STEEL MAGNOLIAS; BRIAN TICKLE, Sale Nomads, THE STEAMIE (771); JOHN CUNNINGHAM, Whitefield Garrick, THE CARETAKER; **ALAN MacPHERSON, Whitefield Garrick, OTHER PEOPLE'S MONEY**

Adjudicator's Discretion (Stockport Guild Theatre Trophy), Cast of THE STEAMIE (771), for excellence as an ensemble, Sale Nomads

Lowry Trophy (Runner Up as Best Production): SHIRLEY VALENTINE, Summerseat Players; **THE STEAMIE (771), Sale Nomads;** OTHER PEOPLE'S MONEY, Whitefield Garrick

Drama Shield (Best Production in Section): THE CARETAKER, Whitefield Garrick

Section B

John Garner Trophy (Best Female Performance): MARIA MASTERMAN as Sally in ME AND MY GIRL (604)M Salford Musical Theatre; KERRY NEWTON as Science Officer in RETURN TO THE FORBIDDEN PLANET (669), Mossley AODS; **IRENE LUNT as Dolly in HELLO DOLLY (79), Farnworth Performing Arts;** ALEX PARKER as Nancy in OLIVER!, St Thomas More AOS.

Ian Armstrong Cup (Best Male Performance): HOWARD CARTER as Ebenezer Scrooge in SCROOGE (181), Whitefield AODS; ADAM BROWN as Billy Bigelow in CAROUSEL(767), Heywood AODS; **JOHN PRESTON as Bill Snibsob in**

ALICE McGREEVEY; BEST FEMALE YOUTH PERFORMANCE, as Cosette in LES MISERABLES (668), also Best Youth Production Awards from both GMDF and NODA

ME AND MY GIRL (604), Salford Musical Theatre; CRAIG LEDBROOKE as Ugly in HONK!, Brookdale Theatre

Certificate of Merit (Best Supporting Female Performance): CAROLE BERNSTEIN as Yente in FIDDLER ON THE ROOF (174), PADOS; **VANESSA RANDALL as Widow Corney in OLIVER!, St Thomas More AOS;** HANNAH GOODINSON as Jackie in ME AND MY GIRL (604), Salford Musical Theatre

Certificate of Merit (Best Supporting Male Performance):RODNEY CADD as Prospero in RETURN TO THE FORBIDDEN PLANET (689), Mossley AODS; **PAUL WEBB as Parchester in ME AND MY GIRL (604), Salford Musical Theatre;** DEREK WARD AS Lord Brocklehurst in THE BOYFRIEND (628), Brookdale Theatre; JAMES ECCLESHARE as Cornelius in HELLO DOLLY (79), Farnworth Performing Arts

June Leech Trophy (Best Female Performance – Youth): RUBY TURNER as Ann in HALF A SIXPENCE (768), Hey Kids; **ALICE McGREEVEY as Cosette in LES MISERABLES (668), Mossley AODS;** JENNY BOWLING as Babe in THE PAJAMA GAME (96), St Philips AODS; SCARLETT CRÈME as Ebenezer Scrooge in SCROOGE, Manchester High School for Girls.

Geoffrey Kellett Cup (Best Male Performance – Youth): MARTIN BRACEWELL as Kipps in HALF A SIXPENCE (768), Hey Kids; **DANIEL**

WINTERS as Vajjean in LES MISERABLES (668), Mossley AODS Next Generation; DANIEL WHITEHEAD as Tony in WEST SIDE STORY (102), CATS; DANIEL BOLTON as Tony in IN GREAT GRANDMOTHER'S DAY. St Philip's Junior Workshop

Certificate of Promise (Best Supporting Female Performance – Youth): JOANNE FARROW as Eponine in LES MISERABLES (668), Mossley AODS Next Generation; **SORAYA MAFI as Hodel in FIDDLER ON THE ROOF (174), PADOS;** CAROLINE GARCIA-COX as Mary in JESUS CHRIST SUPERSTAR (88), CATS

Certificate of Promise (Best supporting Male Performance – Youth): JACK ROBERTSON as Chitterlow in HALF A SIXPENCE (768), Hey Kids; **JONATHAN CUNLIFFE as Pilate in JESUS CHRIST SUPERSTAR (88), CATS;** ROBERT FLITCROFT as Bernado in WEST SIDE STORY (102), CATS; PATRICK LIVERSEDGE as Oliver in OLIVER!, St Thomas More AODS

Wyn Davies Trophy (Best Director): JEAN HORROCKS for Hello Dolly (79), Farnsworth Performing Arts; **JOANNE LORD for both Half a Sixpence (768) and Carousel (767), Heywood AODS;** HOWARD RAW for Me and My Girl (604), Salford Musical Theatre; ANITA STUTTARD for Oliver!, St Thomas More AODS

Ronald Ashworth Trophy (Best Musical Director): DAVID ABENDSTERN for Carousel (767), Heywood AODS**; CATHIE BROOKS for Oliver!, St Thomas More AODS;** KAREN MASSEY for Me and My Girl (604), Salford Musical Theatre; CRAIG SMITH for Hello Dolly (79), Farnworth Performing Arts

Irene Rostron Trophy (Best Choreographer): WENDY ROBINSON for Me and My Girl (604), Salford Musical Theatre; **JULL McINTOSH for Half A Sixpence (768), Hey Kids;** KIRSTEN HAMPSON for Annie Get You Gun (489), Uppermill Stage Society; SHERYL HAYDOCK-HOWORTH for Half A Sixpence, North Manchester AODS

Nan Nuttall Trophy (Best Pantomime): ALADDIN (91), Frnworth Performing Arts; CINDERELLA (722), Sale Nomads; **JACK AND THE BEANSTALK, Carver Theatre;** SINBAD THE SAILOR &39), Tylesley Little Theatre

Joyce Pomfret Trophy (Costume Design and Creation): NORTH MANCHESTER AODS for Half A Sixpence; **PADOS for Fiddler On The Roof (174);** SALFORD MUSICAL THEATRE for Me And My Girll (604); SALE NOMADS for CINDERELLA (722)

John Blackborn Trophy (Adjudicator's Discretion: TYLDESLEY LITTLE THEATRE for their endeavour and originality in WASHBOARD BLUES (743)

John Evans Cup (Best Presentation): LES MISERABLES (688), Mossley AODS; **THE PAJAMA GAME (96), St Philips AODS;** OLIVER!, St Thomas More; FIDDLER ON THE ROOF (174), PADOS

GMDF Youth Trophy (Best Youth Production): JESUS CHRIST SUPERSTAR (88); **LES MISERABLES (688), Mossles AODS**

WASHBOARD BLUES (743); ADJUDICATOR'S AWARD to TYLDESLEY LITTLE THEATRE, for Endeavour and Originslity; seen her, left to right: PAUL WARD (Kenny), PAUL BEARDSWORTH (Johnny) and HANNAH SPEAKES (Gloria).

Next Generation; SCROOGE, Manchester High School for Girls; HALF A SIXPENCE (768), Hey Kids

David Lane Trophy (Best Overall Production); ME AND MY GIRL (604), Salford Musical Theatre

<u>**Section C**</u>

Best Actress: NATALIE CROMPTON as Rita in EDUCATING RITA (98), Phoenix Theatre Company; CATHERINE DILLON as Eliza Doolittle in PYGMALION (377), Northenden Players

Best Supporting Actress: LESLEY BOWERS as Cecily Robson in QUARTET (374), Northenden Players; **HELEN WARD as Angela in ABIGAIL'S PARTY, Players DS;** KRYSTYNA JORGENSSON as Eve in HOLIDAY SNAP, Players DS; ANJI McGREGOR as Dolly in THE STEAMIE, Stockport Garrick

Best Actor: RICHARD ELLIS as Charles Bruno in STRANGERS ON A TRAIN (629), CHADS; **PETER BOWERS as Reginal Paget in QUARTET (374), Northenden Players**

Best Supporting Actor: CHARLIE COOK as Dr Hubert Bonney in IT RUNS IN THE FAMILY (638), Heald Green Theatre Company; JOHN PINFIELD as Mr Szczepansky in THE RAILWAY CHILDRED (630), CHADS

Lauriston Trophy (Best Actress – Youth): RHIANNON LEWIS as Sorrel Bliss in HAY FEVER (637), Heald Green Theatre Company; **JENNY BOWLING as Sheila Birling in AN INSPECTOR CALLS (104), Phoenix Theatre Company;** STEFF SMITH as

PETER BOWERS, as Reginald Paget in QUARTET (374), winning the Best Actor Award; with him MARY DILLON as Jean Horton; Northenden Pleayers

Lucy in THE LION, THE WITCH AND THE WARDROBE, Stockport Garrick

Patricia Hohne Trophy (Best Actor – Youth): SCOTT BROOKE as Edmund in the LION, THE WITCH AND THE WARDROBE, Stockport Garrick; **MATTHEW THISTLETON as Sasha Pesiakoff in BREAKING THE SILENCE (631), CHADS;** NATHANIEL HALL as Leslie in IT RUNS IN THE FAMILY (638), Heald Green Theatre Company; TIM WOOD as Ronnie Winslow in THE WINSLOW BOY (376), Northenden Players

Certificates of Promise: KAROLINE GRADZKA and ROBERT MAY as Queen of the Forest and Sylvester in HANS, THE WITCH AND THE GOBBIN (110), Farnworth Little Theatre

Frances Hargreaves Trophy (Costume Design and Creation); PYGMALION (377), Nothenden Players; **HANS, THE WITCH AND THE GOBBIN (110) and THE IMPORTANCE OF BEING EARNEST (109), Farnworth Little Theatre;** THE LION, THE WITCH AND THE WARDROBE, Stockport Garrick

Frank Hillson Trophy (Set Design & Décor): THE EXORCISM (652) and COMFORT AND JOY (651), Droylsden Little Theatre; **BREAKING THE SILENCE (631) and THE RAILWAY CHILDREN (630), CHADS;** THE STEAMIE, Stockport Garrick

Philip Edwards Trophy (Best Lighting Design): THE LION, THE WITCH AND THE WARDROBE, Stockport Garrick; **COMFORT AND JOY (651) and THE EXORCISM (652), Droylsden Little Theatre;** HANS, THE WITCH AND THE GOBBIN (110), Farnworth Little Theatre

Monica Yeomans Trophy (Best Director); ALAN MacPHERSON for AN INSPECTOR CALLS (104), Phoenix Theatre Company; JOHN PRICE for ABIGAIL'S PARTY, Players DS

Pat Phoenix Award (Adjudicators Discretion): HEALD GREEN THEATRE COMPANY for three brilliant comedies in one season: NOISES OFF (634), THERE GOES THE BRIDE (636) and IT RUNS IN THE FAMILY (638).

Muriel Goodwin Trophy (Runners Up for Best Production):

36 HOURS (525); NEIL BELL as John Cooper Clarke, winner of many Lotta Bottle Awards and also a nominee for Best Fringe Production by Manchester Evening News

ABIGAIL'S PARTY, Players DS; **AN INSPECTOR CALLS (104),Phoenix Theatre Company**

LOTTA BOTTLE AWARDS 2004; made by Salford Studio at the King's Arms on 18 December 2004

Special Thank You Awards: PANDA)Performing Arts Network and Development Agancy}; CRIIS (Creative Industries in Salford); CIDS (Creative Industries Services)

Best Poster: RENNY KRUPINSKI for Bare (04:153); KILLERCHIMP and JAMES FOSTER for Embryo 3 & 4; DEREH HANNA for Life's A Gatecrash; **NEIL BELL for 36 Hours (525)**

Best Costume: THE COMPANY (CUL-DE-SAC) for Endgame (04:265); JESS McGRATHER for Where's Alex (04:211); THE COMPANY (HIT & RUN) for Life's A Gatecrash ; **THE COMPANY (EAT PRODUCTIONS) for 36 Hours (525)**

Best Set: TERRY NAYLOR for Endgame (04:265); **JAMES FOSTER, KEN NORBURY & JOHN SCOTT for The Weir (04:546);** JAMES FOSTER, KEN NORBURY & JOHN SCOTT for Moving Pictures (12); NEIL BELL for 36 Hours (525)

Best Sound: JESS McGRUTHER, JOHN SCOTT for Where's Alex? (04:211); JULIO MARIA MARTINO, JOHN SCOTT for Life's A Gatecrash; **JOHN WEST, JOHN SCOTT for 36 Hours (525);** JOHN SCOTT for Moving Pictures (12)

Best Lighting Designer: KEN NORBURY, PHIL MINNS for The Weir (04:546); KEN NORBURY for Relativity (522); **KEN NORBURY, JAMES FOSTER for 36 Hours (525);** JESS McGRUTHER for Whare's Alex? (04:211)

Best Choreographer: RENNY KRUPINSKI for Bare (04:153); THE COMPANY (THIS THEATRE COMPANY) for Our Daily Bread (04:548); THE COMPANY (VISTA) for Where's Alex? (04:211); **THE COMPANY (EAT THEATRE) for 36 Hours (525)**

Best Director: TERRY HUGHES for Life's A Gatecrash; **JAMES FOSTER for The Weir (04:546)** jointly with **NEIL BELL for 36 Hours (525);** JAMES FOSTER for Moving Pictures (12).

Best Event; 24:7 Festival; **EMBRYO;** Mid West for SUE THOMPKINS; Per Verse for PERVERSE (in Manchester Poetry Festival)

Best Male Actor: WARREN BROWN as Steve in Life's a Gatecrash; JAMES FOSTER as Sid in Life's a Gatecrash; **NEIL BELL as Jim in The Weir (04:546) and as John Cooper Clarke in 36 Hours (525)**

Best Female Actor: LYNN RODEN as Eric and Ensemble in 36 Hours (525); **DENICE HOPE as Anne in Moving Pictures (12);** JO WYNNE-EYTON as Nico and Ensemble in 36 Hours (525); SUE JAYNES as Valerie in The Weir (04: 546)

Best New Writing: MOVING PICTURES by Cathy Crabb (12); **36 HOURS** by Neil Bell and John West (525); RELATIVITY by Claire Berry (522); WHERE'S ALEX? By Phil Minns, Sarah Bacon and Jess McGruther (04:211)

Best Production: THE WEIR (Albino Injun; 04:546); LIFE'S A GATECRASH (Hit & Run); **36 HOURS (Eat Theatre; 525);** MOVING PICTURES (MediaMedea; 12)

Best Embryo Sketch: DRUNKEN STRAIGHT GIRL IN VILLAGE by Cathy Crabb; 36 HOURS (extract, 525) by Neil Bell and John West; **BECKETT FOR CHILDREN by Cathy Crabb;** THE PUB (04: 550) by Terry Hughes

Best Embryo Something Different: DENICE HOPE as Tanya Tray; BUZZ HAWKINS for The Bradshaws Radio Sketch performed Live; **GINO EVANS for Tramp Man – Multi Media;** TERRY NAYLOR for Fish Man, an Ultra Violet Light sensitive Show

Outstanding Achievement Award 2004: AMANDA HENNESSEY and DAVID SLACK for 24:7 Theatre Festival.

MANCHESTER EVENING NEWS THEATRE AWARDS; announced 7 December 2004.

Best Musical: I GOT RHYTHM. Northern Ballet, at Lowry; SWEENEY TOOD (04:604), Watermill Theatre, at Lowry; **TABOO (04:67), Fiery Angel / The Lowry/ Clear Channel/ Adam Kenwright; at Lowry.**

Best Actress In A Supporting Role: LISA EICHHORN as Ouisa Kittridge in SIX DEGREES OF SEPARATION (04:83), Royal Exchange; SHOBNA GULATI as Yellama and Rita in DANCING WITHIN WALLS (04:16), at Contact; JANET HENFREY as Miss Evelyn Whitchurch in THE HAPPIEST DAYS OF YOUR LIFE (04:458), Royal Exchange; **BARBARA MARTEN as Coral Williams in A CONVERSATION (4), Royal Exchange;** ANNE RYE as Lil in KINDERTRANSPORT (04: 136), Bolton Octagon

Best Actor In A Supporting Role: STEPHEN McKENNA as George in HUMBLE BOY (04: 82), Library Theatre; SIMON ROBSON as Rupert Billings in THE HAPPIEST DAYS OF YOUR LIFE (04:458), Royal Exchange; **LEIGH SYMONDS as Wayne in POPCORN (04:135)**

Best Visiting Production: BALLROOM (04:608) at Lowry; **HENRY IV (04:607) at Lowry;** HURRICANE (04: 43) at Lowry; THE LIEUGHTENANT OF INISHMORE (04:23) at Lowry; THE MERCHANT OF VENICE (04: 601) at Lowry; THE STRAITS (04:302) at Contact

Best Fringe Performer: ELIZABETH BESTRODE in Zero Degrees And Drifting (294) at Contact; RANI MOORTHY in Curry Tales (257) at Library; JONATHON PRAM (BEN FAULKS) in Living Room / cassetessac (04: 300, 475), Royal Exchange

Best Fringe Production: THE SANCTUARY LAMP (04:26), Royal Exchange; **COYOTE ON A FENCE (04: 474), Royal Exchange;** 36 HOURS (525), Studio Salford; ZERO DEGREES AND DRIFTING (294), Contact

Best Special Entertainment: CINDERELLA (04: 355), Opera House; THE THREE MUSKETEERS (04:355), Feelgood Theatre; **A STRANGE (AND UNEXPECTED) EVENT (444), Horse and Bamboo;** LOVE ON THE DOLE (545), Lowry.

Best Performance In A Visiting Production: RICHARD DORMER in Hurricane (04:43), Ransom Theatre at Lowry; VICTORIA HAMILTON in Suddenly Last Summer (04:74), Sheffield Theatres at Lowry; RALPH HIGGINS, as and in Richard III (573), KAOS Theatre, at Lowry; **IAN McDIARMID, as and in Henry IV (04: 607), Donmar Warehouse, at Lowry;** BARRY WARD in The Lieutenant of Inishmore (04:23); Royal Shakespear Company, Fiery Angel and Theatre Royal Bath, at Lowry

Best Design; RICHARD FOXTON (Design), THOMAS WEIR (Lighting), ANDY SMITH (Sound) for FOUR NIGHTS IN KNARESBOROUGH (04: 134), Bolton Octagon; **PAUL CLAY for set, video and lighting of PERFECT (04: 86), Contact;** RICHARD FOXTON (Design),

THOMAS WEIR (Lighting), ANDY SMITH (Sound) for KINDERTRANSPORT (04: 136), Bolton Octagon; PATRICK CONNELLAN (Design), THOMAS WEIR (Lighting), ANDY SMITH (Sound) for LITTLE MALCOLM AND HIS STRUGGLE AGAINST THE EUNUCHS (04: 69), Bolton Octagon

Best New Play: MAYBE TOMORROW (04: 202) by Nichola Schofield, Royal Exchange; **PERFECT (04:86)by Kaite O'Reilly, Contact;** SKITTISH (289) by Jonathan McGrath, Contact; 36 HOURS (525) by Neil Best and John West

Most Promising Newcomer;. JULIETTE GOODMAN as Scout in Popcorn (04: 135), Bolton Octagon; **ANDREW GARFIELD as Billy Casper in Kes (435), Royal Exchange**

Best Actress In A Leading Role; BRIGIT FORSYTH in All My Sons (04: 72), Library Theatre; CLAIRE REDCLIFFE in Kindertransport (04:136), Bolton Octagon; JOANNA RIDING in The Happiest Days of your Life (04: 548), Royal Exchange; **DENISE WELCH in The Rise and Fall of Little Voice (04: 459), Royal Exchange;** INIKA LEIGHT WRIGHT in Perfect (04:86), Contact

Best Actor In A Leading Role: DAVID FLEESHMAN in All My Sons (04:72), Library; **0-T FAGBENLE in Six Degrees of Separation (04: 83), Royal Exchange;** MARSHALL GRIFFIN, BEN HULL, GRAHAM McTAVISH, MATTHEW RIXON in Four Nights in Knaresborough (04: 134), Bolton Octagon

Best Production: FOUR NIGHTS IN KNARESBOROUGH (04:134), Bolton Octagon; **A CONVERSATION (4), Royal Exchange;** THE HAPPIEST DAYS OF YOUR LIFE (04: 548), Royal Exchange; SIX DEGREES OF SEPARATION (04:04:83), Royal Exchange

Readers Award for Outstanding Performance of The Year: BRIAN CONLEY in Cinderella (04: 392), Opera House

Alpha Award: 24:7 Festival

MANCHESTER IN-FRINGE THEATRE AWARDS (MIFTAs); Awarded to Entrants in the Manchester Universities Drama Festival (201-208)

It did not prove possible this year to obtain details of these Awards. The presentation ceremony on 16 March 2005 is said to have been most finely devised.

MANCHESTER MUSICAL AWARDS 2005; Chair Person: Gill Lee-White, 15 Fraser Avenue, SALE M33 2TF; 0161-282 6916

Awarded on 11 June 2005

Best Newcomer: DANIEL SHAW as Young Patrick in MAME (688), Altrincham Garrick; MARIA GOOCH as Nancy in OLIVER! (699), Sale and Altrincham Musical Theatre; HARRY HANCOCK as Oliver Twist in

OLIVER! (699), Sale and Altrincham Musical Theatre; KEVIN ELSTON as Buggins in HALF A SIXPENCE, North Manchester AOS; MICHAEL COLLINS as Perchik in FIDDLER ON THE ROOF (174), PADOS

Best Comedy Performance: PAUL WHITTLE as Hines in THE PAJAMA GAME, St Luke's ADS; STUART DAVIES as Lion in THE WIZARD OF OZ, Middleton AOS; TONY ROSTRON as Nicely Nicely in GUYS AND DOLLS (04:752) , South Manchester AODS; JAKKI CLARKE as Flo in HALF A SIXPENCE, North Manchester AOS; **PAUL WEBB as Parchester in ME AND MY GIRL (604), Salford Musical Theatre**

Best Supporting Actress: NICKY MEAD as Maggie in 42ND STREET (640), Stockport OS; **BETH HUGHES as Katisha in HOT MIKADO, All Saints Musical Productions;** AMANDA CRUMP as Chava in FIDDLER ON THE ROOF (174), PADOS; SORAYA MAFI as Hodel in FIDDLER ON THE ROOF (174), PADOS; HANNAH GOODINSON as Lady Jacqueline Carstone in ME AND MY GIRL (604), Salford Musical Theatre

Best Supporting Actor: MIKE SAMMON as Ghost of Christmas Past in SCROOGE (181), Whitefield AOS; RALPH ETHERINGTON as Colonel Pickering in MY FAIR LADY (698), Ttrafford Magaretians; **JAMES ECCLESHARE as Cornelius Hackle in HELLO DOLLY (79), Farnworth Performing Arts;** ADAM PAULDEN as Scarecrow in THE WIZARD OF OZ, Middleton AOS; ROGER DUGDALE as Sir John Tremayne in ME AND MY GIRL (604), Salford Musical Theatre

Best Achievement: HELLO DOLLY (79), Farnworth Performing Arts: for creating New York with out the space in which to create it; THE WIZARD OF OZ, Middleton AODS, for an outstanding display of theatre and technology; **ME AND MY GIRL (604), Salford Musical Theatre, for transferring a major show into theatre in the round**

Best All Round Performance: PATSY ROBERTS as Mama Derring in MAME (685), Altrincham Garrick; JENNIFER TAYLOR as Peggy Sawyer in 42ND STREET (640), Stockport OS; NIGEL MACHIN as Albin in LA CAGE AUX FOLLES (772), South Manchester AOS; **CHRIS GRIXTI as Action in WEST SIDE STORY (647), Romiley OS**

Adjudicator's Award: SORAYA MAFI as Hodel in FIDDLER ON THE ROOF (174), PADOS;

Best Choreographer: SHELLIE-BETH SINCLAIR for 42nd Street (640), Stockport OS; SHARN ALEXANDER for West Side Story (647), Romiley OS; **JEAN ASHWORTH for The Wizard of Oz, Middleton AODS;** CHRISTINE MEADOWS for HOT MIKADO, All Saints Musical Productions; WENDY ROBINSON for Me and My Girl (604), Salford Musical Theatre

Best Musical Director: CLAIRE SWEENEY for West Side Story (647), Romiley OS; **PAUL FIRTH for The Merry Widow, Ashton-Under-Lyne OS;** CRAIG SMITH for HELLO DOLLY (79), Farnworth Performing Arts; NICK SANDERS for The Wizard of Oz, Middleton AODS; STEVEN SANDIFORD for Fiddler on The Roof (174), PADOS

Best Actress: SUZANNE MATHER as Anna in THE MERRY WIDOW, Ashton-under-Lyne OS; LUCY PAGE as Maria in WEST SIDE STORY, Middleton AODS; **JOANNE FARROW as Dorothy in THE WIZARD OF OZ, Middleton AODS;** NATALIE BURKE as Yum Yum in HOT MIKADO

Best Actor: HOWARD CARTER as and in SCROOGE (181), Whitefield AODS; **MARTIN HULME as George in LA CAGE AUX FOLLES (772), South Manchester AOS;** EDIE REGAN as Tevye in FIDDLER ON THE ROOF (174), PADOS

Best Director: JOHN HARRISON for 42nd STREET (640); KATHERINE MACHIN for LA CAGE AUX FOLLES (772), South Manchester AOS; **RON GODDARD for WEST SIDE STORY (647), Romiley OS;** ROBERT MARGOLIS * MARK ROSENTHAL for THE WIZARD OF OZ, Middleton AODS; HOWARD G RAW for ME AND MY GIRL (604), Salford Musical Theatre

Best Musical: LA CAGE AUX FOLLES (772), South Manchester AODS' WEST SIDE STORY (647), Romiley OS; **THE WIZARD OF OZ , Middleton AODS;** ME AND MY GIRL (604), Salford Musical Theatre

Frank Lee-White Lifetime Achievement Award: LIAM SAMMO

NODA NORTHWEST MILLENIUM AWARDS; Made on 1 May 2005, covering the period 1 March 2004 – 28 February 2005.

Best Actor In A Musical: HOWARD CARTER as and in Scrooge (181); Whitefield AODS; **MATIN ROCHE as Sir Percy in THE SCARLET PIMPERNEL (04: 549), Rochdale AOS;** IAN NORTHGATE as Adam / Noah in CHILDREN OF EDEN (04: 676), Mossley AODS;

Best Actor (Drama): STEVE MAXFIELD as Sgt Williams inIT AIN'T HALF HOT MUM (667), Mossley AODS;

Best Actress In A Musical: LEA BOWERS as Nancy in OLIVER! (04: 764), Jewish Theatre Group; ANN BIRCHENOUGH as Marguerite in THE SCARLEY PIMPERNEL (04 549), Rochdale OS; SARAH THEWLIS as Sarah Brown in GUYS AND DOLLS (678), Dukinfield AODS

Best Actress (Drama): JANICE HAUGHTON as Mother in IT MUST BE LOVE (04: 668), Hyde Little Theatre;

Best Supporting Actor In A Musical: GARY DAVIES as Chauvelin in THE SCARLET PIMPERNEL (04:540), Rochdale OS; SIMON HARDISTY as Judas in JESUS CHRIST SUPERSTAR (04: 760), Romiley AOS;

Best Supporting Actor (Drama): ROGER BOARDMAN as Dad in CAUGHT IN THE NET (04:670), Hyde Little Theatre

IT AIN'T HALF HOT MUM (667); one of JOHN BUCKLEY's two Best Staging Awards, for MOSSLEY AODS; seen , here, in the forefront, PAUL FIRTH (Bombardier Beaumont, left) and STEVE MAXFIELD (Sergeant Major Williams)

Best Supporting Actress In A Musical: ELAINX as Aunt Eller in OKLAHOMA! (04:480), East Cheshire aods; ELAINE THOPMSON as Miss Hannigan in ANNIE (04: 534), Congress Players; **MANDY MALLINSON as Miss Hannigan in ANNIE (04:669), Hyde Musical Society**

Best Supporting Actress (Drama): SUE PINDER as Maggie in OUTSIDE EDGE; Whitefield AODS

Best Artistic Direction Of A Musical: JEAN HORROCKS for KISS ME KATE (04:127), Farnworth Performing Arts; **JAMES MASTER for THE SCARLET PIMPERNEL (04:540), Rochdale AOS'** COLIN WARD for CHILDREN OF EDEN (04: 676), Mossley AODS

Best Artistic Director (Drama): JANICE C HAUGHTON for CAUGHT IN THE NET (04: 670)

Best Musical Director: HARRY BUTTERWORTH for THE SCARLET PIMPERNEL (04: 540), Rochdale AOS; **CLAIRE SWEENEY for JESUS CHRIST SUPERSTAR (04: 769), Romiley Operatic Society**

Best Staging Of A Musical:) JOHN BUCKLEY for CHILDREN OF EDEN (04: 676); Mossley AODS

Best Staging (Drama): JOHN BUCKLEY for IT AIN'T HALF HOT MUM (667), Mossley AODS

Best Choreography:BARBARA GRANT for OKLAHOMA1 (83); Bolton CATHOLIC Musical and Choral Society; SHELLEY-BETH SINCLAIRE for 42ND STREET (640), Stockport Operatic Society

Best Pantomime: ALADDIN (769); St Herbert's AD&ES

Best Youth Production: HALF A SIXPENCE (768), Hey Kids; **Joint Winners: JESUS CHRIST SUPERSTAR (88), CATS and LES MISERABLES (668)**

Best Play: IT AIN'T HALF HOT MUM (667), Mossley AODS

Best Musical: CHILDREN OF EDEN (04: 676), Mossley AODS; **THE SCARLET PIMPERNEL (04: 540), Rochdale AOS**

Programme And Poster Competition: BasicClass Programme: THE WIZ (770), Lees Street Congregational Church AMDS; Runners Up: COMFORT AND JOY (04: 115), Farnworth Performing Arts;
Poster: THE KING AND I (04: 684), Ashton-under-Lyne AODS

PARTINGTON PLAYERS ONE-ACT PLAY FESTIVAL; 15 July 2005

Best Supporting Actress:INGRID FOLKARD-EVANSS as Bernice in DRINKING COMPANION (744), Tyldesley Little Theatre

IAN McDIARMID accepts from Frances Barber the TMA Award for Best Actor, for his role in and as HENRY IV (04:607), a title which he also won in the Manchester Evening News Awards

THEATRE MANAGEMENT ASSOCIATION; 32 Rose Street, London WC2E 9ET; 020 7557 6700; THEATRE AWARDS FOR EXCELLENCE NATIONWIDE; Made on 17 October 2004

Best Actress: VICTORIA HAMILTON as Catherine Holly in

Awards

SUDDENLY LAST SUMMER (04:75), visiting Lowry; CARMEN MUNROE as and in MOTHER COURAGE (04:93), visiting Contact

Best Actor: IAN McDIARMID as and in HENRY IV (04: 607), visiting Lowry

Best Actress In A Supporting Role EILEEN O'BRIEN as Eileen in ACROSS OCA (04: 3), Royal Exchange

Best Actor In A Supporting Role: ALEX FERNS as Bobby Reyburn in COYOTE ON A FENCE (04: 474), Royal Exchange

Best Designer: LIZ ASHCROFT for THE RISE AND FALL OF LITTLE VOICE (04: 459), Royal Exchange

Also Available:-

A YEAR IN THE CITY OF DRAMA Greater Manchester 1994

"Reveals Manchester's Finest Talent and Promising New Stars" **Ashton Reporter**

"Enthusiasm Bounces off the Page" **The Big Issue**

"Pretty Well Every Production and Name on Every Stage" **Oldham Evening Chronicle**

"I Have Found It Necessary To Keep the Book Beside the Computer. Every Society Should Have A Copy" **NODA**

ISBN 0 9521502 12 ISSN 1357-6003 £ 6.95

A YEAR IN THE THEATRE:- Greater Manchester 1993

"It really is an excellent publication." **Sir Robert Scott**

"Highly useful. ... all encompassing. ... a snip." **City Life**

ISBN 0 9521502 0 4 ISSN 1357-6003 £ 4.95

Obtainable through any bookshop (quote ISBNs) or direct from **Broadfield Publishing, 71 Broadfield Road, Moss Side, MANCHESTER M14 4WE** 0161-227 9265

Also Available:-

A YEAR IN THE THEATRE:- Greater Manchester 1994-95

"Tells you all you could possibly want to know"
Ian Herbert, Theatre Record

"A very fascinating compilation which I haven't been able to put down" **Joyce Keller, Lord Mayor of Manchester**

"Amateur and professional theatres are well represented, with productions as diverse as MacBeth at Bolton's Octagon and Outside Edge at Tyldesley" **Doreen Crowther, Bolton Evening News**

"An impressive achievement, with an all-inclusive index"
Jim Burke, City Life

"A reminder that 1995 produced theatre of the same immeasurably high standard as the City of Drama" **Steve Timms, The Big Issue**

"Don't miss this book - it's a bargain at only £6.95"
David Lewis, NODA NorthWest News

ISBN 0 9521502 2 0 ISSN 1357-6003 £ 6.95

Also Available:-

A YEAR IN THE THEATRE:- Greater Manchester 1995-96

"Should be under every amateur producer's Christmas Tree. One heart-warming feature of the book is its lack of snobbery about professional and amateur productions. Both are viewed as theatre for their own sake." **Oldham Evening Chronicle**

"Bigger and better: an attention to detail which is awesome." **Bolton Evening News**

"The dazzlingly detailed chronicle of the theatre year, and again its packed with hundreds of reasoned perceptive reviews which make the book a joy to read even if you haven't seen any of the plays covered. If you've seen a play in the last 12 months, **A Year In The Theatre** is indispensable - if you haven't, it'll make you want to find out what you've been missing." **The Big Issue**

"The definitive guide to drama in the county." **Bury Times**

ISBN 0 9521502 3 9 ISSN 1357-6003 £ 6.95

Obtainable through any bookshop (quote ISBNs) or direct from **Broadfield Publishing, 71 Broadfield Road, Moss Side, MANCHESTER M14 4WE 0161-227 9265**

Also Available

A YEAR IN THE THEATRE:- Greater Manchester 1996-97

"Amazing attention to detail ... The publication stands not only as a reference book but as a personal appraisal of theatre in Greater Manchester." **Bolton Evening News**

"Encyclopaedic ..., covering virtually everything that moved on a stage in Greater Manchester: the pros, the amateurs the drama schools." **Manchester Evening News**

"A treasure house of facts, figures and opinions of a multitude of shows. Dramatic societies with a few Christmas shekels to spare should snap up this year's edition." **Bury Times**

"An invaluable source of info, it's a good way of seeing your name in print and your efforts dissected, whether you played Henry V at the Palace or coughed and spat at the back of The Yard." **City Life**

"Immensely readable and written with affection and not a little humour. I particularly like the Journal section, which is a close analysis of the great variety of plays and musicals that have been presented upon the professional and amateur stage." **NODA NorthWest News**

ISBN 0 9521502 4 7

Also Available

A YEAR IN THE THEATRE:- Greater Manchester 1997-98

"One of the most regularly consulted tomes in showbiz around these parts." **City Life**

"Highly recommended; one of the most useful reference works I know; superb Journal Section." **NODA NorthWest**

"Impressive indexing; definitely informative; always a decent read." **Manchester Evening News**

"A Bible for Thespians: As a reference of all things theatrical in Greater Manchester, this book cannot be faulted; amazing attention to detail." **Bolton Evening News**

"Thought your 1998 book the best yet." **JG, Saddleworth**

"I am always astounded by the amount and variety of Greater Manchester's theatrical activity. Extraordinary. I wonder if any compabable area anywhere in the world can match it? I really enjoy trawling through the book - commentary and photographs both fascinating." **DS, Taunton**

"If it was on it's probably there. A supreme example of a project undertaken out of love and respect for its subject." **Bolton Evening News**

Also Available

A YEAR IN THE THEATRE:- Greater Manchester 1998 - 99

"A record of success" **Manchester Evening News**

"Made me extremely sorry that I missed so much excellent fare on the stages of one of the most vibrant theatrical areas in the United Kingdom" **NODA NorthWest News**

"Insightful ... Intelligent ... Inspiring" **Lawrence Till**

"An unrivalled record of theatrical achievement" **Bolton Evening News**

"Unique luxury to be able to engage with such a considered critical response across such a broad sweep of productions" **North West Playwrights Lowdown**

"Covering an astonishing 719 productions" **Bury Times**

"A must - buy" **Oldham Chronicle**

ISBN 0 9521502 6 3

Also Available

A YEAR IN THE THEATRE:- Greater Manchester 1999 - 2000

"As comprehensive as ever. Haworth's own diary of shows he has seen and his very personal reaction to them is again one of the book's highlights, whether or not you agree with his views. His enthusiasm and devotion have made **A Year In The Theatre** pretty much indispensable," **Manchester Evening News**

"It is hard to appreciate the worth of such a detailed record until you want to look up that elusive production, or cast member, or play date - and then this volume comes into its own. The excellent journal section once again proves to be an extremely readable digest of the whole range of theatrical presentation," **NODA NorthWest News**

"If theatre throughout Greater Manchester were not so good, there would be no impulse to record it on such a scale. Although not everything is good, so much of it is that it is appropriate to try to capture the whole panorama," **Bolton Evening News**

"Highly recommended to all theatre devotees," **Area News Today**

ISBN 0 9521502 7 1

Also Available

A YEAR IN THE THEATRE: Greater Manchester 2000-01

A unique publication; the only comprehensive record of Greater Manchester's diverse theatrical life. An invaluable source of information, this chronicle of our city's vibrant performing arts scene is a fitting testament to the wide variety of work that takes place here; both entertaining and extremely good value for money: **www.manchesteronstage.co.uk**

An excellent record of all that is theatrical in the Greater Manchester area. So much information and personal reaction to shows make this engrossing and a very worthwhile purchase: **NODA NorthWest News**

Greater Manchester's unique journal of the past year's theatrical endeavour in both amateur and professional fields is as comprehensive as ever; turns a compilation of names and dates into an enriching experience: **Oldham Chronicle**

ISBN 0 9521502 8 X

£8.95

Also Available

A YEAR IN THE THEATRE:- Greater Manchester 2001 – 2002

This unique journal; more "special than last year as productions from around the world came to Manchester to mark the occasion of the Commonwealth Games. Covering both amateur and the professional stage, it is a complex and impressive record. If you have never bought a copy, it is about time you did! **NODA NorthWest News**

The annual compendium of drama across Greater Manchester **Bury Times**

Manchester's Theatre Bible **The Big Issue In The North**

Percipient critiques; both professional and amateur work covered with the same constructive eye; a testament to the vibrancy of Manchester's performing arts scene; an essential purchase **City Life**

ISBN 0 9521502 9 8